Protect
and
Defend

Protect
and
Defend

A NOVEL BY

Richard North Patterson

HUTCHINSON
London

First published by Alfred A. Knopf, Inc. in 2000
First published in the United Kingdom in 2001 by Hutchinson

The Random House Group Limited
20 Vauxhall Bridge Road, London SW1V 2SA

Random House Australia (Pty) Limited
20 Alfred Street, Milsons Point, Sydney,
New South Wales 2061, Australia

Random House New Zealand Limited
18 Poland Road, Glenfield
Auckland 10, New Zealand

Random House (Pty) Limited
Endulini, 5a Jubilee Road, Parktown 2193, South Africa

The Random House Group Limited Reg. No. 954009
www.randomhouse.co.uk

A CIP catalogue record for this book is available
from the British Library

Papers used by Random House
are natural, recyclable products made from wood grown in
sustainable forests.The manufacturing processes conform to
the environmental regulations of the country of origin

ISBN 0 09 180152 4 (hardback)
ISBN 0 09 179408 0 (trade paperback)

Printed and bound in Great Britain by
Mackays of Chatham PLC, Chatham, Kent

For Katie, Stephen, and Adam
with love and pride

I, Kerry Francis Kilcannon, do solemnly swear that I will faithfully execute the Office of President of the United States, and will to the best of my Ability, preserve, protect and defend the Constitution of the United States . . .

—THE OATH OF OFFICE

PART I

The Inaugural

One

"I, Kerry Francis Kilcannon . . ."

In a high clear voice, carrying a trace of Irish lilt, Kerry Kilcannon repeated the historic phrases intoned by Chief Justice Roger Bannon.

The two men faced each other on the patio which fronted the west side of the Capitol, surrounded by guests and officeholders and watched from greater distances by thousands of well-wishers who covered the grounds below. The noonday was bright but chill; a heavy snow had fallen overnight, and the mist of Bannon's words hung in the air between them. Though Kerry wore the traditional morning coat, those around him huddled with their collars up and hands shoved in the pockets of much heavier coats. Protected only by his traditional robe, the Chief Justice looked bloodless, an old man who shivered in the cold, heightening the contrast with Kerry Kilcannon.

Kerry was forty-two, and his slight frame and thatch of chestnut hair made him seem startlingly young for the office. At his moment of accession, both humbling and exalting, the three people he loved most stood near: his mother, Mary Kilcannon; Clayton Slade, his closest friend and the new Chief of Staff; and his fiancée, Lara Costello, a broadcast journalist who enhanced the aura of youth and vitality which was central to Kerry's appeal. "When Kerry Kilcannon enters a room," a commentator had observed, "he's in Technicolor, and everyone else is in black-and-white."

Despite that, Kerry knew with regret, he came to the presidency a divisive figure. His election last November had been bitter and close: only at dawn of the next morning, when the final count in California went narrowly to Kerry, had Americans known who would lead them. Few, Kerry supposed, were more appalled than Chief Justice Roger Bannon.

It was an open secret that, at seventy-nine, Bannon had long wished to retire: for eight years under Kerry's Democratic predecessor, the Chief Justice had presided grimly over a sharply divided Court, growing so pale and desiccated that he came, in Kerry's mind, to resemble parchment. Seemingly all that had sustained him was the wish for a Republican president to appoint his successor, helping maintain Bannon's conservative legacy; in a rare moment of incaution, conveyed to the press, Bannon had opined at a dinner party that Kerry was "ruthless, intemperate, and qualified only to ruin the Court." The inaugural's crowning irony was that the Chief Justice was here, obliged by office to effect the transfer of power to another Democrat, this one the embodiment of all Bannon loathed. Whoever imagined that ours was a government of laws and not men, Kerry thought wryly, could not see Bannon's face. Yet he was here to do his job, trembling with cold, and Kerry could not help but feel sympathy and a measure of admiration.

". . . do solemnly swear that I will faithfully execute the Office of President of the United States . . ."

The outgoing president watched from Kerry's left, gray and worn, a cautionary portrait of the burdens awaiting him. Yet there were at least two others nearby who already hoped to take Kerry's place: his old antagonist from the Senate, Republican Majority Leader Macdonald Gage; and Senator Chad Palmer, Chairman of the Judiciary Committee, a second Republican whose rivalry with Gage and friendship with Kerry did not disguise his cheerful conviction that he would be a far better president than either. Kerry wondered which man the Chief Justice was hoping would depose him four years hence, and whether Bannon would live that long.

". . . and will to the best of my Ability, preserve, protect and defend the Constitution of the United States."

Firmly, as though to override the old man's hesitance, Kerry completed the oath.

At that wondrous instant, the summit of two years of striving and resolve, Kerry Francis Kilcannon became President of the United States.

A rough celebratory chorus rose from below. Mustering a faint smile, Bannon shook his hand.

"Congratulations," the Chief Justice murmured and then, after a moment's pause, he added the words "Mr. President."

At 12:31, both sobered and elated by the challenge awaiting him, President Kerry Kilcannon concluded his inaugural address.

There was a deep momentary quiet and then a rising swell of applause, long and sustained and, to Kerry, reassuring. Turning to those nearest, he looked first toward Lara Costello. Instead, he found himself staring at Chief Justice Bannon.

Bannon raised his hand, seeming to reach out to him, a red flush staining his cheeks. One side of his face twitched, and then his eyes rolled back into his head. Knees buckling, the Chief Justice slowly collapsed.

Before Kerry could react, three Secret Service agents surrounded the new president, uncertain of what they had seen. The crowd below stilled; from those closer at hand came cries of shock and confusion.

"He's had a stroke," Kerry said quickly. "I'm fine."

After a moment, they released his arms, clearing the small crush of onlookers surrounding the fallen Chief Justice. Senator Chad Palmer had already turned Bannon over and begun mouth-to-mouth resuscitation. Kneeling beside them, Kerry watched Palmer's white-blond head press against the Chief Justice's ashen face. Chad's cheeks trembled with the effort to force air down a dead man's throat.

Turning at last, Palmer murmured to Kerry, "I think he's gone."

As ever in the presence of death, Kerry experienced a frisson of horror and pity. Chad touched his arm. "They'll need to see you, Mr. President. To know that you're all right."

Belatedly, Kerry nodded. He stood, turning, and saw his mother and Lara, their stunned expressions mirroring his own. Only then did he register what Chad Palmer, whose former appellation for Kerry was "pal," had called him.

At once, Kerry felt the weight of his new responsibilities, both substantive and symbolic. He had asked the country to look to him, and this was no time to falter.

Kerry stepped back to the podium, glancing back as paramedics bore the Chief Justice to an ambulance. The crowd below milled in confusion.

Gazing out, Kerry paused, restoring his own equanimity. Time seemed to stop for him. It was a trick he had learned before addressing a jury and, even now, it served.

Above the confusion, Kerry's voice rang out. "The Chief Justice," he announced, "has collapsed, and is on his way to the hospital."

His words carried through the wintry air to the far edge of the crowd. "I ask for a moment of quiet," he continued, "and for your prayers for Chief Justice Bannon."

Stillness fell, a respectful silence.

But there would be little time, Kerry realized, to reflect on Roger Bannon's passing. The first days of his administration had changed abruptly, and their defining moment was already ordained: his submission to the Senate of a new Chief Justice who, if confirmed, might transform the Court. The ways in which this would change his own life—and that of others here, and elsewhere—was not yet within his contemplation.

Two

On a bleak, drizzly afternoon, typical of San Francisco in January, Sarah Dash braced herself for another confrontation.

It was abortion day and, despite the weather, demonstrators ringed the converted Victorian which served as the Bay Area Women's Clinic. Sarah monitored them from its porch, ignoring the dampness of her dark, curly hair, her grave brown eyes calm yet resolute. But beneath this facade, she was tense. This was the first test of the new court order she had obtained, over bitter opposition from pro-life attorneys, to protect access to the clinic. Though, at twenty-nine, Sarah had been a lawyer for less than five years, her job was to enforce the order.

Today, she guessed, there were at least two hundred. Most were peaceful. Some knelt on the sidewalks in prayer. Others carried placards bearing pictures of bloody fetuses or calling abortion murder. With a few of the regulars—the graying priest who engaged Sarah in gentle argument, the grandmother who offered her homemade cookies—Sarah had formed a relationship which was, despite yawning differences in social outlook, based on mutual respect. But the militant wing of the Christian Commitment, the ones who called her "baby-killer," filled her with unease.

Almost always, they were men—often single and in their twenties, Sarah had learned—and their aim was to quash abortion through fear and shame. For weeks they had accosted anyone who came: first the doctors and nurses who arrived to work—whom they addressed by name, demanding that they "wash the blood off their hands," then the women who wanted their services. Before Sarah had gone to court, the militants had effectively shut the clinic down.

Now Sarah's mandate was clear: to ensure that any woman brave or desperate enough to come for an abortion could have one. But the only access to the clinic was a concrete walk from the sidewalk to the porch where Sarah stood. The court's zone of protection—a five foot bubble around each patient—would permit the demonstrators to surround the patient until she reached the porch. To combat this gauntlet, Sarah had designed a system: once a patient called, setting a time for arrival, the clinic sent out a volunteer in a bright orange vest to escort her. All Sarah could do now was hope it worked.

As Sarah surveyed the crowd, she noticed a disturbing number of new faces, men whom she had not seen here before. Their presence, she guessed, was yet another tactic of the Christian Commitment: to use fresh recruits who could claim that the court order did not cover them. But a spate of anti-abortion violence—the murder of a doctor in Buffalo, three more killings at a clinic in Boston—had caused her to look out for strangers more troubled, and more dangerous, than even the Commitment might suspect. It was not the kind of judgment for which her training had prepared her.

Until her involvement with the clinic, the path of Sarah's career had been smooth and without controversy: a scholarship to Stanford; an editorship on the law journal at Yale; a much sought-after clerkship with one of the most respected female jurists in the country, Caroline Masters of the United States Court of Appeals. Her associateship at Kenyon & Walker, a four-hundred-lawyer firm with a roster of corporate clients and a reputation for excellence, was both a logical progression and, perhaps, a first step toward a loftier ambition—to be, like Caroline Masters, a federal judge. And the only volunteer activity her schedule allowed—enrolling in the firm's pro bono program—was encouraged by the partners, at least in theory, as an act of social responsibility.

But after Sarah had taken the Christian Commitment to court, she had felt a clear, if subtle, change. It was one thing for Kenyon & Walker to represent a clinic whose principal service was birth control; another when gratis representation crossed over into abortion, let alone an area this dangerous and inflammatory, and which also had decreased measurably the time Sarah spent on paying clients. The Commitment was formidable: its lawyers were the pro-life movement's most experienced; its public spokespeople the most persuasive; its militant wing—as only pro-choice activists and women in need of an abortion truly understood—the most obstructionist and intimidating.

Despite her success in court, there were rumors that the managing partner was looking for a way to end her involvement. Part of Sarah resented this intrusion; another part, which she admired less, conceded that this might be an act of mercy. Sometimes one's best decisions were made by someone else.

But today's decisions were hers: how best to protect the women who came here; whether to call the police for help. The first patient was due in fifteen minutes.

Scanning the crowd, Sarah noticed a young woman watching her from across the street.

She was a girl, really, with short red hair and a waiflike slimness. But despite the flowered dress she wore, Sarah noticed, her belly had begun to show. Immobile, the girl gazed at the clinic as though it were a thousand miles away.

Two weeks ago, before the court order, Sarah had seen the same girl.

The clinic had been ringed with demonstrators, blocking access. For some moments, as now, the girl had not moved. Then, as though panicked, she had turned abruptly, and hurried away.

This time she remained.

For perhaps five minutes she stood rooted to the sidewalk. Bowing her head, she seemed to pray. Then she started across the street, toward the clinic.

Turning sideways, she entered the crush of demonstrators, eyes averted. She managed to reach the walkway before a dark-haired young man stepped in front of her.

Gently, as a brother might, the man placed both hands on the girl's shoulders. "We can find you clothes and shelter," he promised her, "a loving home for your baby."

Mute, the girl shook her head. Leaving the porch, Sarah hurried toward them.

As she pushed through the bubble, the stranger turned toward her. Sarah placed a copy of the court order in his hand. "You're violating a court order," she said. "Let her pass, or I'll call the police."

The man kept his eyes on Sarah, staring at her with a puzzled half-smile which did not reach his eyes. Softly, Sarah repeated, "Let her go."

Still silent, the man took one slow step backward.

Grasping the girl's hand, Sarah led her past him. The chill on the back of Sarah's neck was from more than the cold and damp. When at last they reached the clinic, the girl began crying.

Sarah guided her to a counselor's office and sat beside her on the worn couch.

Bent forward, the girl's frame shook with sobs. Sarah waited until the trembling stopped. But the girl remained with her face in her hands.

"How can we help you?" Sarah asked.

After a moment, the girl looked up at her.

Though her eyes were red-rimmed and swollen, her face had an unformed prettiness: snub features, rounded chin and cheekbones, a pale, fresh complexion lightly dusted with freckles, and, somewhat startling, blue irises which glinted with volatility. Except for the eyes, Sarah reflected much later, she had looked like a cheerleader in trouble, not a human lightning rod.

"I need an abortion," she said.

Three

Kerry rode down Pennsylvania Avenue in a black limousine, Mary Kilcannon beside him, waving to the onlookers who thronged the street and covered the steps of public buildings. At the suggestion of his advisers, Lara was not with him: before Kerry asked the public to treat her as a First Lady, they opined, she should *be* one. And it was right, Kerry thought, that his mother share this day.

Briefly, she touched his hand.

"I'd say I'm proud of you," she told him. "But that's like saying I had anything to do with this."

He turned to her, a still handsome woman of seventy with steel-gray hair, but the same green eyes which, as long as he could remember, had symbolized love and faith.

"You did, Ma."

Silent, Mary shook her head. In the world of politics, the gesture said, the Kilcannon family served as useful American myth: the two immigrants from county Roscommon, a policeman and his wife, who together had raised a president. But inside this car the myth's survivors could acknowledge the truth—that, at six, Kerry had cowered while his hulking father had beaten Mary Kilcannon; or that the brutality had continued until, at eighteen, filled with anguish and love for his mother and a rage that had never quite left him, the smaller Kerry had beaten his father unconscious.

"The ones that hate you," she told him, "don't really know you."

This, too, Kerry understood without words—his mother's guilty belief that Kerry's heritage of anger, transmuted by self-discipline into an iron resolve to achieve his goals, was as misunderstood by others as the reasons for it. If so, Kerry thought, let it be: he did not believe in calculated self-revelation, or that piercing his mother's fiercely held privacy was the necessary price of public office. His defense was humor, as when a reporter had asked him to describe the traits of the child Kerry Kilcannon. "Sensitivity," Kerry had answered with a smile. "And ruthlessness."

Now, quiet, he took his mother's hand, even as the death of Roger Bannon shadowed his thoughts.

At dusk—after hours spent on a bullet-proof reviewing stand watching his inaugural parade which, by actual count, had included seven hundred thirty horses; sixty-six floats; and fifty-seven marching bands—Kerry Kilcannon entered the West Wing for the first time as President. As he did, he felt the White House encase him: the eight guardhouses with uniformed protectors; the surveillance cameras; the seismic sensors planted on the grounds to detect intruders; the trappings and safeguards which flowed seamlessly from one occupant to another.

At Kerry's request, Clayton Slade and Kit Pace, his press secretary, waited in the Oval Office.

Looking from one to the other, Kerry crossed the room and settled into a high-backed chair behind an oak desk once used by John F. Kennedy.

"Well," he inquired of his audience, "what do you think?"

Eyeing him, Kit suppressed a smile. "Reverence aside, Mr. President, you look like a kid in the principal's office. Your predecessor was six inches taller."

Kerry's amusement was muted; he sometimes resented reminders that he was, at most, five-ten. "They say Bobby Kennedy wore elevator shoes. Maybe you can find some for me."

A smile crossed Clayton's shrewd black face. "Won't help," he told his friend crisply. "Lose the chair before the White House photographer shows."

"'Scandal in the White House,'" Kerry said sarcastically. "'Dwarf Elected President.'" But he got up, closing the office door, and, waving Clayton and Kit to an overstuffed couch, sat across from them.

"I take it he's dead," Kerry said.

Kit nodded. "Massive stroke." Softly, she added, "He might have lived longer if he hadn't despised you so much."

Kerry accepted this for what he thought it was—not callousness, but fact. "Do we have a statement?" he asked.

Kit handed him a single typed page. Scanning it, Kerry murmured, "I suppose it's a mercy, at moments like this, that we so seldom say all we feel." He paused, then asked Kit, "How's his wife?"

"Numb, I'm told. His death's hardly a surprise, but they'd been married fifty-two years. Three kids, eight grandchildren."

"I'll call her before the inaugural balls start." Turning to Clayton, Kerry inquired, "What do we do about *them*?"

"For sure not cancel. You've got thousands of supporters here, waiting for that night they'll tell their grandchildren about. You owe them, and the country, a new beginning. And Carlie"—referring to Clayton's wife—"has a new dress."

Kerry smiled briefly. "So does Lara. I'll just have to find something appropriate to say at every ball, perhaps after a moment of silence. What else?"

Clayton leaned back on the couch. "For openers, you've got a new Chief Justice to appoint."

Once more, Kerry had a moment of disbelief—first that he was President, then that he would be tested so soon. "Not tonight, I hope."

"Soon. We've got a four-four split on the Court—conservative versus moderate-to-liberal—with a full calendar of major cases. And it's not like anyone thought the Chief Justice would be with us that long—our transition team already has a shortlist of names, and they've started up files on each."

"Good. Run them by our political people."

"Your constituent groups will want to weigh in, too," Kit observed. "Hispanics, blacks, labor, pro-choice women, trial lawyers. They all think you owe them, and they're right."

"Haven't they seen the Cabinet?" Clayton rejoined. "We've at least made a down payment." He turned to Kerry. "What we need here is a consensus choice—the Republicans still control the Senate, and Macdonald Gage is laying for you. Maybe Palmer, too, now that he's in charge of running the hearings on whoever you send over. I think we should look for a moderate Republican."

"I thought they were an endangered species," Kerry said dryly. Standing, he told Clayton, "Get me the list tomorrow. Along with a new chair."

Kit frowned, as if unwilling to drop the subject. "Without pro-choice women, Mr. President, you couldn't have carried California, and none of us would be here. As Ellen Penn no doubt will remind you."

At this mention of his feisty new Vice President, formerly the junior senator from California, Kerry feigned a wince; arguably, he owed his election to Ellen, and she would not be shy in pressing her views. "Spare me. I'll be hearing from Ellen soon enough."

"With reason," Kit persisted. "The pro-choice movement is scared to death—you've got this damned Protection of Life Act the Republicans just passed, which your predecessor was too scared to veto. Even you were conveniently absent for *that* vote."

"The pro-choice movement," Kerry answered, "can be too damned hard to please. I was running for President, not auditioning for a supplement to *Profiles in Courage*. One vote in the Senate wouldn't have made any difference."

"Exactly. So pro-choice women gave you a pass, expecting you'd look out for them once you got here. Especially on the Court."

Kerry folded his arms. "I've been President for about five hours, I've got eleven balls to go to, and I'm still struggling to remember what to do if there's a nuclear attack. If it's all right with you, Kit, I'll reserve the Supreme Court for my first full day on the job."

As though to short-circuit Kerry's irritation, Clayton intervened. "Even with Bannon's death," he told Kerry, "people will remember your inaugural address. You made it sound even better than it read. CNN called it the best since Kennedy's."

Kerry smiled, mollified, and noted with amusement that he still needed Clayton's reassurance. At once Kit caught the spirit. "You were terrific," she averred. "The only thing that could have gone better is if the Service had let you get to Bannon before Palmer did. He's gotten too much airtime."

Clayton gave a short laugh. "The most dangerous place in Washington," he agreed, "is the space between Chad Palmer and a Minicam."

As he was meant to, Kerry smiled at them both. But beneath their mordant humor, he understood that Clayton and Kit already saw Chad Palmer as his chief rival, and that this would be the prism through which they viewed everything Chad did. And so, they were warning, should Kerry.

"That's all right," he answered. "Let Chad be the hero. He earned the right, when I was still in college."

Four

"What's your name?" Sarah inquired.

The girl looked down. "Mary Ann."

Sitting beside her, Sarah waited for her to look up again. Then she asked, "How far along *are* you?"

Once more, Mary Ann turned away, as if the question were a rebuke. "Five and a half months," she murmured.

"And you're how old?"

"Fifteen."

So far, Sarah thought, it was as bad as she had expected. "Are you living with your parents?" she asked.

The girl's face grew taut. Her answer, a quick nod, resembled a hiccup.

"If you haven't talked to them . . ."

"Please . . ." Swallowing convulsively, Mary Ann burst out, "My baby's not right. I'm afraid of it."

The moment she saw the technician's face, Mary Ann had known there was something wrong.

A sonogram was routine, the woman had said—afterward there would be pictures and, if Mary Ann wished to know, they could tell her the baby's sex. Her mother, tight-lipped and alert, held her hand: there were times when it felt to Mary Ann that this was her mother's pregnancy.

For a while, the whole thing had seemed like it was happening to someone else, or maybe in a dream. Her first time, in the back seat of Tony's car; crying from the pain of it; feeling abandoned after Tony, with a hurried kiss, dropped her at the corner; resenting the lie she told her parents about seeing a movie with a friend. In her room, she had undressed, studying her body in the mirror. Then she turned out the lights. Alone in bed, she felt confused again, yet proud that a boy so much older and more popular had wanted her. She went to sleep wishing that Tony were next to her.

He never called again. It was like the secret grew within her until it became a baby, and her mother found her vomiting in the bathroom. This time she could not lie.

Her mother took her to the doctor.

Afterward they sat in the living room. Her father, too contained and gentle to rebuke her, explained what they would do: Mary Ann would continue at Saint Ignatius; her mother and father would support her and the baby; with enough resolve and sacrifice the three of them could assure that Mary Ann went to college. Her mother remained silent and stricken. For her parents, Tony's role was done: shamed, Mary Ann tried to imagine that Tony—filled with pride, or perhaps remorse—would come for her.

But Tony would not see her. A few girlfriends were kinder. And it was her mother—whose long silences at the dinner table had been more painful than words—who helped to decorate the guest room for a baby, and who shared Mary Ann's wonder at the stir of life inside her. With each checkup, her mother had become more animated—until the sonogram.

Quiet, the technician stared at it. When her mother stood to see the baby's image on the screen, the woman switched it off.

"What is it?" her mother asked.

The technician remained calm. "Dr. McNally will talk to you," she answered, "as soon as he reviews the pictures."

For the next forty minutes, her mother made forced chatter while Mary Ann wondered what the technician had seen growing inside her. Then a nurse led them to Dr. McNally's office.

The doctor sat at his desk. Fifteen years before, he had delivered Mary Ann; today his avuncular face, a map of Ireland, was troubled. "Can I speak to your mother?" he asked.

This frightened Mary Ann still further. "Why?" she said stubbornly. "It's *my* baby."

McNally gave her mother a glance, then spoke to Mary Ann. "There's a problem, you see. Your baby's hydrocephalic."

In the silence, Mary Ann saw her mother's eyes briefly shut. Margaret Tierney placed an arm on Mary Ann's shoulder.

"In layman's terms," McNally continued gently, "his head is swollen with water. Often, unfortunately, it doesn't manifest until several months into the pregnancy." He looked from Mary Ann to her mother. "Mary Ann is twenty weeks pregnant—within a week or two of viability, on average. Nothing is certain. But the condition tends to impede development of the brain."

Her mother blanched. "'Tends'?" she repeated.

McNally faced her. "There's a slim chance the brain will develop normally. But the condition obscures it: we can't tell from a sonogram what cerebral development is occurring." He paused, his reluctance palpable. "In all likelihood, the baby will die soon after birth. But I'm afraid it's a matter of wait and see."

To Mary Ann, it was like she could not move or speak, yet could hear everything around her. As she fought back tears, her mother moved still closer. "But she's barely fifteen. A head that size . . ."

"Trust in us. We can perform a classical cesarean section, for Mary Ann's protection."

To Mary Ann, his words seemed to arrive slowly, as if from a great distance. She felt her mother kiss the crown of her head; for a time her mother's face rested there, as though Mary Ann were small again.

"What about future pregnancies?" Her mother's voice was tight, a signal of fear. "The risk of not bearing children."

Head lowered, Mary Ann closed her eyes. Softly, McNally told her mother, "I understand, Margaret. Believe me, I do. But these days the risk is relatively small."

"*How* small?"

"Five percent, at most. Probably far lower."

Only then did Mary Ann begin to cry, tears running down her face.

Watching the memory flood the girl's eyes, Sarah envisioned her waking from a dream state.

"When did this happen?" Sarah asked.

"Three weeks ago." Abruptly, the girl stood, as though propelled by anguish. "I'm all alone. My parents are *making* me have this baby, and there's no one else to help me."

Five

"It's a shame about Roger Bannon," Macdonald Gage said, passing Chad Palmer a glass of single malt scotch. "For the best of reasons, he stayed too long."

The two men were alone in the Majority Leader's commodious office, a suite of walnut and leather reminiscent to Chad of a men's club. As always, Chad marked Mac Gage's seamless courtesy: Gage never forgot that Glenlivet was Chad's scotch of choice, or that he liked precisely two shots served over ice in a cocktail glass. These were the kinds of small attentions, combined with an unflagging grasp of detail and a shrewd knowledge of what motivated ninety-nine other men and women, that had made Macdonald Gage the master of the Senate.

"He was dead by the time I reached him," Chad remarked. "Absolutely nothing for it."

Gage grimaced in commiseration, then raised his drink. "To Roger," he said. "He surely served our country well."

Idly, Chad reflected that Mac Gage had carefully polished his public persona to be unctuous and predictable—a series of homilies as unrevealing as his conventional gray suit and striped tie were uninteresting. In some part of Gage's mind, Chad once had conjectured, the world must be a vast, interminable Rotary meeting. But experience had taught him that Gage's manner was intended to lull others into forgetting his unremitting desire to stay one jump ahead.

To Gage, Chad knew, he, too, was somewhat of an enigma, a man to be watched and studied. In looks and manner they were opposites: Gage had the smooth, prosperous look of a provincial worthy in middle age; at forty-nine, Chad was lean, fit, and given to the spontaneous and irreverent. It amused him to know that Gage had nicknamed him in private "Robert Redford," as much for the adoration of the media as for Chad's blond-haired good looks, and that Kerry Kilcannon, with more affection, had labeled him "Harry Hotspur," after the headstrong warrior of Shakespeare's *Henry IV*. Both perceptions, the two men might be surprised to know, suited Chad's purposes just fine.

"To Roger," Chad responded. "And to the new president."

As he expected, the remark induced, from Gage, a frown which he banished at once.

"Our new president," Gage answered, "has a problem. As do we."

So much for Roger Bannon. But then Gage hadn't asked Chad here so urgently, on such a day, to polish the late Chief Justice's eulogy. "I know *our* problem," Chad responded. "We just lost an election. What's Kerry's?"

"That he won by only a few thousand votes, and that *we* control the Senate." Gage sipped his drink. "Our constituent groups, including Christian conservatives, are expecting us to keep Kilcannon in check. The nomination of a new Chief Justice is our chance to lay down a marker."

Chad tasted the rich peaty burn of good scotch. "That depends," he answered, "on who Kerry picks."

"He's got his own constituencies to please. He won't be sending us anyone we like." Gage fixed his eyes on Chad's. "First Kilcannon has to go through *you*. You're the Chairman of Judiciary. You investigate his nominees. You hold the hearings. You decide whether to make things easy for him."

Chad shrugged. "I don't intend to give Kerry a pass. But I'm not going to run a witch hunt either, badgering the nominee to confess that he believes in the theory of evolution—no matter what some of these people want. It's time we noticed that they're one reason we keep losing."

"If *that* were true," Gage retorted, "we could never have passed the Protection of Life Act. Even a Democratic president was forced to sign it." He jabbed a finger for emphasis. "Without Roger Bannon, the whole Court's in the balance. Our obligation is simple—no judicial activists; no liberals on crime; no red hots for abortion." He spread his arms. "You're the first line of defense, Chad. For all we know, Kilcannon pops out a nominee tomorrow. Our people will be looking for us to read from the same page."

"Or sing from the same hymnal," Chad responded with a smile.

Gage's own smile was perfunctory, an effort to appease someone who, his manner made clear, was insufficiently serious. "Will you accept a word of advice?" Gage asked.

"From you, Mac? Always."

"There's been grumbling on our side that you're the new Chairman." Gage's voice became confiding. "Everyone respects you and wants you to do well, so

I've been able to keep it down. But some feel you're too close to Kilcannon, especially after the two of you sponsored that campaign reform bill that most folks on our side—myself included—thought would damn near put the party out of business. You've got amends to make, and this may be your chance."

The message, Chad knew, was clear enough. Once Kerry named his choice, the spotlight was on Chad—fail the test, and his chances of being the party's nominee next time would be severely damaged. It struck Chad that Gage might equally value two distinct outcomes: defeating Kilcannon's prospective Chief Justice, thereby raising Gage's stock as presidential candidate, or arranging matters so that Chad diminished his own. As usual in such circumstances, Chad viewed the challenge with serenity.

"Neither of us gets to be a hero," he retorted, "unless the President gives us an opening, and he's no fool. If he were, he'd still be over here with the rest of the buffoons."

Gage raised his eyebrows. The expression suggested that Chad's contempt for certain of his colleagues, like so many things Chad did, was ill-advised. "Kilcannon's not a fool," Gage countered. "But he's reckless."

"That's what they say about me," Chad replied affably. "And *I've* survived." He did not say the rest—that the flip side of "recklessness" was cowardice, and that its costs were stiffer.

"Look, Mac, I don't want a liberal any more than you do. Or some stealth candidate who turns out to believe only child molesters have rights. If Kerry gets confused enough to ask my advice, I'd make that clear."

Gage produced a fresh smile, to suggest—despite Chad's best instincts—that he was mollified. "Oh, he'll ask, Chad. He'll ask. You've never been as important to him as you're about to become."

Or to you, Chad thought.

In the quiet, Gage fixed him with a bright, untrusting look. At other times Chad would have been pleased to wait him out. Silence no longer bothered him: for over two years of what seemed another life, he had been forced to live, often for days—as best as Chad had been able to measure days—without the sound of a human voice. But tonight he was anxious to get home.

"Can I give *you* some advice, Mac? About the President."

Gage smiled again. "That's only fair, and I'm eager to hear it. You know him so much better."

Chad ignored the implicit jibe. "Kerry may not do what you think prudent. But he's the best intuitive politician I've ever seen, and he plays for keeps." Draining his glass, Chad finished amiably, "You've been here longer than I have. But I think this town may end up littered with the bodies of people who've underrated Kerry Kilcannon."

Gage's smile compressed. *Maybe yours,* Chad could see him thinking, *but not mine.*

Chad stood at once. "Anyhow, I've got to get home. Zip up Allie's dress."

Gage rose from his chair. "How is she? *And* Kyle."

Asking after spouses, and recalling the names of children, was another staple of the Gage persona. Probably, Chad thought, this remark was nothing more.

"Allie's fine. And Kyle's in college now, studying fashion design. If I'm any judge of dresses, she's doing well."

"Good," Gage said firmly. "That's real good."

Driving home, Chad pondered why this last exchange—superficially so meaningless—unsettled him when what went before did not.

Six

"Who *are* your parents?" Sarah asked.

The girl folded her arms, standing stiff and silent and then, as though deflated, sat down again. "My father's Martin Tierney."

She did not say more, nor did she need to. Martin Tierney was a professor of law at the University of San Francisco, a teacher of trial practice and a specialist in ethics, and, by reputation, a formidable advocate for the pro-life movement. Sarah concealed her dismay. "I know who he is," she answered. "And where he stands on choice."

"It's more than that." Mary Ann's voice was soft. "When I was twelve, he and my mother took me to a prayer vigil at San Quentin, the night they executed a man who'd raped and murdered two little girls. They believe that killing is wrong and that life is sacred, no matter who takes it or what the reason is."

"Is that what *you* believe?"

Mary Ann bit her lip. "The Church, my mom and dad, they've taught me that. Before, I just accepted it." She looked up again, voice quavering. "But what if I have *this* baby, and then after that I can never have another one. Even when I'm married."

Her eyes seemed to plead for support, a need so naked it was painful. At this girl's age, Sarah reflected, Alan and Rachel Dash had prized her intellect and encouraged her independence: just as Sarah would not be who she was without her parents, the same, for opposite reasons, was true of Mary Ann Tierney.

"What exactly *do* your parents say?" Sarah asked.

"*He* said an abortion isn't possible." The girl paused, shaking her head. "My mother just cried."

Silent, Sarah tried to sort out her emotions. "Please," the girl implored her, "I need your help."

How many times, Sarah thought, had someone in crisis sought out her supposed calm and common sense. But there was no path open to Mary Ann Tierney which did not promise further trauma, and only one thing that seemed clear—the law. There was no kindness in evading it.

"I'm sorry," Sarah told her, "but you may be too late. At least for the kind of help you're asking for."

Mary Ann's eyes misted. "What do you mean?"

"Congress just passed a law—something called the Protection of Life Act. It reads like it was written for you . . ."

"*Why?*"

"Because you're under eighteen, and by now your doctor would likely say that, in *his* medical judgment, the fetus is—or if it's normal, could be—viable outside the womb. Under the act, you need the consent of a parent before aborting a viable fetus. And even *their* consent must be based on a doctor's 'informed medical judgment' that an abortion is necessary as defined by this law." Watching Mary Ann's face contort, Sarah hesitated before continuing. "Without consent, you have to prove in court that the pregnancy poses a 'substantial medical risk' to your life or physical health. I don't think a five percent risk to future pregnancies will be enough."

Mary Ann's eyes shut. "Even if the baby has no brain?"

"The statute doesn't provide for that." Sarah struggled to stifle the irony and anger she heard in her own voice. "It's one of the things your parents get to decide about."

"But I didn't *know* until the sonogram . . ."

Her protest, plaintive and pitiful, stoked Sarah's sense of frustration. "I saw you here two weeks ago. Why didn't you come in then?"

Mary Ann's shoulders twitched. "I wanted to, but all those demonstrators scared me. One of them was our parish priest."

Mary Ann Tierney, Sarah realized, had become the plaything of Fate. Four months ago, there had been no Protection of Life Act; two weeks ago—given the stage of this pregnancy—another doctor might have questioned viability even for a normal fetus. Now Mary Ann was captive to crosscurrents she neither controlled nor understood, and Sarah shrank from adding to them. But Mary Ann *had* come here, however late, and was entitled to know what chance for her remained.

"There's one thing left," Sarah told her. "It's not clear that this law is valid."

The remark seemed slow to register. Sarah waited until Mary Ann gazed up again, looking so young that Sarah, though pained for her, felt it as a burden. "Under *Roe v. Wade*," she began, "women have the constitutional right to an abortion. But after the fetus is 'viable'—which your own doctor says it is—Congress can ban abortion unless it's necessary to protect the mother's life or health.

"No one knows exactly what that means, and no court has decided yet whether the Protection of Life Act violates a minor's right to decide, with a doctor's advice, what a 'substantial medical risk' means to *her*." Sarah paused, reluctant, then told her the rest. "If the courts find it unconstitutional, there's no law in California to stop you from deciding for yourself."

Fingers tented, Mary Ann stared at the floor, as though trying to absorb this. "It's only fair to tell you," Sarah ventured, "just how hard that would be."

Mary Ann swallowed. "You mean my parents?"

"You may have to face them—in and out of court. At this point, there's no way to conceal an abortion." Sarah's voice was firm. "If you fit within the statute, you'd theoretically be entitled to get an abortion without involving your parents in court, though there's no way afterward they wouldn't know you'd had one. But if you try to get the statute thrown out, that protection may not apply.

"And that's just the beginning. Your lawyer would file the case under a pseudonym, to try and protect your privacy. But if word gets out, the media will be all over it. The same people you saw outside would be picketing the courthouse. The pro-choice activists might try to use you as their poster girl. Because you'd be attacking an act of Congress, the Justice Department will be obligated to oppose you. And because most people believe without much thought that parental consent is good and late-term abortion is inhumane, the political pressures surrounding a challenge to the law could be enormous."

Tears sprang to the girl's eyes again. Sarah forced herself to continue. "Most of all, I worry about you. The weeks you'd spend fighting this law would feel too long, and too short. Too short because there's not that much time until you have the baby. Too long because every day could tear your family apart."

Arms folded, Mary Ann began rocking back and forth, as though her pain were physical. Without much hope, Sarah ventured, "You only need one parent. Is there any way to change your mother's mind?"

Mary Ann shook her head. "You don't understand. It would tear them apart, too."

Her voice trailed off. "Would your *doctor* help?" Sarah asked.

"No." The words were muffled. "He's my parent's friend—they *all* believe abortion is a sin. *You're* the only one who can help me."

The simple anguish in those words broke through the last of Sarah's defenses. My mother would have held you, she thought. Then she'd have found a way.

"It isn't fair," Sarah said. "I know that."

Turning away, the girl shuddered, inconsolable. "I guess court's the only hope . . ."

Sarah drew a breath. "It would be a big case, Mary Ann. I'm just an associate. I can't take any case—let alone for free—without asking the partners' permission."

The girl looked up at her. "Then *ask* them. Please."

Abruptly, Sarah realized how many of her cautions for Mary Ann also applied to herself. And, as quickly, felt a defiant surge of the ego and independence which, in a conservative and hierarchial law firm, she often struggled to suppress.

"At least," Sarah temporized, "I can make some calls. Maybe find someone else."

The girl's face closed, as if at a betrayal. "Whatever."

She was on the edge, Sarah told herself. And she was fifteen: by definition—even before this trauma—unstable, uncertain, untrustworthy, and self-involved. As Sarah remembered all too well.

"Mary Ann," she said succinctly, "we're talking about a lawsuit which could end up in the United States Supreme Court. 'Whatever' doesn't get it."

Chastened, the girl touched her eyes. "I'm sorry . . ."

Now Sarah, too, felt helpless. At length, she said, "Tell me how I can reach you."

Despairingly, the girl shook her head. "You can't. After I got pregnant, my mother took the phone out of my room."

God, Sarah thought. Slowly, she absorbed the full weight of this girl's youth and isolation, and the responsibility this could impose on Sarah. "I'm not saying I'll be your lawyer. But you can call *me* tomorrow, all right? From school."

Mary Ann faced her, tears welling again—as much, Sarah guessed, from exhaustion as from hope. Sarah wondered what would happen if she turned this girl away.

Seven

There were still times, Chad Palmer reflected, when he loved his wife so much it hurt.

She examined herself critically in the mirror of the bedroom, blond head slightly tilted. For Chad, the familiar gesture resonated with the moments of their life together, a hall of mirrors in which Allie's face appeared reflected: the wonder of new intimacy; the image he held fast to in captivity; the surprise of being restored to her again; the nearly eighteen years of evenings since when, with wry resignation, Allie Palmer had appraised the lines which, almost imperceptibly, marked the passage of time. When Chad first met her she had been pretty—pert, blue-eyed, her face lit by good humor, her body slender—but now, twenty-eight years later, he thought her beautiful. The trim figure remained; what time had brought to her face was wisdom, resolve, and, painful to Chad, a certain sadness. But when she saw his reflection watching her, a faint smile appeared.

"Why do you do that, Chad? Watch me?"

Moving closer, he kissed her on the nape of her neck. "Because you're lovely. And because you've forgotten I'm here."

"M-m-m," she said, a sound somewhere between pleased and self-critical. "If I could only forget I'm forty-six."

"Why forget?" Chad said, and moved his hands to her hips.

"Too late. The ball's in an hour, and I'm all made up. For once my hair's doing what it's supposed to."

The familiarity of this complaint made Chad smile again. "The hell with your coiffure," he said. "You're living with a man certified by *George* magazine as the decade's sexiest senator."

"That was the *last* decade. But at least you're not resting on your laurels." Turning, Allie kissed him on the cheek. "Need help with your tie?"

"As usual. I've given up on the damned thing."

Crossing the room, Allie fished a clip-on tuxedo tie from the bureau and slipped it around the collar of Chad's shirt. With great concentration, she arranged it into perfect position. This moment, too, echoed in Chad's mind: when he had returned to her, altered in body and spirit, she had accepted this with a simple kindness that belied how much, in ways they dimly understood, the two years of his captivity had changed her as well.

The woman Chad had met was eighteen, a freshman at Colorado College with no ambition other than to become a wife and mother; the man Allie had met was a senior at the Air Force Academy, the cocky product of an all-male society, whose goal was to fly the newest fighter planes as far and fast as they could go. They had fallen in love—or what Chad believed was love—and married with more optimism than insight. And for the next seven years Chad had continued to be who he was: high-spirited; prone to whiskey and, when at liberty, the seemingly endless number of women who desired him; serious only about excelling as a pilot. Then, Chad's regret had not been what the nomadic career of an air force officer had done to their marriage, but that he had missed Vietnam. Allie's weary resignation, her quiet dislike of their existence—the constant moves; Chad's nights spent drinking at the officers clubs; his casual philandering from California to Thailand—were, to him, unimportant when compared to the convenience of dropping in and out of her life.

Until he could not reach her, and only the thought of Allie kept him alive.

One night in Beirut, filled with scotch, Chad had been snatched off the street by three men speaking Arabic. His journey ended he knew not where, in darkness, a cell. For the first time—endless, minuteless hours and days—Allie was the center of his thoughts, her memory more precious than her presence had been, the hope of seeing her again all that kept him, amidst torture, from wishing to die. Though not—and this still astonished him—enough to make him tell his captors what they wished to know.

And then he was free.

When Chad Palmer came home, more in love than he had thought possible, he found a wife who did not conform to his memories.

Their daughter, Kyle, slept surrounded by his photographs. But Allie had thought him dead. Now she did not seem to need him: for two years Allie had managed her own life.

"You're not the same," she told him. "Neither am I. I'll never be that girl again."

Her distance hurt him. Finally, he said, "I don't think you missed me like I missed you."

She appraised him with a level gaze he had never seen before. "Maybe there was less to miss," she answered.

In some ways, Chad came to realize, he was more lost than he had been in prison. He had returned with a sense of seriousness unforeseeable in him, and rare in any man, to a wife transformed by his disappearance, and a daughter he did not know. The central purpose of his life—to fly—was gone: though his body healed well in time, he could no longer do certain things required to qualify as a fighter pilot. Nor did he know the man he had become by accident: a public figure hailed as a "hero" by the media, the air force, and more politicians than he had ever known existed.

Slowly, from the ashes of his career, Chad constructed a new purpose for his life. Solitude had impelled him to reach conclusions about himself, and the society in which he lived. That was a gift, and so was every day thereafter. And if he did not see himself as a "hero," he was wise enough to know that heroism had its uses and that, in politics, modesty would enhance this all the more. Both parties wanted to use him; he chose the Republicans out of a genuine congruence of beliefs. What he did not tell them, and what they learned only gradually, and to their sorrow, was that Chad was no conformist. He had learned in prison who he was.

Together, he and Allie found a way to reconstruct their marriage. They moved to northern Ohio, where Chad had grown up, and he ventured into politics. He was an image-maker's dream—plainspoken yet appealing, handsome as a film star. After, as Chad sardonically put it, "ten hard months spent proving my fitness for national leadership," he declared himself for senator, and undertook the itinerant life of a candidate for office.

If not enthused, Allie was tolerant. Perhaps it was because she now had a place of her own, and a daughter to love. Perhaps Kyle's problems, appearing in her teens, consumed her. And, Chad thought ruefully, perhaps she still loved him enough to know—and appreciate—that whatever his faults and ambitions, Chad Palmer now loved her far too much to touch another woman.

Allie finished with his tie. "There," she said. "You look handsome enough for your *own* inauguration, God help us."

Chad kissed her forehead. "And *you*," he said lightly, "look hot enough to create a scandal."

"Tonight all eyes will be on Lara. I wonder how it feels to be thirty-one, and have the *Post* calling you 'either the most beautiful about to be First Lady since Jackie Kennedy, or the most scintillating presidential girlfriend since Marilyn Monroe.'"

Chad smiled. "I don't know how *she* feels. But Kerry told me a couple of weeks ago it's like being two teenagers with two hundred seventy million parents."

Allie eyed him curiously. "Do you think he'll really marry her?"

"I don't know—Kerry's not big on revealing himself, especially to someone who may run against him four years from now. But I wonder more if *she'll* marry *him*. Sometimes I think there's stuff going on there I don't quite understand."

"Something personal? Or does she just not want the life?"

"Not sure. The life's hard, as we all know."

Allie looked up into his face. "*Will* you run next time?"

"I wanted to run *this* time, Allie. You know that. So you know what it depends on, and that you're part of it."

She placed a hand on his shoulder. "I do know, Chad. I'm sorry."

"And I understand."

After a moment, Allie turned. "Zip me?"

"Sure." The zipper was no problem, Chad thought—it was the damned eye-hook. "Is Kyle coming?" he asked.

Allie shook her head. "It was sweet of Kerry to ask—especially with all he's got on his mind. But she says she wouldn't know what to say, or who to bring."

Was there anything more crippling, Chad wondered, than lack of self-regard? Or more mysterious in origin? It would ease his conscience, he supposed, to think that Kyle was born this way. But then Chad had too seldom been there for her. Whatever the causes, the Palmers had a twenty-year-old daughter as frag-ile as she was lovely, and the lingering worry for her shadowed Allie's face as she turned to him again.

"What did Mac Gage want?" she asked.

Chad grimaced. "Supreme Court politics. The Chief's not dead three hours, and Mac's trying to position me. Either I use the committee to put the screws to Kerry's nominee—whoever he is—or Mac may try to cause me trouble."

Allie considered this. "When," she inquired, "have you ever avoided trouble?"

Once more, Chad's thoughts circled back to Kyle. "Maybe," he promised her mother, "it's not too late to learn."

Eight

"What would *you* do?" Sarah asked.

"Me? Run like a thief, of course." Turning from the stove, the Honorable Caroline Clark Masters gave her former clerk an ironic glance. "The case you're imagining is a nightmare—legally, politically, and professionally."

They sat in the open kitchen of Caroline's penthouse on Telegraph Hill, spacious and tastefully furnished, with floor-to-ceiling windows which afforded a panoramic view of the San Francisco skyline. Each detail, from the modern art and wire sculpture to the flavorful Chassagne-Montrachet the two women sipped as Caroline cooked, reflected Caroline's tastes, as elegant as the woman, and yet, like the woman, unrevealing. The one personal touch was a photograph of a beautiful young woman with olive skin who, when asked, Caroline had identified as her niece. But Caroline said little else about her: despite her relative celebrity, unusual for a jurist, Caroline remained persistently, sometimes maddeningly, elusive.

The woman herself was striking—tall, erect, graceful, with sculpted features, a long aquiline nose, wide-set brown eyes, a high forehead, and glossy black hair which began with a widow's peak. She looked and sounded like what she was, the daughter of a patrician New England family, except for a touch of the exotic—the darkness, olive skin, a somewhat sardonic smile—which suggested her mother, a French Jewish woman whose parents had died in the Holocaust. Combined with near-flawless diction and a natural air of command, her vivid looks had helped imprint her on the public mind several years before when, as a state court judge, she had presided over the televised trial of Mary Carelli, a famous television journalist accused of murder. By the time Carelli had gone free, after a trial watched by millions, Caroline was almost as well known.

To Sarah, Caroline's every step since—acceptance of a partnership in Kenyon & Walker, then a high federal judgeship—served an ultimate aim so lofty Sarah dared not mention it. Now, though the sound was low, the small television beside the stove was tuned to a replay of the Kilcannon inaugural—as much, Sarah guessed, for its sudden, startling implications for the Supreme Court as for the accession of a new president. In Sarah's mind, no ambition Caroline held could be too great: her year as Caroline's clerk had impressed on her the older woman's integrity and intellectual rigor. Were Sarah asked whom she wished to emulate, her answer would be Caroline Masters.

Why Caroline maintained their friendship seemed less clear. Yet she exhibited an older-sisterly, almost maternal, interest in Sarah's career and life. Perhaps, Sarah had concluded, it was because Caroline had no children of her own, and seemed to regard her only sibling—the niece's mother—with detachment. Whatever the reasons, Sarah was pleased to benefit.

"'Run like a thief'?" Sarah repeated. "Why? Because of the firm?"

"That's *one* reason." Caroline smiled again. "My old partners at Kenyon & Walker may snatch this poisoned cup from your lips before you take a swallow. For once I can hardly blame them. They want to be known as the West Coast's leading corporate firm, not its leading proponent of abortion rights. Any lawsuit to invalidate the Protection of Life Act would be bitter, and the issues are thorny and emotional." Caroline's tone took on its familiar combination of irony and tough-mindedness. "If you have any illusion that this is merely an open and shut case of legalizing 'infanticide,' wait until advocates for the disabled accuse you of wanting to abort fetuses just because they're unsatisfactory—by *your* standards, whatever they may be. You'd better have an answer."

The issue, Sarah realized, had not occurred to her. Taking a sip of her wine, Caroline spoke more softly. "All that I'm asking is that you ponder this with care. The people on both sides of this one, including politicians and activists, have deep convictions and very long memories. Some days I'm very glad to have never ruled on an abortion case."

Or for that matter, Sarah realized, offered her personal opinion about abortion at all—perhaps because Caroline believed that, for a judge, idle chatter about volatile topics was impolitic. And her analysis was depressingly acute: for someone with judicial ambitions, even as nascent as Sarah's, entanglement with issues as inflammatory as parental consent and late-term abortion could be as lethal as denouncing the death penalty. "I keep thinking about the clinic," she answered. "The Christian Commitment nearly shut us down. Now the pro-lifers say they're appropriating the bodies of teenage girls in their best interests, through a 'protective' new law, when what some of them really want is to punish them.

"It's hard not to respect many of the pro-lifers I meet; they're sincere, and their concerns aren't trivial. But the Christian Commitment tries to have it both ways—substantive in public, and scary at the margins. This guy who confronted Mary Ann seemed like a lot of them—marginal, a loner, and resentful of women. I'm sure it's psychosexual: they're so afraid that women will compete with them—or even, God help them, expect an orgasm during sex—that making us have babies is their last line of defense. It would be pathetic if it weren't so scary."

Caroline's faint smile quickly vanished. "It's a mistake to satirize your opponents," she admonished. "Or to be confused about what drives them. Maybe *this* man today couldn't get a prom date. But Martin Tierney is a philosopher."

"You know him?"

"I've seen him, in debates." Turning, Caroline eyed the sea bass she was preparing, and commenced to stir the sauce. "His beliefs—moral and religious—are consistent, well developed, and intellectually compelling. However much you think you've considered the issues, he's considered them more. Add the fact that he *is* this girl's father, and squaring off with him in court would *not* be easy. I know I wouldn't relish it."

It was a benign way of reminding Sarah of her own inexperience: at forty-nine, Caroline Masters had spent twenty more years in the law—beginning as a public defender—and was known as a brilliant trial lawyer. But Sarah felt pride, and stubbornness, overcome her. "In civil trials," she rejoined, "experience is overrated. What you need most is ability and preparation, to make sure the other side doesn't surprise you."

Caroline considered her, wineglass touching her lips. "Actually, I agree with you—at twenty-nine, I was defending indigents accused of rape or murder. The difference is that no one hated me for it, except the survivors. If any." Sipping her wine, Caroline finished, "The times when a judge can duck a case are few and far between. That's not true of a lawyer. For you, I think the standard should be, 'Do I, as a matter of moral choice, absolutely *have* to take this case?' "

Placing her glass on the black marble kitchen island, Sarah leaned forward on her stool, arms folded: as Caroline no doubt intended, her advice had sobered Sarah. "Let me ask you this," Sarah said at last. "Under the case law, what are the odds of winning?"

Caroline shook her head, demurring. "There's a chance, however slim, that this case will wind up in the Court of Appeals, with me on the panel. Even if there weren't, I shouldn't be giving legal advice to prospective litigants."

For the first time, Sarah felt frustrated. There were twenty-one active judges on the appellate court, with three assigned at random to any given case, making Caroline's chances of drawing an appeal one in seven. But Caroline's code, Sarah knew, did not admit exceptions.

Caroline seemed to read her disappointment. "I wish I could be more helpful," she observed gently. "But judges are the opposite of politicians: we're real people who pretend not to be. I'll very much want to know what you decide."

Turning, Caroline returned to the matter of the orange sauce. Beside her, on television, the Chief Justice of the United States was collapsing in slow motion. As if by instinct, Caroline glanced over at the screen.

"Incredible," Sarah remarked. "What was he like?"

"A superior intellect, of course." On the screen, Senator Palmer rushed to the fallen man's aid; watching, Caroline added, "Also rigid, narrow-minded, and as self-serious as a judge in a Marx Brothers comedy. And he made no secret that he despised Kerry Kilcannon. His death must have come as a crushing disappointment—especially to him."

The mordant summary was so like Caroline—a woman who disdained false sentiment—that Sarah found herself smiling. But Caroline was not. Still watching the television, she observed, "This could change the whole Court. Depending on what the President does."

"Because the Court's so divided?"

"Partly. But a new Chief Justice can be much more than just another vote." Caroline's voice assumed the tone of rumination. "Every first-year law student knows that *Brown v. Board of Education* ended legalized segregation in the public schools. But few learn that the first hearing left the Court sharply divided, with Chief Justice Vinson strongly in favor of *maintaining* segregation.

"Before the result could be announced, Vinson died of a heart attack. Earl Warren took his place. The case was reargued, and Warren went to work, using all his skills of consensus-building and persuasion. The result was the unanimous opinion which, some would say, launched the civil rights movement and forced us to confront the issue of race.

"Of course, as bitter as that was, the abortion issues *you're* raising are nearly as divisive, and public life is infinitely more vicious. I don't envy Kilcannon the problem."

"Do you know him?"

"The President? Not personally. My loss, clearly."

Elliptical as it was, this was the closest Caroline had come to admitting the ambition Sarah believed she held. Emboldened, Sarah observed, "But you *do* know Ellen Penn."

"Yes. And I already owe the new Vice President my *current* job." Turning, Caroline fixed Sarah with an enigmatic gaze. "Please, Sarah, don't even *think* about it."

After a moment, Sarah smiled. "I'll censor my thoughts, Caroline. But a girl can dream, can't she?"

Nine

At a little past one-thirty in the morning, Kerry Kilcannon and Lara Costello entered the President's darkened sitting room. Before this moment, she had never been upstairs.

Elsewhere in the White House, Kerry had informed her, were fifty or so people—staff, the Secret Service—who knew where they were. "So now you've seen it," Kerry said. "My new home. The crown jewel of the federal penitentiary system."

Smiling, Lara looked around her, sharing his sense of awe and strangeness. The room was carefully appointed in antiques. At one side was a small plaque left by Jacqueline Kennedy, saying: *This room was occupied by John Fitzgerald Kennedy during the two years, ten months, and two days he was President of the United States. January 20, 1961–November 22, 1963.*

The glossy magazines compared her to Jackie. And it was all so unreal. Lara was no aristocrat: her father, an alcoholic Irishman, had abandoned his family when Lara was eight; her Latina mother had supported Lara and her sisters by cleaning other people's homes; until two years before, when NBC had lured her from the *New York Times,* it had been a struggle to help her mother and pay off her sisters' student loans. And she and Kerry were not married.

Yet here she was at the White House, wearing a stunning Gianfranco Ferre gown, in the President's private quarters.

Hands in his pockets, Kerry stood at the window, watching a light snow fall on the grounds below. Lara touched his elbow. "Hard to believe, isn't it."

Kerry did not answer, and did not need to. He had traveled a path even longer than Lara's: an abusive father; a difficult childhood; his adult self-image as the smaller, less gifted brother of James Kilcannon—a freshly minted Irish-American prince who, until his assassination, had been a senator from New Jersey. At thirty, his brother's accidental successor, Kerry was forced to find his own way. Few, then, had imagined him as President; Kerry never had.

Lara took his hand, watching his face in profile. Lean and fine-featured, every aspect of it was dear to her now, especially the eyes—their green-flecked blue irises were larger than most, giving a sense of deep intuition, of secrets withheld.

"How long," she asked, "before I turn into a pumpkin?"

"Oh, Clayton's commissioned a poll on that. In California, you get to sleep here. But sixty-eight percent of Alabamans want you to leave right now."

"California made you President," Lara retorted. "The citizens of Alabama didn't even want you sleeping here alone."

Kerry's smile was rueful. "True enough. But we've learned about the problems, and long ago."

With their reluctant acquiescence, Clayton Slade had designed rules for the President and his lover: Lara and Kerry must be engaged; she could not preside at White House dinner parties or otherwise presume to act as First Lady; though she had strongly held political views, anything she felt must be said to Kerry in private. And rule number one—Lara could not sleep over. Tonight, of all nights, the White House staff would be careful to log her out.

To others, their reasons might seem obvious. The White House held a special place in the American mind, and the President remained a figure of awe. It would not do, in these merciless times, for Kerry and Lara to seem arrogant or cavalier: from the *Post* to the slick women's magazines, the press was avid for details of their relationship. And if the forces who despised Kerry could find no other way to tarnish him, Lara would do nicely.

This was more than enough. But there was also a deeper reason, dating back several years, a secret which made the rules compulsory: that Lara, then a *New York Times* reporter, had fallen in love with a senator trapped in an emotionless, childless marriage. Kerry was prepared to leave his wife for Lara; loving him, she did not wish to harm his chance of becoming President. When she had become pregnant, Lara, against his wishes, had arranged an abortion and accepted a posting abroad.

Two years of separation—punctuated by Kerry's divorce—had followed, and then, still deeply in love, they came together again. For several months preceding Kerry's election, the media and his political enemies had dogged their present and investigated their past. Though pro-choice as a matter of public policy, Kerry was, like Lara, Roman Catholic: that Kerry had pled with her to keep the child made his feelings about abortion more conflicted, their private history—potentially fatal to his candidacy—more painful and ambiguous. By concealing their affair and her abortion, Lara had freed him to become President, and committed them to do nothing to inspire further inquiry, or to hurt each other still more.

So tonight they had an hour or so. Not enough time to resolve what divided them: his desire to have children as soon as possible; her lingering unease about life as First Lady and the threat posed by their past; their resulting inability to agree on the White House wedding Kerry's media consultant was so desperate for. Just time enough to make love.

"Do you ever miss how we were?" she asked. "Before?"

He cocked his head, a characteristic gesture. "The privacy, you mean."

"Yes. All we cared about was each other. And not getting caught."

Kerry shook his head. "The world of an affair is like that. But we both know better than to call it real life."

Lara touched his face. "And this will be?" she asked gently.

"It's become *my* real life. Only it's like no one else's." His smile, Lara saw, masked worry. "You're not bailing out *already*, are you? I can see the headlines: 'President Sworn In, Shafted.'"

She returned his smile. "No," she answered. "I don't want anyone else. And I always believed you should be President."

"So marry me."

Lightly, Lara kissed him. "Do you think," she inquired, "I could see the bedroom first?"

Afterward, he held her, warm and silent in the dark.

His stillness, so familiar to her, was one of deep thought. As if to acknowledge this, Kerry said quietly, "I was thinking about all I have to do now. About Roger Bannon, really."

This, too, was familiar. Death haunted him, and its randomness was a living presence in his mind. This was more, Lara was certain, than the dark and light of the Irish—it was the legacy of James Kilcannon.

"What about Bannon?" she asked. "That he didn't want you here?"

"That he should have retired before he wore himself out. And that his death was so pointless. Because I *am* here, and the last thing I'll do is put another Roger Bannon on the Court."

"Who *will* you appoint, Kerry? Any ideas?"

"None of my own. But Ellen Penn was whispering in my ear."

"So *that,*" Lara replied, "is why she cut in when we were dancing. I wondered why she'd run the risk."

The remark, as Lara intended, lightened his mood. "It's the new political dilemma," he agreed. "Presidents dancing with vice presidents. Do I lead? Does she follow? Does that make me a chauvinist, and Ellen too vice presidential? She finally decided the hell with it."

Lara's reporter's reflexes might be rusty, but her political sense was still acute. "She must want you to appoint a woman."

She felt Kerry smile at her prescience. "Not just any woman," he amended. "A very particular woman."

PART II

The Nomination

One

"Caroline Masters," Ellen Penn urged Kerry, "is perfect."

She sat beside Clayton in the Oval Office, facing Kerry's desk. If nothing else, Kerry reflected, this meeting would reveal how well his Vice President and Chief of Staff might coexist. In looks and manner they were opposites—Ellen small, bright-eyed, and intense; Clayton bulky, calm, and practical—and their relations were, at best, edgy. Clayton had not favored her selection: intensely loyal to Kerry, he saw Ellen as far too independent, a Roman candle of feminist enthusiasms. Even worse, Kerry suspected with some amusement, Clayton worried that her passions might skew Kerry's judgment: one of his earthbound friend's postinaugural missions was to save Kerry from his own worst impulses.

Part of this, Kerry knew, was born of a friendship so intimate that they could read the other's thoughts. Years ago, Clayton had schooled Kerry in trial tactics; Kerry was godfather to Clayton's twin daughters; Clayton had managed each of Kerry's campaigns—two for the Senate, one for President. Only Clayton knew the truth about Kerry and Lara.

But, Kerry cautioned himself, Clayton's motives were neither simple nor selfless. It was clear he wanted to become the first black Attorney General; after that, Kerry surmised, Clayton aspired to his own spot on the Court. These ambitions depended on Kerry's own success: a failed nomination, brokered by Ellen Penn, would not serve Clayton's interests.

Watching Clayton at the corner of his eye, Kerry spoke to Ellen. "I remember the Carelli case," he said of Caroline Masters. "She handled it well. But 'perfect'?"

"Perfect," Ellen repeated. "You owe California; you owe women. And there's never been a woman Chief before.

"*This* is the woman. She's young, telegenic, and articulate. She's a great witness for herself—four years ago, when she was nominated for the Court of

Appeals, she breezed through the Judiciary Committee on a unanimous vote. Chad Palmer and Macdonald Gage *both* voted to confirm her. What are they going to say *now*—that a woman shouldn't be Chief Justice?

"They'd hardly dare. The Republicans' stand on abortion has repelled women by the truckload. That's why we won, and they lost." Ellen snapped forward in her chair, as if impelled by the force of her own argument. "Chad Palmer knows that, and he also wants your job. Gage wants it, too. You could use a Masters nomination to divide them."

"Why the rush?" Clayton interjected. "This is the most important appointment a president can make."

Ellen did not turn to him. "The Court's deadlocked," she said to Kerry. "That argues for a new Chief ASAP, and creates more pressure on Gage and Palmer to get out of the way. And with Caroline, they've got no weapons. The FBI and Justice vetted her for the appellate court and came up without a negative—no controversial political associations, no drug use, no personal problems of any kind.

"But she's got one more big advantage, at least in the current environment." Turning at last to Clayton, she granted him a smile of benign sweetness. "She has no record on abortion: no articles, cases, or public statements. There's nothing Gage can pin on her."

Seeing Clayton's look of bemusement, Kerry asked, "What is she, Ellen— the Manchurian candidate? I almost believe you about the drug use. For that matter, maybe she's a vestal virgin. But how does a forty-nine-year-old woman have 'no record' on abortion? And what does that say about her?"

Stung, Ellen faced him. "She's not a cipher, Mr. President. She's progressive on the environment, affirmative action, labor issues, and First Amendment rights. But even where she was out of step with Bannon, the Supreme Court never reversed her. And she's called for liberalizing adoption procedures to help minority children find homes. How can the Republicans complain about *that*?"

Kerry gazed at her, then at his desk, lit by a square of winter sunlight. "I want the best, Ellen. Not just the most confirmable. Or even the most congenial to the people who put me here.

"Caroline Masters, if I chose her, could still be Chief when all of us are dead. And her impact on the lives of ordinary people would last far longer than that. I don't want some bloodless technician, even if she turns out to be the darling of legal scholars across America. I want a terrific lawyer who also gives a damn about the world outside her courtroom.

"Maybe she's both. But I need to know much more than what you've told me."

"For example," Clayton followed at once, "how do you know that she's even pro-choice? The last thing we need *there* is a surprise."

The Vice President folded her arms. "She's pro-choice, Clayton. Trust me."

"Did you ever ask her?"

"I don't need to. She's an independent woman, a Democrat, and a feminist. Nothing about her suggests that she'll try to repeal *Roe v. Wade,* or start ordering women to have children they don't want."

Clayton gave her a pensive look. "Does *she* have children?"

"No. But neither does the President, I might point out."

Kerry examined the square of sun again. Evenly, Clayton answered, "That doesn't make it a plus, as the President would be the first to agree. What about marriages?"

"None."

"Then how do you know she's not a lesbian? Mac Gage and his friends have an unwholesome curiosity about things like that."

Kerry looked up at Ellen. Tight-lipped, the Vice President answered, "She keeps her private life private. But I've known her for almost twenty years, since I was a San Francisco supervisor. There's never been a whisper of anything like that." Facing Kerry, she added, "Maybe she's got no children of her own. But her position on adoption speaks to family values."

Ellen was sounding defensive, Kerry knew. Perhaps Clayton and he had pressed her hard enough; she clearly believed in Caroline Masters, and wanted to put her imprint on a new administration. And it could not be easy to subordinate her views to a man who had been her younger colleague in the Senate, and whose election she had helped ensure.

"I'll put Judge Masters in the mix," he told her. "Please make sure the White House counsel's office has everything you've got."

While gracious, this was also a dismissal. Ellen hesitated, then stood. Clayton did not; Kerry watched Ellen register a reality of power—that Clayton Slade would always be the person left alone with Kerry Kilcannon, and no one else would know what passed between them unless Kerry or Clayton wished them to.

"Thank you, Mr. President," she said, and left.

Clayton stood, arms folded. "You weren't just humoring her."

"No."

Clayton glanced back at the door, to make sure that it was closed. "I don't trust her judgment."

Kerry raised his eyebrows. "If she had better 'judgment,' Clayton, she'd have supported Dick Mason for the nomination when he was thirty points up in the polls. Or maybe it's just that we *both* have judgment that is better than you think."

With a faint smile, Clayton considered his friend. "Sometimes."

"So what is it you don't like?"

"This woman's life. You're right about *that* part—it's too sterile. I grant you it's harder for a woman with a family to have gotten this far this young. But, whatever her reasons, she *is* single, and childless."

"So am I." Kerry's voice was soft. "A liability, as you were kind enough to point out."

Clayton met his gaze, unblinking—sustained, Kerry knew, by a friendship tested by time and circumstance. "So why compound it? The same folks who wonder if she's gay will wonder if you're fucking her."

"Now *there's* an option I hadn't considered." Propping his head in his palm, Kerry leaned against the armrest of his chair. "I got three hours sleep last night. So why don't we cut to the merits."

"She's clearly qualified," Clayton answered promptly. "Women's groups like her—the defense in the Carelli case was self-defense against attempted rape, and Masters allowed it. And she could lead the Court away from the judicial grave-yard where Bannon parked it.

"But that's the long view. First we have to get her past Macdonald Gage, who's looking for an opening, and maybe Palmer. It doesn't matter how they voted before—the august duty of the Senate to approve your nominees is never more sacred than for a new Chief. Or more critical to the people who'll help decide whether Gage or Palmer is their choice to run you out of here. That's a lot riding on a woman you know almost nothing about."

"Then find out about her. Soon." Kerry stood. "I'd like to skip the usual vapid Kabuki theater, where we trot in all our interest groups to tell us who to pick, then leak a virtual rainbow coalition of prospective chiefs. We can just say *this* one's the best, period. Whoever it is."

"We'll look naive. Like Jimmy Carter."

"We'll look principled. If people weren't so sick of calculating pols, Dick Mason would be sitting here with his finger in the wind." Smiling, Kerry added, "The more refined calculations appear not to be that at all. Besides, we'd take Mac Gage and his reactionary playmates completely by surprise. That *will* give them something to think about."

. . .

Clayton considered Kerry across the desk.

No, he amended, Kerry was not naive. He was a rare combination of principle with an instinctive, but quite sophisticated, sense of how his principles played out in the world of politics. And a sometimes cold-eyed way of getting where he wanted to go.

"We'll be all right," Kerry said mildly. "Between the two of us, Clayton, we make at least one adequate human being. Maybe even a president."

The comment was at once wry, affectionate, and, if Clayton needed it, a subtle reminder of who occupied this office. Smiling, he answered, "I'll take this on myself, Mr. President."

Two

The head of the firm's pro bono committee gave Sarah a wide-eyed look which combined fascination, amusement, and incredulity.

"We're talking angry clients," Scott Votek said. "Pissed off parents. Picket lines full of Bible thumpers. Rotten publicity. Security problems. In a firm where too many partners still think that 'dead white male' means 'role model.'"

Though disheartening, Votek's list of consequences was not surprising, nor was his satiric tag line. Along with his bright shirts, wire-rim glasses, and ginger beard, Votek cultivated the image of an iconoclast, with a subversive devotion to liberal causes. In the culture of the firm, Sarah counted him a friend, professionally and personally; he was one of the few people to whom she had turned when, a few weeks before, she had broken off her engagement to her boyfriend of three years.

"Sarah," he said flatly. "This case will eat you up."

"What about Mary Ann Tierney?"

"Believe me, I *know*. The Protection of Life Act is bullshit: I'd love to see us take this on—*us*, of all firms." Briefly, he smiled at the thought. "The old guys couldn't show their faces at the Bohemian Club."

"I can live with that, Scott."

"Can you?" Votek exhaled, folding his hands in his lap. "Things are better now, I'll admit, and a fair number of women are junior partners. But it's their elders who can still make you their partner—or blackball you. All it takes is one."

Sarah gazed at Votek's Bokara rug. "Can they still do that?" she asked. "They have to get along with all the other partners, the ones who help decide *their* candidates. In nuclear terms, it's like 'mutual assured destruction.'"

Votek shook his head. "Don't overrate yourself. And I mean that in the kindest possible way. Even Caroline Masters—the only woman superstar we've ever had—didn't find her life here easy."

"She survived, didn't she?"

"She came *in* as a partner, and a celebrity. No one was going to run her out. For her it was a way station—a couple of years with the Establishment, making contacts and rounding out her résumé. And about all she could take." Jerking loose his tie, Votek warmed to his speech. "You've got some real advocates here—me included. But we can't help it if certain other people don't want you. Instead of saying you're 'too political,' they'll use code words. Like 'judgment.'

" 'Abortion lawyers' can take this case, they'll say. It's 'bad judgment' for *you* to want it, and 'bad' for the firm. And if somehow we do take it, and things go south . . ." Votek's tone grew crisp. "The old guys won't try to fire you—that's way too blatant. They'll reach an agreement over lunch in some all-male club: work your ass off for another three years, then pass you over for partner. Because you've got 'bad judgment.' "

If Votek wanted to make her paranoid, he was succeeding—as a woman in a firm still run by men; an associate where partners met in private; a Jew whose parents harbored memories of exclusion. She could not know how matters were decided. "Scott," she said at last, "I'm asking for your help. If you agree with me on the merits, maybe we can do this one together."

Votek tented his fingers, appraising them in an attitude of prayer. "There are other considerations," he answered. "I've always been open about the things we both want here. So you know that our chairman looks upon pro bono as an obligation, not a joy.

"We've been able to do good work because we've stayed below the radar screen—no public controversies, or massive commitments of free time." Looking up, Votek leaned forward on his desk and gazed directly into Sarah's eyes. "They don't like what's happening at the women's clinic, and the Christian Commitment keeps upping the ante. So far I've been able to protect us. But I can't cover for you on this."

Sarah made herself stare back. " 'Can't,' Scott? Or 'won't'?"

A first, faint flush appeared on Votek's cheeks. Watching, Sarah felt comprehension dawn: much of what Scott said about Sarah applied to him. The indulgence of his partners offered him an enviable life: $600,000 a year; treks in Nepal; an ecologically designed vacation house near Tahoe; a collection of Haitian art and costly African masks; an avocation bringing lawsuits for the Sierra Club, protecting wetlands, and limiting ski resorts. And, in return, he personified for Kenyon & Walker its commitment to the public good. Concepts like "infanticide" threatened to upset the balance.

"Sarah," he said firmly, "this one's for the chairman. Assuming you care to go that far."

"What does that mean?"

"You'd have to write a memo laying out the case law, the issues, the witnesses, this girl's family background, and—most important—why *this* firm should take *this* case. I'd advise you to think very hard about *all* those things before you decide to turn it in. Or even spend the time."

Sarah folded her arms. "There *isn't* much time. 'This girl' gets more pregnant every day."

Votek stood. "All the more reason, Sarah, to send her somewhere else. What's good for you is also good for her."

Sarah was staring out the window when her phone rang.

"Sarah? It's me—Mary Ann. What did you decide?"

The rush of words sounded like banked anxiety. "Where are you calling from?" Sarah asked.

"A pay phone."

Mary Ann's voice sounded tight and small. Once more, Sarah was struck by the girl's isolation, then by the fact that, she, too, had entered the surreptitious world of a teenager. "There's a problem," Sarah temporized. "I don't have an answer yet."

"When *will* you know . . . ?"

She was at the end of her resources, Sarah guessed. Then another truth became brutally clear—there was no way Mary Ann Tierney had the time, freedom, or resilience to keep going by herself.

"Call me again tomorrow," Sarah answered. Then, hearing herself, she added without thinking, "Please—don't give up."

Three

"Caroline Masters," Kerry said. "What have we got?"

He sat in the Oval Office with Clayton Slade and Adam Shaw, Kerry's White House Counsel. Lean, graying, and impeccably dressed, Adam epitomized the Washington lawyer with broad contacts in and out of government, and his sense of Caroline would carry weight.

"A lot," Adam responded. "She's among the judges the prior administration kept a rolling file on, in case there was an opening. And the materials from her confirmation for the Court of Appeals fill a drawer: tax returns, financial records, medical data, transcripts of testimony, letters of support.

"Last time out, she had strong endorsements from women, labor, environmental groups, minorities, the trial lawyers—the core of your support. There's nothing in her decisions since to change that. And the opinions themselves are carefully crafted, beautifully written, and sound—progressive, but not radical."

"What about Frederico Carreras," Clayton interjected, "from the Second Circuit? We all know him—he's Hispanic, a scholar, and a moderate Republican." Facing Kerry, he added, "Masters is sounding like a classic liberal, and her personal life—or lack of it—will put Mac Gage on alert.

"There are two ways to get a justice through the Senate: fifty-one to forty-nine, or one hundred to zip. Why risk political capital on Masters when a Carreras breezes through."

"Because Carreras may not be with us long." Kerry turned to Adam Shaw. "Didn't he just have an operation?"

Adam nodded. "Throat cancer. He's a smoker. His friends say the doctors got it all. But why risk a new Chief dying on you? Besides," Shaw added dryly, "it would send the wrong message to our young people."

"Any argument about that, Clayton?"

"No. But at least let's get Carreras's medical records before we write him off."

"There's another reason," Kerry answered. "On some issues I don't *want* 'moderation'—guns, for example. Now that they've collected billions from suing tobacco companies, our pals the trial lawyers are after the gun manufacturers. I know that some of these corporate ambulance chasers are as greedy as the people they sue. But my point of view's Darwinian: if they run the gun industry out of existence, it's a victory for our species. I don't want my new Chief Justice getting in their way."

The blunt assessment brought a smile to Shaw's lips. "There's no way to be sure, Mr. President. But if permitting suits against the merchants of death is one of the criteria, I'd pick Masters over Carreras. Unless he's truly bitter at Joe Camel."

"*I* would be," Kerry said softly, "but you know how vindictive I am. I'm the kind of person who remembers that the gun lobby spent over three million dollars trying to defeat me." *Not to mention,* he did not add, *how my brother died.*

Clayton shifted in his chair. "That's fine in this room," he said with equal quiet. "But not for the Court. The longer I'm in politics, the more I'm struck by the importance of personality. This Court needs a consensus-builder, like Carreras. Masters is the wrong look for Chief—liberal, single, an outsider to the Court."

Kerry turned to Adam Shaw. "How about her written decisions? Does she draw a lot of dissents?"

"Relatively few. Even though the Ninth Circuit, where Masters sits, is sharply divided between liberals and conservatives."

"That suggests she has *some* social skills," Kerry said wryly. "At least for a woman without a life."

"Oh, she's had a life," Adam responded. "Her mother died in a car wreck when she was twelve—drove off a cliff. Her father was a state court judge in New Hampshire and, it seems, a bit of an autocrat. It appears they were estranged: in her early twenties, Masters moved to California and put herself through law school. And never came back."

Kerry considered this. "We all have our fathers, I suppose. I assume the last administration checked all that out."

"Of course. And found no problems."

"I would hope not," Clayton interjected. "If you want to consider her, Mr. President, why not as an associate justice. You can elevate someone who's been there for a while, like Justice Chilton. He knows the other justices, and *we* know he's on our side."

"He's also constipated," Kerry shot back. "Have you ever talked to him, Clayton? It's the nearest thing to eternity you'll experience on earth, and he's got the soul of an actuary. He's part of the *problem* over there." Kerry's voice turned wry again. "You must really be worried to float Chilton. You think I'm falling in love with the idea of a woman Chief."

"Are you?"

"Not yet. And I'm far from committed to Caroline Masters—two days ago, I barely recalled that she existed. But making a woman Chief Justice would send an important message: women still have a ways to go, and I'm determined to get them there. Let Gage chew on that awhile."

Turning to Adam Shaw, Kerry said, "I want Masters back here for a meeting—Clayton, Ellen Penn, and you. No one else. No leaks. Your office gets up everything you need. Then you grill her until there's nothing left to know.

"If your meeting with Masters goes well enough, I may want to see her."

Clayton's brow furrowed. "Seeing her," he interjected, "is tantamount to selecting her. We'd be accelerating the whole process."

"That's why we need secrecy." Kerry paused for emphasis. "I want to find out if Masters has got it, and I don't want Gage to know about it. Or anyone."

Clayton stood. "I'll call her myself, Mr. President."

"It's *Iowa,* Aunt Caroline." Even over the telephone, Caroline could imagine Brett Allen pulling a face. "It's flat, and it's cold."

"New Hampshire's cold," Caroline retorted. "You've been flash frozen your entire life. That's why I wanted you to apply to the creative writing program at Stanford, where they have palm trees."

"It would have been nice," Brett agreed. "And I could have seen you more. But the program here is the absolute best."

"Anything for art, I suppose. That short story you sent me was superb."

"Really?"

"Yes. I've satisfied my appetite for stories where some deracinated male crawls out of bed, brushes his teeth, spends five pages deciding whether to leave his apartment, then doesn't. You're the literary hope of your generation, Brett."

The young woman laughed. "And you're biased, Aunt Caroline."

Caroline smiled to herself. "I hope so," she answered, and then her gray-haired assistant cracked open the door.

"I'm sorry, Judge Masters. But there's a call on line two. From the White House, he says."

Surprised, Caroline stared at Helen, then said hastily to Brett, "Hang on, okay?" Of Helen, she asked dryly, "And who might 'he' be? Surely not President Kilcannon yet again."

Helen shook her head in apparent awe. "Clayton Slade. The President's Chief of Staff."

Caroline felt the first pinpricks of nervousness. "I'd better take this," she apologized to Brett. "Can I call you right back?"

"Sure. I'll be here until four, your time."

"It'll be sooner," Caroline answered, and said good-bye. Looking back to Helen, she directed quietly, "Please close the door behind you."

For a few seconds, Caroline gathered her thoughts. Then she pushed the flashing light on her telephone, drew a breath, and said, "Mr. Slade? This is Caroline Masters."

"Good afternoon, Judge Masters." Though amiable, Clayton's tone was formal. "I'm sorry to interrupt you."

"Not at all," she answered. "When you called, I wasn't dictating the Ten Commandments. Just exchanging gossip with my niece."

This produced a perfunctory chuckle. "In any event," Clayton said bluntly, "your name came up this afternoon. The President would like to know if you're willing to be considered for a seat on the Supreme Court."

Caroline closed her eyes. It was the moment she had hoped for, and feared. And far more astonishing in the event than in the imagining. "As an associate justice?" she managed to ask.

"No, Judge Masters. As Chief."

Caroline gathered herself. "In either case," she answered, "please tell the President that I'd be honored. And that I'm grateful for the compliment implied."

"I'll tell him that. What he hopes is that you'll come to Washington as soon as possible. You'll be meeting with the Vice President, the White House Counsel, and me."

Ellen Penn had done this, Caroline realized. And it was serious.

Standing, she began to pace. "Is three days soon enough?" she asked.

Placing down the phone, Caroline sat, inert. A half hour passed before she recalled that Brett, who consumed her thoughts, was waiting for her call.

Four

"I've read your memo," John Nolan told Sarah, "but I'd like to hear it from you. Given that you want our firm to challenge the Protection of Life Act."

The chairman of Kenyon & Walker was a man of carefully calibrated reactions. His deep voice was typically emotionless; his saturnine mien—black eyes, dark hair, broad face—had a mandarin indecipherability. The result was that the smallest note of sarcasm, a hardening of the eyes, could be as intimidating as someone else's rages. Nolan was a big man, with a reputation built on a devastating skill at cross-examination and an utter lack of sentiment; sitting next to Sarah, Scott Votek seemed diminished, a witness rather than a participant.

"To start," Sarah answered, "it won't take that much time. It can't."

Nolan's eyebrows shot up. "Unless you go to the Supreme Court."

A faint sardonic undertone reminded her of what she dared suggest. But Sarah had prepared herself: she had spent the night in Kenyon & Walker's library, parsing the statute; reviewing the procedural rules for the three federal levels—the District Court, the Ninth Circuit Court of Appeals, and the Supreme Court; reading every relevant case on abortion and parental consent. "Even then," Sarah answered, "the statute requires a District Court ruling within ten days. An emergency appeal should take about three weeks. Ditto the Supreme Court."

"And Miss Tierney is already five and a half months pregnant. By the time you're through, her fetus is seven and a half months old, at a minimum." Nolan's tone was flavored with distaste. "That makes your position rather unattractive, doesn't it."

A sense of unreality hit Sarah hard: they were sitting in Nolan's corner office, with its panoramic view of the San Francisco Bay, talking about a pregnant girl with Olympian detachment. It helped transform her nervousness to passion.

"No," she retorted. "It demonstrates how cynical this statute is in theory, and how cruel in practice. Congress takes a girl with sound medical and emotional reasons to abort, and makes those problems two months worse—because the courts are 'protecting' her from herself. The plain effect is to make underage girls have babies, and to place them at more risk.

"Among the risks in this case is that Mary Ann Tierney will have a hideously defective child, and never have another. I don't think that's right, do you?"

A small frown dismissed this question as too emotive. "What's 'right' may seem clear to you. But some of my partners believe that Congress can, and *should*, limit a fifteen-year-old's ability to abort a viable fetus simply because *she* considers the consequences of her own sexual conduct—pregnancy—distressing.

"Nor do they think it's 'right' to finance a lawsuit which offends their own beliefs just because a fifth-year associate wants them to. Especially when pro-abortion activists would be pleased to take your place."

To Sarah, Nolan's speech was more devastating for its absence of inflection. She felt her own voice rise. "This girl is living with two pro-life parents. I don't think she can hold out if we send her somewhere else."

Nolan raised his head, as though to scrutinize her from greater heights. "In that case, how would you answer the charge of improper influence—that this is *your* lawsuit, not hers? And that you've separated an impressionable girl from a loving family to serve your own political agenda."

This was meant to silence her, Sarah knew. "The way you would with any minor," she came back. "First, I'd ask the court to appoint a *guardian ad litem* to speak for her best interests—"

"A counselor from the women's clinic?" Nolan interjected. "From your memo, she doesn't appear to have some favorite pro-choice aunt."

Sarah ignored this. "Second," she persisted, "I'd engage a psychologist who specializes in adolescents, to testify that Mary Ann understands what she is asking the court to do, and that she believes it's best for her.

"Third, we hire an independent expert—an ob-gyn—to confirm that the medical risks of carrying this fetus to term are real, and that Mary Ann hasn't exaggerated them as an excuse to end an unwanted pregnancy.

"Fourth, we have Mary Ann sign a client consent form which sets out how she met me, the reasons for her desire to terminate, and that she has asked us to bring the suit." Pausing, Sarah softened her voice. "I'm not proposing that we let a teenage girl delude us, or open ourselves to charges of 'improper influence.' Or to let anyone use that as an excuse."

For the first time, Nolan looked nettled—as much by her readiness to answer, Sarah thought, as by her implicit challenge. "One of the reasons I came to Kenyon & Walker," she said evenly, "is that we do pro bono work. If we put other pro bono cases up for a vote, some of the partners wouldn't like *them,* either." Briefly, she inclined her head toward Votek. "I'm sure *Scott* doesn't like it when we represent polluters against the EPA, for money. But we do it—because it's profitable, and because even polluters have a right to representation.

"Whether one agrees with Mary Ann or not, as a principle of our profession even a teenager has the right to challenge a law. That she's so powerless makes the principle more compelling."

"I know something about principles." Nolan placed both palms flat on his black walnut desk, head jutting forward like a prow. "If our commitment to pro bono weren't real, Sarah, you wouldn't have spent so many hours at it. That work is financed by the same partners who have principled reservations about *your* principles—as well as those who, foreign as it may seem, think they have the 'right' to keep you from offending clients."

"The partners who believe in the Protection of Life Act," Sarah retorted, "will be adequately represented by the United States Department of Justice. And the ones who worry about offending clients should ask themselves, 'Which clients?'"

Nolan's gaze became a stare. "What do you mean?"

Sarah hesitated, preparing herself. In the respectful tone of a subordinate, she said, "I'm concerned about clients, too. So I asked Pat Kleiner and some of the other women partners what the effect would be of turning down this case . . ."

"How would *that* get out?"

Sarah shrugged. "Who knows? But the *American Lawyer* has been all over us since we supposedly fired a female associate for an affair with a married partner. Two weeks ago—when they pointed out that we're the only firm in San Francisco still paying for its partners' memberships in clubs that exclude women— they brought that story up again. That makes us vulnerable to more bad publicity, and to questions from some of our clients."

Beside her, Scott Votek shifted in his chair. It was a reminder, if Sarah needed it, of the risks she was running. "What clients," Nolan asked, "do you suppose would care?"

"Our three biggest clients in Silicon Valley have politically active women as General Counsel. According to Pat, in the last year those three women sent us intellectual property and securities fraud cases generating twenty-six million in fees. I worked closely with the General Counsel of Worldscope on two of those cases, and she's deeply involved with pro-choice issues."

Nolan had erased all expression from his face; only his eyes, dark and unblinking, betrayed displeasure. At length he said, "Let's go through the basis for your challenge."

"It rests on the right to privacy," Sarah said promptly. "*Roe v. Wade* extended that right to include a woman's right to choose. But the Supreme Court's 1992 decision in *Casey* also made it clear that Congress can limit abortion after 'viability' *unless* it is necessary to protect the life or health of the mother. In 2000, the Court reaffirmed that decision in *Stenberg v. Carhart.*"

Pausing, Sarah saw that Nolan listened keenly. "The big controversy," she continued, "is whether 'health' includes *mental* health. A companion case to *Roe, Doe v. Bolton,* suggests it does. But pro-life advocates argue that this would legalize abortion on demand right up to the event of birth—that 'mental health' is simply an excuse."

Sarah sat back. "That's at the heart of Mary Ann Tierney's dilemma. The Supreme Court has never clearly resolved whether 'health' includes threats to *mental health*—such as forcing a fifteen-year-old girl to have a baby without a brain. Or even whether *physical health* includes a small but measurable chance of not having further children."

Nolan raised his eyebrows. "What about all the cases on 'partial birth' abortion? Don't *they* affect this?"

Sarah shook her head. "In *Stenberg v. Carhart,* Nebraska tried to ban a specific procedure it called 'partial birth abortion.' The Supreme Court overturned the law because it applied to both pre- and postviability procedures; because the particular procedure outlawed was too vaguely defined; and because it provided no exception for the mother's health. The Protection of Life Act is Congress's first attempt to get around *Carhart.*

"Until now, no statute has given a parent the right to flat-out prevent a minor's abortion by any technique, even after viability, unless there's a narrowly defined medical emergency which expressly *excludes* emotional damage *or* fetal defects—no matter how severe. That's what this statute does: past viability, a court can permit abortion *only* if a continuation of the pregnancy is 'likely' to cause the mother's death, or to 'greatly impair her *physical* health.'

"Any doctor who now performs an abortion on Mary Ann Tierney without the consent of a parent, or permission of a court, faces two years in prison and the loss of his right to practice medicine. That means this girl is stuck." Despite her sleeplessness, Sarah felt a renewed energy. "What I believe," she finished, "is that it violates Mary Ann's right of choice for a parent *or* Congress to force her to have *this* child under *these* circumstances. That's the case I want our firm to bring."

Nolan frowned. "That's very different than suing a landlord who denies hot running water to an indigent old woman."

"I agree," Sarah answered. "It's also more important to more women. Starting with Mary Ann Tierney, and including some of our clients."

Nolan placed a pen to his lips, appraising her in silence. Meeting his gaze, she forced herself to wait him out—this, too, was a test which many others had failed.

"Where would you find the obstetrician?" he finally asked. "And the psychiatrist?"

"The University of California at San Francisco," Sarah responded. "According to the pro-choice groups I talked to, some of the country's top specialists are here, who've served as expert witnesses in other abortion cases. I'm sure I could reach them within a couple of days."

Once more, the swiftness of her response seemed to give Nolan pause. "You're authorized to go that far," he said at last. "And no farther. After that I'll consider whether to trouble our Executive Committee with this. But I'll tell you something right now—they might let pro-choice groups help write your briefs and round up your witnesses. But they will *never* let our firm take them on as co-counsel."

He was giving her time and reason to back off, Sarah knew—to fail to find expert support, or simply to lose her nerve. That way the decision would not be traceable to him; Nolan had not become the firm's head without navigating between competing forces in a way that conserved his power. But she also knew that, from this moment, John Nolan would wish her ill.

She left his office, with Votek at her shoulder. She restrained herself from thanking him, sarcastically, for his support. It was his job to keep her from unsettling Nolan's world, and he had failed; Sarah knew that their relationship would never be the same.

Walking through the halls—the thick carpets, the shiny glass and marble of success—Votek said, "You're making a huge mistake."

She did not turn. "Which mistake was that?"

"You positioned him, Sarah." Pausing, Votek lowered his voice. "He won't forget. If we somehow take this case, your only chance of surviving is to win it."

Five

The day would have seemed bizarre, Caroline thought, had she more time to think about it.

As it was, she was tense and watchful. She had spent the last five hours in a hotel suite near the White House, registered as "Caroline Clark," while one friend, Ellen Penn, and two strangers, Adam Shaw and Clayton Slade, grilled her about the most intimate details of her life and career. But that did not account for her discomfort.

It was now two o'clock, and the room was littered with soft drink cans and service trays. Caroline had long since taken the others' measure: Ellen, warm and encouraging, was her advocate; Shaw—courtly, smooth, and unrelenting— was determined to protect the President; Clayton Slade simply wanted Kilcannon to choose someone else. His questions, though sparing, seemed intended to ferret out details which might make her harder to confirm. That his lack of success was reflected in Ellen's increasing animation only made Caroline more uneasy.

"From your record," Adam Shaw inquired, "I gather you believe in a constitutional right to privacy."

"Not for me, obviously. Or else I would have left by now."

The small joke produced a chuckle from Ellen, a smile from Shaw, and from Clayton Slade, nothing. Caroline faced him directly; in this marathon test, "privacy" was a code word for abortion rights, and a slip could end her chances. "The right was established in *Griswold v. Connecticut.* I think it was reasonable for the Court to infer that we have a zone of privacy, and therefore that the State of Connecticut could no more bar married couples from using condoms than tell them which ones to use.

"But privacy is an amorphous concept and, like freedom of speech, it's not absolute. Whether the right prevails in a given case depends on what *other* interests are at stake." Pausing, Caroline smiled briefly. "As I'll tell Senator Palmer should I be lucky enough to meet him."

The dry aside did, at last, produce a look of amusement from Slade. An unspoken reality was that no one could ask Caroline point-blank where she stood on abortion: they did not want to pin her down, for fear that Palmer's questioning might elicit this fact, and also wished to see whether she was agile enough to avoid this trap on her own. This was the new reality since the Senate had pilloried Robert Bork—it was better to believe nothing than too much. Then Slade asked bluntly, "Have you ever terminated a pregnancy, Judge Masters?"

Caroline stiffened. The startling question, offensive on its face, could be directed at several things—her beliefs; whether she had secrets the opposition might uncover; whether she was heterosexual. "You tempt me," she answered quietly, "to say it's none of your damned business. Because I happen to believe that kind of question isn't—or shouldn't be—the price of a seat on the Supreme Court."

Clayton stared at her. "In theory I agree with you. But I didn't make the rules. So let me assure you that it is."

His tone was distinctly unapologetic. It made Caroline wonder, yet again, about the character of the man Slade worked for. And about her own: after all, she was still here.

"No abortions," she said at last. "Not even one."

"Have you ever been engaged, Judge Masters?"

"No." Caroline's smile, she knew, barely masked her resentment.

"Are you in a relationship?" he asked. "Currently, I mean."

This was enough. "What you mean, Mr. Slade, is, 'Are you gay or straight?' "

The crisp coolness of her answer caused Ellen Penn to smile, and Adam Shaw to glance at Slade. The Chief of Staff folded his arms. "That's your question, Judge Masters. It wasn't mine."

"Then I'll answer both questions," she rejoined. "Am I heterosexual? Yes. It's like being right-handed: because I was born that way, I got spared a lot of nonsense from people who think it's the only way to be.

"Am I spectacular about it? No. Typically, I keep the doors closed."

Ellen, she saw, quickly glanced at Slade. "Do I have a relationship?" Caroline continued. "Yes. Unfortunately at long distance—with Jackson Watts, a state court judge in New Hampshire. We dated in college, and met again several years ago."

"Do you plan to marry?" Clayton asked.

A fiancé, Caroline realized, was much better than a boyfriend—especially at Senate confirmation hearings. "Not now," she answered. "We both have our careers. The virtue of that, from your perspective, is that it leaves us little time for other involvements. So whatever we are is all there is."

Clayton gave her a long, enigmatic look. Shaw edged forward, as though to signal that this exchange had lasted long enough. "Four years ago," Shaw said to Caroline, "you filled out forms for the White House, Judiciary, the FBI, and DOJ, covering every aspect of your life to date—from your family, to your state of health, to whether you've abused drugs or alcohol. Were your answers truthful?"

"Yes."

"And they remain so in all material respects?"

"Nothing's changed."

"Then before we wind this up, Judge Masters, I'd like to know whether there is anything we haven't covered—anything at all—which would embarrass the President if he put your name forward as Chief Justice."

There was no choice but to answer, Caroline knew. And, truly, never had been. She owed this much to Ellen Penn, and, though she did not know him, to Kerry Kilcannon.

Turning to Ellen, Caroline drew a breath. "I'd like to talk with you," she said. "Alone."

Sarah fidgeted in her office, waiting for the phone to ring.

For the last two days she had tried to calm Mary Ann Tierney, fearful of her own parents and what Sarah's firm would do; for the last several hours, consumed by a deposition she was forced to defend, Sarah had run from the conference room during breaks to find another message from the head of obstetrics at UCSF. Three rounds of phone tag had made her frantic.

When the phone rang, she snatched it up at once.

"Sarah? It's Allen Parks. Long time no speak."

Allen was so far from her thoughts that it took a moment for his name to register—her former constitutional law professor, with whom she spoke about once a year. "Allen, how *are* you?"

"Harried, actually—I've taken a job with Adam Shaw, the White House Counsel. I never knew what busy was."

Was this a job offer? Sarah wondered. "If you're calling to complain," she answered, "*I'm* too busy to be sympathetic. Swamped, in fact."

Allen laughed. "Then I'll get right to it. One of my jobs is to review the files on people being considered for appointive office, or maybe some commission or another. I was riffling through some folders and got to Caroline Masters."

Sarah sat straighter. "What's Caroline up for?"

"Nothing specific, as far as I know. But we've got a host of jobs to fill, and I remembered that you clerked for her. It gave me an excuse to call."

Allen was a careful man, Sarah recalled; his explanation, even his tone, were artfully casual. But perhaps what he said was true.

"Okay," she said. "To get right to it, Caroline's terrific—a wonderful writer, great to work for, and the best legal mind I've run into. Except for you, of course."

"How is she on the issues?"

"Which ones?"

"I suppose we're interested in the usual Democratic panoply—immigrants' rights, labor, gender equity, campaign reform."

Quickly, Sarah reflected. "Good on all of them. Her last opinion on campaign reform suggests that limiting these enormous contributions to political parties from interest groups, like the gun lobby, is constitutional. That's the President's position, I know."

"What about choice?"

Sarah hesitated. "I'm sure she's fine," she assured him. "But she's never had a case."

"What does she say in private?"

"To me? Nothing."

There was a first, significant silence. "At *all*?"

The disbelief in his voice underscored the importance of the question and, in Sarah, stirred the first, unsettling doubt about Caroline's views. "Caroline's not exactly Chatty Cathy," she answered firmly. "But you won't find any evidence she's not pro-choice."

Again, Allen was briefly silent, then resumed his casual tone. "Okay, Sarah. Thanks. And, please don't make too much of this—we've got hundreds of names in the hopper, and as many interest groups clamoring for their pets. But that's a good reason, if you don't mind, not to mention this to anyone."

"Sure."

As quickly as Allen had broken her thoughts, he left her with them.

Distractedly, Sarah stared out the window, watching a Japanese freighter, loaded with cars, ease beneath the Bay Bridge toward Oakland. Caroline, she decided, must be on some sort of preliminary list for the Supreme Court. From what Sarah knew of these things, names came and went, briefly flirting with history, then vanishing forever. Still, in another frame of mind, Sarah would have called Caroline right away, to ask what else she might have heard. She would do that, soon—even though their conversation of two nights ago seemed to have happened in another life.

The telephone rang.

"Ms. Dash," the voice said. "This is Dr. Flom, from UCSF. Your phone message said it was urgent."

Six

"She has a *daughter*?" Kerry repeated.

Ellen nodded. "Yes."

By now, little in politics surprised him. But nothing made Kerry unhappier than to peer beneath the surface of someone's life at the anomalies, sad or sordid, which shadowed them. Kerry was too aware of his own secrets not to fear the consequences of this one. Yet, like other personal experiences, this had elevated a bias to a principle: he could not accept that most private acts were so damning that they defined a lifetime. Looking around his study at the others—Ellen, Clayton, and Adam Shaw—he saw them, in their various ways, grappling with conflicted feelings.

"The daughter's twenty-seven," Ellen continued. "She believes she's Caroline's niece."

"The one she defended for murder?"

"Yes."

Clayton turned to her. "Then she perjured herself four years ago. By listing this woman as her 'niece' on the FBI form."

"Which she is," Ellen answered. "Caroline's sister and her husband legally adopted her. Caroline also believes her father had a new birth certificate issued to show her older half sister, Elizabeth, as the biological mother. But whether he did or not, by law Caroline's legal relationship with Brett Allen is that of aunt."

Kerry shook his head in bemusement. "Remember that scene in *Chinatown,* Ellen? Where Faye Dunaway says the girl is her sister, then her daughter, and finally admits she's both? I suppose it's a mercy this isn't incest." Pausing, he gazed absently around the antique-filled room, the light and shadow cast by lamps at night. "Who's the father, by the way?"

"His name was David Stern. He died in a boating accident without knowing Caroline was pregnant. That left her on her own, at twenty-two." Ellen glanced at Clayton. "Her sister and brother-in-law were unable to have children. Caroline thought an adoption was best for everyone. I find that hard to argue with."

Clayton scowled. "Then why not tell the truth four years ago?"

"Because her daughter had been through a lot—more than enough, in Caroline's mind. And she'd spent her life believing that the Allens were her biological parents." To Kerry, Ellen added, "Caroline felt she could tell the literal truth and still protect an innocent young woman. And that it was what she *should* do."

"Then why tell us now?"

"Because the stakes are so high. She knows that we're giving serious consideration to making her the first woman Chief Justice in history. She's worried for *us* if this comes out, as well as for the Allen family." Pausing, Ellen looked at the others. "David Stern was a draft dodger. Caroline didn't know that until shortly before he died—well after she'd fallen in love with him. Caroline's father turned him in, and he drowned while trying to evade the FBI. Caroline feels all this might be embarrassing to us, and distressing to her daughter."

"To say the least," Clayton murmured.

Kerry kept looking at Ellen. "I'm glad I didn't know her father," he said softly. "All in all, I don't think I'd have liked him."

"I liked *her*," Clayton acknowledged. "Partly because she *disliked* me—reasonably enough—and didn't mind letting me know.

"She certainly has her pride, and if you don't like her philosophy you could pass that off as arrogance. But she's obviously gifted, has a real presence, and seems like a decent woman. I could see her making the right-wingers on Palmer's committee look as petty and stupid as they are.

"*But . . . ,*" Clayton paused for emphasis, ". . . a lie is a lie, at least in the context of a Supreme Court nominee. She was right to tell us, and we'd be crazy not to scratch her. I assume no one here says otherwise."

Adam Shaw, Kerry noted, had said nothing. Now Ellen turned to him. "*Is* this a lie, Adam?"

Shaw placed a finger to his lips. "One person's lie is another person's act of conscience. But I've reviewed the forms she filled out, and it's not perjury. As a matter of law Masters told the absolute, literal truth."

Reflective, Kerry sat back to watch the meeting play out.

"That may satisfy us," Clayton told him. "We believe compassion is a virtue. But Macdonald Gage is less forgiving.

"You know Gage better than any of us, Mr. President. Here's what he'll say: If she fudged the truth here, where else? What kind of example are we setting, making this woman the Chief Justice of our highest court, in a legal system founded on the absolute obligation to tell the truth, the whole truth, and nothing but the truth?"

"She *told* the truth," Ellen answered. "Does justice require she proceed to break her word, and ruin someone else's life? Or does justice, in its wisdom, also honor 'acts of conscience'? And, for that matter, do we?"

Clayton shook his head. "Gage would say *this* act of conscience served Masters's own ambition. But another question is how people define morality. On most issues Mac Gage is as cynical as they come. But I think he honestly believes we went to hell sometime in the 1960s—"

"Yes," Ellen interjected mordantly, "back when they started letting women have real jobs, black folks vote, and Catholics become President. All you need is to look around this room to see how *that* worked out."

"The four of us are one thing, Ellen. Premarital sex with a draft dodger is something else. We're the keeper of our nation's morals, or supposed to be— that's why the President has chaperons. 'What about abstinence?' Gage is going to say."

"What about *adoption*?" Ellen shot back. "What Caroline Masters did is exactly what the pro-life people want—to choose adoption over abortion. And then to give her daughter, and her adoptive family, all the love and loyalty she could—at considerable sacrifice to herself, I would guess. That, to me, is a better definition of 'morality.'"

Briskly, Ellen surveyed the room. "Would we all feel better if Caroline Masters were a forty-nine-year-old virgin? Is that what we expect—or even want— from a man? What the hell kind of qualification would *that* be when the President's looking for a Chief Justice who's also a human being?

"Long ago, Caroline Masters proved herself to be an admirable human being. She got pregnant, drew a compassionate lesson, and has lived it ever since—in her own life, and in speaking out for adoption. But Clayton says *that* disqualifies her—"

"What I said," Clayton interrupted, "is that Mac Gage will say that—"

"Then fuck Mac Gage. Because I say it *qualifies* her."

Clayton's tone was even. "If we want a woman this badly, Ellen, there are a dozen capable appellate judges out there who don't have this kind of baggage. A few days into his first administration, the President doesn't need it."

At this mention of Kerry, Ellen faced him, palms spread in entreaty. "This is supposed to be a new day, Mr. President. We campaigned on tolerance—on looking at each person as whole and, in politics, discussing public issues instead of personal failings."

Clayton glanced at Kerry, then said to Ellen, "*We've* done that. But you know the environment we're in—if something personal *can* come out, it likely will. This is exactly the kind of thing Macdonald Gage is looking for.

"Like it or not, politics *is* personal. Maybe the public doesn't grasp legal niceties, but they sure as hell get personal lives—and sex. Gage won't just try to take Masters down in the Senate. He'll use her to tar the President."

Ellen grimaced. "It's not the President's daughter," she retorted. "I think voters are smart enough to know the difference, and fair enough to give us credit for decency and fairness. In fact, one of the President's strengths is that they expect that from him."

"Then let me ask you this, Ellen. Is Caroline Masters prepared to make this public? That way she, and we, at least get credit for candor." Clayton's tone became as dubious as his expression. "After that—maybe—we can spin a sympathetic story of a pregnant girl who opted for life, and proceeded to become a distinguished jurist and supportive aunt. But if it's Gage who breaks this, Masters is just a liar. However Adam defines 'perjury.' "

Ellen frowned in thought. "I don't know the answer to that. She's sat on this for twenty-seven years, and there's her daughter's feelings to weigh."

"Does she want to be Chief Justice?" Clayton snapped. "She was willing enough to be considered."

"Oh, she wants it, Clayton. I'm just not sure at what price."

Clayton folded his arms. "I don't think she can name the price, even for herself. Let alone for us."

At an impasse, the antagonists turned to Kerry. "Where is she now?" he asked Ellen.

"Still at the Hay-Adams, Mr. President. Until tomorrow morning."

Kerry paused, torn between Clayton's practicality and Ellen's principle, more compelling on a personal level than she could ever know. When he made his decision, it was less by reason than instinct. "I'd like to meet her, if nothing else."

Clayton stood, hands jammed in his pockets. "With respect, Mr. President, it's a lousy way to satisfy your curiosity. She's obviously a potential candidate for the Court. If you don't pick her—as you shouldn't—and your meeting gets out, it may look like you rejected her at the eleventh hour.

"That could embarrass her, and be bad for everyone. Because you could never explain your reasons without exposing her."

"The press hangs out at the West Wing," Kerry answered. "Bring her through the east visitors' entrance in an hour, and then up here. No one will see her."

"And if anyone does," Clayton said acidly, "maybe they'll think she's only a girlfriend. At least we can hope."

Kerry smiled faintly. "She told us the truth, at the risk of cutting her own throat. I'd like to give her at least this courtesy."

Turning to Ellen and Adam Shaw, he said, "Thanks for your advice." As was often the case, his dismissal did not include Clayton.

The two friends sat across from each other. For a long time, neither spoke.

"I understand what you were trying to do," Kerry said. "I appreciate it."

Uncomfortable, Clayton shifted in his chair. "I know how much you love Lara. Somehow you two have gotten by—so far. But if you open up the subject of sexual morality, even someone else's, I worry that the press and the right-wing crazies will start looking at your relationship again. There are a thousand reasons, Kerry, that I don't want that for you."

For Kerry, the moment reflected their depth of friendship: that Clayton was the only person he had told about Lara; that, out of affection and respect, Kerry had relieved Clayton of the obligation to call him "Mr. President" in private; that, with equal affection, Clayton reserved this privilege for conversations which were personal; that nothing could be more personal than this.

"I know," Kerry said at last. "But I can't let myself become Mac Gage, treating Masters like Gage would treat me. Lara wouldn't want that, either."

Clayton considered him, and then, on the strength of their relationship, answered, "Do you want Lara to be a symbol of abortion on demand? There's a difference between fear and prudence."

Kerry looked away, then back at his friend. "Caroline Masters," he said finally, "may be one of the few people in town tonight—with the exception of Chad Palmer—who's actually bigger than her own ambitions. That merits my respect."

Clayton met his gaze, and then, after a moment, shrugged. "I'll tell the Service to clear her through."

Kerry stood. "Do that, pal. Then go home, if you can. And please give Carlie my love."

Seven

A young aide led Caroline Masters to the President's study, closing the door behind her.

Kerry Kilcannon was slighter than she expected; his shirtsleeves were rolled up and tie loosened, like a young prosecutor at the end of a tiring day, and his body had a tensile leanness. But it was his eyes which struck her most: an unblinking blue-green, they conveyed the sense that he was absorbing far more than her words.

"Well," he said without preface, "you've certainly made this process more interesting."

Startled, Caroline managed to answer, "Not as interesting as it could have been, Mr. President."

A slight change in his eyes suggested a smile. "For both of us. But what you said to Ellen couldn't have been easy."

With this man, Caroline sensed, nothing but the truth would do. "It was hard," she acknowledged. "There were few days in the last four years when I didn't imagine myself on the Court. But it's not the kind of thing you go around admitting."

"I know—when *my* fantasy got out, a fair number of people were horrified. But here I am." He waved her to a couch. "Please, sit down."

Caroline did that. As Kilcannon sat across from her she realized that, whether from sensitivity or instinct, his directness was helping her transcend the difficulty of the moment.

"Before you arrived," Kilcannon said, "I was thinking about ambition—what it does, and what it costs. About all the men I've known, beginning with my brother, who've wanted to be where I am. Many of them needed it so desperately, and sacrificed so much of value—in themselves and in their lives—that, when they failed, there was no one left inside. In the end, all that was 'real' about them was the president they imagined themselves becoming." He tented his fingers, studying her. "But not you, Judge Masters. I'm wondering why."

Again, Caroline was surprised. She sensed the introspection of a man compelled by circumstance to ponder his own life, and to train the same lens on others.

"It's very simple," she answered. "I love my daughter. Before that, I loved her father. Those two things drove the decisions I made—to have her, but never to tell her—until those decisions, too, became part of me.

"Forty-nine doesn't feel very old. But it's old enough to have reached a few conclusions about who I am, and what that has to mean."

Kilcannon cocked his head. "So you didn't make this sacrifice for the sake of my great crusade?"

Caroline smiled briefly. "I owed you that, of course. But I'll admit it's not the most compelling consideration. I've known my daughter much longer."

Kilcannon's eyes grew hooded. For some moments, he was quiet.

"But suppose," he said at last, "you *were* to explain all this in public. To many people, the decisions you've made would make you seem human and attractive." The same hint of a smile flickered. "It might even leave pro-life Republicans somewhat at a loss for words."

Sadly, Caroline prepared herself to deal the last blow to her ambitions. "I'm not a politician, Mr. President. But I'm not obtuse. So I thought the question might come up.

"This is the confessional age in public life—no sin is too private to confess, no trauma too devastating to exploit. If your opponent had trotted out one more dying relative or Ritalin-afflicted child, I'd have voted for you twice. I'm just glad you defeated him before his guppy expired."

At this, Kilcannon laughed aloud. "I take it you don't approve."

"Not a bit." Caroline sighed. "Honestly, I want this job so much that, in a moment of weakness, I might make myself as big a mountebank as he was. But I don't think it's how public life should be—for anyone.

"For me, there's an absolute prohibition against letting the chips fall where they may: my commitment to the chips." Her voice softened. "I won't undermine everything my daughter believes about her life. If that's not enough, I promised her parents—because that's what they are—I never would."

Kilcannon considered her. "One could argue that your daughter deserves to know."

Caroline found that his matter-of-factness made this most personal of discussions easier to bear. "One could, Mr. President. Selfishly, I wish she did: it's very hard to love a child in secret, and pretend that she's my niece. But I have no right to change that." Caroline hesitated, then finished. "Not even to be Chief Justice."

That would do it, Caroline supposed—it was late, the President was tired, and she was of no further use. The moment of renunciation felt even worse than she'd imagined.

"And yet," Kilcannon said coolly, "you were willing to be nominated. Which means you were prepared to assume the risk that your daughter *would* find out—as long as you had satisfied your personal sense of honor, and we were willing to assume the risk."

Caroline flushed. The analysis was sharp as a stiletto: in that moment, she grasped how tough Kilcannon could be, and how difficult to delude.

"True," she admitted. "It's foolish, perhaps even hypocritical. Perhaps I always *wanted* her to know. But more than that I wanted the job very badly." Her voice became self-mocking. "Why *not* me, I kept asking myself. It isn't fair. The country deserves my talents. Maybe no one but the President need ever know. All the way stations to self delusion.

"But the other truth is this, and I can't leave without saying it—I'd have made a damned good Chief."

Kilcannon cocked his head again. "And why is that?"

"For all the reasons Roger Bannon wasn't. To Bannon, the people he affected weren't real, but chess pieces in some mental game of his own invention.

"All his arid nonsense about deciding cases the way the founding fathers would have—some of them owned slaves, for Godsake, and their wives couldn't vote. American politics in the eighteenth century wasn't driven by mass media and the power of money. The social sciences, including those which explore the impact of parenting and poverty, barely existed. Modern medical science didn't exist at all. All of which are central to how we view the law today.

"Were they alive, the men who framed the Constitution would understand that. It takes a mind like Roger Bannon's to reduce them to flies in amber."

"Bannon," the President countered, "would say that law should be based on fixed principles. Or it's nothing but the whims of the intellectually rootless."

Caroline shook her head. "We're judges, Mr. President. We're supposed to apply the law, not make it up as we go along. But cases don't occur in a vacuum.

"The Supreme Court in 1896 believed that segregation was fine—that 'separate but equal' was not only possible, but all we owed the descendants of slaves. By 1954, the Court could comprehend the withering effects of racial discrimination and therefore that the Constitution, properly interpreted, barred one group of citizens from using the law to degrade another.

"There's a lesson in that. But some of Bannon's allies on the Court seem to have forgotten it."

"Well," Kilcannon said, "now I can dispatch someone to remind them. It's one of the pleasures of victory."

"And I'm very glad of that, Mr. President. I'm just sorry it can't be me."

Kilcannon considered. "So am I," he said at last. "I've even waded through the enormous briefing book Adam Shaw sent over. It was very impressive—including your opinion on limiting campaign contributions. I wouldn't mind a short tutorial on *that*, to help me assess whoever I do appoint."

That she would not become Chief Justice, Caroline decided, left her freer to speak. "I know *your* position," she answered. "You propose to bar interest groups or the wealthy from buying influence through giving either political party these enormous contributions. But legally, you encounter a formidable argument: that the First Amendment makes those contributions a form of 'speech' that you can't touch.

"We don't regulate speech lightly. But one can argue that special access for interest groups drowns out the voices and cheapens the votes of ordinary citizens: How many people can give the Democrats a million dollars to ensure that *you* listen when they exercise 'free speech'?" Caroline flashed a smile. "Not that you'd be influenced, of course."

"That's only the Republicans," Kilcannon said with irony. "I'm above it all. The teachers' unions and trial lawyers have no claim on *me*."

"Naturally. But some people may have missed that. No matter who they vote for, they believe, neither party cares about them. And so they've just stopped voting. Which is how democracy—in the real sense—begins to flicker out.

"That's the cost of treating interest groups as the torchbearers of First Amendment liberties." Pausing, Caroline said emphatically, "Still, it's not a simple question. No judge with any integrity would promise you a result. You shouldn't choose anyone who does."

"It's tempting." Abruptly, the President stood, hands in his pockets, as though he had forgotten all concerns but his own. "For the country to change, the Court has to change. I mean to root out this system of legalized bribery where all of us sell pieces of the government like shares of stock. But I can't do it by myself." Suddenly he stopped, giving Caroline a look of wry self-deprecation. "I sometimes give soliloquies. Like Hamlet."

As she was meant to, Caroline smiled at this. But there was no escaping the scope of his ambitions, or that, like Theodore or Franklin Roosevelt, he tended to see the institutions of government—even the Supreme Court—as extensions of himself. It was fascinating, and a little unsettling.

"I enjoy soliloquies," she responded gently. "But the justices don't work for you, and the role of a Chief Justice is not to dictate change.

"If you simply find a Chief who'll help keep the other justices *open* to change, you'll have done well. Even if the result isn't always what you want."

For a moment, Kilcannon looked surprised. Then he grinned in rueful self-knowledge. "Oh, I know, I know. Sometimes."

This did not require an answer. All at once, their meeting was at an end.

Caroline stood, extending her hand. "Thank you, Mr. President. You were generous to see me."

"Thank you, Judge Masters." Kilcannon hesitated, then added softly, "I regret our current political climate more than you know, and all the more for meeting you. But what you've said is very helpful."

Outside, an aide was waiting. Caroline left, confident she would never see him again.

Eight

The second time Sarah Dash met Mary Ann Tierney was in a cramped, window-less office at San Francisco General Hospital.

It was a Saturday, but the urban tragedies who washed up at a public hos-pital—the AIDS-afflicted, the drug-ridden, the homeless, the maimed—did not receive days off. Mary Ann's frightened eyes registered what she had seen: to Sarah, she looked like a sheltered girl who had taken a detour through purgatory, and now wondered where she was.

"I'm sorry," Sarah said. "I know this isn't easy. But we'll need witnesses if we're going to court. And I wanted you to see a counselor from the clinic."

Mary Ann appeared barely to comprehend this. Sarah did not add the rest—that, no matter what the psychologist and obstetrician said, her firm might not take the case.

The girl studied the paper Sarah had placed in front of her. "Do I have to sign this?" she asked.

She sounded less resistant than dazed. "Our firm needs it," Sarah answered. "And so do I."

Mary Ann looked up at her. "Why?"

"Bringing a lawsuit is a huge step, Mary Ann. If I don't make sure this is what *you* want, then I shouldn't be your lawyer."

"But I *want* you to be."

Even her plaintive tone of voice filled Sarah with doubt. "Please," Sarah told her, "read it carefully."

The girl did this so intently that she reminded Sarah of the times when her own parents had chided her not to read too quickly. At last Mary Ann looked up and said, "It's all true. Can I sign it now?"

Once more, Sarah was struck by Mary Ann's oscillation between vulnerability and challenge. Quietly, she answered, "Before you do, I'd just like to know how you are doing. That matters, too."

Tears sprang to the girl's eyes. "I'm just *so* scared, Sarah. I don't know what's going to happen to me."

This, Sarah suspected, was by far the truest expression of how Mary Ann felt. "What about your parents?"

Mary Ann shook her head. "It's so hard to live with them now. Like we're enemies, and they don't know it. I feel like this *spy*."

So had she, Sarah reflected, when she had been fifteen. But her truancies were small—a brief experiment with dope, furtive petting with a boyfriend. Nothing like this.

"Where do your parents think you are?" Sarah asked.

"At a mall, with Bridget. Looking for birthday presents for my mom."

Sarah suppressed a wince—within the strictures of belief, the Tierneys seemed to rule with a light hand, and now Sarah was party to deceiving them. But the alternative was to make this girl their property, and the doctor and psychologist were waiting.

"Yes," Sarah said, "you can sign the form."

Several hours later, when Mary Ann was gone, Sarah sat at the same conference table facing Dr. Jessica Blake, the psychologist, and Dr. Mark Flom, a specialist in obstetrics who performed late-term abortions. Both Flom and Blake had faced these issues before; both had received death threats; both had gone to court to seek protection. She did not need to mention the risk involved in speaking out for Mary Ann Tierney.

"Well?" Sarah asked.

Blake, a trim, scholarly woman with wire-rim glasses and an incisive manner, inclined her head toward Flom. "You first."

To Sarah, Flom's white hair, fine features, and abstracted look were more suggestive of a poet than a doctor, but his tone was crisp. "I understand the power of belief systems," he answered, "all too well. But I can't believe Jim McNally—or any doctor—would be so sanguine once they saw the sonogram."

"Bad?"

"This is not just hydrocephalus—it's severe hydrocephalus.

"There's water in the ventricle system inside the fetal cortex. It operates to compress and destroy brain tissue and, in the process, prevents us from determining by ultrasound whether there's a chance of tissue developing normally."

He frowned, creating grooves in his slender face. "But when you can't see *any* cortical tissue—as here—the prognosis for the fetus is dismal."

Sarah nodded. "Her doctor said as much."

"Any doctor would. But here's what offends me—the notion of delivering a fetus with a head like a bowling ball by means of C-section.

"Unlike the usual procedure, which is more limited, a classical C-section requires a large vertical incision which opens up the entire uterus. Aside from the emotional trauma to a fifteen-year-old girl, that carries a risk of blood loss, infection, pulmonary embolism, and, in rare cases where something goes wrong, a hysterectomy—risks *twenty times* that of a normal delivery."

Blake turned to him. "But is that the only risk to reproductive capacity—a medical error?"

"I wish it were." Flom grimaced with distaste. "This is a small-boned adolescent. Another risk is a measurable chance, albeit relatively small, of uterine rupture in future pregnancies, leading to the death of the fetus and the removal of the entire uterus."

"Mary Ann's doctor," Sarah ventured, "puts the risk at five percent."

"So that's to be ignored?" Flom's voice filled with disdain. "But I suppose five percent is good enough for government work. Which illustrates the problem with letting those idiots in Congress practice medicine—either they don't know what they're doing, or they don't give a damn about this girl. Or both."

"Is there any chance that, under the Protection of Life Act, a judge would let her terminate?"

"It's hard to see it, Sarah. Under the law, the condition of the fetus doesn't matter, only that it's 'viable.' I question whether you can call *this* baby viable, given how slim its chances are. But what doctor will want to risk prosecution based on that assumption? And forcing her to have a C-section won't establish that a 'substantial medical risk' of physical harm is likely. Just much more likely than before." Flom folded his hands in front of him. "No doctor I know wants to be stripped of his license, sent to prison, and sued by the parents for whatever money he's got left. If you want me—or anyone—to terminate this pregnancy, you'll have to get the Protection of Life Act thrown out."

This was what Sarah had feared. "In any event," she observed, "Mary Ann didn't mislead me about her medical problems."

Flom shook his head. "No. If anything, I'd guess she underrates the problems of delivering this child. She's been living in a pro-life world, cared for by a pro-life doctor."

Sarah glanced at Jessica Blake. "She understands enough," Blake observed. "She's not the most mature fifteen-year-old I've ever met—she's been carefully protected, and most of what she believes has been handed her by her parents.

"I think she was prepared to have a normal baby on autopilot, buoyed by religious doctrine and a substantial dose of fantasy about the child and its father. The sonogram was an antidote."

"Can she make a rational decision?"

"Really, Sarah, the medical problems Mark outlined aren't difficult to grasp. The harder part for her is to weigh that in the face of her upbringing and parental opposition." Blake paused, speaking slowly. "That she marched through a picket line, and then came here, suggests she can.

"Her biggest problem isn't deciding; it's this law. Its hidden agenda is to force pregnant girls—who are likely to be too frightened and ashamed to go to court—to have babies. For their sake, as well as her own, some girl has to take this on. The right one seems to have come to your doorstep."

"Are you willing to say that in court?"

"Yes."

Sarah turned to Flom. "Are you?"

"I am."

"Are you also willing to join as co-plaintiff—have me file the suit on behalf of Mary Ann *and* the doctors subject to the Protection of Life Act?"

Flom nodded. "People need to understand what laws like this do to women and doctors. Right now, they don't."

Among the three of them, Sarah reflected, there was little doubt. She wished she were as certain in the presence of Mary Ann Tierney.

"You'll be hearing from me," she said, and left.

Nine

Twenty-four hours later, awaiting Senator Chad Palmer, Kerry Kilcannon reflected on the plan which was forming in his mind.

Like so many things, it came down to character—in this case, Kerry's estimate of what motivated Chad Palmer. They had been friends ever since Kerry's arrival in the Senate, drawn to each other by a shared sense of humor, a certain iconoclasm, and a preference for candor. In the battle to limit the impact of money in politics, Chad had allied himself with Kerry, winning the scarcely veiled enmity of Macdonald Gage and many in his own party. But, inevitably, Kerry and Chad were rivals: both believed in themselves, and their lives had led them to reach very different conclusions about what the country needed. Not surprisingly, Kerry thought wryly, each man believed what the country needed most was a president like himself.

For several years now, many had predicted a Kilcannon–Palmer race—"the best of America," a pundit had called it. Kerry himself had expected Chad to run the year before: that Chad had not done so made Kerry wonder if he understood his friend and rival as well as he needed to, at least for his plan to work.

Certainly, Chad had taken Kerry's measure with the presidency in mind. Even Chad's oft-quoted compliment—"Kerry is poetry, I'm prose"—suggested a comparison flattering to Palmer. The public Chad was a plainspoken man of straightforward views: pro-defense; pro-life; an enemy of the nanny-state, a friend to personal responsibility. It was this persona, Kerry suspected, which Chad believed might take him to the White House.

But the Chad Palmer whom Kerry perceived was far more complex. Beneath Palmer's cheery admission that "I'm as big a media whore as anyone" lay a deeply serious man. Two years of imprisonment and forced introspection had made him someone who lived by his own standards: a sense of honor was imperative to Chad, and explained his dislike for Macdonald Gage far better than a conflict of ambition.

It was this which Kerry counted on. There was no point in trying to deceive Chad Palmer—Chad would understand what aspects of his character Kerry intended to exploit. But, were Kerry right, this might not matter.

Chad Palmer put down his wineglass.

"She wants to keep this *secret?*" he asked.

They sat in the President's private dining room, replete from a flavorful entrée of Peking duck which, Chad had suggested, must have been the payoff for America's nuclear secrets. "She doesn't even know I'm still considering her," Kerry answered. "But you and I know there are things in your committee files which never see the light of day. And shouldn't."

Chad gazed at the President in open surprise. "Not many."

Kerry leaned forward. "Tell me this, Chad—do you seriously think Caroline Masters's past disqualifies her from becoming Chief Justice? Or that she was required to confess everything in order to become an appellate judge?"

You're really thinking about this, Chad said to himself. It was better to let the conversation play out, to see what Kerry wanted.

"Me, personally? No. Your judge behaved honorably—then, and now." Chad smiled. "I'm pro-life, and I'm not in much position to frown on premarital sex. Thank God I was a little luckier in the area of birth control."

Kerry did not return his smile. "Be that as it may, she's superbly qualified. I'm sick of this 'shoot to kill' environment where both parties exhume someone's tired sins to drive them from public life. I know you don't like it, either."

For a long while, Chad was silent. In the dim light, he contemplated their elegant surroundings—the oil paintings, crystal chandeliers, and, across the table, his friend, whose job he wished to take. A man who understood, quite well, the risks he wanted Chad to run, and perhaps hoped to prevail by daring Chad to be as brave—and unconventional—as he.

"Have you talked to Gage?" Chad inquired.

"Of course not. About *this,* I've got no intention of ever talking to Gage."

"'Of course not.' Instead you want *me* to conspire to conceal a fact which my distinguished leader in the Senate would very much like to know—"

"Which makes it a conspiracy of decency," Kerry interrupted.

"Which makes *you* Machiavelli," Chad retorted. "By telling *me,* you immunize yourself against charges of covering up her past, while exposing me to risk within my party. What on earth, Mr. President, makes you think that I'd relish becoming your shit-shield?"

"Oh," Kerry answered with a smile, "I'll concede this plan has advantages for me. I hardly expected you to miss that—or the possible advantages to you.

"Why am I sitting here, Chad? Women. Even if this comes out, you and I will have risen above politics to give a qualified woman her due."

Chad shot him a skeptical glance. "There are those who think I've risen above politics a little too often."

Kerry tilted his head. "That's because your instincts are better. How will Gage look trashing a gifted woman for preserving an unborn life? How will you look if you help him?"

Chad considered this. "Where *does* she stand on abortion, by the way?"

Kerry smiled again. "Do you think I'm dense enough to ask? And why would you want to make the nomination of the first woman Chief a fight about abortion?"

Chad sat back. "I wouldn't, Mr. President. Gage might."

"He can't. Judge Masters has no record on abortion—none."

"Then she's a Trojan horse," Chad rejoined. "Okay, you won the election. Within reason, I think you're entitled to whoever you want. But you've got no intention of sending over a Chief Justice who sees abortion the way *our* side does."

For a moment, Kerry toyed with his silver napkin ring. "Define 'our side,' Chad. Are you and Gage on the same side when it comes to money in politics?"

"Hardly."

"Hardly. He lords it over the Senate while his old friend and former colleague Mace Taylor collects money from the gun lobby, the Christian Commitment, big tobacco, and all his other clients, then uses it on Gage's behalf—and his own.

"Those two know the drill better than anyone: money buys influence—and laws. Gage lets Taylor write special-interest legislation for Gage to pass, *and* tell him which bills to block or kill. Taylor gets rich, Gage gets big donations from Taylor's clients, and the country—and you—get screwed." Kerry stared at him, though his voice was soft. "You want to run against me, Chad. But Mace Taylor and his friends don't want you to, because they've already bought their candidate—Mac Gage. They'll raise millions to defeat you, and the ads they'll run won't be pretty. So you'll lose."

"Maybe not . . ."

"You'll lose," Kerry repeated. "Which will be fine with me, pal. Gage would be much easier to beat."

Palmer felt a surge of pride and defiance. "You've skipped a step, Mr. President. The one where—with *your* support—I get our campaign reform bill through the Senate over Gage's and Taylor's dead bodies. Choking off their money machine."

Kerry smiled. "*You've* skipped a step—where *my* new Chief Justice helps decide whether your bill is constitutional. And therefore whether you've got a prayer of taking my place."

At this, Chad began to laugh. "She's pro-reform, isn't she."

"I think so, yes. I expect she's also a lot of other things that I like, and you don't. But, as you concede, that's my prerogative." Kerry's tone was cool and emphatic. "Mac Gage is corrupt. Not in the sense that he takes suitcases full of unmarked bills. He's far worse: he's selling the Senate to the highest bidder to perpetuate his own ambitions. And if that means we keep allowing children to be slaughtered with the automatic weapons his NRA friends love so much, that's okay with him.

"I intend to cut off his cash flow and infuse a little integrity back in government, any way I can. After that, you and I can fight it out on principle."

Thoughtful, Chad considered what Kerry was proposing and the man who was proposing it—a complex mix of toughness and idealism, passion and cool calculation. "I'm out front here," Chad said at last. "If this nomination blows up, and I'm on the wrong side within the party, I lose more than you do."

Kerry nodded. "I think that's right. So let's be clear about what I want."

"I don't expect you to support her unless it's a slam dunk. All I ask is that if your investigators dredge up Judge Masters's personal life, you try to sit on it."

Chad sipped his wine again. "That may not be so easy," he admonished. "Not just because the FBI will be all over her, but because of Gage and Taylor."

"Detectives," Kerry answered.

"Uh-huh. Taylor's more than an influence peddler, or even Gage's leading supporter. He's the fucking Prince of Darkness. Through his clients, he controls millions of dollars—enough to fund an army of investigators." Chad paused for emphasis. "You know about those spies who followed Lara around all during the general election, hoping to embarrass you. That was Taylor."

This produced in Kerry the cold gaze, the softened voice, which Chad had learned to associate with anger. "Oh, I do know, Chad. I'm finding it hard to forget."

"Don't. Remember when Frank Keller resigned as Majority Leader, saying that he wanted more time with his family, and how lucky we were to have Mac Gage taking his place?"

"How could I not? Even by the standards of this town it was such patent bullshit I felt embarrassed for him." Kerry gave him a small, curious smile. "So what did Taylor use on him?"

"Prostitutes, rumor had it. A couple of them under eighteen. And it was Taylor *and* Gage, I think." Chad looked at him directly. "If we try to do this, Mr. President, Judge Masters's life is in play. And maybe anyone who helps her."

Kerry shrugged. "My life's an open book, Chad. And yours?"

"Of course," Chad answered calmly. "I'm a hero, after all."

Kerry studied him. In the silence, Chad Palmer weighed the interplay between principle and ambition, his desire to do right against his fear of the dangers it posed. And, as always, his sense of who he must be—the most essential part of him.

"All right," Chad said at last. "If you decide to send this lady over, I'll try to look after her."

Ten

Two nights thereafter, in the chill of winter, Kerry Kilcannon and Lara Costello walked along the ellipse toward the Lincoln Memorial.

It was below freezing, and both wore heavy wool coats. The reflecting pool beside them was covered with ice; their breath misted the air; frost whitened the grass; leaves crackled beneath their feet. None of this mattered to Kerry—after a few short days as President, life in the White House seemed too cloistered. Even his whims were cumbersome: the only people he saw nearby were the shadowy forms of his protectors, a moving phalanx.

"They've given us new code names," said Kerry, referring to the agents. " 'Thumper' and 'Bambi.' "

Lara grinned. "Which one of us is 'Thumper'?"

"Whoever I decide."

Taking his hand, Lara gave him a sideways look of amusement. "You really like being President, don't you?"

"More than I thought," Kerry acknowledged. "After all these years in the Senate, the endless talk, I've got my hands on the levers. It's addictive."

"And you don't feel overwhelmed?"

"I don't have time." Kerry stopped to gaze at the Lincoln Memorial, bathed in light at the end of the ellipse. "Oh, sometimes at night I'll think about all the decisions made in that house, from the Civil War to Hiroshima—lives lost, and history changed. I begin to wonder what decisions I'll be called upon to make. You're acutely aware that you're only a tenant, and that some of the tenants before you were truly great men. And that politics now is uglier, the scrutiny worse.

"But 'the awesome burden of the presidency'? Maybe I feel that drifting off to sleep. But in the morning I can't wait to go to work. So I'm obviously insane."

This last was delivered with a smile which Lara, looking into his face, answered. "At least crazy enough for the job. 'My fiancé, the megalomaniac.'"

"That's me. I think even Chad's impressed."

With that, they began walking again. "So you've really decided?" Lara asked. "Almost."

She gave him a pained look. "Does Clayton know?"

"Not yet." Kerry kept his voice soft. "I'm saving it for a surprise."

Lara glanced over at him. "But you think it's the right thing to do."

"Everything about her checks out. Plus she's got character to burn, and tremendous force of personality—without which, in all immodesty, I wouldn't be where I am." He paused. "I didn't run because I like the sound of 'Hail to the Chief.' I intend to change things. I think Caroline Masters can change the Court."

"And Clayton's reservations . . ."

"Concern her personal life. He's afraid it may only whet the appetite for scandal." The ice covering the reflecting pond, as Kerry gazed at it, was black as onyx. "I understand that this is a risk. But I think there's a deep craving for a president who insists that we judge a person's life with compassion, and as a whole. In fact, I wish that Masters would let us make that case. Though I respect her reasons."

How can you not? Kerry felt Lara thinking. "But if she got it out," she responded slowly, "and the reaction wasn't too negative, you'd be insulated."

"It's more than that. It may sound callous, at least where her daughter's concerned, but I think this works for us even if her opponents bring it out. I'm not sure Masters understands this, but the rest of us could profit politically, even if she loses." Kerry turned to her again. "Sooner or later we'll need to take a stand against using a public figure's private life to destroy him. The politics of scandal has to stop, and the facts involving Caroline Masters are a better platform than most.

"I'd lose the right-wing zealots who want to force pregnant girls to have babies, then kick them out of the National Honor Society for being mothers. But I can live with that."

Lara withdrew her hand, walking with her head down, hands thrust in her pockets. "But there's something you *can't* live with," she said under her breath. "The facts involving us. That's why we're taking this walk."

Kerry touched her arm. "We're taking this walk because I miss you. And because I wanted to know what you think."

Lara shook her head. "Please, Kerry—I made the choice I made, and now I get to live with it. But I don't want to be a part of your calculations."

Her eyes, dark and luminous, held, for Kerry, a painful beauty. "Chad's worried about Mac Gage," he answered. "And Mason Taylor. He's right to be."

"Because it's hard to keep secrets. Only Chad doesn't know *whose* secret you worry about protecting."

Kerry could find nothing to say.

"I haven't met her," Lara said after a time. "I've only seen her on TV, during the Carelli trial. To me, she came across as smart, elegant, and a little supercilious—a bit too Waspy to evoke all the compassion you seem to feel for her. But maybe *that's* not about her, either."

"What do you mean by that?"

Lara turned away. "Well, she had the baby, didn't she?"

"Lara." Kerry's throat felt tight. "For Godsake, let it be . . ."

"Let me finish." Drawing closer, she gazed up into his face. "Politically, I don't know what is the smartest thing for you to do. I can't know how choosing her will affect us. I'm not even clear about why you're doing this—principle, or something far more practical and subtle, which has to do with protecting me in ways that Clayton hasn't thought of. Maybe you even mean to inoculate me by sacrificing Masters, so that people get sick of your opponents dragging private lives into politics. And now you're wondering if I can live with that."

Even now, Kerry thought, her prescience and directness sometimes took him by surprise. He touched her face. "I don't want to lose you, Lara."

"Then you have to accept something—the people who hate you will *always* be after us, no matter what you do. There's no way you can protect me—or us. The only thing you control is who you are."

Kerry studied her—honest, brave, and a little angry. "Be yourself, Kerry," she said softly. "And never, ever ask me anything like this again."

For a moment, Kerry wanted to hold her. And then he remembered their guardians, watching in the darkness.

"Let's go home," he said.

Eleven

She might be present in body, Caroline Masters acknowledged to herself, but her spirit was absent without leave.

Caroline and ten of her colleagues, all men, presided over the marbled courtroom of the United States Court of Appeals for the Ninth Circuit. From the podium before them, a lawyer for the State of California attempted to explain why an indigent prisoner, who claimed to have been beaten and sodomized by his cellmate with metronomic regularity, had no right to their attention. That the state was compelled to explain at all was Caroline's doing.

The en banc hearing was a rarity: eleven appellate judges, a majority of the court's active members, convened to rehear a case previously decided by the customary panel of three. The author of that opinion, Judge Lane Steele, sat three places to Caroline's right, looking ascetic, intellectual, and, on this day, quietly furious at Caroline Masters. In Steele's view, the courts were congested by frivolous petitions from prisoners with rich imaginations and too little to do. His overall solution was elegant—to read into a poorly written federal law technical requirements so complex and obscure that most prisoners without lawyers would never meet them. Its consequence here had been to reject the plea of the supposed inmate-victim—who had sued to impel the prison to protect him—without determining whether his charges of abuse were true.

Caroline's role had begun unobtrusively enough. Indignant, her law clerk had brought the decision to Caroline's attention. Rather than call for a rehearing, Caroline had written Steele and his two colleagues, gently asking that they reopen the case and appoint a lawyer for the inmate. "If," Caroline had ventured, "it is true that Mr. Snipes has no claim because he sued the warden but not the guards, he should at least be permitted a lawyer to help him question the wisdom of such a rule."

Steele's response had been a curt refusal. At this point, Caroline had suggested to her colleagues that the case be reconsidered. That a majority of judges agreed accounted both for the rehearing and Steele's air of deep unhappiness.

But today Caroline had no heart for this. The death of her aspiration to be Chief Justice had left her distracted and depressed: the night before, trying to concentrate on the papers filed by the inmate's appointed counsel, she had been forced to remind herself that disappointment did not excuse indifference. It had not helped much—then, or now.

With unwonted detachment, Caroline took in the scene before her. Having been battered by Steele in his opening argument, the prisoner's court-appointed lawyer, a young man barely out of law school, looked apprehensive; now, the state's lawyer, a blocky young woman named Marcia Lang, argued her case with stolid doggedness. Behind them, sitting on varnished benches, were two black women who, Caroline supposed, must be the inmate's sister and mother. Another hour of justice in America.

"We believe," Marcia Lang was saying, "that this inmate asks far too much."

Steele leaned forward, his high forehead and half-glasses suggesting, to Caroline, a scholar of long-dead languages. "In short," interjected Steele with his usual precision, "your position, Ms. Lang, is that this court is not required to dispense legal advice to assist inmates in suing the state."

Lang nodded briskly. "That's correct, Your Honor. Mr. Snipes insists not only that you allow him to refile his petition, but tell him which defendants to include. We contend that he's obliged to inform himself of the law's requirements before invoking it."

This was vintage Steele, Caroline found herself thinking—a puppet show, in which he led the party he favored through the arguments he wished to make. "And would you also contend," Steele continued, "that the sheer volume of these petitions impels us to impose at least some minimal standards before hearing them."

"We would," Lang answered. "Prisoners' rights petitions burden our office *and* your court."

The smugness of the colloquy roused Caroline from her revery. "Just as," she found herself interjecting, "sodomy might fairly be considered to burden Mr. Snipes."

Surprised, the Assistant Attorney General turned to Caroline. "You assert," Caroline continued, "that Mr. Snipes can't get redress for brutality because he didn't include prison guards in his petition. Where in the statute does it say 'include the prison guards—or else'?"

Lang hesitated. "It doesn't, Your Honor. But that's a reasonable interpretation of this court's decisions."

"Reasonable to whom? Is it reasonable to reject this man's petition without telling him why? Or how to fix that—"

"It seems to me," Steele interrupted, "that we cannot function as a partisan of one side or another. Wouldn't you say, Ms. Lang, that's what this prisoner is asking?"

"I agree, Your Honor."

Caroline glanced at Steele: though restrained by custom from confronting a colleague in open court, he was using Lang as a prop to do precisely that. Caroline turned to Lang again.

"Then you would also agree," Caroline said, "that this judicial game of hide-and-seek will prevent us from determining whether Mr. Snipes has been beaten and sodomized. Or from protecting him if he has been."

"Your Honor, there are standards . . ."

"Whose standards? I certainly don't find them in this law—or anywhere." Caroline's voice was cold. "Just for Judge Steele's enlightenment, and my own, you don't *know* whether Mr. Snipes's rather graphic assertions are true or not, do you?"

Lang hesitated, looking to Steele.

"Answer the question," Caroline snapped. "Please."

Lang planted her feet. "Not on the current record."

"But you do know that Mr. Snipes's petition states that his mistreatment can be verified by a prison doctor."

"It *says* that, yes."

"And you also know the conditions at this particular prison are so abominable that a lower court is considering whether to place it under federal supervision."

Lang's jaw seemed to tighten. "That hasn't been done yet."

Caroline sat back. "Then this court must hope it will be, if we adopt your position. At least those of us who consider systematic sodomy to involve more than some abstract legal theory—however interesting, or mysterious, its origins."

To Caroline's left, her friend and mentor, Judge Blair Montgomery, bent his white head forward to conceal a smile. The enmity between Steele and Montgomery was legendary: Caroline's sharpness, unusual for her, no doubt delighted Montgomery. She told herself to ease off.

Steele stared at her with open dislike. "Isn't it true," he demanded of Lang, "that the statute in question was drafted expressly for the purpose of limiting the number of prisoners' rights petitions?"

Lang seemed to rally. "Yes, Your Honor. The legislative history makes that clear."

"And, if in doubt, shouldn't we interpret its language in light of that purpose?"

"Absolutely."

From her raised bench, Caroline watched the two black women follow this exchange in bewilderment. Congress passes ill-written laws, she thought, and then judges interpret them, with all our biases and deficiencies—including, today, the distraction of a crushing disappointment. And then people like Orlando Snipes have to live with the mess we may have made. Whatever else Snipes deserved, and whatever forces had made him who he was, she owed him the hope of fairness.

"Isn't it also true," Caroline asked in a more reasonable tone, "that Mr. Snipes didn't know he could even *raise* these points until this court granted a rehearing on its own initiative, then appointed a lawyer to help him?"

Lang's eyes flickered toward Steele. "I believe so . . ."

"And that without our intervention, his voice would not be heard today? Or, perhaps, ever."

Lang hesitated, then shrugged in acquiescence. "I suppose that's true."

Caroline leaned forward. "Then perhaps you can explain to me why a process which conceals from Mr. Snipes the means of protecting himself from sexual assault, and *then* conceals his right to question that concealment, is consistent with the ends of justice."

Once more, she saw Blair Montgomery's wisp of a smile. Montgomery seemed as certain as Caroline was, watching the state's lawyer struggle for an answer, that the court would reject Judge Steele's ruling. She did not look forward to still more years with Lane Steele as her colleague.

But Montgomery was inured to this. As the hearing ended, and they exited the courtroom, Montgomery murmured from behind her, "You certainly pulled the wings off *that* particular fly. It was a pleasure just to listen, for once."

Caroline shrugged. "Bad day, Blair. I let him get to me."

Her clerk, Christine, was waiting by the conference room, looking intensely anxious. "What is it?" Caroline inquired with some surprise. "We're about to take a vote."

Eyes bright, Christine motioned her aside. "It's the White House," she whispered. "The President is calling for you."

Twelve

Two blocks from Saint Ignatius High School, a few short hours before going to court, Sarah Dash waited in her car for Mary Ann Tierney.

Sarah had the jitters—too much coffee, too little sleep. The six days since their last meeting had passed quickly, spent consulting pro-choice groups who litigate abortion cases regarding every conceivable issue, lining up the witnesses they suggested, and, most nerve-racking, marshaling support to persuade the managing partner. She had done this in a way which was bound to infuriate him, but represented her best hope: by informing the women partners of the medical evidence that supported Mary Ann. This had engendered emotions which startled even Sarah, culminating in a closed-door meeting between the female partners and John Nolan. Excluded, Sarah knew only that the women had been blunt and insistent, exposing tensions within the firm which until now had been muted. When Nolan summoned Sarah to his office, granting her permission to represent Mary Ann, he made little effort to conceal his anger—or that he blamed Sarah for bringing disharmony to Kenyon & Walker.

"You've managed to force this on us," Nolan had said. "We'll all have ample time to live with that."

And so here she was. All that stood between her and a confrontation with the United States government was the pretty red-haired girl who, glancing quickly over her shoulder, peered through Sarah's car window.

Mary Ann sat next to her, gazing at the affidavit Sarah had given her to sign. Sarah could imagine how fateful it must seem to read its recitations—that she was twenty-four weeks pregnant; that her baby was hydrocephalic; that she risked infertility and other medical complications; that she wanted an abortion; that her parents would not consent. And that, therefore, she was petitioning the court to invalidate an act of Congress.

Mary Ann seemed hardly to breathe. In a frail voice, she asked, "What happens if I sign this?"

The "if" did not elude Sarah. "Let's start with today," she said. "An hour before I go to court, I'll call the Department of Justice to give them notice.

"At around three o'clock, I'll go to the clerk's office, file our papers, and ask to see the motions judge." Sarah kept her recitation clipped, dispassionate. "Justice will have a lawyer from the U.S. Attorney's office waiting for me. Together, we'll go before the judge.

"I'll tell the judge what you want—an order ruling that the statute is unconstitutional, and that you can have an abortion. He'll set a hearing date ten days from now. I'll ask that the hearing be closed, our papers sealed from the public, and your identity concealed . . ."

"Will my parents be there?"

"Not today, I'd guess. But because you're challenging the statute, not proceeding with it, the Justice Department may feel free to contact them—if for no other reason than that they're prospective witnesses." Pausing, Sarah considered her next words with care. "It's possible that, by the time you get home tonight, your parents will already know."

Mary Ann shook her head as though waking from a dream. "Ten days," she murmured. "How long will the hearing take?"

"Several days beyond that."

"And then the court decides?"

"Yes. But if we win, the government will go to the Ninth Circuit Court of Appeals, where I used to work, and after that, they can seek review in the Supreme Court. The Protection of Life Act is an act of Congress, and it's their duty to defend it." Sarah lowered her voice. "The courts will expedite our case, but it will still take several weeks. All that time you'll be getting more pregnant, and living at home."

Mary Ann closed her eyes. *"God . . ."*

Sarah touched her shoulder, speaking softly. "I expect your parents will pressure you to withdraw the suit. If you want an abortion, you'll have to stick with this—in and out of court. Otherwise, it's better to change your mind right now."

Mary Ann slumped in the passenger seat. It seemed to be her characteristic posture when daunted or depressed; looking at the slender girl, her belly concealed by a bulky sweater, Sarah felt afraid for her.

Breathing deeply, Mary Ann took Sarah's hand.

Surprised, Sarah looked down at the girl's fingers, entwined in hers. Suddenly, Sarah wondered if part of her apprehension was for herself and that Mary Ann, sensing this, sought both to give, and receive, comfort.

"It's all right," the girl said.

Closing the door to his office, Senator Chad Palmer took the President's call.

"Let me guess," he said to Kerry. "You're really doing it."

"Yes. This afternoon, in the Rose Garden."

Standing, Chad felt apprehension mingle with anticipation. "Today? You've certainly managed to sit on this one."

"That was the idea, Chad. No one in the Senate knows."

"Not even Gage?"

"Especially not Gage." The President's voice was calm. "I'm hoping to get her confirmed as soon as possible. A lot of that depends on how quickly you can move her through committee."

At once Chad grasped Kerry's strategy—a surprise nomination; a lightning blitz of praise and good publicity; a surge of anticipation for the first female Chief Justice. And with this an inexorable pressure on the Senate to vote before prospective enemies discovered what Kerry and Chad already knew. Chad acknowledged the new president's cleverness: once Chad had entered their conspiracy of silence, he, too, had a stake in its success, a price to pay for its failure.

"Gage won't want that," he answered. "He'll be leaning on me for time to pick her apart. Couched in the usual eyewash like 'all deliberate speed' and 'exercising our constitutional prerogatives.'"

"Mac Gage," Kerry responded, "will die without ever having said a single thing worth remembering. A politician's most dreaded legacy."

Chad was unamused. "Maybe. But someone could get hurt here. Better you—or Masters—than me."

"I understand," Kerry said evenly. "But your ultimate interest is in confirming her, and it's the right thing to do. There are ways to walk the line between Gage and me which help Caroline Masters without hurting you. Starting with your deep concern that the work of the Court not be interrupted . . ."

"By the meddling of senators, you mean? Not so long ago you were one of us. So you know how much we treasure our moments in the sun." Chad paused, and his voice became cool. "I appreciate the heads-up, Mr. President. But I'll run these hearings as I see fit. Don't get so wrapped up in your new office that you forget what you've known about me for the last twelve years."

There was a brief silence, and then a soft laugh from Kerry told Chad he had hit his target. "Actually," the President told him, "I've spent the last few nights designing the Kilcannon Memorial."

"Is it an obelisk? Or does it have pillars?"

"Both." Kerry's tone became sober again. "I appreciate your help, Chad. And I sincerely expect this nomination to wind up being good for both of us."

Once more, Chad felt the small tingle of foreboding. "That's a comfort," he answered. "Someday I'd like a monument of my own."

Thirteen

Moments before the announcement, Caroline waited with her family in the Diplomatic Reception Room of the White House.

The President and Clayton Slade had scheduled the event for Friday afternoon; until Monday the White House could control the news cycle. In the last few hours they had pressed their allies to follow with prompt statements of approval—labor unions, minorities, trial lawyers, environmentalists, women's groups. To disarm the Republicans, they had prepared for the media a bipartisan list of admirers from among Caroline's colleagues, the establishment bar, former corporate clients, and ex-partners at Kenyon & Walker. The White House communications office would prime the press with favorable stories—young women in college or law school inspired by Caroline's appointment; victims grateful for her favorable rulings in cases regarding rape and domestic violence. By Monday, a first impression of overwhelming and well-deserved support would be planted in the public mind.

All of this, Clayton explained, was aimed at Chad Palmer and Macdonald Gage. Administration spokespeople would fan across the Sunday morning talk shows, stressing that both senators had voted to confirm her for the Court of Appeals. Those same shows would be badgering Palmer and Gage to appear; there would be little either man could do except venture cautious praise of a judge who, by Monday, would be one of the most famous women in America.

There would be no escaping her, Caroline thought wryly. Tapes of the Carelli trial would punctuate the news; on Sunday, Lara Costello was hosting a luncheon for Caroline to meet other prominent women; tonight, after the announcement, she and Jackson Watts were dining with the President and Lara at a Washington restaurant, where a photographer and a reporter from the *Post's* style section would be waiting to record the moment. But nothing was more important, Clayton had emphasized, than the first vivid image—Kerry Kilcannon in the Rose Garden, introducing America to its new Chief Justice.

"We want a tableau," Clayton had told her. "You, the President, the Vice President, your friend Jackson Watts, and your family—sister, brother-in-law, and niece."

This comment filled Caroline with misgivings, and not just because Clayton knew the truth. The focus on Brett made her uneasy; her half sister Betty—jealous of Caroline and fearful, even now, that she would somehow reclaim Brett as her own—would be loath to appear. But Caroline was losing control, swept up in Kerry Kilcannon's determination to secure swift confirmation. This was one of its costs.

"I'll call my sister," she had promised.

So here they were—as Caroline had mordantly put it to Betty—"hiding in plain sight." A typical American family: Betty's husband, Larry, a college professor who, Caroline happened to know, had once been involved with a student; Betty, daughter of their father's first wife, who had always despised Caroline's French mother; Caroline herself. A woman who sometimes mourned her youth, and still remembered holding a child in her arms . . .

"Wake up, Dorothy. You're not in Kansas anymore."

Startled, Caroline turned from the window to Brett, her niece by law, her daughter in secret.

Brett was smiling at her; the expression was so like Caroline's mother that, once more, she was grateful that the two had never met. Had Brett even seen a picture of Nicole Dessaliers, she would have seen herself: brown curly hair, a delicate chin, a full, even mouth, slender face, high forehead, vivid green eyes. But Brett's beauty was animated by more kindness than Nicole had been able to muster—for that, Caroline supposed, she had Betty and Larry to thank. For all their flaws, a family.

"Was I that adrift?" Caroline asked.

"A million miles away," Brett answered. "You looked like how I feel when I'm writing a short story."

Caroline returned her smile. "If only I could put my mental absences to such good use. Instead I was experiencing amazement that my prosaic life had come to this."

"I think it's all very cool," Brett murmured in parody of a high schooler. "Except for the President, who's hot."

For Caroline, this moment lightened the occasion, distracting her from the myriad ways in which Brett Allen touched her heart. She looked around them at the oval-shaped room, its wallpaper depicting a panorama of American scenes populated by white males, and at the people who were here on her account. Considerably more awed than their daughter, Larry and Betty were listening to Kerry Kilcannon who, on public occasions, seemed to generate his own electricity, a compound of youth, magnetism, and a certain restless vigor—"hot" was as good a word as any. Jackson Watts was chatting with Lara Costello, who had the dark, perceptive eyes and grave loveliness Caroline somehow associated with Latinas. Near them, Clayton Slade, a bulky African American, towered over Ellen Penn—not only Jewish, but the first woman to serve as Vice President. Taken together, they symbolized the ways in which the face of America was changing, the present century quite different from the last. And now Caroline would be part of this.

Kit Pace, the President's press secretary, bustled into the room and murmured to him. Breaking away from the Allens, Kilcannon crossed the room and said to Caroline with a smile, "Kit tells me it's show time. Are you ready?"

"Yes. And very grateful. Not only for the honor, but for everything."

The look in Kilcannon's eyes showed that he understood her meaning. Briefly, he turned to Brett, including her in his smile, and then to Caroline again. "Oh, the honor's mine," he said. "The first woman to become Chief Justice should also be the best. You are."

The Rose Garden was jammed with dignitaries in folding chairs, reporters, sound equipment, boom mikes, cameras. Seated behind the podium were Ellen, Jackson, Caroline, Brett, Betty, and Larry. Clayton Slade's tableau.

From the podium, Kerry Kilcannon praised her. The words came to Caroline as if in a dream.

"A great Chief Justice must be many things—wise, impartial, respectful of precedent, a person of great character, intellect, and learning. But she must be more than that."

Kilcannon's voice, though soft, carried above the crowd. "When she renders an opinion, a Chief Justice must see more than the words of a statute, hear more than the cloistered quiet of the Court. She must see the faces and hear the voices of people she will never meet, yet whose lives she can alter with the stroke of a pen. For the dream of justice is not the exclusive property of lawyers, nor is it confined to books or laws. It is a dream which has drawn countless men and women to our shores, from the first settlers to the family fleeing oppression at this very moment, believing that their future can be kinder than their past.

"We owe them no more, but no less, than justice."

It was artful, Caroline thought: without demeaning Roger Bannon, the

President was serving notice that the new spirit he had promised the country would also touch the Court.

"Judge Masters," Kilcannon concluded, "personifies that ideal. For all of these reasons—her gifts, and her humanity—it is with great pride and pleasure that I introduce my nominee for Chief Justice of the United States, the Honorable Caroline Clark Masters."

Smiling at Caroline, the President motioned her to the podium. Kilcannon clasped her hand. "Congratulations," he said quietly. "To both of us."

Turning, Caroline faced the crowd and the cameras, the lenses glinting in the pale sun. There was no need to manufacture the humility she felt. But the moment required something more.

"Thank you, Mr. President." Turning to Kilcannon, she smiled. "This morning my niece, detecting my feelings of wonderment, informed me that I wasn't in Kansas anymore.

"Still, it's difficult not to feel a little bit like Dorothy."

There was a small appreciative chuckle from the crowd. "Suffice it to say," Caroline told the President, "that I will do all that is in my power to justify your confidence."

With an air of command, Caroline faced their audience. "I'm also grateful," she told them, "for the presence of my family—my sister, Betty Allen; her husband, Larry; and my niece, Brett. For I know as well as anyone the importance of those who love us, and that few of us succeed—or fail—alone."

The complexity of this statement in her own case, Caroline thought, did not preclude its truth. The myth of family was as deep as the need for it—she could read this in the faces before her, solemn and attentive.

"I look forward," she went on, "to appearing before the Senate, and I should reserve any extended statements for those who bear the responsibility of voting on my nomination.

"Also, like the President, I do not wish to dwell on the obvious—that I'm a woman. We are, I hope, drawing nearer to the time when such a thing is unremarkable."

Pausing, Caroline gazed out at the grounds which surrounded them. "But when I passed through these gates this morning, I realized that, at the beginning of the *last* century, Ellen Penn and I would have been outside them—picketing for the right to vote." Glancing at Ellen Penn, Caroline added wryly, "So I think I can speak for the Vice President in saying that we like *this* century a good deal better . . ."

The audience broke into smiles and applause. We're launched, Caroline thought, and hoped that her quest would end as well as it had begun.

Fourteen

Within minutes of her arrival at court, Sarah's strategy was in ruins.

She had imagined that the process would work as usual—meeting her opponent at the clerk's office; conferencing with the judge in his chambers; debating the date and form of a hearing, with Sarah having the advantage of surprise; securing an agreement to protect Mary Ann Tierney's privacy and, to the extent possible, her emotions. In Sarah's mind, her opponent was a harried lawyer from the U.S. Attorney's office, taking instructions from the Justice Department—which, under the new administration, might not be eager for controversy. The first sign of trouble was when she entered the clerk's office and encountered not a lawyer but a group.

The government lawyer was what she expected—a man barely older than Sarah, whose purpose was to buy time for his superiors in Washington. But next to him was a graying, somewhat theatrical advocate whose specialty was representing the media in seeking broad public access to judicial proceedings. A few feet away, taut and silent, stood a man and woman whose pain was as stark as their discomfort.

The woman, slender and pale, had the haunted look of a mother who blames herself for the loss of a child. But it was the man who held Sarah's attention; tall and slender, he had a fine chiseled face, a high forehead, gray hair swept back over his temples, and blue eyes so pale as to seem translucent. Sarah felt both enmity and intimacy: these two people, so different from her in outlook, were the figures of authority—loved and feared—whom Mary Ann Tierney had asked her to defeat. Ignoring the others, she crossed the room to meet them. "I'm Sarah Dash," she said simply. "I represent Mary Ann."

Margaret turned away. But Martin Tierney answered, "*We* represent our daughter, Ms. Dash. And our grandchild." That this was said with civility made the rebuke seem more harsh than anger would have: at once, Sarah knew that little—today, or afterward—would be as she imagined it.

On the nineteenth floor of the federal building, Judge Patrick Leary's corner office afforded a sweeping panorama of San Francisco, and sufficient room for a sofa, two chairs, a large desk, and a glossy conference table around which the parties sat, with Leary at the head.

"I've read Ms. Dash's papers," the judge said. "Before we go any further, I'd like to know who everyone is, and what their interest is in these proceedings."

"I'm Craig Thomas," the young lawyer answered, "representing the defendant, Attorney General Barton Cutler, for the purposes of this proceeding only. At any future hearing the Attorney General will be represented by the department in Washington."

Leary waved a freckled hand, as though to say he expected this. A pale man with graying red hair and a perfunctory manner, the judge was noted for his conceit that there was no problem so complex that he could not grasp it in five minutes—the approximate time, Caroline had once confided to Sarah, that it had taken her to grasp how dangerous this made him. "And you, Efrem," Leary said to the media lawyer, "to what do we owe the pleasure?"

Efrem Rabinsky smiled with the self-satisfied air of an established courtroom personage. "I represent the Allied Media. Our interest is assuring the broadest dissemination of what promises to be a case of major constitutional importance."

"And I object," Sarah said promptly, "to Mr. Rabinsky being here at all." Tension made her voice higher, her words more rapid. "A fifteen-year-old girl faces a tragic dilemma. She's pregnant with a defective fetus, she wants an abortion, and her parents oppose her. We filed this case as *Doe v. Cutler* to protect her privacy . . ."

Leary raised a hand. "We'll resolve all that later, Ms. Dash. I'm just taking attendance." Turning to the Tierneys, he said with compassion, "And you, Martin? What role are you seeking?"

Tierney clasped his hands in seeming anguish. "I'm here as a lawyer, as well as a father. Margaret and I are requesting leave to intervene in these proceedings."

Alarmed, Sarah turned to the judge. "I sympathize with your concerns," Leary told Martin Tierney. "But according to your daughter's declaration, Ms. Dash speaks for her."

"But who speaks for our grandchild?" Tierney asked. "No one."

"That's not true," Sarah said. "The United States Department of Justice represents your point of view."

Tierney fixed her with his translucent gaze. "Our grandson is not a 'point of view.' If he were delivered right now, he could live outside the womb." Turning to Leary, he said, "Ms. Dash is asking the court to take an innocent life. We're asking to be appointed *guardians ad litem* to the unborn child, with the right to act in his defense: to call witnesses, to make argument, and otherwise do everything in our power to save him."

This was Sarah's worst fear—a hearing in which her opponent was not the Justice Department, but two people speaking with the authority of parents and the zeal of true believers. "With all respect," she said to Leary, "a baby with these defects is unlikely to live at all—now or later. The Tierneys can fully express their concerns as witnesses. But as parties, they're not only unnecessary but—despite their best intentions—will inevitably inflame these proceedings and deepen their own daughter's trauma. Can you imagine a father cross-examining his child?"

"Who better?" Tierney asked quietly. "By what authority do you speak for, and to, our daughter—to the exclusion of the two people who have loved her since before she was born, and will continue to love her when you've vanished from her life? Having pursued the 'best interests' of a girl you've known for two weeks.

"I'm sure you mean well, Ms. Dash. But the arrogance of those who believe as you do never fails to impress me. And never more than now, when you sit across the table from two parents, and tell them that, in the name of their daughter, you mean to bar them from a proceeding you've initiated to secure the death of their grandchild."

Sarah turned to Leary in protest. "Your Honor . . ."

Leary held up his hand. "I've heard enough, Ms. Dash. This is not a visitation case, and Mary Ann Tierney is, herself, still a child under the law. I'm granting the Tierneys leave to intervene on behalf of the unborn child."

The swiftness of events jarred Sarah further. "May I ask one thing, Your Honor? I'd like to know from Mr. Tierney *and* Mr. Rabinsky how they came to be here an hour after I gave notice to the Justice Department. Specifically, who informed them of the case?"

"Does it matter?" Leary asked.

"Yes. It suggests that *someone* is trying to make this case as traumatic for my client as they possibly can. I can only hope it's not the Justice Department."

The young lawyer looked affronted. "You were asking for a TRO this afternoon. I contacted the Tierneys to testify, if necessary."

"And whom did *you* contact?" Sarah asked Tierney.

He shook his head. "This is difficult enough, Ms. Dash. Don't ask me to confide in you who I might have called to help me in what, until your lawsuit, was a private matter within our family."

Once more, Sarah felt defensive. "I'm wondering how *Mr. Rabinsky* got here."

"That's a confidential matter," Rabinsky answered with his usual assurance. "And it's completely irrelevant to the media's right to report on these proceedings."

Tierney had called a pro-life group, she thought, and they had resolved to escalate the pressure on Mary Ann by bringing in the media. Facing Tierney, she asked, "Do *you* want Mr. Rabinsky here? Is that what's best for Mary Ann?"

Gazing down at the table, Margaret Tierney shook her head. Glancing at his wife, Tierney said, "No. We'd like these proceedings to be as confidential as possible. For our family's sake."

Turning to Judge Leary, she said, "That much we agree on. I'd like strict guidelines for the media—no access to our papers, and testimony from Mary Ann given in chambers rather than open court. And any media who report her name or background should be barred from the courtroom. The same protections we accord a juvenile in *any* proceeding."

Rabinsky pursed his lips. "This isn't a case of shoplifting. Of course we agree not to publicize Ms. Tierney's name. But we want full access to all proceedings, including television . . ."

"Television?" Sarah said in anger and surprise. "That's ridiculous."

"Last month," he answered smoothly, "the National Judicial Council lifted its ban on television in federal courts. And it's routinely allowed in major criminal cases.

"This is an issue of far more importance, involving a parent's right to direct their minor daughter's reproductive decisions, and the limits, if any, on the right to an abortion established in *Roe v. Wade*." Turning to Leary, he lowered his voice. "If I may say so, Your Honor, your ruling in this case may well be the most important by a federal district judge in the last ten years. It's vital that the public fully understand the basis for your ruling. Admitting cameras is now within your discretion."

Rabinsky was shrewd, Sarah thought. He had appealed to two of Leary's most salient qualities—his self-image as an incisive judge who ran a model courtroom, and his penchant for excessive courtroom preening.

"I'll save that for last," Leary said. "First, I'd like to know what kind of beast we've got here." Spinning on Sarah, he said, "Let me tell you right now, Ms.

Dash, I'm not granting you a restraining order today—or at all. You're asking that I declare this statute unconstitutional on the spot, which amounts to aborting this baby over the counter. No way am I going to do that."

This much was no surprise. "I understand, Your Honor. But unless we expedite these proceedings, Mary Ann will suffer irreparable harm: emotional trauma, an increased rate of medical complications the longer her pregnancy goes on, and—if we delay too long—a process of hearings and appeals which will force her to have the child regardless of how you rule."

Martin Tierney seemed to awaken from some depth of sorrow; he seemed shocked at what was happening, and at the wrenching ordeal proposed by Efrem Rabinsky. "There's a balance," he said. "I worry for my daughter. But this also involves my grandson. The case against his murder *must* be allowed in full, whatever time it takes."

"For the record," Sarah shot back, "your so-called murder is to protect *your* daughter's physical and emotional health, including the right to bear further children who actually have a cerebral cortex. I refuse to go through the proceeding talking about murder, or treating a girl you claim to love as if she's a human respirator."

To her surprise, Martin Tierney winced. Next to him, Margaret Tierney closed her eyes; gently, Tierney rested his fingers, long and delicate, on her wrist. "To us," he answered, "Mary Ann is hardly a human respirator. Believing strongly that something is right doesn't lessen its pain. What's happened has been agony for us, and now it's come to *this*.

"I think what you're proposing is judicial murder, even more immoral than the death penalty. But that's different from believing you a murderer, or callous, or careless. If I've suggested otherwise, I apologize."

This note of grace surprised her. "So do I," she said. "I hope we can find a way to keep this civil—and no longer than it need be."

"Part of that depends on you," Leary interjected. "You've asked for a hearing in ten days on a preliminary *and* permanent injunction. You've got it—the case won't wait. So who are your witnesses?"

"The co-plaintiff," Sarah answered promptly. "Dr. Flom. Then a psychologist. At least one woman who had a late-term abortion in similar circumstances . . ."

"Why?"

"To show that the statute would preclude a significant number of minors from having emergency surgery to preserve their health." Sarah's voice was emphatic. "I'd also call the mother of a girl who died from an illegal abortion because she was afraid to ask her parents' consent to a legal one."

"That's not the case here," Leary said testily.

"But it will be for *someone,* and soon. We're asking that you find the statute invalid as to Mary Ann Tierney or, in the alternative, as to any teenage girl it could affect." Sarah paused. "Finally, I hope *not* to call Mary Ann. But I may not have a choice."

"What about you?" Leary said to the government lawyer. "Witnesses?"

"I don't know yet. That's up to Washington."

"Well tell them to figure it out within ten days—they're the world's biggest law firm, after all." Facing Tierney, Leary said, "Maybe you can help the government here."

Tierney's brow furrowed. "There are many considerations, Your Honor—including the painful decision as to whether *we* must ask Mary Ann to testify. And I'd like to associate the Christian Commitment: their legal staff has been active in defending the unborn, and has ready access to pertinent witnesses, both expert and lay. According to her papers, Ms. Dash has *pro-choice* groups helping, after all. Even if they won't appear with her in court."

Sarah could only listen. "Certainly," Tierney continued, "we'd like medical testimony regarding both Mary Ann and our grandson, as well as the testimony of a psychologist regarding the trauma of aborting a viable baby. Perhaps—in contrast to Ms. Dash—testimony from mothers who have taken similar pregnancies to term." He drew a breath. "The implication of Ms. Dash's request are more profound than I think she knows. I expect that members of the disability community should also be heard."

It was just as Caroline had admonished her. "On what ground?" Sarah asked.

"You're proposing selective abortion of fetuses because, in the opinion of a mother, they have traits which are less 'desirable' than other children." Pausing, Tierney shook his head in wonderment. "Where would you draw the line, Ms. Dash? Aborting babies because they're female, and a parent—or the state—wants a male?"

Sarah faced Leary. "Your Honor," she urged, "this is about a teenage girl with a hydrocephalic child. Not eugenics."

Leary scowled. "You're asking me to consider throwing the whole statute out—for everyone. And one of your grounds is disability, at least as I read your papers. If someone wants to speak for the disabled, I'll hear them."

"Thank you." Tierney's voice conveyed both gratitude and sorrow. "Also, Margaret and I may well wish to testify—both as Mary Ann's parents and as those who, up to now, have been responsible for her moral instruction. We're afraid of the long-term psychological damage if she contravenes her own beliefs by having an abortion."

Sarah began to absorb the shape of what would come: litigating with Martin Tierney over the best interests of his own daughter, perhaps on television; arguing whether a law which would force a traumatic childbirth on a teenage girl was, instead, a bulwark against the rebirth of Nazi science; clashing with the Christian Commitment, whose tactics—in and out of court—might be far more harsh and devious than Martin Tierney knew; suffering the peremptory and erratic rulings of Patrick Leary—who, Sarah suspected, was more sympathetic to the Tierneys than to their daughter.

"Your Honor," she said, "may I return to the question of the media—and television? If Mary Ann Tierney were a shoplifter, her privacy would be protected. Because she's innocent of any crime, Mr. Rabinsky feels entitled to put her on CNN . . ."

"We can run a three-second delay," Rabinsky retorted. "Beeping out her name, and blocking out her face and that of the Tierneys. It's their circumstances, not their specific identity, which is of the greatest public interest. Not only is this a case of unique importance, but the fact that Ms. Tierney is the daughter of pro-life activists exposes the complex nature of the issue."

"Which is just another way," Sarah rejoined, "of punishing Mary Ann for her parents' decisions. But in this case the Tierneys agree with me. That should be dispositive. Why strip this girl of her privacy for invoking the right to privacy?"

"It's certainly entitled to great weight," Leary answered. "But opening the courtroom not only honors the First Amendment, it demystifies the legal process—especially as to something as controversial as this. Besides, that's a hearing for injunctive relief, heard by the court itself. So there's no question of prejudicing a jury."

No, Sarah thought, it was even worse than that: television would inspire Leary to serve his ego and promote his own career. "Anyone who has a view on this," Leary concluded, "can file a brief by the close of business tomorrow. But I'm inclined to grant Mr. Rabinsky's request, as modified to protect the family's identity."

"Your Honor," Sarah protested, "that's not enough time to brief the matter. Especially with only ten days before a hearing."

"Ms. Dash," Leary retorted in an exasperated tone, "Kenyon & Walker's almost as big as the government. You've got at least four hundred lawyers over there. Turn them loose.

"I've given you the timetable you wanted. So don't complain about it."

It was clear that Leary's attention span, never great, was exhausted. "All right," he announced. "TRO denied, motion to intervene granted, media petition under consideration. No statements to the press until I say so.

"Ms. Dash's brief is due in five days, the reply brief two days later, hearing in ten days—three days for each side's witnesses." He looked sharply around the table. "Anything else?"

No one spoke. "Then that's it for now," Leary said, and dismissed them.

Leaving, Martin and Margaret Tierney avoided Sarah. For this, at least, she was grateful; their exchange felt exhausting and too personal, what lay ahead enormous. She tried to imagine what the night would hold for the Tierneys, parents and daughter, and whether Mary Ann could bear it.

Still shaken, Sarah went to a pay phone to prepare her.

Fifteen

Mason Taylor put his feet up on the ottoman in Macdonald Gage's office, studying the shine of his shoes.

"This is where you draw the line," he said. "It's a power play—the little bastard's trying to blow this woman by us."

Gage sipped his bourbon. Beneath his placid exterior he was sharply attentive—his job, and his hope of becoming President, might well depend on the forces which Mace Taylor represented. More than any man in Washington, Taylor personified the connection between money and power.

Taylor had not always inspired such awe, or such caution. A few years before he had been a second-term senator from Oklahoma with no prospects beyond that. Then the party had made him chairman of its Senate Campaign Committee and discovered his unique gift: Taylor was relentless in extracting special-interest money through promises or threats.

His approach was brutally simple—do you want a place at the table, or the doors to Congress slammed in your face? Favored donors were encouraged to help draft legislation or target bills for defeat; the less generous were banished. Bemused, Taylor's party colleagues found themselves surprised by, then reliant on, the contributions Taylor could produce. Avid to survive, they were fearful of the organization and money the unions and trial lawyers could marshal against them; few could resist more cash flowing into their campaigns, or a suggestion from Taylor that the lobbyist for an HMO or gun manufacturer was too important to ignore. Taylor had made himself the conduit between those willing to use money to assure their favored status and the lawmakers who needed money to keep their jobs. And neither group, they soon discovered, could do without Mace Taylor.

The process changed Taylor, as well. As a senator, he was constrained from sharing in the wealth he had created. Outside, armed with cash from corporations and interest groups, he could charge clients the price of access to senators or representatives who wanted what Taylor could provide. Mace Taylor became an investor in his clients' enterprises, and almost as wealthy as those he served.

But this was only the beginning. With a shrewd eye, Taylor perceived the uses of the scandal culture: the competition among tabloids, cable channels, magazines, newspapers, and internal publications for that sordid private detail through which one might, by destroying a public career, rise above one's peers. To the pragmatists who feared or needed him, Taylor added a second source of cash and power: the interest groups or wealthy zealots willing to fund investigations of politicians whose ruin they desired, or whom Taylor wished to control. Some in Congress were slow to understand this—the prior Majority Leader, resistant to Taylor's instructions, awoke one morning to a phone call describing his sexual behavior with a sixteen-year-old prostitute. The next day he resigned; Macdonald Gage, who had known nothing of Taylor's plans, became Majority Leader because Taylor wished it. It was a lesson Gage never forgot.

But Gage, too, was proud. He had not been bought, he told himself—he had been presented with a force which any man who wished to be President must consider. But there was no question of turning Taylor away. And so Taylor sat in his office, the image of a Washington insider, eyeing the television on which Caroline Masters's face had appeared.

Quite deliberately, Taylor no longer pretended to be the homespun senator from Oklahoma; his Piaget watch, Ferragamo loafers, and Savile Row suit were, Gage knew, a studied reminder of the wealth and power he represented. But the man was the same—slick black hair which gleamed under the lights, a broad face which reflected part-Indian ancestry, shrewd black eyes far better at conveying contempt than warmth—as was his private vocabulary. Even without the context of a Supreme Court nomination, Gage would have recognized "the little bastard" as Kerry Kilcannon, whom Taylor deplored as deeply as the causes Kilcannon represented.

"What do your people say about *her*?" Gage asked.

"That she's a liberal," Taylor answered. "The gun manufacturers have had their eye on her for a while. They think she'll favor lawsuits every time some junkie pops a liquor store owner with a Saturday night special—"

"Yeah," Gage interjected mordantly, "or some sportsman mows down a kindergarten class with an AK-47. Can't be getting in *their* way."

Taylor shot him a look. "Don't you get squishy on me. People need to protect themselves, and the Second Amendment secures the right to own a gun. How long would you last in Kentucky if the NRA put ads on the screen accusing you of taking away their guns?"

Gage smiled. "No chance of that, Mace. I want my constituents to be able to shoot any IRS agent who comes to collect that last hard-earned dollar." He spread his hands. "No argument, either—guns will always be with us, and the gun-control laws never work. But we're not going to use Masters to get Kilcannon by saying she'll let a policeman's widow sue gunmakers. So what else?"

Taylor sipped from his tumbler of the Makers Mark whiskey Gage kept for him. "The heart of it," he said slowly, "is campaign reform. From the looks of her opinions, the Christian Commitment tells me, she believes Chad Palmer's bill is constitutional. It was *their* money that helped you get the Protection of Life Act through, and keep control of the Senate. You can't ignore what *they* want, and what they *don't* want is Chad Palmer, or this woman, trampling all over their First Amendment rights of advocacy."

Gage sat up. The Palmer bill would ban unlimited contributions to political parties, threatening the money flow and, in the process, the role Mace Taylor played in Washington. "Well," Gage answered. "That's a problem."

Taylor looked at him intently. "It surely is. Our friends in the HMOs, the NRA, the pro-life movement, and the tobacco industry would lose their right of speech, while those bloodsucking trial lawyers beat on the gun industry like a gong, and the unions and minorities turn their folks out to help the Democrats take over Congress. What are we going do about that?"

Was this a test? Gage wondered. "Find something else," he answered.

"How do you mean?"

"We're not going to rally the public by saying she'll choke off the cash we need to compete—that's an insider's argument." He paused to reflect. "Where is she on abortion?"

Taylor shrugged. "You've got to figure she's in favor. But the Commitment doesn't know. Still, we wind up with a black eye if we let her on the Court, and then she uses *Roe* to knock down any limit on abortion you manage to get through Congress. Which is probably what she'll do."

"Sure," Gage agreed. "But she's not going to tell us that. By the time she's in front of Palmer's committee, Kilcannon's people will have trained her like a seal."

"Then you have to slow this down, Mac. Until we find something we can beat her with."

"Such as?"

"Anything. You saw that announcement today—no kids or husband, using her sister's family as a prop. Maybe she's lesbian."

The thought filled Gage with genuine unease. Gage had been a poor, unmarried girl's child, adopted by a loving couple, and his affection for his parents, and loyalty to his siblings, was deep; for him, preserving the family was paramount. He had based his life on this belief, from thirty years of fidelity to

Sue Ann Gage—with whom he had adopted a Hispanic girl—to regular calls to each of his grown children. Now the traditional family was besieged by deviance and self-indulgence; he would not knowingly permit a lesbian to be a role model, let alone to lead the nation's highest court. Even if politics allowed.

"I don't think *Kilcannon* would mind," Gage answered. "The question is whether he's that stupid."

"Stupid, no. That stubborn, maybe. You know how righteous these liberals can get."

"So can we," Gage answered. "The difference is that two thousand years of religious tradition and human history says we're right. Or no amount of prosperity will save us from ourselves."

Taking a swallow of rich bourbon, Gage saw his own image appear on the screen. Reaching for the remote control, he raised the volume.

CNN had caught him emerging from his office. Though Masters had been a surprise, Gage was pleased at his unfazed demeanor and measured words, a public face born of much experience. "I commend the President on his promptness," Gage said to the camera. "What the country requires from the Senate, however, is a deliberate process, most particularly in the investigation and hearings conducted by Senator Palmer and his committee.

"We deserve a Chief Justice with a superb judicial temperament, one who strictly interprets the Constitution rather than indulging in judicial activism. I very much look forward to meeting Judge Masters, and to hearing her views . . ."

"You did vote for her before, didn't you?"

"For the Court of Appeals." Gage summoned a benign smile. "Certainly, Candy, I want to give the President's nominee every consideration. But now she has a record as a judge, and the American people expect us to review that record thoroughly before making her Chief Justice."

Lowering the volume, Gage turned back to Taylor. "*Maybe* she's lesbian. But you know the problem, Mace. For sure she's a woman. The party's in trouble with women. And from the look of her, this one's no pushover."

Taylor gazed at the television. "*That* looked like you're holding back, Mac. Letting Palmer take the limelight."

"Sure. Chad loves this—it's a golden opportunity to let the country see him. He needs to remember our constituencies expect him to slow this down, dig into her life and record.

"We've got friends on his committee, like Paul Harshman, who won't like this woman at all. They'll help pressure Palmer without my doing it directly. *My* job is to keep our senators uncommitted until we can give them ammunition."

"It's not that simple," Taylor replied. "Palmer and the so-called moderates may be all the votes Kilcannon needs to confirm her. And Palmer thinks campaign reform would help him beat you for the nomination."

Gage mentally scanned his colleagues: who was worried about reelection; who wanted a change of committee; who had a pet project which required Gage's approval; who depended on the money Taylor represented, and Palmer threatened. "I can keep them from jumping," he said. "At least long enough for you to find holes in her record, or in her character. The moderates have their views, but they don't want to piss me off."

"Except for Palmer," Taylor cut in. "You've never been able to control what he does. The fucking hero business immunizes him."

"And he knows that," Gage rejoined. "When it comes to polishing his own image, he's got the slickest act of all—the uncorrupted man. Who, *we* both know, wants to be President so bad he can taste it."

Pausing, Gage finished his drink. "Chad could fuck up here, alienate the people he needs to pass his stupid bill. He might even carry water for his buddy Kilcannon. That's a complicated relationship—there's no telling what they'd gin up, each trying to serve their own interests."

"So you think Palmer helps you take this lady down, or jumps the reservation and shoots himself in the foot."

"Uh-huh. Either way, I win."

Taylor's cold eyes and hard face became a mask of thought. "The problem," he finally said, "is that Palmer doesn't think like anyone else. It's like two years being kicked in the head by Arabs made him clinically insane. To me, he's the most dangerous man in Washington."

Gage shrugged. "And the most predictable. What you're missing, and what those Arabs figured out, is that he'll do anything to think well of himself."

Taylor met his gaze. "Not 'anything,' Mac."

At this, Gage felt a deep aversion. "I don't like him any better than you do, Mace. But I'd hope never to drop that on him."

Taylor's face closed. "Maybe not over this," he answered. "But sooner or later, he'll make us do it. If only by running for President."

Sixteen

Putting down the telephone, Chad Palmer returned to the living room. "Sorry," he said to his wife and daughter. "That was Mac Gage. The Masters nomination seems to have made me the most important man in Washington."

This was said with wry self-deprecation. The last people he expected to impress were Allie and Kyle Palmer—especially when the two of them were huddled over a portfolio of Kyle's fashion drawings, spread across the coffee table of the Palmer's brick town house on Capitol Hill. But, to his surprise, Allie looked up. "What did he want, Chad—to lecture you on your party obligations?"

Chad glanced at his daughter. Her oval face still gazed at a red dress she had drawn, and she seemed, as often, detached from him. "I'll fill you in later," Chad answered. "I haven't seen the rest of Kyle's drawings."

This time Kyle raised her head. "It's fine," she told him in a flat voice. "We can finish later."

The delicacy of their relationship, Chad realized, left him at a loss. Her tone suggested courtesy rather than any real interest—deliberately so, he guessed. It was the response of a girl who remembered, as her psychiatrist had told the Palmers, hearing from her schoolmates how handsome her father was, and how brave, when what she wanted was a father who paid as much attention to her as the world paid to him. His choice now was to take her offer at face value or, by insisting on his interest in her work, to risk treating her as an emotional invalid. She was, after all, twenty years old.

Allie came to his rescue. "Go ahead, Chad. Kyle doesn't hear much about your work these days."

Chad smiled. "Then why spoil a good thing?" When his daughter smiled as well, he added, "For once, Mac Gage did not explain to me how to be a good Republican. It was even worse—he pretended to take for granted that I was going to help him."

Allie studied him closely. "How?"

"By delaying our committee's confirmation hearings so that our staff, and our constituent groups, can dig up reasons to oppose Caroline Masters."

"Like what?" Kyle asked.

"It could be anything—rulings which are too extreme, an ethical lapse, smoking dope in college. I remember a nominee for the District Court who'd been busted for drunk driving in two different states, Maryland and Virginia, in the same night." Pausing, Chad shrugged. "Mac's even developed the fantastic notion that Kerry may be trying to sneak a lesbian past us."

Kyle wrinkled her nose in disgust. "Why does it have to be like that?"

"Don't look at *me*, sweetheart. Personally, I could care less."

This time Allie smiled fractionally. "You're not saying that in public, are you? A lot of people on the Christian right will think you're encouraging an epidemic of homosexual conversions."

Chad laughed. "It's a risk, all right. People *choose* to be gay because it's such an attractive option—dislike, discrimination, and difficulty in forming families." He eyed his daughter with mock regret. "If some nice man had told me it *was* a choice, I'd be leading Gay Freedom Day parades instead of being stuck with your mom and you."

Smiling, Kyle fell into the spirit of things. "There's hope for you, Dad. You're not nearly the reactionary you pretend to be."

The irony of this comment, Chad guessed, was, for once, innocent. But Allie sat back a little. "What *are* you going to do?"

Chad shrugged. "Not exactly what Mac wants. I'm in the spotlight here—especially because I'm not a lawyer. I'll get all the media time I could ask for. But that's good for me only if I treat Masters fairly, which is what I'd do in any case. She isn't who *I'd* choose, but Kerry's the President, after all."

Allie appraised him. "*You* weren't surprised, were you? Kerry must have told you before today that this was coming."

Once more, Chad realized how good her antennae were—Allie did not love politics, but fear of its consequences had made her alert to nuance. "He did," Chad acknowledged. "He thinks she'll be good on campaign reform."

He chose to stop there: his agreement to help protect the nominee's secret, though Allie would deeply sympathize, would further raise her apprehension. "I know you know this," Allie warned. "But you can't seem too close to Kerry. It will hurt with some of the groups."

His daughter was watching them closely, Chad realized. He selected his words with care. "I can't cozy up to *them*, either. I'm not in anyone's pocket, and I can't let them make it look like I am. Meet with the Christian Commitment, and they'll pressure me by leaking that I'm on their side . . ." His voice trailed off. "I am," he added, "in many respects. Although they've stopped being a cause and become a business—like a lot of their opponents, of course. But they're way too hard-line, and it's scaring off women."

This, Chad thought, was as close to an apology as he could ever make. Allie, silent, glanced at their daughter.

"It's abortion," Kyle said simply.

Chad felt himself tense. This time, he could not glance at Allie to solicit help; his own reflex with Kyle was avoidance. "Anyhow," he said, "the right will be on alert, and I've got a divided committee—ten Republicans and eight Democrats, with at least three of Gage's allies looking over my shoulder. Being a statesman is also my best defense."

"So you won't delay the hearings," Allie said.

Chad shook his head. "Kerry wants them in a month. I'm inclined to give him *that*, at least."

Allie glanced at Kyle. "What about what Gage wants? To dig into the judge's personal life."

Once more, Chad felt on edge—the subject had too much resonance, and he could not tell his wife what he had promised to keep private. "You know how I feel about that," he answered. "If it's relevant to someone's performance in office, that's one thing. But it's another thing to keep running off good men and women for every personal lapse. Or there'll be no end to it."

Mercifully, Kyle chose not to pursue the subject. She seemed much better, Chad reflected, than she had a few short years ago: the fluctuations in weight had diminished; the pallor of her skin was gone; she had stopped changing the color of her white-blond hair. Her eyes, so like Allie's, were brighter and happier. Perhaps they were through the worst.

"Anyhow," he finished with a smile, "I'll be on *This Week* Sunday morning. A great moment for America."

Kyle shot a wry look at her silent mother, then returned her father's smile. "You'll be fine, Dad. Just remember there are women watching—at least two of them."

Seventeen

Mary Ann Tierney lay crying on her bed.

An hour before, her parents had sat on the edge of her bed. "This isn't my home," she had told them. "All you care about is what *they* think of you, and how much I've embarrassed you."

Tears sprang to her mother's eyes. Softly, her father answered, "The Christian Commitment worries about the harm you'd do to other girls, and to their unborn children. We're worried about the harm to you, and to your child."

Though his tone was even, its plaintive note made Mary Ann quiver inside. She gazed at the man who, before this year, had been to her the face of kindness and wisdom. Miserably, she said, "I don't want my life to be over."

He summoned a faint, sad smile. "This isn't the apocalypse, Mary Ann. It's a child."

His forbearance, the sense that he was talking down to her, made her more angry than threats or punishment. Suddenly she wanted to hurt them both. "*You* want this baby," she said to her mother. "You don't care what happens to *me*."

Her mother stood. "We didn't ask you to sleep with that boy. I didn't beg you to get pregnant . . ."

"Oh, no," Mary Ann said in a quavering voice. "You just want me to have a baby for you—no matter what's wrong with it."

Her father strained to keep his voice low. "This is not a good time to talk, Mary Ann. What you've done has shocked and saddened us."

Her mother's dark eyes seemed wounded. "What about *me* . . . ?" Mary Ann asked her.

"What about *you*?" her father cut in. "You've made two decisions in the last half year—to get pregnant, and to bring a lawsuit to kill your own child, our grandchild. And you expect us to live with them both.

"Before, you were happy enough when you imagined Tony would come riding to your rescue—whatever you thought that meant. And it was all right if your mother and I helped care for you and the child. Then your image of perfection was shattered, and now you're desperate to dismember the baby inside you."

He inhaled deeply, steadying his voice, and Mary Ann could feel his horror—at her decision, and at his loss of self-control. "He's not a convenience, Mary Ann, or a fantasy. He's not a perfect child on a greeting card, or some monster of imperfection. He's not just yours, or ours. He's a creation of God, and no one has the right to take his life."

Pausing, her father gazed down at her, and shook his head. "It's unnatural for a mother to murder her child. That's what you're asking us to let you do. And if we refuse, then you'll ask a court to let every girl like you kill any child she considers to be a hardship." His voice became quiet. "I know you're afraid. I hate it for you. But the selfishness of what you're doing—the sheer disproportion of it—sickens me."

The last soft words struck Mary Ann like a slap in the face. She looked at the first man she had loved, his fine features and pale eyes, through a film of tears. "I can't stay with you," she said in a flat voice.

Beside her father, Margaret Tierney shook her head in disbelief. Evenly, her father answered, "You need us more than ever now. You're as lost as any girl I've ever seen. You've lost track of what you believe, or any sense of what you've set in motion . . ."

"Don't you know," Mary Ann cried out, "how it feels to be *me*? I sit here listening to you say how selfish I am, how I don't know what I'm doing. Well, I *know*, all right? I *know* I don't want a baby with no brain. No matter what you taught me, I don't think that's a sin."

In obvious pain, her mother stared at her; for an instant, all Mary Ann wanted was to throw herself into her mother's arms, rely on her as she always had. "I need to go away," she said in a pleading voice. "I can stay with Alice."

Her father sat on the edge of the bed, taking her hand. Until this year, he had always been able to see inside her, and to calm her. "This is your home," he said firmly. "And we're your family. No matter what, you belong with us."

"Why?" Mary Ann answered. "So you can control me?"

"*No.*" It was her mother's voice.

Mary Ann looked up at her. "*You're* afraid you won't be able to stop me from getting an abortion. That's why you want to keep me here."

Her mother flinched. "We don't know what you'd do, Mary Ann. How *can* we know after this?"

Her father, intervening, stood to place a hand on his wife's shoulder. "We'll leave you alone tonight," he said to Mary Ann. "If you want, you can have dinner in your room."

Grateful, Mary Ann nodded. All she wanted was to be left alone.

As if to heal the breach between them, her father, still touching her mother, took Mary Ann's hand again. Gently, he said, "Father Satullo will be along to see you, a little later. We thought it might be easier for you to talk with him."

Mary Ann stiffened. A vivid memory came back to her—Father Satullo, kneeling on the sidewalk in front of the women's clinic, frightening her away.

Without a word her father released her hand. The only sound was the door of her bedroom closing.

Mary Ann looked at the darkened window. At least they hadn't nailed it shut.

Sarah Dash stared at her television.

"If confirmed," the news anchor concluded, "Judge Masters will become the first woman ever to serve as Chief Justice."

"You *made* it," Sarah said aloud.

A surge of elation and amazement brought her to her feet. For a moment, she shed the worry and depression which followed her telephone call to Mary Ann, the weight of her responsibility for a girl who, when told about her parents' intervention, could barely form words between her sobs. Sarah's first impulse was to call Caroline at once; then she realized that Caroline was in Washington, and recalled her reason for watching the news—to see whether the media had begun to report the Tierney case.

She did not have long to wait. *"In federal district court,"* a pert brunette was saying, *"a pregnant fifteen-year-old filed suit to invalidate the Protection of Life Act . . ."*

The buzzer to her apartment made her start.

The first reporter, Sarah thought. Even though the court papers were filed under seal, protecting both Sarah and the Tierneys, someone must have leaked her name—the Christian Commitment, she felt sure. Glancing over her shoulder at the television, she went to her apartment intercom, prepared to tell whoever was waiting below to leave.

"Who is it?" she demanded.

"It's me." The voice sounded wispy, out of breath. "Mary Ann."

Slumped at the door, Mary Ann looked frightened and apologetic. "I couldn't stay," she said without preface. "Father Satullo was coming."

This half-coherent statement, Sarah thought, was shorthand for hours of conflict and confusion. The girl looked pale and drawn.

Taking her hand, Sarah closed her door behind them, leading Mary Ann to the white couch in her living room.

"Tell me what happened," Sarah said.

For a half hour, interrupted by spasms of crying, Mary Ann tried to do this. Sarah's empathy commingled with the strangeness of it—a girl she barely knew now occupied the center of her life and, quite literally, the only private space she had. All that Sarah could think to do—like her mother in times of crisis—was to bring Mary Ann warm milk.

Sarah gave her time to settle down. Quietly, she said, "We need to call your parents."

Mary Ann's eyes fluttered. "I want you to get me an abortion, Sarah. Maybe we can go out of state."

Her desperation hit Sarah hard. "I know you're upset," she answered slowly, "but this is a federal law, remember? It applies to every state. And even if it didn't, something called the Child Protective Custody Act makes it illegal for anyone to help you get an out-of-state abortion against your parents' wishes."

Mary Ann blinked. "What about Canada? I can't go on like this."

Sarah chose her words with care. "Mary Ann," she finally said, "I'm doing all I can to help you by bringing this lawsuit. Your choice is to go to court or to have this baby, however bad that choice may be."

Swallowing, Mary Ann looked around the living room—hardwood floors, colorful rugs, a large-screen TV, an expensive sound system, and plush furniture bought on the installment plan. She was imagining herself in such a place, Sarah guessed—perhaps as Sarah herself, a lawyer with a life of her own. The only sound was the droning of a newsman. Sarah could not bring herself to reveal that the case was already on the news.

"Can I stay with you?" Mary Ann asked plaintively. "Just until I get the abortion?"

Sarah felt herself inhale. Inevitably, the girl saw her as a refuge, a substitute parent, the guide to a freedom exemplified by a safe and comfortable apartment.

"Mary Ann," she said, "you can't. There are just too many problems . . ."

Bowing her head, the girl shook it in a spasm of protest and distress. Suddenly she got up and hurried through Sarah's bedroom. Following, Sarah heard the bathroom door close, the sound of retching.

Sarah went to call the Tierneys.

Eighteen

When the two couples entered Citronelle, Caroline had an immediate taste of how her life had changed.

The restaurant was airy and modern, with an open dining room which offered a clear view of those who entered. A young couple at a table for two was closest to them; the woman, touching her husband's arm, fixed Kerry Kilcannon with a startled, starstruck gaze, then recognized Lara, from her years in television almost as familiar as the President. Seeing Caroline, the woman smiled at her. As Caroline smiled back, another man rose to shake the President's hand, and the electricity of their presence enveloped the room—heads turning, exclamations of surprise spreading until, finally, two couples stood and began applauding. In seconds, like an audience rising in stages at the end of an opera, the applause became general.

"It must be me," Jackson Watts murmured in Caroline's ear.

For a split second, she noticed, Kerry Kilcannon had looked bemused. Then his bright smile flashed and he stood straighter, his confident stride making him seem taller than he was. Hands reached out to him; from the side, alerted by the press office, a photographer from the *Washington Post* began recording their progress across the room.

"If it's you," Caroline whispered to Jackson, "you must be utterly intoxicated. Lord knows *I* am."

After they had offered a few words for the *Post*'s style section about the celebratory nature of their dinner and the historic import of their day, the President stopped to greet the new administration's next-most-glamorous pair, seated nearby—Secretary of Commerce Peter Carey and his striking wife, the documentary filmmaker Noelle Ciano. Then the two couples sat at a corner table.

"We leave nothing to chance," Kerry told Caroline. "If no one applauded, Noelle and Peter were prepared to go it alone."

This wry remark seemed typical of Kilcannon. But Caroline felt as though she had just stepped through the looking glass; in the world of a president, the most seemingly casual moments were part of a performance from which he was never released and which, in some measure, would continue until he died. For Lara to live with this must be stressful; it helped, Caroline supposed, that she was also well known, and so could more easily tolerate this unceasing spotlight. As for Jackson Watts—tall and rangy, with a kind, thoughtful face and hair dappled with gray—he was acquitting with grace and good humor his bit part in this particular play: to establish Caroline's credentials as a practicing heterosexual. "If they want," he had told her earlier, "I'll put my hand on your thigh." This aspect of the play, Caroline reflected, was less drama than farce.

As if reading her thoughts, the President said across the table, "There's nothing like public life, Caroline, to hone one's sense of the absurd."

Caroline smiled. It was pleasant how at ease he put her—this first use of her given name, suggesting both regard and friendship, seemed perfectly natural. It struck her again that their fortunes were intertwined; not only had the President appointed her, but he had done so at some risk to himself.

The head of his Secret Service detail, Peter Lake, appeared at their table, bending close to speak to Kilcannon. "I'm sorry, Mr. President, but Adam Shaw just called. He says it's urgent."

At once, Caroline felt alarmed—the fear of exposure was a new and unwelcome companion. But the President merely raised his eyebrows. "Where's a secure line?" he asked.

"The manager's office."

Turning, Kilcannon excused himself, and left.

Lara's gaze followed him. "I hope he can stay for dinner," she said. "The day was seeming too good to last."

Caroline covered her worry with a smile. "So do I. For me, few days have ever been this good."

Lara studied her. *Of course,* Caroline thought, *she knows.*

"No more than you deserve," Lara answered. "Kerry's positive you'll be a great Chief Justice, which is why he's feeling so cheerful.

"That's what some people don't understand. Kerry decides what he thinks is right and then figures out how to make the politics of it work for him—not the other way around. This myth about ruthlessness makes me livid."

Lara's last remark was spoken with quiet intensity. It enriched Caroline's impression of her: beneath the professional veneer of a public woman was someone who loved Kerry Kilcannon deeply and, as best she could, looked after him.

"It can't be easy," Caroline ventured, "seeing someone you love be picked apart."

After a moment, Lara nodded. "I should be used to it, and mostly I am. But I just got the galleys of a new book about him that Kerry hasn't even seen.

"Dark Prince, it's called—psychobabble by some magazine writer who doesn't know him at all. The central thesis is that Kerry's President only because his brother died, and that he's made calculated use of the so-called American romance with death." Pausing, Lara looked at Caroline. "Kerry *knows* that he never would have been in politics without Jamie, and that he will always evoke his brother's memory."

"That's inescapable," Jackson interposed. "But the President's clearly different from his brother."

Abruptly, Lara smiled. "If I weren't so underemployed doing puff pieces and celebrity profiles, I'd think about it less. It's foolish to expect people in my business to ever acknowledge how hard it is to understand anyone, and how unfair it is to pick apart a life."

Several years before, Lara Costello had distinguished herself as a journalist in Kosovo; now, barred from covering hard news because of her engagement to Kerry, she herself was news, the object of constant scrutiny. But her defensiveness of Kerry was, Caroline thought, also a way of conveying sympathy for Caroline without acknowledging what she knew. Which, though Lara surely did not intend it, reminded Caroline to worry about what was delaying the President's return.

Adam Shaw's tone was hasty, apologetic. "I'm sorry, Mr. President. But something's come up, and I know reporters are there. I didn't want you and Judge Masters blindsided."

It must be the daughter, Kerry thought. Silent, he prepared himself.

"About two hours ago," Adam explained, "a fifteen-year-old girl challenged the Protection of Life Act in the federal district court in San Francisco. It's a complete horror show—her parents are pro-life activists, and Dad's a law professor. They've intervened on behalf of the fetus, saying they'll associate the Christian Commitment. Worse, it looks like the whole trial's going to be televised."

Surprised, Kerry answered, "That's more than inauspicious. It puts abortion back in the headlines, and on the toughest and most ambiguous issues—late-term abortion, and parental consent. I've been happy to avoid them both."

"I know. But Justice has to defend this suit, of course—arm in arm with the Christian Commitment. Someone's sure to ask you about it, and the Senate and the media will be badgering Judge Masters for comment."

"That part's simple," Kerry replied. "Justice can let the Commitment take the lead in fighting a teenage girl—in that way, they're a Godsend. I've never taken a position on this law, and now that it's in the courts, I shouldn't. That goes double for Judge Masters. This could be headed straight for the Supreme Court." Briefly, Kerry tried to imagine what might happen. "As soon as there's a district court ruling, Adam, let me know."

For the first time, Adam laughed. "I won't have to. Your pro-choice friends will be all over this one, including those who've never liked you, like Anthony's Legions. Whoever wins, you'll hear the screaming all the way from San Francisco."

"Not before dessert, I hope," Kerry answered, and rang off.

"So," Kilcannon told the others, "the Protection of Life Act is in court."

Listening, Caroline felt deep concern for Sarah Dash. "Unless I'm mistaken, Mr. President, the lawyer's a former law clerk of mine. I've refrained from giving her advice, except to tell her how awful bringing a lawsuit could be for her. But not this awful this soon. She must feel overwhelmed."

Lara played with her wineglass. "Do you think she might give up?"

"Not Sarah. She's stubborn and she's good—by miles the most able clerk I've had, and very quick on her feet." Turning to Kilcannon, she added, "If she loses, Mr. President, she'll appeal to *my* court, then the Supreme Court. It might well get there before *I* do."

Kilcannon pondered this. "As I read the Court, there's a four-four split on this one. Your ex-clerk might not get a ruling, or even a hearing."

This was likely, Caroline thought, and could only heighten the stakes for her nomination. "Which is yet another reason," she said at last, "for me to express no views on abortion."

Kilcannon gave her a brief, curious glance. *What* are *your views,* she could see him wondering. It made her distinctly uncomfortable.

"It must be time to order," he said. "It certainly is for me."

Nineteen

To Sarah, walking through the Tierneys' door was like entering another world.

Like the home of Sarah's childhood, it felt modest and familiar—a 1950s two-story near the Catholic law school where Martin Tierney taught. But, for Sarah, Mary Ann came from a tradition which evoked images she found alien and frightening: unyielding rules; a paradoxical mixture of mysticism and literal belief; the repression of women; the suppression of dissent, whether philosophical or scientific. Though she thought better of Martin Tierney, he embodied for her the two-thousand-year divide between the religious and the rational which had created so much misery. She wondered how the Tierneys saw her: a secular Jew who, like her family, espoused reason over belief.

They settled in the living room, the Tierneys on a couch, Sarah in a chair. "I'm sorry," she said to Margaret Tierney. "This is the last thing I wanted."

Margaret's brow knit in distrust. She was in her midforties and, though slender and dark-haired, youth seemed to have fled her. It was as though life had become something to be endured, promising more adversity than joy. Perhaps, Sarah reflected, this was also her expectation for Mary Ann.

"What else could you expect?" Margaret asked. "You were the one who made her do this."

"That's not true," Sarah answered. "She began thinking for herself, and couldn't tell you. All I did was describe her legal choices."

A flicker of doubt appeared in Margaret's eyes. Despite the accusation, Sarah felt sorry for her—she had willed her version of Mary Ann so strongly that she attributed this new reality to Sarah's influence. "She could tell me anything," Margaret insisted.

Sarah felt tense. "If she could tell you anything, why were you in court to stop her, instead of protecting her?"

"So a fetus is her property?" Martin Tierney asked. "Not a life, not a creation of God with an animating spirit—but a tumor she can excise at will." In the dim light, his eyes held a quiet passion. "You remember the *Dred Scott* decision, where the Supreme Court ruled that an escaped slave was not a person under the Constitution, and therefore 'had no rights which a white person was bound to respect.' *Roe v. Wade* is even worse—it says that an unborn child is property, to be disposed of as we like. And by helping Mary Ann put her own child to death, you're wounding her more terribly than a problem childbirth ever will.

"In the next five years, abortion in America will take more than the six million lives which perished in the Holocaust." He leaned forward, speaking intently. "The only difference is that *our* murders are committed by the mothers, one child at a time.

"You want to believe that we're the adherents of some outmoded way of thinking. But the slow yet inexorable progress of moral development has taught mankind to value life, and the rapid rush of science has given us pictures of how life develops in the womb, and ways of preserving it we never before dreamed of."

Though he looked at Sarah keenly, his voice held sadness. "You think that Mary Ann ran to you as some beacon of truth. We believe she went to you to hide out from the truth. We're not just trying to protect our grandchild, we're trying to protect *her*—from you."

The depth of his belief, and its cogency, made his concern for Mary Ann more palpable to Sarah. "So you'll pressure her until she cracks."

"Do you expect us to be neutral?" Margaret Tierney asked. The question was more disbelieving than hostile. Sarah felt Martin Tierney regard her closely.

"No," she acknowledged. "I don't. That's the problem with a law which makes a minor subject to her parents' beliefs. *My* beliefs give her a choice."

"In a moral society, murder is not a 'choice.'" Tierney's voice remained quiet. "Our daughter's in your apartment, estranged from anything she's known. It's a parent's nightmare. We love her, and she needs to be with us. Think of us how you like, but we want you to bring her home . . ."

"Please help us." To Sarah's surprise, Margaret Tierney reached out to touch her wrist. "We could have called the police. But instead we asked you here. We don't want this to be any worse for her than it already is."

Sarah felt deeply sorry for her. "Neither do I. Please understand, Mrs. Tierney, that I could go back to Judge Leary tomorrow. Along with a psychiatrist who can confirm how damaging it is for Mary Ann to live with parents who are opposing her in court, and that the best way to preserve your family is to place her with a guardian until this case is over."

Margaret Tierney withdrew her hand, eyes wide in disbelief. Sarah sat back, looking from wife to husband. "Don't you see what's already happening to us all?

"All sorts of people have told me how hard this case will be for *me*—that I'll be humiliated; that I'll make enemies; that you two will bring charges against me; that I might even lose my job. But you may be losing your daughter."

For the first time, Sarah's voice rose in anger and frustration. "I didn't recruit her. I didn't ask her to come tonight. I don't want to be accused of undue influence. I don't want those fanatics from the Christian Commitment picketing my building. I don't want to be her parent, her sister, or her role model. But I *do* care what happens to her.

"This unbelievably stupid, cynical law is tearing your family apart. And that's true whether you fight her in court or succeed in breaking her down at home." Sarah paused, drawing a breath before she turned to Martin Tierney. "Bringing in the Commitment is a huge mistake. You may know them on a philosophical and legal basis—that they have the best lawyers, the best data, the best experts. But I've seen them close-up—they don't care how they win, what they do to raise money, or who they damage in the bargain. All I'm asking is that you consider letting her stay with a friend, or relatives who can see their way clear to leave Mary Ann in peace."

"That's very considerate of you." Tierney's voice, though even, carried its first hint of anger. "Everything that's happened is because *you* explained her 'rights' to Mary Ann, instead of respecting ours."

"I made a moral choice," Sarah answered. "Like you. Now I can't turn my back on Mary Ann unless she asks me to. And I can't do *that* in good conscience if I feel she's been coerced."

A silence fell on the room. Sarah could feel how the absence of their daughter must pain the Tierneys, and how invasive her presence must feel. "So you'd drag *her* to court this time," Tierney said at length, "to say she didn't want to be with us."

"I wouldn't want to. But the judge might need to see her."

Tears filmed Margaret Tierney's eyes. Glancing at her, Martin Tierney said, "*We* couldn't put her through that." Nor, Sarah suspected, did he care to do this to his wife.

With emotions this raw, it would not do to push them. Sarah spoke to Margaret Tierney, "I know this is difficult for you to accept, but I'm trying to do what's best for Mary Ann. I'd far prefer not to be here, or to cause you any pain."

Margaret Tierney's eyes softened fractionally. "You've never been a mother," she answered. "I can remember feeling Mary Ann move inside me. You can't feel what I do. What's more hurtful is to think that *she* doesn't feel what I do. But if she aborts this child, she will."

Perhaps it was true, Sarah thought. Mary Ann was struggling to detach herself from the fetus, and to focus on her own protection. Sarah could accept that this was necessary to her emotional health; to Margaret Tierney, the response was alien.

"Your child was healthy," Sarah answered. "This fetus has more chance of harming her than it does of living."

Margaret fidgeted with the hem of her dress. Sarah found herself wondering if, without the resolve of Martin Tierney, Mary Ann's mother might relent—and at what cost to the marriage. "I don't want her living with a stranger," Margaret said, "some counselor from an abortion clinic. I want to see her every day."

"Aren't there friends?" Sarah asked. "Or relatives?"

Margaret shook her head. "We have no relatives here. And we don't want to take this outside our family."

Sarah found this less sympathetic—the reflex of a family to hide its secrets, common in cases of alcoholism and family violence, seldom served its members. But it might help preserve what chance there was that Mary Ann's identity stay private.

"Right now," she said to Margaret, "Mary Ann's in my guest bedroom, crying and afraid. Do you have any suggestions that don't involve police or the courts?"

Margaret did not answer. At her side, Martin looked from his wife to Sarah.

"That for the next few days we can see her," he said at length. "Just as Margaret says. If that goes well, she can come home for good."

"And where will she stay the rest of the time?"

"If Margaret agrees, with you."

As Margaret turned to him, Sarah felt dismay at her own entrapment. "I'm not set up for a roommate, Professor Tierney, and I'm absolutely not prepared to defend charges of undue influence. Which is exactly where this leads."

"We can prepare a written agreement," Tierney answered in a weary tone. "Better the devil we know than the one we don't know at all. At least we've got a common interest in her privacy.

"You say you care about her, Ms. Dash. The impact of taking a fifteen-year-old to court transcends the courtroom, and makes you more than just a lawyer. Just as you contend that it makes us less than parents."

Once more, Sarah feared entanglement with the Tierneys—the bitterness that clashing in court would bring, the hydra-headed price of her commitment, both in private and in public. She had deluded herself when she thought she had reckoned the cost, and measured the risk. Yet the alternative was to leave Mary Ann with her parents, or take them to court tomorrow.

"Let me think about it," she answered. "And talk to my client, of course."

As she left, Sarah was exhausted. Her elation over Caroline was forgotten. The trial would start in ten days.

PART III

The Trial

One

Resolute yet anxious, Sarah arrived at the federal building with Mary Ann Tierney.

For the last ten days Mary Ann refused to sleep at home. "They wear me out," Mary Ann told Sarah, "even when they don't mean to. I can't stand the way they look at me." Yet the night before, Mary Ann had insisted on coming to court.

"This is about *me*," Mary Ann argued. "My parents will be in court, talking about what's best for me, while I'm hiding from my own case. That would be like saying this law is right."

This observation, Sarah realized, was surprisingly acute. For Mary Ann to be in court was a powerful statement that she knew her own mind; her absence would reinforce the Tierneys' authority to speak for her best interests. And Mary Ann could help Sarah refute the arguments Martin Tierney offered in his daughter's name.

But there were risks. Though a Democrat, Judge Leary was Catholic, and seemed more sympathetic to the Tierneys than to their daughter: the sight of Mary Ann's swollen belly could remind Leary more acutely of the progress of her pregnancy and the nature of the procedure she requested. The trial—which Sarah expected to be angry and emotional—could traumatize her further, or seal her estrangement from her parents. Or she might back down entirely, and change her mind.

Sarah explained this. "If I back down," Mary Ann answered, "then I shouldn't have the operation, should I?"

And so, together, Sarah Dash and Mary Ann Tierney climbed the steps of the federal building. They made an odd pair, Sarah thought—a pregnant waif of a teenage girl, a solid dark-haired woman with Eurasian eyes and the controlled demeanor of a lawyer. What felt so familiar about this escaped her until, at the top of the steps, she saw the cluster of pickets.

It was like the day at the clinic when she had rescued Mary Ann. But now the members of the Christian Commitment, enlisted by Martin Tierney as co-counsel, had come to shame his daughter. Their picket signs were brutally precise: DON'T MURDER YOUR SON one read; another, showing a remarkable photograph from *Life* magazine of a fetus in the womb, was captioned, THIS IS YOUR CHILD AT TWENTY-FOUR WEEKS. What made this even crueler was that the fetus in the photograph was normal.

Flinching, Mary Ann turned away. "It'll be all right," Sarah told her, although, sleep-deprived and on edge, she was far from feeling this. The girl slipped her hand in Sarah's.

In front of the glass door was the man from the clinic.

He stood slightly apart from the others, and held no sign. Seeing him, Mary Ann froze.

"Keep moving," Sarah murmured, and steered Mary Ann around him. For once his tone was conversational, that of a man imparting an interesting piece of knowledge. "They won't just kill him, you know. They'll crush his skull, then tear his arms off like the wings of a chicken. He'll come out of you in pieces."

Jaw clenched, Sarah pushed open the door. As they entered the elevator, Mary Ann was weeping; inside she leaned against Sarah's shoulder. "You don't have to be here," Sarah said.

"No," the girl answered. "I do."

On the nineteenth floor, the elevator opened. As they approached the swinging doors of Patrick Leary's courtroom, the clicking sound of Sarah's heels echoed off the tile floor.

Inside, the benches were jammed with reporters. Three television cameras were trained on the well of the courtroom. Mary Ann stopped; she had never been inside a courtroom, Sarah knew, and the glass eyes of the cameras seemed to signify the ordeal she must now endure in public. Sarah mentally cursed Patrick Leary for his vanity.

"Well," Sarah said in a low voice, "here we go."

The atmosphere had a muted electricity, the sense of things about to happen, of a courtroom awaiting a judge. The defendants' table was manned by Thomas Fleming, a flinty, gray-haired veteran of the Justice Department, and Barry Saunders, a florid Texan who was General Counsel to the Christian Commitment. Standing apart, a somber Martin Tierney whispered to his wife.

As Sarah and Mary Ann walked between the rows of reporters, Tierney saw them.

A range of emotions crossed his face—surprise, anger, grief, love for Mary Ann. Gently, he touched Margaret Tierney's shoulder; as she turned, facing their daughter, her lips parted in mute protest. No words were needed to tell Sarah that the fragile peace they had achieved was shattered.

"Sit down at the table," Sarah instructed Mary Ann. "I've got to talk with your father and mother."

Crossing the courtroom, Sarah saw them as a frieze—stricken mother, a father paralyzed by love and outrage. Under his breath, Tierney told Sarah, "I knew you were young, and self-certain. But I never grasped how cruel you are." His voice rose in anger. "How dare you bring her here. How dare you do this to her—to us."

The cutting words shook Sarah badly. "You can't be *that* surprised," she answered. "Your friends from the Christian Commitment surely weren't. Or did you somehow miss the little show *they* put on for Mary Ann's benefit."

For an instant, Tierney looked off balance. Glancing at his wife, he answered, "We arranged to park underground, and take the judge's elevator. To protect our privacy as we thought you'd protect our daughter's."

"Well no such luck," Sarah retorted. "Besides the usual harassment, there was a sign identifying the baby's sex, and another showing a perfect twenty-four-week fetus, instead of one with a head the size of a bowling ball . . ."

"Stop," Margaret Tierney cried out. Beside them, Sarah saw Fleming and Saunders, the Tierneys' allies, look up from the counsel table.

"You stop," Sarah snapped. "You invited these people from the Commitment. You're so blinded by your own sanctity that you can't see who they are.

"They don't give a damn about you *or* her. Some of them don't like Catholics either. They're here to make a propaganda point, and keep their dollars flowing. Lord help them if they ever win—they won't have anything left to do, like tormenting your daughter. Who you love almost, but not quite, as much as your unique relationship with God and his *other* representatives on earth."

Tierney flushed; the venom in her words startled even Sarah. "Mary Ann's here," she said more evenly, "because she wants to take responsibility for her own actions. Now it's your turn. You've got the power to call off the dogs—*you're* their lawyer's ticket to this morality play. If these pickets are still out there tomorrow, then I won't owe you an apology."

Tierney's effort at self-control was painful to watch; the stained cheeks and fixed stare showed the cost of his forbearance. "Which I wouldn't accept," he answered. "But you can tell me how it affected her."

"She was in tears, of course. But if she has to, she'll go through it again tomorrow."

Margaret Tierney touched his hand. In a low voice, Martin said, "I'll talk to their General Counsel."

Turning, Sarah walked to her table. As she sat beside Mary Ann, her mouth felt parched.

Anxious, Mary Ann asked, "What did they say?"

Sarah took a swallow of water. "That they love you, and that they're sorry you're here."

Mary Ann focused on the table while Sarah watched the harbingers of Judge Leary's arrival—a court reporter settling behind her machine, the lanky courtroom deputy with the John Wayne manner emerging from chambers. Across from them, Martin Tierney murmured to his wife; he took a seat at the conference table, while Margaret, hands tightly folded, sat in the first row. Two of the judge's law clerks drifted into the jury box.

"All rise," the deputy called out. "The United States District Court for the Northern District of California is now in session, the Honorable Judge Patrick J. Leary presiding. God save the United States, and this honorable court."

This somewhat baroque salutation, Sarah thought to herself, had fallen into disuse. But Leary insisted on it, and it had its effect—an awed silence marked his first appearance.

In black robes, Leary walked briskly to the bench and sat, looking from one party to another for a long silent moment, followed, Sarah thought, by a briefer glance at the cameras.

"Good morning," he said. "Before we commence, I'll reemphasize the rules for any media which wish to attend this trial.

"There will be no mention in the media of the minor's name, or that of her family.

"There will be no one in this courtroom without press credentials except for counsel, the minor, and her family."

Pausing, Leary spoke directly to the camera, as though admonishing CNN. "The live television broadcast will beep out the minor's name, and obliterate her face. The same rules apply for her family. I will—I repeat *will*—balance the public's interest in a landmark case against the minor's interest in privacy."

Bullshit, thought Sarah in disgust—the broadcast of the trial would inflame the issue in untold, uncontrollable ways, magnifying exponentially the chances that Mary Ann's identity would be leaked, or betrayed by some biographical fact. Leary had rejected all her arguments; what he had omitted from his recitation then, as now, were the dictates of his own ego. But no doubt his sternness played well on television.

"Except for the minor and her family," he continued, "all witnesses will be sequestered in the jury room until they're called to testify.

"All witnesses, counsel, and the parties will refrain from making public statements until further notice.

"All transcripts of proceedings will use the plaintiff's pseudonym, and any pages revealing her name and identity, or that of her family, will be sealed.

"*Any* member of the media who violates *any* of these rules will be barred from the courtroom.

"The trial will take six days, followed by closing arguments." Leary paused again, surveying the courtroom. "Immediately thereafter, the court will rule, with a written opinion to follow within one day."

At least he had given her that much, Sarah thought—with Mary Ann six months pregnant, swiftness was essential.

Abruptly, Leary turned to her. "Please call your first witness, Ms. Dash."

With this, the trial of *Jane Doe et al. versus Barton Cutler, Attorney General of the United States* had begun.

TWO

Questioning Dr. Mark Flom, Sarah tried to ignore the cameras, Judge Leary's restless fidgeting, the tense scrutiny of Martin Tierney, until it seemed that she and Flom were talking in a vacuum.

Quickly, she established his unique credentials: that he was an obstetrician; that he possessed a law degree; that he was one of the few specialists in postviability abortions practicing on the West Coast. Then she pinned a fetal sonogram to an easel.

Here she paused: the size of the head, grotesquely large compared to its limbs, caused even Leary to sit still. When Sarah glanced at Mary Ann, her head was bowed, and her hands covered her face.

"The fetus is hydrocephalic," Flom told her, "to a one-hundred percent certainty."

"And how does that affect mental capacity?"

Flom straightened his tie. With his white hair, careful demeanor, and sensitive air, he was all Sarah could have hoped for, the antithesis of a callous doctor butchering babies without remorse. He glanced at Martin Tierney, then told Sarah firmly, "It is almost certain that, if born, the baby would have no brain."

"As to life, Dr. Flom, what are the implications of *that*?"

"Grim. Most such babies would die shortly after birth, or within days. Though I am familiar with one who lived two years in an irreversible coma." Flom's measured tone took on a slight, but palpable, edge. "The baby's existence was, in essence, both parasitic and expensive. The mother was sixteen, and couldn't afford the bills. Understandably, no one wished to adopt him."

"Objection," Martin Tierney had stood abruptly. "I move to strike the doctor's last remarks. The reference to adoption is irrelevant in this case—where *we* stand ready to care for the child—and gratuitous in any case."

"Hardly." Ignoring Tierney, Sarah spoke to Patrick Leary. "We're asking the Court to rule this statute to be unconstitutional in *all* cases. The opponents of abortion claim that adoption is a humane alternative. Professor Tierney wants the benefit of that argument without facing its absurdity in the context of this law—"

"Enough," Leary cut in sharply. "There's no jury here. When the trial's over, *I'll* decide what's relevant to my ruling. Move on, Ms. Dash."

This was typical of Leary, Sarah thought, impatient, self-important, and short-sighted; thinking to push things forward, he could guarantee a free-for-all, a longer, sloppier trial where everything was admissible. It would not be pleasant. "Thank you," she said with seeming deference, and turned to Flom. "What other defects might be apparent at birth?"

"Several, some less serious *only* in the most relative sense." Flom began to tick them off on the fingers of one hand. "Heart defects and respiratory defects, both potentially fatal. Spasticity of the lower extremities. Others might include club feet, cleft palate, broad nose and neck, low-set and malformed ears. But the gravest, and insoluble, problem is the absence of a brain."

At the edge of her vision, Sarah saw Mary Ann Tierney cringe. "Insoluble?" she asked Flom. "What about fetal surgery to relieve the hydrocephalus?"

"It's been tried, by using utero-ventricular shunts to drain the fluid. In a relatively small percentage, less than thirty percent, the brain developed normally." His voice lowered. "Of the rest, there was no improvement. Except that they lived a little longer than expected, perhaps in great pain. As a result, our profession has placed a moratorium on such surgery."

Sarah found that Flom's professionalism fed her confidence: his testimony followed the grid they had designed, after hours of work. "Then let's consider," she continued, "the potential effects on Mary Ann Tierney of taking this fetus to term."

Flom nodded briskly. "At term, the hydrocephalic fetus is almost always in the breach position, problematic in itself. But it's the head which poses the greatest risk to Mary Ann."

Walking to the easel, Sarah removed the blowup of the sonogram. As she did, she felt the camera follow her, saw those at the defense table—Martin Tierney, Barry Saunders of the Christian Commitment, and Thomas Fleming of the Justice Department—watching her intently.

Beneath the sonogram was a depiction of a fetus in the womb, feet first. Once more, its head was horribly swollen. "Is this an accurate portrayal," she asked Flom, "of the position and proportions of Mary Ann Tierney's fetus, should it go to term?"

"It is," Flom answered crisply. "In particular, note the head. It's roughly the size of a cantaloupe or, perhaps, a soccer ball."

From the bench, Leary seemed transfixed by the fetal head. "Your Honor," Martin Tierney interjected, "Dr. Flom's choice of language is both inflammatory and inhumane. This is not a 'soccer ball,' it's the head of a living child—our grandchild, our daughter's child. This testimony is calculated to appall while avoiding what Dr. Flom apparently considers the small matter of infanticide. If he considers it at all."

Listening, Sarah was struck by a curious sense of duality. Tierney's demeanor reflected a genuine passion. Yet his rhetoric suggested that he, like Sarah, was well aware of the cameras and their impact on Leary and a potential audience of millions, and therefore saw the trial as both legal and political. If so, she was prepared.

"The living child in question," she told Judge Leary, "is Mr. Tierney's child, Mary Ann. Dr. Flom is testifying to the facts of the birth Mr. Tierney wishes this court to force on her. Which facts include—whether he cares to acknowledge it—the danger to Mary Ann Tierney of a head the size of a soccer ball."

Leary's milk-white face betrayed the flush of irritation: speeches from lawyers offended his sense of a tight courtroom, with himself at its center. Abruptly, the judge asked Flom, "Soccer ball, watermelon, or child of God, what about a C-section? Can't you get this baby out the same as millions of other babies?"

Flom looked momentarily astonished, then recovered. "That depends, Your Honor, on what kind of cesarean section you're asking about.

"To deliver this baby, you'd have to perform a classical C-section. That's no longer performed in the case of a normal fetus—it's too radical and risky in any case, and worse for a fifteen-year-old girl whose body may not have fully matured." Pausing, he moved his hand in a slicing gesture. "You'd have to bivalve the uterus, Judge Leary. That means roughly a twelve percent risk of rupture in Mary Ann's next pregnancy, creating at least the five percent risk to reproductive capacity identified by her own doctor."

Leary hesitated; to Sarah, he appeared to be looking for an exit. "Your Honor," she interposed, "we have an exhibit, premarked as plaintiffs' three, which may clarify this testimony."

Curtly, Leary nodded. Walking to the easel, Sarah removed the fetal diagram. The photograph beneath it was a vivid color.

Leary blanched visibly. With deliberate calm, Sarah asked, "Can you identify that photograph, Dr. Flom?"

"Yes. It's a photograph of a uterus which ruptured following a classical

C-section. Aside from the bleeding, you'll note that it appears to have exploded in the course of childbirth. Which, in essence, it has."

Silent, Sarah let his last remark sink in. Standing beside the easel, she saw Margaret Tierney turn away.

So, apparently, did Leary. "At this time," he said, "we'll take a fifteen-minute break. Please return promptly."

When the trial resumed, Mary Ann did not look at her parents, nor they at her.

"As someone with a degree in law," Sarah said to Flom, "and a doctor who has performed late-term abortions, do you believe it's legal—without this statute—to abort the normal fetus of a healthy teenage girl?"

"Objection." This time it was Thomas Fleming, from the Justice Department. "You're asking the witness to render a legal opinion, which is the prerogative of the court. Not to mention one which is irrelevant: this law, after all, *does* exist."

"Which is why Mary Ann is forced to be here," Sarah countered. "The question is whether it's necessary to stem an onslaught of late-term abortions, or if it simply operates to deny an emergency medical procedure to pregnant minors."

Leary nodded. "I'll allow it," he said to Fleming. "But it's nice to know you're here."

In the jury box, Leary's clerks, both men, grinned at each other. It was one more thing Sarah disliked about Leary: his penchant for showing off, at the lawyers' expense, to his paid gallery of retainers. And though his ruling was apt, his barb at the government's quiescence might make Fleming more active, to Sarah's detriment.

"Can you read back the question?" she asked the reporter.

The reporter did. "Our profession agrees that it's quite clear," Flom answered, "even without this statute. It's illegal, after viability, to abort a normal fetus of a healthy mother. Regardless of the mother's age."

Sarah stood near Mary Ann, one hand flat on the conference table. Beside her, Mary Ann stared at the photograph of the ruptured uterus, which Sarah had left there. "So *you've* never performed such an abortion?" she asked Flom.

"No. Nor do I know any doctor who has." Pausing, Flom gazed at the defendants. "What abortion opponents don't understand—or at least pretend not to—is that late-term abortions are rare: beyond twenty-one weeks, fewer than one in a hundred; beyond twenty-four weeks, perhaps one in a thousand.

"The idea that they're routinely used as a form of birth control slanders my profession. Nor, despite the propaganda otherwise, are doctors snatching babies from the womb moments before birth. Although thanks to this ill-conceived statute, Mary Ann Tierney is getting closer to that circumstance every day."

Watch it, Sarah warned him with her eyes. She waited a moment to ask the next question. "Suppose, Dr. Flom, that a teenage girl came to you in the sixth month of pregnancy, lacking any means of support, and said she wanted an abortion because her boyfriend had abandoned her."

Flom's fine poet's features became emotionless, and the renewed calm of his voice suggested that he had received Sarah's message. "I'd feel profound sympathy. But I'd have to tell her it was illegal, and counsel her on alternatives like adoption."

"Suppose that she'd been raped?"

"I'd feel even more sympathy, Ms. Dash. But my answer would be the same." Flom spread his hands. "Only if there is a significant threat to the life or health of the mother, *or* a severe fetal anomaly, will I perform a late-term abortion."

Sarah glanced at Leary. He seemed to be paying close attention, though she could not be sure what that meant. "Aside from hydrocephalus," she asked Flom, "what are common threats to the life or health of the mother?"

"A cardiac problem, or cancer—any condition where pregnancy delays vital treatment." Following Sarah's cue, Flom faced Leary again. "Often, Your Honor, treatment has already been delayed by other conditions—poverty, lack of insurance, substance abuse, or simple ignorance—which forestall diagnosis and create the need for a late-term abortion. For teenage girls you can add still another: the attempt to conceal their pregnancy."

"In your experience," Sarah asked, "why do they do that?"

"Because, for a host of reasons, they're afraid." Pausing, Flom faced the courtroom, and spoke with quiet emotion. "But that leads to one very frequent reason young girls are afraid, which *also* leads to fetal anomalies. Incest."

Sarah paused a moment. "Is that common?"

"We see it regularly," Flom answered. "And it's a little tough to talk *that* one over with Mom and Dad."

In the silence, Martin Tierney rose. "Your Honor," he said slowly, "I recognize that Dr. Flom sees social problems which are tragic and which we all deplore. Still, a fetus is a life. Nor should the sad facts of one family—or the claims about that family, true or false—deprive other families, such as ours, of the protection of this law."

It was an attempt, however wan, to blunt the impact of this testimony. "Your Honor," Sarah emphasized, "this is *not* a case of incest, and we acknowledge that the Tierneys are loving parents. But many girls subject to this law are not so fortunate."

"All right," Leary told her. "Go ahead."

Facing Flom, Sarah asked, "In the case of troubled families, what are the drawbacks of requiring a parent to consent to a late-term abortion?"

Pensive, Flom steepled his fingers. "The best way to answer," he said at last, "is to tell you a story.

"Last year, I got a call from a teenage girl who lived in another state. She was three months pregnant, and the law in her state required parental consent to *any* abortion. Because California has no such requirement, a women's clinic referred her to me.

"Even on the telephone, she was crying. But I finally found out what else was wrong. Her father, an alcoholic, had raped her, and she was afraid to tell her mother."

Pausing, Flom bit his lip. "She was hoping," he continued, "that someone from the clinic could drive her here. But Congress had passed an *earlier* law. It forbids anyone not her parent to take a minor, without parental permission, out of state for an abortion. One law ordered her to tell her parents, and another kept her from escaping them.

"All I could tell her was to try and get here on her own.

"Three months later, she did. She was tired, and dirty, and hungry, much like the other runaways we see. I asked her what had happened." Flom inhaled and his voice, though still level, was tight with anger. "Thanks to these 'protective' laws, she'd been forced to tell her mother. When Mom confronted Dad, he hanged himself. And so, unfortunately, the mother blamed her daughter.

"The girl ran away. By the time she got here, she was six months pregnant. All that I could do was hope that what was true in so many cases of incest—that testing would show the fetus to be defective—would be true here.

"It wasn't. So instead of aborting her late father's child, I delivered it. Now she's trying to raise him on her own." Once more, he looked up at Leary. "As a doctor I have to ask, Your Honor, why this was necessary. But *Congress* never asked. Instead they passed a law, and now they've passed another. God knows how many more tragedies these laws will force other girls to live with."

There was quiet, and then Leary recessed the trial for lunch.

Three

When the defense commenced its cross-examination of Dr. Flom, it was Barry Saunders, not Martin Tierney, who questioned on behalf of the fetus.

The General Counsel for the Christian Commitment was a large shambling man with small, shrewd eyes, a slightly pursed mouth, and razor-cut hair. To Sarah, he looked like the prototype of a southern football coach, with all the bluffness, calculation, and zeal to win that this implied.

"This procedure"—the word was laden with distaste—"you're wanting to perform on Mary Ann's child, is that what's called a 'partial birth' abortion?"

Flom gave him a measured look. "In medicine, there is no such thing. That's a term invented by politicians and anti-abortion activists."

Saunders placed his hands on his hips. "You mean doctors don't allow the baby to be partially delivered, then crush the skull?"

"Doctors *may*," Flom answered, "if that's the safest technique for saving the mother's life or health. I don't intend to do that here."

"You don't? Then you're meaning to dismember the fetus and deliver it piecemeal?"

Beneath the table, Sarah felt Mary Ann grip her hand. "No." Flom's voice remained calm. "Let's be clear, Mr. Saunders. Dealing with a medical emergency which requires late-term abortion is neither simple nor pleasant, for either the woman or her doctor.

"For propaganda purposes, your group has tried to pass state laws barring procedures which may be the safest for the mother, but can be made to sound the most gruesome. *Those* laws were thrown out—they were too broad for doctors to know what was illegal, and created greater danger to the mother. So now there's *this* law, which governs *all* late-term abortions in *every* state unless the parents consent." Once more, Flom's voice took on an edge. "This bars me from protecting Mary Ann's reproductive capacity by any procedure, including the one I *would* anticipate using. So I suppose it has the virtue of clarity."

Saunders appraised him, then said to Leary, "I realize the witness is ideologically committed to the pro-abortion cause. But he should confine himself to answering my questions. He can deliver speeches on the courthouse steps."

Sarah remained sitting. "When Mr. Saunders deliberately misunderstands the witness," she said to Leary, "and misstates medical procedures, his questions must be placed in context . . ."

"Confine yourself to answering," Leary snapped at Flom.

"Just how," Saunders inquired promptly, "*do* you intend to take the life of Mary Ann Tierney's child?"

Flom glanced at Sarah. "Forgive me," he told Saunders politely, "but perhaps both of us should leave to others whether a fetus without a brain has a 'life' as we understand it—"

"Oh, we'll get to *that*," Saunders cut in. "Just answer the question."

Flom folded his arms. "Suffice it to say, Mr. Saunders, that a medical emergency like this is a tragedy for all concerned. The question is what procedure is safest for Mary Ann. Will you permit me to give you a little history?"

Saunders briefly flapped his arms, miming helplessness and impatience. "Go ahead. Seems like nothing's going to stop you."

At the defense table, Martin Tierney looked down with furrowed brow. Sarah wondered how this performance was affecting him; Saunders's veiled bullying and anti-intellectualism seemed contrary to Tierney's faith in argument and reason. Quickly, she decided to let Saunders do what he wished, and place her trust in Flom.

"First," Flom said, "there's a myth that late-term abortion originated with *Roe v. Wade,* and reflects a particularly barbarous extension of abortion on demand. But as early as 1716, an English medical treatise proposed saving the mother's life by removing the contents of the fetal cranium before delivery.

"In essence, that's what I propose to do here, if possible. Although, in this case, we can expect the cranial contents to be minimal—except for fluid."

Saunders's small mouth grimaced with distaste. "You're assuming a lot, Doctor, about someone else's grandson. Maybe you can tell me precisely how you intend to do away with this life you deem so worthless."

Instinctively, Sarah rose to object, then sat again. "No life is 'worthless,'" Flom responded tartly. "But as a doctor, I'm aware that the same anomaly which renders *this* fetus virtually hopeless threatens Mary Ann's capacity to have normal children. This law prevents me from protecting her by the safest possible means—or any means. And that, as a *doctor,* I resent.

"As a *doctor,* Mr. Saunders, I'm faced with the problem of getting an unnaturally enlarged fluid-filled object, the fetal head, through the opening of a semi-elastic container, the uterus, which is too small for this to be possible without damaging the container or its opening."

Beneath the table, Sarah felt Mary Ann's grip tighten. The court was seized by intense quiet; Leary was quite still, and his clerks had stopped snickering and whispering. "One technique," Flom told Saunders, "of which you apparently disapprove, involves extracting the feet in a breach delivery, then decompressing the skull. The technique which I think safest involves decompressing the skull, and delivering as normal.

"Morally, I don't see the difference. Medically, I've performed this procedure precisely one thousand three hundred sixty-seven times." Looking past Saunders, Flom seemed to speak to Martin Tierney. "Of that number, I've had five hospitalizations for complications, three blood transfusions, no extra surgeries, and no cases of infertility whatsoever. If I'm permitted to do so, I *will* make certain that Mary Ann can have more children. Period."

Martin Tierney's pale eyes were thoughtful. As if to himself, he slowly shook his head and then, rising, asked Judge Leary, "May I briefly question the witness, Your Honor?"

Saunders turned to him, seemingly amazed at this intrusion. For her own reasons, Sarah sympathized—Saunders offered Flom a better foil. Swiftly, she said, "This isn't tag-team wrestling, Your Honor. It's enough for the witness to be questioned by two parties, let alone two lawyers for one party."

"The witness seemed to be speaking to me directly," Tierney replied in mild tones, "as a father, if not a prospective grandfather. I'd like to make some inquiries in that same spirit."

"Go ahead," Leary ordered. "You can sit down, Mr. Saunders."

Without glancing at Tierney, Saunders retired to the defense table, sitting with his chin propped in his hand. Moving toward Flom, Tierney addressed him with quiet intimacy. "It's possible, is it not, that this child could be born with a normal cerebral cortex?"

"Objection," Sarah said at once. "In theory, almost anything's possible. The question is how likely—"

"Are you testifying?" Leary interrupted, "or merely telling the witness how to testify? Sit down, Ms. Dash." As Sarah sat, flushing, Leary demanded, "Answer the question, Dr. Flom."

"It's extremely *unlikely,* Your Honor."

"But medically possible," Leary pressed.

"Put that way, yes."

Leary shot a triumphant look at Sarah; helpless, she wondered whether he had taken such a dislike to her, or to her case, that he meant to undermine her before her client, her witness, and an audience of millions. In any case, she was warned; Flom was on his own.

Facing Flom, Tierney said, "You should also know, Dr. Flom, that any risk of infertility to Mary Ann distresses her mother and me more than we can express. Can you accept that?"

"Of course."

Pausing, Tierney slumped as though burdened by his responsibilities as a parent, and its implications for Mary Ann. "You place that possibility at roughly five percent, correct?"

"I do."

"But that's not a precise figure, is it?"

"No. It's an estimate. It could be more, or less."

"So it could be four percent. Or three."

"Yes."

"And, indeed, some studies place the risk at two percent, or lower."

Flom hesitated; like any good expert, Sarah noticed, he became less voluble when wary of his interrogator. "That's true," he answered. "Perhaps one of our differences is that I wouldn't deem even *that* an acceptable risk for my own daughter."

Tierney gave him a small, bleak smile. "If my grandson were 'normal,' in your view, but the same risk to Mary Ann existed, would you recommend aborting him?"

Flom frowned, unsettled. "That would be highly unusual, Professor Tierney. It's a situation I've not faced."

"Face it for a moment, Doctor. Without this law, the decision would be up to you."

Flom hesitated. "Under those circumstances, I don't think I would."

"So," Tierney pursued, "your decision turns on your belief that my grandson isn't 'normal.'"

"I think it's important, Professor Tierney, to weigh the prospects of a meaningful life for *this* child against the risks of a classical cesarean section."

Tierney moved closer. "But isn't this 'weighing' process of yours a lot like playing God? What standards circumscribe your judgment?"

"The standards of medical ethics—"

"As interpreted by *you*? Suppose there was no risk to Mary Ann, but six months into pregnancy you discovered that she was carrying a Down's syndrome child. If this law did not exist, would you abort the child if she asked you to?"

Flom crossed his arms again. "Under those circumstances," he said at length, "I'm not comfortable with termination."

Tierney raised his eyebrows. "But some would be?"

"I can't answer that, Professor. But instead of the mother deciding whether she can raise a Down's baby, should the *grandparents* decide? I'll leave it to you to explain why that's better." Leaning forward, Flom tried to alter the balance between them. "But we're not dealing with a Down's baby, are we? We're dealing with an anomaly which is infinitely worse, with potentially terrible consequences to your daughter . . ."

"Which you believe constitutes a 'medical emergency,' justifying termination." Pausing, Tierney scrutinized him closely. "What's to keep you, Dr. Flom, from deciding that anyone who wants a late-term abortion faces a 'medical emergency'?"

For the first time, Flom bristled visibly. "My sense of ethics—which is also that of my profession."

"Speaking of your profession's ethics," Tierney replied in unimpressed tones, "didn't I understand you to say that fetal surgery could result in 'normal' births for thirty percent of hydrocephalic fetuses?"

"Roughly, yes."

"But your profession has now banned such surgery."

Flom sat back. "The results in the remaining seventy percent were tragic. Including to condemn a damaged child and its family to several years of pain and hopelessness . . ."

"And so," Tierney pursued, "the ethics of your profession permit you to deny my grandson a thirty percent chance of developing a 'normal' brain. And then permit you to abort him because he poses a very remote threat of infertility."

At the plaintiffs' table, Mary Ann was still; Sarah wondered whether, in her mind, the credibility of Flom versus her parents hung in the balance. "Professor Tierney," Flom said tightly, "we're discussing fantasy, not fact. If you can tell me this fetus has a five percent chance of having a brain, I'd be interested to hear about it. But you won't because you can't. Instead we have this law."

"Which protects our daughter," Tierney rejoined, "and our family. You don't know anything about her, do you? Or us. And yet *you* propose to take our place, without knowing our reason."

"No," Flom answered firmly. "I propose to practice medicine, the best way I know how, and to let Mary Ann decide what to do about this tragedy. For you to take that decision away from her is contemptuous of medical science, and of her."

At this, Tierney hesitated. With fascination, Sarah watched a father weigh a lawyer's dilemma: whether he had accomplished enough, and whether continuing would cause more harm than good—to his case, and within his family.

Sitting beside her, Mary Ann seemed not to breathe. "No further questions," Tierney said.

In a split second, Sarah decided, and was on her feet. "Why do you perform late-term abortions, Dr. Flom?"

Flom considered her with weary dignity. "To protect the life and health of the mother."

"Do you enjoy that aspect of your practice?"

"I do not. It's difficult for everyone—occasionally, I have dreams about it." Glancing at Tierney, he added quietly, "I set out to deliver babies, not terminate problem pregnancies."

"So how did your practice evolve?"

"Because I found out women needed me. Ob-gyns are popular—doctors who perform late-term abortions aren't." He inhaled, then said in a harsher tone, "Do you know why I've performed over one thousand late-term abortions? Because there are only two doctors in California who will."

"Why so few?"

"Because we get harassed by groups like the Christian Commitment. My wife's been confronted at the grocery store, asked why she's married to a baby-killer—"

"I object," Saunders called out. "This is slander, hearsay, and irrelevant . . ."

Sarah spun on him. "*You* object? *I* object to the demonstrators you sent to harass *us* this morning. But I thought *you'd* be proud enough to let the world know." At once she turned to Leary, "If I'm angry, I apologize. But Mr. Saunders implied that Dr. Flom was acting callously, even blithely. Out of decency, I ask that Mr. Saunders at least allow him to complete his answer."

For the first time, Leary seemed to regard her with something akin to respect. "Finish your answer," Leary told Flom.

Turning, Flom addressed himself to Saunders. "There have been death threats—to myself and to my wife. Given the murder of other doctors, I have to take them seriously.

"We have guards at the hospital now. Before I appeared here, I spoke to my family, and polled the members of my clinic. Because my testimony on television poses a threat to *them*."

Slowly, he faced Tierney. "So, no, Professor Tierney—I'm not playing God.

I don't want to play God with women's lives, or the lives of my family or my colleagues. I'd just like to be left alone, by Congress and by your allies, to be the best doctor I can."

Saunders began to protest. Then Tierney grasped his arm, and the courtroom was silent.

"No further questions," Sarah said.

Four

"If we can't get you confirmed," Adam Shaw told Caroline, "without answering a single question about abortion, we're amateurs."

They sat around a long table in a wood-paneled conference room in the West Wing. Her other interlocutors, Ellen Penn and Clayton Slade, smiled knowingly; as an outside adviser, Shaw had shepherded two prior Supreme Court nominees through the gauntlet of Senate confirmation, and understood how byzantine the process had become.

"Responsiveness is risky," Ellen affirmed. "Bob Bork tried to answer questions, and it killed him. If you're careful, the partisan bitterness that's existed ever since the Bork fight won't spill over onto you."

Once more, Caroline felt that she had entered the shadowy zone between law and politics, where candor was a menace and honesty a curse. "So this is not my God-given chance to demonstrate how brilliant I am."

"It's *their* chance," Shaw answered. "Your job is to convince ten out of eighteen senators on the committee, and fifty-one out of a hundred in the full Senate, to vote for you. The more they talk, and you listen, the less chance for you to screw up." He gave Ellen Penn an ironic glance. "As the Vice President knows, her former colleagues will be happy for the camera time. Beginning with Chad Palmer."

"I call it the eighty-twenty rule," Ellen told Caroline. "If they're talking eighty percent of the time, and you twenty percent, you're winning. If it's sixty-forty, you're in trouble. And if it's fifty-fifty, you're in deep shit.

"These hearings can make or break you. Our job, in the next few weeks, is to make sure you're the best-prepared nominee Palmer's committee has ever seen. Like it or not, that means the most well trained."

Clayton nodded in affirmation. "We'll get you briefing books on every conceivable issue. We'll have a platoon of law professors to brief you on new developments. Then we'll put you before some murder boards . . ."

"'Murder boards'?" Caroline inquired. "Like mock hearings?"

"'Murder boards,'" Shaw responded, "captures the spirit of things. At the hearing room doors, the Constitution stops, and Palmer and his colleagues become God. There are no rules of evidence, and some on his committee won't be governed by the rules of decency. Imagine yourself as the star of every bad hearing in the last quarter century." Pausing, Shaw locked his gaze on Caroline. "You could be forced to lay your life bare—like John Tower.

"Your net worth will be exposed—like Nelson Rockefeller.

"Your comments at the water fountain twenty years ago might get thrown back at you—like Clarence Thomas.

"The videos you rent from Blockbuster may be uncovered—like Robert Bork.

"Your confidential medical records will be dissected—like William Rehnquist.

"Your former use of drugs or alcohol could be used against you—like Douglas Ginsburg. Or even your driving record in college—like Dick Cheney. And all this time the committee, the FBI, and any interest group who doesn't like you will be digging for more." Sitting back, Shaw's voice became softer. "Our job is to make sure your answers are as cogent, persuasive, *and* uninformative as you can make them. So that the committee goes back to making speeches instead of asking more questions."

None of this daunted Caroline; nothing was a surprise. What remained unspoken and uncomfortable was the fact of Brett, and Chad Palmer's ambiguous role as Caroline's protector and interrogator. "When will I meet Senator Palmer?" she asked.

"Soon," Shaw answered. "You'll be starting a round of courtesy calls to every member of the committee, beginning with Palmer. We'll tell you who to watch out for . . ."

"But Palmer's critical."

"Yes—and later on, Macdonald Gage. We'll try to get you a meeting with him, too. But the main point there is not to give him ammunition."

Caroline reflected that her confirmation, and more, depended on the complex motives and ambitions of two men she did not know. "You won't be out there by yourself," Ellen told her. "We'll have a team keeping tabs on all the senators. The Minority Leader, and the ranking Democrat on the committee, will be looking out after your interests. We'll be lining up the best witnesses to support your nomination, and a string of endorsements, from the ABA to the AFL-

CIO." Ellen's manner radiated energy and confidence. "Last, and best, there's President Kilcannon. He's made your confirmation the first test of his presidency."

Though meant to reassure, Ellen's words underscored the stakes for all concerned. Wryly, Caroline said, "I'll keep that in mind."

The others, even Clayton, smiled. "But whatever they ask you," Adam Shaw said with equal dryness, "don't act nervous—the TV cameras pick up tics. Whenever they shaded the truth, Al Haig jiggled his knee and Kissinger began picking his nose."

"This brings up the matter of visuals," Clayton observed. "We'll reserve places so that your family and Jackson Watts can sit behind you."

Nodding, Caroline felt her past converge with her present, and the risks that bore. "Is there anything new," Clayton asked her, "that could be a problem?"

Caroline considered this. "Only one thing," she answered. "Our court's about to issue an en banc opinion in the case of a prisoner named Orlando Snipes.

"It could be controversial. Snipes is an armed robber who sued prison officials in California to stop his cellmate from beating and abusing him sexually. The original panel opinion by Lane Steele denied Snipes the right to sue—"

"I'm familiar with Steele," Shaw interjected. "He sees himself as the intellectual heir to Roger Bannon. Only *he* thinks that's an achievement."

"Exactly. When I read Steele's opinion, I asked the full court to vote to rehear en banc.

"They agreed, by eleven votes to ten. Eleven of us heard it, and then reversed by six to five. I was the initiator and, one could say, the deciding vote in both instances."

"Did you write the en banc opinion?" Clayton asked.

"I *would* have, but the day we reheard it the President chose me for the Court. So my friend and mentor, Blair Montgomery, reassigned to himself the job of writing the opinion.

"As senior judge in the majority that was Blair's prerogative. His stated reason was that I would be too busy. His real reason was to save me trouble in these hearings."

"Will it?" Ellen asked. "If you initiated the rehearing, won't that come out?"

"It shouldn't. Some aspects—such as my role, and our deliberations—are supposed to be internal." Pausing, Caroline glanced at Clayton. "Blair was trying to make me look like just another vote in support of *his* opinion. Which, given that he despises Steele and all he stands for, he was more than happy to write."

"Did Steele dissent?" Shaw inquired.

"Yes. Specifically, he accused Blair of 'creating a new hobby for inmates who, deprived of their normal pursuits, can now do violence to the truth.' Lane considers himself a phrasemaker."

Shaw frowned. "It sounds like Montgomery did you a favor. But we should be prepared. We'll need copies of his opinion and Steele's dissent."

Caroline nodded. "Is there anything else I should do?"

"It's more what you shouldn't do." Clayton sat back, folding his arms. "Right now we're set to win this. So between now and the day the full Senate votes on your nomination, pretend that you're the bridegroom at a wedding. The rules are the same: keep quiet and stay out of the way—no speeches, no letters, no appearances.

"We need fifty-one votes. We want one hundred. Because if you get in trouble, and Mac Gage smells it, he could let the right-wingers filibuster you to death, and keep you from ever coming to a vote."

This startled Caroline. "On a Supreme Court nomination?" she asked. "Has the Senate ever done that?"

"Not in living memory, and it would take real balls for Gage to do it now. But never underestimate how much Gage dislikes the President, and how much he wants to undermine him.

"Under the rules of the Senate, all Gage needs is forty-one votes against shutting down a filibuster. That means you could have fifty-nine senators willing to support you, and still never make it to the Court."

Ellen turned to him in surprise. "That's a long shot," she interjected. "No matter how much Gage wants to break the President, that could tear the Senate apart. Gage isn't *crazy*."

"He's not," Clayton agreed. "But I don't think he's a free agent, either. There are people who Gage answers to."

Though she was the focus of the discussion, Caroline felt herself an outsider, about to enter a world she did not fathom. For a moment, Ellen's eyes narrowed in thought, and then she turned to Caroline. "Just follow the rules, Caroline, and learn your lines. We'll take care of the rest."

Five

Watching Siobhan Ryan take the stand, Sarah felt the weight of her own responsibility. As a lawyer, Sarah's sole concern must be for Mary Ann; as a woman, she wished that Ryan was not here. So, plainly, did Barry Saunders.

"Your Honor," he said, "we're very familiar with Mrs. Ryan. She's a professional witness for the pro-abortion cause. Her personal experience was as an adult, not a minor, and her political opposition to this law is notorious. Any testimony she might give is biased, and irrelevant to Mary Ann Tierney."

"It's highly relevant," Sarah retorted, "and Mr. Saunders knows it. The court has already stated its disposition to hear all testimony, and weigh relevance for itself. If it does so here, the true reason for Mr. Saunders's objection will become quite clear."

From the witness stand, Ryan watched this exchange with an air of weary resignation, as if she had become accustomed, if not inured, to castigation. She was in her late thirties, with pale skin, delicate features, round dark eyes, and black hair cut close to her head; Sarah hoped Leary would see her for what she was, a reticent woman who had forced herself to come here.

"If her testimony is irrelevant," Leary told Saunders. "I can cut her off myself."

As Sarah moved toward the witness, she was aware of the camera following her, an unwelcome presence that would change Siobhan Ryan's life still further. "I'm sorry," she had told Ryan in private. "If you don't want to do this . . ."

Sarah's voice had trailed off, and Siobhan Ryan had finished the sentence for her in a soft, clear voice. ". . . it'll go worse for this girl."

Now, perched on the edge of her chair, she reminded Sarah of a sparrow who wished to take flight. "Could you state your name for the record," Sarah directed.

"Yes." Her voice remained wispy. "Siobhan Elizabeth Ryan."

"Are you married?"

"Yes."

Ryan's quiet voice seemed to draw the courtroom toward her. Leary leaned forward, as though to hear each word; only Barry Saunders, grimacing, seemed at odds with the prevailing mood.

"Were you brought up in any religious tradition?" Sarah asked.

"Yes. My parents are Irish Catholic. I was raised and confirmed in the Church."

"Are you still an observant Catholic?"

"Yes."

"Are you also pro-life?"

"Your Honor," Saunders called out. "I object. As her testimony will establish, for Mrs. Ryan to call herself 'pro-life' is an insult to our movement, and a fraud on the court."

Sarah did not condescend to look at him. "We're in a court of law," she said to Leary, "not the Church of Barry Saunders. Mr. Saunders has no power to excommunicate Mary Ann Tierney's witnesses, or to censor testimony he wishes you not to hear."

The remark brought a smile to the judge's lips. This time television helped, Sarah was quite sure; there was no way that Leary would stifle this fragile-seeming woman at the behest of an overbearing man. "Let Mrs. Ryan talk," he told Saunders. "I'll be hearing from you soon enough."

With unsettling amiability, Saunders smiled and sat down; it would be too bad, Sarah thought, if he were shrewd enough to modulate his tone. Once more, she faced the witness. "Yes," Ryan told Sarah firmly. "I'm morally opposed to abortion as a form of birth control."

"Has that always been your view?"

"Always. My parents were, and are, adamant in that belief. When I was a teenager, and our parish priest organized demonstrations at a Planned Parenthood clinic, I was part of that." Tilting her head, her gaze seemed inward, reflective. "I wasn't very tolerant, then. At nineteen, when my best friend had an abortion, I stopped speaking to her. That's something I'm ashamed of now."

"Do you still think your friend was wrong?"

"Yes." Ryan's voice was softer yet. "But deserving of a better friend."

At the plaintiff's table, Mary Ann Tierney looked down; Sarah guessed that she was imagining how her own friends might react. "Are there any adult experiences," Sarah asked Ryan, "which have confirmed your pro-life views?"

Ryan glanced at Martin Tierney. "I'm a pediatric nurse. Almost every day I see the miracle of life, and the advances medical science has made—from fetal surgery to care for premature babies—to preserve it. To me, science has shown us that a fetus is not a clump of tissue, and that our duty is to save it."

That the answer was plainly sincere, Sarah thought, made Ryan's presence here more powerful, and more painful. "Shortly after your marriage," she asked, "did you become pregnant?"

Even now the memory made Ryan pause. "Yes."

"In the early stages of that pregnancy, did you undergo prenatal testing?"

"No. I was aware of all the tests which *could* be done, of course. But I was only twenty-five, well below the age of risk, and my husband and I don't believe in abortion as a response to disability." Once more, Ryan looked toward Martin Tierney; more than Sarah, she seemed to see Tierney as a moral reference point. "We specifically discussed whether we could love and nurture a Down's syndrome baby, and were certain that we could."

Sarah moved closer. "Did you eventually have a sonogram?"

"Four months into my pregnancy." Ryan paused. "It was fine. But they couldn't tell the sex, and my husband couldn't be there to see it. My doctor was a member of our parish, and a friend of my family, so he suggested I schedule another six weeks later."

"In that six weeks, did you perceive any change in your condition?"

"Only that I felt heavier than I expected from seeing other pregnant women, and that my stomach seemed more swollen." Ryan spoke in a monotone, as if to drain her oft-told story of its hurt. "If I hadn't known better, I might have thought I was having twins. But I told myself it was nothing."

At the corner of her vision, Sarah saw Saunders fidgeting restlessly, a portrait of frustration. But Martin Tierney's translucent gaze at Ryan held no malice. "Could you tell us," Sarah asked, "what happened after the second sonogram?"

For an instant, the witness closed her eyes, inhaling visibly. "When we entered his office, Dr. Joyce was staring at the sonogram. I'd never seen a doctor cry before."

At this Saunders rose, more slowly than before, his voice recalibrated to a tone of mournful deference. "Your Honor," he said, "whatever her motives, this testimony is obviously painful. If Ms. Dash has any compassion for her own witness, I'd suggest we stipulate that her testimony be taken by deposition, which need not be televised to be part of the record. There's no need for counsel to put Mrs. Ryan through an ordeal."

The hypocrisy of this suggestion, Sarah thought, was breathtaking: Ryan's impact on their audience could be highly damaging to the Christian Commitment, emotionally and politically, and Saunders was desperate to pull back from the abyss. Swiftly, Sarah stifled an angry retort and placed her trust on Ryan's own feelings about Barry Saunders. In a mild voice, Sarah said to Leary, "I appreciate Mr. Saunders's suggestion. Perhaps we should ask the witness how she prefers to proceed."

The judge turned to Ryan. "Mrs. Ryan?"

There was a film of tears in Ryan's eyes; perhaps only Sarah saw the faint outline of a bitter smile, directed at Saunders, quickly erased by deeper emotions. Softly, she said, "It's a little late now. Years late, in fact. I'm prepared to continue."

The somewhat delphic remark seemed all too clear to Saunders. Sitting, he looked like a man in an invisible cage, perfectly aware of what was happening around him, but powerless to stop it. Only anger, and decorum, kept Sarah from laughing aloud.

"Thank you," she said to Ryan. "What did the doctor tell you?"

"That it was a boy." Ryan bent her head, touching her eyes. "He had severe fetal anomalies, including almost no lung development. After that moment, I never felt our baby move again. It was like he'd heard, and given up."

"Did *you* give up?"

"No. In the next three weeks, Mike and I went to three specialists in fetal surgery. Two said it was hopeless. One said that, with luck, he might enable our son to live a year. But that it would be very expensive."

"Were you willing to do that?"

"Yes." Ryan seemed to swallow. "Mike and I hoped against hope that, if we gave him a year, something more would happen. Some new advance."

"Did you have that surgery?"

"No." Ryan gazed up at the ceiling, as though to disengage herself. "The reason I felt bloated was excessive amniotic fluid. By the time I was scheduled for surgery, my uterus was the size of a woman ten weeks later in pregnancy, and our son's head had begun to swell."

"Did that impact his prognosis?"

"His, and mine." Pausing, Ryan looked at Sarah again. "He had a form of hydrocephalus, potentially impeding cerebral development. To deliver him, Dr. Joyce would have to perform a classical C-section."

"And how did that affect your decision?"

Ryan clasped her hands together. "Perhaps we could give our baby lungs," she said quietly. "But we couldn't give him a brain. Of course, we couldn't be sure he didn't have one, either."

"How did you resolve that?"

Looking away, Ryan gave a small shrug of helplessness. "As a nurse, I knew the risks of a classical C-section. And Mike and I wanted to have more children."

"So what did you do?"

"Prayed." Her voice trembled, and her eyes shone with tears again. "We decided to abort our son."

Sarah gave her a moment to recover. "Did your doctor agree to perform the operation?" she asked.

The quick shake of Ryan's head was almost a twitch. "He refused, and our priest counseled against it. We finally found another who said it wasn't a sin, that God gave us the gift of reason for a purpose."

Martin Tierney, too, slowly shook his head; to Sarah the gesture seemed reflexive, involuntary.

"What did you do then?" Sarah asked Ryan.

"We found a specialist in San Francisco. Dr. Mark Flom. After he performed the procedure . . ."

At this, Ryan stopped abruptly, gazing out at some middle distance where no one could look back at her. But when she resumed speaking her voice was clear and steady. "Our son lacked a cerebral cortex. They put a cap on his head, and gave him to us. We were able to hold him, and mourn him, and bury him."

Sarah paused again, less from drama than decency. "Did your parents support your decision?"

"No. For three years they refused to see me, or speak to me."

"What changed their mind?"

For a moment, Ryan seemed caught in the past. Softly, she answered, "The birth of our oldest daughter."

From over his shoulder, Lara handed Kerry a short drink of Bushmills on ice, and kissed the back of his neck.

"What are you watching?" Lara asked.

"The trial. Unless I'm wrong, the girl's lawyer's about to stick it to the Christian Commitment."

Lara sat on the couch beside him. It was night in Washington; other than the television, the only light in Kerry's study was the dim glow of a lamp. On the screen, Sarah Dash faced the witness.

"Other than estrangement from your parents," she asked, "what were the consequences, if any, of your decision to have a late-term abortion?"

The camera panned to Ryan. In close-up, her eyes were luminous, her expression composed. "Nothing, at first. I was ashamed. Then I met other women who had had the same procedure for medical reasons, all after wanted pregnancies. One of them told me the Protection of Life Act was pending in Congress, and asked if I'd share my experiences with the Senate. That's when it all began."

Watching, Kerry felt uneasy. Though the need to campaign in California had been pressing, it had also been convenient for Kerry to miss the vote: regardless of how he might have voted, the Protection of Life Act could have cost him the election. "I'd pity Barry Saunders," he told Lara, "if only he deserved it."

"What was your purpose," Sarah asked, "in testifying before the Senate?"

Ryan faced Martin Tierney again. "If I'd been sixteen," she answered, "instead of twenty-six, my parents would have refused permission, and the son and daughters I have now might not exist.

"I thought that the senators didn't understand that, and that they risked taking away from teenage girls the hope of having more children. That's what I told the committee." Pausing, Ryan added quietly, "They passed the law anyway. So here we are."

Sarah glanced at Barry Saunders; both hands on the table, he was poised to rise and object. "Did testifying against the Protection of Life Act," she asked Ryan, "have any consequences to you and your family?"

"Objection," Saunders said promptly. "Whatever the witness may claim was done to her, it has nothing to do with the obvious constitutionality of the law, or with its plain intent."

"It has everything to do with this law," Sarah told Leary. "The Christian Commitment is part of a campaign to intimidate women who speak out against it, and the law itself stems from their effort to misrepresent a medical necessity in order to attack abortion rights in general . . ."

"*Your Honor*," Saunders's voice rose in protest. "I object to this calumny in our motives . . ."

"You were quick enough to denigrate Mrs. Ryan's motives," the judge retorted. "Sit down, and take whatever's coming."

To Sarah, Leary's lightning changes of mood were impossible to predict. Swiftly, she moved to exploit this one. "*Were* there consequences to your family?"

"Several," Ryan answered with quiet composure. "The Christian Commitment picketed my daughter's first Communion. Then they published a photograph of our son's grave site on their Web page, with an attack on my truthfulness before the Senate . . ."

"What did they say?"

"That I'd exaggerated our son's medical problems, and my own, to promote abortion rights. And that my son's murder represented the reason they needed more donations to protect the lives of other children." Ryan's tone was cold, and she looked directly at Saunders. "I don't know how much money they raised by exploiting our son. What I do know is that Mike and I received hate mail, and threatening phone calls, and that a couple of my daughter's second-grade class-mates told her we were murderers . . ."

"Your Honor . . ."

Facing Tierney, the witness ignored Saunders. "I share almost all of your convictions, Mr. Tierney, and I don't doubt your sincerity. But these people don't care about your family, or mine. We're just another opportunity for propaganda, and to raise money—"

Leary's gavel cracked abruptly. Facing Sarah, his air of sternness was leav-ened by a hint of humor around the eyes, suggesting an Irishman's amusement at a mordant joke. "I think you've made your point, Ms. Dash. We'll take a fifteen-minute break, and then the defense can have their turn."

"Thank you, Your Honor."

As Leary left the bench, Mary Ann Tierney gazed at her mother, and then Martin Tierney took Saunders aside. He spoke in a low voice, his eyes cold; Saunders listened.

A few minutes later, when Sarah stepped outside for fresh air, the pickets were gone.

Six

When Martin Tierney, not Barry Saunders, cross-examined on behalf of the fetus, Sarah was not surprised: one of the emerging, critical aspects of the trial was who would speak for the pro-life cause. Martin Tierney, Sarah had concluded, was the more principled of the two, and also the more subtle and dangerous. Beside her, Mary Ann watched her father with mixed love and resentment, while Siobhan Ryan gazed at him from the witness stand with a sympathy she did not feel for Saunders. Tierney kept a distance from the witness; combined with his mildness of voice and manner, he conveyed that this circumstance was painful for them both.

"From the moment of conception," he began, "you believe that a fetus is a life."

Ryan nodded. "Yes. I do."

"And so, whatever her justification, my daughter proposes to take the life of her son."

Ryan looked down for an instant, then met Tierney's eyes again. "Yes."

"Do you believe that your situation was the same as Mary Ann's?"

Ryan looked at him with caution. "In its details, or in general? We both faced a classical C-section."

Tierney moved closer. "But you also had excessive amniotic fluid. Didn't that endanger your health still further?"

Ryan nodded. "At the end. I couldn't move or walk, and the fluid compressed my lungs. Because it was hard to breathe, I was afraid to sleep."

"In other words, your condition was potentially life threatening?"

"Yes."

"You're not suggesting, are you, that—had you been a minor—the Protection of Life Act would have made *your* choice illegal."

It was a delicate point. "I have no idea," Ryan answered. "All I know is that my parents would have forced me to find out."

Folding his arms, Tierney paused, gazing at the floor. It was a small, human moment; rather than a relentless cross-examiner, Tierney appeared to be a deeply concerned father, trying to resolve a difference with a woman of goodwill. "Let me ask you to imagine," he continued, "that *your* oldest daughter is now fifteen, and pregnant. You would want to know, wouldn't you?"

"Yes. To help Theresa through it."

A small change of demeanor, the use of her daughter's name, hinted at a parental empathy between Ryan and Tierney to which Sarah felt an outsider. "Suppose Theresa wanted to abort her child," Tierney asked. "Were it in your power, would you stop her?"

"I would try to."

"For what reason?"

"Because I believe abortion on demand to be a sin. I also believe that a sin wounds any person who commits it."

"And were *we,* as parents, to act under *those* circumstances, you'd believe that we were right to do so?"

"Believing as you do," Ryan said carefully, "and knowing your own daughter—yes."

"And so your testimony in Mary Ann's favor is based solely on your perception that her pregnancy poses medical risks?"

"Yes."

"What about the moral and emotional risks? Are *they* different for your daughter than for mine?"

Looking down, Ryan twisted her wedding ring. "Every child is different," she said at length. "But, no, I believe the principles are the same. As well as the potential for psychological damage."

The witness and Tierney had fallen into a rhythm. Grimly, Sarah imagined the impact of this on the millions watching and, more crucial, on Leary. The judge was silent, watching the exchange between his fellow Catholics with respectful interest.

"You've mentioned meeting a number of women," Tierney noted, "who faced late-term abortions. Were there any with whose decisions you disagreed?"

Ryan folded her arms. "One," she finally answered. "Although I like her very much. Her fetus had serious heart problems which made him unlikely to live. She decided that she couldn't bear to watch her newborn baby die."

For Sarah, it was the worst possible answer; she could see too clearly where it led. "And so she took his life in the womb," Tierney said, "to spare herself emotional hardship."

"Yes."

"And you don't think that's justified."

"Not according to my moral beliefs. I think that to pursue perfection, and eliminate the challenges God gives us, is never more wrong than when applied to unborn children. Nor, to me, is the pain easier to bear—quite the contrary. One is God's doing; the other, your own."

"And you would want to spare your daughter, a minor, that same pain."

"If possible. Yes."

Tierney paused. "Suppose, then, that she faced a cesarean section that one doctor, a pro-abortionist, estimated could create a five percent risk of infertility, but conceded might be less. Knowing the trauma of abortion, and believing it the taking of a life, would your decision as a parent be difficult?"

"Extremely." Ryan paused, then added quietly, "I sympathize with all of you."

"Then how can you be certain that, with *our* daughter, you wouldn't decide as we have?"

Sarah started to object, then realized that it would be fruitless. Arms resting on the bench, Leary looked absorbed, his self-regard forgotten. "I couldn't," Ryan said. "But I believe, where a baby has so little chance and future children may be at risk, that a mother's wishes are entitled to great weight. And that for you to override them, and face your daughter in court, has risks all its own."

Ryan paused to fortify herself, then concluded, "I love my mother and father, Professor Tierney, very much. But we fell out in private, and still our relationship has never been the same. I worry much more for yours."

The sad, measured admonition caught Martin Tierney short, accenting the deep silence in the courtroom. From the defense table, Fleming and Saunders stared at him. Tierney had gone from an anguished father to a lawyer with a classic dilemma—overconfident in his rapport with the witness, he had asked one question too many.

Tierney did what Sarah would have done; he sat down.

Allie Palmer leaned back, resting her head on Chad's shoulder. But as Sarah Dash's image crossed their screen, Chad felt in Allie's stillness the slightest withdrawal from him, though she had not moved at all.

"Why *did* you vote for it?" Allie asked.

The question carried the hint of long-ago discord—no longer confronted, and never quite buried.

"Because I believe abortion's murder," he said evenly. "That you and I disagree is the oldest news in our marriage, and the tiredest. I've tried to let it go.

"As I'm sure you understand, I feel some sympathy for this girl's father. I also want to be President, and I've already antagonized half my party over campaign finance reform. Even if I agreed with you—which I don't—voting against this bill would have been as reckless as Mac Gage thinks I am."

Allie laughed mirthlessly. "Big boys, playing big games. What does a teenage girl matter?"

Gently disengaging, Chad stood and left the room.

Seven

Sarah sat at the desk in her bedroom, reviewing her notes for tomorrow's first witness, Dr. Jessica Blake.

It was ten at night and beneath the window of her second-floor apartment, the streets, slick with a chill winter rain, were subdued—scattered voices; the sound of tires spattering water; gusts of wind rattling the glass through which, every so often, appeared the mechanical arms of an electric streetcar run by overhead cables. This respite from the hermetic tension of the courtroom was a relief, as was, strangely, the presence of Mary Ann Tierney, reading textbooks in the guest room after a dinner with her parents which she had described as "silent stress." If she worked hard enough, Sarah told herself, and kept anticipating Tierney and Barry Saunders, her inexperience would not be fatal; so far, her witnesses had been well prepared, and she had made no real mistakes. But fear of tomorrow's errors would keep her working well past midnight.

From beside the desk came the low drone of her television, a cable news reprise of the trial. On occasion, with fascination and disbelief, Sarah would turn to watch herself or Martin Tierney—his face obscured by a screen of electronic blocks, his name deleted by a low buzz. She hit the remote, banishing her image from the screen: the idea that she was becoming famous, or notorious, was both a distraction and too much to absorb.

The telephone on her desk rang. Hastily, she picked it up.

"Sarah Dash?" a man asked.

Sarah hesitated. "Who is this?"

"Bill Rodriguez, of the *San Francisco Chronicle*." The voice was quick, edgy. "We'd like your comment on a report on the *Internet Frontier* identifying the Tierney family by name, and describing their involvement in the pro-life movement."

Startled, Sarah took a moment to answer. "I don't have any comment. This is like rape and molestation cases, where your newspaper has been careful to protect minors. Any report on *this* case violates my client's privacy—"

"That's already happened," Rodriguez interrupted, "and the *Frontier* claims that the Tierneys' identity and background is too important not to print. Millions of people are already watching on television—if we can't report this, we're at a disadvantage."

Surprise yielded to anger; were Mary Ann's name and face exposed, the burden could be crushing. "So the *Frontier*'s your evil twin?" Sarah answered. "If they do the slimy things you'd like to do, you get to do them, too?"

"If your client's old enough for this abortion," the reporter said curtly, "isn't she old enough to speak for herself? Put her on the phone, Ms. Dash. We know she's there."

Sarah fought to control her voice. "So you want a comment?"

"It's a start."

"All right—go fuck yourself." Heart racing, Sarah hung up.

Sitting, she tried to compose herself.

She'd lost it—outrage was no excuse for acting unprofessional, and readiness in court no substitute for diplomacy outside it. The strain was worse than she'd admitted to herself; now the only question was whom she owed the first warning—Mary Ann, Martin Tierney, or the chairman of her firm.

After a moment, she picked up the phone again.

Martin Tierney sounded weary. "Professor Tierney," she said, "this is Sarah Dash. I hope I didn't wake you."

"Wake me?" His laugh was brief and bitter. "After hearing from the *Chronicle*? But you're very kind to worry."

So he already knew. "Other than Barry Saunders," Sarah asked, "who knew that she was here?"

There was silence. "The Commitment's selling you out," Sarah told him. "You called off the demonstrators, and it worried them. They want you committed, and as much publicity as they can get. What happens to Mary Ann doesn't matter—"

"Stop casting blame," Tierney interrupted wearily, "and face up to your own responsibilities. Beginning with what we do tomorrow, when Efrem Rabinsky returns to court."

As Tierney had predicted, the lawyer for Allied Media awaited them, his air of calm self-satisfaction suggesting that he was armored in the people's right to know. When Leary seated them around his conference table, it was Rabinsky who spoke first.

"We all know the situation," he began. "The Tierneys' identity is now widely disseminated on the Internet—regrettable, but a fact. So let me quote the editorial which accompanied the *Internet Frontier*'s story."

Fishing out his reading glasses, Rabinsky read from a computer printout. "*'The heart of the controversy,'*" he quoted, "*'is more than the rights of the unborn, or even who speaks for them. Nor does it lie in case law or expert testimony.*

"*'The single most compelling question is whether a leading intellectual proponent of the pro-life view, who shares with his wife a long history of principled opposition to everything from the war in Vietnam to the death penalty, is entitled to invoke these principles in the case of his fifteen-year-old daughter. For if these parents are not so entitled, parental consent—so popular with Americans at large—will cease to be an element in how we regulate abortion.'*"

Clearing his throat, Rabinsky looked up at Leary. "Whatever their motives, it's a very interesting argument. And if the traditional media can't report this aspect of the story, then our readers, listeners, and viewers will flock to the Internet for news. In other words, to the least responsible sources."

Leary compressed his lips in frustration. *You fool,* Sarah wanted to tell him, *what did you expect?* "These people flouted my order," Leary snapped. "You're asking me to reward them."

"Not so," Rabinsky said. "I'm asking you not to punish those who honored your order, and now find ourselves disadvantaged. In my experience, Judge, the Internet is so hydra-headed as to be ungovernable. Other Internet outlets are following the *Frontier*'s lead. By the time they finish appealing your current order, this will all be academic—"

"Issue a contempt order." Martin Tierney's interruption was uncharacteristic, as was his open anger. "Today, against anyone who's printed our name . . ."

"Anyone?" Rabinsky asked him. "Everyone? There's no putting the genie back in the bottle, nor should there be. When you chose to intervene on behalf of the fetus, then to conduct the case yourself, you made your own identity central to the story.

"Judge Leary has no jurisdiction to find the entire Internet in contempt, let alone private citizens who pass the story on to others. So consider not only whether you've asked for this attention but whether you shouldn't, at least in some ways, seek it. Instead of making the media your adversary, make it a vehicle for your views—"

"Mary Ann Tierney," Sarah cut in, "is not a 'vehicle.' She's a fifteen-year-old girl who wants a personal tragedy to remain personal." Pointing toward Martin

Tierney, she said to Leary, "If she had *murdered* her father for his beliefs, instead of simply opposing him in court, the confidentiality laws regarding juveniles accused of crimes would protect her from exposure. The least this court owes her is to enforce its own orders."

Leary raised his eyebrows. "Mr. Fleming," he asked, "does the Justice Department have any view?"

"This is a constitutional challenge," Fleming answered soberly, "not a teaching opportunity. In our view, which advocates of children's rights would echo, Mary Ann could be severely harmed by being forced to become a public figure. We're happy to resolve this matter without exposing the Tierneys on television."

"Mr. Saunders?" the judge asked.

Saunders folded his hands. "We're here at Mr. Tierney's invitation, Your Honor. We defer to him."

It was hardly a firm statement of support; to Sarah's mind, Saunders was like a political candidate who leaves the dirty work to his minions. But it was sufficient for Tierney's purposes. "All the parties to this case," he told Leary, "are in agreement. The only one who wants my family exposed still further is Mr. Rabinsky, who's here at his *own* invitation."

"You've exposed yourselves," Rabinsky countered. Facing Leary, he said, "While Mr. Tierney's feelings are entitled to some weight—"

"Mary Ann has feelings of her own," Sarah interjected. "What price does she have to pay for an act of Congress?"

"That's the point," Rabinsky said imperturbably. "Both the Tierneys and their daughter voluntarily invoked the legal process to raise matters of overriding public interest covered by the First Amendment. It's clear that this case is inextricably intertwined with the character of the Tierney family itself. Where that information is already on the Internet, to continue obliterating faces and beeping names, or censoring the mainstream press, is futile and unfair."

Raising his hand for silence, Leary squinted at the table, as if a few seconds of concentrated thought were sufficient to slice through the thicket of contention. "All right," he said. "I'm lifting my previous strictures on the media."

Turning to Tierney, he explained, "I'm sorry, but Mr. Rabinsky's position has the unhappy virtue of acknowledging reality. I'll keep the ban for twenty-four hours, so that you or Ms. Dash can appeal to the emergency motions panel for the Ninth Circuit. I believe Lane Steele is the presiding judge this month."

This last information jarred Sarah from her shock at Leary's decision. The month had barely begun; whoever lost at trial must appeal to—or be reassigned by—a panel including the judge on Caroline's court most noted for his pro-life views. But Martin Tierney stared past Leary, bereft.

For once, he did not speak the perfunctory, foolish word of thanks custom requires from lawyers after a ruling, however adverse and peremptory. Tonelessly, Sarah uttered it for them both.

In the corridor between the chambers and the courtroom, Sarah stopped Martin Tierney. In an undertone, she said, "Leary's an idiot. God help us both."

Tierney still looked stunned. "Will you join me in an appeal?" he asked.

"Yes. But I doubt that Judge Steele, or anyone, will see any point in disturbing a trial judge's reversal of his own order." Gently, Sarah rested her hand on his arm. "Let her go, Professor Tierney. Sign the consent."

Tierney paused, pale eyes filled with anguish, then shook his head. "You still don't understand," he answered. "I can't."

He turned from her, leaving Sarah to explain the ruling to his daughter.

Eight

Questioning Dr. Jessica Blake, Sarah felt on edge; though the psychologist was poised and well prepared, her testimony would be crucial. With her delicate features, wire-rim glasses, and hair skimmed back from her face, Blake exuded calm. But Blake's premise—that parental consent laws damaged teenage girls— was incendiary.

"In your experience," Sarah asked, "are teenage girls sufficiently mature to decide between motherhood and abortion?"

"Most are," Blake answered. "As to the rest, one must ask why a girl who's unequipped to choose between motherhood and abortion is equipped to be a mother."

"How does that affect your view of parental consent laws?"

"It's one of several reasons that they do more harm than good," Blake explained, facing Leary. "Up to now our experience is with state parental consent laws for previability abortions, which grant minors far broader exceptions than *this* law allows. Under *those* laws, a judge can either conclude that a girl is mature enough to make the decision for herself, or—if not—that her interests are better served by abortion than by motherhood.

"These exceptions permit a minor to abort in ninety-nine percent of all cases which go to court. But the problem with *any* parental consent law is that many girls are *afraid* to go to court. The result is that they become unwed mothers by default, with all the difficulties that implies for both the minor and her child."

"And how do parental consent laws impact families?" Sarah asked.

"Their stated purpose is to promote family unity. But their actual effect is contrary—"

"I've had teenage daughters," Leary interjected. "Sometimes they didn't like the rules I set. But part of being a parent is helping them make wise choices, sometimes by setting limits. Now that *they're* parents, they thank me for it."

Looking up at him, Blake's eyes narrowed, and she measured her words with care. "If we're talking about makeup, or curfews, or homework—most teenage issues—we're completely in accord. But if you took your daughter to court on national television, and in essence said, 'You're a delivery system for a fetus with little hope, incapable of deciding for yourself how that will affect your capacity to bear more children,' she might be a bit less grateful."

Watching Leary's annoyance, Sarah was torn between amusement and concern; though Blake had reduced him to wordlessness, it might come at a price. Smoothly, Blake continued, "You're well aware, I know, that the normal parental paradigms don't apply to this situation. A girl who lacks the capacity or experience to choose is a poor risk as a mother. And far too often, her 'love' for a child reflects the narcissistic hope that the child's love for *her* will fill an emotional need that her own parents have failed to fill. A far cry from your daughters, I'm sure."

Blake was astute, Sarah realized; she had first put the judge off balance, then given him an out. Taking it, Leary asked, "What conclusions did you reach about Mary Ann?"

"That she's typical for her age and experience," Blake answered promptly. "And, as such, completely capable of making this decision.

"At fifteen, the ability of a minor to understand the impact of abortion versus motherhood is little different than that of young women at twenty-one, or even twenty-five. And a survey of young women after a first-trimester abortion shows that only seventeen percent suffer from any appreciable guilt—"

"Shouldn't they," Leary interjected, "by the third trimester of pregnancy? Which is where Mary Ann Tierney is now."

Unruffled, Blake looked at up Leary. "Where Mary Ann is *now*," she answered, "is in your courtroom. That shows a strength of character which speaks well for her ability to make this decision, then live with it.

"The best predictor of emotional peace with such a decision is the ability to make it for yourself. And one of the two leading predictors of emotional damage is a nonsupportive emotional environment." Once more, Blake glanced at Martin Tierney. "Which *is* what we have here."

Tierney stood at once. "I understand that expert witnesses have latitude," he said to Leary. "But I object to Dr. Blake's bias regarding our family.

"The world of Dr. Blake is a foreordained moral dead zone, where the decision to abort is the only measure of sanity, and parental reservations make us—or any family—dysfunctional. When Mary Ann at first resolved to bear our grandson, it meant that she was narcissistic. When she decided to abort, it meant that she'd become emotionally healthy. And when we objected, we became a 'nonsupportive emotional environment.' But all that really demonstrates is that Dr. Blake's testimony is worthless."

Leary held up a hand. Turning to Blake he said, "In essence, Professor Tierney says you're offering cookie-cutter conclusions, where everyone and everything fits your preconceptions."

"I have no preconceptions," Blake replied. "The seven hours I spent with Mary Ann are informed by fifteen years of seeing other teenagers, and by extensive research—mine and others'. But I base my opinion on Mary Ann herself.

"When Mary Ann first became pregnant, she imagined an uncomplicated pregnancy which would make her boyfriend love her. That's not uncommon, nor confined to teenagers. Add Mary Ann's respect for her parents' opinion, and her passivity is unsurprising.

"The sonogram was a wake-up call. Mary Ann realized that this was not the normal child every mother hopes for, and that complying with her parents' beliefs meant that she might never have another. Which brings me back to whether parental consent laws are either necessary or desirable . . ."

"I know you have an opinion." Leary had begun his regimen of what Sarah thought of as aerobic judging—cocking his head, rocking back and forth, fidgeting with his tie, interrupting and looking more pleased with himself than when forced to listen passively. "What I don't know is what it's based on."

"Research," Blake responded. "From 1997 through 1999, three colleagues and I surveyed seven hundred pregnant minors living at home in California, where there was no state law mandating parental consent.

"Eighty percent of minors involved their parents in deciding whether to abort, suggesting that a functional family doesn't require Congress to force them to communicate. In ninety-five percent of those cases, the parents supported their daughter's decision, regardless of what it was—"

"What about the other five percent?" Leary interjected. "Is the only measure of a healthy family parents who acquiesce in whatever their teenage daughter wants?"

"No," Blake responded coolly. "Another measure is that the father doesn't have sex with her, or beat her, or throw her out for becoming pregnant. And the leading cause of late-term fetal anomalies—those impacted by this law—is incest."

There was little risk, Sarah realized, that Leary's intervention would unnerve Jessica Blake—the risk was that she would embarrass him on television. "What all of these laws demonstrate," Blake told him, "is the shocking—or deliberate—naïveté of lawmakers with respect to dysfunctional families. Imagine explaining to your mother that your father made you pregnant, or watching him beat her for your sins, or selling your body to abusive strangers because you're homeless and have a child to support. We saw those cases, numerous times . . ."

"What about the Tierneys," the judge persisted. "A normal, loving family where the parents will love and support their child and *their* grandchild? Doesn't that happen more often than these difficulties you mention?"

"Where the minor wants an abortion," Blake answered, "and her parents object? No. That's just as well: the unwanted children of unwed mothers have a far greater propensity to drop out of school and to commit acts of violence. Over the long term, an unwilling parent is less likely to be a good parent, regardless of who the grandparents are.

"But that aside—and even in a loving home—the negative effects of having an unplanned child include depression, a lack of self-esteem, and a sense of hopelessness." Blake glanced at Mary Ann Tierney. "That reflects some very harsh realities—statistically, unwed minors have less education, and a far greater chance of being economically marginal. Only five percent of women who have children when they're under twenty-one finish college; *over* twenty-one, and almost half get their degree . . ."

"I'm thinking about adoption," Leary objected. "Doesn't giving a child to a loving home create more satisfaction than abortion? Or is that depressing, too?"

"This case isn't about an adoptable child," Blake responded. "Cases of late-term abortion seldom are. If that weren't so, Your Honor, I'd be asking the very same question you are. Because we're in accord—no civilized society prefers abortion to adoption."

Watching, Sarah blessed the witness; with surprising tact, she had given Leary an exit, defusing their debate. "Could you elaborate," Sarah asked Blake, "regarding the impact of this law on the Tierneys?"

"No one seems to ask how this girl got pregnant in the first place, besides the obvious—a crush on an older boy. So *I* asked." Blake looked at Mary Ann Tierney with concern. "According to Mary Ann, she couldn't talk to her mother about sex, and she knew that—for religious and moral reasons—her parents don't believe in birth control. The one thing she recalls her mother saying about contraception for teenagers is that it promoted sex."

Focusing on Blake, Sarah tried to block out the anguish this testimony must produce, both in Mary Ann and Margaret Tierney. "How does that affect Mary Ann?" she asked.

"Mary Ann," Blake continued, "believes that her parents' 'rules,' combined with their silence, left her unprepared to deal with her feelings for Tony—either emotionally or on the practical level of preventing pregnancy. Add their insistence that she bear the child that's resulted, at whatever risk, and she feels great resentment toward *both* parents."

At the edge of her vision, Sarah saw Martin Tierney gaze at his daughter with infinite sadness.

"Is there any way," Sarah asked, "that the Tierneys can repair the damage?"

Blake frowned. "The two things which could help Mary Ann the most," she answered, "are out of their control. First, that the baby dies at once. Second, that Mary Ann is able to bear more children—which, in the best of circumstances, she won't know for years."

"Will these things help repair the relationship?"

"It's hard to know." Blake's brow knit, and she seemed to study her folded hands. "One thing she said to me is critical: *'I got the wrong parents, Dr. Blake. How many families would take their own daughter to court?'*"

In the quiet courtroom, none of the Tierneys—parents and child—could face each other.

Sarah allowed the judge, pensive now, to regard the stricken people before him. "No further questions," she said, and then Leary called a recess.

Nine

When Martin Tierney rose to cross-examine, Sarah felt a hush descend. Beside her, Mary Ann gazed listlessly at the table.

Tierney himself appeared hollowed out—his eyes were bleak, his bearing less erect. Blake regarded him from the witness stand with an unflinching attention which, Sarah guessed, she maintained only with great effort.

"What," Tierney asked her, "are your religious beliefs, if any?"

Startled, Sarah stood. "I object, Your Honor. The question invades the witness's privacy, and has nothing to do with her testimony."

"This case invades our privacy," Tierney countered with sudden anger. "The media invades our privacy. Ms. Dash and the witness invade our privacy. As for whether religious beliefs are irrelevant, Dr. Blake has treated ours as a symptom of familial dysfunction. It's only fair to ask Dr. Blake what, if anything, she believes in. Besides herself."

"Go ahead," Leary said to Blake. "Answer the question."

Blake hesitated, then faced Tierney. "I was raised as an Episcopalian," she answered tersely.

"And now?"

"I have no formal beliefs."

"Do you believe in God?"

Blake glanced at Sarah. But they had not expected, or prepared for, this line of attack. "Not as a patriarchal figure," she responded. "Beyond that, I believe that there's a balance in nature—that the good we do creates more good, and the evil we do to others harms ourselves. But whether that reflects a divine presence, or what its nature might be, is impossible for me to know. Or, with respect, for you to know."

For a moment, Tierney regarded her in silence. "Do you believe that life is sacred from the moment of conception?"

Blake's brow furrowed in thought. "What I believe," she answered, "is that a fetus is a potential life, worthy of respect. But not inviolate in every circumstance."

"Is it inviolate in *any* circumstance?"

Blake hesitated. "Without an example, I don't know how to answer that."

"All right. Do you believe that a woman—even a minor—has the right to abort a fetus if she wants to?"

"After careful thought, and prior to viability, yes."

"What about without careful thought, Dr. Blake? Does she have the absolute right, for any reason, to snuff out this 'potential life'?"

Blake folded her arms. "I might not approve of her reason. But I believe she has that right."

"Suppose that a woman in the eighth month of pregnancy, with a fully viable and healthy fetus, decided that having a child was too stressful. Does she have the moral right to abort that fetus?"

"Objection," Sarah said at once. "That's not the law, nor is it this case."

"It *could* be," Tierney answered. "Much like her uncertainty regarding the existence of God, Dr. Blake can't know that our grandson won't be 'normal.' And she bases much of her opinion on the emotional damage to Mary Ann—"

"I'll allow it," Leary interrupted. Powerless, Sarah sat.

"The circumstances *are* different," Blake answered. "I'd have to know more . . ."

"But morally you don't rule it out."

There was a long silence, and then Blake shrugged. "Regardless of the woman, or her circumstances? No."

"It seems, Dr. Blake, that you have difficulty imagining *any* circumstances in which abortion isn't a woman's right."

Blake straightened. "No one likes abortion," she replied. "I surely don't. The question is what harm you do by ordering pregnant women to have children. As you're about to find out."

Watching, Sarah felt a wave of relief—Blake was holding her own. Softly, Tierney asked her, "Do you doubt that Margaret and I love Mary Ann? Or that it's possible for us, believing as we do, to love our daughter *and* our unborn grandson?"

"No. I don't doubt either."

"Yet you ascribe to Mary Ann the feeling that we've chosen him over her. Is that a mature reaction?"

Blake adjusted her glasses, and then met Tierney's eyes again. "I wouldn't call it mature or immature. Under the circumstances, I'd call it understandable."

Tierney put his hands on his hips. "And based on seven hours with our daughter, you believe you know—better than Margaret and I—how violating her own religious beliefs would affect her."

"Yes," Blake answered. "Based on that, and fifteen years of experience in treating and studying adolescent girls."

"But Mary Ann is a particular adolescent girl, with whom *we* have fifteen years of experience. For the record, did you try to interview *us*?"

"No."

"Or her teachers?"

"No."

"Or her relatives?"

"No."

"Or her priest?"

"No." Blake's voice rose slightly. "Mary Ann familiarized me with her family life, as well as with the viewpoint of her relatives and priest. If you're suggesting that their opposition will make abortion more traumatic, I'd answer that it's a self-fulfilling prophecy. For which you bear the most responsibility."

Stymied, Tierney seemed to gather himself for a fresh assault; to Sarah, it seemed that all of his anguish and humiliation was focused on Jessica Blake. "Isn't it true," he demanded, "that the emotional impact of late-term abortion is far more severe than in the first or second trimester?"

"It can be, yes. Because it almost always involves severe fetal anomalies in a wanted child."

"Didn't Mary Ann want this child?"

"Before the sonogram? She believed she did."

" 'Believed,' " Tierney repeated mockingly. "So wanting a child is a transient feeling? Might wanting to abort it be a transient feeling?"

Blake hesitated, breaking the rhythm of their conflict. "Professor Tierney," she said, "why don't you turn, and look at your fifteen-year-old daughter. She's gone to court, in the face of your opposition, to safeguard her capacity to bear children. Tell me that's a 'transient feeling.' "

Frozen, Tierney stared at her. It was Leary, in an involuntary reflex, who turned to see Mary Ann gaze steadily at the back of her father's head.

"Do you believe," Tierney demanded, "that adoption is traumatic for the mother?"

"In many instances, yes."

"And in those instances the mother should take the fetus's life, to spare herself more pain?"

"Should? No."

"But she has that right."

Blake hesitated. "Yes."

"So the mother is all, the unborn child nothing?"

"That's not my position," Blake said with asperity. "And no one will be lining up to adopt this child."

"Two people are," Tierney retorted. "Margaret and me. We care about him, and our daughter, more than you can ever know. That's why we're here.

"I don't need you to make me look at her. We don't need you to explain her to us. We've loved her since the day she was born, and we'll love her long after you've forgotten what little you know of her. So never, ever condescend to us the way you have. Let alone flatter yourself that *you* know best."

Blake stared back at him. Angry, Sarah stood. "That's not a question," she said. "It's a speech, and an offensive one."

Ignoring Sarah, Tierney stared at Jessica Blake, as though to underscore her arrogance. "No further questions," he said.

Rising for redirect, Sarah asked, "Do you contend that religious beliefs have no place in the area of abortion?"

"I think they're quite important. The question is *whose* beliefs—mine? Congress's? The Tierneys'? Or are Mary Ann's beliefs the ones that matter most?" Glancing at Martin Tierney, Blake said firmly, "I've concluded that only Mary Ann is capable of deciding what her beliefs are, and what role they play in her decision."

With that, Sarah prepared to sit down.

Blake leaned forward. "I'd like to add one thing more."

"Please do."

"Religion can yield some curious inconsistencies as to how we value life. Recently, my colleagues and I surveyed states with the most restrictive laws to curb abortion—many of which laws were enacted at the urging of groups with strong religious ties." Blake turned to Leary. "What we expected to find was that those states compensated with more liberal programs to support the neediest children, encourage foster homes, provide early childhood education, and facilitate adoption of older children and those with physical or mental disabilities.

"The reality was just the opposite—the states which placed the most restrictions on abortion provided the *fewest* protections for the children that resulted. *This* law provides none at all."

Pausing, Blake considered Martin Tierney, then chose her words with care. "Professor Tierney is fully willing to help sustain his own grandchild. But I've become leery of religious advocacy for laws which only value a 'life' until it's born."

This was the perfect place to end. "No further questions," Sarah said.

Ten

From the moment she met Senator Chad Palmer, Caroline felt an awkward sub-text—her debt to him. When he graciously asked Ellen Penn, her escort, if he could visit with Caroline alone, her unease grew: she had not resolved what, if anything, she should say regarding Brett.

He led her through his suite in the Russell Building to a commodious office in which—unlike those of most public men—the only photographs were of his wife and daughter. Sitting across from him, Caroline reflected that he was one of the few senators whose interest for her transcended how he affected her ambitions.

Palmer was a striking man, with the youthful blond good looks and careless manner of someone who had always excelled without much effort. Yet Caroline knew how dearly Palmer had paid, in mind and body, for his awareness, always lightly stated, that "there are worse things in the world than losing an election." What she found most arresting were his level blue eyes, suggesting a self-knowledge which made possible the surface ease. Edgy, she waited for him to indicate why he wished to meet in private.

"Baseball," Palmer said. "How much do you know about it?"

Caroline smiled in surprise. "A fair amount."

"Then you'll probably be confirmed." Palmer sat back in the chair, stretching his arms as, almost imperceptibly, he studied her. "When Bob Bork came to visit, he had no facility for small talk—I wondered if he'd ever been to a movie. But Justice Kennedy could talk baseball. You'll notice who made it to the Court."

"I know much more than Tony Kennedy," Caroline informed him. "For example, in 1941 Ted Williams hit .406. No one's hit .400 since."

"That's good," Palmer rejoined. "But do you know the best thing about Williams?"

"That he was a fighter pilot?"

"Even *I* can do that—or could." Palmer assumed the mock-heroic tones of a narrator on an old newsreel. "On the last day of the 1941 season, with Williams hitting .401, his manager offered to keep him out of a doubleheader to preserve his average. But Ted Williams refused, and got five hits. The act of a true American."

Though delivered with humor, Caroline sensed that the story had significance to Palmer; Ted Williams had nerve, and his record wasn't cheap. Abruptly, Palmer angled his head toward a television in the corner of his office. "Have you been watching this?"

Turning, Caroline saw Sarah Dash, questioning a scholarly looking woman on a soundless screen. "Of course not," she answered. "If I watched, I might form an opinion. I'm told having opinions is lethal."

Palmer smiled at this. "So the President's people have put you through the blender. Still, do you think this trial should be televised?"

"No. I don't."

He cocked his head. "Why not? You let them televise your Carelli trial."

So this was more than surface patter. "In the Carelli trial," Caroline answered, "the defense requested it . . ."

"And the prosecutor objected, right?"

"Yes. But, for a judge, the rights of the defendant to a fair trial should take precedence. If the defense had objected, that would have been different."

Palmer smiled again. "Then you would never have appeared on national television, Judge Masters. And might not be sitting on the Ninth Circuit—or here."

"At the time," Caroline conceded, "it occurred to me that the exposure might be helpful. I'm sure it's occurred to Judge Leary, whom I know quite well."

"What do you make of him?"

"That he's a man of tremendous confidence, completely unjustified by intellect or ability. If I were him, I'd avoid exposure like Dracula avoids garlic."

This made Palmer laugh aloud. "That's *my* opinion. And I *have* been watching. But I still don't know why TV was right in your Carelli case, and wrong here."

Caroline paused, pondering her answer; with Palmer, it seemed that only candor would do. "After the Carelli trial," she told him, "I searched my soul a bit. A good deal of my decision about television was really about me—about ego, and self-interest . . ."

"But you'd still do it again."

"Probably. I am, as you point out, sitting here." Her tone grew crisp. "But I wouldn't televise *this* case if you promised me the presidency."

"Why not?"

They were edging closer to the subject of Brett. "As I understand it," Caroline answered, "all the parties object. The subject matter—religion, abortion, and family relations—is deeply private. To me, that outweighs Patrick Leary's self-interest. Or even our First Amendment interest in learning about the Protection of Life Act."

Palmer considered her. "Do you think the act is constitutional?" he asked. "Or good public policy?"

"I know *you* think so," she replied, "and I respect that. In my job, I try not to judge an act of Congress until it comes before me." She paused, then added quietly. "The one thing I've concluded about *this* case is that the privacy of the family involved should have been protected . . ."

"Does the right to privacy," Palmer interrupted, "include abortion?"

The directness of his inquiry surprised her. But she had no choice except to answer. "According to *Roe v. Wade,* it does. The Supreme Court says so. As a lower-court judge, it's not appropriate for me to revisit its wisdom, or lack thereof—or prejudge whether it applies to the situations covered by the Protection of Life Act." Pausing, Caroline looked at him directly. "My point's a different one. Whatever rights this girl or her parents have under the law, their personal lives belong to them—not us."

Slowly, Palmer nodded. "That's a fair answer, Judge Masters. Thank you."

Palmer, she realized, did not intend to raise the matter of Brett directly. That decision was hers.

Finding the words, she discovered, was not easy. "The President told me," she said at last, "what you've talked about. Whether or not you vote for me, I owe you a great deal."

Perhaps surprised, Palmer gazed at her, quiet for a moment. "You did the right thing," he answered. "At least by my standards. I don't think you, or she, should suffer for it."

This was palpably sincere. But Caroline could not help but wonder what other calculations, both private and political, informed the civility of this very ambitious man.

"I appreciate that, Senator. Without your understanding, I wouldn't have this opportunity."

Palmer frowned, looking at her keenly. "That may be no favor," he admonished. "There are other senators on my committee—as well as staffers—who'll be turning over every rock, or birth certificate. So will the FBI, the media, and all the interest groups who don't like Kerry Kilcannon or anyone *he* likes. I can try to shape the process, but no one can control it." Leaning forward, he said quietly, "I respect the line you've drawn, Judge Masters. So does my friend the President. But this is not a forgiving town, and these aren't forgiving times. There are a thousand people who could leak this, with a thousand different motives. *If* they ever find out."

Palmer's gaze seemed to turn inward; though Caroline did not know him, she had the intuition that this warning, while delivered to Caroline, was part of a conversation with himself.

Which was all the more reason to heed it. "I know that," she answered. "But I needed to thank you. Both for my sake, and for my niece's."

The word "niece" induced in Palmer a faint smile. "Oh, that's all right," he answered, "I have a daughter, too."

Briefly, Caroline looked down. "In any event," Palmer told her, "*I* wouldn't want to go through this process. So I'll try to move it along, and make it as humane as possible.

"You can help me, Judge Masters. Some of my colleagues beg to be taken seriously; others deserve to be. Give them what they need to make a judgment."

Caroline nodded. "Is there anything else I should know?"

"One thing." Leaning forward, Palmer assumed an air of gravity. "By far the most important. You could be testifying before my committee for several days. So whenever you need to go to the bathroom, touch your left ear. I'll recess the hearing."

Caroline smiled. "That has more value than you know."

"So Allie tells me." Standing, Palmer said, "There'll be reporters waiting. Shall we go feed them?"

By now, Caroline knew Chad Palmer's reputation as a cheerfully self-confessed "media harlot." "You can," she replied. "I intend to imitate Lot's wife."

"A wise policy—for judges. But not for politicians." More seriously, Chad said, "It's truly been a pleasure to meet you, and I wish you luck. If there's anything I can do to help, except shamelessly capitulate, don't hesitate to ask."

He seemed sincere, Caroline thought, and to be as the President described him—an honorable man in a hard profession. "Thank you," she answered. "I will."

Outside, as the Senator predicted, a cluster of reporters and Minicams were waiting. Bob Franken of CNN stepped forward with a microphone. "Can you tell us," he asked, "what the two of you discussed?"

Demurely, Caroline turned to Palmer. "Families," he said with a smile. "And baseball."

Alone in his office, Chad reflected on their meeting.

Caroline Masters was impressive, her concern for Brett Allen affecting. But the image that surfaced now did not involve *her* daughter, but his—a Friday night four years ago, when Allie and Kyle still lived in Cleveland, and he had canceled two appearances in order to fly home unexpectedly.

The decision was driven by worries about Kyle, and the flight from Washington was filled with concern for Allie. Their daughter had taught them a great deal that they had never wished to know—her highs were a frightening mix of giddiness, recklessness, and grandiosity, and her lows left her so lethargic and depressed as to seem autistic. The psychiatrists they consulted disagreed as to the cause: one thought her behavior a form of manic-depression, rare in adolescents; another blamed Chad's absence for an increased need for attention in an already moody girl. Whatever the cause, Kyle had learned to lie without remorse, and to conceal pills or dope or alcohol with the cleverness of a thief.

Therapists, prescription drugs, and counseling for substance abuse did not seem to help. She was draining the life, Chad thought, from her mother, and from his marriage. A child at risk made trust a luxury, each day uncertain, the mere sound of a telephone ringing a reason to flinch.

Would this be the call? Chad could see Allie thinking—fearful of an overdose, or of a car wreck after binge drinking with some ill-chosen friend, or that Kyle had run away from home. Their daughter had become the enemy; with merciless self-appraisal, the habit of two years of solitude, Chad acknowledged that he had come to resent Kyle more than he loved her.

All this had crowded Washington from his thoughts until, on impulse, Chad had driven to Reagan National—less for Kyle's sake than Allie's. A cabbie had dropped him, still preoccupied, in front of their Tudor home in Shaker Heights. "Goodnight, Senator," the man said. "It's an honor. Folks will never forget what you did."

Chad was used to this; as always, his reflex was to deflect it. "I appreciate that," he said with a smile. "But if getting kidnapped were voluntary, I'd have passed it up."

And then he was alone, a man with a suit bag, gazing at the darkened house. Only the porch light was on: Kyle must not be home, and Allie would still be at the symphony. That she did not expect him lent Chad the anticipatory pleasure of surprising her.

He turned the key, stepping softly inside, then stopped.

He had an instinct in darkness, a sixth sense—in his cell, blindfolded or in pitch blackness, he had learned to know when his captors were there. It was a feeling on his skin, at the nape of his neck.

Taut, Chad switched on the hall light.

Kyle lay naked on the Persian rug, staring up at him in startled defiance. On top of her was a boy with lavender hair and a snake tattooed on his back.

Chad could not speak. In a dark fury, he wrenched the naked boy upright by his hair.

"*No,*" Kyle screamed at him.

Chad barely heard her cries. As the boy yelped in primal terror, Chad smashed him against the wall. The boy's eyes bulged, and his lips quivered. "If I ever see you again," Chad said in a tight voice, "your life won't be worth living. I've learned all about that, from experts . . ."

From behind him, Kyle pulled at his suit coat. *"Don't . . ."*

Chad jerked himself away; throwing the door open, he propelled the boy tumbling down the front steps, crying in pain as he sprawled on the cold cement. "On the way home," Chad told him, "buy yourself some clothes."

Closing the door, he faced his daughter, and suddenly wondered what he had done, and what would happen to his family. But by then it was too late.

Eleven

"Before your daughter became pregnant," Sarah asked Abby Smythe, "were you familiar with Ohio's parental consent law?"

A woman of forty with brown hair, snub features, and a quiet voice, Smythe looked like what she was: a housewife from a small town in southern Ohio, imbued with communal values—family, church, volunteerism—which put concern for others before self.

"Yes," she answered. "I'd discussed it with others in my church. Frank—my husband—and I believed that parents, not strangers or the schools, should be responsible for educating our children about sex, and for monitoring their behavior. We thought there were too many degrading outside influences in children's lives, from movies to music, and that a law which reinforced the value and authority of parents was good."

Judging from his expression, Martin Tierney knew about the Smythes and their daughter. He studied her with a self-protective remoteness, as though determined to place distance between them. But Mary Ann, who also knew, leaned anxiously toward the witness.

"Did you," Sarah asked, "have any particular concerns about Carrie?"

"None." The word was emphatic and, Sarah thought, defensive. "She was a cheerleader, an honor student, and worked with our church's community service program, bringing meals to shut-ins. There was never a problem with alcohol, or rule-breaking.

"Other mothers would tell me about what trials their girls were, and I'd say to Frank"—abruptly, Smythe's voice became chastened—"that God had given us the all-American girl."

Beneath Smythe's quiet manner was the echo of endless reexamination, of memory tarnished by hindsight. "What," Sarah asked her, "did you tell Carrie about sex?"

Smythe was fixed on Sarah now, as though to block out how public her confession had become. "That God intended it for marriage. And that sexual relations outside marriage were wrong."

"How did she respond?"

Smythe raised her chin slightly. "That she wanted to be a virgin until she married. I remember telling Frank that Carrie would be a more powerful role model for her sisters than an adult would ever be." She paused, inhaling. "It also reassured me. Carrie had started dating a boy on the football team—Tommy. We felt like she was telling us her values were still in place."

None of this testimony surprised Sarah; she had prepared Smythe with care, and Smythe repeated the same answers with a weary self-condemnation which seemed to have become ritual. But they were edging toward the precipice, where Abby Smythe's life had changed forever, and the part of Sarah not conditioned by the courtroom disliked the need to take her there.

"Did you ever think that Carrie was changing?" she asked. "Or that a distance had opened up between you?"

"No." Smythe shook her head in wonderment. "What did I ever do, I ask myself, that Carrie felt the need to protect me, when I thought I was protecting her?"

The answer haunted Sarah. It was her theory that a teenager's acts of defiance—however vexing or ill-chosen—were steps in the creation of an autonomous adult, and that parents who flattered themselves that this separation was unnecessary did their children harm. But Abby Smythe still seemed not to comprehend fully the tragedy of her daughter's feigned perfection: when they had looked at Carrie's yearbook picture, blond and smiling, Abby had said, "That's how she really was."

"When," Sarah asked her, "did you first discover that Carrie was in trouble?"

At this question, Martin Tierney leaned forward, and Barry Saunders scowled. But Abby Smythe fixed her gaze on Sarah.

"On Friday," she answered, "Carrie asked to stay over with her best friend since first grade, after their double date. Beth was like another daughter, at our house all the time, and her father worked with Frank at the Carver County Bank.

"I said fine, of course. When she left that night I never thought a thing, except to say it was cold out and please to wear a muffler."

Smythe paused, as though clinging to this homely detail, the evidence of her love. "I was in the kitchen," she went on. "I heard them start out the door, and then Carrie hurried back inside, gave me a hug, and said she always felt lucky I cared about her so much . . ." Smythe touched her eyes, then continued in an affectless voice. "I remember thinking if she said that, with all the things I heard from other parents, I must be a pretty good mom."

Judge Leary shifted in his chair.

"When was the next time that you saw Carrie?" Sarah asked.

"In the morning." Smythe's voice was now a monotone. "When Tommy came to the door.

"He was shaking. Then I saw that the rear door of his car was open. Strands of Carrie's long blond hair were spilling from the back seat to the floor . . .

"I ran past him . . ." Smythe bent forward, placing her fingertips to her forehead, then spoke in a choked but louder voice. "There was blood all over her dress, and the muffler was stuffed between her legs. Her eyes were wide, like she was in shock, but they fluttered when she saw me. All she could do was whisper, 'I didn't want to hurt you, Mommy. I didn't want to hurt you . . .'

"She died in the hospital, a few hours later."

Throat working, Smythe stopped. Softly, Sarah asked, "How did Carrie die, Mrs. Smythe?"

"From a ruptured uterus, at the hospital. I couldn't comprehend it." Now Smythe held fast to the same fixed stare, her voice flat, without inflection. "Frank lost his senses. He grabbed Tommy and slammed him against the wall until he told the truth.

"It was kind of a conspiracy. Beth covered for Carrie, and Tommy told his parents he was staying with his friend Ryan. Instead Tommy drove her across the border, to Newport, Kentucky. Somehow he'd found out about a woman who did abortions for girls in trouble."

The sentence came to an abrupt, bitter end. Symthe's sense of betrayal—of shock and disgust at the secret world of teenagers she had thought she knew— seemed to distract her from the drama's central fact: her daughter's pregnancy.

"How long," Sarah asked, "had Carrie been pregnant?"

Smythe was quiet for a moment. "Two months."

"Do you now know what happened after Carrie found out?"

Barry Saunders stood up heavily. "We all feel, Your Honor, great sympathy for a mother's loss. But this testimony is objectionable on at least two grounds.

"First, it's irrelevant—it relates to the Ohio parental consent statute, not this carefully crafted federal law which governs only late-term abortion." Pausing, Saunders flavored his words with quiet disapproval. "Second, the witness is about to give us hearsay. If, as she concedes, she knew nothing about her daughter's pregnancy, she has no firsthand knowledge of the events which caused her death."

The first point was at least arguable, and the second technically correct. But Leary responded before Sarah could. "The court is sitting without a jury, and is well equipped to sort out wheat from chaff. I'd like Mrs. Smythe to answer."

Leary, Sarah realized, did not wish to muzzle a grieving mother on television. Slowly sitting, Saunders assumed a studiedly blank expression, a contrast to Martin Tierney's attentive stillness. At Sarah's request, the reporter read from a piece of steno-tape: "'Do you now know what happened after Carrie found out?'"

"She went to the county chapter of Planned Parenthood," Smythe answered carefully. "When the test came back positive, she sat down with the counselor."

Once more, her words and manner seemed mystified, as though still stunned by the vision of her loving and compliant daughter talking to a stranger about so intimate a thing. "After you learned that," Sarah asked, "did *you* visit Planned Parenthood?"

"Yes. To meet with the woman who'd counseled Carrie."

"What did she tell you?"

Smythe sat straighter, as if preparing herself, though her gaze was far away. "That Carrie was afraid to disappoint me. 'It would kill my mother,' she kept saying."

"Did the counselor tell her she could go to court?"

"Yes." The witness looked down. "She was afraid of that, too. You see, Judge Clausen goes to our church. So she went to Kentucky instead . . ."

With a painful effort, Smythe looked up again, tears streaming from her eyes. "I would have *helped* her," she protested. "I'd have done anything for Carrie. An abortion, anything. But she didn't know that, and I never had the chance to show how much I loved her." Pausing, Smythe wiped her eyes with the back of her hand, and spoke in a stronger voice. "But if a stranger had to be the one to care for her, better a doctor than a butcher.

"This law didn't bring us closer. It didn't protect Carrie Smythe." Turning, Mrs. Smythe spoke to Martin Tierney. "Instead," she finished quietly, "it killed her."

Twelve

To Sarah's surprise, it was Tierney, not Saunders, who rose to cross-examine on behalf of the fetus: questioning Abby Smythe would not be a sympathetic business, and Tierney risked tarnishing his aura of aggrieved father. Beside her, Mary Ann spoke to him under her breath, "Why don't you leave her alone."

With an air of reluctance, Tierney faced the witness. "I don't claim to know how you feel," he began. "But Margaret and I feel for your loss."

Mute, Smythe simply nodded: her air of reticence seemed to combine an acceptance of his statement with the caution of a witness toward a probable antagonist. Gently, Tierney asked, "Are you contending, Mrs. Smythe, that Carrie didn't come to you because of the statute?"

Smythe looked away. "No."

"Wouldn't you like to have participated in your daughter's decision instead of leaving it to an abortion counselor?"

"Of course."

Tierney paused, gazing at her in apparent puzzlement. "And yet," he asked, "your point seems to be that my wife and I should not exercise that same right."

"No," Smythe answered. "I'm saying that the parental consent law drove my daughter to an illegal abortion."

"But that's not the case here, is it? So suppose that Carrie *had* come to you as she should and could have. Would you have left the decision to her, or consulted as a family?"

Smythe stared at her lap. "As a family. We were her parents, after all."

"And, as her parents, did you teach Carrie that abortion was morally wrong?"

"No."

For a moment, Tierney regarded her. "Isn't it conceivable that if Carrie believed that abortion was a sin, she'd still be alive?"

"Objection," Sarah said angrily. "That question calls for speculation. Which makes its patent cruelty gratuitous."

"Gratuitous?" Tierney responded in a mild tone. "Mrs. Smythe has suggested that a parental consent statute caused her daughter's death. But the actual cause was an abortion."

"An *illegal* abortion," Sarah snapped.

"Enough," Leary interrupted. "The question is out of bounds, Professor Tierney. Please take another tack."

Glancing at a notepad, Tierney began anew. "Don't you wish this counselor had told you that Carrie was pregnant?"

"Yes." Smythe's tone held fresh resentment, but not of Tierney. "Of course."

"Then you could have counseled with Carrie. To try to assess all the circumstances, and decide what was best for her."

"Yes."

Torn by indecision, Sarah watched. She could see where Tierney was taking Smythe, and where it ended. But Smythe, imagining her involvement were Carrie still alive, was willing; Sarah's intervention might cause resistance in her own witness.

"And if you and Carrie disagreed," Tierney said, "you would have tried to protect her own best interests—in whatever way you, as parents, believed best."

"That's true."

"Then why would you deprive us, as parents, of that same right?"

In pained silence, Smythe pondered her answer. "I don't want to," she said at last. "And I envy you that opportunity. For whatever reason, our daughter didn't come to us.

"We were a good family, Professor Tierney. What happened to us can happen to other good families. Certainly, it can happen in bad ones. I worry about what happens when the only option for a girl afraid to tell her own parents is to go to court."

The simple dignity of the answer seemed to give Tierney pause. Sarah saw Mary Ann turn to him, as though demanding an answer. "Are you willing to concede," Tierney inquired, "that under this statute a girl might well have second thoughts, and then turn to 'good' parents?"

Smythe hesitated. "In some cases, I suppose that could happen."

Tierney stepped back, resting his palm against the defense table. "And yet you've made opposing parental consent laws somewhat of a cause, haven't you?"

Smythe faced him with renewed calm: the question was expected, and Sarah had prepared her. "Carrie's death," she answered, "is not a cause. It's something that happened to us, and I've tried to give it meaning."

"So now you believe," Tierney said, "that your inability to communicate with Carrie should dictate the relationship of other parents to their daughters."

Wounded, Smythe stared at him, and then she shook her head. "No, Professor Tierney. Your relationship will be whatever it is. *That,* no law can change. Except to make it worse."

Tierney paused, seemingly at war with himself, and then frustration won out. "But isn't it true, Mrs. Smythe, that you're attempting to rationalize your own failure, and salve your grief at Carrie's death, by stripping other parents of their rights?"

The question was so lethal, and so insinuating, that letting Smythe respond was, for Sarah, an act of will. "Salve our grief," Smythe repeated quietly, and Sarah sensed that Tierney, goaded by his own beliefs, had made a terrible mistake.

"Since we began sharing our experience," the witness told him, "someone mailed us a fetus with a coat hanger wrapped around it. Someone else shot a hole in our car window." Tears came to the witness's eyes again. "But for us, the worst was when someone sent us Carrie's picture from the local newspaper with 'whore' written across her face. And now *you* suggest that speaking out is helping to 'salve our grief.'"

"*Nothing* can do that. And nothing can lessen the anguish of what we learned." Her voice, which had risen in anger, softened again. "It's too late for us. But not for you. I didn't come here to help myself, Professor. I came here to help *you.*"

During Sarah's brief redirect, two harried associates from Kenyon & Walker filed an emergency motion in the Court of Appeals on behalf of Mary Ann, challenging Judge Leary's permission for the media crowding his courtroom to publicly expose her identity. By five o'clock, without a hearing, the motions panel presided over by Judge Lane Steele had rejected the motion, along with that of Martin Tierney.

This was no surprise. For the next two hours, while Mary Ann ate with her parents, Sarah considered what that meant, and whether to rest her case tomorrow, or to ask Mary Ann to testify.

. . .

Once she returned, Mary Ann sat heavily in Sarah's living room, legs parted to ease the burden of her pregnancy. Smoothing the shift she wore, she rested both hands on her swollen belly.

"Has he moved?" Sarah asked.

Mary Ann stared at her hands. "That's what my father wanted to know. I said I thought I felt him today—a little."

For a moment, Sarah considered how pivotal this inquiry was: for different reasons, the question of fetal movement, and what it signified, held legal and emotional meaning for both Sarah and the Tierneys. Looking at Mary Ann, who seemed weary and pensive, Sarah added another factor which weighed against calling her to testify—her father's question; his daughter's answer.

"You heard about the panel's ruling, I guess."

The girl nodded. "I'm going to be famous," she said in a flat voice. "My parents asked me if I still wanted to go through with this."

"Do *they*?"

"I asked them that." Mary Ann's voice held quiet anger. "He said yes, and begged me not to testify."

Silent, Sarah wondered whether this was love, or tactics, and marveled at how this law, pitting parents against child, could complicate and pervert the most straightforward of emotions—a father's instinct to protect his daughter.

"Will *they* testify?" Sarah asked. "They've listed themselves as potential witnesses."

Mary Ann rubbed her temples. "They won't tell me," she said at last. "It's like he's playing with my head. Or yours."

This perception, too, was curious: as if propelled into adulthood, Mary Ann had developed an interest, anxious but discerning, in the tactics of the trial. At length, Sarah said, "I don't want to put you on tomorrow."

Mary Ann looked up at her. "Why?"

Sarah could not give the most compelling reason: that she was afraid Martin Tierney, as questioner, would so erode his daughter's confidence that, in the end, he would break her. And no amount of coaching could prepare a fifteen-year-old for a clever and subtle man who also, since her birth, had been the most important figure in her life. "I want to save you for rebuttal," Sarah answered. "After we see what kind of case they put on, and whether your mother or father testifies, then we can decide."

Mary Ann hesitated, as though torn between relief and worry. "What about our case?" she asked. "Have we done enough?"

"I think so." Sarah paused, then admitted, "I don't want to put you on television before we see what your parents do."

This remark, though spoken with dispassion, seemed to renew Mary Ann's disbelief. She was fifteen, and pregnant, and now was fighting her parents, in public, for the right to an abortion. Filled with pity, Sarah forced herself to say, "You don't *have* to testify, Mary Ann. You don't have to continue this at all."

Mary Ann seemed to regard her stomach, and the fetus inside it, with a wistful tenderness. "No," she answered. "I've seen the sonogram, and I do."

Thirteen

"*Who's* calling?" Macdonald Gage asked again.

On the intercom, his receptionist enunciated carefully. "Judge Lane Steele. From the Ninth Circuit Court of Appeals."

Repeating the name aloud, Gage raised his eyebrows at Mace Taylor and, after taking a hasty sip of his morning French roast, hit the button on his speakerphone. "Judge?" he asked.

"Good morning, Senator." Beneath the tone of dry judicial dignity, Gage heard a veiled eagerness. "It's good to talk with you again. You'll remember we met late last summer, at Bohemian Grove."

Glancing at Mace Taylor, Gage gave him a smile which was half grimace. Taylor leaned closer to the speaker box, eyes narrowing with a speculative shrewdness.

"Of course, Lane." That Gage could modulate his southern baritone like a Stradivarius was part of his pride, and his voice infused this use of Steele's given name with welcoming and warmth. "A pleasant respite from my many burdens. Including the chance to visit with you."

"Yes." The dry voice conveyed a guarded pleasure. "For me, as well."

Glancing at Mace Taylor, Gage gave an even more cynical smile and mouthed "Masters" clearly enough for Taylor to nod. "So," Gage said with a mixture of respect and jocularity, "you riding herd on that pack of visionaries out there, helping your brethren—and sistren—follow the tenets of our founding fathers?"

"Would that I could, Senator. With the people he put here, the last president didn't make that easy. Neither, I fear, will this one." There was a brief pause, and then Steele added with near reverence, "We could surely use more judges with Roger Bannon's qualities of mind."

Like you, Gage thought sardonically. Though Steele was edging toward his chosen subject, the Majority Leader decided not to help him; waiting was more decorous, and gave Macdonald Gage more leverage. "Judges like Roger Bannon are in short supply," he answered pleasantly. "Except, I'm informed, for you."

There was silence; the rote courtesy stalled conversation, pushing Steele into a corner. "Thank you," Steele said at last. "I suppose, in a way, that Roger is what compelled me to call. I imagine you've begun to focus on his successor."

With these words, Taylor's expression, amused up to now, became keen. "We've been forced to," Gage responded, "with indecent haste. Thanks to Kerry Kilcannon."

"Yes." There was another pause, and then Steele struck a note of candor and concern. "Frankly, that surprised me."

Once more, Gage smiled at Taylor. "The haste?" he asked Steele with seeming innocence. "Or the appointment?"

"Both." A brief cough echoed through the speakerphone. "Normally, I'd remain silent."

"Of course. But this is Roger Bannon's successor, and our next Chief. Unless the Senate decides otherwise."

"Not a light responsibility." This time Steele's silence seemed deliberate, a signal of reluctance and propriety. "Your staff might want to stay alert to new decisions. Those not yet issued."

Taylor was still, Gage noticed, except for his unconscious rubbing motion of the thumb and forefinger of one hand. "Is there a particular decision?" Gage asked.

He should use a watch, Gage reflected, to time Lane Steele's silences. "There's an en banc opinion coming next week," Steele answered, "*Snipes v. Garrett.* The opinion broadens a prisoner's right to sue beyond what, in my view, Congress intended in last year's legislation. Its failings exemplify that a judge should interpret an act of Congress, not rewrite it."

"Especially if the rewrite favors criminals." Picking up a desk pen, Gage scrawled *Snipes v. Garrett* on a legal pad. "Still," he added in a weary tone, "it's the kind of adventurism we've come to expect from all too many judges on your circuit."

"True." Necessity seemed to make Steele less hesitant. "But not, one hopes, from the next Chief Justice of the Supreme Court."

Taylor's smile, more to himself than at Gage, suggested worldly amusement at an ambitious man's pretence of reluctance. "Do tell," Gage said in tones of wonderment. "Do tell, Lane."

"She's a protégé of Blair Montgomery's, the most radical member of our court. Montgomery wrote the opinion, but *she* called for the rehearing *and* signed on. My dissent points out the manifest weaknesses of their reasoning." Pausing, Steele said with measured sadness, "Some judges try to be scholarly; others lack the requisite detachment. Her first job was representing hard-core criminals, as a public defender, and that seems to have become her religion. She's certainly cool toward religion as most of us understand it."

"A secular humanist, in other words. Pornography in the classroom, but never prayer." Seeing Taylor tilt his head in inquiry, Gage asked, "How's she on abortion?"

"That's rather hard to pin down, like so many things about her. One *knows* what she must believe. But without an opinion with her name on it, there's no way of confirming it."

As Gage watched, Taylor inclined his head toward the television in the corner of Gage's office. "What about this girl's case," Gage asked, "the one who wants to abort a six-month-old fetus? Doesn't that come to your court next?"

Again, there was a long, chaste silence. "One aspect already has," Steele said at last. "I'm presiding over the emergency motions panel. We just turned down her lawyer's appeal to keep her name out of the media, finding that question clearly within the discretion of the trial judge." There was another pause, and then Steele spoke with new boldness. "However distasteful, I think the public will profit from facing the reality of abortion—that we refuse a human fetus the same protection the SPCA accords to wayward cats. And any woman who proposes abortion so close to birth, including a fifteen-year-old, should do so for all to see."

To Gage, the last remark sounded like an audition, a harbinger of pointed opinions and ringing dissents were Steele granted the proper platform. "Does this have any implications for your colleague?" Gage inquired.

This time Steele's quietude was intended, Gage supposed, to signal both reluctance and judicious thought. "Not in the *normal* course," he answered carefully. "Even were she to continue here, we have a complement of twenty-one judges. And, normally, the panel of three are picked at random . . ."

His voice trailed off. "But?" Gage asked.

Gage sensed Steele picking his way through a verbal minefield; perhaps the speakerphone made him even more wary. "This girl's three months from childbirth," the judge answered. "Procedurally, any appeal would have to be an emergency, brought before our emergency motions panel."

"The one you're on."

"Yes. Until the end of the month."

Gage glanced at Taylor. "And the emergency procedure's different?"

"By rule. Our panel can take the case itself, or assign it to another."

Sitting back, Gage stared at the ceiling. "But," he ventured carefully, "even were the case assigned to a panel which included *her*—however that might happen—now that she's got her eyes on the prize, she'd probably find a reason to recuse herself. So, from my perspective, it's better that the Protection of Life Act be upheld. Speaking as a senator, of course, not a judge."

Steele chose not to answer directly. "There's only one other way," he observed in even tones, "for her to hear this girl's case—even in theory. Other, that is, than as Chief Justice of the Supreme Court."

Gage, too, felt himself becoming more cautious. "And what's that?"

"After a panel's decision, a party, or a judge of our court, can ask that the case be reheard en banc, by eleven of our twenty-one active judges—as happened in the Snipes case I mentioned. Or, in a rare case, by *all* of them." Steele paused, then finished. "The odds of either outcome are long. But in a constitutional question as important as this, a little less so."

"How long would such a process take?"

Gage could imagine Steele calculating time. "On an emergency motion," he said at length, "and under the provisions of this statute, a hearing and rehearing would consume about a month."

"But Masters could recuse herself."

"She *could*, yes. After that, the only recourse for the losing party is a petition to the Supreme Court. Which the Court, in its discretion, can either grant or refuse."

Taking Gage's legal pad, Taylor scrawled "How long for *that*?" and held it up to Gage.

Gage repeated the question. "A week," Steele answered. "Perhaps a little more."

Soundlessly, Gage placed down the pad. "Without a Chief Justice, wouldn't you guess that the current Supreme Court would split four to four on whether the Protection of Life Act should be upheld?"

Yet again, Steele paused. "It's not for me to speculate, Senator. But such a split would dramatize the impact of choosing the next Chief wisely." Pausing, Steele added, "Even your question underscores the gravity of this appointment. Which, after considerable reflection, moved me to pick up the telephone."

Once more, Taylor smiled at Gage across the desk. In a pious tone, Gage told Steele, "I count on your patriotism, Judge. And you can count on my discretion."

Switching off the squawk box, Gage said to Taylor, "Amazing—the name Caroline Masters never crossed his lips. Like writing in disappearing ink."

Taylor shrugged. "That was a job application, Mac. He thinks you may become President, and he wants to be on the Court."

Though Gage found this flattering, its truth was too obvious, and too commonplace, to require comment. "She won't keep on deciding cases," he observed. "Let alone one like this. The moment Tony Kennedy was nominated to the Court—from that same damn fool circuit—he made like an ostrich."

"There's also what Steele said about timing," Taylor rejoined. "If we could hold up the vote on Masters, this girl's abortion case might turn out to be useful. If only to dramatize that the new Chief could be the tie-breaker."

"What would help *there*," Gage cautioned, "is for Palmer to stall the hearing. He's been too damned noncommittal."

Taylor sipped his coffee, frowning. "If you still don't want to play hardball, this criminal case could help us. The committee staff should dig into her cases, maybe her time as P.D.—give our allies something to point out to Palmer while we put her life under a microscope. I still think she's maybe a dyke, this beard of a boyfriend notwithstanding."

Though he agreed, Taylor's remark touched a nerve in Gage; however practical it might be, recourse to the personal was too easy for Mace Taylor. As so often before, it reminded Gage that, in politics, riding the tiger—especially in the guise of Taylor—had its own distinct risks.

After a moment, Gage switched on his squawk box again. "Let's call Paul Harshman," he said. "He's our best friend on Judiciary."

"I've got Mace with me," Gage began. "What's going on with Palmer?"

The junior senator from Idaho issued a soft, disgusted expletive. "He's being himself, the Lone Ranger. Narrowing the inquiry by sitting on the staff and the FBI. He's even using his power as chairman to keep us from seeing the FBI's raw data, including interview notes. As usual, only God—and the great Chad Palmer—knows why."

Taylor slid his chair forward. "We don't need the staff, Paul. If we somehow could get the raw data, I can find investigators to follow up. There's money for that."

Gage glanced at him sharply. To his ears, Taylor had come perilously close to suggesting that a senator, a ranking member of Palmer's committee, try to get to the FBI by going around Palmer. On the other end of the squawk box, Paul Harshman remained silent.

"Let's talk about nailing Palmer," Gage interjected, then glanced at Taylor in admonition. "Politically, that is."

Fourteen

From the witness stand, Mary Ann's doctor, James McNally, spoke like a peer to his friend Martin Tierney. To Sarah, Mary Ann looked diminished yet defiant, like a teenager being chastised by her elders for some selfish act. But, in this case, she had become a moral object lesson for millions to witness; though a technician focused the television camera on her doctor, the broadcast no longer censored her face or name. And though Sarah might have invoked the physician-patient privilege to keep McNally from testifying against Mary Ann, his advice was central to her case.

"I brought Mary Ann into the world." Speaking softly, McNally turned his level gaze toward the girl. "I care about her deeply. But, as an obstetrician, my role now is to care for both Mary Ann *and* her child. I simply can't support her claim that an abortion is medically necessary and, for that reason, it conflicts with my obligations as a doctor—morally and ethically."

Though admitting no doubt, McNally's tone expressed more sadness than anger, and he seemed to impress Judge Leary. The two men even resembled each other, though McNally was older and bulkier. Sarah took an instant dislike to him.

"For what reason," Tierney asked, "did you conclude that an abortion was not warranted?" His voice was more a worried father's than an inquisitor's; it was easy to imagine the two friends in the quiet of McNally's office.

"To borrow from the Protection of Life Act," McNally answered gravely, "this child does *not* constitute a 'substantial medical risk' to Mary Ann's life or health."

"What *would* be a substantial risk?"

"Preexisting conditions, as a rule. Cancer, which cannot be treated during pregnancy; heart defects; high blood pressure, which can lead to renal failure;

diabetes, which may cause blindness or kidney failure." Once more, McNally glanced at Mary Ann with an air of sadness and reproach. "Even with these potential difficulties, many women proceed with the pregnancy to see if the threat materializes. But Mary Ann has none of them."

To Sarah, his tone of certainty—of judging the painful choices of pregnant women—translated as far too smug and patriarchal. She noted this for cross-examination.

"Obviously," Martin Tierney said, "we're *also* concerned about our daughter's ability to bear more children."

It was not a question, but testimony; however much he despised the cameras, Martin Tierney seemed acutely aware of his role as father in a domestic drama. Nodding, McNally said, "I know you are, Martin. But even Dr. Flom concedes it is highly unlikely that a classical C-section would compromise fertility."

"When you say 'highly unlikely' . . ."

"Appreciably less than one in forty, in my opinion."

Turning to Sarah, Mary Ann grasped her wrist. "He's lying," she whispered. Nodding, Sarah kept her eyes on McNally.

"It's also conceivable," McNally concluded, "that complications from a C-section could lead to a hysterectomy or other causes of infertility. But that's one percent at most."

Sarah's stare at McNally hardened. Tierney stepped closer to the witness, as though to underscore a critical point. "And in the course of our consultations, what did you advise us as to whether delivery by cesarean section was safer for our daughter than late-term abortion?"

McNally gazed at Mary Ann with a sorrowful expression, and then spoke to Leary. "That late-term abortion posed the greater risk to Mary Ann's life or health.

"The operation proposed by Dr. Flom is more than distasteful. The chance of puncturing the uterus, or some other misadventure, is more serious."

Once more, Leary seemed engrossed. But Sarah felt quiet satisfaction; touching Mary Ann's hand, she scribbled on her legal pad, "That was a *huge* mistake." Conscious of those at the defense table, she did not change expression.

"As I understood you, Doctor, you testified that our grandson *may* have a disability."

"I said *may,*" McNally answered with a judicious air, "because the hydrocephalus, while marked, is not in its severest form.

"Severe hydrocephalus is not compatible with life. But a sonographic measure of this baby for cortical thickness suggests that there is at least *some* reason for hope. It might even be possible to install a shunt, drain the fluid, and save the baby's life. Which is the proper function of a doctor."

Mary Ann was quiet now: McNally's tacit reproof, Sarah thought—that he was acting to protect the life inside her—must resonate with the beliefs she had absorbed since childhood. "What percentage of late-term abortions," Tierney inquired, "represent cases of hydrocephalus?"

"Very few, in my survey of the data—under ten percent. Other cases may include spina bifida, which can be severe, or not severe, or wholly reparable with surgery. And do we start including Down's babies, who many people parent willingly?" Once more, McNally's voice became didactic. "Dr. Flom excoriates Congress. I say thank God it cares. No sane society designates doctors as a special priesthood, charged with deciding what constitutes 'meaningful life.' And even a baby who may well die at birth deserves the compassion of the human community, not"—abruptly, McNally's voice became caustic—"scissors in the back of his head.

"At a minimum, a humane society would pass laws—like this one—to prevent doctors from performing this horrific practice, just as we prevent them from prescribing narcotics without a license; or helping impoverished patients to harvest their organs for sale; or using their God-given skills to *play* God by putting the infirm to death. The pro-abortion argument that—uniquely—the state cannot regulate child-murder is ethically and morally repugnant."

Flinching, Mary Ann turned from him. "But were 'normality' the standard," McNally finished, "I'd give your grandson a ten percent chance of being normal. Which is greater than Dr. Flom's exaggerated claim regarding the risks of a cesarean section."

Tierney seemed to contemplate this with genuine sorrow. "What does that suggest," he asked, "regarding the implications of permitting late-term abortion whenever a doctor claims that it protects a mother's physical health?"

"That 'physical health,' as defined by Dr. Flom, is a slippery slope which brings late-term abortion perilously close to abortion on demand. And that 'mental health'—a stated concern of Dr. Blake's—will take us all the way.

"At *that* point a doctor can conclude that 'mental health' warrants aborting a thirty-week-old fetus to spare a seventeen-year-old girl the trauma of not fitting into her prom dress." Pausing, McNally turned to Mary Ann with an air of avuncular concern. "As a doctor and friend, I'll do anything I responsibly can to care for Mary Ann Tierney. But we're all here today because she chose to have sex, resulting in a pregnancy. That decision—that medical fact—has profound and important implications for *two* lives, not one.

"Mary Ann is here to speak for herself, she claims. But who, then, speaks for her son?"

Despite her feelings, Sarah acknowledged that McNally made a forceful witness; the reporters present had stopped whispering, and were either engrossed or scribbling notes. "To remove a mole from Mary Ann's cheek," the doctor said to Martin Tierney, "I'd require your permission as her father. Yet this procedure has far greater implications."

"Indeed." Martin Tierney's voice, though quiet, had a chilling undertone. "Please describe the procedure through which Dr. Flom proposes to take my grandson's life."

"Very well," McNally answered with distaste. "On the first and second days, Dr. Flom will insert dilators into your daughter's cervix.

"On the third day, he will remove the dilators, and rupture the membrane protecting the fetus.

"At this point, some doctors dismember the child's extremities, while others would partially deliver his feet and legs. Dr. Flom's procedure is aesthetically superior: he will prepare to deliver your grandson normally." Pausing, McNally scowled. "To accomplish this, while lifting Mary Ann's cervix, Dr. Flom will jam a pair of blunt curved scissors into the baby's skull.

"His next step will be to spread the scissors to enlarge the hole. Then he'll insert a catheter, and suction out what's inside. That's an experience Mary Ann cannot escape, and which none of us ever wish her to know."

At her side, Sarah saw Mary Ann's face drain of blood. "Medically," McNally concluded in a tone of devastating quiet, "its only 'advantage' is to guarantee that your grandson—Mary Ann's child—will be dead upon delivery. And that's not why I went to medical school."

Fifteen

Walking toward James McNally, Sarah tried to block out everything but what she had to do.

"Have you ever performed an abortion?" she asked.

McNally folded his arms. "No."

"Because you're morally opposed to abortion?"

McNally frowned. "I'm Catholic, and I follow the teaching of my church. But my beliefs are also based on science, and on a doctor's obligation to save life."

Sarah paused, eyeing him curiously. "As a doctor, have you ever treated a rape victim?"

Quickly, McNally glanced at Martin Tierney. "Yes," he answered. "Several."

"In your observation, did those women find being raped traumatic? *Genuinely* traumatic, that is?"

Sarah saw McNally's mouth tighten. "Yes."

"Have you ever treated victims of incest?"

McNally seemed to draw his body tighter. "Yes."

"What about both, Doctor—where the patient was a victim of rape *and* incest?"

McNally paused. "Once."

"How old was she?"

"Fourteen."

"Did you have occasion to observe how the experience affected her?"

Once more, McNally hesitated. "Adversely, it was clear. She had a hard time talking about it . . ."

"Was she depressed?"

"Depressed? At the least. She reported difficulty sleeping . . ."

"Was she potentially suicidal?"

McNally considered this. "I would have to say she was."

"Your Honor." Behind Sarah, Martin Tierney rose. "I fail to see relevance."

Leary turned to Sarah, arching an eyebrow in inquiry. Ignoring Tierney, Sarah said, "One more question, Your Honor."

"Go ahead."

"You were describing, Doctor, a fourteen-year-old who was sleepless, despondent, and potentially suicidal as a result of being raped by her own father. In your view—moral, religious, and medical—is such a girl entitled to an abortion?"

Grimacing, McNally braced himself. "No," he answered. "However evil her child's provenance, it is, nonetheless, a life."

"And so, even if she asked you for an abortion—a legal, first-trimester abortion—you would not perform it."

"No. Instead I'd try to get her all the support and help I could, including some sort of intervention with the father . . ."

"A little late for *that,* don't you think?"

"Ms. Dash," the doctor said tightly, "I cannot condone abortion, even under circumstances as tragic as those."

"Even if her prom dress didn't fit?"

"Your Honor . . . ," Tierney protested.

Dismissively, Sarah said, "I'll withdraw it," without breaking off her scrutiny of McNally. She was locked in on him now, the questions coming reflexively; watching her, McNally hunched over as though entrenching himself.

"In other words, Doctor, no emotional trauma—whether incest or prospective infertility—justifies abortion."

"That's right."

"In your mind, is there *ever* a situation where abortion is morally justified?"

"Yes. Where it's clear the mother may die."

"Even if the fetus appears healthy?"

"That's a difficult case, Ms. Dash. But where a mother already has children who depend on her, and they're at risk of losing her, the balance may favor saving the mother's life."

"In that case," Sarah prodded, "you think she's free to decide, and that a doctor should be able to proceed. Even though the baby's 'normal.'"

"Yes."

"But *not* when the fetus is unlikely to have a brain, and the threat is not to life, but to reproductive health?"

McNally sat back. "One can always design harsh hypotheticals," he answered. "Ones which touch the heart, and tax the conscience . . ."

"I take it that answer meant 'no.' Even if the girl were *your* daughter, and wanted an abortion?"

The question, though obvious, induced a reflective silence in McNally. "I can see," he firmly answered, "the pain such a conflict can bring. But I hope I would be principled enough to do as Martin Tierney has."

It was a better answer than Sarah had hoped for; quickly, she decided to leave it there. "Suppose," Sarah asked, "that a court granted your daughter that right, over your objections. Would you want the late-term procedure done in the safest possible way by the best available doctor—regardless of your objections?"

"For my own daughter?" McNally's voice held quiet indignation. "Of course. Or for anyone's."

"Do you dispute Dr. Flom's statement that he has performed this procedure over thirteen hundred times, with *no* serious complications?"

McNally's ire yielded to distaste. "I can't dispute it, or confirm it."

"Are you suggesting, Dr. McNally, that Dr. Flom is lying?"

"No."

"Good. Are you aware of any late-term abortion procedure safer than Dr. Flom's, or any doctor more capable?"

"In *that* particular context," McNally answered with disdain, "no."

"Yet you disapprove of Mary Ann Tierney availing herself of that same procedure?"

"Yes. Because it's barbarous . . ."

"But not unsafe."

"No." McNally's voice turned acid. "Except for the baby, of course."

Sarah ignored this. "And yet you told Martin Tierney that birth by cesarean section was statistically safer than late-term abortion."

"Overall, yes. According to the literature."

"'According to the literature,'" Sarah repeated. "What about your *own* experience, Doctor?"

McNally sat back, mouth slightly parted; by degrees, Sarah watched apprehension overtake him. "As I told you," the doctor temporized, "I have no experience with abortion. At any stage."

"But what about cesarean sections?"

After a moment, McNally nodded. "I have performed cesarean sections, yes."

"Including the classical cesarean section which would be necessary for Mary Ann to give birth?"

"Yes."

"They're much more invasive than a normal C-section, aren't they?"

"Yes."

"Yet you say—absent unusual complications—that a classical C-section would be 'unlikely to compromise Mary Ann's fertility'?"

"That's what I believe."

"How unlikely, Doctor? Two percent?"

"Less."

"One percent?"

"Perhaps."

"Would *you* accept a *one percent* risk of infertility for *your* daughter?"

"Objection," Tierney called out.

Still facing McNally, Sarah waved a hand. "Isn't it true, Doctor, that when you first spoke to Mary Ann and her mother, you placed the risk at around five percent?"

"Perhaps." McNally folded his arms again. "But I've since consulted the literature."

"'The literature,'" Sarah repeated. "So we're back to that again."

Before Tierney could object, the witness, stung, countered, "In *my* experience, Ms. Dash, I've never seen a classical cesarean section later cause a woman's uterus to explode, as Dr. Flom described."

"He didn't just *describe* it," Sarah answered. "He brought photographs. But the other risk you mentioned was a surgical mistake in performing a classical cesarean section, correct?"

Once more, the witness studied her with veiled eyes. "Correct."

Softly, Sarah asked, "In your observation, Doctor, has such a mistake resulted in a hysterectomy?"

McNally's lips compressed. "Yes. I mentioned that."

"How many times?"

"I don't know. It occurs, Ms. Dash—just not often."

Sarah moved closer. "How often," she inquired, "when you were the doctor?"

The hurt which showed in McNally's eyes occasioned, in Sarah, a moment's pity. "Twice."

"And, in both cases, you were sued for malpractice—"

"Objection." Tierney's angry voice cut through Sarah's question. "The question is irrelevant, and its clear intention is to humiliate this witness in public—"

"Unlike his testimony," Sarah shot back, "which was intended to humiliate your *daughter* in public." To Leary, she said, "This witness claimed that a late-term abortion performed by Dr. Flom is more risky than a classical C-section. I'm entitled to impeach his credibility."

Leary nodded. "I'm sorry, Dr. McNally, but the question falls within the scope of your direct testimony."

Slowly, McNally turned to Sarah, speaking with a dignity she found far more affecting than his air of moral certainty. "Ms. Dash, I've practiced medicine for thirty years. I've brought countless children into the world and, on occasions, saved lives. But nothing can erase the pain of those mistakes."

"Neither for you," Sarah answered, "nor for the two infertile women, I suppose."

Briefly, McNally averted his gaze. "I suppose not, no."

Sarah nodded, maintaining a few feet of distance. "Isn't it likely, Doctor, that your moral repugnance for abortion affected your medical assessment of the risks to Mary Ann?"

The witness studied his hands. "That's impossible to say . . ."

"So you're not claiming—after all—that a classical cesarean section performed by you is safer than the procedure performed by Dr. Flom? Or even *as* safe?"

Resentful, the witness looked up at her again. "I've made mistakes, Ms. Dash. Doctors do."

"Or that you're certain the risks of infertility aren't closer to your original estimate of five percent?"

"No."

"Or that other risks aren't *twenty times* greater?"

"Certain? No. Though I *believe* they're not."

"Nor are you certain that this fetus has a better chance of developing a cerebral cortex than Mary Ann has of becoming infertile?"

"No." McNally folded his hands. "What I'm saying is that there's no way of finding out unless Mary Ann goes to term. And that, whatever the odds, we should value unborn life."

"*And* that," Sarah followed, "in the case of Mary Ann Tierney, her parents should force her to find out, regardless of the risks."

"I'm saying they *can*, morally."

"Even if you were *certain* it had no brain?"

For a long moment, McNally hesitated. "Yes," he said simply. "In my value system, the life of one patient outweighs the finite risk to the other."

Sarah put her hands on her hips. "Even though such a 'life' would barely survive its birth?"

Quiet, McNally considered his answer. "That's not my province, Ms. Dash. It's God's."

"Except," Sarah retorted, "when the baby is normal, and the life of the mother is at risk. Shouldn't God decide that, too?"

The witness hesitated, caught in a logical inconsistency. "That's the worst possible dilemma," he conceded. "I cannot imagine God sanctioning such a sacrifice for any lesser reason."

"And so it's God who deprives you—and Mary Ann Tierney—of choice?"

"Not in the sense that He speaks to me. Except as He speaks to us all: 'Thou shalt not kill.'"

"Is that a medical judgment, Doctor? Or one which reflects your particular moral and religious beliefs?"

Trapped, the witness searched for a politic answer, then seemed to settle for truth. "Everything I've learned, Ms. Dash, suggests that they're inseparable. Whatever the risks."

Sarah stared at him. "Until they happen," she answered. "And not to you."

Sixteen

Sitting in the Majority Leader's wood and leather office, Caroline Masters wondered at the tug of memory this evoked—she had not been here before, nor met Macdonald Gage. But she had little time to ponder this: Gage compelled her full attention.

His amiable demeanor and courtly air put Caroline on edge; she sensed that his conversation was not meant to convey meaning, but to conceal the traps which lurked beneath. Even his appearance—the frequent smiles; the small, shrewd eyes; the pedestrian gray suit with the Kiwanis pin in its lapel—seemed intended to suggest a small-town mayor, not the master of the Senate, one of America's most powerful men. Their first five minutes together were a minuet of exquisite courtesy, as Gage assured her of his fondness for Kerry Kilcannon, her native state of New Hampshire, and, with the barest hint of irony, San Francisco.

"Seems so far away from home," he said. "How'd you decide to move there?"

Because there were so many gay folks, Caroline considered saying. Smiling, she answered, "Because it seemed so far away from home."

Gage produced his automatic smile, a movement of the jaw muscles which signaled that this, too, was ritual. Though her answer seemed to tell him little, it was closer to truth than anything they had said—at twenty-two, Caroline had fled her father, a tyrant who concealed his insecurities and implacable will beneath the velvet glove of paternal concern.

"Growing pains," Gage remarked pleasantly. "Never wanted to leave Kentucky myself, never doubted where I'd raise my children. Just lucky, I guess."

This did not seem to require comment; rather than utter some banality, Caroline smiled yet again. Reticence was another lesson forced on her by Judge Channing Masters, whose every conversation with the young Caroline had been a subtle probe. And then the dormant memory caused a tremor which broke through to her consciousness: Gage's office was far too like her father's den.

The remembrance caught her short. "Chief Justice of the Supreme Court," Gage remarked with a joking air. "Feel like you're up to it?"

This time Caroline did not smile. "Yes," she answered simply. "I do."

Her decision to scorn the usual platitudes—what an honor this would be, how humbled she was—seemed to throw him off, but only for a moment. "That's real good," he drawled in a contemplative manner. "You know, I can't help thinking of Roger Bannon—his legacy at the Court, the wonderful family he had. America's most preeminent judge should not only be a symbol of jurisprudence, but a model for everyone. Wouldn't you agree?"

The thrust of the question, slightly more pointed, unnerved her. Perhaps it was the thoughts she had carried here, and her burden of concealment. "If not a model of perfection," Caroline responded, "at least of humanity."

The answer, which Gage might interpret as suggesting that Bannon had been less than that, evoked from him a smaller smile. Nodding toward the blank screen of his television, he said, "Speaking of humanity, are you watching the Tierney case?"

The question could have many facets—political, legal, and personal. "No," Caroline answered. "For the same reason I don't go to any trials in the lower court—to avoid appearance of bias."

Though Gage might interpret this as evasive, he nodded his approval. "Yes, indeed, Judge Masters. A wise policy. Especially what with Sarah Dash."

Delivered with surface innocence, the bland remark told Caroline that Gage was delving into her life. Left unspoken was whether he intended to refer to Sarah's clerkship, or their friendship, or to jar loose some deeper admission; what seemed plain was Gage's intention to alarm her. "In *any* case," Caroline answered.

Gage shot her a keen, fleeting glance. Then he settled back in his chair, hands folded across his belly, and gazed at the ceiling as if musing to himself. "Still," he said. "You must have been as taken aback as I was when they challenged this law in court. Who, I asked myself, could be *for* partial-birth abortion and *against* involving parents—even if they believe themselves pro-abortion? But then I realized this trial was a virtual seminar, especially for young women who may face this situation."

Caroline said nothing. Gage lowered his eyes, and then looked directly into hers. "That's why it's good," he said, "that you've been so strong on adoption."

Was this about Brett, Caroline wondered, or another tangent of abortion? Or merely a signal that he was studying Caroline's record as closely as her life. "To be unloved," she answered, "is a tragedy. For the child and, perhaps, the rest of us."

Gage nodded sagely. "A loving family," he said, "is the best social program of all. I learned that from my own adoptive family, and from the little girl my wife and I took in as our own."

This could be either an attempt to ferret out her social views, or a tacit reminder that Caroline had no family of her own, perhaps aimed at whatever hidden vulnerability might account for this. Detaching herself, Caroline considered Gage anew. Every nuance, every molecule, of the persona he had constructed, suggested to her that he should remain in the shadows of the Senate, ruling by indirection and maneuver, rather than run for President. It was hard to imagine this consummate pragmatist inspiring millions, as had Kerry Kilcannon. Though Gage lacked the bedrock dedication to country above all that helped place other men—a Robert Taft or Bob Dole—among history's great Majority Leaders, his gifts, like theirs, were well suited to the intimacy of the Senate. And yet, Caroline knew, powerful forces wanted Macdonald Gage to be the President, and that was how he saw himself. This mismatch between his ambitions and his popular appeal might make Gage that much more calculating, that much more beholden to the interests who promoted him, that much more dangerous to Caroline herself.

"Family," Caroline responded, "can be the best thing that ever happens to us. Or the worst."

Gage's look of piety slowly faded. "Tell me, Judge Masters, how would you describe your judicial philosophy?"

Caroline was prepared for this. "Careful," she answered. "Respectful of precedent. I don't think judges should legislate."

Gage nodded in feigned relief. Smoothly, he said, "So you believe as Roger Bannon did?"

Caroline pretended to consider her answer. "I can only be myself, Senator. Let me put it this way: a Supreme Court which is careless of the law can diminish respect for law. But there are clearly times when what might have been acceptable to Thomas Jefferson becomes unacceptable to us, and whether in 1954 Jefferson might have made Sally Hemings drink at the water fountain marked 'Coloreds Only' becomes irrelevant. At best."

By picking this sardonic example, Caroline placed her response beyond debate—especially by a man whose private club memberships, Clayton Slade had told her, included those which admitted a mere trickle of minorities, and excluded women altogether. With a first fleeting trace of annoyance, Gage asked, "What about the Second Amendment? Think the founding fathers put it there for a reason?"

"Of course," Caroline answered promptly. "At a minimum, it bars the government from confiscating all guns. But is it reasonable to suppose that Thomas

Jefferson contemplated cop-killer bullets, or rocket launchers in the back yard? Once more, the founding fathers seem to have left us on our own."

Gage folded his hands. "As you apparently think they did with respect to laws regulating campaign contributions."

Once again, Caroline blessed Clayton Slade for briefing her: she had parried Gage's first inquiries on abortion and guns—crucial to important sources of money for his prospective campaign—and now, he was moved to be even more direct. "I take it," Caroline answered, "that you read my opinion on the subject."

Gage nodded. "Yes, indeed."

"In which I ruled that a limit on donations in Oregon was legal, but expressed no view on what wasn't before our court—such as the far more comprehensive reform law pending in the Senate. Nor can I now, in simple propriety. Any more than Roger Bannon would have."

This veiled irony produced, in Gage, an amiable smile. "Of course not. I was more interested in your philosophical framework."

His tone of mild interest belied the sharpness of his gaze. "It's more or less the same," Caroline assured him. "The First Amendment protects speech in many forms. Did Jefferson imagine television, endless political campaigns, or million-dollar contributions? Clearly not. Does that mean such contributions aren't protected by the First Amendment? Not in itself. Like any prudent judge, I'll wait to see what comes before me."

Stymied, Gage gave a smile which, to Caroline, seemed deliberately slow in coming. "And I admire that, Judge. It speaks well for you—professionally."

The last word, Caroline sensed, was far from casual. She had shown him that attacking her on principles would not be easy; he was warning her that there were other ways. Her smile, Caroline hoped, was suitably enigmatic.

"Well that's good then." Suddenly, Gage stood. "And it's been just fine to meet you.

"But I have to tell you, Judge, we have our ways in the Senate. Sometimes they're more leisurely than a nominee might want. Some of my colleagues believe 'deliberative' means kicking the tires and turning over every last rock. But I think that's better for the Court, don't you?"

Beneath the words, Caroline heard a second warning: if there was anything she hoped to conceal, which Gage could yet discover or perhaps already knew, she was better off withdrawing.

"I agree," Caroline answered. "Completely."

"Good." Clasping her hand, Gage beamed at her, though his cool gaze of appraisal did not change. "Then everything will be just fine."

He ushered her to the door with elaborate courtesy, and no encouragement.

He was careful to avoid the press—another signal, if Caroline needed one, that Macdonald Gage had resolved to bring her down. Perhaps this was inevitable, but the experience of meeting him left her far more unsettled than she had anticipated.

Alone in her room, she called Brett Allen in Iowa, to say hello.

Seventeen

For most of its duration, the testimony of Marlene Brown was as bad as Sarah had anticipated, but no worse.

The sixteen-year-old girl, Barry Saunders's witness, was a portrait of the rural Midwest—wearing a simple dress, and little makeup, the plump brunette answered his questions with respectful docility. "Could you tell us," he asked, "what happened after you became pregnant?"

"It was hard, at first . . ." Marlene paused, glancing down in modesty. "Mike and I were only fifteen, and all our folks thought we were too young to get married."

"Did you consider abortion?"

The girl nodded. "I thought about everything. But we're very strong in our personal relationship with Jesus Christ. I had to ask myself if Jesus would approve my taking our baby's life."

To Sarah, the skeptic, such pronouncements—serenely certain of the speaker's intimate acquaintance with the Godhead—had a blissed-out, cultlike quality which shortcut the process of thought. But she had learned to accept that this reaction set her apart from countless others, whom she seldom encountered, and, perhaps, from Mary Ann, who listened with bowed head.

"What did your parents say?" Saunders was asking.

Marlene looked away. "I knew it would be hard on them, and I felt real bad about that. But they said that love is infinite—that their hearts could expand to love my baby just like they did for me, their youngest child. *I* was a surprise, too."

Sarah imagined the simple goodness embodied in those words—as well, perhaps, as a clue that Marlene Brown identified with her own unplanned child. "It'll be all right," she whispered to Mary Ann—as much for herself as for the girl.

"Did there come a time," Saunders asked Marlene, "that you learned that there were problems with your unborn child?"

Marlene swallowed, as though the remembered moment were tangible and present. "The doctor told me he had water on the brain—hydrocephalus, they called it. All I knew was, on the sonogram, his head was way too big for his body."

"Or *your* body?"

The witness nodded. "To have my baby, I'd have to have an operation."

"A classical cesarean section?"

"Yes." The witness glanced at Mary Ann. "Even if I did, they said my baby would most likely die—that the water would probably keep it from growing much of a brain."

Saunders nodded in sympathy. "How far along were you?"

"Five months—maybe a little more."

"Did your doctor say that having this baby might keep you from having any more?"

The witness paused, twisting her plastic watch. "He said he thought I'd come out fine, but there was always a small chance I wouldn't."

"What did you do?"

"I mean, my mom was there . . ." Marlene gave a shrug of helplessness; her face and body seemed to reflect whatever emotions she recalled. "For a long time we just cried. It was cold—Iowa's *cold* in December—and a snowstorm had shut down my school. But when my mom called my dad, he left the factory and drove right home." As though by reflex, Marlene turned to Martin Tierney. "They sat next to me, each holding my hand. Finally they both—really my mom, mostly—said that they didn't like abortion, but didn't want me hurt, either."

"And so . . ." Saunders prompted.

"And so they said we should pray on it and consult as a family, and then they'd support whatever I decided to do."

In the context she described—two pro-life parents, a vivid, personified Jesus who loved her unborn child—it was difficult for Sarah to imagine Marlene Brown terminating any pregnancy. "So you prayed?" Saunders asked.

"Yes. We kneeled down in a circle, held hands, and asked for guidance. And then we talked about what would happen if the baby came out wrong."

"What did you decide?"

"That together we could bear it. Even if my baby would die soon, at least I could give him a chance." The girl's next words were quiet but affecting. "So we made a place in my room for Matthew, and waited for him to come."

"When was he born?"

"In July." The girl swallowed again. "They had to put a tube in his head."

Turning, Saunders nodded to an associate who stood by the courtroom door. With a certain ceremony, the man opened it and a woman entered, holding a baby in her arms.

She walked between the rows of reporters, a good-natured-appearing woman in a navy blue pantsuit, with unnaturally brown hair coiled tight to her head. Startled, Sarah stood. Even without an explanation, Sarah knew she was the witness's mother; though Marlene was only sixteen, she had the same profile as the older woman—a prominent nose and softening chin—and her appealing, limpid eyes watched the woman and child with adoration.

"Could we have a bench conference?" Sarah asked.

Leary was gazing upon the scene with a half-smile of bemusement. Distractedly, he said, "Approach the bench, counsel."

As Tierney, Saunders, Fleming, and Sarah clustered before him, the woman paused in the well of the courtroom, and the infant emitted a brief squall. "This is a hearing," Sarah told Leary in an angry undertone, "not a Christmas pageant, or show-and-tell. Or are we going to admit this baby into evidence?

"I'm perfectly willing to accept on faith the witness's assertion that her child exists. It has no place in court . . ."

"*No* place," Saunders said with genuine indignation. "We've seen sonograms of an engorged head and photographs of a ruptured uterus, but this beautiful child 'has no place—'"

"All right," Leary interrupted. "What's your point?"

"That as the one who must choose between life and death, you—the entire country, in fact—ought to face him. Or how can we have the moral authority to decide the fate of *any* child?"

Looking toward the baby, Leary raised a hand, forestalling Sarah's rebuttal. Perhaps, she thought bitterly, he had begun to perceive that, by admitting cameras to the courtroom, he had become an actor in a drama manipulated by others. "Miss Brown can identify the baby," he told Saunders. "That should be enough to suit your purposes. We're not equipped with a changing table."

Saunders nodded, his face a buttery mask of satisfaction. He had outthought her, Sarah knew, and the next few minutes would be terrible. Returning to the plaintiff's table, she saw Mary Ann, like everyone present, regarding the child with mixed tenderness and fascination. As Sarah sat, she touched Mary Ann's hand.

But Mary Ann could not stop watching the baby; nor, it seemed, could the judge. Saunders beckoned the woman forward; in near silence, she crossed the courtroom, and placed the infant in its young mother's arms.

Gently, Saunders asked, "Marlene, is this your son?"

The girl, so pitifully young in Sarah's mind, gazed down at the small face peering back at her from beneath blue blankets. "This is Matthew."

As if to affirm this, the baby raised one hand and made a tiny fist, an infant's reflex. In the fond, protective voice of a church elder, Saunders asked, "And how old is he, Marlene?"

"Just seven months, tomorrow."

"Is he crawling yet?"

With a mother's smile, Marlene kept watching his face. "Trying to. He can get up on his knees now."

"What else does he do?"

Mary Ann's eyes grew wide and receptive. "Oh, lots of things," she answered. "He touches the mobile in his crib, and smiles when I sing to him. His eyes are always following our cat around, like Buster's the most fun thing he's ever seen."

At least until I throw up, Sarah thought. But she knew all too well how effective this was; despite her defenses, she felt the shafts of doubt. Mary Ann seemed to fight back tears; Sarah wondered if Saunders's—and the Tierneys'—true intention was to convince Mary Ann to withdraw her suit.

Perhaps mercifully, Matthew Brown resumed squalling. Smiling, Leary said to Saunders, "Perhaps you should find Matthew a bottle, Mr. Saunders. I think he's had his fill of us."

Smiling as well, Saunders signaled the older woman to come forward. With the competence of long experience, she took the baby from her daughter, nestling him against her shoulder. Matthew's outcries stopped.

Silent, Saunders let the scene speak for him: two generations, filled with love, united to preserve a third. Glancing at Margaret Tierney, Sarah felt her own sense of pageantry increasing; Mary Ann's mother looked as rapt as a communicant at Easter—at least as far as Sarah could imagine this. When at last the older woman carried Matthew from the courtroom, a stately procession through the smiling, curious media, Sarah felt a profound relief at his disappearance.

"No further questions," Saunders said, and then Mary Ann began to cry.

Eighteen

Instead of preparing her cross-examination, Sarah spent most of the break in the rest room, consoling Mary Ann.

Weeping, the girl bent over the porcelain sink. "It's like they're saying I'd have killed that baby . . ."

Yes, Sarah thought, and on television. She did not know who she held more responsible—the Tierneys, the Christian Commitment, Leary, or the media. All that Sarah could do was to make Mary Ann Tierney, the public figure, as sympathetic as she could.

"After I'm finished," Sarah assured her, "people will understand." And then she carried the burden of this promise to the courtroom.

Her task was delicate. Marlene Brown seemed guileless, a pawn of forces who might use her, but could never make this girl as crafty, or relentless, as they. Yet the opportunity this created mirrored its challenges—neither could Sarah appear crafty or relentless. As Sarah approached, Marlene watched her with an expectant sweetness.

Quietly, Sarah said, "Your parents didn't *make* you have Matthew, I guess."

Marlene shook her head vigorously. "Oh, no. We decided as a family."

"And if you'd decided not to take the chance, would your parents have supported you?"

Idly, the witness played with a strand of hair, frowning in thought. "It's so hard, now, to imagine life without him . . ."

"But they said you could decide."

Silence, then a quick bob of the head. "Yes, ma'am."

This term of deference made Sarah smile. "You must feel lucky to have the parents you do."

"Oh, yes."

"Then you've probably noticed that other girls at school aren't so fortunate."

The thought brought sadness to Marlene's open face. In a softer voice, she said, "I surely have."

"Within families, what kind of problems do you hear about?"

Barry Saunders was restive now, Sarah noticed. "Drinking, mostly." The girl's voice sharpened with disapproval. "My friend's father beat her, and she had to run away . . ."

She stopped abruptly, remembering her audience; in the global village, let alone a small town in Iowa, her words would spread quickly. Sarah did not press the point.

"When you first thought you were pregnant, Marlene, why did you talk to your mom?"

The girl bit her lip. " 'Cause she *is* my mom. I mean, it was bad, but . . ."

"You didn't talk to her because Iowa state law required a parent to consent to an abortion?"

For the first time, the girl looked puzzled and defensive; the question seemed beyond her ken. "I didn't know about any law. I talked to my parents because I wanted to."

"And you decided to have Matthew because you wanted to."

"Yes. Definitely." She paused, then added, "And because I believed Jesus, my personal savior, would want me to."

Do you know what He wants for Mary Ann Tierney? Sarah considered asking. But the question was too loaded. Vigilant, Barry Saunders sat forward on the edge of his chair, while Martin Tierney watched Sarah with a cool, knowing expression. "So," she continued, "Matthew was delivered by cesarean section."

"Yes, ma'am."

"Do you know what effect, if any, that will have on your ability to have more children?"

The witness shook her head. "I can't know, yet."

"Would you like to have more children?"

"Some day, when I'm married." For an instant, Marlene looked perturbed, then her face cleared of doubt. "I put myself in the Lord's hands. To give me Matthew was His will, and so's whether I have more babies."

Sarah paused, then decided to take a chance. "I guess Matthew must seem almost like a miracle."

Once more, Barry Saunders stirred. But, Sarah knew, for him to challenge the implications of *this* miracle would unsettle his own witness. "Yes, ma'am," Marlene answered. "They said most babies like that don't make it."

Briefly looking down, Sarah tried to conceal her satisfaction. "So once again," she said kindly, "you were lucky."

"Not just lucky." The girl's voice swelled with gratitude. "It's like of all the babies in the world, God placed His healing hand on Matthew."

Sarah was not so sure of this. She had studied the case, and consulted with Dr. Mark Flom; there was considerable doubt about the range of Matthew's cognitive capacities, or his long-term prognosis. But there was no percentage in parsing miracles, or suggesting to Marlene Brown that her son's might be cruelly finite. It would be enough to ask this girl to step outside her blissful world, and imagine Mary Ann's.

"Would you want Mary Ann Tierney," Sarah asked, "to have a son like Matthew?"

Briefly, the girl looked at Mary Ann. "Oh, yes," she said with fervor. "I surely would."

"I guess you know he'll be born hydrocephalic. So for her son to be like Matthew, and have a brain—that would take another miracle, wouldn't it?"

A shadow seemed to cross Marlene's face. Saunders began to stand, then thought better of it; with a certain bitter amusement, Sarah reflected that he was trapped in his own pageant. "Yes, ma'am," Marlene answered slowly. "I guess it would."

"What if her baby weren't like Matthew, but died, as the doctors expected your son to, and as most such babies do. Would you want her to have another?"

"Yes. Of course I would."

Sarah tilted her head. "What if she couldn't, because of the baby who died? What would you say to her then?"

"It would be hard." The girl tried to imagine this, then said more firmly, "I'd tell her it was God's will, to place her faith in Him."

Sarah paused a moment. "Suppose that had happened to you—that Matthew had died, and you could never have more children. What would you believe then?"

"Your Honor." Rising, Saunders spoke slowly. "Ms. Dash is free to ask Marlene anything about her own experience. But how can she answer about experiences she's never had?"

"Precisely," Sarah told Leary. "I respect Miss Brown's experience. I'm merely testing its limits, and its application to Mary Ann Tierney."

For a moment, Leary looked bewildered, unsure of where Sarah was going. Seemingly as much from embarrassment as insight, the judge said, "You may answer, Marlene."

The girl folded her hands, eyes downcast in contemplation. "I'd believe it was God's will," she said softly. "That I shouldn't question His decision for me. Or Matthew."

"But there was a miracle," Sarah said with equal quiet, "and Matthew's fine."

Marlene brightened again. "Oh, yes."

Sarah glanced at Mary Ann. Her client's wits were keener than Marlene's, Sarah believed, her perspective sharper; though her eyes were still puffy, Mary Ann's gaze at the witness betrayed a tentative feeling of distance. To Marlene, Sarah asked, "Suppose you'd chosen an abortion? Would that have been wrong?"

"Yes," the girl answered firmly. "Definitely."

"So your parents were wrong to give you a choice?"

The question seemed to take Marlene aback. It confirmed Sarah's suspicion that this particular "choice"—so humanizing for the Browns, but now so useful to Sarah's purposes—had been more apparent than real. "Once we prayed," Marlene finally said, "we found the answer together. For me to have Matthew."

"So now you think that's the *only* answer?"

Marlene paused, then bobbed her head again. "Yes."

"And so, if your parents *had* forced you to have Matthew, that would have been morally right."

Taut, Barry Saunders watched from the defense table. But it was Martin Tierney's translucent gaze, trained on Sarah with keen perception, which told her she was scoring points. "Yes," the girl answered. "Matthew's the proof of that."

"So the Tierneys should force Mary Ann to have this child. Even if she *never* has a child like Matthew?"

Hesitant, Marlene paused. In a smaller voice, she answered, "Yes."

The courtroom was very still. Quietly, Sarah asked, "What about the father who beat your friend. Should *he* also have that right as a parent?"

Faltering, the girl looked at Saunders. "Objection," he said angrily. "That's hypothetical upon hypothetical."

"Agreed," Leary said.

Sarah had done what she could. Bewildered, Marlene Brown watched from the witness stand, mired in the tyranny of her own goodness, a girl whose beliefs—having been rewarded by God or good fortune—now formed the basis for how all others must live.

"Thank you, Marlene," Sarah told her. "That's all I wanted to know."

Nineteen

Alone in Sarah's apartment, Mary Ann felt too miserable to cry, too sick at heart to eat.

They thought she was a murderer, and there was nowhere, now, to hide. If she went to school, or even to the corner store, everyone would see this slutty girl who got herself pregnant, by a boy who didn't care about her, in the back seat of a car, then wanted to kill a baby as sweet as Matthew Brown. Now the whole world knew Marlene Brown, and loved her for saving Matthew; the whole world hated Mary Ann Tierney for her selfishness, and thought her parents were right.

It wasn't fair. They didn't know her. Sarah had kept her from testifying, and all that anyone believed about her came from other people. They didn't know what it was like to look at a swollen head on a sonogram; or carry a baby that barely moved at all; or be scared of what would happen when they sliced her open. They didn't know what it was like to be afraid of being sterile, or of telling a husband who loved you that you couldn't have children with him. They didn't know what it was like to have your mother and father decide your whole life for you. They didn't know what it was like to be so helpless.

No one knew. Not even Sarah.

With deep and bitter regret, Mary Ann thought of her life six months ago—her friends, her room, the clothes she could wear, her unquestioning belief in her parents and their love. It all seemed precious and irretrievable, a distant dream—shattered by how dumb she was with Tony, and then more terrible things than anyone deserved. She was not sure that she wanted to believe in a God who was so mean and petty that He would ruin her life for one mistake.

As soon as this thought came over her, Mary Ann was assaulted by fear.

She was *so* alone.

The buzzer to the intercom snarled.

Instinctively, Mary Ann cowered. She could not answer.

It buzzed again.

Mary Ann swallowed, fighting the dryness in her mouth and throat. Maybe it was Sarah; maybe she'd forgotten her key. It felt like Sarah was her only friend.

Sluggishly, Mary Ann stood up. Her belly felt distended, her legs and ankles thick; sometimes it hurt to move, and now she was afraid to love the baby who caused this.

Pushing the button to the intercom, she asked, "Sarah?"

"Mary Ann?" a woman's voice asked in some surprise. "This is Tina Kwan, from Channel Five. Can we talk a minute . . ."

"Go away."

Still Mary Ann kept her finger on the button, as though she feared her loneliness as much as she feared the voice. "All I want is a minute," the woman urged. "For your sake."

Finger still on the button, Mary Ann pressed her face against the intercom.

The voice was soft now. "If you're still listening, Mary Ann, I'd like to help you. No one really knows you."

When Mary Ann opened her eyes, tears filled them. "I know," she whispered. "I know."

When her windshield wipers began to squeak, Sarah angrily switched them off.

She was exhausted. She had enjoyed a brief respite from the trial, a dinner with friends who had ordered up buttons which said FREE SARAH DASH. Once at her office, she was briefed by three associates who had summarized the prior depositions of the Tierneys' proposed expert. But working there—though necessary—involved so many distractions that they amounted to harassment: constant calls from media; the patent disapproval of the chairman, John Nolan; the well-meaning visits of encouragement from women and other friends at the firm; the kibitzers who, fascinated that their peer was fighting a televised trial, dropped in with comments or advice, some of it remarkably insensitive.

"Too bad about that baby," one observed. "Hopefully *yours* will turn out to be a really bad connection." By that standard, the starfuckers—who broke Sarah's concentration merely so they could tell their friends they'd talked to her about the trial—had been a relief.

Drizzle speckling her windshield, she drove into the cavernous garage of her apartment building, grateful for the elevator at its center. She had seen no strangers outside. Her phone number was unlisted; with luck, it would take the media and the Christian Commitment a few days to find out where she lived. Any respite was precious.

But any solitude, she discovered in the empty elevator, allowed too many vexing questions to reemerge.

Was she good enough? She had done well so far, but tension and fatigue, the extreme highs and lows of a trial unlike any others, were sapping her resilience and dulling her judgment. Sarah envied Martin Tierney the partnership, if not the company, of Barry Saunders.

There were other doubts, too, which no lawyer trapped in the savage single-mindedness of a trial could afford to entertain.

What if the baby were normal? Should a woman have the absolute power of life and death over the unborn, when Sarah scorned the Tierneys' assertion of power over Mary Ann? What about Martin Tierney's apocryphal mother, empowered to abort a fetus with the wrong eye color, or one with a "genetic predisposition" to be gay? Was Sarah blind to the implications of her own arguments? And what would become of Mary Ann if she prevailed?

Friends were Sarah's buffer, a touchstone to reality; her dating life was at least a pleasant diversion, which sometimes held the hope of more. But Sarah had no time for either. She was living in a bell jar, with only Mary Ann for company. Although, before, the girl's presence had added to her pressures, tonight it would almost seem a blessing.

Fumbling, Sarah missed the lock with her door key—another sign that she was running on fumes. The second try, inserting the key with exaggerated care, was accompanied by a slow release of breath. Then she opened her door, and looked into the startled face of a stranger.

As the woman rose from her couch, Sarah wondered why she looked familiar. All at once she understood.

Mary Ann remained on the couch, staring at Sarah with startled, guilty eyes, a tiny microphone clipped to the collar of her blouse. Standing next to Sarah's stereo was a technician with a Minicam.

The woman composed herself, extending a hand. "I'm Tina Kwan."

Sarah felt herself shaken by outrage and fatigue. As Kwan crossed the living room, the camera followed her. For a split second, Sarah imagined the scene on television.

Sarah took the woman's hand. "Sarah Dash," she said. "I didn't know you'd turned my living room into a television studio."

The woman seemed impervious. "We're anxious for Mary Ann to tell her story."

"Then let's talk—alone." Without waiting for an answer, she took Kwan by the arm, and guided her from the room. Mary Ann and the technician watched them in surprise.

Sarah led her to the bathroom; she did not want this woman in her bedroom. Pushing Kwan inside, she closed the door behind them.

Kwan stepped back a little. Sarah glimpsed their reflections in the mirror, two profiles above Sarah's vanity, strewn with her makeup, toothpaste, and—unfortunate timing for a trial—an open box of tampons. "You're losing the PR wars," Kwan said. "You can't win this trial without winning in the media."

The woman looked perfect—short hair carefully cut, a glossy black; her face made up to accent her exotic features for the camera. Briefly, Sarah felt off balance, trapped in a hall of mirrors in which this woman's claims were true.

"This isn't a PR war," Sarah answered. "It's a girl's life. I don't want it trashed."

Kwan shook her head. "*You'll* trash it," she retorted, "if you let these Bible thumpers make a Martian out of her."

The woman's bluntness muted Sarah's outrage. "When *I* decide it's right for Mary Ann," she replied, "we'll consider talking to you. But only if you give me whatever film you have, and leave."

Kwan squared her shoulders. "*Mary Ann* wants to talk to us," she retorted. "Why don't you let her decide?"

The woman's aggression took Sarah aback. As though seeing this, Kwan brushed past her, opened the door, and walked back into Sarah's living room.

The camera was aimed at them. "Mary Ann," Kwan said, "your lawyer says no interview. I want people to see you as you really are. Only you can decide."

It was a nightmare, captured on videotape. Sarah composed herself. "They're trying to exploit you," she told Mary Ann. "I'm asking you to trust me."

Mary Ann gazed up at her—by turns frightened, sullen, resistant, and confused.

Abruptly, she rose.

Sarah tensed. With the resistant, angry posture of a teenager, the girl turned her back on everyone and walked to her room. The door closed behind her.

Kwan gazed after her. "Get out," Sarah demanded, and then decided to bluff. "You're trespassing, and I can sue you. Use that tape, and I will."

It took them fifteen minutes to pack up the camera and gear. Sarah stayed in the living room. No one spoke.

.   .   .

Sarah opened the door to Mary Ann's room.

Mary Ann sat on the edge of the bed, arms folded, staring at the wall. Sitting next to her, Sarah sorted out a riot of emotions: shock at this invasion of her home, a feeling of betrayal—that Mary Ann had violated her privacy and abused her trust—and a sense, slower to settle in, of how lost this girl was.

"Why did you let them in?" she asked.

Mary Ann did not turn. "It's my case, not yours. It's *my* baby. It's *my* life."

Beneath the stubborn words, Sarah heard her fright. "They're not your friends," she answered. "You're not ready to cope with them . . ."

"Not *ready* . . ." Mary Ann bolted upright, momentarily staggering with the awkwardness of pregnancy. "You sound like *him*—my father. He makes me look like dirt, and *you* tell me to let him." She stopped, words choking at the beginning of a sob. "What will people think of me, Sarah? Who'll want anything to do with me, after this? Who will my friends be?"

It was the lament of any teenager, Sarah thought—except that, in this case, the lament was terribly real. She tried to put aside her own feelings. "The first thing," Sarah answered, "is what you think of yourself."

Mary Ann stared at her, and then sat down again. Softly, she said, "When I saw that baby . . ." Her voice trailed off.

"I felt it, too," Sarah answered. "Do you think that means you're wrong?"

Looking down, Mary Ann gazed at her own stomach. "What if he *is* okay?" she said. "And I've killed him?"

Sarah pondered the loneliness behind the question. "If you have an abortion," she answered, "you run that risk, however small. In fairness to your father, I think that's part of what he wants to spare you. I don't think he's only worried about the fetus."

For what seemed to Sarah a very long time, Mary Ann said nothing. Would she be relieved, Sarah wondered, if Mary Ann removed the weight she felt, gave her back at least a semblance of the life she had enjoyed—free of the press, and the sense that her own future was moving out of her control? Then Mary Ann shook her head. "I have to do this," she said. "For myself. I hope maybe for my husband, someday, and for our babies."

There was resignation in her voice—a deep sorrow and, with it, a measure of maturity. The relief Sarah felt answered at least one question—if Mary Ann was prepared to go on, this was what Sarah wanted as well.

"I was trying to protect you," Sarah said softly, "not stifle you. When we talk to someone, we'll choose who, and we'll dictate the ground rules. Or else it's not an interview—it's an ambush."

Mary Ann nodded. "Okay."

"So can I tell you what went through my head when I saw those people aiming a Minicam at you?"

Silent, Mary Ann assented with her eyes.

"I thought of all the women I've seen interviewed on television. They've slept with a politician, or shot their husband in self-defense. Suddenly they're famous by accident and forget what they're famous *for*. And then they get hooked by pseudocelebrity until they become a narcissistic joke.

"You're not a joke, Mary Ann, and the media isn't reality. If *you* know you're a good person, no one else can make you a bad one." Pausing, Sarah rested her hand on Mary Ann's shoulder. "You're doing this to get your life back. Don't let this *become* your life. Please."

Mary Ann blinked. Then suddenly she was in Sarah's arms, hugging her fiercely. Sarah's own gratitude was a measure of how tired she felt. Far too tired, it now seemed, to say anything more to anyone.

Twenty

Watching Dr. Bruno Lasch testify, Sarah wished that she had slept better—or at all.

Lasch's credentials were daunting enough: a renowned expert in biomedical ethics, Lasch had taught at Yale, was widely published, and now held a senior fellowship at America's most distinguished center for the study of bioethical issues. But what he personified made him more formidable yet. From birth, Lasch's body had been stunted and bent, his hands lacked fingers, and his legs—more vestigial than functional—had consigned him to a wheelchair, now placed in front of the witness stand. Most striking, though, were Lasch's eyes, blazing with a keen intelligence.

He was now forty-two. Few had expected him to live this long or, so seriously disabled, to forge such a brilliant career. His iconic standing in the disability community was affirmed by the circle of demonstrators, many in wheelchairs, who had greeted Sarah and Mary Ann with signs saying DISABILITY IS NOT A DEATH SENTENCE. Pale, Mary Ann had taken Sarah's hand.

"It seems clear," Lasch now told Martin Tierney, "that the principal basis for your daughter's lawsuit is not the extremely marginal threat to her reproductive capacity, but the 'unacceptable' nature of her child."

His voice was reedy; he paused for breath, twisting his neck to peer at Leary. "By that standard, it's painfully apparent to me that *I* wouldn't be here. And I can't help but be grateful, every day, that my parents were loving enough, and brave enough, to see past their dreams of the ideal, and see *me*."

His voice quavered slightly. "But I shouldn't personalize this, Your Honor. My real concern is not to tell Mary Ann Tierney 'you're talking about *me*.' It's to ask her, and to ask this court, what kind of society we are—and should be." He turned to Mary Ann. "What I believe is this: the assertion that the Protection of

Life Act is unconstitutional unless Mary Ann Tierney can take *this* life demeans the value of *any* life which is perceived as less than 'normal,' by whatever subjective standard the mother uses to define that."

This was not testimony, Sarah thought—it was a lecture, delivered from the impregnable fortress of Lasch's cruelly twisted body. But to object would seem petty and disrespectful; there was no way, now, to point out that God had given Mary Ann's fetus arms and legs but, in all probability, nothing which resembled this man's extraordinary brain. Beside her, Mary Ann gazed at him in awe, biting her underlip, while her father's questions held the reverence of a man addressing a secular saint.

"Could you amplify," Tierney asked, "your concerns about selective abortion of the disabled?"

"Certainly." Once more, Lasch swallowed; he seemed to have trouble breathing, and he sometimes spoke in a painful wheeze. "The first concern is what I call the expressivist argument—that biology is destiny, that the trait expresses the whole. Or, put personally, that my arms and legs are all there is of me."

Sarah winced inside; skillfully, Lasch used himself as an exhibit. "A few years ago," he continued, "there was an anchorwoman in Los Angeles whose hands lacked fingers. She had a loving marriage, a fine career. But when she became pregnant, and it seemed clear that her baby would also lack fingers, many people asked her how she could give birth to such a child."

Lasch grimaced in wonder. "They were upset by the image of a fingerless child, because he violated their idea of beauty, and so should be put to death. As bad, they were telling the baby's mother that she should never have been born. But even our *idea* of disability is subjective: in the nineteenth century, on Martha's Vineyard, deafness was so common that virtually everyone spoke sign language. Which suggests that rather than committing murder, society can—and should—adjust to accommodate difference."

Hastily, Sarah scribbled a note with a star beside it. As compelling—and disturbing—as Sarah herself found Lasch's testimony, she thought it laced with a subtle ingenuousness, which Lasch himself appreciated and intended. And in this, Sarah hoped, might lie the seeds of her cross-examination.

"What," Tierney was asking, "are your other concerns?"

"One is societal, Professor—that we've come to view children as commodities, not gifts to be cherished. All too often, parents see a child as an extension of *themselves,* not an end in *itself.* And so they believe they're entitled to order up a child like something in a catalog—witness the couples who advertise on the Internet for eggs from six-foot blond Swedish volleyball players who double as Miss Universe."

At this, Judge Leary smiled, arching his eyebrows with the bright pleasure of agreement. Though Sarah bridled at this facile linking of rich and fatuous would-be parents with the embattled girl beside her, the media, a reflection of their audience, closely attended Lasch's every word.

Tierney still spoke softly. "Are these problems enhanced by genetic testing for pregnant women?"

"Yes, in ways that I find frightening." Lasch glanced at Leary with a spasmodic twist of the neck. "Genetic testing grows ever more sophisticated. Today, a mother can abort this child for hydrocephalus—or because she prefers a girl.

"Tomorrow, she can abort a child for being blond, or because it's tone-deaf, and can't share the mother's love for Mozart . . ." Lasch coughed, his body racking with tremors. "I apologize, Your Honor. My question is this—how can we let the mother select between desirable or undesirable traits, or 'bad' or 'less bad'? And do we want a world of designer babies?"

Once more, Leary's eyebrows, raised quizzically, seemed to signal agreement. "You've spoken of the mother," Tierney said. "What, in your view, is the obligation of a doctor?"

Lasch turned to him, a jerking of the head. "The medical profession," he answered, "has failed miserably to live up to their most basic oath—to save lives."

The effort of testifying, Sarah noticed, seemed to wear Lasch down—his tone was thinner and, for the first time, held a trace of bitterness. Sarah stifled all sympathy: within the ruthless confines of a trial, a tired, angry witness—disabled or not—served her purposes. "Many doctors," Lasch added harshly, "encourage abortion for any and all anomalies.

"Take Down's syndrome. A typical piece of 'medical advice' is, 'What are you going to say to people who ask how you can bring such a child into the world?'

"They don't give credit to all the ways in which parents and siblings welcome and are nurtured by loving a Down's child, or all the love and joy that child—being loved—returns to them." The anger in his voice faded, replaced by sadness and the strain of speaking. "We've all known such a child. Thanks to the callousness of doctors, there are too many others we will never know. To me, that's more than a crime against the child—it's a tragedy for us all."

Like the best of witnesses, Sarah thought, Lasch had modified his tone, remembering that sorrow, not outrage, helped him cast his intended spell. "Unlike you, Professor, I'm not a religious man—I am, at best, agnostic. But I see so many paradoxes here. In my state, a woman hit by a car on the way to an abortion clinic can sue for the death of a fetus. Yet if she reaches her destination and aborts it, the fetus has no status at all . . ."

Lasch swallowed, then went on. "That's why so many advocates of abortion oppose laws to protect the fetus from the horrible consequences of the mother's drug addiction, by charging her with child endangerment—because those laws suggest that a fetus is something more than the mother's property, to be treated as she wishes. Which is the unspoken premise Ms. Dash is urging on this court—that a disabled baby is a tumor to be excised, with less dignity and fewer rights than a slave before the Civil War."

With great effort, Sarah restrained herself from objecting, watching Lasch with the cold eye of a cross-examiner. Martin Tierney's questions were gentler yet, as though he were pained by Lasch's testimony and how it must tire him. "How do you relate these concerns," Tierney asked, "to the life or death of my grandson?"

Lasch slowly shook his head, his gaunt face and close-cropped hair enhancing the sorrowful appearance of a spiritual man confronting evil. "Must your grandson die, I ask, because he may be born disabled?

"To me, the most persuasive argument is not the existence of a Matthew Brown. It lies in the case of the boy they now call 'Miracle Kid.'

"As one writer described it, he was born with a face like a child's unfinished drawing—only one, unnaturally small eye; the other side of his face blank; his nostrils separated by a deep cleft; no fingers. When the doctor presented him to his mother, she said, 'I don't know what this is.'"

Lasch inhaled, as if straining for the resources to continue. "What 'this' was," Lasch said after a time, "was a baby with a rare disease called Fraser's syndrome. He also had only one kidney, severe hearing loss, and an impaired nerve pathway between the right and left side of the brain. Most nurses refused to have anything to do with him.

"His parents could have let him die. Instead they fought for him through countless operations." Pausing, Lasch addressed the courtroom. "The boy is in school now. He has a first-class mind, a sense of humor, and close friends. Because he exists, people have learned to look past what seems strange about him, to see what is so wonderful. And what is most wonderful is rare and precious in anyone, let alone a child—he's enriched the understanding, and deepened the humanity, of everyone who knows him."

It was a moving story, enhanced by Lasch's struggle simply to tell it. Sarah was not immune to this; nor, plainly, was Mary Ann—to whom Bruno Lasch now spoke.

"The sacrifice those parents made," he told her gently, "was heroic. But the child's death would have been as great a tragedy—perhaps greater—than the death of a Matthew Brown.

"If the hydrocephalus has impaired the development of his brain, Mary Ann, your child will likely die at birth, or shortly after. You'll never be called on to make those kinds of sacrifices. But if he is to die, let it be at God's hands, not yours. Give him every chance you can . . ."

Lasch coughed again, followed by a panting wheeze which brought tears to his eyes. "I know how hard this is," he said with renewed effort. "I know how hard it would be to have a child who dies. But we're very close to eugenics here, with terrible implications for the world *all* children may grow up in. What your parents are doing is an act of love, for you and for your child. In the end, I hope you'll love them more for doing it."

At that, Martin Tierney turned to his daughter with a look of love and pleading. "No further questions," he murmured.

Mary Ann stared at the table; Sarah at her notes, the bare bones of cross-examination.

Twenty-one

Facing Bruno Lasch, Sarah called on her reserves of memory—the accumulation of two nights spent, in the week before the trial, reading Lasch's papers on abortion and genetic testing.

"I'm curious about something," she began. "Do you think that a teenage girl who's been raped by her own father has the right to an abortion?"

From his wheelchair, Lasch studied her with caution. "Yes," he answered, "under most circumstances."

"Then let me give you a specific example. Suppose the girl takes a home pregnancy test, finds out that she's pregnant, and goes to an abortion clinic. Do you think she has that right?"

Lasch hesitated. "Yes."

"Let's take the same girl—except now she's pregnant by her boyfriend. Does she *still* have the right to an abortion?"

At the defense table, Martin Tierney stirred, watching Sarah intently. Swallowing, Lasch murmured, "Yes."

Sarah backed away a little; with this witness—stunted, and confined to a wheelchair—to hover would look like bullying.

"Okay. Take the same basic facts—home pregnancy test, positive result, abortion. Except that the woman's forty, married, the mother of six, and doesn't think her family can support a seventh child. Is *she* morally entitled to abort the fetus?"

Lasch's eyes glinted. "It appears you've read my work, Ms. Dash. If so, you'll know that I've written that abortion to preserve a struggling family is not per se immoral."

"So, again, your answer is yes? On economic grounds?"

Curtly, Lasch nodded. "It is."

"Then—unlike Professor Tierney—you're not morally opposed to all abortion."

Lasch twisted in his chair, as though to minimize his discomfort. "To me," he said quietly, "abortion is always unfortunate. But it goes too far to say that it's always immoral."

From the bench, Leary eyed the witness with new perplexity. "In your direct testimony," Sarah said, "you gave us the example of Martha's Vineyard in the nineteenth century, where deafness was common. Are you aware that the principal cause was incest?"

Lasch blinked. "*One* of the causes," he amended.

Sarah kept her tone quiet, dispassionate. "And you believe that the victim of incest has the right to an abortion."

Lasch pulled himself straighter, staring into Sarah's eyes. More sharply, he answered, "What I said, Ms. Dash, was under most circumstances."

"So tell me when she doesn't."

Lasch swallowed. In a thin voice, he answered, "I can't give you a litany of examples, Ms. Dash. But motivation is important."

Watching, Martin Tierney was taut now. "Then let's go back," she told Lasch, "to the teenage girl raped by her own father. Same home pregnancy test, same positive result. Except this time—just to make sure—she goes to a doctor to confirm she's pregnant. *That* doesn't affect her moral right to an abortion, does it?"

Lasch grimaced. "No."

"Okay. Now let's toss in one more fact." Pausing, Sarah spoke more softly yet. "Through a breakthrough in testing, the doctor predicts that the fetus—the product of rape and incest—is hydrocephalic. Can she abort the child *then*, Dr. Lasch?"

Sarah saw Martin Tierney rise to object, then realize how pointless this would be. Swallowing, Lasch choked, gazing up at Sarah with a look of trapped resentment. His voice faltered. "As I said . . . motivation is important."

"Suppose the testing came out 'normal.' In your moral universe, is a victim of rape and incest entitled to abort a fetus with *no* disabilities whatsoever?"

Pride seemed to stiffen Lasch's body and brighten his eyes. "Yes," he said harshly. "I've told you that."

"So she can abort a fetus on account of incest?"

"Yes."

"Or economic hardship?"

"Yes."

"Or because she's a teenager and single?"

"Yes."

"Or just because she's pregnant, and doesn't want to be?"

Lasch twisted his head, jaw tightening. "Yes."

"For *all* those reasons," Sarah said in a soft, remorseless voice, "or no reason at all. But only as long as she believes the fetus is normal."

The resentment in Lasch's eyes, Sarah supposed, reflected a lifetime of pain, of struggle, of believing—often with justice—that the world of the "normal" looked on him with scorn. "What I believe," he said with palpable anger, "is that abortion should not be used to murder the disabled . . ."

"In other words, the only unwanted children women should be compelled to have are those with disabilities?"

"No," Lasch snapped. "They shouldn't use abortion to weed them out."

"So a woman can have any abortion for *no* reason, but not the *wrong* reason."

"You're twisting my words, Ms. Dash. But, in essence—yes."

"Isn't the only way to ensure that, Dr. Lasch, to outlaw genetic testing? And, for that matter, sonograms?"

"That's not my position . . ."

"But if Mary Ann Tierney never had a sonogram, she wouldn't know she had a hydrocephalic fetus—true? She'd just have the child, and maybe never have another."

Wincing, Lasch crossed his stunted arms. "Genetic testing," he answered, "has humane uses. For example, it can help a mother face the fact of a disabled child."

"The *inevitable* fact, in your universe. Because once she *knows,* she's not allowed to abort the child, correct?"

Lasch's eyelids twitched; once more, he looked painfully weary. "What I believe," he said in a parched voice, "is that selective abortions of the disabled are morally wrong, and socially dangerous."

"And, therefore, that they should be illegal?"

"Yes. Unless the life of the mother is actually at risk."

"So you don't agree with the Protection of Life Act, do you? Because it gives parents the right, on medical grounds, to approve the late-term abortion of a potentially disabled fetus."

"I'm concerned about that aspect, yes."

"In fact, you believe that no parent should have the authority to consent to an abortion because of fetal anomalies?"

"Not if that's the reason."

"And you also don't distinguish between the moral wrong of aborting a fetus with blue eyes, and aborting one with multiple, painful, and hopeless disabilities."

"What I said . . ." Lasch coughed, head lolling helplessly. "What I said," he persisted, "is that one may lead to the other. And that both are morally wrong."

"And yet you believe that abortion for economic reasons might be justified."

"In some cases, yes."

"But not where the economic reasons are the staggering expense to a family—with all the strains on marriage and child-raising—of dealing with a severely disabled child?"

The witness hesitated, wincing at a tremor which caused his body to shudder. Seeing this, Sarah allowed herself a moment of compassion: like anyone, Lasch's beliefs were shaped by his emotions, and thus were flawed by them. But his emotions were bone deep, and to be confronted so publicly could only increase his physical and moral anguish. "I'm not saying they're never justified," he said at last. "Our country, including the pro-life movement, has failed to help families support and nurture the disabled—or to provide a caring surrogate if all else fails. For a specific family the financial burden may be overwhelming."

"And who's the judge of that, Dr. Lasch? The mother—or you?"

"Your Honor," Martin Tierney interjected. "This is the harassment of a witness—who finds the very fact of testimony a challenge to his endurance—by means of hypothetical questions which don't concern our daughter or our grandson. As a tactic, it's deeply unfair to Dr. Lasch . . ."

"And deeply embarrassing to you," Sarah retorted, turning to Leary. "Mr. Tierney hoped to enlist the disabled, and their genuine moral concerns, to help him compel Mary Ann to carry this fetus to term. But he overlooked problems with enforcing those concerns, as well as the latent inconsistencies in Dr. Lasch's worldview. And now he doesn't want them exposed."

Leary nodded. "You may respond, Dr. Lasch."

Lasch faced Sarah again. "No, Ms. Dash, I'm not the sole arbiter here. It's up to society to frame the standards."

"But you can't tell me what those standards are. Or who within this society should frame them."

Lasch stared at her. "That's up to the legislature. With appropriate guidance."

From whom? Sarah wanted to ask. But it was better to move on. "In the absence of 'guidance,' Dr. Lasch, isn't the only way for a woman to escape your moral—and possibly legal—judgment to avoid sonograms and genetic testing like the plague? Because if she knows her fetus is disabled, her motives for an abortion are suspect, regardless of what other reasons she may have."

"I don't think that's a fair interpretation of my position."

"Isn't it?" Walking back to the table, Sarah gazed down at her notes. "Yet you commenced your direct testimony by saying that, quote, *'It seems clear that the principal basis for your daughter's lawsuit is not the extremely marginal threat to her reproductive capacity, but the "unacceptable nature" of her child.'* Clear to *whom,* Dr. Lasch?"

Again, Lasch licked his lips. "Clear," he parried, "from the circumstances—"

"To *whom,*" Sarah snapped.

Lasch hesitated. "To me."

Sarah glanced down at Mary Ann, and was touched by the gratitude she saw. Placing a hand on the girl's shoulder, Sarah faced Lasch again. "Clear to you," she repeated. "But you've never even met Mary Ann Tierney, have you?"

"No."

"So you've never asked her what her motives are."

"No."

"But what you *do* know is that her fetus is hydrocephalic."

"Yes. And that its threat to reproduction is, as I stated, 'marginal.'"

"Marginal to whom?" Sarah asked with quiet anger. "You, again?"

"No. To her doctor."

"All right, Dr. Lasch. I won't bother asking you to wonder whether the risk of hysterectomy or secondary infertility would seem quite so marginal if you were Mary Ann. But we're not talking about a baby with blue eyes, are we?"

"Of course not."

"Or a Down's syndrome child."

"No."

"Or even a child with Fraser's syndrome, like 'Miracle Kid.'"

"No."

"We're talking about Mary Ann Tierney's prospective child—who, according to her doctor, will almost certainly never have a brain. And who, as you yourself assert, will quite likely die at birth."

A flush stained Lasch's hollow cheeks. "Yes," he answered grudgingly.

Sarah remained where she was, beside Mary Ann. "And yet you assert that Mary Ann has no moral right to weigh that child's chance of living against her hope of bearing future children."

Lasch's jaw tightened. "Where her life is not at risk? No, she doesn't."

"But not—in your view—because the baby might be 'normal'?"

"No."

"No," Sarah repeated. "You believe she has no moral right *because* her fetus likely has no brain. That's not the choice your parents faced, is it?"

Lasch grimaced, looking down. His answer, "No," was barely audible.

"Nor were you a threat to your mother's fertility—correct?"

"Correct."

"And when you were born, she was thirty-eight years old."

For a moment, Lasch was silent; Sarah watched him process the fact that she had researched not just his writings, but his life. In the same near-whisper, he answered, "Yes."

"Before that, your parents were childless."

Plainly surprised, Lasch hesitated. "That's true."

"Though they had tried for years to have children."

At the defense table, Martin Tierney gazed at the floor. Lasch's chin rested on his chest. "Yes."

"So just as your circumstances were different from those of this fetus, your *parents'* were far different from Mary Ann's."

Struggling, Lasch raised his head. "Personally," he answered in a clear voice. "Not morally. That may sound harsh to you. But there's a price we pay for a more compassionate society, and someone has to pay it—either the mother, or the child."

Sarah looked at him in surprise; somehow, out of passion and pride, he had found a reserve of strength. "But can't you acknowledge," she asked, "that a more compassionate society can place a value on all life, yet recognize that the absence of a cerebral cortex is ruinous to the *quality* of a life? And that the resulting value of *that* life—to others and to itself—is far different than the value of *your* life?"

Silent, Lasch stared at her. As the quiet stretched, Tierney and Saunders formed a watchful frieze. In a trembling voice, Lasch said, "That's not for us to judge."

It was time to end this. "Then don't judge Mary Ann," Sarah told him, and sat down.

Twenty-two

"I've had some disturbing news," Macdonald Gage announced, "about the Masters nomination."

Chad Palmer sat among his party colleagues in the ornate caucus room of the Russell Building, sipping the strong, black coffee that he favored in early mornings. It was eight o'clock and many of the fifty-four senators looked sleepy and quiescent. Leaning closer, his friend Kate Jarman of Vermont murmured in Chad's ear, "Mac's just found out she thinks we're descended from apes. That'll wake them up."

Chad smiled at this; with her pixie looks and irreverent tongue, Kate—like the other independent souls who gravitated to Chad—shared his jaundiced views of Gage. But Kate knew, as did Chad, that the caucus Gage had called was aimed as much at Chad as Caroline Masters. Standing amidst the others, Gage shot Chad and Kate an admonitory glance.

"Yesterday," he continued, "her court issued an opinion, *Snipes v. Garrett,* which guts last year's Criminal Justice Act, and allows these endless lawsuits by career criminals who claim to be 'mistreated.'

"Not only did Masters vote with the majority but, my sources tell me, she was instrumental in seeking to overturn a prior ruling by a strict constructionist judge." Once again, he looked at Chad. "Bottom line, she looks pro-criminal."

Chad summoned an expression of mild interest. But he felt himself tense; Gage had decided to escalate their war of nerves over Caroline Masters, and was using their colleagues to do it. "That's one troubling aspect," Gage went on, "of an emerging picture. We're all getting bombarded with letters, faxes, and e-mails on this Mary Ann Tierney case—Lord knows I am. The Protection of Life Act is where we've drawn the line with the pro-abortion movement: if we can't protect minors, or ban this kind of butchery, we all should just go home.

"Now Masters says she can't talk about that, and our friends in the White House say she's clean on abortion. Maybe so, but there's a pretty telling clue." Hitching up his pants, Gage adopted the posture of a man with his feet, and his principles, firmly planted. "Mary Ann Tierney's lawyer—a radical feminist named Sarah Dash—clerked for Caroline Masters."

"Oops," Kate Jarman whispered. But her eyes were wary; pro-choice on most issues, Kate had cast her vote for the Protection of Life Act as a political balm, hoping to heal her strained relations with the party's right wing. Quickly, she asked Gage, "Is there anything more than that Judge Masters employed her?"

"I've made some independent inquiries. Seems like Masters and Sarah Dash still see each other." Gage looked from senator to senator, as though gauging their reactions, then back at Kate again. "Maybe you'd give this woman a job, Kate, not knowing. But would you want her over for dinner? Let alone a week before Miss Dash files this grotesque lawsuit? Kind of makes you wonder what they talk about."

This information came from Mace Taylor, Chad thought at once; Taylor had put up the money, and set detectives loose on Masters. His apprehension grew—if they knew who Caroline Masters had dinner with, they could surely find out about her daughter. Though not privy to his secret, Kate Jarman seemed more sober, as if she, like Chad, envisioned blood in the water.

"We should check out their relationship," Gage concluded. "Before we make this woman Chief Justice, we need to know a whole lot more about who she really is."

As always, Chad thought, Macdonald Gage was artful. Gage had not mentioned the confirmation hearings: in the guise of a leader dispensing information, he was hoping to build pressure on Chad from the other senators. Now Paul Harshman from Idaho, Chad's chief antagonist on the committee, asked rhetorically, "What about the hearing, Mac? Seems like that's the key to everything."

"Oh, I'll leave that up to Chad." Amiably, Gage turned to him. "What's the timetable, Mr. Chairman?"

It was all neatly choreographed—this meeting; Gage's concerns about Caroline; his implicit hint of things to come; Harshman's intervention. Casually, Chad replied, "The hearing's two to three weeks off, Mac. The staff has a lot of preparation to do."

"Two to three *weeks*," Gage echoed with mild incredulity. "Not months? Sounds like Caroline Masters is on the fast track to confirmation."

Reflexively, Chad counted votes on the committee: all eight Democrats were with him and, of the ten Republicans, Paul Harshman had perhaps three allies.

"As of now," Chad responded, "Judge Masters looks qualified. I won't belabor the problems our party has with women. It doesn't do for us to look obstructionist."

"Not obstructionist," Gage demurred. "Responsible. Has your staff explored her personal life at all?"

Does he already know about the daughter? Chad wondered. "We have," he answered with studied calm. "But we're more focused on her judicial record, like this new case you mentioned. This gratuitous vetting of personal lives can boomerang on us all."

"It's hardly gratuitous," Paul Harshman interjected. "Not only does Masters have an ongoing relationship with Sarah Dash, but she's never been married. How do we know she shares our values?"

Beside him, Chad felt Kate Jarman stir. "Neither has Kate," Chad retorted, "and no one doubts *her* values. But if it turns out that Caroline Masters is a member of dykes on bikes, I'll give you a heads-up."

An unamused smile crossed Harshman's bony features; behind wire-rim glasses, his eyes narrowed to slivers. *So typical,* his expression said. "You've been sitting on those FBI files," he prodded. "Anything in *there* we should know?"

It was a pincer movement, Chad thought—if Caroline Masters had personal problems, Gage and Harshman were telling him, it was Chad's job to expose them. "There's nothing in the files," Chad said flatly.

This was the literal truth; so far, the FBI had not uncovered the facts of Brett Allen's birth. But Chad felt it lurk beneath the discussion—a ticking bomb which, Chad hoped, he alone could hear. "No one's meaning to be critical," Gage assured him. "But you're not a lawyer, Chad, and this is your first hearing as chairman. The nomination of a new Chief Justice is a lot to cut your teeth on, and we want to give you all the support we can."

This tone of kindly condescension, with its reminder of the stakes involved, would not be lost on anyone. Around them, Chad felt their fellow senators—with curiosity and a calculation of their own self-interests—watching two men who badly wanted to be President. Smiling, Chad answered, "I think I can get by, Mac. I think I can get *all* of us by, and without throwing away the next election."

The pointed response induced a deeper silence; Chad had taken the subject of their conflicting ambitions, their competing claims to electability, and dragged it into the room. "There are rumors out there," Paul Harshman said sharply. "Some believe Masters is sleeping with Kilcannon. There are stories he played around on his ex-wife, you know."

Sure, Chad thought, *just like there are rumors about you and* both *of your ex-*

wives. "So what should I check out first?" he inquired pleasantly. "Your idea that Masters is gay, or the pernicious rumor that she's straight?"

Harshman's face went rigid with dislike. It was another small marker, Chad supposed, in Harshman's increasing resolve to deny Chad the party's nomination by any means at hand. "Maybe in San Francisco," Harshman retorted, "no one cares. But you're getting a little too casual, Senator."

"And politics," Chad rejoined, "is getting a little too rancid. If we're not careful, the voters will start gagging, and then spit us all out."

"Now wait a minute." Gage held up a hand, speaking in a tone of reason. "Paul's concerned that we all avoid a serious mistake. Under the circumstances, I don't think it's too much to kick these hearings back a bit." He summoned a joshing tone. "You won't find Joe McCarthy in *this* crowd, Chad. And you don't want folks like Paul thinking you like Kerry Kilcannon more than him."

So there it was, Chad thought—an implicit accusation of disloyalty, which Chad could refute by postponing the hearings on Caroline Masters. But, for Chad, this marked the point where Gage's imagination failed him: long ago, Chad Palmer had faced far worse.

Until Beirut, it sometimes seemed to Chad that the world had been created just for him.

He had been born outside Cleveland, the oldest of six children in a family of little means. But Chad never felt disadvantaged: gifted with an agile mind, blond good looks, and the sinewy frame of an athlete, Chad became a leader. From elementary school, there had always been someone—a teacher, minister, or coach—to help him to the next rung. By the time he reached his junior year, and conceived the ambition to fly, the local congressman was happy to press for Chad's admission to the Air Force Academy.

His parents had not wanted him to go; they lacked experience with the military, and had visions of the Ivy League. But though Chad's first year was harsh, his pride and resilience helped him survive months of sleeplessness and hazing, and his ambition made him want to. At graduation, Chad was the sixth in his class. But, for Chad, that was merely a warm-up to the first time he broke the sound barrier.

This was not long in coming. Cocky and competitive, blessed with reflexes and hand-eye coordination that even his instructors found astonishing, Chad shot through flight school at the top. Swiftly, he progressed from F-4 fighters to the new F-15, careening through Okinawa, Thailand, much liquor, and the many women who always came so easily, too engrossed in living every moment to value Allie as he might have. His deepest regret was that he had missed out on Vietnam.

In fact, he concluded, his life was a series of near misses with adventure. After a tour in fighter-weapons school, where he mastered a top-secret laser-guided bomb-delivery system—nicknamed "Paved Spike"—Captain Chad Palmer had been sent to Iran. The Shah wanted his air force trained to repel the Russians in Afghanistan; the Shah's real problem, it turned out, was closer to home. Chad was on leave when the Ayatollah Khomeini drove the Shah into exile. The reports which followed suggested that some of Chad's colleagues in the Iranian air force had been tortured for information, then killed.

Which was why Chad Palmer found himself in a smoky bar in Beirut, city of a hundred factions and a thousand temptations, moodily drinking to their memory. His luck had held, he supposed—the Russians, Afghans, and Iranians would want badly to know about Paved Spike, and they would not have treated him with kindness. Quite systematically, he set out to get drunk.

Five scotches seemed to do the job. Chad sat watching the bartender, an amiable Maronite Christian with a crucifix around his neck, chat up a melange of customers—a slim Frenchwoman, businessmen of various nationalities, a couple of Marines. Some other night he would have let the Frenchwoman find him, but tonight he didn't give a damn. He kept thinking about his closest Iranian pilot friend, Bahman, and wondering if he was dead.

As Chad drank, a collage of images engulfed him: the sinuous twisting smoke from a cigarette, the bartender's gleaming cross, the dark-eyed Frenchwoman's sidelong glances. Though they looked nothing alike, her slender body, somehow voluptuous despite her narrow hips, reminded him of Allie's. Except, Chad remembered, that Allie was eight months pregnant.

He had not seen her for the last four of them. In three weeks, Chad was due home; at first dimly, then with increasing vividness, Chad imagined holding a newborn son.

Abruptly, he stood. It must be morning in the States; he would go back to his hotel, shake off his thoughts of death, and call her. He barely noticed the bartender picking up a telephone.

Outside, the air was hot and dense, smelling of exhaust fumes and lamb shish kebab from a restaurant with its doors and windows open. He was more drunk than he had realized, Chad thought. After a few steps he paused to remember the direction of his hotel.

Suddenly, three men emerged from a nearby alley; before he could react, they wrenched him into its shadows. Arms pinned behind him, Chad was fighting to keep his balance when something cracked him over the head.

Then there were only impressions—the foul garlic breath of an assailant, a shooting pain in his shoulder as they threw him into a van. A second sharp blow filled his skull with pain and the darkness with red stars. As the three men bound his arms, Chad realized that he must have been walking in the right direction, and that the bartender must have called them. After the third blow he remembered nothing.

Twenty-three

Chad awoke in darkness, nauseated, remembering only scraps of what seemed an endless journey—drugged and beaten, he recalled being thrown in the trunk of a car, hearing terse phrases in Arabic. Now he could see nothing. He did not know where he was, what time of day it was, whether it was dark or light, whether anyone but his nameless captors knew what had become of him. Filled with disbelief, Chad began crawling, one hand held out blindly in front of him. From beneath came the pungent smell of dirt, and then his hand touched stone.

Allie.

Kneeling, Chad tried to concentrate his mind.

He knew nothing about his captors. But in the Middle East hostages were used as pawns, traded for terrorists in prison. If these men wanted information, he knew only one thing of any use. Paved Spike.

Standing, Chad struck his head against cement.

He fell to his knees, stunned. The cell was designed to limit movement. The only exercise for his legs would be from squatting.

For endless time—there was no way to measure it—Chad squatted or crawled or tried to sleep, or drained his wastes in a corner of the cell.

Finally, a light awakened him.

Startled, he struggled to his knees. It was a flashlight, blinding after the long time in darkness.

"Who are you?" he asked.

"Paved Spike."

The voice was soft, English accented by Arabic or perhaps Farsi. The two words, though dreaded, told Chad what he wished to know.

"'Paved Spike'?" he repeated in a tone of bewilderment. "'Paved Spike'?"

The flashlight drew back, then struck him across the mouth. Stunned, Chad fell sideways, tasting blood, feeling fragments of tooth on his tongue.

"Paved Spike," the voice repeated. "Tell us how it works."

Chad closed his eyes. The Code of Honor was ingrained in him, the duty to give them nothing of value. A second thought swiftly followed: once he told them what he knew, his usefulness might end. And, with that, his life. He lay exposed in the light like a trapped animal.

The door closed, and it was dark again.

To gather strength, Chad tried to sleep. His uniform was so soiled by dirt and sweat and urine that he began to itch.

Sometime later, the door opened again.

In the circle of light, a brown hand held out a metal bowl half-filled with what looked like gruel.

Chad restrained himself from eating until the light went out and he heard the door shut. Then he pawed the lukewarm stuff into his mouth by hand.

He had barely finished when the door opened again.

Now there were two of them, he deduced from their footsteps. With brutal efficiency, they bound his arms behind his back, then jerked his legs backward and bound his feet to his arms. Clamping his jaw, Chad fought to keep silent.

Slowly they began twisting the rope between Chad's wrists with a stick they used as a lever. Chad's arms strained to leave their sockets until, helpless, he cried out.

"Paved Spike," the same voice intoned, and then the cell went dark and silent.

The agony was so severe that Chad was on the brink of passing out. Instead, by degrees, he began to lose feeling in his feet and arms. He wondered what it would be like to lose their use.

They had learned this technique from the Vietcong; a teacher at the academy had described it. Chad prayed these men would go no further. The door opened. Kneeling, the two men hung Chad from a hook in the ceiling by the ropes which bound his hands.

When his arms wrenched from his sockets, Chad lost consciousness.

He awakened to searing pain which made him sob and the same insinuating voice.

"Paved Spike."

Eyes shut tight, Chad tried to remove himself to another place. He focused on Allie, the son he imagined. They were what he had to live for.

"We know you were with the Shah. We know you were trained on Paved Spike."

Islamic terrorists, Chad guessed. They needed to understand our weapons systems—perhaps for Iran, Libya, or the Russians, perhaps to learn what the Israelis already knew. "What's Paved Spike?" Chad managed.

They hung him up again.

After a time, his hands and feet swelled up. Chad tried returning to Allie, imagining her body melding with his. They were making love when Chad blacked out again.

The faceless men continued the slow, relentless breakdown of his body and spirit.

Sometimes they hung him up. Sometimes they beat him with rubber straps which smelled like they'd been stripped from tires. Sometimes they made him sit on a sharply pointed stool with his hands tied behind him, straining his haunches. Always, when he fell off, they would beat him. He was never alone; never did they allow him to sleep.

His mind stopped reasoning. It was hard to know what was worse—the sleeplessness which exploded into hallucination and madness, or the excruciating pain of hanging from the ceiling while curled in a ball, feeling and smelling his own wastes. Though the rubber strap had broken his nose and many of his teeth, Chad preferred it—at least the pain was finite, and he could pass out lying down.

Awakening, shattered and disoriented, Chad felt moist lips against his ear.

"Tell us about Paved Spike," his tormentor whispered, "and we will tell your wife you are alive. Otherwise you will remain for her and your government as you are now—dead."

"Please," Chad implored him. "Let me sleep. I can't tell you anything like this."

They left just before Chad passed out again. With his last scrap of sanity, he allowed his mind to leave his body.

It was a mercy. Waking, he fixed on the Code of Honor. They would find him if he somehow remained alive. They would keep faith with him, if he kept faith with them. What he needed was a story.

The flashlight wounded his eyes like an explosion. "Now you will tell us," the voice said.

His captor started his questioning slowly, faceless behind the flashlight. The questions went on for what seemed like days, punctuated by torture, until at last Chad told them his wife's name, his company commander, the training he had received, and all the places he had served. Everything but what he knew they wanted.

Silence fell. The voice spoke in Arabic, and another pair of hands brought a flat stool for Chad to sit on.

"Paved Spike," the voice said.

When Chad shook his head, they hung him up again.

Time passed. "Enough?" the voice whispered.

"Yes," Chad murmured. "Yes."

They took him down. "Paved Spike," the voice repeated.

Haltingly, Chad commenced his half-formed story, straining to find scraps of information which were true but harmless, others which were plausible but false. What he knew about Paved Spike, he told them, was fragmentary or anecdotal—he had not been fully trained. He said this looking straight into the face of a man he could not see.

The second man rebound his hands and feet and placed a noose around his neck.

Chad felt him looping it through the ceiling hook. Slowly, the rope strained his neck, lifting him toward the ceiling. Eyes shut, Chad tried to recall a passage from First Corinthians: *"There hath no temptation taken you but such as is common to man; but God is faithful, who will not suffer you to be tempted above that ye are able; but will with the temptation also make a way to escape, that ye may be able to bear it."*

Death was his escape. Just before the last air left his lungs, Chad choked out, "There's nothing else."

They dropped him to the floor.

Beating after beating, torment after torment, Chad clung to his story, waiting the release of death.

Death did not come.

The torture went on. In the dark expanses between, Chad created his own world, an alternative to suffering.

He reconstructed books, or movies, or lines of poetry. He relived his life in minute detail. Exhausting that, he conjured imagined futures—first in the air force, then as a farmer, a professional football player, a singer, and a politician. His first campaign for President was so successful that he sailed around the world in celebration.

Topless, Allie dived into the blue Pacific waters from the bow of their sleek sailboat, waving at him to follow. The small boy who watched was as blond and tan as the boy Chad had been at summer's end.

When the door scraped open, the horror of reality banishing his dream, Chad steeled himself to survive.

Time after time, torment on torment, Chad repeated his story like a catechism.

Time vanished.

Now, on occasion, Chad was allowed to wash himself. He tried to exercise. He could not do push-ups; his arms barely seemed a part of him. But he would manage sit-ups or, stooped, walk in circles until his back ached.

Please, he begged of Allie, *I love you. Please love me when I return. Please,* he implored his country, *find me. Please,* he prayed to God, *don't let them learn the truth.*

As months passed—surely, Chad thought, it must at least be months—his body wasted, his limbs atrophied, and his once careless faith in God became deep, profound, mysterious. God would bring him back to Allie. An image appeared to him, bright and concrete as a diamond amidst the blindness of his cell: Allie holding their son.

When he returned to them, Chad wondered, would his eyes still see?

But his captivity was endless. The only landmarks were a tasteless meal, a change of clothes, a carafe of water in which to bathe, the removal of the fetid bucket which held his wastes, a beating—more perfunctory now, meant to remind him of his powerlessness. He had no fellow prisoners; he never saw his captors' faces.

Live, he willed himself. *Live, and you can love her as you never have. Live for her, and for your son.*

But Allie's face grew distant. Inexorably, Chad lapsed into despair.

To pass the time, and to mark it, he began to count the number of times his cell door opened and closed.

Chad counted three hundred and twelve.

Hands reached out for him, gently lifting him up. In unaccented English, a man said, "Let's get you out of here, Captain."

The next few moments were fragmented. The man dragged Chad from the cell into a tunnel where, strangely, he could stand, the effort straining the muscles of his back. Barely able to walk, Chad let the man prod him up wooden stairs which led to a trapdoor, a shed, then into a piercing light.

He stood on a parched earth baked by the sun, so blinding that Chad cried out. He knelt to the ground, shielding his eyes, and stared into the face of a dead Arab with a bullet through his eye.

His gaze sweeping the ground, Chad saw two more bodies.

"They took their time telling us where you were."

Chad looked up then. The man was American—alert and hard-eyed, with short black hair. "Where are we?" Chad asked.

"Afghanistan."

"How long have I been here?"

Surveying the wreckage of Chad Palmer, the man's eyes softened. "Two years," he answered.

"Do I have a son?"

"A daughter. Her name is Kyle."

She was almost two.

Looking at Macdonald Gage, it was Kyle that Chad thought of now.

For Chad, to speak of the value of life was not a political tactic, or a religious inheritance, but something far deeper and more personal. And never more than when that life was defenseless.

As for himself, there was little Chad worried about besides his family, his sense of honor, his need to make his own life mean something. Material things barely interested him; a beautiful day, which others might take for granted, reminded him that each moment of life was precious, tomorrow promised to no one. His resolve was to be informed, but not defined, by his suffering, and to live in the future rather than the past.

Others saw him as a hero. Chad saw himself as a careless drunk who never should have been captured and, having been, had cost his family dearly. But, having been, he had done all he could. That knowledge left him with a measure of peace which few others would ever know.

He did not like to discuss these things and, except with Allie, rarely did. Once Macdonald Gage—out of puzzlement, and also to disarm a rival—had said to Chad, "I never could have done that."

Chad gazed at him, his blue eyes distant. "Maybe you could," he answered. "And maybe you couldn't. But don't bother wasting your time on it. Because you'll never know."

Now, facing Gage in the caucus room, he felt Kate Jarman watching them.

Once more, Chad worried about what Gage might know, and not just about Caroline Masters. But he also felt, in spite of this, a degree of fatalism and, for Gage, a contempt he could not banish.

"So," Gage said heartily, "can we count on you here, Chad?"

"To be fair? Always. But kicking back the Masters hearings is not a good idea."

Gage's eyes went cold. "According to whom?"

"Me," Chad responded. "As chairman of the committee."

Twenty-four

"My opinion," Dr. David Gersten said solemnly, "is that parental consent laws can prevent serious emotional damage. And never more so, Professor Tierney, than in the case of Mary Ann."

Listening, Sarah felt depressed. She had survived Bruno Lasch only to crash over the lunch hour, the victim of an adrenaline surge which, once spent, left her flat and unfocused. And Gersten's first few minutes of testimony suggested that he would be effective: a psychologist who had studied the response of adolescent girls to abortion, Gersten was neither affiliated with any pro-life groups nor morally opposed to abortion. And, unlike Lasch, he *had* met Mary Ann Tierney—for five hours of interviews, by order of the court.

Martin Tierney seemed buoyed by Gersten's presence; his voice was firm, his posture straight. "Could you explain the basis for your opinion, Dr. Gersten?"

"Sure," Gersten answered crisply. "I'll start with you, Professor. We've spent several hours together. You and your wife are mature adults in your midforties, with well-developed moral views and the wealth of perspective and experience which can only be acquired—regrettably—by growing older." He smiled briefly, patting his ample stomach. "It's one of the compensations of middle age, which punishes us in so many other ways."

At once, Gersten's face grew serious again. "Fifteen-year-olds," he continued, "lack practical experience, and the wisdom it brings. That's why the suicide rates for teenage girls are so abysmally high. Every new experience is a matter of first impression—often they don't know how to handle it, and give way to despair. Or they make a decision, unable to fully gauge its practical and moral consequences, and can't live with the results." Now Gersten frowned; round and bearded, with appealing liquid eyes, his mobile face humanized his testimony. "That adolescents kill themselves—where adults don't—shows how dangerous it is for parents to abdicate their responsibilities."

From the front row, Margaret Tierney glanced hopefully at Mary Ann; it was sad, Sarah reflected, that these caring people hoped that a stranger could explain them. "How do you relate that," Tierney asked, "to Mary Ann's desire to abort her child?"

Gersten folded his hands. "The decision facing Mary Ann is complex, medically and morally.

"Medically, there are some weighty considerations to balance. Although it seems that Mary Ann has reacted more drastically to one aspect—the risks of a classical cesarean section, including infertility—than she might as an adult."

Sharply, Sarah looked up from her legal pad; Gersten's air of certainty had begun to strike her as insensitive. "Morally," he continued, "an abortion is far different from a tonsillectomy—for which, ironically, she *would* need your consent by law. Mary Ann herself knows the moral difference."

Gersten glanced at Mary Ann with seeming concern. "The decision to abort, once carried out, is irretrievable. I worry about terrible guilt and severe depression."

Shoulders slumped, Mary Ann stared at the table; Sarah, tired as she was, was the only one, at least within the courtroom, who could speak for this girl. It was time to buck up.

"Is your concern for Mary Ann," Tierney was asking, "supported by your experience with adolescent girls?"

Gersten nodded. "Two things emerge.

"First, that the ability to make moral decisions—and to appreciate their consequences—does not develop fully until age eighteen or older.

"Second, that excluding parents undermines that relationship and, as a result, retards the growth of personal competence which parental involvement brings. Which, in turn, can damage the capacity to form healthy relationships of *any* kind."

Frowning, Sarah scribbled her first note: "opinions too sweeping," followed by "incest—the game the whole family can play." As if anticipating her, Tierney asked, "Have you assessed the effect on *Mary Ann* of failing to involve us?"

"I have. But let's also consider the consequences of conforming to your wishes.

"Her child's disabilities—if they exist—mean that the practical consequences of having him will be quite short-lived. On the other hand, should

Mary Ann be blessed with a normal child, as enlightened grandparents you'll help them both in every way you can. In either case, your love for Mary Ann—as well as her love for you—will help the process of healing."

Sarah was far from certain; listening, Mary Ann frowned in resentment. But Gersten went smoothly on. "On the other hand, her act of defiance could create a breach which, in her immaturity, she may find difficult to close.

"And yet—and this is crucial—the nature of *this* abortion means that she will need you all the more. According to one study, over half the women receiving late-term abortions report severe emotional trauma. That's particularly true when the aborted chid was, at least initially, a *wanted* child."

Tierney hesitated, as though weighing his next question. With obvious reluctance, he asked Gersten, "How did your interviews with Mary Ann affect your views?"

"It confirmed them." Gersten gave Mary Ann a small, embarrassed smile. "I liked her a lot—she's very bright, and shows promise of developing into a fine adult. But she's not one now." Facing Tierney, he continued in a firmer voice. "What Mary Ann is *now*, Professor, is stubborn, sometimes immature, and not fully able to consider the consequences of her actions. Such as that unprotected sex can lead to pregnancy."

This condescending answer, Sarah saw, made Mary Ann redden. "At fifteen," Gersten went on, "girls are trying to differentiate themselves. They seek autonomy by defying their parents and—quite often—casting them as the enemy. Unfortunately, Mary Ann's defiance involves something far more serious than curfews: sex, and the prospect of this abortion."

Tierney continued to look chary, as though sensing that each question placed more distance between himself and his daughter. "What role," Tierney inquired, "do you believe Sarah Dash plays in our daughter's defiance?"

Putting down her pen, Sarah stared at Tierney in surprise. "Ms. Dash," Gersten answered, "is indispensable."

At this, Sarah started to object. The hearing had leapt all boundaries—it had become personal, too slanted, and potentially too ugly. But these same reasons stopped her: as the subject, Sarah could not complain without seeming whiny and defensive.

"In my opinion," Gersten went on, "there's no way that Mary Ann would be here without the encouragement of Sarah Dash. It's like a crush.

"Ms. Dash is a twenty-nine-year-old woman who's obviously gifted and, one might say, ruthlessly determined. And of particular appeal to Mary Ann, Sarah Dash—at least by outward appearance—seems utterly indifferent to the dislike or disapproval of those who disagree with her."

Retrieving her pen, Sarah felt her fist close around it; the characteristics Gersten described, those of a trial lawyer, applied equally to Martin Tierney. But Tierney was using Gersten to suggest that Sarah had hijacked Mary Ann, ideologically *and* emotionally, and the impact could be devastating. From the bench, Leary gazed at the witness with keen interest.

"But Mary Ann," Gersten was saying, "is *not* Sarah Dash. The same things that make Ms. Dash such an attractive surrogate in Mary Ann's war with *you* make imitating her not only foolish, but dangerous.

"*And* hopeless. When this case is over, Mary Ann will be who she was before—a young girl who believes that a fetus is a life. Taking that life could damage her immensely."

Furiously, Sarah began scribbling notes. "The Protection of Life Act," Gersten told Martin Tierney, "gives you the chance to stop this. I commend your courage in trying."

"Not a good afternoon," Kerry Kilcannon remarked to Clayton and Lara, "for Judge Caroline Masters's ex–law clerk."

Clayton was there to brief him on the Masters nomination; Lara for cocktails and dinner. Now that both had entered his study, Kerry clicked off the television.

"Or for us," Clayton rejoined. "If this case goes all the way, Caroline's the swing vote, and everybody knows it."

In Kerry's mind, Lara's glance of amusement at Clayton held an edge his Chief of Staff must surely feel. Less pragmatic, Lara was also far more pro-choice; Clayton, though he wished them happiness, was adjusting to a woman whose closeness to Kerry not even he could match. "Where's Caroline now?" Kerry asked.

"Back in San Francisco, being a working judge." Clayton glanced at Lara, careful to include her. "By all accounts, her grand tour of the Senate went as well as possible. But Gage is clearly lying in the weeds."

Nodding, Kerry finished his thought. "Because unless Chad pushes this through committee, the Tierney case may get to Caroline's court before *she* gets *here*."

Clayton sipped his scotch. "Not much worry there," he answered. "Any appeal goes to a motions panel run by a clone of Roger Bannon. And even if he assigns it out, and against all odds gets Caroline on the panel, she's got a good excuse for recusing herself—that Dash used to be her law clerk."

With this, Kerry sat down on the couch; Lara sat next to him, Clayton in the chair across. "Speaking of 'lying in the weeds,'" Lara observed, "your Justice Department lawyer at the Tierney trial isn't saying a word. Is he catatonic?"

"It's the drugs," Kerry answered with a smile. "Each morning, our emissary from the CIA slips quaaludes into his coffee—"

"The last thing a new administration needs," Clayton interjected for Lara's benefit, "is a fight over the Protection of Life Act. It would give Gage ammunition to take us down, and put our entire legislative program at risk."

"I'm dimly aware of that," Lara answered wryly, "and I don't want Macdonald Gage picking on my sweetheart. I was just curious about how you two moral leaders think this trial *should* come out."

"I was curious, too," Clayton said with equal dryness. "So I asked our pollster to whistle up some numbers. I thought it might be useful in steering Caroline through the process."

This, though a surprise to Kerry, was typical of his cautious friend. "What came back?" he asked. "A landslide?"

"About what you'd expect," Clayton answered with a shrug. "Sixty-one percent for the parents, and thirty-nine for the daughter."

"That's closer than I'd have thought," Lara observed. "Maybe this trial is making people think."

Clayton turned to Kerry, as though gauging his subtle chemistry with Lara. Smiling faintly, Kerry told her, "It's even making *me* think a little. Whenever I can find the time."

Twenty-five

Anger was not an emotion Sarah enjoyed feeling, but it had its uses. Facing Dr. David Gersten, she no longer felt tired.

"Don't worry," she said quietly. "I won't come any closer. I don't want to seem too ruthless."

Gersten summoned a tentative smile, which Sarah did not return. "Or was it 'ruthlessly determined'?" she asked.

His smile vanished. "All I said, Ms. Dash, is that you seemed that way."

Sarah cocked her head. "Have we ever met?"

"No."

"So you don't claim any insights into my dark nights of the soul. Or, for that matter, my upbringing."

Gersten pursed his lips. "I was talking about what you model for Mary Ann Tierney—independence and autonomy."

"Would you agree, Dr. Gersten, that becoming 'independent' and 'autonomous' is a developmental process?"

"Definitely."

"And that this process begins in childhood?"

"Begins? Yes."

"So you're not suggesting that I magically became what I *seem* to you at sixteen, or twenty-two, or last year."

Gersten touched his chin. "No. That involves, as I said, a process."

"And that process includes fifteen-year-old girls, doesn't it? I mean, it doesn't just skip the fifteenth year."

At the defense table, Martin Tierney looked up from his notes. Gersten's smile seemed wan. "Of course not, Ms. Dash. That was never my position."

"But it *is* your position that Mary Ann's pregnancy confirms her immaturity?"

Gersten crossed his legs, seeming to jiggle on the witness stand. Carefully, he said, "It *suggests* that."

"Well it certainly suggests something." Sarah's voice was harsher, implying repressed anger. "Do you believe that the parents of a fifteen-year-old girl should talk to her about sex? Or should that be left to chance?"

At the corner of Sarah's vision, Martin Tierney seemed about to stand. Sitting back, Gersten said, "I think at least some information is appropriate."

"Some? Such as that sex for a teenage girl may actually involve a teenage boy?"

"I don't know what you're driving at."

"You don't think much of the maturity of teenage girls. Would you assert that when it comes to sex, teenage boys are more mature, judicious, and far-sighted?"

Gersten's smile was without humor. "No," he said with elaborate patience. "Their hormonal drives are very strong."

"Really?" Sarah's voice filled with mock incredulity. "Strong enough to cause them to actually *mislead* a teenage girl in order to have sex?"

Gersten braced his shoulders. "Boys go through a process, too, before they become sexually responsible. If ever."

Sarah paused a moment, deliberately gazing at Martin Tierney. "Then shouldn't 'loving' parents with a 'wealth of perspective and experience' discuss that with their fifteen-year-old daughter?"

Gersten, too, glanced at Tierney. Softly, he said, "It would be helpful, yes."

"Or, failing that, at least bring up birth control."

"It depends on the family, Ms. Dash. But it's certainly something a fifteen-year-old can handle."

Martin Tierney bit his lip, pale eyes focused on Sarah. "Then would you also agree," she asked Gersten, "that a parent's failure to discuss sex with their fifteen-year-old might, in your words, 'retard the growth of personal competence which parental involvement brings'?"

Pondering his answer, Gersten pursed his mouth. "Some families," he said, "for reasons moral and religious, prefer to treat all premarital sex as wrong. Which may limit discussion."

"So when should *their* 'parental involvement' kick in? After the girl gets pregnant?"

Gersten offered the same forced smile. "In my view, parental involvement at any stage can be quite beneficial."

"Including forcing a fifteen-year-old to have a child because of sex they never prepared her for?"

Once more, Tierney started to rise. "It would depend," Gersten answered, "on the dynamic within the family."

"Okay. In all your hours with the Tierneys, did you ever ask *them* if they discussed sex with Mary Ann?"

"No," Gersten answered slowly. "I did not."

"Well, it's too late now, isn't it? Especially for her."

"Your Honor," Tierney said in an angry voice. "Ms. Dash is distorting our family—"

"I apologize," Sarah said with sarcasm. "I wouldn't want this to resemble Dr. Gersten's remarks about your daughter. Or, for that matter, me . . ."

"All right," Leary told Sarah. "If you want to make a point, ask a question. And you, Professor Tierney, can sit down."

Turning to Gersten, Sarah said evenly, "You've interviewed both Mary Ann and her parents. Is it your understanding that the Tierneys have ordered Mary Ann to have this child?"

Gersten glanced at Tierney. "They're trying to stop an abortion, if that's what you mean."

"And their objections are religious, aren't they?"

"Yes. And moral."

"That objection has nothing to do, does it, with whether the Tierneys are better qualified than Mary Ann to decide?"

"No. Except, as I said, that the Tierneys' moral beliefs are well considered and well formed."

"Well formed enough, in fact, to order their fifteen-year-old to have a child without a cerebral cortex."

Gersten frowned. "They also believe—quite reasonably—that aborting this child will harm their daughter emotionally."

Sarah looked at him in feigned bemusement. "In your expert opinion, Dr. Gersten, is Mary Ann able to grasp the fact that her fetus will likely lack a brain?"

"Yes."

"About *that,* she understands what her parents understand, right?"

"Yes."

Pausing, Sarah cocked her head. "By the way, have you ever undergone a classical cesarean section? Personally, I mean."

There was a small ripple of laughter from the media. Forced to smile, Gersten answered, "It's an experience I've missed."

"Me too. But do you share my understanding that—however you calculate the odds—a classical C-section can possibly lead to infertility?"

"Yes."

"And is Mary Ann Tierney as capable of grasping that as you or I?"

Gersten nodded. "As I said, she's focused on it."

"So she understands both medical risks—hydrocephalus and infertility—just as well as her parents do?"

"Yes."

Sarah turned, walking back to Mary Ann. "So why can't Mary Ann Tierney decide not to risk a classical cesarean section for a child likely doomed at birth?"

Gersten considered Mary Ann, whose own expression—to Sarah's satisfaction—commingled anger and challenge. "The issue," he said at length, "isn't her medical cognizance. What concerns me is the potentially severe emotional consequences of late-term abortion, in violation of her deep belief that a fetus is a life."

"An *inviolate* life?" Sarah asked. "Under all circumstances? She's never faced these circumstances before, has she?"

"No. But her Catholic faith remains strong."

"Are you seriously telling me, Doctor, that from childhood Mary Ann had the unalterable religious conviction that fifteen-year-old girls should deliver hydrocephalic fetuses by means of a cesarean section—at whatever risk of infertility?"

Gersten shifted in his chair. "We're talking about broad principles, Ms. Dash. Which, in the ethic in which she was raised, apply to this pregnancy."

"Isn't a fifteen-year-old," Sarah pressed, "capable of deciding—as to this difficult situation—that her beliefs differ from her parents'?"

"Intellectually, perhaps. At least in theory. But I still worry about the emotional impact."

"What about the impact of being forced to have this child? Wouldn't *that* be traumatic to Mary Ann, and devastating to the family?"

Pensive, Gersten paused to sip from a glass of water. As he did, Sarah noticed Margaret Tierney, hands clasped in anxiety.

"In the short term," Gersten said, "it's harmful. But I think the Tierneys will be healed by love and shared beliefs."

"Short term? What about the birth of a severely disabled baby, who then dies, leaving Mary Ann infertile for life? Would you say all bets are off?"

Grimacing, Gersten wagged his head from side to side. "Infertile for life?" he repeated. "That would present a much larger problem. *If* that's how things turn out."

"Then let's talk about a more immediate problem." Glancing down at Mary Ann, Sarah finished, "This trial."

"How do you mean?"

"You're a noted expert, Dr. Gersten, with a sensitive grasp of the emotional life of adolescent girls. Wouldn't you say that her parents—by having you portray her as immature, minimally competent, and a virtual pawn of her lawyer—are doing serious damage to their relationship?"

Martin Tierney sat straighter, watching Gersten intently. "This trial," Gersten answered, "was forced on them, as is the need to address the issues you raise . . ."

"Forced on them? The *United States government* was ready to defend this case."

"The United States government," Gersten rejoined, "is not her parents. In my mind, their intervention is an act of courage . . ."

"Answer the question," Sarah snapped. "Is your portrayal of Mary Ann potentially humiliating to her, and toxic to her relationship with her parents?"

Gersten frowned. "Toxic? I don't know if I accept that. Nor do I accept that it's the Tierneys' fault—or mine."

"Oh? Then it must be Mary Ann's. Or—better yet—mine."

Gersten exhaled. "At this juncture, there's no point in assigning fault. This trial will certainly leave scars."

Sarah nodded. "Then let's move on. Are you aware that, in 1989, C. Everett Koop, the Surgeon General of the United States, advised President Reagan that the psychological risks of abortion are virtually nonexistent?"

"I am. But that was *all* abortions . . ."

"And that Koop reported that the prior research on psychological risk—including the study you rely on—was so inept that it could not support either side?"

Gersten folded his arms. "My own experience suggests that late-term abortion is qualitatively different. Especially when it conflicts with the woman's own beliefs."

"Might not that supposed trauma, at least to Mary Ann, be relieved by the hope of preventing infertility?"

Briefly, Gersten examined his fingernails. In grudging tones, he said, "It could. I don't know that it will."

"Wouldn't it *further* minimize any trauma if the Tierneys gave her love and support—even if she chose abortion?"

"Again, it could."

"So your prediction of trauma is a self-fulfilling prophecy, based on the Tierneys' permanent disapproval."

Gersten glanced at Martin Tierney. "It will be hard for them, given their deep beliefs, not to feel wounded . . ."

"What about the wounds they've inflicted on Mary Ann?" Resting her hand on Mary Ann's shoulder, Sarah spoke each word with precision. "In your opinion, do the Tierneys love their daughter enough to forgive her for violating their beliefs?"

Stricken, Martin Tierney turned to Mary Ann. "They love her," Gersten said at last. "Of that I'm sure. But the question of forgiveness is beyond my sphere of competence."

Grim-faced, Mary Ann looked away. "Indeed," Sarah said. "Yet you say the Protection of Life Act serves a salutary purpose. Would that be true if the Tierneys were physically abusive?"

"Perhaps not."

"Or where the father rapes the daughter?"

"No—not then."

"Or if the parents are fundamentalists, and want to punish their daughter for having sex?"

"No."

"Or come from a culture which views a daughter's sexuality with shame?"

Gersten hesitated. "Shared cultures," he said, "often have shared values—"

"Congress," Sarah interjected caustically, "didn't make those fine distinctions, did they?"

"No." Gersten folded his hands. "But in each case you mention, Ms. Dash, the minor child can go to court."

As before, Sarah summoned an artificial expression of surprise. "So a minor too immature to choose abortion has the maturity to select a lawyer and file a lawsuit?"

Gersten started to speak, then stopped himself. Tentative, he said at last, "Mary Ann Tierney did."

"Really?" Smiling faintly, Sarah skipped a beat. "I thought I dragged her here."

Perplexed, Gersten stared at her, unable to find an answer. Glancing at her watch, Sarah told him softly, "Make up your mind, Dr. Gersten. I'll give you all the time you need."

Twenty-six

Waiting in her office for Martin Tierney, Sarah treasured the silence, a few moments respite.

It was past nine o'clock; the corridors were empty, and the lights tracing the span of the Bay Bridge glowed against the inky darkness below. But, in late afternoon, when Sarah had returned, pickets from the Christian Commitment surrounded the building, and a hysterical woman had chained herself to a leg of the reception desk on one of Kenyon & Walker's seven floors. John Nolan had hastily hired security guards for each floor; a few of the older male partners expressed their anger at Sarah by ignoring her.

On her desk were several stacks of letters—some admiring, many not, a few anti-Semitic or overtly threatening—and her voice mail was clogged with interview requests and hate-filled tirades. In a vain but kindly effort to buffer this assault, her secretary had left a favorable clipping from the *New York Times* in which legal experts, evaluating her trial skills, referred to her as a "twenty-nine-year-old legal superstar."

She had become famous without noticing, Sarah supposed, because she had no time to notice. Nor did she have time now. A trial required tunnel vision: introspection was a waste of time at best, perilous at worse. She could not look past tomorrow.

Her telephone rang.

It was the security guard on the first floor. Martin Tierney was in the lobby.

Tierney scanned her office, noting the mail strewn across her desk with a look of bleak acknowledgment. "Have you been inundated, too?" Sarah asked.

"Of course." He sat, his fine scholar's face filled with sorrow. "I contemplate

Patrick Leary, and I wonder whether he has any concept of the cruelty he's per-petrating. Or even the capacity to imagine it."

"Leary," Sarah answered, "can't see past the mirror. But he's got no patent on cruelty."

Tierney's pale blue-gray eyes regarded her. "You want us to rest our case tomorrow."

Sarah did not directly answer. "She's over six months pregnant," she told him. "This afternoon, I called Mark Flom. He's afraid that the stress of a trial may cause Mary Ann to deliver prematurely. She's trapped in the legal process like a prisoner while the whole country watches, waiting for Judge Leary—or you—to let her go—"

"You will *never* understand," Tierney interrupted. "All three of us are prison-ers in a death watch far more terrible than a vigil at an execution. Tomorrow, or the next day, or the day after that, Patrick Leary may sentence an innocent life to death. And then *you'll* do your damnedest to make sure that sentence is car-ried out.

"You act as if we were being stubborn, as though our defense of life is optional, a matter of foolish pride." Tierney's voice thickened with emotion. "I can see—I can *feel*—the price all of us are paying for it, and there's no good end-ing. Only a choice, between the moral and the immoral, right and wrong."

Against her will, Sarah acknowledged the immutability of his beliefs and the justice of his words—if this was murder, pure and simple, Martin Tierney was as entrapped as Mary Ann. "All the more reason," Sarah answered, "not to testify tomorrow."

Tierney folded his hands. "And end the defense of our grandson's life with Dr. Gersten."

"Gersten was a choice," Sarah retorted. "I didn't make you call him. Why should *Mary Ann* pay the price for *that*?"

Tierney did not flinch. "It was a mistake . . ."

"A *mistake*?" Sarah echoed. "Maybe for you. Maybe for your grandson. But not for Barry Saunders and his friends.

"This trial's great for them—all the fundamentalists will be sending their grocery money to the Christian Commitment, to stop the kind of antifamily outrage inflicted on Mary Ann's martyred parents." Sarah's voice rose. "Saunders sees this trial as a telethon: 'Send your money to Barry's kids.'"

To her surprise, Tierney expelled a short, bitter laugh, more eloquent than speech.

"The final boost for his ratings," Sarah finished, "would be the aggrieved, pro-life parents testifying against their wayward daughter. You might take time out to wonder if Saunders suggested Gersten to force your hand."

Tierney's returning gaze betrayed, to Sarah, acknowledgment, resignation, and fatalism. "Whatever was meant," he said, "it's done."

Watching him, Sarah felt despair. "Don't testify, Martin. Please. Because if *Mary Ann* wants to win, you may force her to take the stand."

Tierney could not be surprised. But pain showed through his self-control. "You'd put her on."

"After *you've* testified she's incapable of deciding for herself? She'll demand it. I'm her lawyer; you may leave me with no choice." Sarah's voice remained quiet. "And if either of you testifies, I'll go after you. You've thought about that, I'm sure—how I'll do it, and what I know."

Tierney stared at her. "You're offering a deal. If we don't testify, she won't."

"Yes. We both rest on what we have. Before all of us reach the point of no return."

Tierney placed a finger to his lips, eyes downcast in thought. Sarah tried to imagine the personae warring within him: the protective father; the concerned husband; the moral philosopher bent on saving his grandson's life; the litigator forced to calculate his chances. His conflict was as tangible to Sarah as the strength of his principles. "Margaret won't testify," he said at last. "But I will. In fact, I must.

"You think I'm speaking against my daughter. To me, it's my last chance to speak *to* her, in the only place where she still listens."

The sadness of this admission silenced Sarah, as did his concession of how much he had lost. But as it always seemed with Martin Tierney, nothing he did or said was simple—his choice of himself as witness over Margaret, Sarah knew, was also the calculated decision of a clever adversary. "What's to keep me," she retorted, "from calling Margaret as a hostile witness? If I were you, I'd worry for them both—your daughter *and* your wife."

Tierney's smile signaled his anger, tightly controlled. "I thought you might threaten that. Or even *do* it to divide us—as you've been hoping for all along." He stood. "You talk of choices, Sarah. *That* choice is up to you, and to your conscience."

Sarah rose as well. "I'm sorry," she said. "More than you know."

Tierney let the ambiguous remark linger for a moment, then nodded. "On some level, I suppose you are."

Turning, he left her there.

Twenty-seven

Taking the stand, Martin Tierney first looked toward his wife.

Despite her anger, the small moment made Sarah think of her parents. However deeply they loved her, there existed between them an understanding—built on years of compromise, a shared affection, a tolerance for the other's weaknesses, secrets which Sarah could not know. Watching the Tierneys' eyes meet, Sarah sensed their tangible connection, the fruits of twenty years. But Margaret's reflexive glance toward Mary Ann was filled with apprehension.

The girl sat beside Sarah, taut and still. As Mary Ann looked at her father, Sarah read her loss of innocence. No longer could she feel that her parents' love was unconditional: as she grew older, Mary Ann might appreciate their dilemma, but in her deepest heart, Sarah believed, she would always feel betrayed. As if seeing this, her father turned away.

Barry Saunders's questioning began slowly, eliciting from Martin Tierney the dimensions of his faith.

"What are your beliefs," Saunders asked, "regarding the death penalty?"

"I'm opposed to it," Tierney answered. "I believe that life is granted by God, and that we have no right to take it."

"And yet you served in Vietnam."

"Yes. But as a medic, not a combatant."

"And why was that?"

Tierney folded his hands. "I don't object to all wars. But I certainly objected to that war. Becoming a medic gave me a chance to save lives, not take them."

Tierney, Sarah thought, made no claims for himself beyond that he had beliefs too deep to treat as a convenience. "And your wife shares these beliefs?" Saunders asked.

"Long before she met me." Tierney gave his wife a fleeting smile. "Together, we were going to eradicate capital punishment. From the look of things, we've got a ways to go."

The understatement carried a hint of irony and sadness: their ideals were at risk within their own family, and might fail even there. "And has Mary Ann," Saunders asked, "also believed in the sanctity of life?"

"Always." Tierney remained quiet, contained. "The idea of defenselessness, or that someone could take the life of another, seemed to touch her deeply."

Silent, Mary Ann stared at the table, no more able to look at Martin Tierney than he could look at her. That cameras recorded this filled Sarah with disgust.

"When Mary Ann became pregnant," Saunders inquired, "how did you react?"

"We felt many things." Tierney narrowed his eyes in thought, as though straining to give an answer as complete as it was honest. "Angry and deluded, the reaction of parents when a child's conduct shocks them. Resentful, as unready to be grandparents as Mary Ann was to be a mother. Above all, we felt deep worry for our daughter. She was just so terribly young.

"Mary Ann imagined a life partnership with the boy who was the father. All *we* wanted was for him to be decent to her, to treat her with compassion." He paused, glancing at his wife, then added quietly, "So we went to talk to him, and to his parents."

At this, Mary Ann looked up, as astonished as Sarah herself. "What did they say?" Saunders asked.

"The parents were as adamant as their son, and *he* wanted nothing to do with Mary Ann. We've allowed her to believe that we wanted to exclude him." Hesitant, Tierney spoke more softly still. "In truth, he refused to see her. On any terms."

Mary Ann went crimson with shock and humiliation, and then her eyes filmed over. Sarah stared at Tierney in outrage; still Tierney did not look at them.

"On the way home," he finished, "we were overcome with regret. She'd gotten into something she didn't understand—for which, plainly, we had failed to prepare her. We simply could not bring ourselves to make that any worse by telling her."

Perhaps, Sarah thought, this revelation was a perverse form of pleading, a father straining to tell his daughter how much he loved her; if so, its tacit cruelty betrayed how badly Tierney had lost his way. But Patrick Leary's look of commiseration bespoke the sympathy of one father for another.

"Did she ever ask about abortion?" Saunders asked.

"Never," Tierney answered. "Mary Ann may have fantasized about this boy.

But she knew that her reasons for bearing this child were far more profound, and far less transitory. At no time did she question that."

To Sarah, this had the ring of truth, though she believed that the reasons for Mary Ann's silence were different from what Tierney proposed. "And how," Saunders asked, "was that affected by the sonogram?"

"All of us were devastated." Tierney's pale eyes sought out his wife. "I found myself wondering if this was God's way of sparing Mary Ann. But it was agony for her mother, and it has plainly spared our daughter nothing."

At this, Margaret Tierney briefly closed her eyes; Sarah scrawled her first note—"fear of infertility." Face radiating sympathy, Saunders moved closer, "When you speak of Mary Ann . . ."

"She was depressed, more profoundly than I'd ever seen. She couldn't stop crying. Finally, she told us that she didn't want a baby with no brain."

All at once, Sarah understood where this was going. "Could you talk to her?" Saunders asked.

"No. The shock was just too great, I think." Tierney's voice became even quieter, more pensive; to Sarah, his recitation, however heartfelt, seemed rehearsed. "This was the only time I'd seen Mary Ann's concern for innocent life fail her. Which is so unlike her that now she seems a different girl. I fear the day she has an abortion and then awakens to what she's done."

Saunders, too, looked troubled. "Between the sonogram and the day Ms. Dash filed this lawsuit, how much time had passed?"

"Three weeks."

"And in those three weeks, did Mary Ann *ever* express a fear of infertility?"

"No." Tierney's voice was melancholy. "Never."

With this, the thrust of Tierney's testimony struck home: Mary Ann was committing euthanasia—not from fear of infertility—but out of horror at a defective child. "And what," Saunders asked her father, "does that compel you to conclude?"

"That our daughter's groping for a plausible reason. That far too much has happened to her, far too quickly, for her to absorb." Now Tierney turned to Sarah in accusation. "And that she's being used by others, whose beliefs at heart she does not share, who can never comprehend the harm that they will do her."

In the silence, this time extended by Saunders, Sarah's fingertips gripped the table. "Is that why you intervened?" Saunders asked.

"We had no choice. What kind of world would we live in if parents ignore a moral wrong which only they can stop?" Once more, Tierney's voice became lower. "But principles in such a case are cold comfort without love. We deeply love our daughter, and we know her. And so we *know* that, in the depths of her soul, her son will always be a life. And that to take his life will traumatize her forever.

"But it's not just *his* life. It's the countless lives which will be lost if she succeeds in bringing down this law."

At last, Martin Tierney faced his daughter. "Because of this trial, Mary Ann will never live in privacy. And—if Ms. Dash should prevail—Mary Ann will bear the weight of *every* child who dies. Death upon death, abortion on abortion, they will drive her to despair."

In shock and anger, Sarah felt each word come down on Mary Ann: a father's judgment, more punishing than blows. Turning, she saw the girl's lower lip tremble as she tried to fight back tears.

Her father gazed at her, and then turned to Patrick Leary. "Unless *you* stop this," Tierney finished. "That's what I'm asking, Your Honor, as a father who loves his daughter more than life. Because winning this case will destroy her as surely as it destroys her son."

Twenty-eight

Walking toward Martin Tierney, Sarah saw no one else, felt nothing but the need to take him down. On the stand, Tierney watched her with cold dislike.

"That was quite a speech," she said. "Very Old Testament. So let's start out with a catalog of sin."

Silent, Tierney waited. "Do you believe in birth control?" Sarah asked.

"No."

"Because it's a sin?"

For an instant, Tierney looked annoyed, then composed himself. "Because life is a gift from God."

"And so," Sarah persisted, "birth control is a sin."

Tierney pulled on the lapels of his suit coat, straightening its line. "I believe it's wrong."

"So it also would have been wrong to tell your daughter about birth control."

"Yes."

"Does *she* believe that's wrong?"

Tierney hesitated. "So I've always thought."

"Did she form that belief when she was ten?"

"I don't know . . ."

"Or fifteen?"

Tierney sat straighter. "I can't assign a time, Ms. Dash. Obviously, the older one gets, the deeper the context of one's beliefs . . ."

"Or the greater one's opportunity to change them?"

Tierney gave her the guarded smile of an adversary. "Hopefully, one's sense of right and wrong is less elastic."

"Such as beliefs regarding abortion."

"Yes."

Sarah cocked her head. "Do you believe that abortion is justified in cases of rape or incest?"

"No. Regardless of its genesis, a fetus is a life."

"Does Mary Ann believe that?"

Tierney glanced toward his wife. "I always thought so."

Sarah raised her eyebrows. "Really? When did she form *that* belief?"

Tierney folded his hands. "I can't give you an hour, Ms. Dash. Or a day."

"Or a year?"

"No."

"So you don't know whether, at age seven, your daughter believed that incest did not justify abortion?"

"Objection." Saunders called out. "This is nothing more than badgering the witness."

Holding up her hand, Sarah kept her eyes on Martin Tierney. "Does Mary Ann also oppose the death penalty?" she asked.

Once more, Tierney paused to straighten his suit coat. "Vehemently."

"How do you know that?"

"Because I'm her father," Tierney answered with weary patience. "I've talked with her about it, read her school papers on the subject . . ."

"Read them, or wrote them?"

"Objection," Saunders called out.

"Sustained," Leary said promptly. "Please accord Professor Tierney more respect."

Like he accorded Mary Ann, Sarah wished to add. "Mary Ann attended prayer vigils," she said to Tierney, "outside San Quentin. When did *that* start?"

"At age eleven, I believe."

"Did Mary Ann *ask* to go?"

This time, Tierney glanced at his daughter. "Margaret and I took her. We believed that it was part of her moral education."

"So her appearance at San Quentin was compulsory."

Tierney frowned. "For a child to learn," he answered, "parents have to teach. And Mary Ann was willing."

Sarah appraised him. "In your view, does a proper 'moral education' also include a commitment to nonviolence?"

Tierney paused; Sarah guessed that he was wondering whether she had read his writings. "Yes. With rare exceptions."

"Then let me ask you a philosophical question. If this were 1940, and you could assassinate Hitler—knowing of his plan to annihilate Jews—would you do it?"

Tierney gazed back at her, his pale eyes unblinking. "No," he answered.

"Any more than I would murder an abortion provider, despite my belief that—like Hitler—he's performing legalized murder. Because I *also* believe in passive resistance, as practiced by Gandhi and Martin Luther King."

"I won't quibble with you, Professor, about whether sit-ins could have stopped the Holocaust. But I would observe that your beliefs regarding life are unusually rigorous and demanding." Pausing, Sarah cocked her head. "When did you form them?"

From his expression, combining discomfort and defensiveness, Tierney understood where this might lead. "It began in college," he finally answered. "And continued in graduate school, deepened by reading both philosophers and theologians."

"And was further deepened by your service in Vietnam, I believe you've written. Because of the brutality you witnessed."

"Yes."

"So you didn't form this belief when you were ten."

"No."

"Or fifteen?"

Tierney's gaze became a stare. "No."

"So is it fair to conclude, Professor, that your beliefs respecting life were formed as a result of maturation, education, and difficult personal experience?"

Tierney crossed his arms. "In my case," he answered. "But that's not the only path—"

"Isn't it possible," Sarah interrupted, "that Mary Ann has come to *her* belief regarding this tragic situation as a result of maturation, education, and difficult personal experience?"

"A *transient* belief . . ."

"Specifically," Sarah continued, "by being fifteen and not eleven; by exposure to beliefs different than *your* beliefs; and by facing the difficult personal experience of a hydrocephalic fetus."

Tierney stiffened. "As I was trying to say, Ms. Dash, people come to their beliefs in different ways. As an adolescent, I was on my own. But we helped Mary Ann form *her* beliefs from an early age. Her confusion *now* is transient . . ."

"Is it? Why on earth, Professor Tierney, is the threat of infertility at age fifteen more 'transient' than you dragging her to a prayer vigil at age eleven?"

A flush stained Tierney's pallid cheeks. "*This* experience is too colored by emotion . . ."

"Unlike *your* experience in Vietnam? Isn't what's happening that Mary Ann's begun to form her own beliefs, and *you* can't stand that?"

"No," Tierney snapped, then contained himself. "Her mother and I are acting to protect her . . ."

"By putting a virtual curse on her head on national television—that your fifteen-year-old daughter will 'bear the weight of *every* child who dies'? Isn't the trauma you're *really* concerned about *not* to Mary Ann, but to *you*?"

"That is *not* true."

"Isn't it?" Sarah said with real anger. "Isn't this entire trial a massive case of parental projection?"

Tierney paused, forcing himself to take a swallow of water. "It is not," he answered with a show of calm. "That you imply I so lack self-awareness—that I've pursued this trial to meet my own emotional needs—is an insult. It's an *insult*, Ms. Dash, that zealots like you can use to disparage any parent who, loving his child, charts a different course than whatever pleases *you*."

Sarah stared at him, then chose her next weapon. "Did you and Mrs. Tierney want more children?"

To Sarah, Tierney's eyes resembled chips of ice. "Objection," Saunders called out. "What possible relevance does *this* have?"

"Oh," Sarah said to Leary, "Professor Tierney knows. If you'll let him answer the question, *he'll* establish relevance."

Leary seemed to study Tierney's expression. "You may answer, Professor Tierney."

"Yes." Tierney seemed to bite off the word.

"Why didn't you?"

"Because Margaret couldn't."

"Because she'd had a classical cesarean section, you mean?"

Silent, Tierney glanced at his wife. "Specifically," Sarah pressed, "wasn't your wife told that—as a result of the C-section required to give birth to Mary Ann—further childbirth was a serious risk to health?"

Slowly, Tierney nodded. "Yes," he answered in a weary tone. "But the medical facts were different."

"Really?" Sarah placed her hands on her hips. "Was Mary Ann aware of her mother's cesarean section?"

"Of course she was."

"Did she also know that her mother had been advised to have no more children?"

"Yes."

"That must have been painful for your wife."

"Yes. It was."

Sarah paused a moment. "And how was it for you, Professor?"

For a moment, Tierney looked resentful, as though—ironic to Sarah—his daughter had betrayed their privacy. Then he answered calmly, "It was painful for us both."

"Yet you made quite a point of saying that Mary Ann was appalled by a defective fetus, and never mentioned infertility as grounds for an abortion." Pausing, Sarah shook her head in wonder. "But it was entirely unnecessary, wasn't it, for Mary Ann to discuss with you her *own* fear of infertility."

"There was nothing to stop her . . ."

"In fact," Sarah went on, "from the moment they both saw the sonogram she knew her *mother* also was afraid for her."

Briefly, Tierney hesitated. "I assume so."

"And she also knew how distressed you were that you couldn't have more children."

Tierney glanced toward Mary Ann. "We both tried very hard," he answered, "not to burden her with that."

"And yet both of you also told her that she *must* give birth to a hydrocephalic child. Despite the risk of infertility."

Tierney crossed his arms. "There are times," he said succinctly, "when what is morally right is trying, even harsh. But this child is a life, and therefore inviolate."

Sarah stared at him in incredulity. "Didn't Mary Ann have a very compelling personal reason—her fear of repeating her mother's sad experience—to reach a different conclusion?"

"She never once invoked that . . ."

"Why should she have to? She'd seen the sonogram dredge up for her own mother the disappointment that followed *her own* birth. And *Mary Ann,* unlike her mother, was unlikely to get a normal baby in return." Sarah paused, finishing in a lower voice. "She *knew* all that, and yet both of *you* insisted that she take this pregnancy to term. So talking to you about infertility was pointless, wasn't it."

Tierney folded his hands in front of him. "If you think we haven't agonized as parents—both of us—you're completely wrong.

"As parents, we're striving to act for her well-being, and to balance the long-term emotional damage against her more immediate distress. That includes the very hard task—made infinitely more terrible by *your* lawsuit—of hewing to a belief in the value of life which Mary Ann has always shared. And, we are confident, still does."

"'Confident,'" Sarah repeated. "But Mary Ann's not even *living* with you, is she? Because she finds it impossible to live with you while you're opposing her in court."

"Only for the duration of the trial . . ."

"And also because, in her eyes, you're putting your own beliefs above her fear of infertility."

"If that's *her* belief, it's far too harsh."

"Yet your expert, Dr. Gersten, testified that a central purpose of this law is to promote closeness within the family."

Tierney's expression was bleak, his voice diminished. "What Dr. Gersten meant was 'over time.' Not over the last eleven days—"

"Isn't it true," Sarah cut in sharply, "that *your* decision to invoke this law is destroying your own family?"

At this, Tierney straightened, half-rising from the witness chair. "My decision?" he asked. "*You* brought this lawsuit . . ."

"It's not *my* lawsuit," Sarah snapped. "It's Mary Ann's. It's long past time to credit her with thinking for herself."

Abruptly, Tierney drew a breath, his effort at self-control so visible that Patrick Leary stared at him. "Someday," he told Sarah, "you may be a mother. If that day comes, you can call me to apologize."

"Why?" Sarah countered. "Because it takes a mature and loving parent to impose on Mary Ann the risk which caused both of you such pain?"

For a time, Tierney studied her. "No," he said at last. "Because you'll realize that parenthood is not permissiveness, and love a far more complex matter than respecting a child's 'rights.' Then perhaps you'll *also* understand the reasons— despite all you've done—that we'll have a loving family again."

Sarah gazed at him, drained. There was much, she believed, that he did not yet comprehend, including the likelihood that he had just compelled his daughter to testify. "I hope you're right," she answered. "But I think the apology will be *yours* to make, to Mary Ann."

Twenty-nine

"I hope this girl won't testify," Vic Coletti said. "It just keeps getting worse."

The senior senator from Connecticut—and ranking Democrat on the Judiciary Committee—sat in the Oval Office with Kerry Kilcannon. The two men relaxed in overstuffed chairs; it was past seven o'clock, and the windows were dark, the President's formal schedule done with. As often in his spare time, he was tending to the Masters nomination.

"Not to mention tragic," Kerry answered. "This trial makes you wonder if any of our friends in Congress had a clue what they were doing."

"No point wondering," Coletti told his former colleague. "Gage knew what *he* was doing—giving the Christian Commitment value for their money, while choosing issues most people think they agree with. You'll recall he passed this sucker with twenty votes to spare. Including mine."

Coletti's take was, as usual, shrewd and pragmatic. Stocky and balding, with a beaky nose and energetic manner, Coletti was addicted to public life and almost comically ambitious; Clayton Slade was fond of saying that, at his own funeral, Vic would pop out of the casket to announce he was running for reelection. But Coletti's devotion to the dictum that politics, like rust, never sleeps, made him a valuable source of insight and information.

"Politically," Kerry asked, "how does the Tierney case play out for us?"

"Television's the killer, Mr. President. Every day this trial goes on ratchets up the pressure on Caroline Masters. You know: 'As Chief Justice, will you stand up for the family and against dismembering babies?' or 'Can a Chief Justice with no family look out for our family?' For us, this trial is like being hit by a moon rock."

It was sobering, Kerry thought, to experience how much of being President lay not in careful planning, but in coping with the unforeseeable. "Clayton's run some polls," he said. "Support for Mary Ann Tierney is up to forty percent."

Coletti gave an earthy snort of skepticism. "And the rest want to brand a scarlet *A* on her chest—for 'abortion.' But the real problem's money. Yesterday, the Christian Commitment started sending out a mailer with her picture next to one of that other teen mommy, Marlene Brown, asking for money to fight the pro-abortionists who 'would murder the nearly born.' That's millions for TV spots in the next congressional elections, hurting us and helping Gage—just as long as Mac behaves."

"So," Kerry said, "Gage tries to string out the Masters hearings."

"Sure. He's got to figure that everything that happens in the Tierney case— Leary's ruling, the appeal to Masters's court, then maybe to the Supreme Court—enables him to say how careful they have to be before confirming her. That can justify anything short of a blatant witch hunt, and there's not much you can do about it."

"Except depend on Chad."

Coletti rolled his eyes. "That's a hell of a comfort. Considering Palmer wants to run you out of here so he can take your place."

Kerry chose his answer with care. As the ranking Democrat on Palmer's committee, Coletti was the only other senator who knew Caroline Masters's personal secret, and that Palmer was protecting it. But although Coletti might make shrewd guesses about Chad's motives, Kerry had not disclosed their conversations to anyone, let alone that Chad felt that, as Chief Justice, Caroline might serve his rivalry with Gage. "I've never known Chad to break his word," Kerry said simply.

At this, Coletti smiled. "You don't suppose our hero thinks that Masters will vote to uphold his campaign reform law, and choke off Gage's money supply? Including, perchance, all that cash from the Christian Commitment?"

No, Kerry thought, *Vic Coletti was not a fool.* Shrugging, he replied, "I can't help what Chad thinks."

Coletti's smile became cynical, a silent signal of disbelief. "It *would* help explain their caucus the day before yesterday."

"They invited you?"

Now Coletti laughed, with a pleasure as close to childlike as such a maneuverer could ever manage. "No. But I've got friends."

Kate Jarman, Kerry guessed. That the senator from Vermont disliked Mac Gage was no secret, nor that she and Coletti traded votes on occasion. "I never doubted it," Kerry said amiably. "So what do your Republican confidantes tell you?"

"Gage tried putting the screws to Palmer, get him to delay the hearings. So far, Chad's resisting."

The phrase "so far" was enunciated with distinct reserve. "But?" Kerry asked.

"Chad's position is worse than yours. As chairman, he's on the firing line—the Tierney case creates mounting pressure to delay, especially from the pro-lifers in his own party. And before Chad beats you for President, he has to beat Gage for the nomination. If the right wing turns on him, he's sunk."

Once more, Kerry shrugged. "Chad's got cover, Vic. He's always been pro-life, sincerely so."

"Sure. But is he truly devout? Does he go to bed at night dreaming of the unborn? He's already pissed off the Christian Commitment over money. Face it, Mr. President, when Chad told you he'd sit on Masters's private life, he didn't figure on Mary Ann Tierney. Or that Masters's ex-clerk would be her lawyer."

"Not helpful," Kerry acknowledged. "Which makes your Republican colleagues in the middle that much more critical."

Coletti pursed his lips. "Now *there's* a wobbly bunch."

Kerry smiled. "You don't happen," he said in a tone of idle curiosity, "to know where your friend Kate Jarman stands?"

Coletti raised his eyebrows, as though reminded that Kerry Kilcannon also was no fool. "Kate? She's not standing, Mr. President—she's hiding out with the rest of them, watching Gage and Palmer."

Kerry considered this. "I'd bet on Chad," he answered. "But give him all the help you can."

"I hope I didn't interrupt dinner," Kerry said.

On the other end of the telephone, Chad Palmer laughed. "Of course you did—this is when normal people eat. Allie's giving you five minutes."

"Then I'll make it quick. I hear Gage is looking for dirt on Caroline Masters."

There was a brief pause, and then Chad said mordantly, "Just Masters? The other day that rocket scientist Paul Harshman suggested you were fucking her."

Kerry emitted a mirthless laugh. "Tell Harshman she's too tall—that's why I'm putting her on the Court." In weary tones, Kerry added quietly, "Do you ever wonder about your teammates, Chad?"

"All the time. But as long as Harshman's chasing *you,* and not what's real, I can live with it." For a moment, Chad was quiet. "I guess you wonder if I'm putting off the hearings?"

Pausing, Kerry chose to sound surprised. "Are you?"

"I gave you my word," Chad answered with asperity. "You've got four minutes left, and you're wasting them."

It was a fresh reminder of how much Chad disliked having his honor questioned, even by implication. "It's not about your word, pal. I'm wondering if you can control them. Gage must be all over them—and you."

This remark went not to Chad's honor, Kerry knew, but to his pride. More evenly, Chad answered, "I've counted the votes. I'm sure Coletti's got all eight of his, and I'll hold at least half of my ten. Keeping the Masters hearing on the front burner will cost you one week, tops."

Briefly, Kerry tried to calculate the course of the Tierney case. "That's fine."

"*I* thought so. But understand I don't want to be seen with you any time soon. Or even have it known how often we talk."

There was a new sharpness in his voice, hinting at the pressure Chad felt. "I'm well aware of that," Kerry answered.

"But don't lose sleep." Chad's tone became sardonic. "Mac Gage is right, Mr. President. I always liked you best."

Thirty

When Sarah arrived home, picketers stood in front of her apartment building, holding candles which flickered like fireflies in darkness. Glancing up through her windshield, she saw Mary Ann framed in the window of her second-floor apartment.

Baby-killer . . .

The picketers chanted in unison. As Sarah stopped in the mouth of the driveway, waiting for the garage door to lift, they circled her car.

Baby-killer . . .

A face pressed against the window on the driver's side, inches from hers, separated only by glass—the man from the clinic, she thought. When the garage opened, three teenage girls lay down in Sarah's path.

Baby-killer . . .

The man's mouth began forming words. All around her candlelight danced, distorting the faces which surrounded her. Above them, Sarah could see Mary Ann, palms pressed against the glass.

Baby-killer . . .

Sarah reached for her car phone to call the police. The massed bodies to each side began rocking her Honda.

Baby-killer . . .

Fighting to control her voice, Sarah told the dispatcher where she was. The car kept rocking. Hanging up, she turned her stereo up so loud that her Carlos Santana CD drowned out the shouting and made her eardrums throb. The car seemed to rock with the music in a clumsy, ponderous rhythm; the open mouths and contorted faces of the men and women who trapped her became hallucinatory. Startling streaks of red flashed across their faces, and then the police sirens cut through the throbbing bass.

As Sarah turned, two squad cars stopped behind her, then a third, then a wagon. Sarah released a breath.

The faces started receding. Seven cops—five men and two women—began lifting the limp bodies blocking her to clear a path to the garage. Sarah turned off the stereo.

Silent, the dark-eyed man still stared, his breath condensing on the window. A cop pulled him back, and his face vanished.

Shaking, Sarah eased the car into the garage. Tendrils of her curly hair lay damp against her forehead.

"Fame is hell," Sarah said.

At most times she drank wine sparingly and, when in trial, almost none. Tonight, before collapsing on her couch, she had poured herself a generous glass of cabernet.

Sitting across from her, Mary Ann gazed down at her stomach. From beneath them, a disembodied chant rose to the darkened window.

Baby-killer . . .

"Were you scared?" the girl asked.

Sarah sipped her wine. "Was. Am. Will be for a while."

She did not tell Mary Ann about her mother's phone message, begging her to be careful, or that—after much probing by Sarah—her mother had admitted receiving a threat. The caller had been watching Sarah on television, he informed them, and held her parents responsible for the fate of Mary Ann Tierney's child. His voice had been unnaturally calm.

After reassuring her mother, Sarah had called a private security firm. She could not return to court without knowing they were safe.

Baby-killer . . .

"I'm sorry," Mary Ann told her. "I never thought . . ."

"Why should you have? And it wouldn't have stopped me."

Sarah hoped that this were true. But Mary Ann seemed to believe it, and her blue eyes shone with gratitude.

"Without you," she said, "I'd be nowhere."

Sarah knew these were the words that parents, teachers, or coaches cherished all their lives. But after Martin Tierney's testimony, Sarah could not.

"You'd be somewhere," she said. "Maybe you'd be home. Maybe you wouldn't have gone through what your father did today."

Mary Ann rubbed her temples with the thumb and forefinger of one hand. After a time, she murmured, "I think I need to testify."

Sarah finished her wine. Her limbs felt sluggish, inert; the chants continued unabated.

Baby-killer . . .

"Let's get some air," she said.

The roof was another six stories up. A light breeze swirled from the bay, and the cries of the demonstrators were faint.

They sat down in plastic chairs bolted against the wind. To their left the lights of commodious houses—brick, wood, or stone—dipped and rose on the gentle sloping streets of Pacific Heights. A half-mile in front of them the Golden Gate Bridge spanned the narrow opening from the Pacific to the black oval of the bay; beyond that, more lights dotted the hills of Marin County. The roof was quiet, a place Sarah came to think.

Mary Ann's voice, soft and almost indistinct, broke her reverie.

"I can't live with them anymore."

There was a pitiful quality to this which pierced Sarah's heart. The Tierneys had done their daughter great damage; had Sarah's parents done this to her now—unthinkable to Sarah—she, as an adult, would be free to decide that this was unforgivable. But Mary Ann was helpless; she had nowhere else to go.

"I know it's hard to imagine," Sarah said. "That's why I wonder if you should testify."

"*He* did." Mary Ann sounded angry now. "The great authority—St. Martin, the judge of how everyone should live."

Sarah studied her. From some other girl, this remark might seem typical of a teenager, her resentment transitory. But not for Mary Ann. Sarah guessed that— well before her pregnancy—her father's moral certitude had begun to grate on Mary Ann; perhaps the sonogram had hastened, and deepened exponentially, a breach which lay in ambush for them. And, perhaps, as well, for the Tierneys' marriage.

"What about your mother?" Sarah asked.

Mary Ann looked away. Her anger seemed to vanish in regret, perhaps even guilt.

"What if I put her on the stand," Sarah persisted. "If I pressed her hard enough, would she still support him? Suppose they parted company . . ."

"*No.*"

It was said with sudden intensity. Surprised, Sarah modified her tone. "*She* wouldn't? Or *you* don't want me to?"

Now Mary Ann, too, spoke more evenly. "I don't think she would, Sarah. And I don't want you to. I know him, and it could ruin them."

This simple statement was filled with a depth of feeling and perception which startled Sarah. In the crucible of the trial, Mary Ann seemed to have grown, becoming less blind to consequence, more compassionate in her choices, than her father's beliefs permitted him. *He doesn't deserve this much compassion,* Sarah wanted to tell her—*neither of them do.*

Mary Ann seemed to square her shoulders. In profile, she was slight, a silhouette with a stomach so distended it looked painful. "So," she said coolly, "I really have to testify."

There were many things Sarah could have said to discourage her—that Mary Ann would harm her family further, that she might win without speaking for herself. What stopped her was respect.

"Yes," Sarah answered. "I think you do."

Thirty-one

"Did you want to get pregnant?" Sarah asked.

Mary Ann Tierney sat on the witness stand, wearing a floral print maternity dress which hung loosely, partly concealing the shape of her belly and, Sarah hoped, the unsettling nature of a late-term abortion. To Sarah, she looked like what she was—a young girl overcome by circumstance, dragged from the secretiveness of teenage life to explain herself to the world.

The courtroom was preternaturally still—even Patrick Leary was subdued, his only motion to fidget with a pencil. Martin Tierney's gaze at his daughter was penetrating, yet deeply sad. From the front row Margaret watched them both with wounded eyes, her manner veering between protectiveness toward Mary Ann and shock that she would testify against them.

"No." Mary Ann's voice was wispy. "I was scared of that."

Sarah nodded her encouragement. Gently, she asked, "Why didn't you use birth control?"

Mary Ann gazed at the floor, choosing a middle distance well short of her father. "I didn't know how, or where to get something, and Tony said it wouldn't feel good. When I was with him, I tried not to think about it. Just about him."

"What about asking your doctor?"

Mary Ann blinked. "He was *their* friend, not mine. Even if there was something I could use, I was afraid to have it." Pausing, Mary Ann looked at Sarah in exhaustion; they had stayed up late rehearsing her testimony, then tried in vain to sleep, and her eyes were as puffy as Sarah's felt. "My mom was the one who cleaned my room," she explained in a reluctant voice. "I always thought she looked for things, even in my purse."

Whether this was true or not, Sarah reflected, the Tierneys' regulation of thought and action had left Mary Ann with little sense of privacy, except in those moments—as with Tony—when she secured it through deception.

"Did *you* believe using birth control was wrong?" Sarah asked.

"I didn't know. I just knew we couldn't talk about it."

"After you found out you were two months pregnant, Mary Ann, did you talk about *abortion*?"

"Never. My father believed it was a sin. So did Father Satullo, the people at my school, everyone I knew . . ."

"What about your mother?"

"She believed that, too." Sadly, Mary Ann glanced toward Margaret Tierney. "At first it was hard. But after a while she started buying baby clothes, decorating the guest room. She even bought a diary, so I could write down what was happening to my body. When I didn't feel like writing in it, she'd ask me questions, then write down things herself."

Sarah had first heard this last night; for her, it sharpened her sense of a girl whose life was, to an unusual degree, the product of her parents' iron beliefs and subconscious desires.

"Did you feel ready to be a mother?" Sarah asked.

"It didn't matter," Mary Ann said softly. "I *was* one. I knew I'd always love my baby, and protect him."

The words were not rehearsed, and reminded Sarah that, however blind she thought him, Martin Tierney knew that this abortion would cause Mary Ann great anguish.

"What changed your mind?" Sarah asked.

"Not just the sonogram." Still Mary Ann's tone was soft. "The look on my mother's face when the doctor said what it meant. The sound of her voice when she asked if I could have more babies. And I knew—all at once, I just knew—that I shouldn't try to have this one. Because he wouldn't live, and I might never have another."

"Could you tell your parents *that*?"

"No." Mary Ann looked down at her stomach, tears filling her eyes. "I knew what they'd gone through for me, what having me had cost them. Telling them felt too selfish." Mary Ann's voice became husky with misery and protest. "That's what my father called me when I finally said what I wanted—'selfish.'"

Martin Tierney stared fixedly at the defense table, as though shamed by the exposure of so intimate a moment. Quietly, Sarah asked, "Would knowing you were afraid of infertility have changed their minds?"

Mary Ann shook her head. "They know *now*," she answered. "And look at where we are."

Glancing at the camera, trained on a fifteen-year-old girl by his own order, Leary seemed chastened. Martin Tierney seemed to gaze into a void: he was sorry, Sarah supposed, for implying that Mary Ann was fixated on perfection, not the threat of infertility. But nowhere near as sorry as Sarah intended to make him.

"So what made you defy them?" she asked.

"My mother. I mean she had these beliefs, but sometimes she was just so sad." Mary Ann stopped, as though moved by an indelible memory. "After the sonogram," she finished, "I found her in the guest room just staring at the crib, tears running down her face. That was when I knew for sure I had to do this."

At the corner of Sarah's vision, Margaret Tierney closed her eyes. Facing Mary Ann, Sarah silently implored her not to notice, or retreat. "How did you know where to go?"

"I didn't. Then I remembered that Father Satullo—our priest—led prayer vigils outside an abortion clinic. Looking up the address was all I knew to do."

"How pregnant were you?"

"Five months." Mary Ann's voice trembled. "When I went, Father Satullo was there, kneeling on the sidewalk . . ." She paused again, voice trailing off.

"So you left."

"Yes. After that, it was like I was trapped. My mother used to talk about how I moved inside her. All I could think about was that my baby never did."

"Is that why you came back to the clinic?"

Mary Ann's cornflower blue eyes, though wide, seemed to have turned inward. "I kept remembering my mother, crying. She needed to believe in something so much that she was suffering, all over again, by helping him make *me* suffer."

Mary Ann kept surprising Sarah: there was a lucidity to her thoughts, a rueful clarity, of someone reaching her own terms with life. "Then you met me," Sarah said. "And said you wanted an abortion."

"Yes. So you told me about this law. About what I'd have to do, and how hard it all would be. Especially having to face my parents in court." Pausing, Mary Ann seemed to squirm, perhaps at the discomfort of her pregnancy, perhaps at confronting her parents. "I didn't *want* to face them. I didn't want to go to court."

For a moment, Sarah let this linger. "Did I ever say you *should*?"

"No. Only that if *I* wanted an abortion, that court was the only legal way. Whether to go was *my* decision."

Sarah hesitated, giving Mary Ann a brief respite; the girl was visibly tiring, and Sarah wished to make her point, then sit, leaving Mary Ann with the reserves of mind and spirit to withstand cross-examination. "After you filed," Sarah inquired, "did your parents tell you to drop the lawsuit?"

"Yes." Mary Ann's voice held a quiet vehemence. "They *both* did."

At this, Margaret Tierney seemed to blanch.

"What did *I* say?"

"That if I wanted to bail out, I could. You treated me like a person, not a puppet." Now Mary Ann looked directly at her father, speaking clearly and distinctly. "My *father* made me come here. *He's* the one who says I don't know what I'm doing, that I'm not even capable of seeing what's happened to my own mother. But when I listen to him talk about me, it's not like *me* at all, but some-one he made up."

Pausing, Mary Ann took in a breath and her voice was thick with emotion. "Now he says that all I cared about was having a perfect child. *That's* the worst part—they're *still* calling me selfish, and I was trying not to hurt them."

From the defense table, Martin Tierney stared at his daughter with an expression close to wonder. "How could you keep from hurting them?" Sarah asked.

Mary Ann seemed to gather herself, turning from Margaret Tierney's stricken look of comprehension. "By not talking about my mother," she said with weary finality. "Not to them, or even to you. I didn't until my father testi-fied against me."

As the courtroom fell silent, Margaret Tierney bent her head.

Seeing this, Sarah fought back her own regret. "No further questions," she said, and went back to her chair.

Thirty-two

For Sarah, the recess—a mere ten minutes—felt endless.

She sat in a bare witness room with Mary Ann, watching a schoolroom-style clock measure out the time before the girl faced her cross-examiner. That so much of this experience involved her mother's trauma was devastating to both parents and child, and Mary Ann's exposure of her family's wounds seemed to have left her listless and depressed.

"You were good," Sarah encouraged her. "All you need is to stand up for yourself for one more hour."

Mary Ann's eyes flickered, the only sign that she had heard. Sarah could feel her absorb the aching knowledge that her relationships with both parents, and theirs with each other, were being changed forever.

This brought Sarah face-to-face with her own responsibilities. She had made decisions as a lawyer would, marshaling evidence and hammering at the Tierneys' weak points without remorse. As a lawyer, she found little in herself to fault. But though Sarah could tell herself that Congress had written this conflict into law, she could not escape her role in bringing it to this climax. Now the best she could hope for was that Saunders or Thomas Fleming, not Martin Tierney, would cross-examine Mary Ann.

Glancing at the clock, Sarah said. "It's time."

Approaching his daughter, he stopped at a respectful distance with his hands shoved in his pockets. As she watched him with apprehension, the exquisite cruelty of the moment made Sarah wince.

"Mary Ann," he said softly, "I'd like to apologize."

The girl's vigilant expression softened, then stiffened again. Sarah wondered at the skewed intimacy she witnessed—a loving father, so estranged from his daughter that he must broach his regrets on television—even as she questioned the motives of the complex man who was her adversary.

"You've never been selfish," Tierney continued. "I was too emotional, it seems, to see how much you wanted to protect your mother, and worried for us both. I, who should know you better than anyone. Except, perhaps, your mother."

Hope and distrust fought for control of his daughter's face. "Would it have changed your mind?" she asked.

Tierney shook his head. "Not my mind. My heart. To have been so blind shames me, and my failure to understand your fears, and to comfort you, is beyond excuse. Forgive me, please."

The spectators were rapt—torn, Sarah suspected, between sympathy and the desire to look away. Perhaps only she was detached enough to credit Martin Tierney not just with love, but with the diabolical cleverness granted only to parents: to know the means of undermining his daughter's resolve.

Slowly, Sarah stood.

"Your Honor," she said in muted tones, "I appreciate Professor Tierney's sentiments, and fully sympathize with his regrets, however belated. But this is not cross-examination, nor does it address the issues raised by his intervention. Unless his apology includes consent, my client is trapped in this trial, and in a tragedy we should bring to a close."

Tierney faced her, his translucent gaze level. "No one, Ms. Dash, wants to end this more than Margaret and I. But you're an advocate, concerned with winning—as is your privilege. We're *parents,* and cannot be so single-minded. No result would compensate for our prior failings toward Mary Ann, or our failure to seek forgiveness sooner." Pausing, he added, "But I'm through now."

Sarah was filled with relief, believing that Martin Tierney would sit again, sparing his daughter the worst. Then, turning, Tierney said to Leary, "I'll ask my daughter only what I must."

In disbelief, Sarah stepped forward. "A father cross-examining his daughter? What apology can compensate for that?"

"Who better?" Tierney rejoined, and faced Leary yet again. "We're a family, with a shared history of fifteen years. With respect, neither Mr. Saunders nor Mr. Fleming—nor Ms. Dash—knows the questions a father should ask his own child."

From the stand, Mary Ann watched this colloquy in bewilderment. "Of course," Leary answered somberly. "That's your right, Professor. And, one might think, your duty."

There was a note of reproof in Leary's voice—not for Tierney, but for Sarah. She had no choice but to sit and watch.

Turning, Tierney faced his daughter. "Do you love your child, Mary Ann?"

The girl blinked. In a near whisper, she answered, "Yes."

"And before he was part of our lives, you believed that taking *any* innocent, unborn life was wrong."

Mary Ann hesitated, and her voice fell to a whisper. "Yes."

"Do you *still* believe your son is a life?"

Involuntarily, Mary Ann glanced down at her stomach. "Yes," she answered. "But he probably won't *have* a life."

Now her father paused. "Do you think that you should take his life, Mary Ann, because God may have given him a disability?"

Mary Ann stared at the floor, as if penitent. "No," she said. "Not if that's the only reason. But it isn't."

Tierney looked back at her, his face expressing so perfectly his puzzlement and doubt that Sarah had a startling, swift perception—that, whatever his feelings, Martin Tierney had an actor's gifts. "So now you would take your own son's life out of God's hands, and into yours? And, having done so, end it?"

Now Mary Ann looked up. "They don't think my baby has a brain," she answered. "But God gave *me* one, to make decisions. I don't think it's a sin to want more babies who will live."

She was holding her own, Sarah thought. But Tierney seemed undaunted; armed with a father's knowledge, he had another question for every answer. "Like Matthew Brown?" he inquired.

Mary Ann's lips parted. "That was a miracle," she answered. "His mother said so herself."

"Matthew's mother," Tierney responded, "left him in God's hands. Do you think she was wrong?"

Not if that was her choice, Sarah willed the girl to answer. But Mary Ann looked down again. "No," she said.

At once Tierney's face became a portrait of compassion and concern. "Suppose that you take this baby's life, and then discover that he had a normal brain. How will you feel then?"

Mary Ann still could not look at him. "Terrible," she said in a trembling voice. "Worse than that."

Angrily, Sarah turned toward Margaret Tierney. *How can you sit there?* she wanted to ask. But the girl's mother, though pale, watched her husband without flinching.

Tierney moved closer to their daughter. "You'd wish you hadn't taken his life, wouldn't you?"

"Yes."

"To you, *that* would be a sin."

Mary Ann hunched on the witness stand, as if protecting herself against a chill. "I wouldn't *mean* to do it," she protested. "What it means is that I had to make a choice."

"No," Tierney responded, "you *don't* have to. Do you understand now, Mary Ann, that your mother and I are trying to spare you the terrible consequences of *making* such a choice?"

Slowly, Mary Ann looked up again. "Maybe you are," she answered. "But it's also about your own beliefs. They're so strong, and *you're* so sure, that what *I* believe doesn't count."

This sudden challenge begged a question which, though palpably reluctant, Tierney was forced to ask. "And what do you believe, Mary Ann? Or think you believe."

She sat straighter, drawing from a reserve of strength that Sarah had not been sure remained. "*This* baby doesn't have much of a chance," she answered. "But if I have him, maybe he'll be the only baby I'll ever have, and I'll have to watch him die. No one but *me* should make me live with that."

Though firm, Mary Ann's response had, to Sarah, the sound of the girl approaching the limit of exhaustion. "Do you remember," her father asked, "what Dr. McNally said? That there may be as much chance your son will be normal as there is of infertility? And that any risk is extremely remote."

Mary Ann looked down again. "I remember," she said stubbornly, and then suddenly she faced him, bursting out, "I understand as well as you do—even better, because it's *me*. You say I don't, because I'm fifteen. You want to force me to take that chance. You want to tell me what's 'remote.'

"That's *not* about me—it's about you. You, and what happened to my mother. You, and what *you* believe.

"Maybe I'll have the abortion and feel terrible. Maybe the baby will be another miracle. But how will *you* feel—*and* my mother—if I can't ever have more children?"

Taken aback, Tierney stood taller. "That's not the question."

"You never asked yourself that? Did you ever ask my mother?"

The silence, total now, felt stifling to Sarah. "Yes," Tierney answered. "How can you think otherwise?"

Face ashen, Margaret Tierney closed her eyes. "Maybe you *asked* her," Mary Ann responded, "but I *watched* her."

Helpless, Sarah had the sudden sense of too many truths being spoken. "I watched her, too." Tierney answered with the sadness of reminiscence. "When you were born, and in all the years since."

Mary Ann turned from him, resistance seeping out of her in the shame of having said too much. "I want to have more babies," she murmured in a plaintive voice. "Please."

Irresolute, Tierney stood between his daughter and his wife, mirror images of agony. He seemed to weigh his choices, the volatility he risked in speaking further, then said at last, "No further questions."

After a moment, Leary turned to Sarah. In reluctant tones, he asked, "Anything more, Ms. Dash?"

"No," Sarah answered. "Nothing."

Thirty-three

On the morning Judge Patrick Leary would render his decision, Sarah Dash stood up to make her final argument.

The courtroom was quiet. After the raw emotions of the two prior days, with father pitted against daughter, Leary appeared less crisp, as if the burden of ruling had overtaken his pleasure in presiding. Fresh-faced, Mary Ann Tierney looked apprehensive, yet hopeful, sustained by several hours sleep with the aid of a mild sedative. Both Martin and Margaret Tierney feigned an air of calm, as though pretending—in the sad way of families at odds—that nothing remarkable had happened. But their tension, like Mary Ann's, showed in their stillness, the inability of parent and child to look at each other. As for Sarah, she tried to ignore the pressures bearing down on her—her doubts about Leary, the invisible audience of millions, the stakes for countless other young women—to focus on drawing the judge into Mary Ann Tierney's experience.

"This case," she began, "is about a fifteen-year-old girl who—five months pregnant—finds herself staring at a sonogram.

"On that sonogram is a fetus with an enormous head.

"Almost certainly, it has no brain. And there are only two ways it's coming out of her—by abortion, or by cesarean section.

"If aborted, the fetus will die. If delivered—almost as surely—the fetus will die. The difference is this: if Mary Ann delivers by cesarean, there is a small but measurable possibility she will *never* have a child again."

Listening, Leary looked pinched, unhappy; it struck Sarah that he preferred imagining himself as the parent, rather than the child. Intent, she pressed on.

"All this she's known for just a minute. But there's one *other* thing she's known for most of her life: that her own birth left the woman comforting her—

her own mother—unable to have more children. But though she shares this frightening prospect with her mother, Mary Ann remains silent."

Sarah turned now, facing Martin Tierney. "She knows her parents' principles all too well. Never speak of sex. Never speak of birth control. Never, ever speak of abortion. And—because she knows too well what these principles have cost them—*never* hurt your mother by saying you're afraid you'll end up sterile, like her."

Though Tierney met her eyes, his cheeks were concave hollows, hinting at a steely effort. "But she is afraid," Sarah told him softly. "So, in desperation, she asks her parents—*begs* them—for permission to abort. What she gets back is the cold comfort of their principles, and her father's heartless accusation that she's 'selfish.' And she absorbs the saddest lesson for *any* child to learn: that to disagree with *this* mother and father is to go through life alone."

Tierney looked down, then renewed his emotionless stare at Sarah, who faced the judge again. "Now Mary Ann Tierney has *no one*. The only refuge she can think of is a women's clinic; the only reason she knows of it is that her priest is trying to shut it down. And when she goes, she sees him there, and runs away.

"It takes two weeks for her to return. Two weeks to muster the courage it takes for a fifteen-year-old to fight through a crowd of demonstrators who believe as her parents do. Her reward is to discover that—perhaps in those two weeks—she has become the first subject of the Protection of Life Act. That she has lost the right to protect her physical and emotional health. That her only hope is to challenge *that* law, and *these* parents, in *this* court."

Pausing, Sarah stood taller. "She tries to imagine how hard it will be. That she will face her parents' anger. That she has to challenge a federal law. That strangers will hate her for it. That others will exploit her. That she will unleash political warfare she can but dimly understand." Once more, Sarah lowered her voice. "The one thing her lawyer never imagines, and so never thinks to tell her, is that the court from which Mary Ann must seek protection will put her on national television."

Leary reddened. Quickly, Sarah added, "The court has its reasons, I know. But Mary Ann Tierney is still here, asking for its protection. And I do not think that this court can, any longer, doubt her independence or resolve.

"But if doubt remains, consider what her parents have put her through. On national television, they've made their own daughter the whipping girl for every constituency with a point of view.

"The antichoice movement.

"The Christian right.

"The disabled.

"The embittered."

Sarah's voice turned sardonic. "Not to mention Mary Ann's own doctor, and—last and worst—themselves.

"And under what authority do they heap abuse on their fifteen-year-old daughter?" Sarah paused again. "The Protection of Life Act—the purpose of which, they tell us, is to help parents 'protect' their daughters.

"Nothing can discredit this statute more completely than the Tierneys' invocation of it. This law has allowed them to impose their will on their own daughter—at whatever peril to her health—backed by a babel of conflicting voices, with every conceivable agenda except Mary Ann's well-being.

"All *this* has happened to Mary Ann Tierney for the most arbitrary reason— *who* her parents are." Once more, Sarah glanced at Martin Tierney.

"Or, the Tierneys' witnesses would say, how very *admirable* her parents are. So let's consider all the *less* 'admirable' parents this court will empower if it upholds this law in the name of Martin and Margaret Tierney.

"Fathers who rape their daughters. Or beat them. Or throw them out for becoming pregnant. Or are too alcoholic and dysfunctional to care. Or"— Sarah stopped abruptly—"who will murder their own daughter if she tries to go to court."

Leary shook his head. "You go too far."

"I think not," Sarah shot back. "Congress can legislate all it likes, but no law can create a Norman Rockwell family, or give most teenage girls the courage or resources to protect themselves. This law *will* create more emotional trauma, more physical abuse, more teenage mothers denied appropriate medical attention. More girls *will* give birth to their own brothers or sisters. And, yes, more young girls *will* die.

"And for *what*? Because forcing a minor to abide by her parents' orders will make them 'closer' as a family?" Sarah inclined her head toward Martin Tierney. "This court has seen for itself the impact on *this* family. I need not dwell on that.

"So let's turn to the final justification for this law: that Congress has balanced a woman's life and health against society's interest in protecting the potential life she carries, once that life is viable.

"The facts are these: late-term abortions are one out of six *thousand*. They occur when there is a threat to the mother's life or health, or when there are severe fetal anomalies. And, in all likelihood, both.

"*That*, Your Honor, is why Mary Ann Tierney is here.

"One can start by asking whether such a fetus is 'viable' within any humane meaning of the word, or whether the 'life' it 'enjoys' on delivery—whether measured in seconds, minutes, hours, or days—is a life as we understand it. But the more basic question is, who decides, and at what cost?

"Congress?

"The Tierneys?

"Or"—Sarah faced Mary Ann, lowering her voice—"the fifteen-year-old who must live with the consequences."

As Mary Ann gazed resolutely at the judge, Leary looked away. "A young woman," Sarah told him, "who has shown herself thoroughly capable of weighing that decision, then making it. A young woman who has had to justify herself in court, in front of millions, as no mother—adult or minor—ever has."

Slowly, Sarah turned to Leary. "A law that denies her right to decide is irrational.

"A law that says a cesarean section is not a risk to physical health is inhumane.

"For either reason—and both—this law violates the right of choice established in *Roe v. Wade*. As, I submit, does a law which imposes the *emotional* scars of a break with her parents, the ordeal of a court proceeding, and the risk—perhaps the reality—of a life without children of her own." Pausing, Sarah spoke with quiet scorn. "For a woman, Your Honor, this involves something more than the inconvenience of altering a prom dress."

Now Leary was quiescent, eyes focused not on Sarah or Mary Ann, but his notes. Apprehensive, Sarah wondered if this was because he had written his opinion and now—faced with her arguments and Mary Ann herself—felt chastened. She waited until he looked up again, his expression blank and unrevealing.

"This law," she told him, "is a tragedy in the making. Only this court can end it."

Sarah drew a breath. "On behalf of Mary Ann Tierney," she finished, "and every minor girl in America, I ask the court to declare the Protection of Life Act unconstitutional."

Thirty-four

"U.S. Content to Watch in Tierney Case," the *New York Times* had headlined its article. So Sarah was not surprised when Thomas Fleming told Leary that the government would rest on its carefully constructed brief supporting the statute; citing a "senior adviser to the President," the *Times* had reported that the "new administration does not wish to squander any goodwill in this bitter dispute between parent and child, particularly when Judge Masters is certain to be grilled by Senate partisans of both."

Sarah's remaining question—who would argue for the fetus—was answered when Barry Saunders stepped forward. "Your Honor," he began, "Martin Tierney will speak on behalf of his grandson. But, in fairness, someone should speak for the Tierneys.

"To paraphrase Ms. Dash, this case is not about rape, *or* incest, *or* parents who are brutal and indifferent. It is not about *any* of the unseen horrors she would have us believe are commonplace." He turned, symbolically drawing in the Tierneys with a broad sweep of his hand. "It is about two parents so devoted to their daughter that they have risked her anger to protect her soul. And so—in Ms. Dash's perverted logic—their act of love becomes yet *another* reason why no *other* parents should be allowed to invoke this statute."

Apprehensive, Sarah glanced at Leary; the argument was shrewdly pitched to his sense of parental prerogatives. Saunders continued with an air of weariness. "Of course Mary Ann is angry. Of course there's a terrible strain between this young girl and her parents. Because like good parents everywhere, every day, they love her too much to please her.

"How many of us, as parents, have had an angry son or daughter slam a bedroom door in our face? How many of us have endured those terrible words—*'I hate you'*—from the person we'd give our life for? How many of us live for the day when our teenager becomes an adult, and a parent, with the wisdom to say, *'I never understood how much you really loved me'*?"

Mary Ann, Sarah noticed, averted her eyes from Margaret Tierney. "As parents," Saunders continued, "we pray for the gumption to protect our children from themselves, to place their best interests above the transient ease of capitulating to some passing but dangerous desire. We hold fast to the highest duty of parents: to deliver our child to adulthood whole—in mind, in body, and in spirit.

"But *never* have I seen two parents as brave as *these*.

"Faced with the scrutiny of millions, and an attack on their motives more cruel and twisted than their worst nightmares could anticipate, their love has endured. And today they express that love in its purest form: *'No.'*

"They do not want to. They wish they didn't have to. Their deepest wish is to somehow turn back time, to be as they were on Mary Ann's fifteenth birthday. But that is not their fate as parents—*this* is. And so they come before the court and say, 'Help us deliver our daughter to adulthood whole.'"

Stepping back, Saunders stood beside Tierney. "This man and woman know their daughter better than Sarah Dash ever can. If *they* say that this abortion will damage her more surely than childbirth ever could, believe them. Do *not,* Your Honor, make these best of parents the basis for depriving *other* loving parents of their rights."

They were making her the issue, Sarah saw—the feminist lawyer who had come between the Tierneys and their daughter. But more disturbing to Sarah was the look which passed between Leary and Martin Tierney, the compassion of one father for another.

At the podium, Tierney fished out reading glasses, then fumbled with his notes, nervous gestures that even Sarah found humanizing. Fearful that Saunders's florid but effective speech had already swayed the judge, she braced for more attacks.

"In my daughter's name," Tierney began, "Ms. Dash advances an implicit but chilling goal: abortion at *any* time, for *any* reason, if *any* part of the child remains inside the mother."

It was so distorted that Sarah had to stifle the urge to protest. "I say 'Ms. Dash,'" Tierney continued in a voice thick with emotion, "because I cannot believe that this is the considered wish of my fifteen-year-old daughter. More than any impact on the law, *she* is our deepest concern. But because this arises in the context of law, I first must speak of law."

With an abruptness that Sarah found unnerving—and, she thought, must have always daunted Mary Ann—Tierney the loving father became the cool and methodical debater. "Under *Roe* and its progeny," he continued, "Congress has the power to regulate, and even forbid, the abortion of a viable unborn life. The *only* restraint on this power is that any restriction not place at risk the mother's life or health.

"The Protection of Life Act does *not* narrow the law—it merely codifies it. It allows abortion if there is a 'substantial risk to the minor's life or *physical* health.' And if her *parents* do not acknowledge such a risk, a *court* can authorize abortion on that basis.

"So what is Ms. Dash's argument? That a risk need not be *substantial,* or even *tangible.* That parents have no business meddling in these questions. That *any* law which provides otherwise violates the right of an adolescent to settle these matters alone."

With each use of her name, Sarah bridled at Tierney's pretense that she, not Mary Ann, was petitioning the court. Turning to Sarah, Tierney continued. "As she has so thoroughly brought to light, there is no way to quantify our agony as parents, or our fears for Mary Ann. We know far better than Sarah Dash the pain of infertility. But to make a one or two percent risk of infertility grounds for an abortion means abortion on demand: there will always be some doctor, somewhere, willing to shrug his shoulders and say, 'One percent? I guess so.'

"But even *that* loophole," Tierney continued, "does not satisfy Ms. Dash. To her mind, any statute which does not specify 'mental health' as grounds for abortion is not merely unconstitutional—it is cruel."

Tierney's voice hardened. "What is cruel, Your Honor, is to sanction this barbaric procedure—this infanticide by dismemberment—any time that a doctor declares that motherhood will damage a minor's emotional well-being.

"According to whom? Measured by what? One percent?" Tierney's voice became soft again. "And while mother and doctor decide his fate, the unborn child awaits their judgment, with no one to protect him."

Despite her anger, Sarah felt with dismay how skillful Tierney was: by making Sarah the target, then stretching her arguments to their breaking point, he distracted Leary from Mary Ann's dilemma. "Do I exaggerate?" Tierney asked rhetorically. "Then consider this case.

"The one likelihood Ms. Dash can point to is that our grandson will lack a cerebral cortex, and even *that* is less than certain. But there is no case, anywhere, which allows us to murder a viable fetus because it may not live.

"Not only God's laws, but the laws of science, argue against such arrogance.

"Every day, new procedures save the lives and health of fetuses who once were hopeless. Every month, medicine lowers the age at which a premature child can live outside the womb. Every year, the march of science confirms God's love for the unborn.

"By acting to protect our grandson, we also protect *them*—and our daughter." Pausing, Tierney shook his head in sorrow. "If, someday, some young woman must look in the mirror, and wonder how many adoptable babies have been sacrificed on the altar of her 'mental health,' we do not want that woman to be Mary Ann.

"She is *our* daughter, and *we* know her better than anyone. And Ms. Dash summons in our place a phantom army of rapist fathers, alcoholic mothers, and brutal siblings."

At this, Leary raised his eyebrows in seeming challenge. Resolute, Tierney told him, "I do not deny these tragedies exist. Nor can *Ms. Dash* deny the reality of many more loving parents. Do not—I implore you—deny *their* right to act upon that love at the most critical moment of a daughter's life."

Leary's eyebrows lowered, replaced by his former look of empathy. "Nothing in *our* daughter's life," Tierney finished quietly, "tells us that she can murder our grandson without killing her own soul. And God help her if the doctor's scissors pierce a normal brain."

Next to Sarah, Mary Ann closed her eyes. In the silent courtroom, Martin Tierney bowed his head. "God help her," he repeated with prayerful softness. "Because Sarah Dash cannot help her then. Nor, I fear, can we."

Thirty-five

Kerry Kilcannon was picking up the telephone when his secretary appeared in the door to the Oval Office. "Clayton just buzzed me, Mr. President. The judge is announcing his decision."

Kerry put down the phone. "Where are they?" he asked.

"The small conference room."

Kerry hurried through the corridors, creating the stir of excitement—raised heads, faces gazing out from offices—that now attended his smallest movement. Entering the conference room, Kerry found Clayton Slade, Adam Shaw, and Kit Pace watching a television placed on the lacquered table. On the screen, Patrick Leary was taking the bench.

"Any bets?" Kerry asked.

"One," Kit answered. "The ratings will be the highest since the O.J. verdict, and half the country will go nuts."

"Which half?"

"The pro-choicers," Clayton opined. "This judge isn't dumping on Mom and Dad."

That was right, Kerry guessed. He had begun as a lawyer, prosecuting tough domestic violence cases, and had developed an unerring knack for reading both judges and juries; his long-distance sense of Patrick Leary was one of patrimony, a reflexive belief in the wisdom of fathers. "Just as well," Adam observed. "For us, the less controversy, the better."

Kerry sat beside Kit. The group fell silent; across the country, he supposed, similar scenes were occurring—clusters of people who, their emotions aroused by the trial, now awaited its resolution. Kerry's own tension surprised him.

"This case," Patrick Leary began, "confronts the court with painful choices . . ."

· · ·

For once, Sarah thought, Leary seemed daunted by his power to change lives; he did not preen, and his voice was dry and scratchy. Taut, Sarah felt Mary Ann's fingers slip into hers.

Across from them, Martin Tierney watched the judge with a rigid intensity. However complex his motives, Sarah guessed, for Tierney this moment had a stark simplicity—life or death for his grandson. Her fingers tightened around Mary Ann's.

"In the Protection of Life Act," Leary continued, "Congress faced the difficult task of balancing our interest in protecting unborn life against the right of the mother to protect her own life and physical health.

"To this delicate equation they added a separate but central concern: fostering our societal interest in parental involvement . . ."

Sarah did not like the sound of this; Leary's framing of the issues sounded too deferential to Congress, too sympathetic to the Tierneys. Reading from the text, Leary paused but did not look up.

"After the deepest consideration," he announced, "this court finds the following:

"First, that the Protection of Life Act does not abridge *Roe v. Wade*.

"Second, that the potential harm to the plaintiff does not involve a 'substantial risk' to 'life or physical health' . . ."

"No," Mary Ann whispered. "No."

"Third," the judge concluded, "that Martin and Margaret Tierney personify the wisdom of Congress in mandating parental involvement . . ."

"Shit," Kit murmured.

Among the four of them, Clayton realized, it was the first expression of partisanship. Staring at the television, Kerry said nothing.

"It would be the height of arrogance," Leary proclaimed from the screen, "to substitute our judgment for theirs . . ."

"Boilerplate," Adam Shaw remarked. "Mom, Dad, and apple pie."

"Maybe," Clayton answered. "But they'll question Caroline about every line, as if it were chiseled in marble." Turning to Kit, he added, "We'll need some boilerplate of our own."

"The 'rule of law'?" she answered sardonically. "Or does the President, like all good presidents, believe in 'letting the judicial process take its course'?"

"Both," Clayton rejoined. And then he noticed that Kerry, still silent, had not taken his eyes off the screen.

PART IV

The Appeal

One

Lost in memory, Judge Caroline Masters gazed unseeing at the briefing book in front of her.

Chad Palmer had kept his word: in three days, her confirmation hearings would begin, and there was still much preparation to complete. But her sister's call had taken her back to the moment, twenty-seven years before, when she had placed her infant daughter in the arms of Betty's husband . . .

"They've been here," Betty had reported that morning. "The FBI."

Her sister's voice, bitter and accusatory, held an undertone of paranoia. The theme of Betty's life was dispossession—the death of her own mother; their stern father's marriage to Nicole Desalliers, the French-Jewish interloper; his preference for their daughter Caroline, bright from infancy and as dark and exotic as Betty was pallid; Betty's inability to have children of her own. From the moment she became Brett's mother, Betty had feared that Caroline would somehow reclaim the girl for herself. That this badly misread the stern tenets to which Caroline held herself was indicative of Betty's inner landscape: to her, Caroline was the embodiment of everything she feared.

"Of course they came to see you," Caroline said with a trace of irony. "Besides my niece, you're my only living relative."

"I expected some of this, Caroline. But I don't like the government crawling all over our personal lives. Let alone the strangers who've been poking around town." Her sister paused. "There must still be people at the college who remember when Larry brought her home . . ."

"They don't know about *me*," Caroline interposed. "And *I'm* who all this is about. I doubt the FBI is heartless enough to inform Brett for no reason that she's adopted—or that, in itself, her adoption is of any interest to anyone. Although why you choose to deceive her on *that* point escapes me."

Stiffly, Betty responded, "We wanted her to be secure."

No, Caroline thought with a certain pity, *you wanted someone of your own.* "Satisfy my curiosity," she said. "Precisely what *did* our father do about a birth certificate?"

Betty hesitated. "There was a new one issued. On Martha's Vineyard."

"With you and Larry as the birth parents, of course."

"Yes."

"Then you are." Caroline felt her irritation yield to compassion. "I'm sorry about your visitors, Betty. But the hearings will be over soon, and so will this . . ."

But her sister's call had touched wounds which had never quite healed and, Caroline knew, never would.

She looked about her chambers at the trappings of the life she had built: the twenty-foot vaulted ceiling, the stained-glass windows, the elaborately carved marble fireplace. More fundamental were the bound volumes of her legal opinions, carefully crafted and closely reasoned—the best work of Caroline's heart and intellect.

She had not thought to make this bargain, a daughter for a life preserved in law books. But with all the rigor of an honest mind, she felt her life a worthy one. And if she became Chief Justice . . .

With this, she returned to the briefing book, just before Judge Blair Montgomery appeared.

By now, even her mentor's familiar knock, tentative and courteous, evoked fond feelings. When he entered, Caroline looked up from the binder, and smiled.

"Care to quiz me?" she asked. "I've never quite grasped patent law."

Blair smiled in return. "Who does? Except, I keep hoping, at least one of my clerks."

Caroline waved him to a chair. "Then perhaps you can distract me for a minute."

As Blair slowly sat, she examined him; she had begun to accept that she might be moving on, and to hold small moments in her mind. Blair Montgomery was a slight, neat man with white hair and horn-rimmed glasses who, in his midseventies, seemed to be shrinking by the day. But, in Caroline's estimation, his stature was considerable: appointed by President Ford, he had served on their court for a quarter century, evolving into a staunch defender of personal liberties, lionized and vilified in equal measure.

Through it all, Blair remained unruffled, a font of kindness to those he liked. Early on, he had seen in Caroline the potential to go further yet, and had used his seniority to win her friends while sparing her his enemies—assigning her opinions where she had the chance to shine, writing the most thorny and controversial decisions himself. Only in private did he vent his deep frustration at what he viewed as their court's—and the Supreme Court's—inexorable drift to the right. He would not be troubling her today were not something troubling him.

"How resourceful," Blair inquired with some hesitance, "is your former clerk?"

He did not need to specify *which* clerk. "Sarah?" Caroline answered. "Very, as I understand she's made apparent. Why?"

"Because our friend Lane Steele has hijacked the Tierney appeal."

Surprised, Caroline paused to consider the workings of their court. "Steele's presiding over the emergency motions panel this month?"

"He is." Blair's voice was quiet with disgust. "Ms. Dash moved his panel to expedite the appeal—with the Tierney girl over six months pregnant, she had no choice. Steele generously granted the motion to expedite the appeal, then assigned it to himself."

Caroline felt sympathy for Sarah—to have been forced to file her motion before Steele was the worst imaginable luck. "He'll need an ally," Caroline noted. "Who else is on the panel?"

Blair scowled. "Klopfer. And Dunnett. The only question is whether Dunnett has the guts to dissent."

Blair was right, Caroline knew at once: a hard-line social conservative, Carl Klopfer was the former attorney general of Oregon, chiefly noted for his crusade to ban "gay literature" from the state's public libraries. "For Steele," she agreed, "Klopfer's a lock. He'll be agitating to write the opinion."

"Not a chance. Our court will express its considered wisdom in yet another jeremiad by Lane Steele." Blair shook his head in frustration. "He's running for the Supremes himself, Caroline. He won't pass up the chance to ingratiate himself with the Senate by transforming Pat Leary's shallow reasoning and meager prose, and proclaiming the Protection of Life Act the greatest social document since *The Federalist Papers*."

Caroline gave him a thin smile. "Maybe it is, Blair. I've done my damnedest not to think about it."

For an instant Blair looked curious, then softened his tone. "You're on the spot, I know—this case is dynamite, politically. I don't suppose you have a glimmer of what's running through Ms. Dash's mind."

"None. I never even watched the trial. Did you?"

"Enough of it. Judge Patrick Leary in *Father Knows Best*. And now Steele." Blair folded his hands, gazing at the briefing books on Caroline's desk. Almost shyly, he added, "Sarah Dash has a time problem—her client could deliver a child at any moment, with whatever risks that may involve. Once Steele shoots her down, she can petition our full court for a rehearing, taking up a couple more precious weeks. Or she can go straight to the Supreme Court. That's not an easy call."

All at once, Caroline perceived her friend's unstated purpose. She had no doubt that Blair was curious about the potential workings of Sarah Dash's mind, nor that he sympathized with Mary Ann Tierney and was quietly furious about the course of her appeal. But he was also warning Caroline. Sarah might seek to persuade a majority of the twenty-one active judges to grant her a rehearing en banc—and, if not, Blair might initiate such an effort himself. In either case, Caroline must consider her course of action.

"If I were Sarah," Caroline answered, "I'd petition for rehearing. But that would take nerve."

Blair smiled faintly. "Yes," he agreed. "It would."

Two

Entering the Court of Appeals, Sarah tried to focus on her argument.

The corridors were jammed with cameras and reporters. Mary Ann remained at Sarah's apartment, sluggish, despondent, and bloated by the fetus which—despite its probable impairments—kept growing inside her. That she persisted in this appeal was a tribute to her resolve and, as important, a reflection of her fears. But Sarah had discouraged the listless girl from appearing: the ripeness of her pregnancy might unsettle the panel, and Judge Lane Steele would surely dishearten her still more.

Ignoring the reporters shouting to her, Sarah made her way toward Courtroom Two. On some other day, she would have stopped to savor her return, for she had always believed this one of the most beautiful public buildings in America. With its grand marble columns and vaulted ceilings adorned with sculpted cherubs, intricate mosaics, and classic tracing, its design evoked a Renaissance palazzo, a feeling enhanced by the meticulous craftsmanship of Italian artisans and the opulence of its materials—a rich variety of marbles, mahogany, redwood, bronze, colored venetian glass, and bright porcelain tiles.

Sarah's mentor, Caroline Masters, had pointed out each feature. For Caroline, a student of history and a connoisseur of architecture, this grandeur and exuberance expressed the pride and optimism of America on the cusp of the last century. A bit grand, Caroline had wryly added, for twenty-one divided and fractious judges at the beginning of the next. The Ninth Circuit was beset by factions, feuds, and rivalries, that between Blair Montgomery and Lane Steele being the most notorious, and the most rooted in principle. That was Sarah's problem now.

When she entered the courtroom, Fleming, Saunders, and Tierney were already there. But there were none of the perfunctory greetings that routinely attended such a moment—the divisions between Sarah and her adversaries were too visceral. Remote and drawn, Martin Tierney bore the deepest wounds of all: since Patrick Leary's decision, Mary Ann refused to see him.

Sitting at the appellant's table, Sarah ignored the phalanx of reporters jammed in the benches to the rear. Courtroom Two was a small gem: the mahogany bench was inlaid with red numidian marble, and the marble walls featured intricate designs and an ornate gold clock. But today the mass of bodies and their cacophony made it feel stifling. Sarah tried to focus on the index cards she had taped to a manila folder, the outline of her argument; for the last time, she reviewed the carefully wrought chain of reasoning which, she hoped, might compete in the other judges' minds with Steele's stringent logic.

"All rise," the courtroom deputy announced.

As grim as inquisitors judging a conspiracy of heretics, the three jurists emerged from chambers and took their seats, with Lane Steele in the center, flanked by Klopfer, stolid and sturdy, and Joseph Dunnett, an African American with round, inscrutable features. When Steele looked up at last, it was with a glint over his half-glasses which Sarah recognized very well—the pleasure of a man who, all too often, expressed his emotional needs by asserting his intellectual superiority.

"Counselor," he said in a peremptory tone. "You may begin."

With trepidation and resolve, Sarah stepped to the podium.

Sarah had fifteen minutes to open. But she was still arranging her notes when Steele's voice cracked the silence like a whip.

"Isn't it true, Ms. Dash, that the Supreme Court in *Casey* held that Congress can forbid postviability abortion?"

Startled, Sarah looked up; though she expected heavy questioning, the usual protocol would allow her at least to commence her argument. "Except," she amended, "where the mother's life or health is at risk."

"Isn't that precisely what this statute provides?"

"Yes, but . . ."

"Indeed, *this* statute is more liberal than that." Steele was leaning forward now, eyes keen, body taut, voice hectoring. "*This* statute allows parents, not just the courts, to approve abortion if a doctor believes their child's health is at risk."

"It also allows parents to *forbid* abortion," Sarah answered. "Regardless of the minor's life or health."

"Then she can go to court," Steele snapped. "The parental consent provision simply gives her an additional path to an abortion. Indeed, couldn't we delete it altogether, and *still* have a law consistent with the right to *regulate* abortion found in *Roe* and *Casey*?"

Apprehensive, Sarah wondered whether Steele would permit her any argument at all. "If a teenage girl's only recourse," she rejoined, "is to an abusive parent or a distant court, many *will* place their lives or health at risk . . ."

"Isn't that their *'choice,'* counsel?"

Steele's tone was ironic, and he gave the word "choice" a disdainful weight. Sarah's only choice, she abruptly decided, was to give herself freer rein. "Hardly," she shot back. "A fifteen-year-old doesn't 'choose' to have a brutal father. A fourteen-year-old doesn't 'choose' whether she possesses the courage to go to court. To pretend that these are adults is incorrect . . ."

"Precisely," Steele interjected with muted triumph. "So why are they fit to decide whether to abort a viable fetus?"

"Because they are facing a threat to *themselves,* determined by a doctor. They are *not* free to abort for any reason . . ."

"Really? By what higher standard do we judge an amorphous claim of risk to emotional health?" Steele held up his hand, foreclosing Sarah's answer. "Let me read you the pertinent language from *Casey,* quote, *'subsequent to viability, the state can regulate, and even proscribe, abortion except where it is necessary, in appro-priate* medical *judgment, for the preservation of the life and health of the mother,'* unquote.

"That reads *'medical* judgment' doesn't it—not psychological judgment."

Inhaling slowly, Sarah steadied herself. "Psychiatrists are doctors, Your Honor, and physical and emotional health are often medically related." Quickly, she turned her attention to Carl Klopfer. "The phrase 'medical judgment' also implies that the judgment should be a doctor's, not a court's or parent's . . ."

Brow furrowed, Klopfer seemed to ponder this. "Doctors can always enlighten us," Steele interjected. "Judge Leary had the benefit of ample medical advice. As did the Tierneys."

It was now apparent that Steele had no intention of permitting Sarah to persuade anyone. "The Tierneys' judgment was moral," she rejoined, "not medical. That's why they've intervened against their daughter. And by requiring a 'substantial medical risk' to physical health, this law bars a doctor from protecting Mary Ann Tierney against a measurable risk of infertility . . ."

"By *what* measure?" Now Steele's voice was etched with contempt. "Let's define *your* standard.

"If some doctor finds a one percent chance of infertility, he can abort a fetus moments from birth.

"If a doctor believes terminating a healthy eight-month-old fetus will brighten a mother's mental outlook, he may.

"If his youthful patient finds some prospective 'abnormality' distressing, then the fetus is expendable."

"No," Sarah protested. "That's not—"

"*No?*" Steele persisted in a relentless tone. "Doesn't your argument come down to this: that *any* minor can abort *any* viable fetus if she finds her pregnancy upsetting?"

Desperate, Sarah glanced at the others. But Klopfer was watching Steele as though deferring to his better, and Dunnett remained expressionless. "You've yet to hear my argument," she told Steele. "With respect, it's not the argument you've invented for me . . ."

"Really." Nettled, Steele overrode her, voice tight with anger. "Then the fact that I extrapolated it from your brief must betray my waning powers of perception." Abruptly, he seemed to catch himself, choosing a more reasonable tone. "Does it occur to you, Ms. Dash, that having sex sometimes involves consequences—even hard ones? Or is the purpose of this court to serve as a *very* belated morning-after pill?"

With this, Joseph Dunnett intervened at last. "In the course of answering," he told Sarah pleasantly, "you might offer up those arguments you've yet to make. You only have five minutes remaining."

Turning, Sarah addressed herself to Dunnett. "Thank you, Your Honor. The central point is this: a law which forbids Mary Ann Tierney to protect herself from a classical C-section by aborting a fatally impaired fetus violates *Roe v. Wade*—"

"Are you quite certain," Steele interrupted, "that the fetus *is* impaired?"

Once more, Sarah prepared herself to respond. Then she noticed Carl Klopfer, his silent nod seconding Steele's question, and knew that she had lost.

Three

On the day of the Tierney argument, Judge Caroline Clark Masters made her first appearance before the Senate Committee on the Judiciary.

The Old Senate Caucus Room was airy, ornate, redolent of history and past confrontations between prior nominees and this committee. Caroline sat at the witness table, facing a single row of eighteen senators who looked down on her from a raised bench. Crowded behind her were the media; her White House support team; a few members of the public; and—seated in the first row, to reaffirm her as a heterosexual—Jackson Watts.

By mutual agreement, Betty and Larry had not come, nor had Brett, the unwitting source of their shared anxiety. Caroline found her sister's absence a further relief, one less thing to worry about; at this, the climactic moment of her career, Chad Palmer and his colleagues impelled her full attention.

Dressed in a severe blue suit, she mustered her characteristic air of poise which, today, masked an apprehension unrelieved by her depth of preparation. The White House had briefed her on each senator, and she knew their predilections well. Palmer would be neutral but helpful; Vic Coletti, sitting to Palmer's immediate left, would ask prescripted questions directed to her strengths; to Palmer's right, Paul Harshman fixed her with a gelid stare which confirmed him as her chief antagonist. Sitting beside Caroline, the senior senator from California, Betsy Shapiro, spoke her last graceful words of introduction.

After Caroline testified, a parade of favorable witnesses, agreed upon between Senator Palmer and the White House, would endorse Caroline's acumen and humanity. But none of them would matter unless Caroline, in the three days set for her appearance, survived other senators' probing for reasons to oppose her.

The stakes for Palmer, she well knew, were almost as high. He had accelerated the hearings over Gage's objections, and worked with the President to protect Caroline's secret from discovery. The first sin had riled many of his colleagues; the second—if discovered—might derail his own ambitions to be President. Yet Palmer appeared outwardly serene: with his chiseled film-star features, his bright blond hair barely touched by gray, he seemed perfect for the cameras poised to broadcast the proceedings. And despite the worries he must have, these hearings—as Clayton Slade had pointed out—gave Palmer an opportunity to impress himself on the press and the public as a potential President of the United States, more statesmanlike than the partisan Macdonald Gage. If in the process he helped Caroline become Chief Justice, then both might be well served.

The room was quiet with tense expectancy. Quickly turning, Caroline shared a fleeting look with Jackson. Chairman Palmer glanced at the Democrats to his left, his fellow Republicans to his right, then smiled down at Caroline.

"Do you have a statement, Judge Masters?"

The polite question had a wry undertone: in front of Caroline were five typewritten pages, words of confidence mixed with the appropriate humility, and carefully vetted for distribution to the press.

"I do," Caroline replied in a calm, clear voice, and her hearings were under way.

Her statement was followed by Palmer's own, a reasoned disquisition regarding the Senate's duty of inquiry and the standards expected of a Chief Justice.

This, too, was theater, designed to impress their larger audience while reassuring his colleagues that Palmer would not passively acquiesce to Caroline's confirmation. And for the next several hours, Palmer and Caroline played a foreordained game of thrust and parry, where Chad attempted to pin her down to positions, and Caroline politely but eloquently pleaded a jurist's obligation to maintain an open mind.

This reached its climax when Palmer grilled her regarding the jurisprudence of abortion: watching, Paul Harshman registered his frustration through scowls and shakes of the head which Caroline and Palmer pretended not to notice.

"It seems," Palmer observed at last, "that you're not inclined to repeal *Roe v. Wade*. However much you may doubt its reasoning."

Caroline paused, choosing her words with care. "I do believe, Senator Palmer, that there's a right to privacy. Unless judges are careful not to substitute their prejudice for precedent, law descends from principle to bias. With that in mind, I must await the particular cases which come before me."

Palmer's look of faint amusement seemed to acknowledge that, however hard he tried, she was playing her part as written. "Very well," he said briskly, "let's turn to cameras in the courtroom.

"In the Carelli case, you allowed gavel-to-gavel coverage on CNN. Yet many believe that television contributed to the circus atmosphere of the O. J. Simpson trial. Where do you stand now?"

"Pro," Caroline answered promptly. "Properly regulated, televised trials educate the public. For example, its response to the Carelli trial led to the admission of prior rapes as evidence of the accused's predisposition to commit the rape in question. Which, in turn, allows us to protect future victims."

This, too, was expected: Palmer's question enabled Caroline to stress her concern with law enforcement, while addressing a subject important to many women. "But what about the Tierney case?" Palmer asked.

Caroline shook her head. "Absolutely not," she said bluntly. "The privacy of a minor trumps television. Whatever educational value it may have is far outweighed by the sheer cruelty of dissecting this girl and her family for the sake of our enlightenment—or entertainment."

At this, Paul Harshman frowned again: in his moral code, Caroline suspected, Mary Ann Tierney deserved whatever shame accrued to her, and Caroline's expression of sympathy might suggest a pro-abortion bias. Glancing at Harshman, Chad Palmer inquired, "But if you were Chief Justice, Judge Masters, would you advocate television in the Supreme Court?"

Caroline nodded. "There, I would. Generally, the more the public knows about how our institutions work, the better. There's great misunderstanding of how the Court makes its decisions. It's time to let the sunshine in."

Of course, Caroline told herself wryly, if the sunshine in the Tierney case extended all the way to the private maneuvering of her own court, the public would see how human judges really are. But Palmer nodded his satisfaction. "I agree," he said amicably. "Would you also agree that it's time for lunch?"

Caroline smiled. "I'm as hungry, Senator Palmer, as you want me to be."

Despite the ripple of laughter that followed, Paul Harshman did not smile.

It was midafternoon before Harshman could commence his questioning.

From the beginning his tone was cold. "Senator Palmer, I must say, questioned you with great courtesy. But I'm not satisfied with your responses regarding the rights of the unborn."

He stopped, his silence demanding a comment from Caroline. "I regret that," she said simply. "I thought we were discussing the right to privacy."

Arms folded, Harshman craned his neck to peer down at her. "Do you believe, Judge Masters, that the unborn have a right to life?"

Unbidden, a thought leaped to Caroline's mind: *I believed my daughter did.* The nearness of Brett to her consciousness, and conscience, evidenced a fear she could not suppress. Pausing, Caroline retrieved the answer she had rehearsed.

"According to *Roe* and *Casey*," she told Harshman, "they do. Once the fetus is viable, Congress can regulate—or ban—abortion. Subject only to the woman's life or health."

Harshman held up a hand. "'Health' can mean something," he said cuttingly, "or anything the pro-abortionists want it to mean. What does it mean to you?"

They were dangerously close to the Tierney case. "I've not had to decide the question," Caroline answered. "And ethically, I can't prejudge it . . ."

"Come now, Judge Masters. Under the Constitution, does 'health' include *mental* health?"

Caroline could almost feel the gaze of Clayton Slade, watching her on C-SPAN. Carefully, she formed her answer. "In a footnote to *Doe v. Bolton,* a companion case to *Roe,* the Court suggested that a woman's mental health is a factor to be considered. But in the three decades since, the Court has never amplified this point—or even addressed it. Which, to me, makes it an open question."

Harshman's eyes narrowed in frustration. "Do you support a constitutional amendment to ban abortion?"

Do you think I'm fool enough, Caroline wanted to say, *to answer* that *one?* "I support the right of the people, through their representatives, to amend the Constitution. That's how women got the right to vote . . ."

"But *do* you support an amendment protecting life?"

"That's a political question, Senator, not a legal one. As a judge, my job is to follow the Constitution—including any amendments. Expressing a personal bias on abortion is antithetical to that."

"Do you believe," Harshman persisted in an angry tone, "that parents have the right to consent to the abortion of their minor daughter? Or to refuse consent?"

This was, unambiguously, an effort to commit her on the Tierney case. "The Supreme Court says they do," Caroline answered. "The Court has consistently upheld a parent's right to consent to a previability abortion. Provided that a minor *without* consent then has the right to persuade a court that she's mature enough to decide for herself, or that an abortion is otherwise in her best interests—"

"Loopholes," Harshman interjected, "which judges routinely use to rubber-stamp a child's abortion regardless of what her parents say. Are *you* saying *that's* sufficient to protect life?"

Caroline looked at him evenly. "I'm saying it's the law . . ."

"But you concede, Judge Masters, that Congress has the right to protect a fetus *after* viability. Does Congress *still* have to provide these gaping loopholes for any minor child who wants to abort a viable fetus?"

Caroline smiled. "The outside world has a way of intruding, Senator—even for those of us preoccupied with this hearing. It's my understanding that, even as we speak, a panel of my colleagues is sitting to determine the constitutionality of the Protection of Life Act.

"The Tierney case may well come before the Supreme Court. Moreover, I think it unseemly to give my three colleagues on the Ninth Circuit advice they've neither asked for nor require."

Thwarted, Harshman leaned back, conferring with a slim, blond-haired woman Caroline presumed to be his aide. He nodded to her, then turned to Caroline again. "The questions aren't *that* novel, Judge Masters. In *Stenberg v. Carhart,* the Supreme Court struck down a state law barring partial-birth abortion of viable fetuses. Do you agree with that?"

Caroline's voice took on a slight edge. "Whether I agree or disagree doesn't matter. The Supreme Court has already ruled."

Harshman bored in, jabbing the lectern with his finger. "But do *you* believe *those* rulings mean that the Protection of Life Act must also be struck down?"

"No," Caroline answered bluntly. "The Nebraska law in *Stenberg* made no allowance for a mother's health, and so the Court found that it unduly burdened the right to an abortion established in *Roe* and affirmed in *Casey*—for abortions *before* viability as well as after. In addition, Nebraska purported only to ban *certain* late-term procedures but—in the Court's view—defined them so vaguely that a doctor might not know he was performing a criminal act.

"The Protection of Life Act responds to *Stenberg*—one might think of it as the second generation of such laws—and applies to *all* postviability abortions, and *only* postviability abortions. No doctor can be confused by *that*." Pausing, she concluded mildly, "So the Tierney case presents different questions. To which, as I've already said, I cannot speak."

Silent, Chad Palmer turned to Harshman. *She's beaten you,* Palmer's expression seemed to say. *Quit making us look like zealots.*

Harshman said, "Ten years ago, Judge Masters, you ran for election as a state court judge—correct?"

At once, Caroline discerned his intentions. Calmly, she answered, "Yes."

"And isn't it also correct that you were supported by the Harvey Milk Democratic Club, a group of gays and *lesbians*?"

His deliberate emphasis on the final word, Caroline reflected, was remarkably unsubtle. "That's true." Fleetingly, she smiled. "As well as by the Chamber of Commerce and, I believe, the Fraternal Order of Police . . ."

"Do you support the lesbian lifestyle, Judge Masters?"

Caroline paused again, this time to suppress her anger. "My role as a judge isn't to support 'lifestyles,' Senator. And the term 'lesbian lifestyle' has no more meaning to me than 'police lifestyle.'

"My job is to be fair, which is all I ever promised anyone. The fact that so many diverse groups supported me suggests that I was."

Harshman cocked his head. "You have no children, correct?"

The directness of the question startled her. *Does he know?* Caroline wondered. Quickly, she groped for an innocuous evasion. "I've never been married, Senator."

Tense, Caroline awaited the next fateful question, or perhaps Harshman brandishing an ancient birth certificate. Instead, he asked, "Then how can you appreciate the special problems of parents?"

Through an act of will, Caroline restrained herself from telegraphing her relief. "You and I," she answered, "aren't people of color. But I hate to think that the only experiences we can imagine, or care about, are those we share in common."

This time it was Harshman who paused; Caroline's response, a veiled jab at Harshman's opposition to affirmative action and third-world immigration, left him visibly annoyed. He checked his notes and, bristling with renewed aggressiveness, leaned forward again.

"Do you support, Judge Masters, the right of all Americans to keep and bear arms?"

No, Caroline wanted to answer, *I support the right of all Americans to keep and arm bears.* Stifling her dislike, she answered, "I believe those rights are protected by the Second Amendment . . ."

"But do you mean to respect those rights, Judge Masters? Or to narrow them?"

It was time to stop trimming, Caroline thought. "What I have very little respect for," she answered, "is extremism. I question those advocates of gun control who pretend that the Second Amendment doesn't exist. I also question those who say that a two-hundred-year-old amendment, referring to a 'well-regulated militia,' means that we can never regulate cop-killer bullets, cheap handguns, or the assault weapons too often used to slaughter children."

Harshman stiffened. "The *problem* isn't guns—it's the murderer who uses them. Once we start chipping away at the Second Amendment, where would you draw the line?"

Guns don't kill people, Caroline thought to herself, *slingshots do. And lesbians.* She cautioned herself to conceal her contempt, as well as her sheer bemusement that any state could choose this humorless and angry man to represent them. "Drawing lines," she answered, "is the job of Congress—"

"And reviewing those lines," Harshman interrupted, "will be *your* job. *If* you're so fortunate to be confirmed."

"True," Caroline answered mildly. "I simply note that the right to life does not end at birth. *And* that—just as for viable fetuses—Congress may have the right to protect the 'born' from psychopaths who acquire guns at will, or weapons the founding fathers never dreamed of . . ."

From behind her came a sudden spattering of applause. As Senator Palmer banged the gavel, Harshman flushed, reminding Caroline to leave him with his dignity intact. "You raise an important question," she added in a more deferential tone, "the particulars of which I can't prejudge. In the case of any law, the Court's duty is to scrutinize with care its effect on Second Amendment rights."

But Harshman did not seem mollified. Caroline felt herself, as tired as she now was, hovering on the edge of a misstep which might enrage him further. Glancing at Palmer, she lightly touched her ear.

Noting this, Palmer turned to Harshman. "Excuse me," he inquired pleasantly, "the Chair is wondering how much more you have for Judge Masters."

In obvious anger, Harshman spun on Palmer. "Are you trying to cut me off, Senator?"

The accusation did not, in Palmer, occasion a change of tone, or even expression. "Not at all. I'm just asking how much time you need to finish."

"Hours," Harshman snapped. "Maybe days. Judge Masters wants *us* to make *her* the leader of the highest court in the land. Yet her studied evasions raise so many unanswered questions that I can't predict in good conscience *when* I'll be through."

"In that case," Palmer suggested with an unruffled air, "why don't we adjourn until tomorrow at ten, out of courtesy to the witness. Seeing how it's already past four-thirty."

Harshman glared at him, resentful and plainly anxious to continue. "That's only fair, Mr. Chairman," Vic Coletti smoothly interjected. "It's been a long day for all of us."

The passive subject of this tense exchange, Caroline could only watch, wondering whether it might be better to go on, and what Paul Harshman—given the night to work and reflect—might present her with tomorrow.

"Fine," Harshman told his colleagues with a sudden indifference, and the first day of hearings was over.

Four

At nine o'clock the next morning, a messenger brought the panel's opinion to Sarah's office.

Sarah flipped to the last page and, with more anger than surprise, saw *"Judgment Affirmed."* The opinion was unanimous.

Composing herself, Sarah reviewed the decision more carefully.

Steele's language was cool, surgical, and crafted to survive challenge. Late-term abortion, Steele ruled, is not protected by *Roe* absent a substantial threat to physical health, which requires more than the mere risk of infertility. "Mental health" is a code word for abortion on demand. And the parental consent provision has the benign effect of promoting family consultation; only when a family cannot agree need a court determine whether a minor can abort a viable fetus. Only the final paragraph was harsh:

"It makes no sense," Steele wrote, *"to invalidate an act of Congress because a fifteen-year-old girl, having displayed the lack of mature judgment necessary to become pregnant, rejects the guidance of two exemplary parents because her own child may turn out to be—according to her latest exercise of judgment—unsatisfactory.*

"If that were our standard, we would have no standards at all."

Heartsick for Mary Ann, Sarah wondered how she would receive this, and how much more the girl could take.

Mace Taylor was sampling the coffee in Macdonald Gage's office when an aide delivered a fax with a cover page headed *"From the office of Judge Lane Steele."*

Gage felt a deep but quiet pleasure, the flow of events beginning to conform to his design. "It's Steele's decision," Gage told Taylor wryly. "His valentine to Caroline Masters."

Taylor did not smile. "Is it good? Saunders told me Steele reamed the girl's lawyer."

Intent, Gage read without looking up. Reaching the end, he murmured, "We'd better make sure Harshman gets this. He's been waiting to put Judge Masters in a vise."

At noon, Paul Harshman entered the third hour of his second day spent questioning Caroline Masters.

The first two hours had been a standoff. Frustrated, Harshman asked, "Are you a judicial activist, Judge Masters?"

Caroline repressed a smile: to confess to "judicial activism" would be, in Harshman's view, on a par with embracing evangelical lesbianism. "No," she answered simply.

Irritation showed in Harshman's narrowed eyes and rising voice; plainly he had expected to provoke a deeper anxiety. "No?" he repeated. "Then explain your decision in the *Oregon* case, holding that the First Amendment doesn't protect political speech."

Chad Palmer's expression became keen. "All we held," Caroline corrected, "is that *Oregon* struck a proper balance between unlimited 'free speech' for the wealthy—like giving a million dollars to a political party—and public concern that the donor is buying influence. Our court simply followed the Supreme Court's precedent in the *Missouri* case . . ."

"Which is ill-conceived," Harshman snapped, "and due to be overruled."

She had a decision to make, Caroline knew. The subtext was Chad Palmer's proposed law forbidding such contributions, bitterly opposed by those who had mortgaged themselves to interest groups—notably the Christian Commitment and the NRA—in exchange for money to finance their campaigns. "'Judicial activism,'" Caroline calmly rejoined, "would be to ignore Supreme Court precedents. Or to lobby for promotion by pledging to overrule them."

Though blandly delivered, her answer was so pointed that the spectators emitted nervous laughter, and Palmer's quick smile seemed to further stoke Harshman's outrage. "'Judicial activism,'" Caroline concluded, "treats law as the tool of one's political beliefs. I agree with you that judges should *apply* the law, not reinvent it."

Harshman flushed, stymied by a statement with which he could not quarrel. "You began your career," he said flatly, "defending accused murderers, rapists, robbers, and child molesters. Frequently you sought their acquittal on the basis of so-called police misconduct—illegal searches and the like. But most of those people were guilty, weren't they?"

Caroline smiled faintly. "I certainly hope so."

Harshman's head snapped forward, as though offended by her flippancy. "Why would you say *that*?"

"Because most of them were convicted."

There was more laughter, less apprehensive than before. "That vindicates the police," Harshman snapped, "doesn't it? And exposes your pro-criminal bias as unfounded."

Now Caroline did not smile. "The simple truth, Senator, is that most people a criminal lawyer defends *are* guilty. If most were innocent, this country would be Libya—or China. The accused in those countries *have* no rights. Which makes injustice possible."

Harshman shook his head in disgust. "That's a far cry from getting a child molester acquitted on a technicality, leaving him free to molest again. Do you remember *that* case, Judge?"

Caroline did, all too well: the face of his alleged victim, the man's stepson, had haunted her for years. "I do, Senator. The judge—a former prosecutor—concluded that the police had coached the boy so thoroughly that he could not be believed . . ."

"After you asked him to so rule."

Caroline felt tense: the most difficult aspect of a lawyer's life, and the hardest to explain, was that upholding the rights of the guilty helps prevent the conviction of the innocent. "Under the Constitution," she said, "we protect defendants against coerced confessions and fabricated evidence. Sometimes that means that we free the guilty with the innocent. I wish that we, as humans, were capable of perfection. But we're not—"

"That must be why," Harshman interrupted, "you support these endless habeas corpus petitions that keep prisoners on death row for decades."

Caroline cocked her head. "I support the death penalty, fairly applied. But in numerous cases DNA testing has proven that men awaiting execution are innocent. Typically poor, black men—often with inadequate representation." Her voice became ironic. "One lawyer was drunk throughout the trial. His finest hour was when he fell asleep.

"His innocent client came within three days of execution. And killing the innocent is murder, whether committed with an ax or by the State of Illinois . . ."

Harshman's eyebrows shot up. "Your compassion does you credit, Judge. But your devotion to prisoners' rights transcends death penalty cases. Are you familiar with *Snipes v. Garrett*?"

Of course, Caroline mentally answered. *I read it again last night, certain that you'd bring it up.* "It's a recent en banc case. Our court held that an inmate who claimed that he was beaten and sodomized should be given a chance to prove that—"

"Specifically," Harshman cut in, "you voted with Judge Blair Montgomery—a noted judicial activist. Despite a dissent by Judge Steele which correctly cited the intent of Congress to limit frivolous suits by inmates."

Caroline shifted in her chair, trying to relieve the ache in her lower back. "Anyone who knows California's prisons," she answered, "had reason to worry that Snipes *was* being abused. The majority of us shrank at turning away a semiliterate prisoner because he failed to name the right defendants on the first try . . ."

"Don't you hold these people to *any* standards, Judge? Or did being a convicted felon give him more rights than the rest of us?"

Harshman's obtuse, badgering tone had begun to fray Caroline's patience. "The man was sentenced to twenty years in prison. But that doesn't mean he deserves anything he gets there." Pausing, Caroline added softly, "Twenty years of sodomy, Senator, falls outside the sentencing guidelines."

The last remark caused Harshman's face to redden. From the body language of his colleagues, conveying a studied neutrality, Harshman was gaining no ground. Turning to Harshman, Palmer raised his eyebrows in silent inquiry.

Frowning at his notes, Harshman seemed relieved when the blond aid materialized at his shoulder, placing some papers in front of him. As she whispered, Harshman listened intently, and then, apparently revitalized, faced Caroline again.

"This morning," he informed her, "your court affirmed Judge Leary's opinion in the Tierney case, upholding the Protection of Life Act *and* the grandparents' right to protect their unborn grandson. Seems like Mary Ann Tierney's only recourse is to petition your court for an en banc rehearing—like in your Snipes case—or go to the Supreme Court. Would you agree?"

At once Caroline was on edge; Blair Montgomery had been right to warn her. "So it would seem," she answered.

A grim smile appeared on Harshman's face. "Then would you also agree, Judge Masters, that you should disqualify yourself in *any* such proceeding?"

Pausing, Caroline tried to guess where he was headed. Coolly, she inquired, "On what grounds?"

"Bias." Harshman's tone was accusatory. "Specifically, your relationship with Mary Ann Tierney's lawyer."

Caroline was taut with fury: Harshman had been careful to leave "relationship" undefined. "You refer," she responded, "to the fact that three years ago Sarah Dash served as my law clerk. Our rule is that—absent unusual circumstances—the need for recusal ends one year after the law clerk's term of service."

Once more Harshman produced a knowing smile. "Define 'unusual circumstances,' Judge Masters."

Caroline's mind flashed back to her meeting with Macdonald Gage, his elliptical reference to Sarah. "'Unusual' means just that. A familial relationship, for example, or an economic one . . ."

"Or," Harshman interjected idly, as if possibilities were only now occurring to him, "if the judge and the lawyer were romantically involved?"

Caroline forced herself to smile. "*That*," she answered, "would certainly suffice."

"What about the *appearance* of a relationship which strikes others as too close?"

What "appearance" did he mean, Caroline wondered, and how might he decide to twist it? Answering, her voice was tighter than she wished: "A judge's 'relationships,' Senator, are very often rooted in his or her professional life—law school classmates, law partners, others whom we've worked with. Including former clerks." Seeing Harshman raise his eyebrows, Caroline spoke more firmly. "But I *am* a judge, and my job is to be impartial. If I were so sentimental and weak of mind that regard for a former clerk would sway me, I'm unfit for the job.

"I've no opinion about the Tierney case. I've never watched it on television. I've never discussed it with anyone. *That's* what's required of a judge."

"So what you're saying," Harshman persisted, "is that there's no personal factors which would keep you from ruling fairly. Either on your court, or as Chief Justice."

With appalling swiftness, Caroline saw the trap into which she had fallen. If she backtracked, she would be admitting her "closeness" to Sarah and, in Harshman's reading, her sympathy for—even her collusion in—Sarah's cause. But if her answer was "yes," she would open herself to possible involvement in any en banc petition, or to becoming the potential swing vote in the Supreme Court itself—at whatever cost to her chance of confirmation. The sudden attentiveness of the other senators, particularly Palmer, betrayed that they perceived this as well.

Cautiously, Caroline ventured, "Nothing I'm aware of . . ."

"Wouldn't you be 'aware,'" Harshman asked with incredulity, "of any reason a fair-minded person might consider grounds for bias?"

Caroline squared her shoulders, "I'm aware of the facts," she said succinctly. "I'm aware that I'm unbiased. The only bias I can't account for belongs to others."

Harshman's smile became enigmatic, but his eyes were keen with pleasure. "That's all I have, Judge Masters. For now."

Five

Sarah was weighing hard choices when the chairman of Kenyon & Walker appeared in her office.

Without ceremony, John Nolan said, "I've read the Steele opinion."

Sarah was surprised; Nolan, too, must have had it messengered. "Not great," she answered.

Nolan sat down with the leisurely air of a man who intended to stay. "What Steele managed to do, Sarah, is bring out everything that's unattractive about Mary Ann's desire to abort this child. Which a good many of my partners mention with regularity."

Even on this difficult day, Nolan did not bother to feign compassion. Waiting him out, Sarah said nothing.

"How well," Nolan asked, "do you think you've served your cause?"

The question was not merely condescending, but pointed. Tired, Sarah tried to control her frayed emotions. "It's not my cause," she said evenly. "It's Mary Ann's."

"And yours. Or you wouldn't have pushed us so hard to take it. At this juncture, some mature consideration of the outcome is in order."

This nettled Sarah too much to hide it. "When there *is* an outcome, I'll consider it."

Nolan settled deeper in the chair, as though to overcome her by his sheer adamantine power. "The best lawyers," he answered, "review the endgame before they get there. I'm not referring to the partners you've antagonized, but to your impact on the pro-choice movement.

"This morning, the Ninth Circuit upheld the Protection of Life Act: it now applies to the roughly twenty percent of the country covered by the circuit. If you lose in the Supreme Court, the act will be the law for every minor in America." Nolan folded his arms, speaking with the authority his peers found so impressive. "You chose a weak case, Sarah—a girl with two respected parents, and a claim of 'physical harm' which is too thin to prevail. So you lost. If you force the Supreme Court to uphold this law, a girl with a more attractive claim will have no chance to prevail. The ruling in Tierney will be the law for everyone."

This troubled her greatly, Sarah conceded. To Nolan, she said, "I don't represent the pro-choice movement. If I drop this now, my client goes to term . . ."

"A sacrifice which prevents her from making binding precedent—at least in the forty or so states outside the Ninth Circuit's jurisdiction. Don't you have any discretion here, Sarah? Are you really going to let a fifteen-year-old invite the Supreme Court to make 'bad law' nationwide?"

Whatever else, Sarah thought, Nolan was canny and pragmatic; it might help her process of decision to hear him out. "Why do you think I'll lose, John?"

Nolan scowled at her shortsightedness. "Caroline Masters isn't confirmed yet. Without her, the Supreme Court likely splits four-four in Tierney—at *best*.

"Someone like Macdonald Gage not only knows that, but worries that Masters might vote *with* you once she's there. So he simply stalls her confirmation until the High Court's ruled on your emergency petition. As the Court stands now, they'll refuse to hear it. Or—if the pro-lifers have a majority—they'll take the case and shaft you."

Listening, Sarah recalled that Nolan had begun his career as an aide to California's then senior senator, and retained close ties to Washington: either his assessment reflected guesswork born of experience, or more concrete information regarding Macdonald Gage's intentions. "In that case," Sarah answered, "I should petition the Ninth Circuit for rehearing en banc."

Nolan's face reflected the jaded amusement of a man one jump ahead. "Explain the virtues of *that*."

"All twenty-one active judges," Sarah answered promptly, "will vote on Mary Ann's petition. Many—perhaps a majority—don't share Steele's views, and some don't like him, either.

"If eleven of twenty-one active judges vote in favor of rehearing, then eleven are selected at random to actually decide the case. Depending on the luck of the draw, I've got a chance to carry six of them. Which is all we need."

Nolan smiled. "Do your twenty-one active judges include Caroline?"

In the few hours since receiving Steele's decision, Sarah had not fully considered this. "Unless Caroline's been confirmed," she answered.

"She won't be. And you must not be answering your phone." Nolan no longer smiled. "I just watched a little of her confirmation hearing. You're playing with matches, Sarah."

"How so?"

"Your name came up." Nolan leaned forward. "Specifically, Senator Harshman asked Caroline if she'd disqualify herself based on her 'relationship' with you."

Startled, Sarah felt her skin tingle with anxiety. "Because I was her clerk?"

"Harshman left it open." Nolan's tone remained dispassionate. "When it comes to Supreme Court nominees, the Senate can be brutal. Harshman forced Caroline to deny bias, or any reason she couldn't sit in Tierney.

"Your case is growing tentacles. File for rehearing, and politically Caroline's only choice—other than recusal—is to vote against you. And if she's selected to hear reargument, and votes *with* you, I don't think Kilcannon could save her. Or would want to." Pausing, Nolan finished, "It's no secret that Caroline and I weren't exactly soul mates. But it would be good to have the new Chief Justice be a former partner of Kenyon & Walker. And too bad if we kept her from it."

Silent, Sarah absorbed the shock of unintended consequences: the course she chose could threaten Caroline's chances or, because of that, lessen Mary Ann's. Quietly, she said, "I'll have to think this over. But I guess my situation's like Caroline's. However she might vote, she can't shirk her duties. And neither can I."

"Consider that, Sarah—carefully." Nolan's voice was low. "You've become part of a very clever dynamic which Harshman—and probably Gage—has set up for you and Caroline. Depending on what one or both of you does, they improve their chance of influencing the outcome of the Tierney case, or of keeping Caroline off the Court. In political terms, either suits them fine."

Once more, Sarah wondered whether Nolan's awareness of the Senate was more intimate than he admitted, and whether he was bearing a message from those who pulled the strings. She felt herself teetering between naïveté and paranoia.

"Thank you," she said simply. "It's good to have your advice."

Mary Ann was curled on Sarah's couch, tears coming to her eyes. The court's opinion slipped through her fingers and scattered on the rug.

"I thought he loved me," the girl mumbled.

"Your father?"

"Tony. I never *knew* . . ." Mary Ann shook her head. "My parents. The baby. What this judge says about me. All because I slept with him."

There was no point sharing her own worries, Sarah thought. Compounded by shame and disbelief, Mary Ann's burden was bad enough—it might be crushing to mention Caroline, or the complexity of Sarah's role.

"Don't blame yourself," Sarah said. "Whatever mistake you made, you don't deserve what's happened."

Mary Ann massaged her stomach, as though feeling for the baby inside. Softly, she answered, "Then nobody does."

The room fell silent; when the telephone rang, Sarah ignored it. "You've got two and a half months left," she said at length. "Maybe less, if you deliver prematurely. We've got to decide what to do."

Eyes downcast, Mary Ann was slow to react. "What choices do I have left?"

"Only three. Petition for rehearing. Petition the Supreme Court. Or deliver by means of a classical cesarean section."

For a long time, Mary Ann said nothing. Sarah let her mind drift to the world which enveloped them—the unanswered phone messages, many regarding Caroline; the media clustered below; the demonstrators with their signs and slogans.

At last, Mary Ann looked up at her. "I still want you to help me."

Then there it was. Sarah was, after all, her lawyer. "That leaves the Supreme Court," she answered. "Or taking the time to try for a rehearing first."

Mary Ann touched her eyes. "What do you think?"

The answer was now clear to Sarah. Without Caroline on the Supreme Court, their chances of winning seemed dim. Rehearing held out a bit more hope and—should Mary Ann not deliver prematurely—the time consumed might be long enough for Caroline's confirmation. The political perils of rehearing could not be Mary Ann's concern.

"We should petition the Ninth Circuit," Sarah replied. "Soon."

Six

Eight days later, Caroline Masters sat in her chambers, watching C-SPAN.

On television, the hearing room appeared less daunting than she remembered it. She supposed this was akin to the difference between playing football—the sweat and effort and danger of mischance—and merely viewing it on the screen. But the tension of the hearing was fresh in her heart and mind.

On the surface, the intervening days had been quiet and uneventful. Caroline owed this to Chad Palmer: in private, Palmer had squelched Paul Harshman's proposal to subpoena Sarah Dash, arguing that it would seem spiteful and gratuitous. Far more ominous, the FBI had uncovered what it called a "rumor"—that sometime in the 1970s, on Martha's Vineyard, a young woman resembling Caroline Masters had delivered a baby girl.

For Caroline, several nights of broken sleep ensued. But the "rumor" remained a passing remark on a scrap of paper, seen only by two members of the committee—Palmer and Vic Coletti. As before, the chairman had used his prerogative to keep all other senators, including Gage and Harshman, from reviewing the FBI's raw data. To help ensure this, he had discouraged the FBI from pursuing the "rumor" any further.

Senator Palmer's final achievement had been to resist the pressure from Gage and Harshman to prolong the hearings. Now, as Caroline watched, he looked calmly at the Republicans on his right, then the Democrats on his left. With deceptive blandness, he directed the clerk to call the roll.

"All those who favor sending the nomination to the full Senate with a favorable recommendation, please signify by saying 'yes.' All opposed, by saying 'no.'"

Thirteen in favor, Palmer had predicted to Kerry Kilcannon. As the voices called out in turn, Caroline counted: to Palmer's right, four out of nine said yes, as did all eight Democrats to his left.

Paul Harshman pronounced an emphatic "No," followed by four of his party colleagues. The ten Republicans—again as Palmer had foreseen—were equally divided when Palmer added his "Yes."

In the same even tone, the senator announced, "By a vote of thirteen to five, the committee forwards the nomination of Judge Caroline Masters to be Chief Justice with a favorable recommendation." Only then did Caroline emit a sigh.

She had made it to the full Senate without mischance. All that remained was for Macdonald Gage, as Majority Leader, to schedule a vote.

When her private line rang, she answered it herself.

"Congratulations," Clayton Slade said without preface or, to Caroline, any discernable elation.

Am I missing something? she wanted to ask. Instead she answered, "Thank you. *And* the President." Pausing, she added, "Please thank Senator Palmer, as well."

"Palmer *did* hold half the Republicans on his committee," Clayton observed. "That wasn't easy. But if they split like that on the final vote—which, as of now, is reasonable to expect—you'll be confirmed by roughly seventy-five to twenty-five. Not terrific, but good enough."

"What would make it better?"

"Nothing. The question is what would make it worse." Clayton's tone remained level. "Your statement of impartiality was helpful. But Gage will sit on this awhile; to him and people like Harshman, you smell like a liberal, and they want more time and latitude to keep digging through your life. So if you see any controversy coming, and can reasonably avoid it, do that."

Clayton Slade was far too discreet to suggest that she recuse herself from a specific case, or vote in a particular way. But his message was clear: don't help Mary Ann Tierney if you want to be Chief Justice, or even to avoid any more scrutiny of your personal life. Caroline suspected that the President had approved this word of caution, and was using Slade as his buffer.

"If I see trouble coming," Caroline said in a noncommittal tone, "it'll have to find me."

For a long moment, Clayton was silent. "Good," he responded coolly. "The President's got a lot riding on this. As do many others."

Including Brett, Caroline thought. When she hung up, her relief at the committee's vote had faded.

．　．　．

"Congratulations," Blair Montgomery said with a fair show of cheer. But his smile was perfunctory and, though raising his wineglass to mark the moment, he seemed distracted.

They occupied a corner table at Ovation, a carefully appointed restaurant with the decor of an Edwardian club, and tables spaced to facilitate private conversation. The suggestion that they dine here had been Blair's.

Caroline touched her glass to his. "Thank you," she answered. "Maybe the worst is over."

This last remark was a probe—which, from the look in her mentor's blue eyes, he recognized as such. At length, he said, "Steele's motion panel turned down Mary Ann Tierney's rehearing petition, of course. Which leaves pending her request for a rehearing en banc."

Putting down the glass, Caroline gazed at the china place setting, tented fingertips grazing her lips. "How soon," she asked, "will it come up for a vote?"

"Very soon. Given the girl's condition, it's an emergency." Sipping his Bordeaux, Judge Montgomery added mordantly, "Rather like a petition from an inmate two days from execution. Although who the victim might be in this case depends on one's point of view."

Caroline was quite certain how Blair Montgomery would vote and that, among his fellow judges, he would do all he could to secure Mary Ann Tierney a prompt rehearing. She was also certain that this was not his purpose here.

"So," Caroline said, "you think we'll vote on her petition before the Senate votes on me."

"I *know* so." Montgomery swirled the red liquid in its generous, pear-shaped glass. "If I were inclined to conspiracies, I might think that Lane Steele's haste in ruling was meant to put you in a bind. Unless it suggests an unwonted sensitivity to the Tierney girl's dilemma."

"Oh," Caroline said with a smile, "I always figured Lane for the baby's father."

"Now there's a vision." At once, Montgomery's answering smile vanished. "Rather than attacking Steele, those who support Ms. Tierney would do well to argue that her petition presents issues of national importance, to which a majority of our court should speak. That's their best chance to get Mary Ann a rehearing. But the vote will still be close."

It was her day for elliptical admonitions, Caroline reflected. Blair's overt warning contained two unspoken ones: that Caroline's vote could be decisive, and therefore that she must choose between self-interest and her sympathy—if any—for Mary Ann Tierney's legal arguments. To this Caroline added one further consideration—a judge's individual vote on Mary Ann's petition would not be public. Only if rehearing were granted, and Caroline were named at random to the en banc panel, could the Tierney case entangle her in controversy.

Yet Caroline suspected that Blair pondered complications of his own. Though ordinarily he would seek her vote in favor of rehearing, he did not wish to jeopardize her confirmation. But if Caroline were inclined to oppose Mary Ann's petition, Blair would far prefer that she recuse herself beforehand.

"Truth to tell," she said bluntly, "I don't know how I'd vote. I didn't watch the trial, and I haven't read the briefs. Only Steele's opinion."

"What did you make of it?"

"Typical. But that doesn't mean, in this case, that he's wrong."

Blair's smile was more than a little wintry. "True. But consider the odds."

Finishing her wine, Caroline did not answer; the conversation had gone as far as she wished. Perceiving this, her friend turned to other topics.

Only after dessert did he reach into his briefcase. "I ran across something yesterday," he said with a casual air. "One of my all-time favorite opinions, *Pierce v. Delamater*—legal reasoning at its finest. At least in 1847."

"What was the issue?"

Blair smiled. "Whether a Judge Greene Bronson, after being promoted to an appellate court, could review his own decision."

Caroline raised her eyebrows; once more, their conversational minuet was edging toward the Tierney case. "How did it turn out?" she asked.

Picking up the pages, Judge Montgomery donned his glasses and commenced reading with mock solemnity:

"*There is nothing which makes it improper for a judge to review his own judgments. If he is what a judge ought to be—wise enough to know that he is fallible, and therefore ever ready to learn; great and honest enough to discard all mere pride of opinion, and follow truth wherever it may lead; and courageous enough to acknowledge his errors . . .*" Pausing, Montgomery interjected, "and here's the kicker—'*he is then the very best man to sit in review upon his own judgments. If right at first, he will be confirmed in his opinion; and if wrong, he will be quite as likely to find it out as anyone else . . .*'"

"How very male," Caroline ventured dryly. "Who wrote the court's opinion?"

Blair's smile flashed. "Judge Greene Bronson—who then affirmed his own decision, removing all doubt as to its rightness. Otherwise, he probably wouldn't have been able to live with himself." Her mentor's eyes sparkled at this paradigm of judicial folly. "The poor plaintiff, Mr. Pierce, foreswore a petition to the Supreme Court. He might have feared it would provoke Bronson's elevation to Chief Justice."

Caroline laughed at this. "As upright as he was, *Chief Justice* Bronson might have reconsidered."

"No doubt. Fortunately, I don't believe this is the law anymore. But I thought you'd find the opinion an amusing oddity."

And useful, Caroline thought, for its implicit suggestion of another means of escape: to claim that she should recuse herself from any case which might later come to her as Chief.

"Thank you," Caroline answered. "It is."

Seven

"Blair Montgomery," Judge Steele said, "is pushing for a rehearing en banc. Which puts Masters on the spot."

To Macdonald Gage, Steele's voice sounded tentative; though Gage assured the judge that no one else was present, Gage's squawk box plainly made him nervous.

"Suits me," Gage said comfortably. "Still, how stupid can she be?"

"She's not stupid, Senator. But our vote on the petition isn't public. And you can never underestimate her arrogance and self-regard."

Or yours, Gage thought. "Oh, I've seen it," he assured the judge. "She won't be making Paul Harshman's Christmas card list this year. So what are the chances this rehearing petition gets granted?"

In the silence, Gage felt Steele's hesitance; reluctantly, the judge was edging away from his pose as cloistered jurist, drawn by ideology and ambition into Gage's design. "In my count," Steele said at last, "we're evenly divided, or within a vote or two. But even if she participates—and even if the petition's granted—only eleven out of twenty-one of us will be drawn to hear the case."

Gage glanced at the memo on his desk, reviewing his Chief of Staff's research. "Refresh my memory," he said with seeming casualness. "Been years since I practiced law, and that was in Kentucky. But I recall you saying that your circuit provides for a rehearing en banc by *all* the active judges?"

"That's extremely rare." Steele stopped abruptly, as though the thrust of Gage's question had just now overtaken him. "I can only recall three or four instances. Also, a vote on a full court en banc call would be taken, and a hearing by all of us held, only *after* a decision by the eleven-judge en banc court."

"But," Gage asked cautiously, "could you skip the eleven-judge hearing and go straight to the full court?"

Steele thought for a moment. "It could be argued that time doesn't permit two en banc hearings here, and that the issue is so important that the entire court should hear it. Of course, a judge would have to make the case for extraordinary action."

Yes, Gage thought sardonically, *a judge would.* "But if a judge *did* ask," he said musingly, "then right up front Masters knows that if it's granted, she's forced to hear the Tierney case. Unless she decides to recuse herself, I guess."

When Steele did not answer, Gage scanned the memo further. "So think along with me," he continued in the same tone of discovery. "Seems like to stay out of trouble, Masters would *have* to recuse herself, or maybe vote against. Which increases the chance that *your* original opinion gets upheld. Am I right?"

"Yes."

"But if she doesn't recuse herself, and rehearing is by the entire court, she's stuck. Then *she* has to vote to uphold your opinion—which is fine—or to declare the Protection of Life Act unconstitutional. Which, I can assure you, would change everything for her back here."

Sitting back, Gage could hear Lane Steele thinking, could feel temptation at war with his sense of rectitude. Gage had seen this in the Senate many times.

"All that's true," Steele ventured at last.

Gage glanced at his watch: it was close to noon in Washington, nine in the morning in San Francisco. Steele would have all day to ponder.

"Well," he said amiably, "thanks for walking me though the process, Judge. Just *thinking* about it is interesting."

Shortly before *Air Force One* landed in Newark, Kerry Kilcannon gazed out the window.

The perquisites of office still bemused him. As a senator, he had flown back and forth from Newark to Washington in economy class, the natural and expedient choice for the son of Irish immigrants who had not forgotten his roots. But now, though he savored his return to Vailsburg, the neighborhood of his birth, his manner of arrival seemed strange. All air traffic had stopped; below, the airstrip was cleared, and the trappings of power awaited—the Secret Service, the press, the local dignitaries competing for attention, the line of black bullet-proof limousines, the police escort. It was at once heady and disconcerting; idly, Kerry wondered how it would be the day that all of this, and all of his power, vanished in an instant.

Would it be so much a part of him that the loss would leave him empty? Given his hopes for a future with Lara, the family they might have, he assumed not. But he had begun to understand how desperate presidents became not to have their days in office foreshortened by rejection, turned to four years instead of eight.

Next to him, Clayton Slade settled into an overstuffed chair. "Remember the other time I flew with you as President?"

"Sure. To Michigan."

Nodding, Clayton smiled. "I was first off the plane, and there were all those people waiting. It felt so heady I nearly started waving to them. At the last second, I remembered they weren't out there waiting for *me*."

Turning, Kerry gave him a long look: they had known each other for so long, and so well, that his friend had an uncanny gift for divining Kerry's mood. "Oh, well," he replied. "Consider yourself Newark's second most beloved figure."

"The first in Carlie's mind, I hope. Though she always liked you, oddly enough. Considering the havoc you create."

Kerry smiled. It was rare to have his Chief of Staff travel with him, though both men welcomed it; the reason Clayton had come with him was that Carlie, his wife of twenty-five years, had not yet found a permanent home in Washington. This was one of the many sacrifices that Kerry's ambitions had called forth from the Slades—he was fortunate, Kerry thought, that Carlie's affection for him was so deep. "I always liked Carlie," Kerry answered lightly. "But she was already taken. So I decided to be President instead."

Like the flipping of a switch, this seemed to return Clayton to the deeper reason he had broken Kerry's musings. Glancing at the congressman and senator from New Jersey, and finding them preoccupied with each other, Clayton murmured, "I'm a little worried about Masters."

At once, Kerry's mind became alert, unsentimental. "How so?"

"I delivered the message yesterday—as clearly as I could without leaving fingerprints on the scales of Justice." Once more, Clayton looked around them. "It wasn't that she didn't get it. But her response was, shall we say, reserved."

"Wouldn't yours be? If I read her right, Caroline's developed some attachment to the notion she's a judge."

Clayton frowned. "Not a foolish attachment, I hope. Why risk your credibility, and a quarter century as Chief Justice, for the sake of a fifteen-year-old girl?"

This baldly stated, Kerry guessed, the question was less rhetorical than exploratory: Clayton had begun to wonder about Kerry's own sympathies in the Tierney case, and was reminding his friend—in case a reminder was needed—to curb them. "She shouldn't," Kerry said coolly. "For many reasons. Beginning with the fact that she owes me, and what she owes me for. Which is why she won't be reckless."

· · ·

"I've known him forever," Clayton told his wife that night. "But here I am still worrying about him, and then he stops me short."

They lay in the dark, in the commodious comfort of their Tudor house in South Orange, so deeply woven into the fabric of their family—the laughter of their twin girls, the death by accident of their only son—that they had decided hours before not to part with it. "How?" Carlie asked him.

"The way he looked when he said it. He likes Masters for her integrity, and probably *dislikes* the Protection of Life Act—though he won't say. But his eyes were absolutely cold.

"He's staked too much on her. And he's thought out to the core why she won't get herself in trouble over Tierney: that she's afraid for her daughter. And that's just fine with him."

"And that surprises you?" Carlie's voice held its own trace of wonder. "Most times, I just want to put my arms around Kerry and hug him. Now and then I can even see the lonely little boy peek through, the one who loved his mother, feared his father, and lived in his brother's shadow. But other times he scares me a little."

Head on the pillow next to Carlie's, Clayton fell quiet, a signal of assent. "But we're still with him," he said at last.

"True." Carlie's dry chuckle was that of a spouse privileged to speak the truth. "Because we love him, warts and all. And because you want your own place on the Court."

The next morning, Blair Montgomery appeared in Caroline's chambers. With a jerky motion—disgust combined with advancing age—he tossed some papers on her desk.

Alarmed, she asked, "What's this?"

"Another gem of legal reasoning, a good deal less amusing than the last. Lane Steele's request for rehearing by all twenty-one active judges. Immediately."

He did not have to name the case. Silent, Caroline stared at the papers. "I've never seen this," she said at last.

"I've been here since 1975, Caroline, and we've always held the normal en banc first." Abruptly, Montgomery sat. "Steele's rationale, like mine, is the overwhelming import of the issue. But to him it's so important that—if we hear it—all twenty-one of us should speak to it, rather than a mere eleven drawn at random."

"Bizarre," Caroline said slowly. "You think he'd simply oppose you."

"You would, wouldn't you. But then *you* might not be forced either to recuse yourself, or participate." Montgomery frowned. "There's no way to prove that, of course. And no other explanation, though I'd have credited him with more integrity."

Leaning forward, Caroline rested her forehead on the fingertips of one hand. She made no effort to conceal her dismay.

"Before our dinner," she told him, "Slade called me to suggest caution, in the voice of a cop reading a defendant her rights. He also mentioned that Gage was holding up the vote."

"So I guess I don't have to draw you a picture."

"No." Still Caroline did not look at him. "What's the likely vote on Tierney's petition?"

"For rehearing en banc, as opposed to by the full court? My guess is ten to ten—the same as Steele's, I expect."

"That's without me?"

"Yes." Montgomery paused. "Steele complicates it a bit. Now we'll have two votes tomorrow—on my request, and his.

"If our colleagues who favor rehearing came to believe what *I* believe about him, they might vote for rehearing by eleven judges, but not all twenty-one. But it's a hard thing to accuse a colleague of colluding in Supreme Court politics. And, when it comes to Steele, even my most fervent admirers sometimes doubt my objectivity."

For the first time, Caroline looked up at him. Softly, she said, "I don't doubt your insight, Blair. And I've never doubted your wisdom."

Though Montgomery gave her a self-deprecating smile, his tone was serious. "Your only flaw, Caroline. I've seen no others."

In this moment, Caroline felt the depth of her mentor's kindness. It seemed to strip her of defenses, the need to conceal her own vulnerability and fears. Except for those regarding Brett, which Blair Montgomery did not know.

"As a judge," she asked with real despair, "what would you do?"

Now Blair, too, seemed burdened. Gazing at the floor, he fell silent, then looked up at her at last.

"As a judge of this court," he said simply, "I want you to vote in favor of Mary Ann Tierney.

"As someone who cares about the future of our highest court, I want you to become Chief Justice." His voice softened. "And as your friend—which, to me, is more important than anything else—I want you to do what you think best for you. And what you best can live with afterward."

Caroline felt a tightness in her throat. At length she said, "I suppose, at least, that I should read the papers. I've got the night to decide."

Eight

Shortly after ten o'clock at night, Caroline finished her last cup of black coffee.

She sat in her kitchen, papers spread on the marble counter. Randomly, her mind moved between the case at hand and the vision, as tangible and tantalizing, of all that lay before her.

She could do such good. She had imagined herself on the Supreme Court—though for years it had seemed a foolish dream—for most of her adult life. A life without a family and which, by accident and design, had become dedicated to being the best lawyer, then the finest judge, she could be.

And now the dream was very near reality. "The Masters Court," scholars would call it: for the next quarter century, Caroline could help shape the laws for generations after.

And who better? she thought without false modesty. She could bring to bear all her training in the law, and all her experience of life. For though many saw her as a patrician, she had started in the law at its seamiest and most gritty—defending those molded by poverty and abuse—and had lived a far more complex life than they knew. She felt the impact of law on ordinary people much too keenly to imagine the Supreme Court as a temple, or the rendering of justice a mere exercise of intellect. A judge's fidelity must be to law, but also to fairness, for those it touched were not pieces on a chess board.

And that was the problem here.

From the polished words in front of her had emerged a picture of a fifteen-year-old girl, who because of the binding force of law would represent other girls. Yet Mary Ann Tierney had become incidental, the plaything of forces much larger than herself—the President, Macdonald Gage, and the warring interests they represented—all focused on whether Caroline Masters would become Chief Justice. And now the girl's only hope might rest in Caroline's hands.

Could Caroline—even if she tried—judge fairly? It was a difficult case and, despite herself, Caroline resented Sarah Dash for placing it before her. Sarah was not obtuse: she would understand all too well the consequences to Caroline. And though the risks Sarah herself had taken—hostility within her firm, a lifetime supply of enemies outside it—were considerable, the risk she asked of Caroline was enormous and immediate. This was Caroline's chance; to destroy it might turn all that had gone before to ashes.

Yet Sarah had done no more than Caroline would have, had Mary Ann Tierney come to her. Sarah had played her role as advocate, and now asked Caroline to play hers—as judge. Four years ago, Caroline Masters had taken an oath to serve as a judge of the Ninth Circuit Court of Appeals and, as best she could, to render justice. The resentment Caroline felt toward Sarah was, in truth, a resentment of the obligations she herself had assumed and, conversely, of her own desire to shirk them. And this quandary was where she questioned her objectivity as a judge.

At bottom, she had no other grounds for avoiding the Tierney case. Caroline could claim that Harshman's questions in themselves raised an "appearance" of bias which she should avoid. But, in truth, Caroline would cut Sarah Dash no slack. And though she also could assert that the case might come before her as Chief Justice, it was moving far more quickly than Caroline's confirmation, even if Macdonald Gage were not wedded to delay. So while these might serve as excuses, that was all they were.

This, at last, brought Brett Allen, ever present, to the surface of her mother's thoughts.

Caroline did not know, in the clash of contending forces, what dangers the Tierney case might pose to Brett. But Caroline's ambitions now had made her powerful enemies, whom the President and Chad Palmer had kept at bay at some risk to themselves. If she placed herself on the side of Mary Ann Tierney, her enemies would be enraged, and her friends might no longer be willing to protect her—or Brett. Given all that Kerry Kilcannon had done for her, and Chad Palmer as well, Caroline would hardly blame them.

But that placed Brett's future in her hands. Caroline did not know what the truth—that Betty was not her mother, or Caroline her aunt—would do to Brett. But Caroline's decision to have her, and then to give her up, had led to a lifetime of deceptions, and now Caroline had no right to unravel them. What would she have done, she wondered now, had she foreseen all this at the moment of Brett's birth?

She had been barely twenty-two, and alone. But this memory, in turn, brought her back to Mary Ann Tierney.

The girl was much younger, her dilemma far different. But, except for Sarah, it was clear that Mary Ann Tierney also was alone. And this touched Caroline's conscience.

Harshman was right, in his way: no judge comes to judgment without bias, be it Caroline or Lane Steele. Caroline had attempted to delude her senatorial antagonist on that point and, to some extent, herself. This case exposed that starkly—her ambitions pulled her one way; her life, another.

As for the case itself, the path of justice was by no means as clear to her as it seemed for Blair Montgomery. Morally, there was much to be said on either side. Her own decision to have Brett, while she did not see it as the paradigm for all women, had ripened into a silent love which, in retrospect, made abortion unthinkable. On a larger scale, Caroline honestly wondered whether abortion, unquestionably to her mind the taking of life, contributed to a coarsening of conscience which, over time, would make all life less valued. But neither consideration could obscure the point on which Blair Montgomery undeniably was right: the case was important—indeed, at the heart of how we define our values—and Lane Steele's conclusory opinion, while written well, did not truly address the questions raised. The Ninth Circuit owed more.

Perhaps, Caroline told herself suddenly, she was mired in needless melodrama. This case was not about *her* and, with luck, Steele's suggestion of rehearing by the full court would fail. And Caroline herself was far from resolved to vote with Blair Montgomery—even if, in the worst of luck, she was drawn to hear the case. If not, a vote for Blair's suggestion—a rehearing by half the court—could turn out to be nothing more than a cost-free vote of conscience, preserving both her self-esteem and her glorious future in Supreme Court jurisprudence.

But why take the chance, when so many interests—hers, the President's, Chad Palmer's, and, most of all, Brett's—might be placed at risk? Only because, Caroline answered herself, she was who she was—or, more precisely, had willed herself to become. A judge.

Still, sleepless and pursued by memory, she did not decide until morning, in the quiet of her chambers.

At four in the afternoon, Caroline received a call from the en banc coordinator, whose job it was to keep the active judges abreast of such proceedings.

"We have what you might call mixed results," John Davis told her. "Judge Steele's suggestion for a rehearing of all active judges failed by twelve to nine."

She was almost free of this, Caroline thought; she guessed that Blair had voted with her to defeat Lane Steele's request. "And Judge Montgomery's suggestion?"

Davis hesitated; as an observer of the court, he surely understood the significance of this vote. "Ms. Tierney gets her rehearing, Judge. By a vote of eleven to ten."

Alone, Caroline closed her eyes. She barely managed to thank Davis for his call.

For the next hour she questioned herself ceaselessly, thinking of her obligations to Kilcannon, Palmer, and Brett Allen. But it was too late for recusal: Caroline's vote in favor had determined the fate of Mary Ann Tierney's petition. Now her only hope was that she not be drawn for the en banc panel.

Shortly after five, John Davis called again, to give her the schedule for the Tierney rehearing. Among her ten colleagues would be Blair Montgomery and Lane Steele.

"You must have voted against Steele's petition," Caroline said. "Trying to keep me out of this."

Sitting in Caroline's office, Blair Montgomery looked old and very tired. "I wasn't sure you'd vote at all," he answered. "But, knowing you, I thought you might. I owed you at least that much, and I wasn't at all convinced a full court rehearing would go the way I wanted."

This combination of compassion and practicality underscored, for Caroline, the ambiguities of her role. "I wanted to stay out of it, Blair. But recusal seemed like cowardice."

Her mentor's smile was brief. "A lot that seems like cowardice to you, Caroline, is commonplace for others. What you did is admirable."

Even this compliment, Caroline found, depressed her. "No," she answered. "It was stupid. I just lost the lottery. Or, worse, gave back the prize."

"Not yet." Blair drew himself up, sitting erect in the chair, and spoke in a much firmer voice. "I don't usually do this kind of thing. But let me tell you what your duties do *not* involve.

"First, opening your mouth at the hearing. The courtroom will be crawling with press, and I'll have more than enough questions to keep Martin Tierney occupied."

Despite her gloom, Caroline smiled at this. But Montgomery did not: his eyes had the look of command, impelling her attention. "At conference," he continued briskly, "when your turn comes to speak, don't. Tell them you're reflecting, and prefer to hear the wisdom of your colleagues. And don't let Steele bait you.

"By the time we go around the table, you'll know how the votes shape up. If the Tierney girl's losing anyhow, vote against her—at that point, your only obligation is to become Chief Justice. A vote for the Protection of Life Act would leave Gage and his allies with next to nothing."

That was right, Caroline thought. "And if there's an even split? What would you advise me then?"

Blair looked down. "Perhaps, by then, you'll be persuaded that the statute passes muster."

What he was telling her, Caroline sensed, was that he would never judge her. No one could know if she had acted from self-interest, or belief. And if Caroline had not voted for rehearing, Mary Ann Tierney's petition already would have failed; if now, in the moral equation, Caroline decided to vote for herself, and not Mary Ann, that decision was no worse than recusal.

"Even," Blair said at length, "if you come to believe the statute flawed as to *this* girl, you can reserve for another day whether it's flawed for *all* girls. A narrow decision, applying to Mary Ann alone, might be less open to reversal. Or attack."

Caroline gathered her thoughts. "Which leaves only," she said dryly, "my emphatic vote to throw the whole thing out."

Blair chose not to answer, or to look at her. After some moments, he said quietly, "I can't advise you on what course is the most expedient—or the wisest. I merely note that until the moment you cast a final vote, your slate in the Senate is clean. This morning's vote isn't public."

Even in her despair—for herself and perhaps for Brett—Caroline felt a deep fondness for Blair Montgomery. Much of this conversation went against his deepest instincts as a judge and yet, for her sake, he had resolved that they should have it. To thank him would be much more than he wished.

Instead, she chose the lightest tone she could muster. "Before we get there, Blair, I have to explain this to Clayton Slade. And, by extension, the President. Perhaps you could suggest the nicest way to do that."

Nine

Kerry Kilcannon looked astonished, and then began to laugh, his tenor and expression by turns rueful and—surprising to Clayton—sardonically amused at his own miscalculation.

"I certainly earned *this* one," the President told him. "It's exactly what I liked her for—this quaint notion that she's larger than her ambitions. Even, it seems, her fears."

"We can always pray," Clayton offered, "that she's decided to vote against the girl, and for the act. *That* would get her confirmed by about one hundred to zero."

Kerry's look of amusement vanished. It was nine at night; in the dim light of the study, he looked as tired as he had at the end of the campaign. "No," he said at last. "*She* may not think she knows yet, but *I* do—at least if there's a split. She didn't pass on recusal just so she could pick up more Republicans, or get *us* off the hook.

"This is about Caroline's idea of herself. That's what prompted her to tell Ellen Penn about her daughter and, however politely, tell *me* to take a hike after I started angling for a commitment on campaign reform." Kerry gave a brief, ironic smile. "If she votes to overturn the Protection of Life Act, she'll offer to withdraw. It would have been so much easier to have taken her up on that the *last* time."

"The days of innocence?" Clayton said. "*Before* you cut a deal with Palmer—putting *you* in his debt and *him* in trouble with Gage—for what may turn out to be nothing? Or merely before the vote you think she'll cast, inflaming the abortion issue and maybe costing you much more than you can afford to pay."

This last reference, though coded, brought home for Clayton how angry he himself was at Masters's arrogance, and how concerned for Kerry that Lara Costello's abortion, if discovered, could destroy him. But Kerry's response was an opaque silence, behind which his deepest thoughts often seemed to vanish.

"What about Gage?" he said at length.

"He set Masters up to self-destruct. He had Harshman corner her on recusal and Sarah Dash. Now he's holding up her confirmation until she votes."

The President shrugged. "That's just hardball. It's what you'd expect him to do. And what the Christian Commitment is no doubt telling him to do."

"Fair enough," Clayton rejoined. "But consider the rest: first, this Judge Steele assigns the case to himself, and then he turns around to call for a rehearing by the entire court. It's like Gage is pulling his strings."

As Kerry considered this, his expression became chill. "Life is long," he answered softly. "If we can ever prove that, I'll make Gage's feel like eternity."

At ten o'clock, amidst a debate on the new telecommunications bill that threatened to go past midnight, Macdonald Gage pulled Chad Palmer off the Senate floor.

"We need to talk," Gage said brusquely. "It won't keep."

To Chad, the only business which could be so pressing was Caroline Masters. He awaited an explanation, wondering whether someone with the FBI had improperly leaked the "rumor" regarding the birth of a daughter. But Gage did not speak again until they reached the underground subway between the Senate and the Russell Building.

"Let's go to your office," Gage suggested. "Less likely for the press to see us." But though the media was covering the debate closely, the tunnel in the bowels of Congress was empty; when Chad and Gage got in the open car, they were alone.

"What's the problem?" Chad inquired. "Did Paul Harshman find out that Masters is a registered Republican?"

As usual, Gage frowned at his colleague's levity. "They've granted a rehearing in Tierney. Masters has been named to the panel."

Maybe it *wasn't* the daughter, Chad thought with relief. "When did *that* happen, Mac? I hadn't heard a thing."

Gage hesitated. "It's not public yet," he answered tersely.

Then how do you know? Chad wanted to ask. Instead, he maintained his pose of ingenuousness. "How could Masters let that happen?"

"Maybe because she's a true believer, like Paul was saying." Gage's tone became harsher, cutting through the clatter of the car as it moved through the bleak gray corridor. "The kind of liberal who wants to keep parents out of their children's lives."

Instinctively, Chad bridled at this oversimplification, the sort of political red meat more suitable to a fund-raising letter than to reality. He reminded himself that, with Gage, partisan rhetoric often concealed a deeper purpose. "Unless Masters is voting *with* us," Chad replied.

"That's the only way," Gage said pointedly, "she'll ever be confirmed. The Protection of Life Act is fundamental to our political base."

And your financial base, Chad thought. It was cynical of Gage to suggest that they had a common need to propitiate the Christian Commitment, while ignoring the complex realities which divided them. Four years hence, Gage would need the Commitment's financial support to defeat Chad for the party's nomination, and then wrest the presidency from Kilcannon: in the service of defeating Masters, he wanted Chad to collaborate in his own destruction. "Sometimes," Chad observed, "it's hard to tell a 'base' from an anchor."

Gage pursed his mouth: the remark not-so-tacitly suggested that the Christian Commitment, and Gage, would cause their party to lose to Kilcannon. "Christian parents," Gage intoned, "are entitled to keep their children from taking an unborn life."

At similar times, Chad had thought with some contempt that Gage had the soul of a Russian apparatchik, who cloaked his endless machinations beneath a string of pious bromides. But this particular bromide, and Gage's willingness to advance his goals by any means at hand, reminded Chad to be wary. With renewed courtesy, he inquired, "What do you suggest I do?"

Gage turned to him. "Stop protecting her," Gage said bluntly. "If she votes wrong, you'll need to help me pull the plug on her. For your sake as well as our party's."

This was so abrupt that Chad wondered again what Gage might know. "I can't believe she'll do that," he found himself temporizing. "She has her pride, but Caroline Masters is too smart to stick it to us."

Gage shrugged, eyes narrowing behind his glasses. "We'll see, Chad. We'll just see about that."

Beneath the Russell Building, the car rumbled to a stop. Gage beamed at him brightly, an expression he managed without opening his lips to smile. "We've only just arrived," he said in his most comradely tone, "and our business is already done. Why don't you pour me a drink, and tell me all about Allie and Kyle."

· · ·

It was not until morning that Sarah Dash learned that her petition had been granted, midafternoon before she picked up Mary Ann at school.

They sat in Sarah's car. As she listened, the girl's mouth parted, her expression oscillated between hope and worry. "What happens now?" she asked.

"In three days we'll have a hearing. After that, they'll decide as quickly as they can." Gently Sarah placed her hand on the girl's wrist. "Dr. Flom thinks you should stay quiet and in bed. He doesn't want anything to go wrong while we're waiting for a ruling."

Quiet, Sarah watched Mary Ann absorb a distasteful paradox: the risk of premature delivery without permission to abort; the need to rest so that she could take her child's life. A legal "victory" had never felt so painful and ambiguous.

Ten

Entering the courthouse, Sarah felt the Tierney case becoming part of history.

The ornate building was besieged by Minicams and demonstrators—some in wheelchairs—carrying signs supporting the Tierneys or their daughter. In the Great Hall leading to Courtroom One, more media thronged, their calls to Sarah echoing beneath the vaulted ceiling as they had two weeks before. But today the landmark case which would decide the fate of Mary Ann Tierney and her unborn child might also determine whether Caroline Masters would become the most important legal figure of her time, or a melancholy footnote—the woman who had lost her chance to be Chief Justice of the United States.

As for Sarah herself, her cause seemed fated, but not doomed. Among the eleven judges were several, including Caroline, whose leanings were uncertain. To persuade them, Sarah must use the time allotted her with firm resolve and keenness of mind, keeping Mary Ann Tierney ever present in their consciousness. Sarah was as rested and calm as possible: buffeted by notoriety, hostility, and the legal blows dealt by Patrick Leary and Lane Steele, she had found within herself a determination and resilience that distinguished her from the young lawyer who, seven weeks ago, had watched a red-haired girl brave a crowd of pickets.

"Sarah," someone called out, "what are you expecting?"

To do my best, she thought. Silent, she entered the courtroom.

In the robing room, Judge Caroline Masters removed her black robe from the ornate wooden coatrack.

She was the last judge to do so. Beneath the fluted lamps, her colleagues waited in silence. Today there were few jocular quips, and the quiet chatter which preceded even the most contentious hearings was lacking. This monastic air was due, Caroline knew, less to the unprecedented crush outside the courthouse than to the tension inside this room: her colleagues were well aware of the unique importance of the case and Caroline's role in it. Sitting at the conference table, Lane Steele propped his chin on folded hands and stared at the polished walnut, as though marshaling his energy and intellect. Only Blair Montgomery—raising his eyebrows and slightly smiling at her as he cracked open the door to listen—seemed more or less in character.

Caroline glanced at the wall clock. The second hand, circling, marked ten o'clock. Chief Judge Sam Harker, a courtly Arizonan in his late sixties, looked around him at the others. "Ready?" he asked. When no one demurred, he nodded toward Blair Montgomery.

The door opened slowly, and then the eleven judges filed into court.

"All rise," the courtroom deputy called.

As the fourth most junior, Caroline sat on the left of the lower of two benches. Standing at the table reserved for her, Sarah Dash stared straight ahead.

From her own experience, Caroline knew what Sarah must see. She could still recall her only en banc hearing as a lawyer, early—as with Sarah—in her career. Now, as then, the lawyers faced two banks of silent judges, a first bench of eight, the higher bench seating only three: the Chief Judge flanked by the two most senior judges—Blair Montgomery, in this case, being one.

The courtroom itself was overwhelming in its extravagance, a lavish melange of marble mosaics, carved Corinthian columns, plaster cupids and flowers, and stained-glass windows filtering a golden light which augmented the intended sense of awe. Garlands of fruits and vegetables carved in marble around the columns and door frames portrayed the bounty of California, and the marble panel behind the two benches had an intricate design expressive of Native American art. The upper bench was marred by a colorful piece of history—the ricochet from a bullet fired by a defendant who, in 1917, had murdered an adverse witness. But the fresh history being made was evidenced by the novel presence of two cameras, broadcasting the hearing on the motion of Judge Lane Steele—who had cited, with seeming relish, Caroline's own responses to Chad Palmer on the virtues of televised proceedings.

Three chairs to her left, Steele peered at his notes, then at Sarah. Her counterparts each presented a different aspect: Thomas Fleming looked as gray and recessive as a diplomat hoping to draw but minimal attention; Barry Saunders personified the glazed reverence of a lawyer straining to show his respect; Martin Tierney appeared weary, spectral, and, somehow, self-martyred. When Caroline glanced at Sarah, their eyes met briefly, and then the younger woman averted her gaze. Caroline resolved not to look at her until she rose to argue.

Much like Sarah, Caroline supposed, she did not know what would happen.

As the parties sat, she realized that her hands were clasped tightly beneath the bench.

"Ms. Dash," the Chief Judge said politely, and the hearing began.

Afterward, still feeling the adrenaline rush which made the hearing seem like disjointed pieces of a dream, Sarah sorted through her most vivid impressions.

Lane Steele's face and voice were imprinted on her mind. For the first ten minutes, his piercing voice had interrupted her with question upon question:

"With the advance of medical science, Ms. Dash, won't a cesarean section soon become no more problematic than having one's tonsils out?"

Then:

"Are you asking us to sacrifice a life on the altar of a mother's mental health?"

Then:

"Does an anomaly in a fetus automatically equate to emotional distress in the mother?"

Then:

"If all we have to go on is some unverifiable claim of angst, aren't you asking this court to sanction eugenics?"

"We're not advocating eugenics," Sarah recalled objecting. "We're trying to protect a minor's reproductive health—"

"At least one percent of it," Steele interjected in caustic tones. "What would you say to us if your abortion yields a normal—albeit dead—child . . ."

"Forgive my interruption." Speaking from behind Steele, Judge Blair Montgomery had used a mild voice which seemed to underscore his disdain. "If I might suggest this to my colleague, the remaining ten of us are quite familiar with the substance of his written opinion. That's why we're here.

"I, for one, am interested in a fresh perspective. Perhaps even Ms. Dash's."

The directness of this challenge left Steele groping for a retort less venomous than the look he shot Montgomery. With a smile of encouragement, Montgomery said to Sarah, "I'm sure you can incorporate an answer into the body of your argument. Which we, and the country, remain anxious to hear."

This clear reference to the camera had seemed to seal his adversary's silence. Sarah's argument commenced at last, gaining strength, punctuated by questions posed in more civil tones. But Caroline Masters asked nothing.

Martin Tierney's principal memory, Sarah supposed, would be of Blair Montgomery.

Unlike Steele, Montgomery bided his time. His first question, asked several minutes into Tierney's argument, was unexpected:

"Would you say, Professor Tierney, that a mother's prospective loss of an arm is a 'substantial risk' to physical health?"

Tierney hesitated, plainly surprised by the question. "Under the Protection of Life Act," he answered, "there is room for a parent—or a court—to so conclude."

"But wouldn't you agree," Montgomery asked, "that at least some women would rather lose an arm than lose the capacity to bear children?"

Once more, Tierney paused. Watching, Sarah had wondered whether he was thinking of his own wife, and whether Blair Montgomery had intended that he do so. "They might," Tierney conceded. "But fear is one thing, reality another. When a minor becomes pregnant, a parent, or a court, can determine whether any threat to infertility is substantial, or marginal . . ."

"Then let me ask a real-world question: Should a battered wife determine whether a minor daughter should bear her own father's child? Or does the added fact of incest suggest that the girl and her doctor should have a greater role?"

Challenged, Tierney retorted, "These horrors surely happen, however isolated. But under this law such girls can go to court."

"Go to court?" Montgomery repeated in a tone of incredulity. "The thirteen-year-old daughter of an abusive and incestuous family?"

"Truly, Professor, I wonder if life often conforms to the tidy patterns you're constructing for us: loving parents, benign judges, and teenage girls too immature to have an abortion, yet resourceful enough to hire a lawyer and proceed to federal court. Which, in the case of girls in this district, may be as much as two hundred miles away."

"Your Honor," Tierney responded, "any rule which prevents tragedies may, in rare cases and by inadvertence, make others possible. I submit to you that the protection of a viable late-term child is far *less* tragic than the exceptions which might result."

Montgomery sat back. "The 'exceptions,'" he observed, "are girls you will never meet, or even know to pity. But please continue, Professor Tierney."

Sarah glanced at Caroline, wondering how she registered Martin Tierney's deflation. But, though intent, Caroline remained expressionless. In watchful silence, she observed her colleagues questioning Tierney, then—during rebuttal—Sarah.

And then, quite suddenly, it was over, and Caroline and the others had turned their backs and were filing toward the conference room.

The spectators stirred to life, trading comments and speculation. Amidst the din, Sarah tried to imagine the deliberations which would now begin, the thrust and cut of argument among the judges. All but Caroline Masters had asked at least one question: though Sarah understood her reasons, she could not help but feel betrayed.

In the Oval Office, Clayton turned from the screen.

"Hardly a distinguished performance by our putative Chief Justice. But at least she's learned the virtue of silence."

The President shrugged, speaking in the shorthand he often used when the two of them were alone: "Television."

"If she meant to give Gage nothing," Clayton observed, "she succeeded brilliantly. How do you suppose they'll rule?"

Kerry stood. "There are two votes with Montgomery," he ventured, "and three, I think, with Steele. The others didn't tell me much."

"You should hope they're in Steele's pocket, Kerry. That could be the best for all of us."

The President did not answer. Instead he drifted to the window, gazing out at the grass lit faintly by pale winter sun.

After a time, Clayton, the only person besides Lara who would feel comfortable asking, inquired what the President was thinking.

For some moments Kerry did not answer. Then, quite softly, he said, "I was recalling why I have such mixed feelings about all this. And wondering about Caroline's."

Eleven

The conference room dated to the 1930s and had a stark and disconcerting authoritarian aspect, emphasized by gilded plaster eagles on the wall and—to Caroline's continuing amazement—swastika-like emblems in the labyrinthine pattern of the ceiling. The effect was ascetic and austere: in the harsh lighting from recessed cans, the eleven judges sat around a long walnut oval, resembling, but for the presence of two women, a conclave of monastics. Their expressions were as grave: all of them must guess, as Caroline did, that the court was closely divided, each vote potentially fateful.

The process was fixed by long tradition. The judges would speak in order of their arrival on the court, from the most junior to the highest in seniority, with the chief judge speaking last. The result of these exchanges was a preliminary vote which, if it held, entitled the senior judge in the majority to write a draft opinion, or assign the opinion to another who concurred. The author of the opinion would circulate the draft for review and, should it still command a majority, the court would issue it as written or as modified. The author's name appeared beneath the caption; as with most judges, Caroline took great pride in the cogency of her writings, the body of decisions which reflected her life in the law.

Schooled in patience by necessity, Caroline had come to enjoy the process, from the clash of argument to the slower pace of reconciliation and refinement. But today was different. The case was an emergency, made so by the state of Mary Ann Tierney's pregnancy—the inflammatory element which had focused national attention on this room, and on Caroline's vote. Within forty-eight hours the court would issue its opinion to an explosion of headlines and a cacophony of newsbreaks, and both the fate of the fetus, and of Caroline's nomination, might be sealed. As they waited for the Chief Judge to begin their ritual, her colleagues' body language was repressed, their glances at Caroline more covert.

"Well," said Sam Harker dryly, "here we are." Turning to the most junior judge, he said, "Mary?"

Mary Wells—blond, trim, and a Democratic appointee—was noted for her brevity and, with only a year on the court, her deference. "This is a hard one," she said. "But it illustrates the problem with drawing narrow rules restricting medical decisions, then taking those decisions out of the hands of doctors.

"Because the physical health exception is too narrow, the problems it creates are too broad. The fact that we're quarreling about whether a chance of infertility is one percent, or five, suggests that. What's enough—ten percent, or twenty? And who decides?" Wells paused, glancing at her notes, less to review her conclusion than to find the resolve to speak it. "The act unduly burdens the right to an abortion found in *Roe* and *Casey*. To me, it's unconstitutional as to Mary Ann Tierney, *and* on its face."

Caroline felt a tingle of anticipatory tension. Though Mary's opinion did not surprise her, her incisiveness did—to throw out the Protection of Life Act altogether was the boldest and broadest ruling. Mary had shaped the discussion which would follow, laying down a marker for the others. Across from Caroline, Lane Steele, too, looked tense.

"José?" Sam Harker asked.

Next to Mary Wells, José Suarez gathered himself. A lawyer from Phoenix, José had been passed over in Caroline's favor four years prior, and his accustomed courtesy toward her did not entirely conceal his resentment. In this case, José was a puzzle: though inclined toward women's rights, he was a devout Catholic, and his ambivalence was apparent.

"I would not sweep so broadly," José began with care. "I'm concerned with Ms. Tierney's well-being, but also with invalidating an act of Congress which has the salutary purpose of protecting a viable fetus." Turning to Mary Wells, he said, "I'm open to persuasion here. But I think the best way to proceed is by upholding the Protection of Life Act, then interpreting its 'physical health' exception to include the risk of infertility. That would give Mary Ann Tierney her abortion."

True, Caroline thought. But legally it would be a mess: in trying to make the narrowest ruling—confined to Mary Ann—he was expanding the statute in a way that Congress plainly had never intended. Lane Steele, too, perceived this; he smiled grimly at the table, as if to say that this was no more than he expected from Judge Suarez. The first two votes for Mary Ann Tierney, Caroline thought, lacked a common thread; were Sarah Dash here, she would consider the votes expected, but their differing rationale worrisome.

"Judge Bernstein?" The Chief Judge spoke the more formal title with added decorum, signaling that Marc Bernstein was the only judge present whom Sam Harker truly loathed. Harker was not alone. In Bernstein's view, a razor-sharp mind licensed him to be acerbic: with the exception of Lane Steele, his dissents had derided the intellect of every conservative at this table, as well as that of most others present.

"Congress," he began in clear rebuke of José Suarez, "may not know what it's doing. But it surely meant for Mary Ann Tierney to have this baby *if* her parents want her to.

"This is an anti-abortion statute, dressed up in deceptive platitudes like 'bringing our families closer.' So let's treat it like what it is, instead of rewriting it so we can pretend it's something else." Pausing, he spoke to Caroline, as if to challenge her. "Congress is practicing medicine—badly. And all this rapture about 'family' defies reality. This law is unconstitutional, and has to go."

It was, Caroline conceded to herself, a reasonably succinct—if one-sided— condemnation of the social policy which underlay the act. But it was short on law, and long on ego: effectively Marc Bernstein was asking Caroline, whom he acknowledged as his equal in intelligence, to match him in clarity and courage. The fact that this might doom her as Chief Justice no doubt accounted for Bernstein's edgy smile.

"Caroline?" Sam Harker's voice was tentative. "Your turn."

Ignoring Bernstein, she turned to the Chief Judge, feeling her colleagues' stares. It was not every day, she supposed, that they could observe a Supreme Court nominee teetering on the precipice.

In a tight voice that embarrassed her, Caroline said simply, "I'll pass for now, Sam. I'd like to hear more."

At once, Lane Steele jerked his head up, eyes bright, mouth forming a skeptical smile. "Pass? Surely, Caroline, you can favor us with *some* thoughts."

The inquiry was made more scathing by what the others knew of her—that she almost always enjoyed the chance to persuade, and came with her arguments carefully marshaled. Caroline felt herself flush; restraining her pride even as she recalled Blair Montgomery's warning, she instinctively made a chess move, though to what end she was not sure. "Oh, I have *thoughts*, Lane. Several. What I can tell you now is that I'm very interested in what José had to say."

Down the table, Suarez looked surprised at this implicit compliment, then pleased. Lane Steele—far more guileful—studied her with open skepticism, as though to divine what her strategy might be. But Steele had little time to wonder: in the order of seniority, the conservatives' turn to speak had come.

This, Caroline knew, reflected one of the ironies of life as a federal judge. The eleven judges in this room were, in theory, impartial and nonpolitical. But they were appointed by a president with the concurrence of his party and the interest groups which supported it. With exceptions, Caroline's colleagues represented, in geologic layers of seniority, whether the administration which had appointed them had been Democratic or Republican.

Almost uniformly, Democratic politicians favored abortion rights; overwhelmingly, their Republican counterparts upheld the rights of the unborn. This divide had seeped into the courts, and now would decide the fate of Mary Ann Tierney under a statute designed to unify the Republicans in Congress and—because even many advocates of choice considered parental consent benign, and late-term abortion distasteful—to divide their Democratic rivals. Now the moment to speak had passed to four judges appointed by Republicans: the most senior, and their leader, was Lane Steele, who knew full well how loudly their decision would reverberate in the Senate, which had passed the Protection of Life Act, and which would vote on Caroline Masters.

"Your turn, Carl," the Chief Judge told Judge Klopfer.

Breaking from his scrutiny of Caroline, Carl Klopfer said flatly, "I concurred with Lane's original decision. I still do. So I'll defer to him."

On a legal pad, the Chief Judge marked this down. Three to one for Mary Ann Tierney, Caroline thought, though José Suarez was shaky.

The next two Republicans—Mills Roberts and Joe Polanski—fell in line with Steele. The vote now stood three to three.

"Lane?" Sam Harker asked.

Steele arranged the sheets before him, the bones of his argument. But it was clear he did not need them.

"This statute," he said bluntly, "is constitutional, and to overturn it is to overstep our bounds.

"*Roe* is a sloppy exercise in judicial legislation, expanding an amorphous 'right to privacy' found nowhere in the Bill of Rights. But even under *Roe,* Congress can regulate the abortion of a viable fetus.

"That's what Congress did here. That's how democracy works; if the people don't like the law, they can petition Congress to change it." His tone sharpened. "*Congress*—not the judiciary, in our self-appointed role as philosopher kings. 'Unwise'—even if you think that's what this law is—does not mean 'unconstitutional.'

" 'Unconstitutional' is not even a question here: the law provides exceptions for life and physical health, while 'mental health' is so amorphous that it means abortion on demand. Which even *Roe* and *Casey* conclude is inappropriate after a fetus—like Mary Ann Tierney's fetus—becomes viable."

Caroline listened with respect: at his best, as now, Steele was arresting and persuasive. But at the end of the table, Blair Montgomery stared at the wall, concealing his distaste behind indifference.

"As for 'unwise,'" Steele continued, "that's a matter of social policy, not law. But I personally think the policy a salutary one, as personified by the Tierney family. A girl whose sense of social history extends to the erection of the latest shopping mall should not compel us to further sanction a taking of life—which if it occurred in a camp, and not one-by-one in the privacy of abortion clinics, would be perceived for what it is: a holocaust.

"If *that's* the right to privacy, we should have none of it."

Abruptly, Steele was silent. Two of his compatriots nodded; a moment passed, and then the Chief Judge wrote down the vote. It was four to three against Mary Ann Tierney, and in favor of the law.

"Franklin," Sam Harker said wryly to Judge Webb, "care to follow *that*?"

The touch of humor was surely an attempt to lighten an increasing division, but might also, in its tacit compliment to Lane Steele, be a clue to the Chief Judge's leanings. If so, Caroline reflected, Mary Ann was one vote from defeat.

Franklin Webb, a grizzled African American and the appointee of a Democrat, returned the Chief Judge's smile. "I was thinking about fishing," he answered. "Salmon, mostly. Or rainbow trout."

This mild pleasantry elicited perfunctory and nervous laughter, which neither Caroline nor Steele joined. "As soon as we finish here," the Chief Judge responded, "you're free to go. But first you have to vote."

"Oh, *that.*" Webb furrowed his brow. "I'm torn, frankly. I've got some sympathy for Ms. Tierney's position, and also for Lane's argument that we're not the legislature—or God.

"José has pointed one way out. Another is to find the statute unconstitutional as to Mary Ann Tierney—because it ignores a proven risk of infertility to *her*—but not to throw the whole thing out for *every* girl in every circumstance.

"That leaves the law in place, and Congress free to address the infertility question if it wishes." Glancing at Caroline, Webb smiled again. "I think our pals on the Supremes will appreciate our restraint. They're as divided as *we* are."

Sam Harker nodded. "Is that where you sit?" he asked.

"Yup. At least for now."

Though skimpy on analysis, Caroline thought, the proposal reflected one of Franklin Webb's many virtues—pragmatism. But this piecemeal approach would leave the law, and those affected by it, in confusion.

Nonetheless, Mary Ann had gained a vote, however tenuous, and the count was four to four. But the votes against her were firm: two of those for her were wobbly and too inconsistent in their reasoning to support a consensus opinion.

That left three judges: Blair Montgomery, the Chief Judge—and Caroline herself.

"Blair?" the Chief Judge murmured.

Leaning forward, Montgomery addressed Franklin Webb. "I appreciate your concerns, Franklin. But you'd also leave some basic principles unclear. Let me suggest a few."

Though strained with age, Montgomery's voice was firm. "I'll start with the right to privacy. Here"—Blair glanced at Steele—"I disagree with Lane.

"There *is* a right to privacy, and the fact that the Bill of Rights doesn't contain those exact three words ignores the obvious." Pausing, Blair's tone became harder. "There are some places the government doesn't belong. Because if a court can order a minor to have a severely defective fetus—at whatever risk to her—it can order her to abort one. And none of us believes in that.

"Lane would tell us that there's a difference—the government can protect 'life,' not take it. But at what cost? The Bill of Rights doesn't say the government can't sterilize minor girls at will, and yet we *know* they can't. So why, in an area as private as this girl's reproductive capacity, can the government place her fertility at risk against *her* will?"

Despite her apprehension, Caroline repressed a smile: whether one agreed with Blair Montgomery, his power to provoke fresh thought remained undiminished. She sensed the waverers listening closely.

"The government should not do so," Blair continued. "And a statute which requires that will impinge on a host of *other* judgments better left to girls and their doctors.

"*Not,* I might add, to their parents. Healthy families may have many virtues, but Congress can't create them. Let alone convert an abusive family into the Brady bunch." With an ironic smile, Blair turned to Lane Steele. "As for Professor Tierney's manifest virtues, Lane, they lie in the area of moral debate. But it is possible that moral passions can blind the best man to injustice—even one right under his nose. The fact that a *different* father might perceive that suggests how arbitrary this statute really is. And why it can't be saved."

Caroline watched Steele's jaw tighten. The vote stood at five to four in favor of Mary Ann, with the Chief Judge coming next.

"Well," Sam Harker said with real humility. "This *is* a hard one, the kind I've gotten too old to enjoy. Especially when what I remember most clearly are my mistakes.

"But," he continued in a reluctant tone, "I'm forced to agree with Lane.

"We can't function as a legislature. If there are anomalies, they should be addressed by Congress. That's my bottom line."

And so it was, Caroline thought. Sam Harker was a man of kind intentions, but no one had ever accused him of profundity.

Now it was down to Caroline.

Around the table, the others faced her. She felt her heart beating faster.

She took a sip of water, then turned to José Suarez. "Where do *you* sit, José? In cement, or on the fence?"

Suarez gave her a prim smile. "I'm Don Quixote," he answered, "in search of an honest compromise."

Caroline nodded, facing Franklin Webb. "What about you, Franklin?"

Amidst the general nervousness, Webb summoned a smile. "Still on the fence," he said. "Hoping I don't fall and crack my skull."

No help there. In the end, what happened would be *her* doing. As she had always suspected.

Caroline inhaled. "Here's the problem," she said to Webb and Suarez. "At least as I see it.

"The two of you are trying to save the statute on a very narrow point—by 'clarifying,' or by rejecting, a specific requirement drafted to be more stringent: a 'substantial risk to physical health.' But that won't become the consensus of this court. We have five judges supporting the law as written, and three who say there's no way to fix it on several different grounds. And even Franklin believes there's no way to fix it when it comes to Mary Ann."

Nodding, Webb acknowledged this reality, while José Suarez regarded her with apparent suspicion. "And so?" Suarez asked.

"And so," Caroline answered, "if we're going to have a majority opinion, one or both of you will have to decide which approach you're least unhappy with: Blair Montgomery's or Lane Steele's. Otherwise, we'll have one of those messes the current Supreme Court is becoming famous for—a plurality opinion, with so many conflicting voices that, while Mary Ann Tierney either wins or loses, going forward no one *else* will know what we've really said. And, therefore, what the law is."

At this, Franklin Webb leaned forward, eyes alight with curiosity. Across the table, Caroline saw Lane Steele tensing.

"True enough," Webb told her. "But if *you're* voting with Lane, our two lousy little votes won't matter. There would be six votes in favor of the law and against Ms. Tierney, and I really *can* go fishing."

Caroline felt her chest tighten. But she was as she was.

Facing Webb, she manufactured a fair facsimile of a smile. "I guess I forgot to mention that," she answered. "I'm voting with Mary Ann Tierney. So I suppose we'd better talk."

Twelve

Two hours later, after an intense and often contentious discussion ended in a vote of six to five, Caroline had assumed that the senior judge in the majority would assign to himself the task of writing a draft opinion. And so she was surprised when Blair Montgomery announced that—given the complexity of the case and the initial divergence of views—he wished to reflect on the assignment. But, after a few moments reflection of her own, she was distinctly unsurprised when her old friend appeared at her door.

Though his eyes were grave, he summoned a smile. "If it weren't for what's at stake here, I'd thank you for the single most entertaining moment in my quarter century as a judge. Lane Steele's face was a study."

Caroline, too, smiled. But the reality of what she had done, kept at bay by the stimulus of debate, had left her tired and dispirited. "A study in contrasts," she answered. "The outrage you saw was followed by sheer rapture at the thought that, however much he deplored my vote, I'm not going anywhere. He imagines being able to taunt us both for years."

Blair sat down wearily. "I don't have years—I don't even buy green bananas anymore. But it was never more apparent that you'd have been a great Chief Justice."

"Why the past tense? Have I died?" Discarding all attempts at levity, Caroline softened her tone. "Looking back on it, I never really had a choice. No doubt it's vanity, but I'm hung up on the concept of what a judge is supposed to be. The judge I've always imagined would not put this girl's health at risk just to serve her own needs."

Blair considered her. "So some of us believe," he answered with equal gravity. "But there'll be hell to pay in the Senate. The only question is how much, and what you can do about it."

"Very little, I think. I'm going to offer to withdraw, and I expect the President to take me up on it. A few weeks into his term, he doesn't need a lot of controversy. Let alone a firestorm."

"Maybe. But I'd like to do what I can to save you."

Caroline smiled at his doggedness. "It's a little late," she said dryly. "Or are you suggesting that I change my vote?"

"No. I'm suggesting you write the opinion." Pausing, her mentor gave Caroline an intent look which, even more than words, compelled her attention. "If you're to be condemned, it should be for your words, not mine. *Your* words, I would like to believe, might cause a few fair-minded senators to take a fresh look at the issues. And at you."

Caroline cocked her head. "A brief for the defense, you mean?"

"In part. But it's also what's best for this court. You were kind enough not to mention it, but I'm part of the problem you were addressing in there—I probably hold the record for brave dissents, and sweeping opinions which command only a plurality.

"You're a consensus-builder, Caroline. That's why you got Webb and Suarez to go along. But if *you* don't write the opinion, there's only a vote behind closed doors, reflecting nothing of the qualities that persuaded those two men to join with you." Leaning forward, Blair finished quietly, "So do this as a favor to me. And to yourself."

Touched, Caroline at first could find no words. "I probably should," she finally answered with a trace of humor. "To tell you the truth, I've always thought you were too much of a 'judicial activist.'" When her mentor smiled, Caroline's tone grew serious. "I'm grateful to you, truly. For so many things. Including this."

After Blair left, Caroline sat back, closing her eyes. But only briefly, for there was far too much to do.

First, she would call Clayton Slade to warn him, and to offer the President her withdrawal. Then she must clear her mind of everything; ahead, well into the night, lay hours of thought and writing.

Thirteen

At a little before eight o'clock at night, Caroline put aside all other concerns—her fears for Brett; her offer to withdraw—and wrote the first few passages of her opinion:

"Whether Congress can bar all postviability abortions for minors absent a 'substantial' risk to life or physical health is a question of first impression. Equally of first impression is whether this important judgment can be made by a parent, or a court, rather than the minor or her doctor."

Pausing for a moment, Caroline thought of another young woman who had borne a child against her father's wishes, and of the vibrant woman that child had become. But the mother, she reminded herself sternly, was now a judge.

"We start by affirming," she continued, *"two core principles:*

"First, absent concerns for a mother's life or health, Congress has the power to ban all postviability abortions, whether for minors or adults.

"Second, under existing Supreme Court precedents, in most circumstances Congress can require the consent of one parent before a minor child obtains an abortion, if the law provides the minor with a safe and accessible judicial alternative . . ."

It might take a little work, Caroline thought dryly, but at least it *sounded* like a judge. The hard part lay ahead.

Thirty-two hours later, Judge Lane Steele's voice echoed with genuine indignation through Macdonald Gage's squawk box. Listening, Gage sipped coffee, glancing at Mace Taylor.

"She starts," Steele reported, "with whether the 'substantial risk to physical health' requirement violates *Roe v. Wade*. Listen to this:

"*'Generally, judges should defer to Congress; certainly they should refrain from imposing their own beliefs. In turn, Congress must not curtail certain fundamental rights unless it has an especially compelling reason to do so.*

"*'These rights include not only those expressly enumerated in the Bill of Rights, but other rights fundamental to their exercise. One such right is privacy. And nowhere is the right to privacy more important than in the area of procreation . . .'*"

"It's the same old song," Gage interjected caustically. "Infanticide is the woman's business, not ours."

"Precisely," Steele agreed. "But she's been very clever about turning that around. For example:

"*'Privacy means more than the right to contraception—the right of a woman to decide when to have a child, or not to have children at all. It must also mean the right to protect her ability to have children if she chooses.*

"*'No humane definition of physical health can exclude procreative health. And when a woman's doctor determines that she faces a measurable risk of infertility, it is for a woman and her doctor—not the Congress—to determine whether this risk is acceptable to her . . .'*"

"I guess any old risk will do," Gage observed. Sitting next to him, Taylor—whom Steele did not know was there—nodded with a tight smile.

"She throws us a bone here and there," Steele replied. "Let me read a little more:

"*'Abortion on demand of a viable fetus is not protected by* Roe—*nor, given our societal interest in preserving life, should it be. But Congress should not be empowered to force Mary Ann Tierney—or any minor child—to run* this *risk. Or, for that matter, the other risks inherent in a cesarean section.*

"*'That Congress has done so here is in little doubt. According to the legislative history,* "substantial medical risk" *limits abortions to those* "necessary to prevent the death of the pregnant minor, or the likelihood of a grave and irreversible impairment of physical health." *This* "more likely than not" *standard would seem to preclude an abortion for Mary Ann Tierney, and for any other minor child for whom the risk of infertility exists but is not, it is clear,* "likely"—'"

Abruptly, Steele interrupted himself. "Without legal standards," he complained, "or judicial supervision, a minor can always find *some* doctor to gin up *some* level of risk to health. It's not much better than aborting eight-month fetuses to protect her psyche."

It occurred to Gage that, if it was seven o'clock in Washington, it must be 4:00 a.m. in California. He imagined Steele in his pajamas, looking like a disgruntled grandfather forced to read a particularly banal bedtime story. Gage, too, viewed the opinion with deep aversion. But it also held the key to his consuming ambition: to defeat Caroline Masters, thereby tarnishing Kerry Kilcannon and moving one step closer to the presidency.

"How," Gage inquired, "does she get around to throwing this law out for every girl who gets herself pregnant?"

"By trusting to her powers of invention. *This* should give you a flavor:

"*'Admittedly, this is a difficult case. But it also exemplifies how hard it is to draw bright-line rules in areas of complex medical and personal judgment. For it is not hard to envision other cases which, if anything, would be far more complicated and agonizing.*

"*'In this case, the prognosis for the fetus is dismal, but not hopeless; infertility unlikely, but possible. One can conceive of an even more painful case, where the fetus appears normal; or a distasteful one, where the mother uses a relatively remote risk of infertility as an excuse to cover her dislike for the gender of the fetus.*

"*'Yet we can also imagine a case where the fetus is without hope, and the prospect of infertility not one to five percent, but twenty. And the progress of medical science will inevitably bring us to this: a pregnant minor at risk for infertility, but hopeful that the anomalies of her fetus can be cured by fetal surgery, will be forced by this law to abort* prior *to viability. Why? Because once viability occurs she cannot act in her own protection—even if it becomes clear that her fetus will die at birth, and that the chances of infertility are greater than they first appeared.*

"*'A statute which impels such trade-offs—between preserving fetal life, however challenged, and a minor's health—cannot stand.'*"

Halting, Steele said in an acrid tone, "She has a wonderful literary imagination. But that's not law."

"It's emotive crap," Gage shot back. "*That's* what it is. Why not nominate Oprah Winfrey." Pausing, he glanced at Taylor, then asked, "Can you fax that to me, Lane?"

From California, there was silence. "This isn't public yet," Steele replied at length. "It won't be until nine this morning."

"And I surely respect that," Gage assured him. "This is for my internal use only. I just need to think through our strategy before the phone starts ringing."

There was a last hesitance—like the feigned virtue of the piano player in the whorehouse, Gage thought sourly. "Very well," said Steele. "I can fax from here at home."

Turning, Gage gave Taylor a grim smile. "You're a true patriot," he told Steele. "I won't forget this."

"You needn't thank me, Senator. It's a matter of conscience."

Quickly, Gage ended the conversation.

"Palmer," Taylor said at once.

"Yeah." Gage put down his coffee. "We better get to him before the press does."

In the Oval Office, Kerry and Clayton bent over Kerry's desk, scanning the faxed copy Caroline had sent. "The least she could do," Clayton murmured. "This is a fucking nightmare."

Kerry shrugged: that much went without saying. "What does she say about the parents?" he asked.

Clayton flipped some pages, then stopped. Kerry began reading:

"We start by noting that the Protection of Life Act creates two classes of minors: those whose parent consents to an abortion, and those whose parent refuses. The former are entrusted to a doctor's care; the latter are directed to federal court.

"Demonstrably, those consigned to court face obstacles which put them at greater risk. Refused consent, a child must—in defiance of her parent—retain a lawyer and proceed to court, often situated far from her home. It is likely that many girls will risk their health, or even life, because this requirement seems too daunting.

"For some, it will seem impossible. And these burdens will fall disproportionately on the poorest, the least educated, the most geographically distant . . ."

"True," Kerry said. "All of it."

Clayton grunted. "Maybe so. But she's already admitted that the Supreme Court has upheld parental consent laws."

Kerry scanned the opinion, then placed his finger on a passage, raising his eyebrows at Clayton:

"While some of these drawbacks also pertain to state parental consent laws upheld by the Supreme Court, there is a fundamental difference. Those laws apply to previability abortions, and require merely that a minor show that she is sufficiently mature to make the decision to abort, or that abortion is otherwise in her best interests.

"This statute governs a medical emergency, where the minor's health is at issue. Given that distinction, the justification for a consent requirement—which effectively denies some girls an equal opportunity to act in their own protection—must be exceedingly persuasive.

"One rationale offered is that the law promotes familial closeness. But as a practical matter, if a trusting and supportive relationship between a parent and child has not already been established, it is unlikely that Congress can create in a moment of crisis what the family could not develop over the course of the child's life. Certainly, the Tierneys offer no persuasive evidence to the contrary.

"Indeed, their painful and public rupture with Mary Ann suggests the oppo-

site—by pitting parent against child, this law has driven a wedge between them which may never be repaired . . ."

Pausing, Kerry wondered where the judge was molded by the woman: Caroline's breech with her father had never healed, with terrible consequences for all concerned. But this was what he had asked for—a judge whose view of the law was informed by her compassion, and her life.

He began reading again.

"Another supposed justification," his nominee had written, *"is that the statute protects minors. According to the experts who testified on behalf of Mary Ann Tierney, the opposite is true. The consent required falls hardest on those girls who are the victims of incest, abuse, and other familial dysfunction. As for those girls whose families function well, most will not require an act of Congress to seek the counsel of a parent . . ."*

At this, Kerry recalled the misery of his own childhood, and then his first domestic violence case, culminating in a murder of the mother by the father, witnessed by the child. Again his finger jabbed the passage. "She's nailed it." The President's tone was soft now. "And you know how well I know that."

Clayton turned to him. "That's fine," he said coolly. "She's an admirable woman, and she's got a job in San Francisco for life. But 'right' and 'admirable' don't translate to confirmable.

"In less than four hours, Kerry, this town will be a war zone. Caroline Masters has to go."

Gage threw the pages on Palmer's desk. "Your friend Caroline Masters," he said brusquely, "has punched you in the shorts."

Behind the mask of outrage, Chad observed, Mac Gage considered him shrewdly, no doubt wondering if Kilcannon had warned him. But Gage did not ask, which was just as well—the President had called Chad as soon as he knew.

"That's why I wear a protector," Chad answered. "What's in here?"

"Liberal garbage." Though Gage's tone was peremptory, his veiled appraisal continued. "I thought you'd be particularly interested in her take on parental consent."

With a cool deliberation which belied his pose of anger, Gage began turning pages. "Here, I underlined some passages for you."

And in red, Chad thought, in case their significance eluded him. He began reading:

"The dissent asserts that the Tierneys are concerned and loving parents. No doubt they are. But Judge Steele's argument proves too much: if a statute unduly bur-

dens the rights of a minor whose parents are well-intentioned, it inevitably will foster tragedies where the family is a seedbed of pathology. The horror of forcing a minor to ask her father for permission to abort the product of his own act of incest—a common cause of fetal anomalies—cannot be justified in the name of Martin Tierney . . ."

"She's got it backward," Gage said flatly. "Because *other* parents may be bad, good parents have no rights. There's going to be a tidal wave, I can promise you."

It was true, Chad thought with apprehension. His best hope was to avoid the undertow.

Quiet, he continued reading.

"The Tierneys, were they so inclined, could not legally force their daughter to abort this child. Can they then compel her to give birth because they think this best for her? Mary Ann's testimony provides ample evidence that she understands the dilemma she is faced with, both medical and moral, and is capable of resolving it.

"A central paradox of this case is that Mary Ann Tierney is entitled, without a parent's consent, to protect her own health in almost every other way. She could, on her own, secure treatment for drug and alcohol abuse, rape and sexual assault, sexually transmitted diseases, mental and emotional difficulties, and all manner of medical assistance related to her pregnancy—including, ironically, a cesarean section. Her parents' antipathy to abortion should not preclude her from making this more difficult, but medically warranted, choice."

Softly, Gage said, "You've been as big an advocate for parental consent as anyone, Chad. You know why this can't stand."

Chad picked up the opinion, flipping to its conclusion. But he no longer truly read; instead he thought of the thing he could never tell Macdonald Gage, and could only pray that Gage would never know. Chad's short-lived pleasure in the chairmanship, his calculated alliance with Kerry Kilcannon, had turned to dust.

"There's no choice now," Gage told him. "Kilcannon either dumps her, or we'll have to take her down."

Scanning the opinion with shock and elation, Sarah stopped briefly at the footnote headed "Mental Health":

"Because we declare the statute unconstitutional on other grounds, we need not resolve the vexing question of whether concerns for emotional health can ever justify a postviability abortion. We share the apprehension that this could lead to abortion on demand: any such abortions, if allowed, should contemplate emotional damage which is demonstrable and severe.

"We note, however, that courts routinely assess mental condition in other contexts, such as criminal culpability. And no precedent exists which would foreclose the authors of future legislation from a careful consideration of this issue. See Doe v. Bolton, 510 U.S. 179 (1973) at 191–92."

Even here, Sarah thought, Caroline had shown more courage than was required.

She sat on the couch, Mary Ann next to her. Rapt, the girl asked, "What else does she say?"

Voice thick with emotion, Sarah began reading:

"'Professor Tierney argues that abortion of this fetus—his potential grandson— would be a way station to eugenics. He summons the prospect of abortion based on eye color, or the absence of musical talent, or because genetic testing may indicate a predisposition to homosexuality. When these problems present themselves, as they inevitably will, we hope that the law—and more important, our societal sense of ethics—will be equal to the challenge. But we should not prevent a future harm by creating one in the present.

"'When we discuss these issues, it is well to remember that this case involves a real person—a fifteen-year-old girl. She does not advocate eugenics. She does not seek abortion on demand. She does not even propose to abort this fetus solely because of its anomalies. Rather, she seeks to ensure that, in the course of her adult life, she may bear another child with a better chance of living.'"

Breathing deeply, Sarah read the final ruling:

"'Does Mary Ann Tierney have that right? Under the Constitution, she does. And so does any minor facing a decision so fundamental and profound.'"

When Sarah looked around, Mary Ann was feeling her stomach. Tears ran down her face.

But Caroline had been impeccable to the last, though it took some moments for Sarah to explain this to Mary Ann.

"Because of the gravity of the issues," Caroline had written, *"and the prospective termination of fetal life, we stay Mary Ann Tierney from securing an abortion until seventy-two hours after the entry of this order. In that time, the government, or the Tierneys, may petition the United States Supreme Court for a further stay pending consideration of a petition for certiorari."*

Stunned, Mary Ann could only ask, "Then it's not over?"

"Not if they petition the Supreme Court. But Caroline Masters has written a wonderful opinion, and the Court could deny your parents a hearing. Suddenly their legal position is a hard one.

"A single justice can grant them an emergency stay pending a review of their petition. But that's a matter of a few days, tops. After that, the full Court can grant a further stay only *if* it decides to take the case . . ."

"My parents will *never* quit," Mary Ann said in despair. "They'll try to keep this going until he's born."

"They can't—they've got a week, maybe two at most, and then the Court will have to rule." Sarah hesitated, then resolved to say the rest. "Right now, there are only eight judges on the Court—they don't have a Chief. It takes only four to decide to hear a case, but *five* to stay you from having an abortion until they do. Without five votes for a stay, Caroline's opinion stands. There's nothing your parents can do."

Swallowing, Mary Ann stared at her, bewildered. "You mean the Court can decide to hear the case," she asked, "but I still could get an abortion before it ruled against me?"

"Yes. If so, we'll have won no matter what."

Sarah stopped there: she could see Mary Ann begin to imagine the further mass opprobrium which might await her. But it was this very potential—exposing a fractured Supreme Court—which made matters worse for Caroline Masters. Even as Sarah's heart went out to Mary Ann, some part of it went to Caroline.

The country was about to explode.

PART V

The Vote

One

An hour after the opinion became public, the White House was buffeted by faxes and e-mails, and its telephone lines were clogged. Pro-life leaders were demanding that Kerry Kilcannon withdraw the Masters nomination, and the Christian Commitment had scheduled a rally in front of the White House. In response, several pro-choice spokeswomen had leapt to Caroline's defense, calling her decision "courageous" and asking the President to reaffirm his choice. But an instant poll on MSNBC was running two to one against the opinion, and several key Democratic senators, reserved in public, had expressed their anxiety to Clayton Slade.

"As long as she's in play," Clayton said to Kerry Kilcannon, "*this* is what you're going to be about."

They sat in the Oval Office—the President, Clayton, and Ellen Penn—waiting for the Senate Minority Leader, Chuck Hampton. "Where's Chuck?" Ellen asked.

"Meeting with Gage," the President answered. "I gather Mac has a message for us."

It was a moment, Macdonald Gage reflected, when power hung in the balance, testing the nerve and sinew of President and Majority Leader alike. But much depended on a third man, Minority Leader Charles Hampton, with interests of his own.

Gage and Hampton shared four years of warfare, compromise, and resentment, with Gage holding the majority and, therefore, the upper hand—doling out committee chairmanships, controlling the Senate calendar, rewarding his constituencies while stinting Hampton and the Democrats. Chuck Hampton wanted the majority, and the five seats he needed to win it, with all the passion of a competitor who had learned that, until then, every defeat would taste like bile. And Mac Gage knew that well.

Hampton sat across from him, lean, scholarly, and intense; filled with distrust for Gage, with apprehension about Caroline Masters. He did not want a fight over the Masters nomination, Gage was sure, and must worry that if the President and Gage commenced one—through either calculation or mischance—it could cost the Democrats dearly.

"Chuck," Gage offered in a fraternal tone, "you need to remind our old colleague of the yawning gulf between difficult and impossible. He may have forgotten who he's left behind."

Hampton's eyes glinted. Gage's comment was a tacit reminder that Kilcannon's election had done nothing for the Senate Democrats—the Republicans' edge, fifty-five to forty-five, remained as it was before November. "Some of us," Hampton answered, "thought it was impossible for Kerry to become President. He hasn't forgotten that, *or* that he is."

Though he felt edgy, Gage chuckled in appreciation. In the Democratic primaries, Hampton had supported Kilcannon's opponent, the incumbent vice president, and now must work with a president whose memory was long. "That doesn't mean," Gage responded, "that he's got nothing left to learn. You can keep him from learning that by hard experience."

"At your hands?"

Gage decided to get to the point. "I haven't had time to count, Chuck. But I'll round up the votes to beat her . . ."

"Including Palmer's?"

It was a shrewd thrust. "Chad will be there," Gage answered firmly.

Hampton studied him, plainly noting that Gage did not claim Palmer's firm commitment. "I admire your confidence."

Gage maintained an unruffled air. "Chad has ambitions. No Republican with ambitions favors dissing parents and dismembering babies. Nor does any Democrat with sense.

"Bottom line, you can't get Masters fifty votes. Why blow up the Senate trying?"

Hampton considered him. "And that's what you want me to tell the President."

Gage spread his arms expansively. "Why build rancor and spend capital in a losing cause, which will only bring more discord to this body? There's nothing in it for Kilcannon—or you.

"You end up losing, pissing off my party colleagues, and leaving you with

scars Kilcannon will be too weak to erase with some great record of accomplishment. All over a woman who placed the thrill of voting for infanticide over sure
confirmation as Chief Justice." Gage's voice rose in amazement. "Anyone with
the IQ of a rutabaga would have ducked that vote. And if Kilcannon hasn't lost
his political judgment, he won't ask you to walk the plank for a judge who has
none."

Hampton wiped his glasses, buying time. "You know the President," he ventured dryly. "He's been known to act on principle . . ."

"Principle?" Gage summoned a sardonic smile. "Like cutting your nuts off?

"I *know* you, Chuck. If Kilcannon can give you something positive to talk
about, you'll be running around the country to all of your contributors, saying
you need money and votes so your noble but embattled president can beat old
Mac Gage and all those right-wing troglodytes who whore for gun nuts and polluters and tent-show revivalists. Why, it might even work." Gage lowered his
voice. "It might *even* get you the majority. But not if you shill for Caroline
Masters.

"She's Rosemary's baby, Chuck. The President needs to drive a stake
through her heart. Tell him that."

Hampton put on his glasses, then placed his hand to his own heart. "I'm
deeply touched, Mac. You're *worried* about me. Never in our years together have
I felt such compassion."

Gage covered his own tension with brisk sobriety. "I'm worried about us
both," he answered. "We've got business to do, and Caroline Masters is in the
way. It's your job to help get rid of her."

"He's not sure about Palmer yet," Chuck Hampton told the President. "That
may be why he wants her gone without a fight."

Kerry studied him, letting the silence build long enough to put the Minority
Leader on edge. "So I'm supposed to get him off the hook."

Quickly, Hampton glanced at Clayton and the Vice President. "Where *does*
Palmer stand?" Ellen asked.

"I don't know yet," the President answered. "But I will."

His tone suggested that Palmer was *his* responsibility, and no one else's. "If
you're going to withdraw her," Hampton inquired with care, "does Palmer matter? And why do you think you can hold him now?"

This question was more than rhetorical, Kerry knew; Hampton sensed that
the President and his potential rival had an arrangement, and he wanted to
know what it was. Instead of answering, the President asked, "How *was* Gage?"

Hampton pondered this. "At his best—confident, relaxed, expansive. Which means *he's* worried, too. He thinks he'll win, but he isn't sure he wants to find out what'll happen along the way."

"He'll come out against her," Kerry predicted. "Today. That way, if *I* take her out, he'll get to claim the credit with his people, but won't look so anti-woman to everyone else. It's Gage's favorite tactic: getting others to screw themselves on his behalf . . ."

"It's not screwing yourself," Clayton interposed. "Masters already did that."

This bluntness, which only Clayton used with the President, cast the others into silence. "You admire her courage," Clayton continued. "And her opinion—as legal craftsmanship—confirms you weren't off base on *that* score. But Gage is right: *no one* needs this. Especially us.

"You've got a big agenda, Mr. President, and you just squeaked through last November. Most people agree with Gage that parenthood is sacred, and late-term abortion tantamount to murder." Clayton's tone became satiric. "I can't wait to see us selling *that* one. What's our slogan going to be: 'It's not a baby 'til it's born'?"

"Unless Mom and Dad say it is." Kerry murmured this, as if to himself. "Which is particularly touching when Dad's the baby's father."

"The 'incest defense,'" Clayton retorted with repressed exasperation. "This isn't about the merits, Mr. President, *or* morality. The moral—and practical—thing to do is to preserve your political capital for things like health care, gun control, campaign reform, and saving social security. *They're* why you're here, *not* late-term abortion." Clayton stood. "It's bullshit to say if we fold on this, we fold on everything. And where do the pro-choice folks have to go—Mac Gage? Even *they'll* understand the problem . . ."

"What exactly," Ellen Penn interjected, "are they supposed to understand? That Caroline Masters applied *Roe,* and followed the law? That if Gage and the right wing back us off, *Roe* isn't the law anymore? That we're only here because pro-choice women voted for us?" Sitting on the edge of the couch, Ellen leaned toward Kerry, her dark eyes and quick speech underscoring her intensity. "She stood up for them, they're telling me, and *you* should stand up for *her* . . ."

"This isn't about her," Clayton objected. "It's about *this* President. She's at *his* disposal, not the other way around."

Silent, Kerry turned to Ellen: Clayton's point was essential, and he wished her to remember that. "I understand," she told him with quiet urgency. "But the pro-choice groups will work their asses off for you. They'll lobby senators, hold rallies, run ads if you want them to . . ."

"All of which," Clayton told Kerry, "is a mixed blessing. A whole lot of people hate them, and *they* can't get you the votes you need. Only *you* can."

Pausing, Clayton glanced at Hampton. "I mean no disrespect to Chuck. But even the senators on *our* side will have a price—a worthless dam, a crop subsidy, some hack they want to be a judge, or maybe ambassador to New Guinea.

"Even *that* won't be enough. To keep all the Democrats in line, you'll have to mobilize the civil rights groups, the trial lawyers, the AFL-CIO." Clayton began pacing. "The fucking trial lawyers," he concluded, "will want the right to sue everyone for everything. And I can't wait until you call Sweeney at the AFL-CIO."

Despite, or perhaps because of, Clayton's vehemence, Kerry found himself smiling. "I can't either. So tell me what he'll say."

"Something like 'If you think most of my members give a damn about this crap, you're nuts. So why should *I* squander all the juice we earned last fall supporting some embattled moron of a senator by pressing him for a vote as dumb as *this?*'"

"Oh," Kerry answered quietly, "I think he'll be more respectful. The *last* risk he took was coming out against me in the primaries."

To the President's satisfaction, Chuck Hampton shifted uncomfortably in his chair. "Sweeney," Clayton countered, "was there for you in the general election. To support you on Masters—if *that's* what you want to ask him for—he'll need to go back to his people with something big. Like that he owns you on free trade." Clayton stopped pacing. "And *these*," he finished, "are your *friends*."

Kerry smiled grimly. "Which brings us to Palmer, I suppose."

"It surely does. You need fifty-one votes, Mr. President. Even if you and Chuck could hold every Democratic senator, that only makes forty-five. At least six Republicans will have to defy Macdonald Gage, and the price for *that* will be high—compromises on a lot of your agenda, and weapons built in their home states that the Pentagon doesn't want, until we've got billion-dollar submarines cruising the Great Salt Lake.

"You'll be paying on the installment plan, forever. And every favor done for your enemies—even Palmer—will alienate your supporters. All for the judge who created this mess."

With this, Clayton fell quiet, as did the others. Kerry read their faces: Clayton's concerns were deeply sobering, as was the task before them—determining the fate of a Supreme Court nomination and, by extension, the character of a new administration.

Facing Clayton, Kerry spoke as though they were alone. "So you say just let her withdraw. Quick and clean, with a statement of mild regret, and deep appreciation of her decision to spare the country such trauma."

"That's the best way," Clayton answered imperturbably. "Two days and it's over. The only other rational choice is to leave her hanging there, and lose."

Kerry smiled, but only with his eyes. "Don't withdraw her," he said flatly. "Just pass the word that we're not playing to win, and that our friends can vote their own self-interest. That way we don't mortgage ourselves, but don't look quite so craven in public. And we can say it's *Gage,* not us, who's taken down a qualified and courageous woman."

Clayton shrugged. "At least there's *something* to recommend it. Trying to salvage this has nothing."

"Nothing?"

"About as much as Vietnam. A bloody fight, waged by green troops, with no simple way out. Until you've completely lost perspective." Clayton's tone was soft and serious. "We've all seen it happen—people so caught up in winning the presidency that they forgot where power ends, and arrogance begins. I don't want that to be our story."

Kerry was silent: because others were present, Clayton had not mentioned the worst of it—not Caroline's secret, but Kerry's own. Yet Kerry could read his thoughts.

"Don't do this," Clayton told him. "There's no good end to it."

Two

Caroline Masters gazed out her penthouse window at the jagged San Francisco skyline.

The late morning sun seeped through haze and fog, and the towers of the city seemed distant, a mirage. Her apartment was quiet, and she was alone; the only sign that she was the center of a national furor came from the drone of a cable news reporter.

"At this hour, demonstrators have already begun gathering outside the White House. Press Secretary Kit Pace has told us that Judge Masters retains the President's confidence, but that he will have no further comment until he studies the opinion."

Which meant that she was hanging by a thread. Perhaps she should depart with dignity, by insisting on, rather than merely offering, her withdrawal. For *that*, Kerry Kilcannon no doubt would be grateful.

The telephone rang.

It was the media, Caroline thought at once. Then she realized it might be Clayton Slade, or even the President himself. Walking to the kitchen, she answered with a curt, "Hello."

"Aunt Caroline? It's me."

Caroline took a moment to find her bearings. With relief she said, "I thought you were a reporter. I'm glad I decided to answer."

"Me, too. I wanted to see how you are."

Alone, Caroline wished to say. *Clinging to a foolish hope, unable to let go.* And then it struck her that she teetered on the brink of self-revelation which, once begun, she was uncertain she could stop. "Fairly lifelike," she answered dryly, "for a corpse. When Jackson called to say how brave I'd been, I felt like I was attending my own memorial service." Pausing, Caroline tried to put a smile in her voice. "I suppose it's hard to keep all this attention from going to my head."

Brett did not laugh, and her tone was soft. "You're trying to sound like it doesn't bother you. But I know it must."

There was compassion in her voice, and a hint of frustration, as though she wished to penetrate her aunt's reserve. "It does," Caroline said finally. "Quite a lot. But there's nothing I can do."

"Is there something *I* can do?"

Come see me, Caroline thought. But Brett was not her daughter, and never had been. She had her own life.

"You already have," Caroline told her. "But you might send me another short story. The last one was sublime."

"Starting with her daughter," Ellen Penn told Kerry, "she's acted with complete integrity. Especially when she wrote the opinion. So let me ask you this: Do you think she was wrong?"

When Clayton began to interrupt, Kerry held up his hand, eyes fixed on the Vice President. "No," he conceded. "I don't."

Ellen expelled a breath. "Okay, then. She stood up for what you both believe the Constitution says. For that, we propose to dump her. Because it's 'smart.'"

"That's not how you got here, and *I* don't think it's smart." Glancing at Chuck Hampton, she said, "Chuck can tell me if I'm wrong. But Reagan didn't suffer for standing by Robert Bork. And I'd guess the senators in our party are waiting to see what kind of president you are. They can live with a vote of conscience now and then, as long as you take the lead. But first you have to ask."

"A vote of conscience is one thing," Clayton objected. "But this is like gays in the military. A complete nonstarter, politically. However we might accept the principle."

"It's nowhere close to that," Ellen retorted. "If we frame *this* principle right—standing up for a woman of integrity—we can bring along the women and swing-voters.

"Dump Caroline now, and we disappoint our friends, draw the contempt of our enemies, and tell all of them we're gutless." Once more, she turned to Kerry. "Even if she loses, we've got an issue. Let's see how much taste Gage has for turning this into a jihad, or for looking like the kind of paternalistic creep women are thrilled they didn't marry. Or, even worse, *did* marry."

"This isn't just a game of chicken," Kerry replied. "Winning matters. If the only 'upside' is losing, I'll pass."

"I think you *can* win." Pausing, Ellen angled her head toward Clayton. "I understand Clayton's point about the AFL-CIO. But the last thing they want is Gage with a stranglehold on the Senate. If you can bust him on this one, *they* win."

"True enough. But that gets us back to Palmer. The AFL-CIO cuts no ice with him."

For the first time, Chuck Hampton intervened. "I'm not spoiling for a fight here, Mr. President. But Chad knows elections are won in the middle, and he wants to sit where you're sitting. I doubt he thinks he gets there by blindly following Gage, and I'm damn sure he doesn't want to. If you can manage to keep Palmer neutral, and build support, maybe we've still got a shot at getting Masters on the Court.

"Split Palmer from Gage, and it's easier for us to pick off the remaining votes we need—Republicans from swing states. They may be scared of Gage, but it's the voters who keep them here. They're Chad's people, and they may hope he'll give them cover."

Kerry concealed his surprise. He had expected Hampton to counsel surrender; now he wondered whether the Minority Leader was trying to prove his mettle—or, perhaps, was probing the complexities of Kerry's relations with Chad Palmer.

"For Chad to risk that," Kerry answered, "we'd have to accomplish more than he thinks we can—or should. Turn the country around on late-term abortion."

"We can do what Sarah Dash did," Ellen suggested promptly. "Give the issue a human face. We roll out real women to talk about how late-term abortion got them three kids down the road, or kept the kids they already had from becoming orphans. That means being shameless—bringing them to the White House, putting them on talk shows, and using their husbands, too. We can even give them their own Web site.

"It's one thing to talk about disassembling babies. It's another thing to have two loving middle-class parents look America in the eye and say, 'We *know* how tough this is—it happened to us.' With that kind of platform, we can start reaching out to the high-end media—editorial pages, and news magazines like *Nightline* and *20/20*." Buoyed by improvisation and inspiration, the Vice President added, "That's where Lara would be perfect."

Kerry felt Clayton's glance of warning. Quietly, the President said, "That's for her to decide."

Ellen seemed to wait for some elaboration. When there was none, she said, "Then talk to her, because we need her. We could also use some religious leaders to say that protecting a mother's life, health, and fertility is moral, and helps keep families intact. That would hit Gage where he lives. And it may help keep Palmer from coming out against her.

"Remember, you have to make the case to an audience of two hundred seventy million before you reach an audience of one: Chad Palmer." Glancing around, Ellen included the others in her peroration. "One of his charms is that he's actually open to argument—especially if it serves his interests. As for our interests, consider what *you* gain by winning."

Kerry smiled. "And what is that, precisely? You've raised so many dazzling prospects I forget."

Ellen gazed at him, unsmiling. "You get Caroline," she answered. "And you—not Gage—get to run the country."

"Remember your advice about juries?" the President asked Clayton. "Back when I was a rookie lawyer?"

The meeting was over, and the two men were alone. Accustomed to silence, Clayton had waited for his friend to think aloud.

"I told you a lot of things," Clayton answered brusquely. "About half the time, you listened."

"I always *listened*," Kerry responded. "What you said was, 'Don't try to be someone you're not.' And you were right. My worst day in the campaign was when I ducked the vote on the Protection of Life Act. I looked like a kid caught in a lie."

Clayton shrugged. "It was necessary."

"I agree. But it was also a moment when Gage understood me perfectly. Because I was doing what *he'd* do in my place." Kerry sat back. "And if I take Caroline Masters down, Gage will understand again. Because it's the percentage move.

"But that's *not* why people sent me here. They expect me to keep my commitments, and act from core beliefs. Which is exactly what I came here for, or I've missed the point of my own campaign." Kerry's tone grew harder. "*That's* when I scare Macdonald Gage. Because he's not sure then what drives me, or what impact that will have on him. He may not want an all-out war with someone quite that incomprehensible."

"And if he does?"

"Maybe I beat him. If not, I'll make him pay the price for beating me— letting the country get a good look at him."

"They'll take a good long look at everyone," Clayton admonished. "A nomination in trouble is a magnet for all the scalp hunters in the media. They'll be scavenging for leaks from the committee files and the FBI, putting garbage from private investigators on the Internet, grubbing for *anything* in Caroline's background . . ."

"All of which," Kerry finished for him, "puts her daughter at greater risk. *And* Palmer."

"Of course. Palmer's already sitting on the 'rumor' that Caroline has a daughter. Your 'all-out war' increases exponentially the chance that Harshman breaks Palmer's stranglehold on the files, or that some right-wing group digs it up on their own."

"Maybe. But that's Caroline's problem. And Chad's."

Clayton looked at him in some surprise. "You don't care?"

"Not nearly as much as they do. I promised I'd protect her, and I have. But Caroline made 'a decision for life,' as Gage is so fond of saying. If she'd have let me, I'd have made it public myself."

"That was *before* the hearings," Clayton retorted. "Remember Harshman's question—'How can you understand families if you don't have kids?' They'll say she lied to him."

Kerry shrugged. "Let them. Let them reopen the hearings. *You* saw her testify; if some old white guy like Harshman starts beating on her for *that,* he'll come out the loser. And having her explain why she didn't abort a talented girl with a working cerebral cortex would be a welcome change of subject."

Clayton's gaze became a stare. "And if they all blow up," he answered coolly, "so does Gage."

Kerry nodded. "It's a little like playing with matches. A smart man keeps his distance."

"Including *you,*" Clayton shot back. "Tell me you're not going to do this."

"I don't know yet. But by tomorrow morning, I will. That's all the time I've got."

Slowly, Clayton shook his head. "Your instincts have always been good, Kerry—in ways that still surprise me. But this one worries me, for *you.* It really *is* a game of chicken, and that's risky for a president. Especially a new one."

Kerry considered him, grateful for his concern, uncertain of who was right. "*This* President," he said quietly, "means to *be* President. Macdonald Gage or no, I chose Masters to be Chief Justice."

"And you can *unchoose* her," Clayton answered stubbornly, "like every president before you. What can I say to talk you out of this?"

All at once, Kerry felt the weight of his decision, the warmth of Clayton's loyalty. "You already have," he assured his friend. "Don't think I won't consider it."

Clayton fell quiet. "While you're doing that," he said at length, "consider Lara."

Three

"Only you can stop this," Sarah said.

In the cramped confines of his office, she faced Martin and Margaret Tierney; though the USF campus was tree-lined and commodious, to Sarah the room at night felt like a prison, allowing the tension between them no release.

"By not appealing?" Tierney asked quietly.

"Yes. In thirty-six hours, the stay will expire." Sarah kept her own voice low. "You've been true to your beliefs, Martin. But that's not been enough."

Behind his bare wooden desk, Martin Tierney steepled his fingers; sitting next to Sarah, Margaret Tierney stared at the tile floor. Such close proximity felt uncomfortable to Sarah, but all other choices—the Tierneys' home; Sarah's apartment; the offices of Kenyon & Walker—were patrolled by the media and demonstrators from the Christian Commitment. Caroline's ruling, Sarah reflected, seemed to have unleashed forces which had overwhelmed them all.

"It's not that simple," Tierney told her. "Even if we withdraw, the Justice Department will petition the Supreme Court. This is an act of Congress, and it's the government's duty to defend it—no matter what *this* President may want."

Sarah glanced at Margaret Tierney, who now watched her husband with pained intensity. "There's another way to end it," Sarah ventured. "However hard that might be."

Tierney's spectral eyes fixed her with a bleak stare. "Consent to an abortion?"

"Yes. That should moot the case—there'd be nothing for the government to stop, even if it were willing to risk an adverse ruling." Sarah turned to Margaret Tierney. "This already has marked your daughter for life. Now she's caught in the middle of a Supreme Court nomination. Either *she'll* be the reason Caroline

Masters withdraws, or the President will decide to fight—in which case all hell breaks loose."

"What happens to the President," Tierney interrupted sharply, "*or* Judge Masters, is no concern of ours."

Margaret Tierney still gazed at her husband in what Sarah hoped was a silent plea. "But Mary Ann is," Sarah countered. "If you don't stop them, she'll never get her life back. She'll be like Patty Hearst by a multiple of ten: in twenty years, some rag will put her on the cover with a caption like 'The Girl Who Changed Supreme Court History—Where Is She Now?'"

Sarah paused, looking from husband to wife. "Where she is now," she finished, "is waiting. For me to come back to my apartment, where *she* now lives. For you to say that you love her, and forgive her, and hope for *her* forgiveness. And that you'll allow her to protect herself as she thinks best."

At this, Margaret Tierney turned from her husband to Sarah, her voice tremulous, "How *is* she?"

Sarah searched for the most honest answer. "Scared," she said. "Damaged. Hoping against hope you'll change your mind.

"Part of her still thinks about how all of you were before the pregnancy, and wishes she could go back. Sometimes she wakes up, she says, and she's that girl again. And then she remembers she can *never* go back." Sarah softened her voice. "I know you love her. But do you have any idea how much you've hurt her?"

"Oh, a little," Margaret answered with quiet sadness. "We're the parents who denied her birth control, and I'm the mother who never spoke to her about sex. Which, unfortunately, isn't true . . ."

Surprised, Sarah stifled a question.

"Yes," Margaret told her. "I told her much, much more than 'just say no.' I suppose, perhaps understandably, that she wishes to forget that. And who would believe a mother who wants to pass on the curse of her own infertility?" She quickly closed her eyes, as though clearing them of tears. "We're the adults, and she's the child. Who I love, and hurt for, more than you—or Judge Masters— will ever know."

Heartsick and confused, Sarah recalled the different versions of a family which sometimes divided her from her parents—the events, so vivid to one, which another recalled quite differently. But here she foresaw something more fateful: the possible disintegration of this family and, perhaps, this marriage. "If you love her," she urged Margaret, "you'll need to let that transcend your own beliefs. All it takes is one of you to consent, and the other to forgive."

Margaret's lips parted. "Beliefs are hard," she said at last. "Betraying them is worse. I don't want that for Mary Ann."

The telephone on Tierney's desk rang.

It made Sarah start, breaking her silent connection with Margaret Tierney. Irresolute, Tierney stared at the blinking light. Then, with palpable reluctance, he answered.

"Yes?"

Listening, he seemed to sag. "I'm sorry," he finally said, "I can't talk to you right now. We're meeting with Ms. Dash."

Through the telephone, Sarah heard a voice rise in alarm, tinny and indecipherable. Gripping the phone to his ear, Tierney listened for some moments, in obvious distress.

At length, he interrupted. "Barry," he said tightly, "I will have to call you back."

In the moment which followed, Tierney's face was blank. "Yes," he promised. "Soon."

Without awaiting an answer, he put down the phone.

Margaret Tierney watched her husband, tension creasing her forehead. "They'll never let you alone," Sarah told them. "Not until your family's destroyed. Unless one of you puts an end to this."

There was silence, and then it was Martin Tierney who answered. "An end to our grandson, you mean. Of all the actors in this miserable drama, we're the only ones who are trying to save them both." He shook his head, as though to clear it. "We need to be alone, Sarah."

In mute appeal, Sarah turned to Margaret Tierney.

For an instant, the pain etched in her face gave Sarah hope, and then she turned away. "Please," she murmured.

Without speaking, Sarah left.

Four

Lying in bed, Kerry heard the sound of water running in the bathroom, Lara showering. From his television, Caroline Masters gazed back at him.

The Christian Commitment had used selected photographs from the hearing, transmuted into a grainy black-and-white to make Caroline look imperious and remote. The text for the thirty-second spot was blunt:

"Ninety percent of Americans," the woman's voice said, *"oppose the barbaric procedure called 'partial birth abortion.'*

"This *woman supports it.*

"Call President Kilcannon and tell him that a judge who favors infanticide is unfit to be Chief Justice of our highest court."

The Commitment, Kerry realized, must have cut the ad before the ruling became public—no doubt because of a leak from the court itself. Now they meant to ensure that he abandon Caroline Masters: according to Clayton, the spot was running hourly on NBC—Lara's employer—and the three major cable news networks.

Fretful, Kerry snatched his bedside phone and hit the "redial" button. Three rings were followed by Allie Palmer, reciting the message which tonight Kerry had learned by heart.

"This is the Palmer residence . . ."

When the message ended, Kerry said simply: "Chad, it's Kerry again. You know the number. Call me no matter how late."

When Kerry hung up, the picture had changed.

A live broadcast on CNN showed a candlelight vigil at the Lincoln Memorial. The camera focused on a handmade sign: LINCOLN FREED THE SLAVES—NOW FREE THE UNBORN. In a haunting, near-religious tableau, the demonstrators huddled like communicants before the monument: a grave and massive Lincoln, lit a yellow-bronze, seated behind white pillars.

Kerry's enemies would leave nothing to chance, he knew. And they would use any weapon they uncovered.

He had not picked this battle; it was the last he would have chosen—and the worst, Clayton insisted—on which to stake his presidency. That had been the focus of today's tense and sometimes testy meetings: Kerry as President. Yet now, alone, he thought of those other people about whom, except for Lara, he had spoken of as chess pieces: Caroline Masters, who as a judge had chosen to face an issue which might shatter her ambitions. Her daughter, whose life as a result might be cruelly altered. Chad Palmer, who out of honor and self-interest had conspired to prevent this, and now risked enraging those set on besting Kerry. And Lara, whom Kerry feared losing more than he feared defeat.

But there were others, as well. Mary Ann Tierney, whom Caroline Masters had saved—at least for a time—from what Kerry believed was a grievous wrong. The nameless girls, all too real to Kerry, who were lost, abused, mistreated. He had been marked from childhood by the shock of seeing his mother's bloody and broken nose, hearing her cries from the bedroom; as terrible as that had been for him, Kerry knew that it was essential to the man he had become. For he could never be like Macdonald Gage, who believed that his own good fortune was a reflection of virtue, which others could emulate if they wished.

Nor could Caroline Masters.

She had proven that—in her rulings in favor of the brutalized prisoner, and now with Mary Ann Tierney. The Supreme Court Kerry meant to leave behind would know that law without compassion was a shortcut to injustice. For this, he could not have chosen better than Caroline; if he chose to fight, that would be why.

Kerry knew himself; he would not be President without that. He was as capable of ruthlessness and unsentimentality as Gage. But Kerry needed a larger cause than power; the belief that he was bettering the future of those who relied on him, and of a country he deeply loved, whose ideals had helped raise Kerry himself, the son of immigrants, to become its leader. Armed with *that,* he acknowledged with withering honesty, there might be little he would not do to make Caroline Masters the next Chief Justice.

Before him, candles flickered around the monument, the electronic image of a reality less than a mile away. If he went to the window, Kerry could almost see it. Instead he watched the screen, and wondered what his course would be.

By tomorrow morning, he would know, and so would the country.

As Kerry reflected, the bathroom door opened.

The shadow of a woman crossed the room, pausing by the screen, her nude body illuminated by its light. She registered the candlelit images, then turned to him.

"On?" she asked lightly. "Or off?"

In the darkness, Kerry smiled. "Off."

Lara walked to the bed, pulling down the cool sheet, sliding close to him so that her nipples grazed his chest and the slim line of her body touched his.

Kerry closed his eyes. Until the night they had become lovers, so surprising and yet, it now seemed, so inevitable, he had forgotten that it was possible to love someone so much that it frightened him. This was different from loving a child, surely, but the feelings must be akin—to place this much at risk, to lose control, so that the life of another was essential to your own. In childhood, Kerry had learned the pain of loving; it had hurt to love his mother yet be unable to protect her. But it was that vulnerability, the melding of his emotions with those of someone else, which had made him who he was, so different from his cool and self-protective brother. And it was Lara who had taught him that he, not Jamie, was—after all—the fortunate one.

Softly, she kissed his neck, the wisp of her breath warm on his skin. "What are you going to do?" she asked.

"Right now? Just be with you."

Her laugh was knowing. "Unless Chad calls."

"Timing," he answered, "is everything."

With his free arm, he swept aside the covers, leaving them exposed.

Gently, he kissed her and then, lips parted, again. His mouth, sliding to her throat, began a leisurely progress down her neck, her nipples, her stomach . . .

"I'm sorry, Chad," he heard her whisper. "He's busy."

Afterward they lay in the dark, warm and damp, Lara's body flung carelessly across his. They had not spoken in some minutes.

"What *will* you do?" Lara asked.

"I don't know yet." He gazed at the ceiling, pensive. "A lot depends on Chad."

For a time, Lara was quiet. "And on me?" she finally asked.

It was this conversation which, though necessary, Kerry dreaded. That her secret could destroy his public career stirred in Lara both worry and resentment, a volatile mix which—in the crucible of his presidency—Kerry feared could put an end to them. Silent, he pondered the complexity of love, in which selflessness was inseparable from selfishness. He feared for Lara, and feared losing her.

"The last time we discussed this," he told her, "we were walking toward the Lincoln Memorial. As I recall, it didn't go very well."

"What you mean," she answered with a trace of humor, "is that I acted like a bitch."

"That's not how I remember it. I do remember you saying to leave all that behind us—for good. And, about Masters, to do what I damn well pleased."

Her tone retained its irony. "And that wasn't clear enough?"

Still gazing upward, Kerry expelled a breath. "Since then, Caroline's changed the equation. Now she rises or falls on abortion . . ."

"So tonight you have a vision. I'm on the *Today Show,* discussing my Vera Wang bridal gown. Jealous of my youth and beauty, Katie Couric asks if I aborted the President's child when he was a married senator and I was covering him for the *Times.* And the best I can say—at least truthfully—is, *'Kerry didn't want me to.'"*

There was no avoiding this. "If not Katie," Kerry answered, "someone. They got damned close to it during the campaign. And Gage and the Christian Commitment play to win."

"A *triple* play, actually. They get Masters, you, *and* the 'liberal media.' Through me."

"Yes," Kerry said with reluctance. "Something like that."

"Short of *that* disaster," Lara continued, "you'll have pro-lifers holding rallies and news conferences, crawling all over talk radio, and elbowing each other to get on Rush Limbaugh, Charlie Rose, Ted Koppel, and every other interview show in America. There'll be mass mailings of anti-Masters propaganda, a tidal wave of protest on the Internet, and a statement by all the bishops, archbishops, and cardinals of our church, denouncing the Tierney decision and, implicitly, you for being a rotten Catholic. And the *next* ads on 'partial birth' will be a lot more gory. Not to mention that Gage may find out that Caroline has a daughter." She paused, speaking more quietly. "Of course, Clayton's already told you that. And you—knowing you as I do—told *him* you're willing to live with it. All that's slowing you down is Chad. And *me.*"

The summary was so trenchant that Kerry emitted a mirthless laugh. "So," Lara finished, "I guess you want my opinion. Whether or not I want to give it."

Kerry was silent; there was no need to answer.

"The first time we talked about Caroline Masters," Lara told him, "I said she struck me as a supercilious Wasp—not worth the trouble. In fact, I accused you of being drawn to her because *she'd* had *her* baby.

"Of course I hadn't met her yet, but why let *that* stop me. And, of course, I *was* being a complete bitch." To Kerry's surprise, she kissed him. "So now I'm apologizing."

"Why?"

"Because Caroline really is that good. And because she stuck her neck out for a teenage girl, whatever the risk to her own daughter. And to her.

"How am I supposed to feel, Kerry, if you drop her because of me? And what will *that* do to us?" She rested her forehead against his. "I love you, more than I can say. But I can't live like I'm being blackmailed. So if you decide you can't stand by her, make sure it's about the risk to *you*. Not me."

Curling his fingers, Kerry grazed her cheek. "And us?"

"I know I've been worried about becoming First Lady, perhaps too much. So there's something I said last year, which I need to tell you this last time." Pausing, Lara pressed his hand to her face. "If the worst happens, I can hold my head up—if you can. It was my choice, after all."

There was nothing else for Kerry to say. Or do, except to hold her.

"You should call Chad again," she said at last. "It's getting late."

Five

Lying next to Allie, Chad Palmer ignored the telephone. "Whoever it is," he told Allie, "I don't want to hear from them. Unless it's Kerry, telling me he's pushed her off a bridge."

Allie's bedside lamp was on; neither could sleep. "It's really *that* bad."

Chad nodded. "Unless Kerry backs off. Gage wants me to reopen the hearings. Turn them into a morality play on partial birth abortion, with Masters in the role of baby-killer."

Propped on her side, Allie regarded him with green-flecked eyes which expressed the worry of a wife and mother confronted with forces she could not control. "*Will* there be more hearings?" she asked.

"Not if I can help it. They'd be a nightmare—it was risky enough the *last* time, keeping the zealots who wanted to crawl through her life from seeing our own files." Chad's tone became sardonic. "At least *that* secret involved sex with a man. Harshman's latest idea is that Masters and Sarah Dash are lovers, and her ruling in favor of Mary Ann Tierney was actually a crime of passion. Imagine *that* interrogation on national TV."

Allie's lips compressed in worry and distaste. "But you're the chairman. Can't you stop him? Or at least stop him from investigating Masters?"

"Not with Gage egging him on. I told Vic Coletti that the President ought to withdraw her. Not simply to avoid defeat, but also humiliation for both him *and* her."

"Does Vic agree?"

"I hope so. He certainly sees why *I* don't want more hearings, and not just because he knows I've been covering for her. Once I reopen them, we'd have to send her back to the full Senate with a positive or negative recommendation, or no recommendation at all. Unless I try to kill the nomination in committee without ever bringing it to the floor—which may be what Gage ends up wanting me to do." Chad's voice hardened. "That way her blood's on *my* hands, not his.

"The pro-choice groups understand that. So they want *me* to stand in his way. All day they were like a recorded message: Gage may be a right-wing lackey, but I'm not, so I should let him be 'anti-woman' by himself. Some Republican pro-choice women even hinted they support me for President—as if me becoming their poster boy isn't exactly what Gage wants."

"And the pro-lifers?"

There was no point, with Allie, in telling less than the truth. "Were worse," Chad acknowledged. "*They* want to know why I supported an antifamily judicial activist, and want *me* to know I'll never be President if she gets on the Court. In case I missed that, Barry Saunders sent black lilies. The only question is whose 'death' he has in mind—Mary Ann Tierney's baby's, or mine."

Allie took his hand. "These people have always made my skin crawl, Chad. But now they really scare me."

Chad gazed at their hands, locked together, and felt the complexity of their bond, the fear that neither spoke aloud. "With good reason," he said quietly. "They'll use anything they dig up, on anyone who's in their way. This is one they can't afford to lose.

"The media knows it, too. Bob Novak inquired if it's true I'm stiffing Gage, and wimping out on the right to life—cued by Mac himself, no doubt. Then Tony Lewis called to ask if I'm preparing to confront the Commitment head on. They're looking for me to drive the story."

Chad felt her hand squeeze tighter. "*Those* guys I can deal with," he told her. "It's the sleazemongers who could hurt us."

Involuntarily, it seemed to Chad, Allie glanced at Kyle's picture. "Do your friends see any way out of this?"

"They're only focused on the politics, of course. Tom Ballinger says the Christian Right is losing ground, and that anyhow there's nothing I can do to please them. But Kate Jarman thinks there's no way I win the nomination without helping the Commitment get Masters." Chad's tone became mordant. "Kate asked a pungent question: What happens to me if the Tierney girl has an abortion, and her fetus turns out to have a cerebral cortex?"

For an instant Allie appeared stunned. "They'd find that out?"

"The Commitment would surely try, so they could give it to the press. Unless I help take Masters down, that *would* ruin me." His voice softened. "I can see the spot they'd run against me in the primaries, showing the Gerber baby with an *X* across his face."

Though Allie was quite still, Chad could see the tension in her body. Torn between hope and doubt, she said, "Kerry wouldn't risk *that*, either."

Chad shook his head. "Don't be too sure. Suppose the fetus turns out to be a mess. Then *we'll* have gone after Masters for protecting a fifteen-year-old girl, and Kerry will go after *us* without a trace of mercy.

"I know him—he's already thought about that. It may not look good for Masters now, but Kerry's a nervy bastard. No one in American politics can raise the furies like he can—pro *or* con. And he doesn't know what that might mean to us."

Fearful, Allie asked, "How can you avoid that?"

"The best way is to oppose her, then somehow persuade Gage to put her to an immediate vote on the Senate floor, rather than send the nomination back to my committee. That might put an end to this before anyone else gets hurt." Chad's voice became clipped. "Maybe Mac will see the virtue of pursuing a summary execution. If he strings this out too long he may get a baby without a brain, instead of Matthew Brown."

Allie glanced sharply at him. "I know," Chad reassured her in a milder tone. "We both hope for this girl's sake that her son *is* hopeless, so this isn't even worse for her. But whatever he turns out to be, it won't be Mary Ann's private tragedy. It'll be a political land mine, throwing shrapnel everywhere. All I can do is try to keep us out of the way."

Allie's face softened. "I'm sorry, Chad."

Her husband mustered a smile. "At least for a politician, you mean."

"At least." Gently, Allie touched his face. "You knew someday it might haunt you, and still you put our daughter first."

The moment was burned into Chad's memory: the naked boy stumbling across the darkened lawn; turning to his daughter, who was naked as well, and shivering with fear and anger. He could smell the wine on her breath.

"You *fuck*." Kyle's voice was slurred. "I love him. *Him,* not you."

Like a burst of light, the horror of what was happening cut through Chad's fury. "Kyle," he said in a tightened voice, "you're drunk. Get dressed."

There was a sound behind him. From the shadows of their living room, Kyle gaped at the front door.

Turning, Chad saw his wife. She stared at them, trying to comprehend.

"That weasel Eric," Chad managed to say. "I found them on the rug . . ."

"You *humiliated* me," Kyle screamed. "You shit . . ."

"Shut up." Chad turned on her, anger spinning out of control. "I find you fucking him in our living room like some slut in an alley, drunk out of your mind. You've humiliated *us*—and yourself. That boy is scum . . ."

In hysteria, Kyle whirled, grabbing a vase off the coffee table. As she jerked her arm back to throw, Allie stepped between them.

"Stop it," she demanded. "Both of you."

"Eric *loves* me," Kyle burst out. "He's the only one who does."

"He'd 'love' anything," her father snapped, "that spread its legs for him. And you're pathetic enough to do it."

Allie turned on him. "*Stop,* Chad." Her voice was choked, but still controlled. "I'm telling you to stop."

Chad could see the desperation in Allie's eyes, and a mother's instinctive resolve—somehow she would salvage this, if only she could stop them now. Chad's shoulders sagged.

Seeing this, Allie turned to Kyle. Softly, she said, "Go upstairs, and get dressed. I'll be up to talk to you."

Irresolute, Kyle stared at her parents, torn between shame and fury. "Go ahead," Allie told her.

Slowly, the girl turned and started up the staircase, gripping the banister for balance. After a few steps, she turned to her father. "You *ruined* it," she said.

Allie gripped Chad's arm. The girl climbed the stairs.

Silent, Allie flicked on a light, staring in disbelief at Eric's clothes on the living room rug. "You pushed him out the door," she said in wonder. "Naked . . ."

"Somehow," Chad retorted, "I don't think his parents will be calling to complain."

"What about *Kyle* . . ."

"What *about* her?" At once Chad felt the raw misery Kyle had brought them—the lying, the drugs and self-absorption, and felt the visceral wish that she had never been born. "*Look* at what she's done, what she's doing to us. She's become this sinkhole, dragging both of us down with her."

Allie gripped his shoulder. "*Don't,*" she spat. "Don't say anything more." After a moment, voice low again, Allie continued, "She's our daughter. She's our daughter, and we'll have to find a way."

Looking at his wife, her face haggard with emotion, Chad felt a terrible weariness. "How?" he asked. "A new psychiatrist? Or just this endless, helpless, hopeless patience, where we're social workers, not parents, and she's responsible for nothing."

"I don't know." Allie's tone had a repressed shrillness. "I don't know. All I know is that I'm gone for three hours, and I come home to find you here, and more damage than Kyle could do alone." Pausing, Allie tried to control her voice. "Why are you here, Chad? I thought you were in Washington."

"I was." Remembering his impulsive flight home, his pleasure at imagining

Allie's pleasure, Chad felt the foolishness of his own words. "I wanted to surprise you."

Allie closed her eyes. "You did, Chad. You surely did. And now you can go back."

Chad flinched. The unfairness of it hit him hard, the sense of separateness ever since his release from captivity, of having become superfluous. "If she's our daughter," he answered, "then I must be her father. You can't just fire me—or is that what you want?"

Opening her eyes, Allie gripped the lapels of his suit coat. "No, Chad. It's not what I want. What I want is time to deal with this, before you two hurt each other even more. Please."

In the morning, Chad was gone. When next he saw his daughter, she was pregnant.

Kyle sat at the kitchen table. Bending, he kissed her forehead. She did not look up at him, or speak.

Turning to Allie, Chad saw her nod toward the sunroom. He followed her there.

He closed the glass doors, and they sat on the sofa. The Saturday morning was bright with spring; on their lawn, which Chad saw through the window, two squirrels ran up an oak tree. A frayed rope still hung where Kyle's tire swing once had been; Chad could recall pushing her, her childish shrieks of delight.

"What now?" he murmured to Allie. "What now?"

She looked at him guardedly. "An abortion, Chad—to start."

Chad's returning gaze was steady. "I don't believe in it . . ."

"That's politics, Chad. This is Kyle."

"It's not just politics. I happen to believe this is a life, even if the father's an evolutionary cul-de-sac." Chad felt a sudden, visceral anger. "Where *is* good old Eric, by the way? Has he found the clothes, or the guts, to show his face? Or is he making her deal with this alone?"

"Yes." Allie's voice was tired. "He's dropped her, as you predicted. Kyle's devastated."

"For which she blames me, I suppose."

Though she regarded him with a straightforward look, Allie was silent.

"Whatever she thinks of me," Chad said at last, "this isn't wart removal. If there's anything I learned in prison, it's how precious life is, and how careful we should be about assuming the right to take it.

"I'm as sick for Kyle as you are. But this has to do with how we value life, and how we—*including* Kyle—take responsibility for what we do. It's more than an inconvenience, and we don't fix it by what, to me, involves murdering the innocent victim of her mistake. *Kyle* was once a fetus, you'll recall."

Allie's voice, though level, was faintly accusatory. "She was also wanted." At least *then,* she did not need to add.

Chad took her hand. "I'm not trying to punish her, believe me. I wish she weren't pregnant. But either we can care for this child, or find someone who will—God knows there are enough very sad couples out there, who've been trying to do for years what Kyle and Eric managed to accomplish in an instant." He softened his voice. "If there's any good to come of this, that would be it. Abortion would be just one more ugly, irresponsible act, with us as aiders and abetters. I don't think *that's* good for any of us."

Allie bit her lip. "No, Chad. However you feel, it would be best for our daughter. If I thought an abortion was irresponsible, or that she could withstand pregnancy and motherhood, that might be an option. But she's on the brink already—to the point of harming herself. To be abandoned, and then pregnant, would damage her even more. And adoption would be traumatic . . ."

"For *whom*?" Chad retorted. "Is this *all* about Kyle, and nothing else?"

"For me, it has to be." Her voice was thin now. "She's the one I love, Chad. She came to this decision after hours of talking with me—*and* Dr. Blevins.

"Kyle understands what this involves. But it also involves the child of a girl who was using drugs and alcohol, and who doesn't have the strength to go through an adoption. And Dr. Blevins worries that forcing her to have a child would drive a wedge between us which we might *never* fix. I can't risk that—for her, or us."

"Dr. Blevins," Chad answered, "may think that treating a fetus like a wart is good for Kyle's moral development, and no doubt for mankind in general. But I don't agree—on either point."

Allie squared her shoulders. "I know you don't. But this is a family, not a conclave of the Christian Commitment, and no one's treating abortion like 'wart removal.' It's what she wants and needs, and what I as her mother believe is best . . ."

"So once again, I'm irrelevant. As her father, my highest and best purpose is to stay out of the way."

"That's *not* what I'm saying."

"Allie," Chad said, "that's the kind of empty thing someone says when it's *exactly* what they're saying. So let's skip the verbal foreplay, and get to what you plan to do."

Allie's face was rigid. "There's a parental consent law, Chad. I'm planning to support our daughter and protect you. With whatever misgivings, I intend to sign the form . . ."

"Regardless of what I think."

"One parent is all it takes, and I'm willing to be that parent." Allie's voice became quiet. "Dr. Jacobs is my high school classmate. This will be confidential, and she more than understands our needs."

Chad stood. "Do you think *that's* what I'm worried about?"

"No." Allie's demeanor was calm now. "But I don't think it's fair that you pay the price for my doing this. I accept that you feel differently . . ."

"That's very gracious." Chad felt a fresh burst of anger and frustration. "Others, if they ever find out, won't be quite as large-spirited in absolving me. But, as I say, for me *that's* the least of it."

Allie stood, resting her hands on his arms. "But not for me," she said quietly. "I know you hurt, and I know she hurts. I don't want either of you hurt anymore."

Chad shook his head. "Your friend can hide the form in her files. But kids talk. *Eric* talks—knowing him, he's probably proud of his achievement. Especially one for which he'll bear no responsibility at all."

Allie bent her head. "You're right. And I'm sorry. There aren't any guarantees. There's no guarantee even that abortion is what's best for her. All I can do is listen to her, make the best judgment I can, and pray it's right."

With this, Chad felt her burden, the resistance seeping out of him. "I'm sorry, too."

"Then do something for me, please. Tell Kyle you still love her." Allie looked up at him again. "Please, Chad. You may not believe this, but that would mean more to her than anything I can say. Or do."

Chad studied her. "There's something I want from you," he said at last. "And it's relevant to all of this. Including the fact I've become an outsider, so that I don't trust myself with her, and you don't either. To the point you drag me off to the sunroom so Kyle doesn't hear us."

"What is it?"

"I want you to move to Washington. Both of you."

Allie gazed at him in open surprise. "Why?"

"It would be a fresh start for Kyle—and for us." His tone was calm and clear. "You say we're a family, but I'm a weekend father—I pay the price of family, but I'm not part of it. And there's no argument, anymore, that staying here is good for her."

Allie's brow furrowed. "This is very new, Chad."

"Not to me. It's what I should have done, after I was released. Instead, I picked up where I left off—even though life as an itinerant husband wasn't what I wanted anymore. I'm tired of collaborating in my own uselessness."

He touched her face and spoke softly. "I'll work with you, Allie. I want to, very much. But you'll have to accept me as a father, in more than name."

Allie leaned her head against his chest, taking a deep breath. When she looked up, there were tears in her eyes. "Then go to her. Please."

Chad did that.

It was not easy, and never quite became so.

After her abortion, Kyle had good days, and others where her depression, as before, seemed close to suicidal. After the move, Allie hewed to her closely— through a new therapist, new private school, and, gradually, a friendship or two, which Allie nurtured with anxiety and care. Slowly, Kyle's mood seem to lift, and her presence in their home became less like a ticking time bomb, then less volatile altogether. To Chad, this felt like a collective release of breath.

Kyle would never be as close to him as she was to Allie. But what they achieved was a kind of peace, in which Chad, teaching himself an unwonted patience, served the family as a steady presence.

His efforts, Chad reflected, must have helped. For years, Allie still suffered when Kyle went out the door, fearing a mischance that would drive her back into despair, or even take her life. But Kyle's bouts with drinking, while they still occurred, became rare, and drugs vanished from her life. For whatever reason, their move to Washington seemed to have worked.

Yet they took nothing for granted. Chad became invested in their new success: although pressured to run for President in the election just won by Kerry Kilcannon, Chad had demurred—it was too soon, he calculated, to separate from his family once again, or place Kyle in the spotlight.

"She knows you feel that," Allie told him. "And so now she's sure you love her. She never was, before."

If this was so, Chad thought, then he had accomplished something. Certainly his daughter had. Though he often wondered what would have happened had Kyle kept her child, all he could know was what had happened once she did not. And now she was in a local college, studying fashion design, and her every small accomplishment was something Chad Palmer carried with him.

In his own life, too, Chad was changed. He remained pro-life, a belief at once too genuine to discard and too necessary to his survival as a Republican. Still, he was quieter about it—out of sensitivity to Kyle and concern for himself, and to a degree, because of the questions Kyle's experience had planted in his mind. On *this* point, he had no wish for attention. But there was no way to escape it altogether: the Christian Commitment, while it could not fault his voting record, had begun to question his zeal.

Its scrutiny deepened another belief Chad had always held: that the private life of a public figure should be his—or hers—alone. It was that, even more than

Kerry Kilcannon's blandishments, which had secured Chad's commitment to protect Caroline Masters. And the fact that Caroline acted as Chad wished Kyle could have, and had a daughter of her own, left him with no real choice.

"The things that matter most," he had said to Allie, "transcend politics."

But now Masters was the center of a firestorm, and he had to find a way out for them.

"This," he told Allie, "is where the politics of abortion meets the politics of investigation. Everyone, not just Caroline Masters, will become fair game.

"Our daughter had an abortion. That makes me a total hypocrite—to pro-choicers because I remain pro-life, to pro-lifers because I acquiesced, to everyone because I'm silent about whatever I may have learned. And God help us if Macdonald Gage finds out." He shook his head. "I don't want Kyle to become the next Mary Ann Tierney. She's too fragile."

Allie touched his wrist. "The files are confidential," she said. "How would they ever know?"

"Files get stolen, or leaked." Seeing her worry, Chad hesitated before adding, "Eric's still out there, Allie. If he thinks it's time to tell his story, there's nothing we can do."

Allie's lips parted. "Can you resign the chairmanship?"

This, Chad thought, was a measure of her fears. "Now?" he asked her gently. "Deciding not to run for President was one thing, but resigning really *would* bring the hounds to our door. All I can do is quietly fall in line with my colleagues, and hope that Caroline Masters is gone soon."

Silent now, Allie kept her hand on his wrist. "It's too bad," Chad mused aloud. "I may not agree with Masters, but I like her a great deal. Same with Kerry. More and more, I tend to like the people who don't believe as I do more than the ones who do. The Christian Commitment has made me wonder— some of those fanatics don't understand how complex life can be. You're either good, or bad."

Allie managed to smile. "You're good, Chad. Because you *are* complex."

Looking into her face, Chad felt reality closing in on them. "What I am," he told her, "is chastened. You hurry along, eyes on the prize, and then something forces you to see how selfish and delusional politics can make you. Yesterday I was the powerful chairman of Judiciary, at the top of my game. And now . . ."

His voice trailed off.

Beside them, the telephone rang again.

Six

"I thought you'd died," Kerry said with a trace of humor. "You don't usually hide out so long."

"I've been busy," Chad answered, "taking calls from Judge Masters's new admirers. Both of them. I assume Coletti told you what I think—that you should pull the plug."

"Because she's right?"

"She's *not* right." Over the telephone, Chad sounded testy. "And it doesn't matter if she is."

Kerry felt Lara's hand, gently resting on his shoulder. "It matters, Chad. It matters to women. It matters to me."

"With all respect," Chad countered, "you don't matter anymore. This is going to be dirty, and you and Masters are going to lose. Unless you back out now."

Kerry kept his voice even. "Before the Tierney decision, she was the best qualified to be Chief Justice. She still is. You're asking me to dump her over a single vote . . ."

"A single disastrous vote. Don't be a Boy Scout, Mr. President—or a megalomaniac. This isn't just about *you*, and what you want." Chad's tone was clipped. "You signed me on to cover for her. But not through *this* mess."

With deliberate calm, Kerry asked, "Are you breaking your word?"

There was silence. At length Chad said, "You *owe* me on this one, dammit. If you push it, chances are what's in the file gets out, and gets worse. Which puts me at more risk."

Turning, Kerry glanced at Lara; she watched him with eyebrows raised, mirroring his concern. "Maybe so," he told Chad, "but I can't explain that to the American public—or to Gage. All they'd know is that I dumped Judge Masters."

"Then that's the price of honor . . ."

"The price of honor," Kerry snapped, "is keeping your word when it's hard. Or do you want to expose the daughter yourself."

Chad emitted a harsh, cynical laugh. "You know I can't—not without people wondering *when* I first found out. And I know you wouldn't mind that much if I did oppose her. So cut the crap, Mr. President . . ."

"You too, pal. Your party is losing women, and you want to be President. However you play abortion, you don't want to be the symbol of an antichoice crusade. Not if you want *my* job."

"I do," Chad shot back. "And so does Gage."

"Gage," Kerry said with scorn, "is mortgaged to the far right, who've got a fucking death wish. If you want to compete for votes in *that* fever swamp, be my guest. I'll get reelected without ever leaving home."

There was another silence, briefer now. "Just what," Chad inquired in an unimpressed tone, "do you propose to do?"

They were in a war of nerves, Kerry knew; if Chad decided to oppose Caroline with all of his considerable force, there was no way to save her, and little point in trying. "I propose to keep her," Kerry said evenly. "And let you Republicans define yourselves . . ."

"You'd create a train wreck? Just for the hell of it? I don't think so. Or you wouldn't have already called me three times."

Kerry felt his chest tighten. Softly, he said, "I want to win, Chad. I want Masters on the Court. And I'll do whatever I need to put her there."

Listening, Chad was appalled. If Kerry waged a war, not just a pro forma effort, there might be no containing the damage.

"That's crazy," Chad said. "You can't win this."

"Oh, I'll *win*," the President answered. "But how I win depends on you. If *you* don't go all out against her, she's got a chance. If you do, then you'll look like Gage—another running dog of the religious right who takes down a qualified and courageous woman. Which I'll be happy to road test for the next campaign."

Quickly, Chad tried to assess all he knew about Kerry Kilcannon. But Kerry's essential character offered Chad no certainty. Kilcannon was a risk-taker, unafraid of controversy, and his intuition often ran against the grain. Now, as President, he might consider it necessary to meet Gage head-on.

Evenly, Chad asked, "What part do I play in this fantasy?"

"The loyal—and temperate—opposition. I don't expect you to support her. But if you oppose her, please do it quietly. Don't lobby for votes—"

"Gage," Chad interjected, "wants me to reopen hearings."

"Fine," Kerry said with surprising calm. "That gives you an excuse to play the statesman—as chairman, you shouldn't head a lynch mob. And Caroline would have an opportunity to defend herself . . ."

"Bullshit. It would string this out for the scandalmongers—and increase exponentially the chance that the daughter gets exposed, along with our little game of footsie." Chad's voice rose. "If that's what you want, I'll make sure to sink her first . . ."

Kerry's forehead was damp. Beside him, Lara moved closer.

"New hearings are a risk," he conceded, "but they could give you cover, and me time to build support for Caroline. I'm not sure they wouldn't backfire on Gage . . ."

"Wake up," he heard Chad snap. "Gage may try to force me to kill her in committee. She could never even get to the floor."

Kerry knew this. What was telling, and puzzling, was that Chad seemed not to sense when Kerry was fencing. The pressure of his new chairmanship, and Caroline's secret, appeared to be fraying him to a point that Kerry found surprising.

"So," he asked, "what would you suggest?"

"Dump her."

Kerry gripped the telephone tighter. "Other than that."

In Chad's silence, Kerry felt the visceral intimacy of their contest. "You want me to keep sitting on the daughter," Chad said at last. "You want me not to take the lead in opposition. You want a fucking lot, frankly."

Eyes narrowing, Kerry waited for more. But Chad had finished. Coolly, Kerry asked, "And what do *you* want?"

On the other end, Chad expelled a breath. "Tell your people—especially in the Senate—to oppose more hearings. Then challenge Gage to bring this to an up or down vote, quickly."

Briefly, Kerry pretended to consider this. "I need time to build support. Otherwise, she loses—"

"Otherwise," Chad interrupted, "I'll do my damnedest to beat you and win the plaudits of my party.

"That's my price, Mr. President—no hearing, quick vote. Then you and Macdonald Gage can fight it out alone."

Kerry hesitated, just long enough to seem reluctant. "Fair enough," he answered.

. . .

Rolling on his back, Kerry exhaled.

"He believed you?" Lara asked.

"Yes," he answered. "If he hadn't, I'd have pulled her." Taking her hand, Kerry allowed himself to feel his own misgivings. "But he misread me. So now we'll get to live with the results."

For an hour, the Palmers lay sleepless in their darkened bedroom, Allie curled in Chad's arms, thinking of the daughter who knew nothing about the calculus of power and, they hoped, never would.

"I did the best I could," Chad murmured.

Allie burrowed her head on his shoulder. "I know," she said. "I know you did."

Seven

"Remember," Kerry asked Carl Barth, "when you endorsed Dick Mason in the primaries?"

On the other end of the line, the director of the *New York Times* editorial page was momentarily silent. "Of course, Mr. President. I wrote that editorial myself."

"You said then that I wasn't tough enough in defending choice. But now I'm defending Caroline Masters. I'd like your help."

Barth hesitated. "Actually," he said, "we're considering a piece on that."

"When will it run?"

"We're not sure yet. Maybe day after tomorrow."

"Tomorrow would be much better. If you don't counter fast, the ground could slip right out from under her." Kerry glanced at his notes. "In an hour, Katherine Jones of Anthony's Legions will be faxing a piece for your op-ed section, refuting the Christian Commitment's claim that late-term abortion is used as birth control. I expect you'll receive a copy, and hope you can commend it to the editor of your op-ed page."

"I'll look out for it," Barth promised. "I must say, Mr. President, you're taking a very active interest in this."

"I don't mean to lose," Kerry answered. "Any more than you would want me to."

With that, Kerry got off the phone.

He glanced out the double-arched window of his private living room; through the glass the baroque structure of the old Executive Office Building, lit by winter sun, looked like a child's gingerbread cake built to grotesque proportions. Then he scanned the list of names beside him.

The list had several columns: "Media," headed by the *Times,* the *Washington*

Post, and CNN; "Senate," including members of Chad's committee and the Republican moderates he needed to dissuade from committing to Gage; and "Interest Groups." Looking up at his silent television, he saw the ad excoriating Caroline Masters running on MSNBC. Hastily, he searched under "Interest Groups" for the name he wanted, and stabbed out the telephone number next to it.

In Los Angeles, it was not yet seven o'clock. After several rings, a voice, though thick with sleep, answered with the pompous "how dare you" tone of a man whose notion of importance began and ended with himself.

"Good morning, Robert," the President said crisply. "Too early to be out suing someone?"

In the silence which followed, Kerry had the image of Robert Lenihan—with his chaotic blond curls and the belly of a pouter pigeon—absorbing that the distinctive voice which had awakened him belonged to the President of the United States. But his surprise, Kerry knew, was merely prelude: swiftly, Lenihan would conclude that this call was just another acknowledgment of his unparalleled stature among the plaintiffs' lawyers of America.

"Mr. President?"

"None other. I'm calling to ask you to exert your influence in a righteous cause. Within the next hour or so, I hope you'll raise two million dollars for an ad campaign supporting Caroline Masters." Kerry's voice, though bantering, had a certain edge. "For you, Robert, that's a phone call or two. Unless you just decide to write the check yourself."

"Two million?" Kerry could hear surprise mixed with Lenihan's calculation of the benefits, as well as the sheer pleasure of having the President in his debt. "That's expensive fun."

"For lesser men. But you've made half a billion suing tobacco companies, and now you're after the gun manufacturers for billions more." Kerry's tone was pleasant, but brisk. "We've got Villela-McNally in New York cutting the ads, and we need to put them on the air by tomorrow morning."

"That's not much time . . ."

"I don't have much time. The Christian Commitment is in its second day of spots, and my pollster tells me that they're working."

There was a brief silence, induced, Kerry supposed, by his own failure to pay more tribute to Robert Lenihan's consuming ego. But time was short, and asking Lenihan for money was distasteful enough.

"I'll need to reflect, Mr. President." Every syllable dripped with self-regard. "Before you nominated Masters, you never solicited my advice. If you had, I'd have expressed my reservations about a lawyer who spent much of her career defending large corporations. Frankly, you've caused me grave concerns."

"That's nothing." Kerry's instinct about how to handle Robert Lenihan merged with genuine irritation. "You want to sue the gun manufacturers. You want punitive damages. Mac Gage wants to pass laws shutting all that down, and he's got a majority in the Senate."

"But you can veto that, Mr. President."

"Yes, that's how the Constitution works. So without a friendly Supreme Court, the only thing between Gage and you is *me*. Assuming I decide that a veto serves the public interest."

Now Lenihan sounded faintly indignant. "You're as against guns as I am."

"More. But some people don't think lawsuits are the answer.

"You supported me in the general election because you had to. But you raised money for Dick Mason to oppose me in the primaries—a lot of it. So I don't have any illusions I'm talking to a loyalist." Kerry's tone softened. "This is your chance to change that, Robert."

This time, Kerry supposed, the silence suggested an element of worry. "Tomorrow," Lenihan temporized, "is quick."

"Not for us. We've got the ad company, the script, and a schedule for running spots. All you need to do is form 'Lawyers for the American Way,' funded with two million dollars, and Caroline Masters is on the air." Kerry's voice turned cool. "Then we can both consign Dick Mason to the dustbin of history."

There was a last, brief silence. "All right," Robert Lenihan answered slowly. "We want your friendship, Mr. President."

Putting down the telephone, Kerry Kilcannon pondered the costs of such a call.

With or without Robert Lenihan's help, he intended to veto Gage's bill. More fundamentally, Kerry loathed the corrupting role of money in politics, the dishonesty of the thirty-second TV spot. But he would have to fix *that* problem later—the Christian Commitment had given him no choice. There were no spending limits on its anti-Masters campaign; the first task was to confirm her, the test of strength on which so much else depended. It was, as he had told Caroline Masters, a matter of principle—and more.

Consulting his watch, Kerry saw that it was ten o'clock.

In the East Room, Ellen Penn was presiding over a press conference. Orchestrated by his media advisers, it featured pro-life Catholics who agreed that Mary Ann Tierney faced a medical emergency; women who might have died without late-term abortions; and a mother from Ohio—a witness in the Tierney case—whose daughter had chosen an illegal abortion over parental consent, and bled to death. But to get them the maximum exposure, his own appearance was essential.

Kerry made two more calls—to Minority Leader Chuck Hampton and Senator Vic Coletti—and then headed for the East Room.

It was elegant but sparsely furnished, and its parquet oak floor and Bohemian cut-glass chandeliers made it a classic setting for dances and receptions. But today it hosted a reprise of the Mary Ann Tierney trial; as Ellen Penn hovered protectively by the podium, a teenage girl spoke to a room jammed with reporters crowded in folding chairs or standing at the rear.

Kerry took his place beside Ellen—unnoticed, it seemed, by the girl.

"My father raped me," she began in a near whisper.

His staff had found her, Kerry realized—the fifteen-year-old victim of rape and incest mentioned by Dr. Flom at the Tierney trial. She was slender and pallid, with circles beneath her eyes and legs as thin as sticks, and her youth seemed to have fled. Ellen Penn placed a hand on her shoulder, lips forming words inaudible to Kerry. As painful as this was to witness, Kerry reflected, it would not make pleasant viewing for Macdonald Gage.

The girl's eyes were downcast, and she spoke in a halting murmur. "My father made me promise never to tell. He said he'd kill me . . ." She choked now, and then said brokenly, "After he hung himself, I ran away . . .

"It was too late, the doctor said. Because I was healthy, and they thought my baby was, too."

The room was hushed; the reporters watched, transfixed, too professional to look away. *What have politics come to,* Kerry wondered; he watched, stricken as the others. "My baby's retarded," she said softly. "Retarded and blind . . ."

The girl shook her head, unable to go on. As she turned from the reporters, shamed and sickened, she also turned from Ellen.

Instead, she saw the President. She hesitated, then she went to him.

She felt like a stalk. *I'm sorry,* he wanted to say. *We shouldn't have asked you to do this.*

But even before he heard the whir of cameras and the bustle of photographers, the President knew that this image would lead every news broadcast and dominate every paper. Perhaps *that* had been what he wanted.

"I'm sorry," he murmured. "I won't let you down." Moving closer, a reporter wrote this in her notebook.

Eight

On CNN the girl closed her eyes, her face pressed against Kerry Kilcannon's shoulder.

"There are days," Macdonald Gage murmured, "when I still can't believe that people buy this crap."

Mace Taylor eyed the screen. "It's his favorite tactic—the politics of victimhood. Sort of like group therapy, where we all get to feel someone's pain. It'll wear off before the next election."

"Maybe. But he's good at it." Turning from the television in disgust, Gage faced his former colleague, who was sitting on the couch with a glass of iced tea in his hand. "If he makes this all about women, we've maybe got an image problem. For me, it's better to take the high road, and let Paul Harshman trash her."

Taylor still watched the screen. "No reason you can't do 'more in sorrow than in anger.' Let our spots do the damage—we've got enough money from the Commitment and the gun folks to run them from now till doomsday."

"Kilcannon will put spots up, too," Gage answered. "He'll dredge up the money somehow, maybe from those bloodsuckers who want to sue the gun manufacturers and need our beloved President to help them. Now that he's committed himself, Kilcannon will go for our throat."

"The people who hate him—*them* we can count on. But there's a whole slough of voters out there who don't give a damn about anything but the Dow—including that thirty years of sexual license is bringing us down." He pointed at the screen—the girl and the President, foreheads nearly touching, Kilcannon's lips moving in silent consolation. "Before the little bastard's through, he'll have a lot of folks forgetting how the Tierney girl got pregnant. Or that the *real* victim is her baby."

Taylor sipped his tea. "You need Palmer," he said tersely.

"What we need," Gage rejoined, "is to widen what's at stake beyond abortion, finesse Kilcannon by giving people broader reasons to believe that Masters is unfit. Using Sarah Dash could open up the Tierney case into an ethics issue—that Masters never should have heard the appeal, that this woman's been seen at her apartment." As he spoke, Gage felt distaste overcome him. "Who knows what they did in there? Talk about the case in bed?

"Point is that we'll never know, which makes it wrong. Which makes it about *ethics*. And we don't want an unethical judge—maybe a lesbian unethical judge—replacing Roger Bannon."

Taylor's narrowed eyes conveyed suppressed impatience. "Like I said," he repeated, "you need Palmer."

Briefly, Gage considered the lobbyist's meaning. "What *Palmer* says," Gage told him, "is that we should force a vote. Take her down before Kilcannon can rally opinion, or the baby turns out to have no brain. As of now, the polls are with us."

Listening, Taylor's expression was cynical. In a flat tone, he said, "And you think Palmer's right."

"No. A quick vote would look too arbitrary, a rush to judgment. I've told Chad that. And I don't have fifty-one votes committed yet . . ."

Taylor grunted. "You've got *forty*-one, don't you?"

This, Gage sensed, was less a suggestion than a test, intended to make him confront his paucity of choices. But Taylor's only interest was in money and results; for Gage, who wished to be President, pursuit of his aims required a certain elegance. "A filibuster," Gage answered coldly. "That's a fine idea, Mace—use forty-one out of a hundred senators to deny Judge Caroline Masters the courtesy of a vote. That would make me the dark practitioner of hardball politics, who reduced a matter of principle to a cheap parliamentary trick. All to shaft a woman.

"Kilcannon would like that almost as much as winning. Next election, he'd jam it up my ass. I don't owe *that* to anyone, and anyone who wants it is a fool."

Taylor's lips formed a faint smile which did not touch his eyes. "Then you need more hearings. You need a flat-out inquisition into this lady's life, using Dash and ethics as a reason.

"Harshman can't wait to do it, the whole nine yards—drugs, sex in college, lesbian lovers. To him, she's an ethically challenged, antifamily baby-killer, who corrupted the legal process because her lover gives good pillow talk." Pausing, Taylor sipped his tea, mouth pursed, eyes distant. "You can keep your distance, Mac. Then if Harshman sells *that* scenario—or any part of it—you just step in, the statesman, and save the country from Kilcannon. But first," Taylor finished softly, "you need Chad Palmer."

The insistence of this mantra had begun to make Gage edgy. "And Palmer doesn't want hearings," he reiterated.

Taylor shrugged. "What was the name of that movie—*Dead Man Walking*? That's what I see whenever our heroic friend starts posturing: a dead man. Dead, and he doesn't know it."

Gage stared at him. "I don't want to use that," he said bluntly. "No matter what I think of Palmer. And it might come back to haunt us."

Staring back, Taylor's eyes were devoid of feeling. "Then make him Harshman's love slave, any way you can. That way he can live a little longer."

"I don't like her decision," Chad Palmer said, "but I don't like crawling all over her life, either." Reaching across his desk, he handed Macdonald Gage a printout from an Internet gossip column by a marginal journalist named Charlie Trask. "Have you seen this, Mac? Without quite saying so, it implies that she and Dash are lovers."

Gage did not pick up the paper, or take his eyes off Chad. Calmly, he answered, "Maybe they are."

Palmer felt the tug of worry: the reason he doubted this—his knowledge of Caroline's daughter—could arouse the enmity of the forces opposed to Masters. "And probably they're not," he answered. "Not that this sleazemonger knows, or cares. Which is why Trask is the conduit of choice for trash like this."

Gage's silence signaled his irritation. "You don't think it matters if our Chief Justice is a lesbian?"

Chad weighed his response with care. "For us to ask the question," he replied, "is to answer it. There've been too many of these personal smears—the public doesn't like it, good people wind up hurt, and it makes politics a snakepit for the rest of us." Pointing at the printout, he asked, "Any notion where this comes from, by the way?"

The thinly veiled accusation produced an expressionless stare. "No," Gage answered. "But now that it's out there, our constituents will damned well expect your committee to investigate. Don't you think it's funny that Dash visited her apartment, alone?"

The rumor had Mace Taylor's fingerprints on it, Chad guessed with disgust, ferreted out by investigators who were financed by his clients. But Chad also took it as a warning: their intrusions on Masters's privacy were intended to compel further intrusions by Chad's committee and, should he anger Gage and Taylor by objecting, Chad might face intrusions of his own. "You and I are alone right now," he retorted. "With the door closed. Do you suppose people will say we're in love?"

There was a glint in Gage's eyes. "That would be a slander on your family, Chad. On Allie, and on Kyle. Masters has no family."

Chad felt his anxiety sharpen—first about Kyle, and then about Brett Allen. "That doesn't make her gay, Mac. Nor does having women friends."

"Suppose she was lesbian back in college," Gage rejoined. "That would put her 'friendship' with Dash in a very different light." His gaze was vigilant, as though searching Chad's face for clues. "Chief Justice is not just a legal position; it's a moral one. Our constituents expect a justice—or a senator—to exemplify those values . . ."

"By conducting a witch hunt."

"It's not a witch hunt." Gage's voice rose, the sign of tension. "It's an inquiry about ethics. Even if we can't prove they're lovers, Dash was Masters's law clerk."

How, Chad wondered, could he hope to fend off hearings. "That was over three years ago . . ."

"It's part of a pattern," Gage snapped. "Employee, friend, maybe more. And you want us to act like ostriches."

Chad reined in his temper. "Five judges on the en banc panel," he said evenly, "voted with Caroline Masters. They're not all part of some homosexual cabal—they're simply wrong.

"*That's* our argument: the opinion is wrong, and speaks for itself. Let the full Senate have an up and down vote, without hearings and innuendo. We can beat her on the merits."

I'm giving you fair warning, Gage thought with mounting anger. *Get yourself out of the way.*

"Chad," he said with exaggerated gentleness, "you're a proud man. You have your own notion of integrity, and I admire that. But do not fuck with this."

For the first time, Chad hesitated. "You've got my vote," he answered, "and I'll speak against her on the floor. No one will be able to fault me—or you."

"But they will, Chad. They will. They'll fault us both. The pro-life forces hate Masters on abortion, the groups who give us money to watch out for them hate her on campaign finance reform, and the folks who worry about moral decline wonder who and what she is." Gage's voice remained quiet. "For them, what we do here is defining—the Court is hanging in the balance—on both issues, and on countless others. It's defining for us, as well. Put the future of the

Court aside, and there's still one more question to be answered: Does Kilcannon run the Senate, or do we?

"If you help him protect this woman, you're disloyal. I've counted votes, Chad: if you side with the Democrats, you may keep me from getting the fifty-one votes I need to recommit Masters to your committee for more hearings. But I'll make you do it, in front of God and everyone—including our supporters. They won't forgive you. And that could be the end of you in presidential politics."

The baldness of this threat induced in Palmer a surprised and contemplative stare. "If we make this a public burning," Chad finally answered, "it could do that to us both. Remember Anita Hill? Suppose we come up dry, and turn Masters into Joan of Arc . . ."

"Not if you handle it right," Gage interrupted. "You're not presiding over a kangaroo court, but a serious inquiry into the moral and ethical fitness of a judge . . ."

"'*Serious*'?" Palmer shot back. "Paul Harshman's ready to wave a bloody shirt. And we're probably days away from an abortion. What does Harshman say if the fetus turns out as hopeless as most doctors think it will be? What will the American people say? And what will Kilcannon say about us *then*?" Pausing, Palmer leaned forward. "This could blow up on us all, Mac. Including the Republicans on my committee, and any senator you convince to vote for recommitment. For everyone's sake, leave this lesbian stuff alone."

Gage fought to stifle his own doubts, show Palmer a calm resolve. "And if I don't? Are you prepared to oppose me?"

Palmer's gaze was veiled now. Gage was fascinated by the sense that he was watching a man unwittingly endanger his career and the future of his family; the moment induced contempt for Palmer's hypocrisy, and a measure of pity. Then Palmer looked up at him with his customary directness. "If *you're* prepared to risk losing, Mac. So I suggest we both take a day to search our souls . . ."

Palmer's intercom buzzed.

He glanced at his phone in irritation, then picked it up. "I'm with Mac Gage," he said.

Palmer's caller seemed undeterred. As Gage watched, his rival's face turned pensive. "How many days?" Palmer asked. After another pause, he put down the phone, his expression grave.

"Justice Kelly," he told Gage, "has entered a stay in the Tierney case, barring an abortion until the full court decides whether to hear Martin Tierney's petition. Which would require them to grant a further stay."

Gage felt a rush of satisfaction. "That stretches things out, doesn't it. And highlights the stakes for the Court."

"And for us," Palmer answered. "It also gives us our day to reflect."

"A stay of our own?" Gage's smile was grim. "All right, Chad. We'll talk again tomorrow."

Clayton Slade hurried into the Oval Office. "If it's about Justice Kelly," he told the President, "I've heard."

Kerry shook his head. "Chad Palmer called. He's getting worried. He thinks Gage will call a vote on recommitment to Chad's committee, and maybe win. Which means open-ended hearings."

Clayton looked unsurprised. "What's the pretext—a seminar on the horrors of late-term abortions, with color photos of the end result?"

Kerry winced. "Partly," he answered. "But our friends have found a new tack—Caroline's ethics. Specifically, her relationship to Sarah Dash."

Clayton grunted in disgust. "I could have told her that. In fact, I tried to."

Kerry smiled without humor. "But did you tell her she's a lesbian? Ironic, isn't it."

"*That's* their angle?"

"Oh, they'll start with a simple 'friendship.' But what they're trying to float is a lesbian affair."

Clayton sat heavily. "*That*," he said at length, "could be a problem."

Nine

"Mr. President," Frank Lenzner told Kerry the next morning, "there's a sensitive matter we need to raise with you. No one here wants to take you by surprise."

From his tone of voice, the editor of the *New York Times* was as reluctant as his words implied. Kerry was silent: ever since Lara's abortion, some subconscious part of him had awaited such a call. The fact that it came from Lenzner, and outside normal channels, confirmed that this was not a standard inquiry.

"What is this about?" Kerry asked.

"It concerns Judge Masters." Another silence afforded Kerry a moment to experience both relief and apprehension. "Most of the reporting has been done by Julia Adams. Can we include her?"

Was it the lesbian rumors, Kerry wondered; for the two days since the Internet report, they had spread just below the surface of mainstream journalism. "Of course," he answered.

Kerry heard a click as Adams picked up a second line. "Good morning, Mr. President," she said briskly. "Thank you for speaking to me."

"I'm delighted. I think."

Adams did not respond to this. With a trace of nervousness, she said, "We believe, and are about to print, that Caroline Masters has a daughter."

For Kerry, a split second of surprise was followed by rapid calculation. "Based on what?"

"A confidential source. This person told us that the FBI had uncovered 'rumors' that, when Masters was just out of college, she gave birth to a child on Martha's Vineyard."

Adams was fencing with him; her opening seemed to assume that Kerry was not surprised. "You don't print rumors, Julia."

"We found the nurse within an hour," Adams replied bluntly. "An hour or so later we found records confirming that Masters was a patient at the Martha's

Vineyard hospital. The date coincides with the birth of her sister's supposed daughter, Brett Allen. According to our source, she's actually *Masters's* daughter."

That assertion, Kerry knew, was not in the FBI notes which Palmer had suppressed—the principal reason, along with Palmer's intervention, that the FBI had not known to match the rumor to the timing of Brett Allen's birth. "Why," Kerry asked, "does the *Times* think this story—even if true—is news?"

"Any number of reasons." Now Adams's tone matched her persona; tensile and aggressive, she was among the most thorough of the Washington press corps. "Arguably, Judge Masters misled Congress. *And* you."

Kerry stood. He had little time to choose his course, but long experience in politics, and his own preferences, told him he should not dissemble. "Okay," he said evenly, "let's go off the record. What I'm about to tell you, you can't use, unless and until I say you can. Agreed?"

Adams hesitated briefly. "Yes."

Kerry began to pace. The sunny morning, casting light on the White House lawn, seemed deceptively mild; any misstep might dwarf the bitter controversy already surrounding Caroline Masters. "I did know," he said simply. "Judge Masters told me, before I nominated her. When I decided to proceed, she asked me to protect Brett Allen.

"She acted with complete integrity. And I agreed that this was private, completely irrelevant to her fitness to be Chief Justice. I still do." Kerry's voice, though quiet, was forceful. "So if the idea that she deceived me is your rationale for damaging her—or her daughter—you'll have to find another one."

"There's *also* Senator Palmer, Mr. President."

It was unraveling quickly, Kerry thought. "What about him?"

"According to our sources on the committee staff, he restricted access to the files. No one saw the memo."

Which implied, Kerry thought, that the source was not the staff; if so, the FBI was among the dwindling possibilities. "What difference does it make?"

"A big difference," Adams retorted. "Because it suggests that *Palmer* knew as well. Perhaps, like you, before the FBI found out. Perhaps because you told him."

Kerry felt a rising dismay—he did not want Chad dragged into this. "What's your point, Julia? That Chad Palmer's a decent man? That's hardly breaking news."

"No. But it *is* news when a Democratic president and a potential Republican nominee agree to withhold from the Judiciary Committee information that many other senators would find relevant. To say the least."

Kerry strained for a tone of patience. "I can't speak for Senator Palmer, even off the record. What does *he* have to say?"

Adams hesitated. "We haven't reached him yet."

"Then let *me* suggest another way of looking at this. You're implying that, somehow, Chad Palmer 'conspired' with me to suppress something—which makes that 'something' news. But does it matter to you *what* we were supposedly suppressing, or whom it hurts if you report it?" Kerry's voice became sharp. "It's become far too easy for the media to find some reason to expose a public person's private life. This 'conspiracy' you imagine is a rear-guard action against indecency—in this case, yours."

"Mr. President," Adams said with unwonted sharpness, "are you telling me that this story doesn't serve your political interests?"

The first seeds of suspicion began to grow in Kerry's mind. "If I wanted to leak this," he rejoined, "why would I ask you not to run it?"

At this, Adams laughed. "Perhaps because you're right about us. You already know we will."

"Fuck," Chad Palmer murmured into the telephone.

"The FBI," Kerry told him. "Who else could have done this?"

"Who else?" Chad responded coolly. "Anyone who knew."

Once more, Kerry felt unsettled. "It sure as hell wasn't me."

"Then take her down, dammit. That's the only way to kill this story."

Kerry stared out the window. "It's already too late to kill it, I'm convinced. And withdrawing her would look like I was caving in to the forces of reaction."

"We surely can't have *that*," Chad retorted. "So instead you'll hang me out to dry—the pro-life senator who conspired with the Antichrist. Which might also serve your long-term interests."

Torn between defensiveness and regret, Kerry hesitated. "I didn't give you up," he insisted. "The *Times* doesn't even know we talked."

"Don't they? Doesn't it strike you that they're awfully well informed?" Chad's voice became flat. "I'm not going to lie to them. And it would be stupid to try."

Kerry reflected. Chad Palmer was a resilient man, both confident and fatalistic, but today he seemed weary. "Not everyone in your party," Kerry told him, "will want to pillory her for *this*."

"No," Chad snapped. "They'll pillory *me,* if Mac Gage has his way. I've betrayed our brotherhood for a libidinous pro-abortionist. Speaking of whom, Mr. President, is *she* prepared to go through this?"

"We're trying to reach her at home. No one answers."

"I wonder why." Pausing, Chad's tone combined resolve with resignation. "Time for me to face the firing squad. But you'd do yourself a favor by arranging one for *her*. Because the only way for me to atone for my sins is by helping Gage defeat you."

This was what Kerry had feared. "I understand," he said. "But let's see how it looks when this is out."

"I know how it'll look," Chad said with a trace of bitterness. "What I don't know yet is who leaked it."

Before Kerry could respond, Clayton walked into his office. "Masters," he mouthed, "line two."

"She's on the other line," Kerry told Chad. "I'd better go."

"So should she," Chad answered crisply, and hung up.

Kerry pushed the flashing button. "Caroline?"

"I'm sorry, Mr. President." Caroline's voice was arid. "But I'll have to call you back. Right now I'm talking to my daughter."

Ten

Caroline had imagined this moment a thousand times—with dread, hope, despair. But what she had not appreciated was the depth of her inadequacy.

"Are you my mother?" Brett asked.

"Yes," Caroline said softly. "I am."

Brett sounded stunned, as though awaking to her feelings of confusion and betrayal. "When they told me, I knew it must be true. It explained so much about both of you. But I didn't even know who to call—you, or Betty." Her voice turned quietly bitter. "You remember her, 'Aunt Caroline.' The woman formerly known as Mom."

On the other end, Caroline closed her eyes. "I'm sorry . . ."

"Sorry." Brett's voice tremored with emotion. "I've just found out the basis of my entire life—twenty-seven years—is a lie. That my father isn't my father . . ."

"He was *dead,* Brett. Before you were even born . . ."

"My mother is my aunt, my aunt's my mother, and the three of you cooked up this Gothic nightmare and then lied and lied and lied to me." Brett stopped—holding back tears, Caroline guessed. "I had to hear the truth from some reporter. Why didn't any of you respect me enough to tell me?"

Through her grief and shame, Caroline felt a deep anger toward the unknown person who had called the *Times.* "Sometimes I wanted to . . ."

"Sometimes? I didn't even see you for twenty *years.*"

"You already *had* a mother. And a father." Caroline stopped, feeling anew the anguish of her sacrifice. "Giving you up was the hardest thing I've ever done. I couldn't trust myself to see you and not *want* you, couldn't trust myself not to tell you. I never imagined that the *New York Times* would do it for me." Fighting her own bitterness, Caroline felt it turn back on herself. "I was selfish," she finished. "As selfish as trying for the Court, knowing this might happen."

"But you *did* try." Her daughter's voice betrayed a quiet anger. "It's why they've done this to me, isn't it."

"Yes."

"So what do *you* plan to do, Caroline? Now that our mutated 'family tree' is public knowledge."

Caroline paused, trying to pick through the maelstrom of her own emotions. Her dream of becoming Chief Justice, she acknowledged bleakly, was so strong that even this act of cruelty had not quite killed it. But she did not want Brett dragged through this battle any further. "Of all the things I've thought about," she answered, "that hasn't been one. I expect I should withdraw . . ."

"Why?" Brett asked sharply. "For me? Haven't you 'protected' me enough?"

Caroline flinched. "It's not just you, Brett. There are a lot of reasons. They'll accuse me of dishonesty—"

"Then that's *your* problem," Brett interrupted. "But it's a little late to be worrying about *my* feelings, isn't it?

"You wanted this, Caroline. Whatever you are to me, and whatever else you've done, I'm here because you also wanted me.

"I don't know if I'll ever be able to unravel this. But I refuse—absolutely refuse—to be any part of the reason that the people who hate you drive you out. That would be no help to me."

Caroline felt twenty-seven years of blocked emotion breaking loose inside her, as palpable as her need to cry alone.

"I love you," she managed to tell her daughter. "I always have. But you really should call your mother . . ."

"Sit down," the President said coldly.

Eyes vigilant and wary, his oldest friend sat across from him, saying nothing.

"Are *you* going to try to tell me," Kerry asked, "that the FBI leaked this to the *Times*?"

Clayton's own gaze did not waiver. "That's not a question you should be asking, Mr. President. You might become responsible for knowing the answer."

At once, Kerry understood the reporter's skepticism, her inference that he was playing a cynical game. His feelings of anger and betrayal made it difficult to speak. "Don't you see what's been done to these people—*all* of them?"

"Fuck these people." Clayton's words, though harsh in content, were spoken in a monotone. "This isn't about Caroline Masters—or Chad Palmer. It's about whether you succeed."

Kerry felt comprehension seep through his outrage. "So I'm like King

Henry in *Becket,* saying *'Can no one rid me of this meddlesome priest?'* Is *that* your excuse?"

Still Clayton did not flinch. "Not quite."

"Well it damned well better not be. When did you reinvent me as some palace plotter, giving cues with winks and nods." Kerry's voice became caustic. "English isn't my second language. If I'd wanted to screw Palmer, Masters, and the daughter, I'd have said that flat out. Or I'd be telling you now to find out whoever leaked this, and cut his throat."

Clayton looked down, then faced the President again. "Do you want to consider the benefits? Or don't they matter now?"

"'Benefits,'" Kerry repeated softly. "What might they be?"

"Start with this—the daughter you were hiding is the best thing you've got going for you." Clayton smiled with a certain grimness. "Disclosing Brett Allen turns Masters from a closet lesbian into an object of sympathy—a woman who chose to bear a child rather than abort it, then gave it a loving family which included her own sister.

"If Gage goes after her for that, he steps on his own propaganda—not to mention his own biography. And the professional pro-lifers won't know *what* to say. *You've* always seen that." Clayton's gaze was steady. "There might be other reasons, too. But they'd be even harder for you to talk about. Or act on."

Kerry propped his chin in a cupped hand. "I'm still listening," he said.

"The right wing has its dirt now—the secret daughter. They'll be distracted, trying to figure out how to play it." Leaning forward, Clayton spoke intently. "Without a diversion—and with abortion as their line of attack on Masters—it's far more likely they'd dig up the truth about Lara. And ruin *you.*"

"So Caroline," Kerry said with disgust, "has become my shit-shield . . ."

"Not just a shield. A weapon." Clayton's tone was cool. "With Masters a much less plausible lesbian, Gage will be forced to argue that she's a liar, and that protecting her child—twice—disqualifies her for the court. Which in terms of Christian charity is distinctly unappealing.

"And who's the real embodiment of Christian ideals—her defender, the advocate of compassion, adoption, and family values in the truest sense? *You.*" Irony entered Clayton's tone. "*You* protect her from this right-wing vendetta. *You* draw the line against trashing the private lives of public figures. *You* call on the righteous outrage of the American public against those who'd use a youthful indiscretion to destroy a decent woman." Pausing, Clayton looked at Kerry intently. "In the process, you inoculate yourself against an attack on Lara. The American people are far more forgiving than a Mace Taylor or Macdonald Gage—after *this,* they'll be sick of dirt and dirtmongers."

Kerry stared at him. "And everyone will think Gage and his friends leaked this. While I just sit back and enjoy the joke. Not just on Mac, but Palmer."

"I know you'd never do this," Clayton said. "But as matters stand, Palmer will have to agree with you that private lives should be private—he committed himself when he agreed to sit on Masters's secret. And with Masters and her daughter as the victims of reactionary viciousness, you've *still* got a chance to get her on the Court.

"You'll have to be careful about how you play this, of course—*if*, as you believe, the leak came from inside the White House, the *Times* might reveal their source if you *then* suggest this came from Masters's opponents.

"But if you end up taking the hit for this leak yourself—and if you go around asking questions, you may well—you lose to Macdonald Gage. And perhaps lose everything."

It was as cold-minded an analysis as Kerry could imagine, and it was absolutely right. Unless Kerry paid more dearly than his presidency could afford, his closest friend had imprisoned him in a strategy as amoral as it was shrewd. And, for that, the two of them would never be the same.

Watching, Clayton seemed to sense this. "I know you, Kerry," he said with an air of fatalism. "If you decide to, you can turn this into magic. But if you want to hold someone here responsible, I'll resign. That risk goes with my job."

A complex of emotions—hurt, rage, a sheer, appalled astonishment at his friend's presumption—overcame the President. "Because you can't trust me on my own, is that it? I'm not quite up to the job without you to sell my soul for me." Circling his desk, Kerry stood over his Chief of Staff. "Who in hell do you think you are—or I am. What kind of role reversal makes me your fucking ward. And what kind of president accepts that.

"If I decide that my presidency requires a bargain with the devil, I'll make it on my own. *I've* earned that right, goddammit—*I* won this job, not you. No matter what you think." Kerry's voice turned chill. "You'll resign when it serves my interests. But right now that would draw too much attention, and I've got some serious business to attend to. I am, as you say, the President. So you'll play the loyal soldier until *I* tell you to go."

Still sitting, Clayton stared up at him. Though a wounded resentment flashed in his eyes, he did not protest. "Will you tell her what you suspect?" he asked.

Kerry crossed his arms. "No," he said softly. "As you point out, that wouldn't be terribly helpful, would it. After all, I've got a nomination to save."

．　．　．

"How did it go?" the President asked.

Sitting at the kitchen table, Caroline groped for words. "Hard," she said at last. "Inexpressibly hard."

"Will she be all right?"

"In what sense?"

There was silence. "I'm sorry this happened," the President said at last. "But I hope you'll stand with me. If this didn't disqualify you before, it can't now. I want you on the Court, and it's time to draw a line."

Silent, Caroline reflected on Brett's final words. "I'll probably lose," she said at last. "But that's all they can do to me, isn't it. I've written my opinion, and they've exposed my daughter. There's nothing left to fear."

Again, the President was quiet. "You'll need to put out a statement," he told her. "Brief, and dignified. I'll get Clayton on the line."

Eleven

"Masters Admits to Secret Daughter," the *Times* headlined the next day. But such was the speed of events that, by midmorning, two cable news networks were conducting instant polls, Macdonald Gage's office had been flooded with faxes and e-mails, and Gage himself was struggling to craft a response between incessant calls from senators, reporters, and supporters across the country. In self-defense, he was letting his phone ring through, though its constant jangling made him feel more harried.

"It's blown the dome off the Capitol," Gage complained to Mace Taylor. "My people are scrambling for solid ground, and that sonofabitch Palmer has known from the beginning."

Taylor looked up from Gage's draft statement, riddled with handwritten deletions and corrections. "So now it's time."

Gage did not respond. Instead he asked, "Where did this come from?"

Gage watched the calculation flicker in Taylor's eyes; knowledge was power and, even with Gage, Taylor did not care to divulge the breadth of his clients' activities or, conversely, that their machinations had any limits. At length, the lobbyist answered, "Not from us, I don't believe. Not from anyone on Palmer's committee, either. Our friend utilized the greenhouse technique—keep us all in the dark, and feed us shit. Him and Kilcannon, a cozy little conspiracy."

There was enough bitterness in Taylor's denial of complicity to carry the ring of truth. "Chad sure wouldn't leak this," Gage said flatly. "Now that it's out, some of our party colleagues want to cut his nuts off. Not to mention our supporters."

The telephone rang again. Thoughtful, Taylor squinted at Gage's favorite photograph—a much younger Gage as a freshman congressman, looking awestruck in the presence of Ronald Reagan. "What about Kilcannon?" he asked. "One of his people leaks it to the *Times,* which has to keep their sources confidential. Then Kilcannon attacks 'the forces of intolerance.'"

Gage smiled in sour amusement. "That," he said, "would be the act of a true professional, and a total prick. Float this, then blame us by implication— Palmer, too. And no one can ever prove it."

"*That,*" Taylor echoed, "is why it's the perfect play. He's reserving time on all four networks—nine o'clock tonight." Glancing toward the pile of faxes and e-mails stacked on Gage's desk, Taylor asked, "What are you hearing?"

"It's all over the map. Some say she's the apotheosis of the sixties—self-indulgence, illegitimacy, moral flexibility. Some others say she did what unwed mothers are supposed to do." Once more, a bilious humor tugged at one corner of Gage's mouth. "A couple of folks reminded me that Masters did the same as *my* birth mother, God rest her anonymous soul. Of course, that was back before *Roe v. Wade,* when she couldn't just go to an abortion clinic and have me sucked out with a vacuum hose . . ."

"Or," Taylor interrupted, "tear you to pieces if you got too big to murder so efficiently. I know for a fact the Christian Commitment isn't confused, and the other committed pro-life groups won't be either. Same with the NRA, and everyone who hates her on campaign finance reform . . ."

"I know all that," Gage said with impatience. "So here's what we have to say. Masters did the decent thing *after* she got pregnant—which, of course, we acknowledge. But pregnancy outside marriage is the total opposite of the message we want to send our young people. We can't turn around and *reward* her for it by making her Chief Justice."

Gage picked up the draft statement, brandishing it like a weapon. "But," he continued, "we have to find the right way to say something more: she's a woman with secrets, who swapped a child for her career—then *lied* about it. She *lied,* and Kilcannon—and Palmer, if he doesn't get out of the fucking way—covered up for her. This isn't about human frailty, or personal privacy. It's about judicial *integrity.*"

"That's all fine," Taylor said. "But you need more hearings, time to build the case. You need a parade of law professors saying what she did was perjury. That way we're not just some right-wing moralists.

"We get some editorials going, sway opinion. And we keep looking into who she really is. There's nothing about getting pregnant thirty years ago that proves she doesn't like girls better. I mean, why do women like her and Dash flock to San Francisco? For the weather?"

"For the sisterhood," Gage said with sarcasm. "You're right about hearings. It's time to continue my little chat with Senator Palmer . . ."

"It's time," Taylor said trenchantly, "to drop the daughter on him."

At once Gage's thoughts slowed. "That's radioactive," he cautioned. "I can't get within five miles of it."

"You don't need to. All you need is to be prepared." Taylor's voice was emotionless. "His own kid's abortion turns Palmer from the protector of privacy into a pious hypocrite. At least Masters didn't abort *her* baby—as soon as *his* daughter gets pregnant, all his alleged pro-life beliefs mean nothing.

"He'd be done for, Mac—through in presidential politics, and a eunuch on the committee. Completely out of your way." His tone took on an unwonted softness, the lilt of pleasure. "A shell, reduced to begging the good folks of Ohio to keep his job."

Silent, Gage stared past him. He despised Chad Palmer, but Taylor relished this too much—the cycle of destruction, once commenced, was not easily controlled.

Taylor's voice broke his thoughts. "*Look* at him," he said. "Just look at him."

Glancing up, Gage saw Chad Palmer on CNN, facing a cluster of reporters in the Capitol rotunda. Taylor turned up the volume.

Palmer's clear blue eyes conveyed candor and sincerity. "Throughout the morning," he began, "I've been asked a single question: 'Did you know?'"

The reporters fell silent. Pausing, Palmer looked into the camera. "Yes," he said simply. "I knew.

"Twenty-seven years ago, Caroline Masters made a private decision: to have a child. Well before the hearings, she acknowledged that in confidence. I admired her honesty, and the decision itself—a commitment to life. And part of that commitment was to protect a daughter who grew up in a secure two-parent family, unaware of the circumstances of her birth.

"In Judge Masters's place, I might have decided otherwise. But Judge Masters was wholly candid with me. And what she wrote on the disclosure form was not only intended to spare her daughter needless hurt, but was, quite literally, true: as a matter of law, this young woman is who she was raised to be—her niece . . ."

"I'd love to see *that* genealogy," Taylor interjected mordantly. "Not a tree, but a circle . . ."

"There are good reasons to oppose Judge Masters," Palmer continued. "On the basis of the Tierney decision, *I* oppose her." Pausing, Palmer raised his head, speaking slowly and emphatically. "But for any who believe she should have risked wounding her own daughter, do not blame her. Blame *me*."

"Mac," Taylor said in a low voice, "I'm tired of his heroics. This piece of phony candor makes me vomit. He held out on you, and now the press will drool all over him, like always—America's last honest man. And we know his entire act is bogus.

"We've known for years—we've got the form; we've got the daughter's drugged-out boyfriend. It's time to pull the trigger."

Gage felt temptation course through him: the vision of a swift and startling end to all of these unflattering comparisons—Mac Gage, the soulless pragmatist; Chad Palmer, the hero of matchless character. How pleasant it would be to escape the cringing feeling that, whatever his own talents, he had never been tested as Chad Palmer had. But Gage's own self-knowledge went deep, and he paused at another queasy sensation, remembering the morning he had awakened to find the *last* Majority Leader linked to a sixteen-year-old prostitute, the path to leadership open before him. And knew at once—though Taylor had never acknowledged this directly—that he owed his rival's ruin to Mace Taylor. *Knew* that, and then had accepted Taylor's support, a tacit bargain Taylor never mentioned, and would never forget.

"Mace," Gage said coldly, "I'll handle Palmer in my own way, in my own time. He can be as self-righteous as he wants on CNN, but he cannot—and I mean flat cannot—oppose new hearings now."

Frustrated, Taylor jabbed his finger at the television. "*Look* at that, goddammit. He's hanging out a mile . . ."

"So leave him there." Gage's voice brooked little argument. "You can always get him later. For *now,* he can front for us. A much-needed lesson in humility."

As night fell, Sarah Dash looked up from the scraps of prior briefs, scattered beside her on the living room couch, which she was cobbling together for the Supreme Court.

Even by her recent standards, the last forty-eight hours were devastating. They had begun with Justice Kelly's stay of Mary Ann's abortion; since then, emotionally exhausted, Mary Ann had remained in her darkened bedroom, trying to avoid a premature delivery induced by stress. Now an Internet columnist named Charlie Trask had made the first of several similar inquiries, this one by e-mail: he was aware, Sarah read on her screen, that she and Caroline Masters were lovers, and hoped she would use his column to humanize their relationship. Sickened, Sarah retreated to her apartment: it was there that she learned with astonishment that Caroline's niece—the striking young woman in the photograph—was, in fact, her daughter. Amidst all this, she had to draft the opposition to Martin Tierney's petition for a full Supreme Court reversal of Caroline's ruling.

She had little time to ponder the deeper mysteries of Caroline Masters, a woman whom Sarah once had flattered herself she knew, or to vent her own outrage at being used to smear Caroline for the Tierney decision. But she doubted that they would—or could—ever be friends again.

One emotion was clear to Sarah: a deep loathing of all that public life had become. Yet the unfolding spectacle of the Masters fight had a terrible fascination, combining the savagery of modern politics—in a time when multiple media fought for every titillating scrap of news—with the inexorable corrosion of privacy. Twenty-four hours ago, Sarah surmised, some right-wing operative had decided to ruin Caroline Masters. In rapid succession the merciless spotlight had moved from Caroline to Palmer to Macdonald Gage—who, moments before, had declared Caroline Masters unfit to be Chief Justice—to President Kilcannon, who now must answer.

Reaching for her remote, Sarah turned up the volume.

Minutes later, the door to the guest bedroom opened. "Did something happen?" Mary Ann Tierney asked.

Sarah looked up at her—pallid, her belly distended, her eyes bright and a little feverish. It was hard to accept that, less than two months ago, this girl had appeared at the clinic, setting in motion all that was about to take place.

"It's the President," Sarah said, and then Kerry Kilcannon materialized on her screen.

Twelve

Moments from commencing his speech, Kerry Kilcannon gazed into the lens of the camera.

He disliked this sense of isolation; he was at his best when he could see faces, feed off the reactions of a crowd. Even from the Oval Office, speaking to a piece of glass felt artificial.

But then, so did he. His passion to defend Caroline Masters—while genuine—was eroded by his knowledge that the latest damage to her had originated in the White House, and his cynicism in letting others take the blame. Still, the damage to his sense of self went deeper yet. For seventeen years, he had taken for granted Clayton's absolute loyalty; even amidst the maneuvering of politics, the self-serving and slippery alliances, this had been a constant, the standard by which he had always defined friendship. For all that people were drawn to him, the essential Kerry Kilcannon was a solitary man—his love and trust, when given, were profound, but they were given to few. That was what hurt.

Weeks ago, he remembered, Lara had asked if he felt the loneliness of power. Then, he had answered lightly. Now the Masters nomination—the stakes, the risks, the self-doubt, the playing God with others' lives, the breach with Clayton—would have made his response far different.

But there was little time for self-reflection. He had wanted this job, and now there were millions who relied on him to do it. That he was right—about Caroline Masters, about the Tierney case, about the politics of scandal—he believed to his core. He was equally convinced that he, not Macdonald Gage, spoke to the better nature of his countrymen. So, as seconds passed, he called on the trick of imagination which always served when he could not see his audience: to envision a face, or faces, to whom—or for whom—he spoke.

Tonight, the faces which appeared to him were women: the damaged girl from the press conference; Mary Ann Tierney; Caroline Masters. And, most of all, her daughter, Brett.

At this moment, Caroline Masters wished that her two closest friends were not judges. Though both had called several times, Jackson Watts was presiding over a murder trial in New Hampshire; Blair Montgomery was hearing cases in Seattle. With the wounds of the past reopened, knowing that her future might rest on the response to the next half hour, she watched Kilcannon alone.

As before, he seemed—at least to Caroline—startlingly young for a president. But his voice was calm and clear; somehow the camera caught the tactile intensity of his presence.

"The issue," Kilcannon insisted, *"is clear: whether the Senate will reject Caroline Masters for two acts of enormous courage—one as a judge, the other as a young woman, twenty-seven years ago . . ."*

Had *that* been courage? Caroline wondered. Such had been the intensity of her love—for David, for the child he had left inside her—that snuffing out this life would have felt like the death of her own soul. There was no way to explain this, and she had never wanted to try. But now she must, if only to Brett. Just as, somehow, she must try to mitigate the devastation her own ambitions had wrought on her own sister; for all her jealousies and flaws, Betty had done nothing to deserve this trauma. A trauma attenuated, Caroline must acknowledge, by her own resolve to brave the furor which it created.

"As a judge," Kilcannon continued, *"her qualifications are superb. Two short weeks ago, by an overwhelming majority, the Committee on the Judiciary recommended that the Senate confirm her as Chief Justice—the first woman to so serve.*

"What happened?" Pausing, Kilcannon's voice took on a note of irony. *"Three days ago, joined by five of her colleagues, Judge Masters held that the Protection of Life Act violated the United States Constitution.*

"It was the one thing Caroline Masters could do to jeopardize her nomination.

"She knew *this ruling would create controversy.*

"She knew *that her opponents could use it to defeat her.*

"She knew *that the subjects of late-term abortion, and parental consent, are widely misunderstood.*

"She knew *that the case of Mary Ann Tierney had aroused passions across America.*

"She knew *all that, and then decided this: that her obligations as a judge— to render justice to a fifteen-year-old girl—are more important than her own ambitions.*

"*For* that," Kilcannon said with scorn, "*the forces of the far right—whose cynicism knows no limits, and whose compassion has* every *limit—have resolved to defeat her by any means at hand.*

"*They know that—as a judge—Caroline Masters cannot speak for herself. They hope that, in her silence, they can destroy her through distortion, and through smear. And so I will speak for her . . ."*

Caroline sat back. Whatever else might happen, Kerry Kilcannon did not intend to make her a sacrificial victim. They were going down together.

"He's going for it," Gage murmured. "The little bastard's going for it."

"The little *demagogue*," Paul Harshman amended. "Whenever I hear his version of the 'truth,' the term 'Orwellian' pops to mind. And people buy it."

"Not this time," Gage promised. He felt the others, a small group of allies clustered in his office, noting this exchange. Chad Palmer was conspicuously absent, but Gage had invited a potential waverer—Kate Jarman—in an attempt to seal her loyalty. She watched the screen intently.

"*Late-term abortions,*" Kilcannon said, "*are perhaps one in a* thousand.

"*They do not threaten the healthy fetuses of healthy mothers—that's illegal in all fifty states. Rather, they arise from medical emergencies. And, of the women who must face this tragic situation, only a fraction involve girls like Mary Ann Tierney— minors living with their parents.*

"*It is for them this law was written.*

"*I do not doubt the good intentions of those who helped to pass it . . ."*

"Oh, no," Gage said satirically. "We're only the cynical, heartless, right-wing conspiracy, the fifth column for a pack of inbred child molesters with vacant eyes and sloping foreheads."

Kate Jarman gave him an edgy smile. "In Kentucky," she said, "don't you call those folks the 'swing vote'?" Harshman kept his eyes on the screen.

"*But,*" Kilcannon continued, "*the Tierney case has made us face hard questions:*

"*Does a good family—the great majority of our families—communicate because Congress tells it to?*

"*Should a minor child be forced to bear a child of her own—no matter how doomed or damaged—at the risk she can never have children again?*

"*Should the victim of rape and incest be forced to bear her father's defective child, adding this trauma to the trauma of abuse?*" Kilcannon's voice softened. "*And what would those who vilify Caroline Masters say to the fifteen-year-old girl I held in my arms here at the White House, after she risked humiliation to describe how she was forced to bear a son who was blind and severely retarded? Because he was also her brother . . ."*

Kate Jarman no longer smiled. "You may not like it," she told Gage. "But it's effective."

"The truth is harsh," Kilcannon went on. *"But it is indispensable to judging Caroline Masters. That's why her opponents don't want you to hear it, and why it's so important that you do.*

"Two days ago, at the White House, I gathered women who had lived the truth of late-term abortion at first hand, and girls who had suffered the unintended consequences of parental consent laws.

"All of those women wanted children. None of their children would have lived. Nor might several of the women. Two wondered who might care for the children they already had. One girl—the girl I mentioned—was the victim of the most terrible betrayal a father could visit on a child. And another woman, who loved her child immeasurably, lost that child to an illegal abortion because her daughter was afraid to disappoint her . . ."

"A real Jerry Lewis telethon," Harshman said with scorn. "Doesn't he know any normal people? You'd think we're a country of two hundred seventy million victims." But Kate Jarman ignored him, watching Kilcannon intently—an intimation, if Gage needed one, that there might yet be problems in the Senate.

"But another girl," Kilcannon continued, *"could not be there at all. Nor could her mother speak for her.*

"Her name was Dawn Collins. When she was thirteen, her father raped her." Kilcannon's voice turned flat, staccato. *"Ashamed, she tried to keep this secret. But pregnancy was one secret she could not keep.*

"So she asked her mother for permission to abort—as required by Idaho law. And then her mother questioned her until she learned the truth.

"With Dawn hiding in the bedroom, her mother confronted her father. He was drunk. In a rage, he shot and killed his wife. Then he murdered Dawn as he had threatened, for betraying him." Kilcannon's voice went quiet again. *"And when I heard that, I resolved that I would never avert my eyes, and sign a law, rather than face the truth.*

"That—in essence—was the choice that Caroline Masters faced. You may not agree with her decision; I do not ask that. Instead I ask you this: is it right for the Senate to deny our country her services because of a single act of courage?

"And this." The President's voice turned harsh. *"How on earth did we reach the point where such a question is asked at all?*

"The answer, I'm afraid, is the day that abortion ceased being a moral question, and became a political issue. The day that groups like the Christian Commitment

ceased being a cause, and became a source of funding for right-wing office-holders . . ."

"Whoa," Kate Jarman said under her breath. Beside her, Paul Harshman's face reddened in anger.

"In the pursuit of money and power," Kilcannon went on, *"the opponents of Judge Masters have turned morality on its head.*

"One can reasonably debate the morality of ending first-trimester pregnancies as a means of birth control. But that's a woman's right by law—one which, with whatever personal reservations, most Americans support.

"And so, to defeat Judge Masters, the far right perpetuates a lie—that healthy children are being aborted by callous doctors and selfish mothers a few short moments from birth." Kilcannon slowed his voice for emphasis. *"It's a lie with terrible consequences: in no other area of medicine does the law—like this law—criminalize a doctor for protecting a minor's reproductive health, and her hope of children in the future. Because, even now, there lingers in our society a pervasive insensitivity toward women . . ."*

"So now we're sexists," Harshman said. Once more, Gage noted, Kate Jarman did not respond.

"In 1954," the President went on, *"the Supreme Court decided in* Brown versus Board of Education *that legalized segregation violated our Constitution. Today, if any judge flouted* Brown, *there would be a universal outcry. And whether or not we agree with* Roe, *it is—like* Brown—*the law of the land.*

"Those who oppose Judge Masters ignore that; ignore the tragedies she was compelled by duty to address; ignore the superb qualities she offers to the Court. It is time for us to ask why such unfairness—to this woman and all women—is somehow still acceptable.

"It is not acceptable," Kilcannon said succinctly, *"to me."*

"He didn't call us sexist flat out," Gage told Harshman. "At least not by name. But the night is young . . ."

"I've read Judge Masters's words with care, and thought about them deeply. And I've learned. No longer can I accept that it's the proper role of government to tell a minor child—no matter how harsh her circumstances—that she no longer matters." Kilcannon raised his head, a gesture which combined a calm resolve with a touch of defiance. *"For these reasons, I have today instructed the Solicitor General not to oppose Mary Ann Tierney in the Supreme Court of the United States . . ."*

"We *passed* that law," Paul Harshman snapped. "It's his duty to uphold it."

With this, Kate Jarman broke her silence. "I'll be damned," she murmured, and then turned to Gage. "He could have left it with 'right or wrong, don't punish her for one decision.'"

In his own surprise, Gage was slow to answer. The President had placed his moral authority squarely behind Caroline Masters and, by doing so, risked everything.

"No one ever said," he told his colleagues, "that the little bastard lacks for nerve."

"It's so good," Sarah said in a thick voice. "The President just said your father's wrong."

Mary Ann's grip tightened on Sarah's hand. "Will it help us?"

"Psychologically, it does. Even Supreme Court justices are human." *And it helps* me, Sarah did not add; for the first time in days, she felt less tired.

"*But I have something more to say.*" Pausing, Kilcannon softened his tone. "*Today, the* New York Times *revealed that Caroline Masters has a daughter of her own.*

"*Within hours, the Senate Majority Leader, Macdonald Gage, declared her 'morally unfit' to be Chief Justice. He never asked her to explain. He never asked me what I knew. He never paused to ask himself whether this was fair or just. He took one piece of a woman's life, and proceeded to condemn the woman.*

"*I think we can do better.*"

Kilcannon paused. "*Imagine Caroline Masters,*" he said quietly, "*not as the distinguished judge she is today, but a young woman of twenty-two.*

"*It would have been simple to terminate her pregnancy.*

"*But she could not. She believed that this decision involved a life other than her own.*

"*She had little to offer a child but that belief.*" Briefly, Kilcannon let the image linger. "*But there was one thing she could give her: a sister and brother-in-law who desperately wanted children.*

"*A few weeks before her daughter was born, they asked to adopt her child.*

"*They offered two parents, and a loving home. All they wanted in return was to raise the child as theirs.*

"*This was not what she had planned. But she faced the facts with the same unsparing honesty which impelled her to have this child. And she knew it was best that her child be secure.*

"*Three days after the child was born, her brother-in-law came for her.*"

"That explains so much," Sarah said, less to Mary Ann than to herself. The girl watched the television, transfixed.

"*So Caroline Masters,*" the President continued, "*started a new life. She could never talk about what had happened; she'd promised her sister that. She could never know her child. But she knew that the girl was well, and that her parents loved her.*

"For Caroline Masters, that knowledge justified her sacrifice, and her silence . . ."

Turning, Gage observed Kate Jarman, watching the screen as though her political life depended on it.

"For twenty-seven years," the President continued, *"she kept her word.*

"She protected her daughter and the adoptive family.

"When I considered her for the Court, Judge Masters made it clear that if damaging her daughter and her family was the price of being Chief Justice, she would not pay it.

"I could not quarrel with that. Nor can I quarrel with the choices made by Caroline Masters and her daughter's adoptive parents.

"I have met that daughter. She is an intelligent and accomplished twenty-seven-year-old woman." The softness left Kilcannon's voice. *"And she is a compelling argument for the virtues of adoption, which Caroline Masters's chief opponents assert so often but which she herself has lived . . ."*

"So now she's a pro-lifer," Gage observed. "Amazing."

"It's shameless," Harshman snorted with contempt. "He's going to trot out the daughter, the new poster girl for adoption . . ."

"And now, within hours of this painful disclosure, Senator Gage asserts that her daughter's very existence disqualifies Judge Masters. I can only assume that Senator Gage is not referring to Caroline Masters's courage in preserving her child's life, and then giving her up—since, as the Senator invariably points out, he, too, is adopted . . ."

"Kerry," Gage said quietly, "you truly know how to hurt a fellow . . ."

"Perhaps," Kilcannon continued, *"he believes that Caroline Masters is disqualified because, twenty-seven years ago, she made the same mistake many young people make."* Here the President paused, his voice taking on an ironic lilt. *"To Senator Gage and his allies I say this: a mistake-free life is not a prerequisite for public office. And if Caroline Masters's opponents claim that it is, they present the Senate with a choice—between her grace and dignity, and their sanctimony and hypocrisy . . ."*

Kate Jarman turned from the screen. Dryly she said, "What do you think, Mac? Sound like a toss-up to you?"

"She's a *liar*," Harshman interjected. "That's the whole point."

"There are those," the President continued, *"who assert that Caroline Masters misled them. Why? Because, despite having told the legal and literal truth, they claim*

she owed it to them to break her promise and wound her family by disclosing in pub-lic the private details of this young woman's life.

"*Instead,*" the President said firmly, "*she disclosed them to me.*

"*I concluded that her debt was to her family, and no one else. So I stand with Senator Palmer: if there's anyone to blame, blame me . . .*"

"Of course," Harshman said. "Use your pal Chad for cover. He *likes* that."

"*For my part,*" the President continued, "*I am proud of this nomination—of the person who protected one young woman from the moment of conception, of the judge who protected another at risk to her own ambitions. Her performance in the Tierney case reflects the highest traditions of the law, and the deepest values of her life. No president can ask for more.*

"*Nor, I believe, can you.*

"*You, I know, are better than those who—through smear and innuendo, through degrading rather than disagreeing—would take the low road to power. You, not they, represent a country which is tolerant in spirit, generous in understanding, and gracious in forgiveness. And, always, willing to value a person for the whole of who she is . . .*"

No, Gage thought to himself; it would not be easy. Ahead were days of close maneuvers, a fight for every vote. Kilcannon saw the stakes as Gage did, and was determined to break his control; Gage was facing a politician of considerable gifts, not the least of which was ruthlessness.

"*So I ask the Senate,*" he concluded, "*to confirm Caroline Masters as Chief Jus-tice. And if you join me in that effort, it will.*"

"Will we, now," Gage murmured. But Kate Jarman did not look at him.

Thirteen

The next twelve hours, Gage reflected, were a sobering reminder of the power of the presidency.

By the time Mace Taylor came to his office for rolls and coffee, an overnight poll by CNN-Time showed that, among the estimated fifty million adults who had watched Kilcannon's speech, forty-two percent favored Caroline Masters's confirmation, with thirty-three percent against, and the balance—a significant twenty-five percent—undecided. Some quick calls to his whip and a few key senators suggested that Kilcannon had succeeded in freezing votes in place: though Gage's best estimate was that he had forty-one votes, he did not yet know where the next nine or ten were coming from. And of the Senate Democrats, though some from border states and the South were inclined to opposition, none had publicly broken with their president.

"The forty-one against," Gage told Taylor, "are solid. But some of them won't support a filibuster. So I can't just shut her down, and calling a vote is risky."

"Kilcannon knows that. The longer this goes on, the more support he can try to build: women's rallies, rooms full of adopted kids—hell, I bet he's got Barbara Walters lined up to interview the daughter. An exercise in lacrimony." Gage spread his hands in frustration. "In the age of confessions, there's no underrating the bad taste of the American people. I can imagine Masters and the daughter's newly proud dad reunited on Jerry Springer. Whoever *he* might be."

With a surprising fastidiousness, Taylor pursed his lips to sip coffee from Gage's china, displaying starched French cuffs and silver cuff links. "The father," he said. "*That's* the only detail Kilcannon spared us—we're not even sure if it was a man, or a turkey baster."

"They're not saying," Gage responded. "It's 'private.' But someone has to know."

"We'll try to find out—just in case the guy dropped LSD with her when she was pregnant." Taylor put down the cup. "All we know is she was dating Watts in college, and no one ever saw her using drugs, or holding hands with another girl. Sort of makes you wonder how we could miss a baby."

"It does," Gage said pointedly. "It surely does."

Taylor looked up at him. "Don't blame us, Mac. Blame Palmer. You've gone too easy on him." His voice lowered, an implied warning. "I know you've heard from folks like Barry Saunders. They want this lady gone, and they don't want Kilcannon rolling us. Seems to me like it's gut-check time. For you, and for Palmer."

One by one, Gage felt his options closing. He could not yet call a vote, and time might be his enemy. He did not have Kilcannon's platform, or his talent for swaying the public mood. And the Tierney case was heading to its conclusion—which, in the worst case, might reveal that the fetus had no cerebral cortex, and no prayer of ever living.

"I have a plan," Gage said. "One way or the other, Palmer will see the light."

"We need more hearings," Paul Harshman told his colleagues.

All fifty-five Republicans were gathered in the Old Senate Chamber, an ornate amphitheater suited to their numbers. But the reactions of most interest to Macdonald Gage were those of Chad Palmer and Kate Jarman, bellwethers of party moderates.

"We have a woman," Harshman continued, "whose latest and greatest ruling is pro-abortion, whose personal life is dubious, whose ethics are in question, and who—skip the fancy words—lied to us about all of that.

"'Oh, no,'" he said in mocking imitation of Masters, "'I've got an open mind. Sarah Dash is nothing to me. Oh, and isn't my niece just lovely.'" His voice filled with scorn, he gazed at Palmer, "And we just lapped it up . . ."

"No," Chad Palmer interjected pleasantly. "I did. You, Paul, were on the cutting edge. I can only regret my folly, and wonder what might have been."

With Harshman, Gage reflected, Chad could not seem to help himself. Though a few of their colleagues smiled, Harshman's bony frame seemed to twist in indignation. "You may find promiscuity and lying funny, Senator. I can assure you my constituents do not.

"There are fifty-five of us in this chamber. I think you'll find that the great majority want to reopen our committee's hearings—in great measure because of what the nominee, *and* you, chose not to 'share' with us."

Chad shrugged. "You've heard my reasons. All of us know how ugly politics has gotten. We can sit here in this hermetically sealed room sounding righteous, but it seems like a lot of the country agreed with Kilcannon's speech—at least about privacy. If we react like lemmings to whatever interest groups want her head on a platter, they may get sick of us all." Pausing, he looked around him. "Do we really think the public wants a spectacle—"

"They want the truth," Harshman interrupted. "In these morally equivocal times, perjury may not seem important to *some* of us, even perjury by a nominee for Chief Justice. But the core of our supporters, thank God, retain their moral bearings."

Palmer rolled his eyes. For a dead man, Gage thought, he looked remarkably unrepentant, and this concerned him—for some of his colleagues, Chad's devil-may-care persona held a certain charm.

"I think you'll find," Gage interposed, "that you're both in agreement on the bottom line—Caroline Masters has to go. Chad feels his responsibilities *there* as keenly as anyone."

The remark, intended to remind Palmer of his lapse, clearly struck its target: as often when cornered, Chad Palmer's eyes grew hooded, as though to conceal his resentment.

Walking to the front of the room, Gage thrust his hands in his pockets, speaking with studied solemnity. "This is that rare moment," he began, "when a vote has constitutional significance. The President has challenged us. *Each* of us has to decide how we value unborn life, how we value truth, how we value the Court, and how we value ourselves as senators.

"The vote on Masters must be a vote of conscience. We're facing an opponent who is castigating us before we've even voted. So I don't want to add to your burdens with pressures of my own."

Pausing, Gage surveyed the blank faces of politicians who, while appearing to accept this piety, knew better: they knew the stakes for Gage and Palmer, and the infinite variety of ways—from bad committee assignments to pet bills which died without a vote—through which Gage could punish them without a word. Kate Jarman, her head back, seemed to smile at the ornate ceiling.

"But Paul's right," Gage went on. "Process is important, and many unanswered questions have arisen since the committee recommended we confirm her. Our constitutional obligation is to probe these issues thoroughly." Pacing, Gage spoke more rapidly. "Two months ago Kerry Kilcannon was one of us. He was elected President by a sliver. The voters didn't make him some demigod we suddenly should bow and scrape to. Many of our constituents expect us to control his excesses, as is our *duty*.

"Will we abandon our pro-life principles? Will we shrink from raising questions of character because Caroline Masters is a woman?" Turning to Chad, Gage spoke quietly. "If we do, we'll be complicit in a cover-up, even if we were never privy to it."

This remark, a thinly veiled reference to Chad's protection of the nominee, induced from Chad a faint but defiant smile. "Whatever we do," Gage went on, "we should do it as a united party. That's why I called this meeting—to see where we stand on new hearings. Because if most of us want them, but can't get them through the Senate, we'd look pitiful indeed."

For this, Gage believed, he had the votes. So, apparently, did Chad: that he understood the true purpose of this exercise was apparent in the skeptical gaze he focused on Macdonald Gage. "Mr. Chairman," Gage said to him, "any thoughts? After all, the hearings would be yours to run."

Chad smiled again. "Not if I can help it." He turned to the others, eyes sweeping the room. "I've got no illusions about the sentiments here, or the pressures we all feel. Despite," he added wryly, "Mac's best efforts to spare us.

"I don't doubt, either, that some of you question my judgment regarding Caroline Masters. I respect that, and I suppose I'll have to live with it.

"What I'm not sure any of us can live with are more hearings." He glanced at Harshman. "Paul and I have had the pleasure of meeting Caroline Masters at first hand. But we seem to have different perceptions of that experience.

"What I saw is a woman who's very resourceful, and extremely clever. What she isn't, always, is sympathetic." His tone turned dry. "But we have it in our power to fix *that*.

"If we start pounding her about protecting her daughter, or—frankly—implying that she's lesbian, she's smart enough to kill us, and savvy enough to do it in a way that makes the public glad she did. And *then* we'd have to go to the Senate, and try to vote her down." Chad's voice rose. "Better to do it now. It's one thing to vote against her. It's another to make her a martyr. Remember how we looked after Anita Hill? Masters and Kilcannon will make that look like a stroll in the park.

"We've all read the Tierney decision. We all know about the daughter now. We *always* knew Dash clerked for her. What else do we need to know?

"Time won't make this better. And the resolution of the Tierney case—in brutal fact—may well make it worse." Once more, Chad turned to Gage. "You've got my vote against her, Mac. Round up the remaining votes you need, and bring her to the floor."

Nettled, Gage felt the others divining a truth they had only suspected—he did not yet have the votes to defeat the nominee. "I'm not convinced," Gage answered, "that new hearings will make Caroline Masters more—rather than less—attractive. And the time they'd take has virtues of its own. Vote now, and we look peremptory. After more deliberations, we're statesmen." He smiled at Kate Jarman, whose indecision was obvious. "And -women."

From the expressions of his colleagues, this observation sealed the result. Supporting a motion to recommit—even if not fatal to the nominee—was a vote to postpone the day of reckoning, the better to judge the volatile and swiftly changing public mood, while buttressing the reasons to oppose her. There would be time enough to face the ultimate test and—though the others did not yet know it—for Gage to force Chad Palmer's hand.

"Let's have a vote," Paul Harshman called out.

"Why don't we do that," Gage said promptly. "What's the sentiment for recommitment?"

As he paused, looking around the room, people began to raise their hands— a cluster at first, then others less decisive and more scattered—until, as Gage had hoped, all but four had joined in: Chad Palmer, Kate Jarman, and two others.

Palmer looked around him. With an air of resignation, he said, "That's pretty clear, isn't it. So when we vote to recommit tomorrow, we should make it unanimous. No divisions in the ranks."

Satisfied, Gage surveyed the room. "Is that all right with everybody?" When no one spoke, he added, "We're all set, then."

With this, the meeting broke up. As the others left, Gage touched Palmer's elbow, steering him aside.

"Artfully done," Chad murmured.

"We need to talk," Gage said bluntly.

They sat in Chad's office. Coolly, Chad said, "We can shit-can the Gilbert and Sullivan now. You want me to kill her in committee, don't you."

Gage managed to cover his surprise: never, he admonished himself, should Chad's cavalier manner distract him from the man's hard intelligence. "You owe me," Gage answered. "You owe *us*."

"Because I covered for this promiscuous judge?"

"Yes." Gage's tone was factual. "I made you chairman—I could have induced Joe Silva to stay, rather than head up Labor. And your very first move is to sell me out to Kilcannon.

"I can speculate on your reasons, Chad. But the party faithful don't give a damn. Did you hear Rush Limbaugh this morning? He called you the Benedict Arnold of heroes." Gage held up his thumb and forefinger, a millimeter apart. "On the national level, you're *that* close to being through in our party. Unless you step up *now,* the people who make or break candidates will never forgive you."

Across the desk, Palmer surveyed him with the dead calm that Gage found so frustrating. "That's quite a penance, Mac. I've been a senator since the age of thirty-four. In all that time, I've never seen the Judiciary Committee block a Supreme Court nominee from coming to the Senate floor."

"I don't know that it's *ever* been done. A negative recommendation—sure. But just say to Masters, *'Sorry, we're not even sending you to the Senate'?* Unheard of."

"Really. Then why did it trip off your tongue so quickly."

Picking up a pen, Palmer idly played with it, still eyeing Gage. "I know you, Mac. I was watching you just now. You're not sure you can win. And if you lose, the 'party faithful' will be saying that *you* don't have whatever it takes. So what's the magic bullet? To kill her without a vote.

"You don't want your fingerprints on *that* one. Kilcannon will murder us with it—we'll be the right-wing lackeys who thwarted democracy. But we've got a ten-to-eight majority on the committee. Unless Jesus appears to testify on her behalf, you figure Harshman and seven others will vote to kill her no matter what. That leaves Kate Jarman—and me."

"That leaves you," Gage said evenly. "Nine to nine would kill it." Gage's voice was quiet but firm. "It's a chance for you to show leadership, and make amends. You'd have my full support."

A brightness in Chad's eyes bespoke a lingering amusement. Then it vanished: as Gage watched, he could see, almost feel, the progress of Palmer's thoughts. Chad did not want to do this, and disliked being pushed, but he was not immune to political reality. He had allied himself with Kilcannon—now he faced deep trouble in his own party, and knew it.

Palmer exhaled, too absorbed in his dilemma to conceal its weight. "I'll ponder it," he said. "But I can't promise to kill her before we've even conducted hearings. I'll have to see how she looks *then.*"

"See what?" Gage said with some impatience. "See if she starts looking like a lesbian again?"

At once, the resistance reappeared in Palmer's eyes. "Frankly, Mac, I don't give a damn if she's a lesbian. Harshman has persuaded me that caring makes you stupid."

Gage felt a flash of irritation, followed by a deeper, grimmer feeling. It was in his power to destroy this man, and only compassion and a certain caution had kept Gage from it. Soon compassion might be a luxury, and the power to prevent this might slip from Gage's hands.

"We're not friends, Chad." Gage spoke quietly, each word deliberate. "We'll never be. But I'm speaking for your own good.

"I came to you on this twice before, and came up empty. For my own sake as leader, I can't accept that forever. Please understand that."

Palmer scrutinized Gage with care. It was an acknowledgment that they had never spoken like this before and, perhaps, of something more—the fear Chad Palmer must feel, knowing the forces arrayed against Masters, for himself and his family.

"I understand," Chad said.

Fourteen

When Caroline Masters returned to Washington, she was greeted by a press corps so aggressive and disorderly that it seemed to her she was in the eye of a mob. They called out questions about Brett as she moved through the airport, head high, saying nothing. At a newsstand, her face stared back at her from the covers of *Time, Newsweek, People,* and *U.S. News and World Report,* with captions such as "What Is Moral?" and "Fit to Be Chief?" The *Washington Post,* with encouragement from the White House, was running a series on adoption; on the *Tonight Show,* Jay Leno characterized the Judiciary Committee as "one woman, and seventeen guys who are grateful extramarital sex doesn't make men pregnant." And, to Caroline's surprise, Lara Costello began appearing on selected talk shows, repeating the line of attack begun in the President's speech.

Though the hearings were two days off, Caroline's schedule was full. Spaced between preparation sessions were a White House reception with a plethora of celebrities, members of Congress, and prominent women from the worlds of politics, athletics, and a variety of charitable endeavors; a meeting with Senate Minority Leader Chuck Hampton and several female Democratic senators; a breakfast with a group of pro-choice Republican women who had broken with their party to support her; lunch with Lara Costello and other women from the media. The one woman who seemed to be missing—because Caroline refused to ask her—was Brett Allen.

But Caroline's first meeting was the most symbolic: a stroll with President Kilcannon on the grounds of the White House, to be duly photographed by the White House press corps and the hoard shoving lenses and Minicams through the bars of the iron fence. "So much of it is theater," the President remarked as they walked. "Reagan wasn't the only actor to be President, just the only one with screen credits."

It was the first time she had seen him since the Tierney decision. Though his outward manner was unconcerned, there were bruises of sleeplessness beneath his eyes, and he already looked subtly older. Caroline trod carefully; though the late-March weather was mild, the grounds were wet. "I don't mind costarring in a silent film," she answered. "But taking a pratfall in high heels just won't do. I've caused you enough trouble already."

The President stopped, smiling a little. "I can't say it's been no trouble. But there's a certain freedom in saying what you believe. And the opposition seems to find that worrisome."

Caroline shook her head. "Still, I never imagined reading that the future of your administration rides on me. That feels much bigger than I am."

The President shoved his hands in the pockets of his suit coat, his gaze serious and inquiring. "Bigger than what's happened to you?"

Caroline looked down; since the revelation, Brett had been secluded, avoiding the media, politely refusing to see either Caroline or Betty until she came to terms with her own feelings. The freshest image Caroline had of her was a fuzzy picture from the cover of *US Magazine* showing Brett, captured by a telephoto lens, putting out the garbage at dawn. "Maybe to me," Caroline said. "Not to her."

The President was quiet. "I'm sorry," he told her. "I wanted to protect you both."

Caroline met his eyes; suddenly, he looked more troubled than she had expected. "Well," she said, "I can't say you didn't warn me. It happened because I wanted the job."

Kilcannon paused again, staring intently at the ground, as though considering whether to speak. Then he seemed to shrug. "We'd better keep walking," he said, "or we'll look like a couple in crisis. Besides, standing next to me in heels, you seem as tall as I am. Kit Pace is very sensitive to that."

Smiling, Caroline began walking again, though with care. "Brett," the President asked. "How is that now?"

"For me? Hard. I entertain these selfish fantasies . . ." Abruptly, Caroline stopped herself. "As for her, I imagine a young woman going backward in time, reinterpreting the chapters of her life—how Betty spoke of me, or didn't; my estrangement from her grandfather; crosscurrents where she imagined something was not quite right, but didn't know what it was. Why the family albums contained no pictures of my mother—who, *US Magazine* was kind enough to reveal, looked so much like Brett that it's haunted me for years.

"She's a sensitive young woman, and, I think, a wise one." Caroline glanced at the photographers ringing the White House grounds. "She's leaning on her friends, I'd guess, trying to come to terms with this before she faces the rest of us, and all of *this*. Her life will never be the same, and I doubt she wants to start with a misstep."

Walking beside her, the President simply nodded. Though she did not truly know him, and he had said relatively little, Caroline felt his empathy, the same surprising sense of comfort she had felt at their first meeting.

"I guess it's pointless," the President said at length, "for me to say how difficult these hearings could be."

Though this seemed a change of subject, Caroline guessed that it was not. "I have an inkling, Mr. President. I noticed with regret, though not surprise, that Senator Palmer isn't on my schedule."

This seemed to make the President pensive. "Chad can't see you," he answered. "He's in trouble in his party—your opponents see him as our co-conspirator. He'll barely talk to *me*."

The President's regret sounded as personal as it did professional. "I keep wondering where it came from," Caroline said. "The leak."

The President shrugged again, squinting in the afternoon sun. "No point in wondering, Caroline. It's done."

After a time, Caroline nodded. "I suppose we took our chances, both of us. But Senator Palmer did, too, and I find myself feeling bad for him."

"So do I," Kilcannon said. "Believe me."

Caroline looked across at him; for the first time, she wondered if the President knew—or guessed—more than he was saying. But she had to trust her sense of him; she did not believe that Kerry Kilcannon would betray a promise, to Palmer or to her.

"From what you say," the President ventured, "I suppose Brett won't be coming here."

"I haven't asked her, Mr. President. And I won't—to expose her, or to use her, is more than I can stand." Caroline paused, softening her tone. "Whatever else comes out of this, I want a relationship with her. I can't start it with another act of selfishness."

They stopped again, this time by the Rose Garden, while the President pretended for the cameras to point out some new plantings for the spring. "Perhaps she'll come on her own," he murmured.

Despite her firm intentions, Caroline felt a spasm of hope. With great resolve, she squelched it. "Then she will. But I truly hope she doesn't."

At this, the President smiled slightly. "Really?"

"Really."

Kilcannon seemed to study her. "Suppose *I* ask her."

Caroline stood straighter. "Don't do that," she said. "Please. It's not what's best for her."

The President cocked his head. "But isn't that the problem? Everyone decided what's best for her, except her."

Caroline looked at him evenly. "I don't want to be difficult, Mr. President. But regarding Brett our interests aren't the same.

"I have a daughter I love, and who I hope will grow to love me. You're looking at your nominee for Chief Justice, about to face some very messy hearings, with your own prestige on the line. And you can't help but imagine how much better it would be if Brett came out here, and told the Senate and the world how much she values the gift of life, and appreciates that I acted out of love.

"I hope she gets there. But she'll have to come to that on her own. And if you call her, she'll think it comes from me. Or that we're both playing politics."

Kilcannon studied the stalks of roses. "Perhaps not," he answered. "Sometimes the political can serve the personal." Facing her, Kilcannon still spoke softly. "That's the wonder of being President, I find. Some may impugn my motives, but everyone takes my calls. And even, on occasion, listens."

"Damn him," Harshman said without preface.

Gage looked up from a series of tracking polls, a survey by the Republican National Committee showing sharply polarized opinion over the Masters nomination. "Damn who? Kilcannon? Or Palmer?"

"Martin Tierney. Saunders tells me he still won't testify without a subpoena. The man says his family's had enough."

"Now?" Gage said with faint derision. "Isn't it a little late for him to revirginify?"

Harshman sat. "Tierney never wanted the trial on television, so the Commitment had to go behind his back. Saunders says he's always been difficult—he finds the good professor's principles a little hard to parse. But whatever they are, they don't include committing to a media blitz on Masters, or even testifying voluntarily. And goddamned Palmer won't get on the phone."

With rising irritation, Gage pondered Chad's latest dereliction. Though Gage had satirized Masters's new supporters as "a pack of R-rated Hollywood liberals who think marriage is a 'sexual preference,'" it was hard to counter Kilcannon's glittering lineup with fundamentalist ministers, Christian music stars, and the aging former movie hero who served as figurehead for the NRA. "If Chad won't call him," Gage inquired, "will he send him a subpoena?"

"No. He says that would be harassment, and the family's suffered enough. Some crap about respecting their privacy—as if they had any left."

Gage scowled, thoughtful. "If the man's dug in," he mused, "a subpoena might be trouble. Guess you want *me* to call him."

Without answering, Harshman fished a slip of paper from his shirt pocket, and passed it across the desk. Scribbled on it was the name "Martin Tierney" with telephone numbers for home and work.

Both numbers, Gage discovered after dialing, were set to ring once, then switch to a message machine. "Professor Tierney," he told both machines, "this is Senator Macdonald Gage. When it's convenient, I wonder if you might call me. Don't worry about the hour."

He repeated his home and office numbers, then put down the phone. "All I can do, Paul."

Harshman's mouth set. "We need him."

Glancing at his television, Gage saw the President and Caroline Masters intently talking in the Rose Garden, the President's hand placed lightly on her shoulder. "I know that," Gage said. "I surely do."

By eleven that night, Martin Tierney had not returned his call, and Mac Gage was at home.

Or, he amended, what passed for home. It was a furnished efficiency apartment in Crystal City; his wife had never taken to Washington, and Gage returned to Lexington every weekend, where they had raised their children and where their grandchildren lived now. One of the grandchildren was African American; it seemed ironic, even to Gage, that three generations of his family had made adoption their tradition, commenced by the unknown woman who had been his mother. Reflective, Gage looked at their pictures on his wall, the sole adornment of the sterile living space, barely better than a dormitory room. Gage had never exploited his office for personal gain; anyone looking for his riches, he thought, would find them on this wall.

Lying down on his bed, he reluctantly replaced the faces of his grandchildren with those of his colleagues, riffling them through his mind like flashcards as he counted votes and debts, with question marks for Senate moderates or those facing close elections. He envisioned a handful cowering between Kilcannon and himself—or bargaining with each. He was certain of forty-five votes now, with three more leaning. But even counting those, the last three votes he needed were uncertain, and Kilcannon had prevented the rush for cover which would have doomed his nominee. No Democrat had defected—though, as with the Republicans, ten were undeclared. And all twenty neutrals, Gage was certain, would watch the hearings closely before taking a firm position.

The hearings might decide this. And if Palmer did what he should, the neutrals would have nothing left to wait for, and Caroline Masters would be done.

Which brought him back to Martin Tierney.

Tierney could give Palmer cover, and help them all—an agonized and loving father to offset the incest victims and movie stars. Even as Gage thought this, the telephone rang.

In the life of a Majority Leader, his caller could be anyone. But, guessing it was Martin Tierney, Gage paused before answering, summoning all his resources of guile and persuasion.

"Senator Gage?" The man's voice was familiar from television.

"Professor Tierney," Gage answered, in the welcoming tone his wife wryly called "Southern Comfort." "I've been wanting to make your acquaintance, but I've hesitated to call. I know how hard all this must be."

"Yes," Tierney answered. "It has been. And is."

His tone was pointed, hinting at resistance to what he surmised must be Gage's purpose.

"Well," Gage said somberly, "I don't know how much it helps, but you have the admiration and gratitude of millions of Americans. Including me."

Tierney's voice softened a bit. "Thank you, Senator. I appreciate that. I also have a wife who finds this devastating, and a daughter who barely speaks to us."

"That's a high price to pay," Gage acknowledged. "Even for an hour, or a day. In all honesty, I don't know if I could do it. Which makes it so impressive that you have."

"Believing as we do," Tierney answered, "we had no choice. But there are days when I wonder, as a husband and a father, whether I could have gone to court if I'd foreseen this moment. And I ask myself why God put this on our doorstep."

Gage considered musing aloud about the imponderables of faith, the mystery of God, and rejected this approach as inutile. Tierney sounded too weary and untrusting. At length, Gage said, "I guess you know why I'm calling, Professor."

"Yes."

Gage felt his tension rising; the one-word answer was not promising. In tones of sympathy, he said, "It must seem like too much for you, at times. Going the last mile."

"*All* the time." Tierney's voice was even. "I don't see myself as a martyr, Senator, suffering for principle. I see my daughter, and my wife."

"I understand." Gage kept his voice soft. "But they're not who the country's seeing now—or you. Between Judge Masters and the President, your healthy and loving family has been replaced with drunken and incestuous fathers, indifferent mothers, and pitiful daughters. And your grandson has been altogether lost.

"You've gone this far. But now it's about the future of the Court, and of the pro-life movement. As well as what it's always been about—your daughter and her baby." Gage's voice rose in peroration. "All of us, Professor—you, and the movement—are in danger of losing everything."

"The movement," Tierney answered softly, "put my family on television. Or do they think that's escaped me."

Surprised, Gage called on his reserves of calm. "I'm over my head here, Professor. I don't know what issues you may have with the Commitment. Although, in my experience, they're as good and honorable a group of folks as I can think of . . ."

"How fortunate for you," Tierney answered with asperity, and then seemed to force on himself a more even tone. "You're about to ask me to rise above any personal antipathy, and put our common principles first.

"I've done that—throughout the trial. I'll do it in the Supreme Court. But I'll be damned if I'll excoriate my daughter in the Senate, on television. Or even attack Judge Masters." The vigor vanished from his voice, replaced by a deep fatigue. "I loathe her opinion. She may well have signed my grandson's death warrant. But now I've heard her story, and I can't quite summon the level of animosity required to blind me to the further damage I'd be doing.

"The judge has done her damage already. My grandson's only hope lies in the Supreme Court, not the Senate."

Gage felt his temples throb. Quietly, he said, "I understand the stress you're under, believe me. But as you've said yourself, it's not only about this baby, but *all* babies. If Masters is confirmed, it's not just the Court which will change. The whole pro-life movement will be weakened, and the most pro-abortion president in our history will be emboldened." As he spoke, Gage felt his own political interests merge with the truth of what he said. "This is an epochal moment, Professor. I beg you to consider that."

There was a long silence. "I'm sorry," Tierney answered quietly. "My family has done enough for the movement. We'll leave the rest to you."

Gage hesitated. "While I don't feel this way," he began, "others want to serve you with a subpoena . . ."

"So the Democrats can subpoena Mary Ann?" Tierney's voice was cold. "Tell the 'others' this: If they send me a subpoena, I will come, and state my beliefs as I always have. I'll also call a press conference, repeat this conversation, and tell the media that I implored your party not to do this. You and Mr. Saunders can decide, Senator, whether that serves your purposes."

Startled, Gage hesitated. "Maybe," he said warily, "you should talk to your wife. Or perhaps I could . . ."

"Goodbye, Senator." The phone clicked off.

Fifteen

Two hours before the hearings recommenced, Caroline Masters breakfasted alone in her suite at the Hay-Adams.

It would, she knew, be a long and emotional day. There had been an influx of death threats; by order of President Kilcannon there were two Secret Service agents in the hallway. A small army of reporters and Minicams awaited her below, and on Capitol Hill crowds were gathering to demonstrate for or against her confirmation. For the next hour or so, she would try to find the serenity to face whatever came.

There was a knock on the door. Surprised, Caroline wondered if—oblivious to the drama of the moment—the hotel intended to restock her minibar. She rearranged her robe, then cracked open the door.

The first face she saw belonged to Peter Lake, head of the President's protective detail. Beside him was her daughter.

Brett regarded her with a gaze at once tentative, reserved, and avid for detail; it struck Caroline that this was Brett's first experience of seeing her and knowing who she was. Caroline felt her stomach constrict.

"Thank you," she said to Peter Lake. Brett stepped inside.

Silent, they faced each other.

"The President?" Caroline made herself ask, though she hoped this was not so.

"Yes. He called me, and then sent *Air Force One*."

Brett's voice was uninflected. She did not move, but seemed to soak up Caroline's features with Nicole Dessaliers's startling green eyes.

"I'm sorry," Caroline said.

She meant many things: that she was sorry for leaving her; sorry for a lifetime of deception; sorry that Kerry Kilcannon was the reason Brett had come. And sorry for the time and manner of her appearance, surely the President's doing. With any warning, Caroline might have discouraged her daughter from coming, or arranged a meeting more private and less dramatic: were she to switch on CNN, Caroline would no doubt see a film clip of Brett arriving moments before, emblazoned with the words "breaking news."

"I'm sorry," Caroline repeated, "for everything."

Brett said nothing. Nor could Caroline seem to find more words. Twenty-seven years evanesced: she reexperienced the last moment of holding the new-born Brett, smelling her fresh skin and soft wisps of hair, before placing her in Larry's arms.

"So much to say," Caroline ventured in a wan attempt at humor, "so little time. This isn't how I wanted it."

Brett gazed into her face. "That's what the President said. But he also said you needed me here."

Caroline drew a breath. "Personally?" she asked. "Or politically?"

"Both."

Caroline looked down. "Then you must know how this is bound to hurt your mother. You, on television, coming to me."

"Yes." Brett's voice was soft, but controlled. "I explained the President's call as best I could. And that *your* needs seem to have a deadline."

At this, Caroline felt ashamed. "How did she take that?"

"It's hard to know. She breaks down on the phone, and I feel for her. But it's hard to get much out of her—about how she felt, what she thought, why she couldn't at least tell me I was adopted."

Caroline paused. "Of the two of us, Brett, I think your mother's wounds go deeper. Perhaps too deep to explain."

Brett stared at her, reluctant to speak, yet, to Caroline, so hungry for comprehension that she felt obliged to try. "I was never an easy sister," Caroline said. "Our father deeply loved my mother—at least for a time—and saw himself in me. I was always treated as the smart one, the important one, until I became as reflexively dismissive of your mother as *he* was.

"Betty had lost her mother, and then her place in the family. She wanted her own child desperately, and couldn't have one." Caroline's voice softened. "At twenty-two, I didn't care much, but *could*. Whoever said 'life is unfair' must have had Betty in mind."

Brett considered her, silent. Even now, Caroline realized, she could not talk of Betty without a touch of condescension. "Listen to me," she told Brett, "and you'll feel how wounding I am to her, even now. My best efforts at compassion turn to pity."

This, despite the painfulness of the moment, evoked from Brett a faint ironic smile. "That must be why you're so low on *self*-pity, Caroline. You reserve it for lesser mortals."

The truth of this, and the solitude it suggested, left Caroline without words. "I wanted to tell you," she said at last. "So much. But long ago I realized people are what they live. Betty was your mother, and you're her daughter. Now I can only hope you'll forgive me for how this is playing out. In public, and in the worst conceivable way."

Even as she said this, Caroline remembered that their time alone was running out fast—in little more than an hour, she had a date with the United States Senate. Brett looked into Caroline's eyes without censure or sentimentality. "But you still want this, don't you—to be Chief Justice."

If Brett could face the truth without flinching, Caroline resolved, so must she. "Yes," she answered. "As I said, people are what they live. Twenty-seven years ago, I stopped being your mother. Instead, I became a lawyer, then a judge. This is about who I turned out to be."

Caroline paused, meeting her daughter's gaze. "But it's not *all* I want. Now that you know, it's nowhere close. That's why I worried so much about your coming." Caroline paused, then finished quietly, "More than anything, Brett, I hope you'll come to love me."

This statement, so uncharacteristic in its admission of need, caused her daughter's eyes to shut. With equal quiet, she answered, "I came here, didn't I?"

An hour later, Brett and Caroline walked the few short steps from the hotel—shepherded by agents and surrounded by media—to a bullet-proof limousine.

Once inside, the young woman seemed to ignore the reporters' questions, shouted through the glass. To Caroline, she seemed to enter a private zone of self-possession which reminded Caroline of *her* own mother until, with some surprise, Caroline recognized it in herself.

The limousine cruised toward Capitol Hill, the crush of media receding from view. Along Pennsylvania Avenue more Minicams recorded their progress; gazing at the Capitol, framed in the front window, Brett seemed to withdraw more completely, as though preparing for their arrival.

They cruised to a stop in front of the Russell Senate Office Building, which housed the Old Senate Caucus Room. In the bright morning sun, more cameras waited, along with the phalanx of agents assigned to protect them. The car door opened. When they stepped from the car, Brett first, the cacophony began.

For Caroline, time seemed to stop. Then the two of them, surrounded by agents, entered the building.

Sixteen

Once more, Caroline Masters faced the Senate Committee on the Judiciary.

Much was the same—the bank of eighteen senators with aides hovering behind them; the television cameras; the standing-room-only mass of reporters. The difference lay in the level of intensity, and the reasons for Caroline's recall. The one restraint on Caroline's adversaries—at which they were demonstrably uneasy—was Brett Allen's watchful presence in the first row.

It was a little past eleven. For the first hour, Chad Palmer had questioned her about the Tierney decision, leaving the matter of Brett and Sarah Dash to others. Palmer had been persistent but fair; coolly, Caroline had summarized her position.

"*Roe* and *Casey*," she had told Palmer, "permit a ban on postviability abortion absent extraordinary circumstances. Some might call rape and incest extraordinary. Some might call severe fetal anomalies extraordinary. Under our decision, neither is—in itself—sufficient grounds. But these tragedies are often accompanied by a third extraordinary factor: a threat to the mother's life or health.

"Whether by accident or design, the Protection of Life Act deprives young women and their doctors of the right to deal with significant risks to health, including infertility, typically arising from one or both of the other factors I've mentioned. In the case of Mary Ann Tierney, the threat to her fertility arose directly from a fetal anomaly, hydrocephalus, which rendered it highly unlikely that the fetus would survive."

Pausing, Caroline had surveyed the committee. "Pregnancy is that rare condition where two lives—mother and child—are inextricably intertwined. My colleagues and I concluded that a statute which barred Mary Ann Tierney from protecting her physical health, under these circumstances, unduly burdened a minor's right to an abortion under *Roe v. Wade*.

"There are those who disagree. I respect that; I found the case a difficult one. But whatever the outcome of these hearings, I'm comfortable that we fulfilled our obligations, and applied the law."

Shortly before eleven-thirty, Senator Vic Coletti, the ranking Democrat on the committee, yielded to Senator Harshman.

Though she did not turn, Caroline was acutely aware of Brett, the heightened tension in the room. Feeling her shoulders stiffen, Caroline took a deep breath. There was dampness on her forehead.

Leaning on his elbows, Harshman peered at her over the raised bench, his glasses glinting with light.

"You have a child," he said bluntly.

Caroline folded her hands, expelling a silent breath. "A biological daughter," she answered, "who is my niece by adoption and by law."

Briefly, and it seemed involuntarily, Harshman's gaze flickered to Brett Allen. "You've never married, correct?"

"Correct."

"And so you had the child out of wedlock."

Once more, Caroline felt a piercing regret—not for herself, but Brett. *"That,"* she answered tersely, "would seem to follow."

Harshman's neck twisted forward, a symptom of anger. "Do you know who the father was?"

Turning, Senator Coletti stared at his colleague, his rough-hewn face a mask of disgust. Between them, Senator Palmer gazed at the papers in front of him. Caroline drew herself up.

"Yes," she answered. "I do."

"Can you tell us?"

Caroline paused. "No."

Abruptly, Palmer's head snapped up. "Why not?" Harshman demanded.

Caroline met his eyes. "I'm here to answer your questions, Senator. In that spirit, I'm willing to discuss matters I regard as personal. But I don't believe that this particular invasion of my privacy—and that of the young woman you see behind me—is in any way pertinent to your inquiry. That's a subject for the two of us, and no one else."

With this, Palmer turned to Harshman, lightly touching his arm. A whispered colloquy, which clearly irritated Harshman, ended in a scowl. It was not hard for Caroline to guess what had happened—Palmer had told Harshman that he would not direct her to answer.

After a moment, Harshman resumed with greater calm. "It *is* true," he said, "that you never acknowledged this young woman as your daughter."

"It is."

"And, in connection with your appointment to the Court of Appeals, you designated her as your 'niece' in forms provided by the FBI."

"Yes."

Harshman's voice rose. "Again, in connection with your nomination for Chief Justice—the presiding judge of our nation's highest court—you wrote that Brett Allen was your '*niece.*'"

Caroline stared at him. The others seemed to recede; the exchange felt visceral now, and very personal. "Which she was—and is. Shortly after her birth, Brett was adopted by my sister and her husband. We all thought that was best—"

"Especially," Harshman interjected, "for you."

Caroline concealed her anger with a shrug, the smallest movement of her shoulder. "In some ways, yes. In others, no." Her voice grew stronger. "I decided that adoption was best for Brett. Both you and I, Senator, advocate adoption as social policy. No doubt some of the many birth mothers you've met have mentioned how hard it is to give up a child."

Harshman tented his fingers, eyes narrow. "Some also acknowledged publicly that they *were* birth mothers. You chose not to."

"True. As, for a variety of reasons, do many others."

"Put bluntly, Judge Masters, they didn't lie to the United States Senate."

Caroline drew a breath. "I assume not, Senator. I know *I* didn't."

Harshman flushed, the reddening of his high forehead an alarming contrast to his thinning white hair. "Don't bandy words with me, Judge Masters. You perjured yourself in forms submitted to this Committee."

Caroline gathered herself. "No," she reiterated. "I did not.

"I told the truth. As a matter of law, and for her entire life, my niece was parented by Larry and Betty Allen . . ."

"That's sophistry," Harshman interjected. "If *that's* the standard of truth you'd impose on our courts . . ."

Caroline held up her hand. "Let me finish, Senator, please.

"It's true that I didn't write down that my niece is also my birth child. With good reason: *she* never knew until five days ago, and in those five days she has been through more than should be required of anyone.

"You can quarrel with my decision, Senator Harshman. And you're certainly within your rights to ask these questions. But I ask you one simple question: What would you have done?

"Would you expose your daughter—or your niece—to the kind of publicity your questions create?"

"Judge Masters," Harshman interrupted angrily.

Caroline's voice rose, the release of her own outrage. "Would you," she demanded, "expose someone you love to a humiliation akin to what this young woman has been forced to endure?

"Would you make her a plaything for the media, and for political partisans?" Pausing, Caroline subdued her tone. "I've no formal right to an answer. But I'm sincerely interested in knowing, Senator, what *you* would have done."

Harshman's jaw worked, but his voice was level and authoritative. "Then I'll tell you, Judge. If I were you, I would not have allowed the President to nominate me, and if I were *he,* I'd not have done so.

"You have a biological daughter. If you couldn't tell the truth about that—the truth, the whole truth, and nothing but the truth—then you are unworthy of presiding over a system of justice which rests on that commitment."

It was a good response; at once, Caroline regretted having pushed him. "I told the truth," she insisted, "and all I believe anyone was entitled to—"

"As a member of the Senate," Harshman cut in, "I don't agree. In fact, I believe you owe me an apology."

This interruption was a mercy, Caroline thought; just when he had squelched her, Harshman had gone too far.

"I regret your feelings," she answered. "For my own part, I believe that—under these circumstances—matters private to our family should have remained private.

"If you intend to vote against me for that reason, that's your right." Lowering her voice, Caroline looked at him directly. "But I'm afraid you'll have to do so without an apology from me."

On television, the image was striking: the composed and dignified judge; the beautiful young woman directly behind her, staring at her mother's antagonist.

"That last bit was a slip," Clayton told the President. "But she's held up well. And the two of them together are worth a thousand thirty-second spots."

They were alone in the interior conference room. Turning, Kerry said sharply, "That's no cause for rejoicing. They're there because of us, and don't know it. I hope that bothers you at least a little, because it bothers the hell out of me."

Clayton met the President's eyes. Since their breach, they had barely spoken; they were alone now only because several others—Ellen Penn, Adam Shaw, and Kit Pace—had been called away by emergencies. To Kerry, acting as if nothing were wrong was a level of pretense too painful to endure, the final death of friendship.

"Personally," Clayton answered, "I'm very sorry—about her, and about you. Politically, I think Masters is about to hand Paul Harshman his head. She couldn't do that if she knew . . ."

"*Twenty-seven years ago,*" Caroline continued, "*I made the decision I believed was right. At least I got to make my decision in privacy, and to protect our family's privacy—until, mercifully, the young woman we all love in common is the adult you see today.*

"*Which brings me back to* her, *and to Mary Ann Tierney. Both of whom have been stripped of all privacy and used as pawns.*" Folding her hands, Caroline addressed Harshman calmly. "*Our court's decision in* Tierney, *like* Roe, *is premised in the constitutional right to privacy. That right is well established. But whether you agree with it or not, the entire conduct of that case on television is a tragedy for this young girl.*

"*Not only did she face a compulsory childbirth—and still may—but she was compelled to seek redress in public. Because, it appears, the very forces who claim to be acting to protect her have decided that they prefer her to be a public object lesson.*

"*They've decided the same, it appears, regarding my niece.*" Caroline's voice was firm. "*I don't know about you, Senator, but that offends my notion of public decency . . .*"

"Bingo," Clayton murmured.

"Demagoguery," Gage said in disgust. "Lying as the highest morality. If that's the standard of truth she'll bring to our justice system, God help us all."

Mace Taylor kept watching the screen. "I think Paul's going to drop the hammer on her."

Frustrated, Gage turned to him, feeling a growing disquiet about where events were taking them. "What hammer?" he inquired with an edge of sarcasm. "Your people couldn't find anything new about her. Or even who leaked this business about the daughter."

Caroline faced Harshman. The room felt hot and close.

"Speaking of decency," Harshman said with ominous softness. "Do you know a lawyer named Sarah Dash?"

Caroline steeled herself. "I do, Senator. She was counsel for Mary Ann Tierney."

"Indeed she was," Harshman said primly. "And she was also your law clerk, you've acknowledged."

"Yes. Three years ago."

"And you formed a friendship."

"Yes. As I testified before."

Harshman's eyebrows shot up. "A *close* friendship?"

Caroline met his gaze. "I don't know if one would call it that. We're well apart in age. But Sarah remained a friend."

"A good enough friend, Judge Masters, to visit your home."

For a split second, Caroline imagined detectives combing through her life. But discipline turned her outrage to coolness. "From time to time."

Harshman folded his hands. "Alone?" he asked. "Just the two of you?"

At that moment, Caroline became aware of Chad Palmer, leaning back from Harshman in silent disassociation, his face betraying a fleeting expression of distaste, followed by blankness. "Sometimes," Caroline answered dryly. "I enjoy cooking, Senator. If I'm fortunate enough to live in Washington, I promise to fix you some veal *piccata*."

Sitting beside Palmer, Vic Coletti turned to Harshman with amusement and curiosity, as if wondering how his colleague would react. Nettled, Harshman said, "What was the nature of these visits, Judge Masters. Were you merely exchanging recipes?"

Caroline felt herself stare at him, her voice turn wintry with repressed anger. "Ms. Dash isn't much of a cook, I don't believe. So we weren't 'exchanging' anything."

Harshman hesitated. Across the twenty feet which separated them, their eyes met. *I dare you,* Caroline silently told him. But, as she suspected, Harshman chose to leave his implication dangling.

"Did you ever exchange *thoughts,*" Harshman asked, "about the Tierney case?"

Caroline composed herself, briefly rehearsing the response she had prepared. "Since the filing of the Tierney case, I've neither seen nor spoken to Ms. Dash. So the answer is no." Pausing, Caroline spoke with renewed strength. "But for the sake of completeness, I should tell you that—the last time I prepared dinner—Ms. Dash mentioned meeting Mary Ann Tierney. I told her that, inasmuch as any case which resulted might come before my court, I didn't want to hear about it, and wouldn't discuss it."

Harshman stared at her in skepticism and surprise. "And you're saying *that* was the entire conversation."

"Not quite." Caroline's voice was cold. "I told her that the partisans on both sides of the abortion question had long memories, and that it would be better for her to avoid this altogether. Although I *never* anticipated the inference you've raised this morning."

The room was hushed. Angry, Harshman leaned forward, jerking the microphone close to his mouth. "I'm entitled to an inference of bias, Judge, when you have private tête-à-têtes with counsel for Mary Ann Tierney. You did not choose to disqualify yourself, did you?"

"Obviously not. If I had, I wouldn't be sitting here."

Once more, Palmer turned to Harshman. "In fact," Harshman continued, "you voted to grant Ms. Dash's petition en banc."

"Ms. Tierney's petition," Caroline corrected. "That vote is private by rule of our court, so I'd be curious to know where you acquired your information. But the fact is that I voted for rehearing."

"And then wrote the opinion, invalidating the statute."

"Yes. I thought that's why we were here—"

"And you did *all* that," Harshman said in a prosecutorial tone, "at the behest of a friend who often visits your home—alone."

Kit Pace, Adam Shaw, and Ellen Penn had gathered now. Adam and Kit flanked the President; Ellen—too intent to sit—stood next to Clayton with her hands flat on the conference table.

On the screen Caroline had regained her calm. *"As I remarked the last time, every judge has friends. I've lived and practiced in San Francisco for over twenty years and so, like many judges, most of my friends are lawyers.*

"As for former clerks, our rule—as I also said—is to recuse ourselves from their cases for one year after their clerkship. There are many former law clerks who practice before us; were the period any longer, our court would be paralyzed.

"I don't know any of my colleagues who would put a relationship with a former clerk above their duty to be impartial. When I was here before, you asked me that very question—and I answered, truthfully, that I would not." Pausing, Caroline remained composed, almost professorial. *"Our other obligation is to ensure we avoid the* appearance *of partiality. We believe a one-year period satisfies that need."*

"Even in a case as important as this," Harshman persisted, *"with a clerk who's also a friend?"*

Intent, Kerry watched the screen. Softly, he said to Caroline, "It's time."

Caroline appeared to gather herself. *"Yes,"* she answered. *"Perhaps the best analogy I can offer, Senator, is one which you'll find familiar: the Senate rule which permits former senators to lobby members one year after they leave.*

"*After a year, the Senate has concluded, there is no inference of any undue influence . . .*"

Watching, Kerry heard Ellen Penn's knowing laugh of delight. "*For example,*" Caroline went on, "*I've become aware that your former colleague from Oklahoma, Senator Taylor, represents the Christian Commitment in urging members of this body to defeat my nomination.*

"*Obviously, no one here believes that Senator Taylor's advocacy is in any way improper, or that those senators who might oppose me are acting from anything but conviction . . .*"

"Catch Harshman," Kit Pace remarked. "He looks like he gargled with vinegar . . ."

"*Or,*" Caroline continued blandly, "*that his activities in raising money for your party are any other than a legitimate exercise of his First Amendment rights of speech.*

"*Were it otherwise, Senator, surely* you *would have taken the lead in changing the rules which permit Senator Taylor to come here . . .*"

Sitting beside Harshman, Chad Palmer turned away, obviously attempting not to smile.

"It's all too funny," Mace Taylor said to the screen. "It's all too funny, Chad." Angered and dismayed, Gage said nothing.

"*Are you questioning my integrity?*" Harshman demanded with genuine indignation.

Caroline's expression did not change. "*To the contrary,*" she said, "*I was affirming my belief in your integrity. I believe you were questioning mine.*

"*I hope I can change your mind, though I don't presume I can. Beyond that, I can only hope that all ninety-nine of your colleagues have the chance to judge me for themselves . . .*"

"Kilcannon saw us coming," Gage said abruptly. "He primed her. They know we're trying to kill her in committee."

Taylor scowled in disbelief. "Bullshit, Mac. Palmer *told* him—or her."

On the screen, Paul Harshman hesitated, and then spoke with weary disdain. "*Very well, Judge Masters. Let's take your Tierney opinion on its so-called merits . . .*"

Seventeen

The Senate was running late that evening, caught in a debate over gun control, and so Chad Palmer and Kate Jarman sneaked out for a quick dinner at the Oval Room.

They had a corner table, and the dim-lit elegant surroundings lent a sense of privacy. After looking about, Kate asked quietly, "What are you going to do about her?"

Chad did not need to ask whom Kate meant. She studied him, her thin face and light blue eyes betraying a keen intelligence which grasped the essence of Chad's dilemma—he was a potential candidate for President, caught between his party base and his own sense of what was right. "Tell me how it went today," he parried, "and maybe I'll know."

Kate smiled. "From where *I* sat—five chairs away from Paul—I was glad I wasn't next to him. People watching might think we're friends."

"It was *that* bad?"

Her smile became skeptical. "You *were* sitting next to him. Which moment did you enjoy least: when Harshman asked who Dad was with her daughter looking on, or when she stuck Mace Taylor in his ear? Gage should issue Paul a regulator." She lowered her voice. "It's one thing to vote against her. But I hear Mac wants to kill her in committee."

Chad did not bother to deny this. Sipping from his Stolichnaya on the rocks, he answered, "Did you hear he mentioned you?"

Kate stopped smiling. "He doesn't have to run for reelection in Vermont, where gays have civil unions and one of our congressmen's a literal socialist. I won't get my ticket repunched by pandering to the far right.

"And then there's what Paul would call the merits, which seem worthy of some attention. About the daughter, I think Masters has the high ground—she's a class act, and I don't think calling her a 'liar' is going to work, especially when her chief accuser ends up sounding like Cotton Mather." Kate played with the straw in her gin and tonic. "About the Tierney case, I think she's probably more right than wrong. But for anyone in our party to say that is a risk—I don't want a primary challenge from some nut job."

Looking up, Senator Jarman fixed Chad with a level glance. "Kilcannon's figured all that out," she finished, "including what Gage is up to. Mac's underrated him—before this is over, it could be a bloodbath."

His own situation, Chad reflected, was growing more perilous by the hour. "So what are you telling me?"

"I could probably get by with voting against her. But I wouldn't vote to kill her without having you for company. And even that's unlikely to persuade me."

Though disheartened, Palmer smiled: Kate had given him early warning, so he could calibrate his moves. "You're an honest woman, Kate. Thanks for letting me know."

She studied him with open curiosity. "What *will* you do?"

"Tread water." Briefly, he looked around them. "I think the hearings will sort themselves out. We'll get a sense of public opinion, and how hard Gage wants to push this. Maybe he'll back off."

Slowly, Kate shook her head. In quiet tones, she said, "You're forgetting who his stockholders are. I don't think Mac's a free agent here—even if he thinks so. If I were you, I'd watch my back."

The next morning, alone in his office, Chad pondered Kate Jarman's warning. He was studying a photo of Kyle smiling at him—an airbrushed version of family history—when his private line rang through.

"Hello, Chad. Mac here."

Chad sat back. "Morning, Mac," he answered. "I guess you're calling to congratulate me on this morning's CNN poll."

"Haven't seen it."

"Well," Chad said, "maybe you should look it over. Among those who watched yesterday's hearings, Masters has roughly a ten point spread."

"It's those damned TV spots," Gage complained, "paid for by the fucking trial lawyers. There's an ethical problem in itself—they're purchasing a Chief Justice on the installment plan."

The spots were fresh in Chad's mind: a handsome Caroline Masters, with Paul Newman's distinctive voice asking, *"Isn't this who we want as a judge?"* "You coin a nice phrase," Chad answered, "and the Kilcannon ad blitz hasn't helped. But neither did our colleague, Senator Torquemada.

"She's not a lesbian, Mac, or you'd have found out by now. And she acted to protect her daughter. Objecting to Tierney is fine. But burn her at the stake in committee, and you'll create a martyr."

"Chad," Gage said in exasperation, "we've trod this path before."

"No," Chad snapped. "We're treading it now, and it's a bed of hot coals." Hearing himself, he moderated his tone. "Know where CNN's ten percent came from? A twenty percent edge among women.

"That's where Kerry ate our lunch four months ago. Now he's found a way to make that worse—suburban women *hate* this kind of thing." Pausing, Chad strained for a tone of politeness and sincerity. "When I was protecting her, I was protecting us. Fight her on the merits, Mac. Not on her personal life."

There was a long silence. "This is a time," Gage said, "when our base expects action."

"From whom? George Armstrong Custer?" Chad felt his anxiety rising. "There are four more days of hearings, Mac. Show me something, and I'll reconsider. But yesterday was a disaster."

Conversation ended, Gage slowly put down the phone.

"Well?" Taylor asked.

Gage looked into his colleague's face—the hammered cheekbones, the frontier squint of his eyes—and briefly wished, despite his frustration with Palmer, that he did not have to answer.

"We'll have to see," he said at length. "But it's time to squeeze Kate Jarman. I don't think Palmer's going for it."

Four days later, after chairing a virtual colloquium by law professors and ethicists on the legal definition of perjury, Chad Palmer summoned the Republicans on Judiciary to his office. Kate Jarman, he noted, sat as far from Harshman as possible.

Quickly, Chad surveyed the others: Jim Lambert of Alabama, dark, sleek, and guarded; the shrewd and amiable Cotter Ryan of Indiana; Jerry Deane of Georgia, looking, as always, red-faced and short of breath; Frank Fasano of Pennsylvania—young, ambitious, and wholly without humor; Bill Fitzgerald of Florida, chewing gum in his perennial fight against nicotine addiction; Dave Ruckles of Oklahoma, mean as a snake, with the sincere voice and constant eye contact of an evangelist or a stockbroker; Madison Starkweather of Mississippi, eighty-five and running on fumes and staff assistance, who had yielded the committee chairmanship in preparation for death. Somehow, Chad reflected, people elect us all—a truism he tried to remember in his unceasing fight with his own impatience.

"Here we are," Chad began. "We vote Monday, and the Supreme Court has yet to rule in the Tierney case. So we know all we're going to know before we're forced to take a stand."

"We know plenty," Paul Harshman said promptly. "This woman lied; she has a history of promiscuity and God knows what; the trial lawyers have purchased her at auction; her ethics are in question; and she has now acknowledged a radical pro-abortion agenda. She doesn't belong on the Court."

Chad felt himself smile. "You surprise me, Paul. So what do we do?"

Harshman looked at the others, and then at Palmer again. "We vote not to send her to the floor, Senator. And end this farce."

For once, Chad did not want to take the lead. His glance at Kate Jarman was a signal—it was time for her to give him cover.

"Killing a Supreme Court nomination in committee," she said to the others, "would be extraordinary. Apart from Masters's testimony, there's nothing new: the law professors have quarreled, though no one made a persuasive case for perjury; the interest groups have said what they've always said; and the Tierney opinion is what it is.

"We've all had our chance to hyperventilate in public. But we've changed no minds—except those we've changed against us." She paused, looking about the room. "I'm sure Mac's talked to all of us. I know he's talked to me. What I told him is that I won't take on a suicide mission."

Harshman stared at her. "Mac says he'll speak out for us."

"Which," Kate answered dryly, "is an enormous spiritual comfort. But it won't help me in Vermont."

Harshman looked at the others. "The rest of us," he remarked to Kate, "don't come from a people's republic."

"True," she answered with a smile. "But even *you* let women vote."

The lines were being drawn, Chad saw, where he always feared they would. Six of their seven colleagues came from conservative states; the seventh—Frank Fasano—was a committed pro-lifer whose national ambitions would rise and fall with the power of the Christian Commitment. And in no case were they prepared to defy Macdonald Gage.

"Chad," Fasano said, "I count eight of us for voting Masters down: everyone but Kate—and you. Nine is all we need."

Gage had orchestrated this neatly, Chad thought. "All *you* need to do," Harshman told him, "is vote with us. For once."

He was trapped. In his mildest voice, Chad answered, "What you're suggesting, Paul, might have been possible four days ago. Until you decided to go after her—"

"The woman was arrogant," Harshman interjected.

"And now she's sympathetic. Far more than you, in candor. Or any of us white guys who all ganged up on her, and now propose to kill her off in our own version of a smoke-filled room.

"That," Chad told the others, "would be a coup for Kerry Kilcannon. And it would harm the next Republican president—if we can ever elect another.

"But forget the women we're offending, if you like, and remember Robert Bork. The liberals trashed him, totally unfairly—as a person and as a judge. They nearly brought down Clarence Thomas, based on allegations about private conduct no one could prove or disprove.

"After Bob Bork went down, he said to me, 'They'll never choose another judge who has opinions.' How much farther do we want to go down *that* road? Especially when it hurts conservative judges at least as much as liberals." Standing, Chad placed his hands on his hips. "It's not good for the party, or the country, for Supreme Court nominations to continue as guerrilla warfare. If we want to vote down Masters, fine—let's do that. But out in the open, on the Senate floor, with all one hundred of us voting. Not like *this*."

Harshman stared at him with contempt. "Payback's a bitch," he said. "But if it's all that bad, let's spare our party colleagues a vote. Show some guts for a change."

"I think they can step up to it," Chad said evenly. "That's what we're elected for." Once more, he faced the others. "I'm willing to take the lead. I'll vote to send her to the floor with a negative recommendation."

By prearrangement, Kate Jarman said promptly, "So will I."

Glancing from Kate to Chad, Harshman's eyes reflected his brief and bitter smile. "What about the eight of us?"

Chad sat again. "You don't have the majority, Paul. There'd be the eight of you voting to kill her, then Kate and me, and then all eight Democrats—so Vic Coletti tells me—voting for a positive recommendation. I'd rather join them than reap the whirlwind." Though his heart was not light, Chad smiled back at Harshman. "Viewed that way, I'm offering you a deal, and Gage a weapon. A ten-to-eight recommendation against."

The characteristic flush appeared on Harshman's forehead; some day, Chad thought, the man would have a stroke. Biting off his words, Harshman said, "Seems like we're stuck."

For a triumphant moment, Chad reflected, this gave him far less pleasure than apprehension. Somberly, he answered, "Seems like we all are."

Eighteen

A few hours after the Judiciary Committee sent the nomination of Caroline Masters back to the full Senate, Clayton came to the Oval Office.

Kerry looked up from a summary of pending legislation. For the first time since their rupture, Clayton had the glint of amusement. "Gage just called," he said.

"About Caroline?"

"Yes. He wants to see you."

At once, Kerry understood his friend's expression. He felt a fleeting sense of satisfaction; perhaps, as President, he was proving more formidable than Gage had expected. "We have his attention," Kerry observed. "Now that he has to beat us on the floor."

"What should I tell him?"

Kerry smiled. "That I'm a busy man—what with running the world, and battling the forces of reaction. But I can always make time for my old friend from the Senate."

Ceremoniously, the two men shook hands. Then Kerry closed the door behind them and waved Gage to an overstuffed chair in front of the marble fireplace.

Kerry felt each taking the other's measure. Less than four months ago, they had been colleagues, with Kerry, a youthful two-term senator, subject to the velvet tyranny with which Mac Gage ran the Senate. Then, in the wondrous quadrennial act of community, the vote of a free people, the voters had made Kerry Kilcannon the most powerful man on earth, the occupant of an office Macdonald Gage desperately wanted. And so, while Gage remained "Mac," Kerry had gone from the "little demagogue" behind his back and "Kerry" to his face, to "Mr. President."

It threw Gage off, Kerry sensed—the Majority Leader disliked having to recalibrate their relationship so drastically, and beneath his smooth and faintly avuncular manner was a novel trace of uncertainty. The White House press were clustered outside, Kerry knew, speculating on what it meant that Macdonald Gage—as Kit Pace had promptly informed them—had asked to see the President.

"It's been a while," Kerry said pleasantly. "Since the inaugural, in fact."

Gage nodded, conveying with his actor's range of expressions both his pleasure in seeing Kerry, and the sadness of this particular memory. "Since Roger Bannon's passing," he said solemnly. "A lot has happened in these few weeks."

Kerry saw no reason to replicate Gage's mournful aura. Pleasantly, he said, "It surely has. Now and then I realize how long it's been since I've last seen my old friends."

This veiled jibe—a reference to Gage's long-distance war against Caroline Masters, marked by their absence of contact—induced in Gage a shrewd, appraising look. "My fault, Mr. President, no doubt about it. I haven't wanted to impose myself. But we're overdue for a visit."

"I certainly agree."

At this comment, a shade more pointed in tone, Gage leaned forward, closing the space between Kerry and himself. It was an old Senate trick—Gage using his bulk to assert dominance—and it conveyed without words that they were engaged in a struggle for power. "Overdue," Gage repeated. "And now we have a problem."

Kerry smiled. "Which one?"

Gage's eyes widened, conveying mock surprise. "Why Caroline Masters, Mr. President." His voice was soft. "The Honorable Caroline Masters."

"Well," the President answered, "she's certainly that."

Over the smallest of smiles, Gage's eyes were combative. "It depends on your point of view." He paused, his tone becoming reflective, statesmanlike. "She's turned into plutonium, Mr. President. We're about to invest a lot of resources in a contentious battle over whether she should lead the Court. No matter how it turns out—and I'm confident I *know* how—it will leave a legacy of rancor which will taint everything else the Senate tries to do." Gage leaned closer, looking into Kerry's eyes; but for his new status, the President sensed, Gage would have put a hand on his shoulder. "And for what, Mr. President? For what?"

Kerry's own gaze was unblinking. "For the nominee I think best."

Gage frowned. "That's fine, of course. That's the privilege of your office. But there has to be a political point to it all, or it's sort of like the war in Vietnam—a lot of carnage and bitterness, for nothing."

Kerry had resolved not to be defensive, or to explain himself. "Not for 'nothing,'" he answered. "For a principle."

"What principle is that?" Gage's voice was patient and sincere. "I have the sense, Mr. President, that you foresee some permanent residue of outrage should Caroline Masters meet an adverse fate. With your instinct for the public pulse, you can't *just* be doing this based on the unlikely hope she'll win. So I'd like to offer my perspective on reality."

At this the President smiled. "Yes," he said, "tell me about *your* reality."

"All right," Gage answered crisply. "In *my* reality, we've got one year and eight months until the next congressional election, and two years beyond that before we next elect a president. Americans are a blessed people, and among the things they're blessed with is forgetfulness.

"That's even more true of women than it is of us men—there's a school shooting, and some pollster says how fervently the 'soccer moms' support new gun laws, but when it comes right down to it they don't vote the issue. It's much the same as abortion, though I doubt most women are nearly as pro-abortion as you liberals seem to think." Abruptly, Gage's tone became tough and practical. "But you know who *does* remember? Folks who are *angry.* Folks who believe that as a nation we're headed in the wrong direction—whether it's abortion, or taking their guns away, or this general degradation of our culture by music and films portraying violence, or everyone having sex with everyone else."

For emphasis, Gage jabbed a finger at the space between them. "*Those* folks vote. I hear from them, by the thousands. They wouldn't shake hands with Caroline Masters. They don't want to be in the same room with her. They'll never forgive you if you try to push her down their throats. And they'll never forgive *me* if I don't try to lay you low.

"So, what do we have? A nominee who's likely doomed, and who'll be forgotten by most people come election time. Except by millions of angry citizens who'll see you as the Antichrist. Literally."

Kerry smiled without amusement. "A grim prognosis, Mac. And very complete. How do I spare myself?"

This small irony produced a sigh from Gage. "Let her withdraw," he said solemnly, "as gracefully as you need her to. Then send us someone who's a little bit more reasonable.

"I don't mean someone I'd appoint—*you're* the President. Just someone I could vote for without embarrassing myself, or the party, with the millions of folks who rely on us to maintain some sort of balance.

"*That's* what's gotten lost here—a spirit of cooperation. You called Palmer before you nominated Masters, but never said a word to me. The Senate could have used a little deference from the new president—*you* know how we are. And now you and I have to deal with the mess." Gage's voice was soft. "We'll never agree on policy. But we can have a constructive relationship, getting things done where we can, and disagreeing without being disagreeable. All we need is to remove the sty of Caroline Masters from our collective eye."

Kilcannon listened, still and watchful. Though Gage credited the President with lightning—occasionally lethal—flashes of political intuition, he still struck Gage as unseasoned, mercurial, too young for the office. It was like awakening from a coma to learn that Brad Pitt was President.

"I agree," Kilcannon said reasonably. "I should have called about Judge Masters—before I nominated her, and several times in the last few weeks. So, Mac, mea culpa . . ."

Gage raised a hand, a gesture of self-deprecation. "Plenty of blame, as I say, to go around."

"That's very gracious of you. In that spirit, I should make amends by sharing *my* reality." Kilcannon's voice was mild. "Those angry people you mention will never vote for me. They hated my brother, and they hate me. In fact, a lot of them hope some committed patriot will come along and blow *my* head off, too . . ."

"Not so," Gage objected, startled less by Kilcannon's feelings than his willingness to express them. "These are loyal Americans . . ."

"Who despise me, and everything they think I stand for." Kilcannon's tone remained cool. "I don't worry about pissing them off. The angrier they are, the more useful they are to me. If you try to do their bidding, I'll hang them around your neck like an anvil, until all those forgetful people you mention stop forgetting.

"Every kid who dies in a school shooting, you'll hear from me. Sooner or later, you'll conclude that being a wholly owned subsidiary of the NRA does not serve your best interests. And that *will* happen, believe me."

Gage felt his face become a mask; surprised and angry, he forced himself not to interrupt.

"Let's turn to Masters," the President went on. "My reality is this: You're wrong about the Tierney case. You're hypocrites on adoption. You've tried to use her daughter against her *and* smear her as a lesbian. You've tried to vilify her as a person in every way you can. And, having done that, now you want me to make a deal with you.

"We'll deal with each other, Mac. But first we have to define our relationship, and this is the time and place." The President's eyes turned cold. "For years in the Senate, I sat in the minority, watching you kill bill after bill—gun control, campaign finance reform, what have you. If you wonder why I wanted this job so badly, look in the mirror.

"You've tried to kill Masters in committee. Having failed, you want me to do it for you. But you're going to have to take her down yourself.

"Before you try, listen well." Now it was Kilcannon who leaned forward, though his tone, belying the intensity of his stare, was conversational. "What you've done to Caroline Masters is unacceptable to me. This is a woman who can better the lives of millions of Americans, long after we're both dead. My job is to make her the next Chief Justice. And if I lose, to make you pay."

Listening, Gage was appalled and, briefly, unnerved. Despite his long experience in judging men and motives, he could not tell whether this was a highly convincing act, or whether the man in front of him had somehow escaped his comprehension. But he was certain of one thing: there was no hope of dissuading Kerry Kilcannon, and trying might embolden him still more.

"Mr. President," he said simply, "this is a grave mistake."

The President smiled. "Yes. But whose?"

"Well?" Clayton asked.

Though Kerry's instinct to confide in his Chief of Staff was reinforced by the tension of the meeting, he hesitated to renew their intimacy. Finally, Kerry said, "He's wondering if I'm crazy, and he's not quite sure. Of course, neither am I."

"What's he going to do?"

Pondering the question, Kerry felt an odd jumble of emotions—fatalistic, determined, depressed, uncertain. "Anything he can to beat her. He's gone too far to back off, and doesn't believe he can. He's too mortgaged to the Commitment and the others on the right."

Clayton folded his arms. "I talked to Chuck Hampton—he gave us a list of Democratic undecideds, senators you need to call."

"How many now? Seven?"

"Six. He thinks we've got the other thirty-nine. He also thinks Mac's still stuck at forty-seven."

"Including Palmer and Jarman?"

"Yes. But Palmer won't actively help Gage, and Vic Coletti says Kate isn't happy where she is. So we maybe could still flip her."

"If *we* know that," Kerry answered, "so does Gage."

With that, Kerry fell silent, thoughtful. He remained at his desk, chin propped in his hand, almost forgetting that Clayton was there.

At length, Clayton ventured, "You're thinking Gage might try a filibuster."

Kerry looked up. "Yes," he acknowledged. "It's never been done that *I* know of. But neither was trying to kill a Supreme Court nomination in committee, and Gage nearly pulled *that* off.

"Gage may still worry he can't dig up the four more votes he needs to get to fifty-one. All he'd need to sustain a filibuster is *forty*-one, and the willingness—or desperation—to sink the knife between her shoulder blades himself."

Clayton shoved his hands in his pockets. "A lot could depend on Palmer."

Kerry did not need to mention to whom he owed Chad Palmer's distrust. Tersely, he answered, "I'll call him. I'm sure he'll be thrilled to hear from me."

Nineteen

"To start," the President told Chad Palmer, "I wanted to say thanks. You could have killed her in committee."

"Not easily." Palmer's tone was cool. "Harshman's main reason—the daughter—was something *I* knew from the beginning. If I didn't think it disqualified her before, I can't very well say that now, can I?"

The implicit accusation suggested that Kerry had ordered the leak, making Chad's position untenable. But it was also self-deprecating: within his own party, the best thing for Chad would have been to go along. "Whatever the reason," Kerry answered, "I understand you have to oppose her, at least as a formal matter. But I'm wondering how far you mean to go."

"I mean to vote against her—period. I've said that." Chad paused, then asked bluntly, "What is it you want, Mr. President?"

"Not me—Gage. He asked to see me."

"So your press people made clear. And?"

"He's getting a little anxious, I think." Kerry paused, then decided on frankness. "I know you're pretty well hemmed in, Chad, and I think Gage is about to make things worse. I thought you should know."

"We've done our part," Barry Saunders told Gage. "We've taken on the Tierney case, raised three million dollars in a month, and put up TV spots opposing Masters for almost two weeks. That on top of giving over two million to your party in the last presidential campaign. We wonder what we're getting for it."

Sitting to one side, Mace Taylor looked from Saunders to Gage. The counsel for the Christian Commitment had demanded a meeting, and Taylor had arranged it; now the lobbyist's glance at Gage conveyed a warning—with respect to Caroline Masters, both men needed to come through. But Gage felt resistant; the President seemed to have darkened his mood.

"What you got for it," Gage answered, "is Kilcannon. He uses you as a foil. You should have heard him today—you'd better pray we win next time, or you've really got some problems." He paused, choosing a more ingratiating tone. "Believe me, Barry, we're grateful for all your help. We need it. But if we're to realize our agenda—*your* agenda—we can't look like you're handing us our lines on marble tablets. That can cost us votes."

Saunders pursed his lips in disappointment, his shrewd eyes fixed on Gage. "You're sounding like Senator Palmer, Mac. You really are."

It was time to remind this man, Gage thought, how limited the Commitment's choices were. "If I were Palmer, you wouldn't be sitting here. At best, Chad has granted God diplomatic relations—He's fine as long as He knows His place. Chad feels somewhat less enthused about you."

Saunders gave the smile of a poker player in a two-man game. "When we go looking for a president, it won't be Palmer. We were sort of hoping it'd be you."

"So was I," Gage said comfortably. "So was I . . ."

"We can't have this woman," Saunders said abruptly. "Not only did she undo all our work in the Tierney case, but she'll clearly favor this campaign finance reform Palmer and Kilcannon love so much. It would keep us from being players—*and* from helping you." Abruptly, Saunders snapped his fingers. "Those millions you'll be wanting next time? Up in smoke."

Gage felt something—pride, or caution—keep him from delivering the answer which Saunders was expecting. Taylor gave him a puzzled glance, then said soothingly to Saunders, "Mac has a plan."

With reluctance, Gage said, "I'm looking at a filibuster. All we'd need to keep Masters from coming to a vote is forty-one determined senators refusing to close debate." He paused for emphasis. "But that's a far riskier vote, Barry, than just saying you're against her."

Saunders considered this. "Undemocratic, you mean."

"The *Senate's* undemocratic," Taylor rejoined. "That's the beauty of Mac's leadership position. All he has to say is that the Senate's 'working its will.'"

Though directed at Saunders, Taylor's remark, Gage knew, was intended to prod him. "Except that," Gage amended, "the Senate's never 'worked its will' on a Supreme Court nominee in this particular fashion."

Seemingly dissatisfied, Saunders glanced at Taylor. "I'm sure Paul Harshman would be willing to step up to the plate."

"Sure he would," Gage said. "And that's precisely what Kilcannon wants. Paul has his virtues, but he's far too easy to caricature. That's not the image we need to put forth." His voice grew firm. "I'm with you, Barry. I want her gone. But we have to do it just right."

"Sometimes," Saunders replied with equal conviction, "you just have to do it—period. You can't treat us like some girl you're seeing on the sly.

"You're still not sure about your fifty-one. So go make sure about your forty-one. That's ten votes easier." Saunders's voice abruptly lowered. "Don't lose this one on us. Our people vote, *and* give you money. You can't win without us."

"Or with you," Gage said gently, "if Kilcannon has his way. So where will you go, if not to us?" He raised a hand, forestalling an answer. "We're all together here, my friend. It's just a matter of approach."

Saunders stared at him, unmollified. "Maybe Kilcannon thinks Paul's amusing," Taylor said to Gage. "But he wouldn't laugh if Palmer were out front, would he?"

As Taylor had surely intended, Gage felt his freedom of action slipping away. The Christian Commitment wanted his pledge to defeat Masters by any means at hand; Taylor wanted a final reason to destroy Chad Palmer as a future candidate for President. And as wary as all this made him, both men spoke to Gage's first ambition—to secure his party's nomination, and run against Kerry Kilcannon.

"We'll find a way," Gage told both men. "The first thing is talk to Palmer."

Even as the meeting began, Mac Gage sensed that he would look back on it as a symbolic turning point—though symbolic of what, he was not sure.

It was late afternoon, and the half-drawn curtains in Palmer's office admitted thin rays of pale sunlight, turning his yellow walls a muted gold. Palmer greeted him pleasantly, if cautiously; Gage's eyes were drawn to the photograph on his desk, Chad and Kyle Palmer smiling at each other. If only our lives were as simple as we pretend, Gage mused; even in his own family, the most fortunate and upright, his fourteen-year-old granddaughter was experimenting with drugs and alcohol. Yet this was all the more reason, Gage affirmed to himself, for those in power—whether senators or parents—to draw lines.

But his mood, despite the tension, was also faintly elegiac. In this spirit, he stopped to examine his colleague, his rival. For all that he had been through, the years seemed to have touched Chad Palmer little: he was still trim, blond, blue-eyed—the golden boy, as youthful and as lucky as the country which he served. Except in the shadows of his family: perhaps it was this that accounted for the reserve with which Chad—who usually treated the most difficult moments with at least a show of blitheness—had greeted him.

"So," Chad said at length. "Masters."

"Yes. Does it sometimes feel to you, Chad, like Caroline Masters has always been with us?"

Chad smiled in acknowledgment. "She's made quite an impact on us all, in a few short weeks." His voice turned dry. "Of course a bit of that's my doing."

Equably, Gage nodded. "A lot of it, Chad. With a considerable assist from the President."

Chad shrugged. "Our entente cordiale—if that's what you'd call it—has expired. I opposed killing her in committee because I think it's wrong. But I'm voting against her on the floor."

This much Gage knew—and therefore, he supposed, was Palmer's way of sparring. He sensed this visit was no surprise, that Palmer had anticipated him. Quietly, he said, "I'd like your help, Chad. Beyond that."

Chad's lips formed another smile which did not reach his eyes. "A fiery speech?"

Gage prepared himself. "Yes. Against a cloture motion. I want you to help me round up the forty-one votes we need to maintain a filibuster."

To Gage's surprise, Chad laughed aloud. "A filibuster," he said. "Our new president is such a clever boy."

Gage felt mild alarm. "In what way?"

"He called a while ago. Predicted, in fact, that you'd be coming around to see me on this very subject." The transient breeziness in Palmer's manner yielded to seriousness. "Remember at the beginning of all this, when I told you not to underestimate him? It's all coming true."

Gage fought back his alarm. "Specifically," he answered in his most pleasant tone, "you predicted this town would end up littered with the bodies of folks who'd underrated him. I'm afraid I didn't take your warning for the kindness that it was." Gage paused, taking the smallest sip of the bourbon Palmer had poured him—it would not do to dull his wits. "What else did Kilcannon say?"

"That it's never been done. That if we take her down with a minority, we'll look like tools of the far right. That he'll say every vote against cloture is a vote *for* Masters, and that we've kept a nominee supported by a majority of senators from having a vote . . ."

"That's rhetoric. We'll all survive that."

"He also said that two can play—that with forty-five Democrats in the Senate he can filibuster anything we want to pass. That presidential vetoes will start falling like autumn leaves. In other words, that he'll use the power of his office to fuck you."

Palmer sat back. "On a somewhat higher plane, he warned that you'll set a precedent for *future* Supreme Court nominations by Republicans. Specifically, that you'd 'reduce the Senate to a Hobbesian state of nature.'"

Palmer's tone, Gage noted, was dispassionate, neutral. "Do you agree with that?" he asked.

"Some of it."

"Enough to oppose our filibuster?"

Chad placed his palms on his desk, bending forward to look into Gage's eyes. "Mac," he began, "years ago, we let people like the Christian Commitment in the tent. We never thought they'd *own* the tent. Now they do, or think they do.

"Politics requires compromise, a messy process conducted to achieve a common good. But *their* belief system precludes compromise, and it's changed our party for the worse."

Palmer, Gage realized with alarm, was speaking from the heart. "I know you think I'm pious," Chad continued, "a self-anointed truth-teller. But I honestly believe what's bad for our country can't, in the long run, be good for us.

"Some moments are defining, Mac. This is one. *How* we defeat Caroline Masters—if we do—is more important than *that* we defeat her.

"Maybe I'll make the religious right unhappy. Maybe they'll keep me from becoming President." Briefly, Palmer smiled. "If so, it would be a damned shame for America. But at least I can respect myself.

"What about you, Mac? Is that kind of Faustian bargain worth it to you?" Palmer's tone was even. "As you recently pointed out to me, we're not friends. We both want the same job, and have different views of how to get it. But, at bottom, I have too much respect for you to think you want to sell your soul to them. Or won't regret it if you do."

It took a while for Gage to respond; he was restrained by a sense of foreboding, combined with the knowledge that—although Gage believed it too simplistic—Palmer's view of the world contained a core of truth. "So," Gage compelled himself to say, "to be clear about your position . . ."

Palmer looked disappointed, then resigned. "I'll oppose her. But I won't support a filibuster. We beat Masters straight up, or not at all."

Gage folded his hands. He had never liked Palmer, and did not care for him now. Nor was he squeamish about the requirements of political life. But in this moment, he felt regret, and something akin to desperation.

Softly, he said, "Get out of the way, Chad. For your own sake."

For an instant Palmer seemed startled, and just as quickly recovered. "Are you telling me something, Mac?"

For a moment as fleeting as Palmer's alarm, Gage considered telling him the truth, then realized he never could. "No," he answered. "Nothing you don't already know."

Twenty

The President's day was tightly scheduled—telephone calls to senators, a speech to a lawyers' group on the Masters nomination, a strategy meeting with Chuck Hampton—and the last-minute intrusion annoyed him almost as much as its source. With repressed impatience, he said to Katherine Jones, "Clayton tells me this concerns the Masters nomination. And that it's important."

Jones nodded brusquely. "Not just important. Critical."

The touch of self-importance irked Kerry further. Of the major pro-choice leaders, women whom Kerry generally admired, Jones was the only one he disliked. She reminded him of a Buddha without the compassion: gimlet-eyed, heavy-lipped, and self-satisfied, with a mindset so adamant that Kerry found it counterproductive. Her militant group, Anthony's Legions, had demonstrated against Kerry in the primaries, and though he could not prove it, he believed Jones was personally responsible for spreading rumors about his relationship with Lara Costello. Their truce since then had been, at best, uneasy. Only her urgent request that they meet alone, and his knowledge she would not lightly exhaust her limited chances for a private hearing—gained solely through her support of Caroline Masters—had secured her this appointment.

Now, despite her assertiveness, Jones appeared nervous; sitting in the Oval Office, she traced with an index finger the edges of the flat letter-size envelope she held. "'Critical'?" Kerry repeated. "How so?"

Standing, Jones passed the envelope across his desk. With an unwonted softness of tone, suggesting hesitance and, perhaps, discomfort, Jones answered, "Read this, and you'll understand."

Though Kerry could not imagine what was inside, he paused before opening the envelope and withdrawing the two pieces of paper it held. He looked at

Jones: her gaze, rapt and tense, remained on the paper in front of him. Then he began to read.

He first perceived the nature of the document, and then whom it pertained to; disbelief was followed by a slow, stunned acceptance which altered his sense of human motivation, at least in one instance, and of the dynamics he had been playing with in ignorance.

For some moments, staring at the first piece of paper, he did not speak. Looking up at last, he softly inquired, "Where did you get this?"

Jones's eyes remained on the document; it was a ploy, the President guessed, to keep her from meeting his stare. "In the mail," she answered.

"From whom?"

"I have no idea. But the next page is a typed list of names, with a description of who they are and how they know. It's like a witness list."

The President flipped the page. The list included addresses and telephone numbers—the work, he was certain, of a private investigator. "You have no idea," he repeated.

"None."

"Oh, but they know *you,* it seems. And perhaps think they know me, as well."

The edge in his voice forced Jones to look up. "What do you mean, Mr. President?"

"Let me ask you a question first, Katherine. What do you propose I do with this?"

Jones seemed to maintain eye contact with difficulty. "This is critical information, Mr. President. I thought you needed to know."

Kerry felt distaste becoming anger. "What," he asked calmly, "do you expect me to do?"

Jones did not answer. "I see," the President said. "This is the act which dares not speak its name. But 'blackmail' comes to mind."

For an instant, Jones's jaw clamped tight. "I could have leaked this," she answered. "And didn't."

"Instead, you came to me." Kilcannon's tone was flat. "For you to leak it would merely ruin him. But if he knows *I* know, think how malleable he'll become. Especially about Masters."

Jones crossed her arms. "They leaked Masters's daughter, Mr. President. It's time for us to fight back.

"I didn't ask for this—it just arrived. It's not for me to decide what to do with it. But he's never been a friend to us, and isn't now." Her voice rose, defensive. "Masters is critical, Mr. President. To all of us."

"Indeed." Kilcannon's coolness seemed to unnerve her more than anger. But he was far too conscious, as Jones could not be, that he, through Clayton Slade, had unwittingly caused this moment. "Critical enough," he continued, "for you to think I'd use this on him. So before you leave, I want you to know precisely what I will do."

Pausing, Kerry placed his finger on the document. "If this comes out and I think it comes from you, you've sat in this office for the last time. If it's *you* who dug this up in the first place, the Justice Department will turn your organization inside out, until you feel like you're living in the grand jury room. And if whatever you've done to get it isn't a federal crime, I'll make sure that we invent one."

Jones stared at him, mouth slightly opened. Abruptly, Kerry felt his disgust at her turn upon himself.

"You've done what you came to do," he said. "And now I know. I'll deal with this from here."

He wished he had more time. But being President, he had discovered, often left too little time to reflect, and even less to feel.

He could see now what had happened. Chad was cornered, and Kerry had helped corner him. Only now did the President understand how complex Chad's response had been to his own maneuvers and yet, at heart, how simple. But there was nothing simple about the decision Kerry faced.

To tell him, the President realized, would be in itself a form of blackmail— for the fear it would create, the debt it would imply. Chad might well believe, with justice, that this was another trick of Kerry's or even, though the President hoped not, that this information had been uncovered at his instance. But if Jones had received these papers, others would, or could: in the end, the President's only option was to warn him.

And so at last, ignoring the list of undecided senators, Kerry picked up the telephone himself.

"I hope this isn't about Masters," Chad told him. "We've used up my nine lives."

"It is," Kerry answered tightly. "I have to see you, ASAP."

The President's tone of voice produced a brief silence. "We can't play footsie anymore . . ."

"Come here after hours," Kerry interjected, "through the east visitors' entrance."

"You're dredging up painful memories," came the sharp retort. "The last time we did this, you'll remember, I got burned."

Once more, Kerry felt deep regret. "I know," he answered. "But your problem's much worse than that." He hesitated, adding quietly, "This is about Kyle, Chad. And Allie."

For a time, as the President looked on, Chad Palmer simply stared at the document.

It was dark; in the dim light of the President's study, Chad's expression had a painful intensity. Kerry found it hard to watch.

Softly, he asked, "Do you know where this came from?"

When Chad looked up, he was pale, but composed. "No," he said. "Do you?"

Kerry felt a flash of indignation, which died as quickly. Palmer had good reason to blame him for the leak regarding Caroline's daughter; in the hall of mirrors which the Masters nomination had become, he could offer no assurance—even to himself—that the document had not come from a source closer to him than he knew.

"No," the President answered. "I don't."

Distrust merged with distaste in Chad's cold-eyed expression. "Then what do you want?"

"Nothing." Kerry maintained his calm with difficulty. "I've shown this to no one. I've made no copies. Once you leave, we'll never talk about it again. It won't exist for me."

Palmer's expression did not change. Their meeting, Kerry knew to his regret, was fraught with ambiguity; whatever he intended, he was placing Palmer in his debt, and Chad would leave here knowing that the President had the means to destroy him. Nor could Palmer be sure, or Kerry assure him, that this was not the President's intention—or even that he had not uncovered this document himself.

"I'm not asking for your help," Kerry told him, "and I don't expect it. So before you pin *this* one on me—or my source—consider the motives of whoever mailed this.

"He doesn't just want your vote, or he'd find another way to use this. Instead he sent it to a group which supports Masters, one willing to put this in my hands." As he spoke, Kerry leaned toward Chad, as though to emphasize his words. "Why, I keep asking myself? One answer is that he may think I exposed Caroline and her daughter, and won't hesitate to use *this* as well.

"Whoever did this wants to ruin you as a person and a presidential candidate. If I blackmail you into voting for Masters, you're damaged within your own party. And if *then* they feed it to the media, you're finished. Which, in combination, is far more lethal than just exposing you at once."

Once more, Chad gazed down at the document. Kerry could imagine all too easily how it felt to see—perhaps for the first time—Allie's signature on the consent form for their daughter's abortion. He found himself wondering if Chad had even known: though he assessed Chad's marriage as a good one, he was too aware, from his own failed marriage, how much could be concealed, from a partner and from others.

To Chad, the President looked haunted. But whether this was because of what he had learned, or what he had done, Chad could only guess. The exposure of Caroline Masters's daughter, and Kilcannon's skillful use of it, had left no room for trust.

"Before you decide it's me," he heard the President say, "or one of her supporters, consider who else might try to use us as a cutout."

Chad looked up sharply. "Such as."

"Ask yourself who—other than me—doesn't want you to run for President. Someone you've offended." The President's voice became softer. "Someone who sees you as a threat, and who's ruthless enough to do this."

"Get out of the way," Gage had told him. *"For your own sake."*

"Are you telling me something?" Chad had asked.

"Nothing you don't already know."

Chad felt darkness shroud his thoughts. In years past, given a choice between trusting Kilcannon and Gage, he would not have hesitated. But now he must. "Or," Chad said coolly, "I can ask myself who's desperate enough to try and launch me at Gage's throat."

"If you still think I'd use this," Kilcannon answered with genuine anger, "I've wasted my time on you. Just pray I've managed to keep it quiet. Though that's nothing I control." The President stopped himself. "I don't want anything from you. Just watch out for your family, and hope that whoever leaked this shares my special quality of mercy. Although I wouldn't count on that."

If Kerry was telling the truth, Chad knew, this last prediction was surely true. His enemies, whoever they were, did not care about what they did or whom they hurt. All at once, Chad felt the weight of his family—Kyle's fragility, Allie's desperate love for her—and the harshness of his own solitude.

He had never told anyone what had happened, nor voiced his doubts about himself as a father. Before the last two weeks, he might now have found an odd comfort in Kerry Kilcannon's knowing what had happened; with his curious blend of toughness and sensitivity, Kerry might have helped to ease his burden. Now, Chad could only wonder what becoming President had done to the man in front of him. Presidents might grant favors, but few of them were free.

Folding the two pieces of paper, Chad put them in his coat pocket, and left.

Kerry could hardly blame him.

Since Clayton's act of cynicism, which Kerry had exploited, there was no way to expect trust. As President he could not explain to anyone what had happened; in the harsh and unforgiving environment of Washington, it would amount to a self-indictment, and doom Caroline Masters.

For Kerry, that was the worst of it; the realization that Chad must have concealed Caroline's past, at least in part, from empathy—Caroline had acted to protect her daughter, as Chad had his. Just as Chad's belief that personal lives should be private had turned out to be deeply personal.

And so was Kerry's. If he could have told Chad Palmer why, Chad would have to believe him—the pain and risk for Kerry would have left no doubt. But for many reasons, beginning with Lara, he could not. So both men would remain where they were, hemmed in by their secrets, each trying to protect themselves and the people they loved most.

The envelope mailed to Katherine Jones remained in his desk. Opening the drawer, the President studied it. Then he returned to the list of undecided senators, and began placing calls.

Twenty-one

Two nights later, Kerry was back in his study, still telephoning senators on behalf of Caroline Masters. But he had solidified the Democrats: forty-one had declared their support for Caroline; the other four, though formally undecided, had pledged the President their votes if this could supply the margin of victory. The latest national poll now showed a plurality favoring Caroline Masters—forty-seven to thirty-eight—with the difference reflecting a twenty percent edge among women. Directed by Clayton, the administration was orchestrating speeches and articles which stressed the role of an independent judiciary, and called the opposition to Caroline Masters an attack on judicial integrity.

This was having its effect, both on opinion leaders and, through them, on the Senate. In the closely scrutinized battle for Republican moderates—covered by the media like a horse race—Macdonald Gage had not added to his total of forty-seven, four short of what he needed. He was in a difficult position, Kerry estimated: without fifty-one committed votes, Gage could not risk calling a vote on the nomination; with every day of delay, Kerry seemed to gather strength. And, beyond anyone's control, a great imponderable hung over the process: the imminent Supreme Court decision on whether to hear Martin Tierney's appeal, and the abortion which would follow should it decline.

All of this, the President understood, increased the pressure on Gage from his party's right wing to defeat the nominee by the only other available means: if Gage could persuade forty of his forty-seven loyalists to support a filibuster, keeping Caroline Masters from coming to a vote, the nomination would be dead. For the last two days, Kerry knew, Gage had been sounding out support.

For the last two days, Chad Palmer had been silent.

Other Republicans, looking to Chad for cues, received none. He took no position on a filibuster. He did not reiterate—or withdraw—his opposition to Caroline Masters. He said nothing in public.

Nor did he contact Kerry Kilcannon. Once or twice, Kerry had imagined Chad's painful conversation with Allie. Only later did Kerry learn that Chad—trying to spare his wife and daughter anguish; hoping to find his way through the maze without making them feel responsible for what he chose to do; believing there would still be time—had delayed two days in telling them.

It was a mistake the President would not have made.

But on this night, Kerry tried to banish Chad from his thoughts.

"So, Mr. President," Leo Weller was saying, "you want my assurance that, if necessary, I'll vote to shut down a filibuster. Despite the wishes of my leader."

Kerry heard this for what it was—a testing of the waters, Weller's efforts to ferret out the highest bidder. Amiable and crafty, the senior senator from Montana faced a tough fight for reelection: only a president could reward Weller's supporters with appointments, or sign or veto bills important to their interests.

"You can have it all," Kerry answered easily. "You can vote against Judge Masters once she comes to the floor—after you vote to make sure she *gets* a vote. It's the democratic way."

On the other end, Weller chuckled softly. "It's interesting strategy, is what it is. You start by inducing a few of us who oppose her to help get her a majority vote. Then you try to get at least five Republicans to vote for her, to get you to fifty. At which point, Ellen Penn comes down to preside over the Senate, and casts the deciding vote."

"Neatly summarized," the President replied. "So consider your alternative. Gage gets forty of you to sink Caroline Masters. We've got forty-five: I'll use them to shut down votes on everything he wants—tort reform, tax cuts, you name it. And I won't make helping *you* a top priority, either.

"So consider, Leo, just what it is Mac offers you. Besides a deck chair on the *Titanic.*"

"Lots of things," Weller answered cheerfully. "The chairmanship of Agriculture, my bills called up for a vote . . ."

"Only if you're still in the majority, and Gage is still the leader. I wouldn't bet on either: as a political matter, opposing Masters is dumb—you look like toadies for the Christian right."

"Maybe so, maybe not." Weller's voice was cool now, the pose of relaxation abruptly gone. "You're talking about shutting down the Senate, Mr. President . . ."

"I'm talking about making sure Gage never tries this again. The only way out for your side is to make sure it never happens in the first place." Kerry's tone was calm, analytic. "Gage wants to be President, and thinks he needs the Christian right. So he's overlooking your more immediate problem—reelection. You've got a tough race next year, and you need something for your people."

"With all respect, Mr. President, my people don't give a shit about Caroline Masters. They're too busy with their lives to care about editorials and noble speeches . . ."

"But some of them do care about grazing rights. You've got a bill pending that would expand them into public lands. The environmentalists want it blocked—or vetoed. Which, as of now, I'm inclined to do."

"Fine," Weller said in an unimpressed tone. "Do that, and the kid your party's putting up against me won't have a prayer."

"If you say so," Kerry answered blithely. "I'm sure when he calls you a dinosaur, and asks what you've done for Montana lately, your current forty percent favorable rating will carry you to victory. Perhaps a landslide."

Weller gave a terse chuckle of acknowledgment: the President could imagine his cherubic face become shrewd, lips pursed in calculation. "So I vote for cloture, and get my grazing rights."

"It's fair to say," Kerry answered, "that you'd find me more impressionable."

There was silence, Weller weighing the benefits of an amenable president, the detriments of offending his almost equally powerful antagonist, a man whom he must live with day-to-day. At length, Weller said, "There's also the matter of a judgeship. I'd like to do something for my last campaign manager . . ."

Kerry glanced at the memo in front of him. "A guy named Bob Quinn, to be specific. I'm told his only flaw, besides being a conservative, is that he's a truly mediocre lawyer. None of which suggests that he wouldn't make a brilliant judge."

Weller gave another short laugh. "You're very well informed, Mr. President. Except that Bob's perfectly well qualified . . ."

"For the District Court, perhaps. The Court of Appeals—which I'm informed you want for him—is pushing it."

"Bob," Weller countered bluntly, "has his heart set on the Court of Appeals."

Kerry paused, weighing the balance of power, replaying Weller's tone of voice. "Tell your old friend Bob," he answered, "that I have a soft spot for him. I, too, was once a mediocre lawyer . . ."

"I doubt that, Mr. President."

"But that my fellow-feeling ends at the District Court," Kerry continued crisply. "So ask your friend if that will do."

Once more, Weller was silent. "If it has to do," he said at last, "I think it will."

"Which brings us back to Mac Gage's filibuster."

"If it comes to that," Senator Weller said slowly, "I'm willing to oppose it."

The President felt a relief his voice could not betray. "Do that, Leo, and you can pass on the good news to Mr. Quinn. And to all those cattle, too."

Putting down the phone, the President saw Lara standing in the doorway. With a smile, she said, "Impressive."

She was wearing leather gloves and an overcoat, and her skin retained the flush of cold. "How long have you been here?" he asked.

"The last few minutes," she answered. "Your man Bob Quinn sounds like the next Cardozo. I only hope his district has more cows than people."

Kerry smiled. "One does what one must. You're staying for a while, I hope."

Crossing the room, she bent to kiss him. "These days," she told him, "it's the only way to see you. 'She also serves who lies in wait.'"

Kerry gazed up at her. "It's been hard," he said. "I'm sorry."

"Don't be. I understand. I'm getting used to you being President."

Kerry wished that his calls were done. More than that, he wished that he could pause to tell Lara about Chad Palmer. But he had no time, and Chad's story had such resonance for them that he was reluctant to share it.

"I won't be that long," he said. "Unless India bombs Pakistan, perhaps another hour."

Lara shrugged off her coat, draping it over a chair. "That's fine. I've got some calls of my own to make, and I left the new Stephen King on your nightstand."

Kerry smiled again. "Marry me," he told her, "and maybe you can finish it."

At 8:00 p.m., typical for Chad, he was driving the few short blocks to his town house for a late dinner with Allie. Perhaps, tonight, he should tell her.

Two days had passed, with what seemed to Chad an eerie silence hanging over him. Perhaps some of the eeriness was from his own silence with Allie; after so long together, no matter how painful the subject, it was hard to withhold something so central to their lives.

Pulling from the parking lot, he stopped for a moment, gazing back over his shoulder at the dome of the Capitol, glowing marble-white against the night sky. When he had first arrived—even with the bitter hardship which had gone before—the dome at night had seemed symbolic, a dream of America. But tonight the dream felt soiled: he had risen here, and now his wife and daughter might pay for it.

Over the last two days, he had contemplated this with a numbing disbelief, as though, despite his hard-earned knowledge of the ways of power, he had felt himself immune. How many others, he thought now, had shared this illusion and then found themselves ruined, ghosts from another life.

As he turned onto East Capitol, Chad's cell phone jangled.

Though he was used to this, Chad started. It could be anyone, he reminded himself; he made a point of being accessible, and his aides, colleagues, and key supporters had his number. And more than a few reporters.

"Chad?"

To his relief, it was Allie. "I'm just a few blocks from home," he answered. "Two minutes."

"I've been trying to reach you." Chad suddenly grasped the tension in her voice. "Someone from the *Internet Frontier* called, whatever that is. He said it's personal, and urgent—that he needs to see you at their offices, now."

Chad felt her tension like a contagion; the *Internet Frontier* had first revealed the identity of Mary Ann Tierney. "Why now?" he asked with deceptive calm.

Allie's voice rose. "He's on deadline, he said—the editor, Henry Nielsen. They're running a story in three hours, and he wants to talk to you first."

Allie sensed what was happening, Chad realized—years of worry had taught her what this must mean. He steered over to the curb, and stopped. "Where's Kyle?" he asked.

"I don't know. I just tried her apartment."

"Is her number listed?"

Allie hesitated. "No," she answered, in a voice filled with bewilderment and fear.

"Good. Leave her a message not to answer the phone, or talk to anyone . . ."

"Chad," Allie demanded with tenacious self-control, "what's this all about?"

"Not on the cell phone," he snapped. "Just call her. I'll be home as soon as I can."

Twenty-two

The *Internet Frontier* did not waste money on decor. Its floor plan was open, stark, principally decorated with posters for movies and rock concerts, reflecting its self-image as lean, mean, liberal, and iconoclastic. But Henry Nielsen's office at least had walls, sealing Chad and the editor in chief from the eyes and ears of those who looked up from their desks as Chad walked quickly through the floor.

Closing the door behind him, Nielsen motioned Chad to a chair. In the fluorescent light, Nielsen's caramel hair and pale skin made him look bleached out. But his quiet aggressiveness reminded Chad of the first time the *Frontier* had come to his attention: as the source of rumors about an unnamed senator—in fact Gage's predecessor as Majority Leader—who embraced "family values" but sexually exploited teenage runaways.

Silent, Nielsen placed a Xeroxed document in Chad's hand. Chad found himself staring, once again, at Allie's signature.

"We've found the boyfriend," Nielsen said.

Chad felt a last moment of disbelief that the world of predatory journalism, in which private lives were grist for journalistic competitors, had now ensnared his family. Rather than resisting, Chad asked simply, "How?"

"A list came with that. Names, addresses, telephone numbers."

It was the same list the President had given him, Chad knew, no doubt provided by the same source. This fact did not preclude deception by the White House itself—warning him first, then providing Nielsen with the document. But, at least until recently, such callousness ran counter to Chad's assessment of the President. And there were other possibilities: the President's anonymous source; enemies within his own party. The only certainty, he knew with a miserable clarity, was that—in days, if not hours—Allie and Kyle would be exposed.

"We're satisfied," Nielsen told him, "—in fact, we *know*—that four years ago, with your wife's consent, your daughter had a first trimester abortion."

At great cost, Chad imposed on himself a stony calm. "Have you talked to Kyle?" he asked.

"We can't find her."

For this much, Chad felt grateful. But whatever Nielsen felt was unclear; he talked with the clinical air of a doctor describing a course of treatment. "We're aware she had emotional difficulties," Nielsen told him, "problems with drugs and alcohol. We'd like your perspective for our story. In fact, we'd like *her* perspective—to us, it would give dimension to what, as of now, is just another dreary instance of political hypocrisy."

Reigning in his temper, Chad assessed his tormentor's motives and perceived the germs of a bargain—access to Kyle in exchange for better treatment. But there was not much time to probe this, and the prospect filled him with loathing and despair.

"So that's your hook," Chad said bitingly. "Hypocrisy—with you as the protector of public sanctity. What does my daughter count for, when you're wearing the First Amendment like a Communion dress." Suddenly, Chad's emotions slipped out of his control. "What's twenty years of her life, or her mother's endless worry about her, or all the things which go into who she is that you can't possibly understand, and don't give a shit about. Any more than the damage you inflict matters to you at all.

"You've got advertisers to solicit, readers to titillate, competitors to beat. Whatever maggot sent you this knows that all too well. They *know* you, pal—we all do. You're part of the ecology remaking public life into a cesspool—the willing tool of politicians and interest groups to destroy whoever's in the way." Chad's voice became commanding. "Tell me who gave you this."

For an instant, Nielsen seemed to recoil. "I can't do that, Senator. We have to protect our sources."

He was not claiming, Chad saw at once, that the document had arrived by surprise in this morning's mail. More quietly, Chad said, "They know *that*, too—that you'll let them destroy someone from ambush. At least consider their motives."

Nielsen folded his arms. "We do."

"Really. Like you did when you made Macdonald Gage Majority Leader."

"That wasn't our intention." Though clearly tense, Nielsen summoned a note of patience. "We never revealed the senator's name. We merely published what we believed to be true, and suddenly Gage's predecessor resigned. Confirming the accuracy of our story." Nielsen fixed Chad with a pointed stare. "As for its relevance, hypocrisy seems to be a common vice. The senator had accused the Secretary of Transportation of lying about an affair with a subordinate who at least had the virtue of being past the age of consent."

"So," Chad said with disgust, "I'm the moral equivalent of a liar or a statutory rapist. Or both."

Nielsen glanced at his watch, as though to remind Chad that their time was running out. "What you are is a key player in the most controversial Supreme Court nomination in memory, of the first woman to be named as Chief.

"It turns on two legal issues, late-term abortion and parental consent; a personal one, the decision of a pro-choice judge to have a child out of marriage; and an ethical one—whether she lied about it, or at least was obliged to say more than she did.

"Now let's apply all that to you." As if swept up in his own argument, Nielsen's voice became prosecutorial. "You supported the Protection of Life Act. You oppose Judge Masters. You say abortion is, effectively, murder. Yet you—or at least your wife—consented to the 'murder' of your prospective grandchild. Unlike Martin Tierney, I might add . . ."

"Whose name," Chad snapped, "you made public for his pains. Was he a hypocrite, too?"

"Not at all," Nielsen shot back. "He was a prominent pro-life advocate, opposed by his own daughter, which made it news. But when it came to your own daughter, you said one thing in public and did the opposite in private. Which suggests you were obliged to say much more than you did—exactly the sin with which Harshman and the right seek to pillory Caroline Masters." Nielsen's tone became soft but skeptical. "Unless you're saying this comes as a complete surprise."

He was trapped, Chad realized. He would not lie to protect himself, nor ask Allie or Kyle to lie for him; to protect *them,* his only choice was candor, his only hope delay. In an even tone Chad said, "Let's go off the record."

Nielsen settled back. "All right."

"You're right about Kyle, Mr. Nielsen. She did have problems with substance abuse. But that's just symptomatic.

"From childhood, she's had emotional problems—moments of elation, days of terrible depression, a crushing lack of confidence. For a time we thought she was bipolar, and someday we may find out that she is.

"For certain, she was starved for love and affirmation." Pausing, Chad forced himself to continue his painful admissions, stifle his contempt for his listener. "No doubt some of that was my fault. Until this happened, I was pretty much an absentee father. Among the substitutes she found was a boy who used both drugs and alcohol—*and* her.

"Kyle was barely sixteen, and a mess. As soon as she got pregnant, the boy ditched her.

"Parental consent means just that—a parent can consent. My wife believed Kyle couldn't withstand having a child, and that abortion was the only means of saving her. I couldn't stop her, and didn't try. That's all there is."

Nielsen regarded him with, it seemed, a measured sympathy. "Then you could have told that story, Senator. Instead of continuing to vote and speak as if nothing had happened."

Chad sighed. "Mr. Nielsen, my beliefs never changed. But I did become much quieter about them . . ."

"To protect yourself?"

"To some degree. But mainly to protect Kyle." Chad paused, remembering his helplessness. "After Kyle's abortion, if I talked about 'taking life,' I became a distant and disapproving father. There'd been too much of that already."

Nielsen considered him. Chad had an uncomfortable sensation: though very different from the darkened cell in which he had spent two years of his life, the blank white walls and harsh fluorescent light made him feel entrapped, diminished. "Your account at least lends nuance," Nielsen said. "I urge you to tell it, and have your wife and daughter do the same. Otherwise, the facts appear in their harshest light."

Once more, Chad felt a visceral loathing: at once judge, executioner, and father confessor, Henry Nielsen—perhaps ten years out of journalism school—offered public humiliation for Chad's family as balm for Chad's own political ruin.

"Print this story," Chad said, "and you'll damage our daughter much worse than Allie *or* me. She's made *progress,* Mr. Nielsen—can you possibly know what that means to us? And she loves me now, as I love her.

"If you do this to her, you'll do more than dredge up an awful time she's started to put behind her. You'll make *her* mistake the reason for *my* political ruin." Chad's eyes bored into Nielsen's. "I don't know, truly, what the guilt and shame of that will do to her. And if I don't, you can't."

Nielsen folded his arms. "What are you proposing, Senator?"

"That you think harder about who gave this to you, and what their motives are. And about whether their desire to use her against me is a reason to punish a fragile young woman for what happened when she was sixteen years old."

Nielsen placed curled fingers to his lips, and slowly shook his head. "Their motive may be interesting. But that doesn't change the facts, *or* their public relevance.

"All I can offer, Senator, is the chance for you and your family to help shape what's in our story. But if we don't run this, our source will feed it to someone else. You don't have much time."

"*No* time," Chad retorted. "Like you, we tried to reach Kyle, and we couldn't . . ."

"How do I know you're not hiding her?"

Chad leaned forward, staring into Nielsen's eyes. "Because I say so, damn you."

After a moment, Nielsen looked down at his watch again. "When can you talk to your family?"

"My wife, immediately. Kyle, as soon as we can find her."

"Will you ask them to speak with us?"

"I'll ask them to consider it. If you'll promise to hear them out, and reconsider whether to run this."

Nielsen began drumming his fingers on the desk. "You've got twenty-four hours," he said.

"We can't control this," Chad said quietly.

He sat with Allie in the brick-walled living room of their town house on Capitol Hill. But, for Chad, the moment resonated with another conversation, four years prior. Then Allie had spoken with the quiet ferocity of a mother protecting her daughter; now, she looked frightened for Kyle, distraught for Chad, desperately intent on bearing up. It was, Chad thought, like so many moments in Allie's life as a wife and mother—she would think about herself later, if at all. With instinctive stubbornness, the unwillingness to accept something so unnatural as Kyle's exposure, she said, "Do we have to involve her? I can't stand to think of Kyle on the cover of a magazine."

Chad reined in his impatience: it was his fault, after all, that she was unprepared for this. "Someone else could break the story," he told her. "Something else could set it off. I don't know where this is coming from, or what their motives are. I don't know how to please them, whom to please, or if there's any way." He strained to keep his tone gentle, reasoned. "I don't want Kyle ambushed, or made to sound like some irresponsible, self-indulgent girl. The best way to protect her is to tell her story—once—and then hope it dies as soon as possible.

"All we can do is try to influence *how* the story turns out. That's the only way to help Kyle get on with her life."

Despite his efforts, Chad heard the despair in his own voice. Allie looked down at the coffee table, and then at Chad again. "Do you blame *me*, Chad?"

"No. You did what you thought was right. For Kyle, it probably was."

"But not for you."

"As a candidate for President?" Chad's voice was quietly bitter—this dream of the future, once so vivid, was suddenly part of his past. "No. But that's why we're here, isn't it. Because I wanted to be President."

"I'm also a father, Allie. We're a family. So we have to take what comes together." He softened his voice again. "I've experienced much worse, sweetheart. I'll be all right."

Tears came to her eyes. Chad imagined her reviewing the moments of their life together: falling in love with more optimism than insight; the awakening of a young wife to her husband's selfishness and infidelity; the uncertainty of his capture; learning to cope as a mother on her own; his return, refined by suffering, to a woman who had changed and a daughter he did not know; the dawning awareness of Kyle's problems; her desperate—and, it must have seemed—solitary struggle to save their daughter's sanity and even life; her fateful consent to an abortion; the slow renewal as a family with two parents who cared deeply; the revival of Chad's ambition to be President.

"I don't tell you nearly enough," she said in a muffled voice. "I always think it, and so seldom say it."

"What's that?"

"How much I love you. How kind you are." She managed a somewhat shaky smile. "I must have known that, from the beginning."

This touched him. "That makes you a rare woman," he answered. "But then you are."

They both fell quiet, cocooned for a moment from the reality about to overtake them. As if awakening herself from a dream, Allie went to the kitchen to call Kyle again.

Edgy, Chad waited. Allie returned, silently shaking her head.

Chad felt his tension rise. "We don't have much time," he said. "Either we bring her to their offices, or tomorrow afternoon the *Frontier* goes with what they've got."

"I know." Allie sounded defensive now. "You told me."

Chad replayed her tone of voice. In the manner of a husband who knew his wife so well that words were superfluous, he fixed her with a steady, mildly reproving, gaze of inquiry.

"Kyle has a new boyfriend," Allie said at last. "She might be there."

Chad felt a familiar and unhappy emotion, the sense of being an outsider, a stranger to the intimacy between mother and daughter. Had he time to dwell on it, he would wonder who this boy was, whether he was good for Kyle, why he did not know. But all he said was, "Do you have his number?"

"No. Of course not." Allie's voice was tired. "Kyle's a woman now, Chad. Or trying to be."

Another memory came to him: Allie waiting up for Kyle, hour after anxious hour during one or another of the drug or alcohol-fueled disappearances which, they both feared, might end in her death. As if sensing this, Allie said gently, "She's all right now. Really."

It was becoming hard for Chad to sit. "I hope so," he murmured.

Twenty-three

At nine o'clock the next morning, after a sleepless night in which Kyle did not call, Chad Palmer answered his telephone.

"Chad?"

Recognizing the voice of his Chief of Staff, Chad sat down heavily at the kitchen table. In a wan imitation of his usual manner, he said, "Morning, Brian. What's up?"

"The Supreme Court just ruled in the Tierney case. I'm faxing you the opinion."

Chad heard an anxious undertone in Brian Curry's normally phlegmatic voice. "What's it say?"

"It's pretty unusual," Brian answered. "Actually, I've never heard of anything like this."

Clayton placed the opinion on Kerry's desk. "A four-to-four split," he said. "Four justices voted to grant a stay, and to hear the case; four judges opposed both."

"Where does that leave us?"

Clayton turned a page. "Justice Fini," he said, "goes out of his way to explain that. And I mean *way* out of his way—Adam Shaw tells me he's never seen a justice comment on a decision whether or not to hear a case."

Fini, Kerry knew, was the justice closest to the late Roger Bannon, an outspoken conservative and pro-life advocate. Quickly, the President began reading:

"Under the 'rule of four,'" Fini had written, *"the votes of four justices are sufficient to grant certiorari; in this case, to hear Professor Tierney's appeal on behalf of the fetus. However, five votes are required to extend the stay granted by Justice Kelly, and prevent an abortion until the appeal can be heard . . ."*

"No stay," Kerry murmured.

"Just keep reading."

"Therefore, the four justices who favor a full hearing are unable to preserve the life of the intervenor's unborn grandchild.

"Currently, the Court is without a ninth member, the office of Chief Justice being vacant. We do not express an opinion regarding the wisdom or propriety of Judge Masters's participation in the rehearing en banc. However, such participation clearly disqualifies her from considering this petition, even if confirmed . . ."

Kerry looked up. "Very nice," he said. "Fini makes it seem like *she's* the reason they can't hear this." When Clayton's only answer was a bleak smile, Kerry read further.

"Those of us," Fini continued, *"who favor a full hearing regret our inability to address the important legal issues presented, including the value our society places on viable life, and the role of parents in helping minors face a moral choice so permanent and profound. But such is the harsh reality of our procedural dilemma.*

"Without a further stay, this abortion will be performed, and the case mooted. None of our brethren opposed to a hearing on the merits will vote to grant such a stay. Put baldly, we have the four votes necessary to decide whether a life should be spared, but not the five votes required to spare it until we decide.

"With great reluctance, we are forced to acknowledge that granting Professor Tierney's petition would be pointless . . ."

The President looked up at Clayton. Softly, he said, "So it's Caroline's fault."

Clayton nodded. "What Fini's done is blatantly political. Read how Justice Rothbard responds—you can almost see the blood in the margins."

Avowedly pro-choice, Miriam Rothbard was the only woman on the Court. Turning the page, the President began reading:

"I regret," Rothbard had said, *"the extraordinary statement by those colleagues who favor a grant of certiorari.*

"The statement is unprecedented: it is a political, not a legal, document, calculated to inform the Senate and the public that we appear to be deadlocked on the issues presented, including the constitutionality of the Protection of Life Act. The effect can only be to insinuate this Court into the Senate's deliberations regarding the nomination of Judge Masters as Chief Justice.

"The issues posed by this appeal are best left for another day. The statement of our colleagues would have best been left unwritten . . ."

"If anything," Clayton said, "it makes matters worse. Far worse."

Kerry pondered this, wondering what role his decision to withdraw the government's support for the Protection of Life Act might have played in the outcome. "Maybe for us," he answered. "But not for Mary Ann Tierney."

A little after 6:00 a.m. in San Francisco, Sarah took the last page off the fax machine in her bedroom.

It was over—the law, if not the consequences for Mary Ann, Caroline Masters, Sarah herself. Despite the startling nature of what she had just read, the Tierney case was consigned to history. As a lawyer, Sarah had done all a lawyer could do. She had won.

After some moments, she went to the kitchen to make coffee, absorb what had happened. She thought of herself two months ago, sheltered from the misty drizzle, watching a nameless red-haired girl cross a line of pickets, to begin a process which now had transformed both their lives.

It felt enormous; together, they had brought down an act of Congress, defined the law for whoever followed Mary Ann, at least within the Ninth Circuit. But Sarah felt no elation. Perhaps her reward would be a deep satisfaction, years from now—especially if Mary Ann Tierney prospered.

Finishing her coffee, Sarah went to awaken Mary Ann, imagining as she did the same moment in the Tierney household, Margaret and Martin Tierney awakening to the end of the case, trying to imagine a future which included—for them—facing the literal loss of a grandson, and the estranged daughter who had caused this. Standing over Mary Ann, Sarah hesitated, as if by pausing she could delay the pain to come.

The girl's eyes fluttered open, blank at first, then focusing on Sarah. In them Sarah read fear and hope; she knew that Sarah would not awaken her without reason.

Sarah took her hand. "We've won," she said. "The Supreme Court has refused your parents' appeal."

Mary Ann looked stunned and then, to Sarah, as frightened as she was relieved. Sarah could imagine how complex "winning" must seem: victory must carry with it the fear of sin, an imagined whiff of hell. Two months could not erase the girl raised in her parents' home.

Sarah knelt by the bed. "When the time comes," she promised, "I'll be there with you."

Reflexively, the girl felt her rounded belly. Then she covered her face, and began to weep.

For Caroline, the news had come from Clayton Slade, his call breaking a restless sleep. She sat up in bed, heartsick.

What Justice Fini had done felt like a blow to the solar plexus. *We don't want you here,* his statement told her. *We do not want you here, and we want the Senate to spare us your presence.* If there had been any doubt as to how divided the Court was, and how divisive Caroline might become as Chief, that doubt was gone.

In two months her life had been exposed, her daughter wounded, her own reputation damaged. Her only consolation was that she had acted as she felt a judge must act, and faced the consequences as they came.

And so she would, until the Senate voted.

In Washington, Macdonald Gage, too, felt leaden. Even Mace Taylor, the most cold and practical of men, was reduced to a contemplative silence. At last, Taylor said, "You're out of time."

Gage looked up from his coffee. "The baby, you mean."

"The baby. If it turns out it never had a brain, there'll be more sympathy for Masters. You might not get the last few votes you need." Taylor's voice was quiet, sober. "Tony Fini left you in as good shape as he could. But that may be a matter of days, or hours."

Gage stared at his carpet. "I could call a vote tomorrow," he said. "But Kilcannon would scream bloody murder about 'surprise tactics.' And I may not have the votes to win . . ."

"And a filibuster?"

"Might take us past when the girl has her abortion. Some of our own people are getting real vague on me, like they've been cutting deals with Kilcannon." Gage felt a rising unease. "The dumbest thing in the world, Mace, is for a lawyer to ask a question he doesn't know the answer to. Except for a leader to call a vote that you don't know you'll win, when there's nothing to gain by losing, and the greatest harm you'd be doing is to yourself. And then there's Palmer." Pausing in his reverie, he looked up at Taylor. "Always, there's Palmer."

Taylor watched him, his thoughts imponderable. "So there is."

Gage studied him. "If I call the vote tomorrow," Gage said at length, "Chad's the wild card."

Now it was Taylor who contemplated the carpet with veiled eyes. "You willing to gamble on the baby being normal?"

His tone was cool. "No," Gage answered. "That's something to hope for, but surely not to count on."

Taylor looked up at him. "Then call the vote," he said. He did not mention Palmer.

. . .

Shortly before eleven, Chad Palmer heard a click on his line, the signal for call waiting.

"That may be her," he said to Henry Nielsen. "Hang on for a moment."

Hastily, Chad hit the flash button.

"Senator Palmer?"

It was a man's voice, high-pitched and, to Chad's ears, invasive. "Yes," Chad answered tightly.

"This is Charlie Trask."

Startled, Chad took a moment to steel himself, feeling surprise turn to dread: a call from the gossip columnist, the man who had implied that Caroline Masters was a lesbian, was, on this morning of all mornings, something to fear. In an even tone, mustered with difficulty, Chad inquired, "What can I do for you, Mr. Trask?"

"I'll get right to the point. We know about your daughter's abortion, and I'm about to go with it on-line. I thought you'd want to comment before I do."

Sickened, Chad felt his hope of protecting Kyle slip away, Henry Nielsen waiting on the other line. "Yes," he managed to say, "it's not relevant . . ."

"Don't even try relevance, Senator. This morning's pronouncement from the Court makes it doubly relevant. And Senator Gage just called a vote. So do you have anything to say, or not?"

Chad forced himself to pause, thinking of Kyle. "Not to you," he said softly.

Chad hit the flash button, and banished him.

Twenty-four

It was twilight before Kyle Palmer returned to her apartment.

On impulse, she and Matthew had decided to just blow off the day—their classes, his part-time job, pretty much anything which had to do with the outside world. She felt kind of guilty about that. But then it wasn't every day you figured out that, just maybe, you were falling in love.

Matthew was a film student, tall and bearded, with ruddy cheeks, gentle brown eyes, and a smile so genuinely happy and unaffected that it transformed his face entirely. They could talk so easily; in between making love—wonderful in itself for his tenderness—they had pretty much talked all night. She could imagine his parents now, his teenage twin brothers, the six-year-old sister Matthew clearly adored. Kyle was still careful about what she told him; she didn't want him to look at her and see damaged goods. But if this kept up she could imagine, someday, telling him almost everything—he seemed that good. Kyle prayed that he really was.

This was what she wanted: something of her own—a career in fashion design, but also a husband she loved who loved her, an understanding between the two of them that they were the central thing in each other's lives. Though Kyle loved her parents, she wanted something different in a marriage; with tenderness, yet guilt, she knew that *she* had been the most important person in Allie Palmer's life, and that her father was born to be a hero, at home in the larger world—adored by those who barely knew him, and millions more who only knew his name. Kyle wished to be safely anonymous, with a husband she would spend her days and nights with.

She turned the corner onto her street in a kind of dream state, driving by memory and instinct, her imaginings of Matthew more vivid than her surroundings. So that the men and women clustered in front of her apartment, the snug basement of an old house, struck her as unreal.

Parking across the street, Kyle walked toward them. Only then did she see the Minicams and know that, though she did not know why, they had come for her.

They scrambled toward her. The red-haired young woman in front, a local news reporter, was calling out. "Tell us about your abortion, Kyle. Did your father support your decision?"

Kyle froze, immobilized by disbelief.

"Your father," the woman persisted, "says you had problems with drugs and alcohol . . ."

"Your boyfriend," another voice called, "claims you were emotionally unstable. Was having an abortion right for you?"

Kyle felt shaky, sick. *"Go away,"* she said in a trembling voice. Then she began running across the lawn, circling the house to the rear. As she fumbled for her keys to the basement door, she heard them running after her.

Slamming the door behind her, Kyle haltingly descended the stairs into the basement.

She sat on the edge of the bed, skin clammy, staring at the white rectangle which was her home. She barely noticed the blinking red light on her answering machine. From outside came the faint sounds of a commotion.

Thank God there were no windows.

Dully, she crossed the room and saw that her machine had recorded sixteen messages. She made herself push the button . . .

"Kyle." Her mother's voice sounded strained. *"Please call . . ."*

Each message added to the story, a tortured sequence in which the truth teased itself out, climaxing with her father's halting explanation of what was happening, then the questions of reporters who had somehow discovered her number.

Tears ran down Kyle's face.

Someone had betrayed them. They knew of her abortion, her mother's consent. Eric had given an interview describing her father's "brutality" to him, their sudden move to Washington, her parents' collusion in the breakup of their "relationship" and the "cover-up" which followed.

"Please," her father's voice had pleaded. *"As soon as you get this message, come home."*

Eric.

Her father had been right. Eric was a sleaze. He had used her, then abandoned her. Now he was back in their lives—probably for money as well as for notoriety—to shame her mother and destroy her father. Because of *her.*

The telephone rang.

Standing by the answering machine, Kyle hesitated.

"Kyle?" It was her father. She had never heard him sound so hopeless, so humiliated. He was *Chad Palmer,* in Kyle's mind so impervious to pressures . . .

Shaken, she turned from her father's voice.

"Kyle?" he asked again. "Are you there?"

She could not bring herself to answer this new Chad Palmer—so pleading, so unfamiliar, that it devastated her. Hands covering her face, she sat on the bed again.

Matthew. Her whole life would be exposed to him, and to his family. Kyle Palmer, the drunken, druggy, crazy girl who had ruined her father's career and made her mother's life a living hell. Now she would be that girl forever; such was her agony, the wrenching feeling inside her, that all she wanted was to escape. But she could not—the reporters outside imprisoned her.

On the table was a bottle of cheap Chianti.

In his innocence, unaware of the reasons Kyle did not drink, Matthew had left it here. She found herself staring at the bottle.

She should not touch it. But this did not seem to matter now—it was an escape, the only one available. Right now she wouldn't care if she were dead.

Shakily, Kyle filled a coffee mug with wine.

There were shadows on the wall, cast by the lamp on Kyle's nightstand. The room receded, became unreal; stunned by alcohol—the shock to a system now unused to it—Kyle was motionless save for pouring wine, placing the mug to her lips. Repressed images surfaced from the past, vivid and immediate—Eric on top of her, her father's rage, her mother holding her hand while the doctor slipped the tube between her legs. Memories she now shared with the world.

Her father had been right about Eric, about her. She was a fuck-up, an albatross, flawed from birth. Her mother and father would have been better off if she'd never been born—how vividly she remembered the silent fear in her mother's eyes, the wary, probing look behind the mask of serenity which fooled everyone but Kyle . . .

Her poor mother, who loved so much and tried so hard. She did not deserve this.

No, Kyle thought with a jolt. *She did not deserve* this.

In a moment of strange clarity, she saw herself as she was—hiding in her room, drunk, the ultimate betrayal of her parents and herself. Her hand shook as she held the wine bottle; with a ferocious act of will, she flung it against the painted stone wall. Shattering, it made her flinch and then, abruptly, stand.

Reeling, she went to the bathroom and stripped.

The shower was cold, a punishment. She hunched, shivering beneath the icy spatter, the shock to her skin which would help her confront her life again. Stepping from the shower, her hair was moist ringlets, and her skin felt blue.

Her parents couldn't see her like this, she couldn't call them like this. Naked, she paced the apartment, straining to get sober, stepping over the jagged glass with the exaggerated care of intoxication. When the phone rang—this time her mother—she did not answer; when Kyle got to them, she would be better.

At last, fingers stiff and fumbling, Kyle dressed again, disguising the wine on her breath with mouthwash. Her car keys were still in her jeans.

When she cracked open the door, she heard nothing.

Outside it was dark and chill; a thin sleet hit her face, the dying fall of March. Like a nightmare, the reporters had vanished.

She would go to her parents.

Walking to the car, a plan came to Kyle. She would drive the long way, with her windows open, along Rock Creek Parkway. By the time she reached her parents, maybe they would not know—that, now, was the only way she could help them. As capable as they were, they needed that: her father, who had never needed anything, needed the best that she could give.

Sitting in the car, she envisioned him. Her handsome father, whom she had always worshiped, whose approval she had always needed, even when she hated him.

She loved him now. That, and a fierce desire not to worry him, were all she had to give. She imagined draping her arms around his neck.

At last she started the car.

The streets seemed a maze—once or twice, memory failed her, and she missed a turn. But her instincts were good; eventually, she found herself on Rock Creek Parkway.

Though the parkway was quiet, she drove with care; the pavement was slick, and she did not trust her reflexes. Time passed. She craned her neck, peering out at the moving patch of asphalt illuminated by her headlights. To her right, the dark forms of trees slipped by, sloping toward the creekbed. Through her open window, sleet misted her face.

She was almost fine now.

At the edge of the headlights, something moved. Kyle squinted; back hunched, a squirrel, scrambling, stopped suddenly, frozen by her headlights.

Kyle stabbed the brake.

The car shimmied, then began to skid sideways. She wrenched the wheel, and lost control entirely. For Kyle, the next moments were like watching a film; as she left the road, the looming trees seemed insubstantial. The first few seemed to slip by her; then—in a moment vivid with reality and horror—she saw the massive trunk in her windshield.

The car stopped with a sickening crunch. Kyle did not; hurtling toward the windshield, she wished her seatbelt were fastened. And then knew nothing.

As reported to Chad Palmer by the police, the facts were stark. Their daughter was dead; it seemed she had been drinking.

Only in the morning did her grieving father enter Kyle's apartment. The rug was covered with green shards of glass; on the table was a coffee mug half-filled with wine. Her message light was blinking.

Numb, Chad pushed the button.

Before the last message—the haunting sound of his own voice, telling Kyle he loved her—were messages from three reporters, mentioning Eric's name and her abortion. And he knew for sure that whoever wished to destroy him had murdered Kyle Palmer.

Twenty-five

It was a day when Washington stopped.

For Kerry Kilcannon, it had begun the night before, when Lara Costello called to tell him what NBC News had just pulled off the wire. As hours passed, the sequence of events began to emerge, and the media's role in the death of Kyle Palmer became bitterly clear.

Kerry could not sleep. When Lara arrived, drawn by the pain she had heard in his voice, he quietly outlined his role in the events which now had led to tragedy: Clayton's exposure of Caroline Masters, and of Chad's efforts to protect her; his own awareness of Kyle's abortion, the revelation of which—shortly thereafter—had precipitated her death. Gravely, Lara listened.

"You don't know where it came from," she finally said. "And part of you is afraid to know."

Kerry found it difficult to say this. "Yes," he acknowledged. "I'm no longer sure of anything."

They sat together in his study, silent in the wake of his admission. It was difficult to articulate, even to Lara, the emotions at war inside him: grief for Chad, Allie, and a young woman for whom, Kerry had always sensed, her father felt such deep concern; an empathetic horror of what it must be to lose a child; a deep, immutable anger toward whoever had used her in their pitiless design; the fear that those responsible had acted in his name.

"That's a lot to live with," she said at last.

Perhaps she was simply responding to his confession; perhaps, to his breach with Clayton, the wounds which must remain. "I have to find out," he told her. "No matter who gets hurt."

From her expression, Lara knew he did not say this lightly. "And you think it may hurt *us*?" she asked.

Kerry nodded. "What was done to Kyle," he answered simply, "could be done to us. And if I pursue this, it might well."

"Then it will."

The equanimity in Lara's voice, Kerry realized, reflected an outrage of her own. And, more than that, her understanding of what Kerry must do to restore his moral balance, as well as her desire to heal, at last, the lingering breach between them. "I don't want you living with this," she said gently. "Not alone, at any rate."

Even in his sadness for the Palmers, Kerry noted the moment, for its implications were both subtle and profound: Lara no longer wished to stand outside his presidency, wary of its consequences. When he briefly smiled at her, mostly with his eyes, she came to sit beside him.

That Kerry was capable of an anger which could give the most jaded politician pause was well known to his enemies. But what they could not comprehend was how completely Kerry, the adult, had subordinated the childhood rage implanted by an abusive father—an ordeal known only to Lara and Clayton—to a cold assessment of its uses. Kerry was a practical politician and, even at this terrible hour, the resolve to make Caroline Masters the next Chief Justice never left him. Though he did not yet know how, his intuition told him that this ambition was conjoined with the death of Kyle Palmer.

But the immediate connection was obvious. When Lara left, he awakened Chuck Hampton. Kerry allowed the Minority Leader a moment to express his own shocked humanity, and then implored him to ensure—by any and all means necessary—that Macdonald Gage would postpone the Masters vote, adjourning the Senate out of deference to a grieving colleague.

Hanging up, Kerry removed a postmarked manila envelope from his drawer. Then he shaved, put on a suit and, after walking the shadowy West Wing at a little past 4:00 a.m., called Clayton to the Oval Office. As Kerry had instructed Kit Pace, printouts of every article regarding Kyle Palmer's abortion were spread out on his desk.

Awaiting Clayton, he studied them, from Charlie Trask's first bulletin to the crescendo which so quickly followed. For half a day, the story had run through the media like a fever: it had taken roughly nine hours, Kerry calculated, to consume Kyle Palmer. In the margins of the "Trask Report," Kerry began making notes.

When Clayton appeared, Kerry took a moment to look up.

"Did *you* do this?" he asked.

Clayton required no explanation. He sat, his own face implacable. "No. And I don't know who did." Pausing, he asked, "What do you take me for?"

Kerry could receive this as a simple declaration of core decency, or a more pragmatic statement that, while exposing Caroline Masters carried clear risks and benefits, exposing Kyle Palmer was more distasteful, the potential rewards less clear. Or both.

"Chad Palmer," Kerry said, "could have been President."

"But you are." Clayton's voice remained quiet. "You reminded me of that, quite recently. I haven't forgotten."

Habits die hard. The chief habit of Kerry's adulthood had been to trust Clayton Slade. It was painful to step outside this, to watch Clayton with detachment.

"Whoever did this," the President told him, "I'm roasting on a spit. You can help me, or not."

In another man, Clayton might have taken this for bluster. But the two had met as prosecutors; both knew what a prosecutor could do, and how the power to investigate could engender fear and uncover truth. What it took was a relentless will; a chess player's guile; a field general's breadth of vision. All of which, Clayton years ago had learned, Kerry Kilcannon possessed. Nor would mercy give him pause—Kerry had a long memory, and there were acts he did not forgive. For him, retribution should come in this world, not the next.

In a voice without emotion, Clayton said, "What do you want me to do?"

"Call the director of the FBI. I want them to get a subpoena and search Charlie Trask's office for any piece of paper with Kyle Palmer's name on it . . ."

"The press," Clayton interjected, "will scream bloody murder."

"Let them. I want Trask's files, and I want him scared. I want them to interview the boyfriend, learn how whoever did this found him, and who he talked to. I also want them to interview Kyle's doctor." Kerry's voice softened. "If the director wants to know why, tell him to call me. By the time he does—*if* he does—I want Adam Shaw here with a plausible list of every conceivable federal crime committed by the person who leaked this story, and anyone who conspired with him. Starting with how a consent form supposed to be confidential wound up in an envelope mailed to Katherine Jones." Pausing, Kerry picked up the envelope he had secreted in his desk. "This envelope, to be precise."

Though he was silent, Clayton's eyes seemed to widen, as if he were slowly comprehending the dimensions of what Kerry had withheld from him. "Jones gave the form to *you*?"

"And I gave it to Chad. But kept this. I want it fingerprinted." Kerry tossed the envelope in Clayton's lap. "I'm not up on the latest technology, but I imagine by now some bright crime technician has figured out how to lift prints off paper. And our database of fingerprints should have a wide universe of suspects. Including all former and current federal employees."

The irony of this last remark was not lost on Clayton. He stared at the envelope in his hands.

"If they only find your prints on that," Kerry said evenly, "but not on whatever they get from Trask, you may be in the clear."

Speechless, Clayton stared at him. "Tell the director," Kerry ordered, "that I want the fingerprint results by tomorrow. In case Trask hasn't revealed his source by then."

There was one call Kerry did not mention—the call he made himself, to Henry Nielsen.

"I was wondering," Kerry began, "how you feel about yourself this morning."

Nielsen, Kerry guessed, had been awake, though it was not yet six o'clock. But it took some moments to register that the President indeed was calling, and to absorb the import of his question.

"In candor," Nielsen said quietly, "not too great."

Kerry did not push this. "From your article, it's clear you didn't find the consent form under a cabbage leaf. Someone gave it to you."

"Yes."

"Who?"

Kerry heard an audible sigh. "I can't tell you, Mr. President. You know that. As a matter of First Amendment principle, we can't reveal sources."

"Yes." The President's tone was flat. "Your principles. I'd forgotten." Kerry paused. "I assume that whoever it was gave this to *you*, in person."

"Yes." Nielsen struck a firmer tone. "No one else was there. No one saw us. No one on my staff's involved."

"I'm not looking for martyrs," the President answered softly. "The document will do for now. Specifically, the original of whatever this person gave you."

Nielsen hesitated, sounding less certain. "As a First Amendment matter, that document may also be confidential."

The President stood. "I doubt that. The person you're protecting is a blackmailer who caused a death. Kyle Palmer paid too dearly for your principles." Once more, Kerry paused. "I'm willing to grant you absolution. This morning the FBI will come to your office, subpoena in hand. Give them the original, then have your lawyers file whatever motion they care to. All I want is a day or so."

In the silence, Kerry imagined Nielsen trying to reconcile the demands of his profession with remorse at where they had led, the dawning awareness of what purpose the original might serve. "A day or so," he finally answered. "Under protest, of course."

Only then, the process started, did the President face the melancholy task of calling Chad and Allie Palmer.

He found a woman who could not stop crying, a man nearly inarticulate with grief and anguish. Kerry could not tell him that he knew what they were feeling, only that he was deeply sorry, and would do whatever he could. What that might be, or whether it would matter to them, he could not yet know.

Twenty-six

Two days later, on the morning of Kyle Palmer's funeral, Kerry awaited a call from the director of the FBI.

The day itself was gloomy, with a dismal and persistent rain seeping from dark skies. Out of deference to Senator Palmer, the Senate was closed, the debate on the Masters nomination scheduled to commence on the following day. The vote count seemed frozen: all forty-five Democrats were in favor, forty-eight Republicans—including Chad Palmer—were opposed, with the last seven uncommitted. Of the forty-eight opponents, in Kerry's estimate forty or forty-one would support a filibuster—a crucial difference, as forty-one votes were necessary to prevent the Masters nomination from reaching the Senate floor.

Feverishly, Kerry had worked the phones to keep the seven Republicans from committing to Gage, and to chip away at the support for a filibuster. But no one dared approach Chad Palmer; no one knew how, or whether, Kyle's death might affect his vote. Just as no one outside the White House was certain what Kerry intended by the subpoena to the *Internet Frontier,* or the FBI's seizure of Charlie Trask's files.

There had, of course, been the predictable protests. The *New York Times* had denounced these actions as "chilling" and "a raid on the First Amendment." The White House had greeted the protest with stony silence; on the President's instructions, Kit Pace gave the press corps a clipped response—that this was a "criminal matter" on which she could not comment. This remark, along with the death of Kyle Palmer, seemed to impose an unusual and uneasy quiet on the members of the Senate. And hanging over all of this was the latest Gallup poll: forty-nine percent now supported the Masters nomination, and thirty-seven were opposed. The fact that this reflected a swing toward Caroline Masters among suburban women, a crucial voting bloc, seemed to stall Macdonald Gage's pursuit of the last three senators needed to defeat her.

Kerry was gazing out his window, thinking of Chad Palmer and the battle to come, when his telephone rang.

The director of the FBI, Hal Bailey, was a career federal prosecutor who had made his reputation bringing organized-crime cases in New York City. Though Kerry's impression of him was favorable, he had not yet indicated whether Bailey could keep his job, the pinnacle of his career, and Bailey's term would soon expire. This, the President knew very well, had now become useful. In his bland, professional way, Bailey seemed prepared to please.

"I'm sorry it took two days," the director told Kerry. "But the fingerprint base is extremely large."

"You were able to get prints?"

"A number of them, including yours—the sheer volume most of the problem. To extract the prints we used a chemical called ninhydrin, which is extremely reliable. From there it was a matter of determining whether the same set of prints recurred on your envelope, Trask's documents, and those we got from the *Internet Frontier*." He paused, voice lowering in what sounded like discomfort. "The prints offer the only definitive evidence, Mr. President. Whoever gave the boyfriend cash also gave him a false name, and the kid doesn't seem to know or care who sent this guy. As for the doctor, it appears that someone got into her office, copied the consent form, and left. She didn't even know it had happened."

For Kerry, this confirmed his fears—the persons responsible for Kyle Palmer's death had been thoroughly professional. "But you were able to match up prints."

"Yes." The reluctance in Bailey's voice returned. "One set appeared on every document."

"Whose?"

Bailey hesitated. "If you don't mind, Mr. President, I'd prefer to give you the report in person."

Thirty-five minutes later, Hal Bailey was in the Oval Office. Dark-eyed and balding, with the short haircut and lean intensity of an ex-Marine turned fitness fanatic, Bailey perched on the edge of his chair. With seeming reluctance, he glanced at Clayton Slade, who sat at his side.

"I thought," the President explained calmly, "that Clayton should hear this."

Hesitant, Bailey gave Clayton a sidelong look, and then passed five single-spaced pages to the President. "I typed it myself," Bailey said. "I didn't want this leaking before you saw it."

Composing his face into an expressionless mask, Kerry began to read. He forced himself to work through Bailey's prose—three pages of bureaucratic throat-clearing which described each step—without flipping to the end. It took some moments to reach it.

Staring at the final page, Kerry made no effort to mask his emotions.

"Who is it?" Clayton asked.

For a moment, Kerry simply nodded at the report, feeling his anger merge with a sense of the inevitable—that yes, in the end, only *this* made sense. Then he looked up, into the face of his oldest friend.

"My esteemed ex-colleague," Kerry answered. "Senator Mason Taylor."

A few minutes later, the two men were alone.

Clayton's expression remained grim. And yet, beneath this, the President saw a certain brightness, a satisfaction which matched his own.

"Stupid," Clayton said. "For a man that smart."

"I think I follow his reasoning," Kerry replied. "Whatever he did, there were risks. He didn't want a go-between, anyone who could flip on him. He couldn't ask a secretary to mail it. To fax it might be traceable. So that meant handling it himself—ninhydrin must not be on his radar screen."

Clayton stared at him. "If it's Taylor," he said finally, "it's Gage."

"I expect so. But we can't prove that yet."

"You've got a vote tomorrow." Clayton's tone was filled with an anxious determination. "Busting Gage could make the difference."

"Yes," Kerry replied with the same quiet. "I've considered that. From the beginning."

"Then what will you do with this?"

"I don't know yet."

But perhaps he did, Kerry thought to himself. Perhaps he had known all along. Perhaps he pretended otherwise so as not to face—at least until he had to—how far he was willing to go, and whom he was willing to use. But until he crossed that threshold, a trace of doubt remained.

"I don't know," he repeated.

And, as he entered the cathedral for Kyle Palmer's funeral, it seemed, at least for a moment, that this was so.

Lara was beside him and a cluster of official Washington was there, includ-ing, the President noted with dark irony, a somber Macdonald Gage. For a moment, Kerry wondered why Chad had not barred them all—left to her own devices, Kerry was sure, Allie Palmer would have done so. But, in many ways, official Washington was their family. And if in Chad Palmer's mind, some of its inhabitants shared the blame for Kyle's death—or at least in the cycle of vicious-ness which had placed her private struggle in public view—Chad might want them to bear witness.

Chad carried himself with the grim composure of a warrior faced with a bit-ter and ineradicable sorrow. He appeared gaunt and, though Kerry perhaps imagined it, his shirt collar seemed loose, as if he had begun shrinking from the inside out. Beside him, Allie was waxen, her face drawn, and her eyes puffy from crying. If he had seen Allie on the street, Kerry might not have recognized her.

Following Kerry's gaze, Lara squeezed his hand. Like an electric current, this surfaced an even darker thought: besides Lara, of all those present, perhaps one other person knew what Kerry knew. But Kerry alone could decide what to do with it and thus, quite possibly, alter the fate of both the guilty and the innocent, here and elsewhere.

The service was muted and, to Kerry's mind, lacking in catharsis. Chad Palmer shed no tears. Standing beside his daughter's casket, he seemed to have receded so completely that Kerry could feel how shattered Chad was. His brief words to Kyle, a father's simple, helpless assurance of love, stirred emotions Kerry found difficult to bear; when Allie told her daughter that "a part of me died with you," Kerry felt the simple truth of this. And, with finality, felt the weight of his responsibility, the choices which awaited.

For a time, the dark and somber church receded. The Palmers faded into shadows; the touch of Lara's hand was light as a sparrow in his palm. His most vivid image was of a man he could not see—Macdonald Gage, seated behind him in the second pew.

Determinedly, Kerry forced himself to focus, as he should, on Chad and Allie Palmer, standing beside the beflowered casket which held the body of their only child. It was in his power to change forever the chemistry of their grief, turn this to his purpose. But did anyone—president or not—have the right to tamper with their lives when another man already had altered them so cruelly?

Unresolved, this question haunted him through the moments which remained. Then the pallbearers bore Kyle Palmer from the church, her parents following, and Kerry and Lara, flanked by the Secret Service, emerged into the rain.

There were police cars in front, barriers, more agents—a reminder of the cumbersome machinery constantly devoted to his protection. Looking to his right, he saw Macdonald Gage, his gaze moving from the funeral hearse to Kerry's vigilant protectors, and wondered at the flow of his thoughts.

As though feeling his scrutiny, Gage turned to him, his face sober and, to Kerry's embittered mind, arranged in formulaic piety. Gage hesitated, and then took a few steps forward, to speak to him quietly.

"A sad day, Mr. President."

Kerry placed a hand on Gage's shoulder. "Mac," he said softly, "I think you have no idea."

Silent, Macdonald Gage watched Kerry Kilcannon disappear into his black limousine.

No, Gage corrected, he had an idea. The President had dispatched the FBI himself, Gage calculated; helpless, he could only wonder what Kilcannon—a vengeful, ruthless man on the best of days—knew, or thought he knew, and which the Majority Leader of the United States Senate wished never to know for sure. But there was one thing Kilcannon could not know—the depth of Gage's regret at the death of Kyle Palmer, the fervent wish that whatever caused it could be undone.

Yet it was done, and Gage must somehow consign the burden of what he *did* know to the recesses of his mind. Some day, Macdonald Gage himself might be President. But first there was a nominee to vanquish, a president to defeat. Tomorrow, power lay in the balance: to Gage, Caroline Masters personified a contest, though sometimes murky in its particulars, between what was best for the country and what was not.

Gage returned to his office, to work.

Silent, Kerry and Lara followed the funeral cortege. Aided by Kerry's escort, the line of cars drove steadily toward Arlington, the splash of rain beneath their wheels a low whisper.

"What will you do?" Lara asked.

As with Clayton, Kerry did not answer. Lara took his hand again.

They stood by the grave site in Arlington National Cemetery, relatives and a few close friends, beside where Chad would someday lie. Given the sensitivity of veterans to the sanctity of Arlington, Kerry had called key veterans groups and the appropriate chairman in Congress, to ensure that Kyle could be buried there. Perhaps, Kerry reflected, that was why Chad had suggested he could accompany them on his daughter's last journey.

A little apart from the others, the President and his fiancée watched the clumps of earth cover Kyle's resting place.

In the end, it was Chad who approached him.

With a few soft words, Lara moved away, leaving them alone. "I'm sorry," Kerry told him.

There were tears at last in Chad's eyes, though his voice was flat. "This never should have happened," he murmured. "They never should have done this to her."

Nodding, Kerry paused, looking into his ravaged face. Then he placed a hand on Palmer's arm. "I know how hard this will be," he said at last. "But I'd like to see you tonight. I think there's something you should know."

Twenty-seven

It was past ten o'clock before Chad Palmer came to the White House.

Entering the President's study, Chad looked haggard. Kerry closed the door behind him.

"How's Allie?" the President asked softly.

Chad looked down, then shook his head. "Sedated," he answered.

For Kerry, the single word conveyed Chad's helplessness; his inability, even now, to fully grasp what had become of them; his discomfort at having left his wife with others. His presence seemed an act of will.

He sat, looking weary and detached from his surroundings. When he spoke again, it was with a kind of disembodied patience, as though he accepted that Kerry would not have asked him to come unless it was important in ways that Chad Palmer, at this moment, could not imagine or care about.

"What is it?" he asked.

Kerry considered offering some sort of apology, or explanation, or account of how much he had agonized before making this decision. But any words which came to him seemed pointless and self-serving. Without preface he took the FBI report from his desk, and handed it to Chad.

Chad began to read.

After a moment, Kerry saw a subtle change: Chad's air of exhaustion replaced by utter stillness. He did not speak, move, or look up from the report. More than any words or gestures, this drove home to Kerry the weight of what he had just done. As Chad turned the final page, Kerry watched, silent.

When Chad looked up at last, tears ran down his face. "What do you want for this?" he asked.

"Nothing. It's yours."

Slowly, Chad nodded. Without saying more he stood, cheeks still stained with tears, and left.

Alone in his darkened sitting room, Chad began living with the truth.

The last relative was gone; alone, Allie still slept. There was no one with whom he could share his guilt.

He had not protected Kyle. He had risked too much with Gage; gone too far in helping Kerry Kilcannon. Some of that had come from ambition, some from ego of another kind—that Chad Palmer did what was right, no matter what the consequences. Now his pride had helped to kill his daughter; with merciless clarity Chad saw that his fingerprints, too, were on the envelope.

That Taylor had acted with Gage's knowledge he had no doubt; in his way, however oblique, Gage had tried to warn Chad. But in the end Gage had acquiesced—or more—in the act of cruelty which led to Kyle's death.

Chad replayed the last few weeks, like a film the end of which he knew but could not change. From the funeral he could retrieve but a few dazed images, as though he, too, were sedated. The most vivid impression was the soft echo of the first clump of earth, Chad's own, spattering on Kyle's casket.

What acts of his now, he wondered, could possibly do justice to his daughter?

Suddenly, the thought struck him as pitiful. Nothing Chad could do could help his daughter or, he was certain, fully restore the woman in their darkened bedroom to who she had been before. And so he sat alone, living with all the pointless, thwarted love of an imperfect father whose daughter was now a memory.

There was nothing he could do. Except try to act with honor, to hope that tomorrow there was something, if he could find it, which might send some ripple of good into the future, to commemorate the woman Kyle Palmer could have been.

Clayton sat where, moments before, Chad had read the FBI report. Unsettled by this memory, Kerry paused before speaking.

"Did you call Sarah Dash?" he inquired.

"Yes. The abortion's set for tomorrow morning."

Kerry gave a grim smile; no comment was required. "What will Palmer do?" Clayton asked.

"I have no idea." Kerry's voice was soft. "It was all I could do to watch him."

Clayton gave him a complex look of sympathy and concern. "Does he know what *we* mean to do?"

"He will. Once he thinks about it." Kerry's voice assumed a tinge of irony. "Do it the way you did with Caroline Masters. Only this time it's the *Post*'s turn."

Twenty-eight

At seven the next morning, Sarah Dash sat outside an operating room at San Francisco General, waiting for Dr. Mark Flom to abort Mary Ann Tierney's seven-and-a-half-month fetus.

They had come in secrecy, before dawn, in an ambulance dispatched to conceal Mary Ann's arrival. Mary Ann was composed yet frightened; she had rejected her father's agonized last appeal, but her fears were both spiritual and physical. Still, her deepest fear, repeated to Sarah in the middle of the night, was, "What if he's normal, Sarah? What if he would have been all right?"

Sarah did not tell her about the call from Clayton Slade.

The call did not surprise her—by now, nothing did. Nor was she offended: she was grateful to Kerry Kilcannon, and admired his advocacy of Caroline Masters. But she found the Chief of Staff's blunt practicality unnerving.

"The debate begins tomorrow," he told her. "If the fetus turns out to be abnormal, we hope you'll make that public right away."

"And if it's not?"

"I can't tell you what to do," Slade answered calmly. "But from your client's perspective, I would think that the less said, the better."

So now Sarah waited, fearful for Mary Ann, pondering her obligations. She could not help but visualize the procedures taking place behind closed doors. The pro-life forces had been clever: they had targeted a procedure the visceral horror of which obscured the medical reasons for it. Understanding this, Sarah had used all of her skills to bring Mary Ann to this moment. But now, like Mary Ann, she was consumed by fear that—despite the medical odds—inside the operating room they were ending the life of a viable, healthy child.

Still, this was not all that worried Sarah. Two days before, Mark Flom had said to her, "People can argue all they want. But when it's all said and done, there are times when this procedure is necessary.

"It's also quite difficult—not many doctors can do it. With every week, it becomes that much harder. The Tierneys have made it two *months* harder, on us all."

Now, while the extraction of the fetus proceeded, Sarah was overcome by the consequences—not only to Mary Ann, but to others. Glancing at her watch, Sarah calculated that it was past ten in Washington, and that the Senate had begun debating whether to advise and consent to the nomination of Caroline Clark Masters as Chief Justice of the United States.

Distractedly, she read her *New York Times*. On the eve of the vote, the lead article reported, it was unclear whether Macdonald Gage had the forty-one votes needed to support a filibuster. If not, both Gage and President Kilcannon presently were at least two votes short of the fifty-one required to defeat or sustain the nomination. A final complicating factor was Senator Chad Palmer: despite the avalanche of reporting which surrounded his daughter's death, no one knew whether Palmer would emerge from his seclusion.

No, Sarah thought, she could not blame Clayton Slade for calling. But this was the last piece of Mary Ann's public exposure—that, after all the trauma she had suffered, the outcome of the Masters nomination might hinge on the condition of her fetus.

Above all, Mary Ann was who Sarah cared about. It had been easy for Sarah to become who she was: her parents were secular, liberal, enamored of their daughter's intellect and independence. But Mary Ann's courage—and stubbornness—were almost inexplicable. In two months, Mary Ann had become so central to Sarah's life that she both resented this responsibility, and would not have passed it on to anyone. Now she wished—for both the girl's sake, and her own—that she believed there was a God to pray to.

Sarah closed her eyes.

An hour passed. Staring at the floor, Sarah heard Dr. Flom approaching.

With trepidation, she stood. Still in surgical dress, Flom looked exhausted; perhaps he, too, had suffered from the weight of his public involvement.

"How is she?" Sarah asked.

"Fine. Still unconscious from the anesthetic, of course." He paused. "The delivery was normal, Sarah. Mary Ann can have more children. Which was the point of the exercise, after all."

Feeling a shudder of relief, Sarah hesitated. "And the fetus?"

A look of gravity crossed Flom's fine features, and he slowly shook his head. "Hopeless. When I sutured the head, to drain it, there was almost nothing there. No way he could have lived."

Arms folded, Sarah swallowed, looking down. For a moment, she fought to control her emotions—there was one decision yet to make, and no time to ask Mary Ann. Once again, she weighed her obligations to her client, to Caroline Masters, and, in a sense, to the President.

"If I authorize it," she said, "are you willing to make that public?"

Flom smiled faintly. "It seems to be of some moment, doesn't it. And not just to Mary Ann."

Twenty-nine

At ten o'clock, the President and Clayton Slade began watching the Senate debate on C-SPAN.

They sat in an interior conference room, with a telephone at Kerry's right hand. For the moment, they had done all they could; the two greatest imponderables—Mary Ann Tierney's abortion, and Chad Palmer's actions—were beyond their control. In the hope that Chad would turn on Gage, they had delayed leaking the FBI report until a few minutes before: the story would not appear until tomorrow, giving Chad one day to act on his own.

That he would do so was Kerry's fervent wish. "Following Gage makes senators feel practical," Kerry observed to Clayton. "Following Chad makes them feel they're more like *him.*"

But all he knew was that Chad was in the Senate, having arrived in grim silence to a horde of media. For now, Macdonald Gage held the floor, beginning his last assault on Caroline Masters.

"Look at him preen," the President murmured. "How convenient it must be to have no conscience."

Macdonald Gage stood in the well of the Senate.

It was the apogee of his power, a day on which he would challenge the President himself. All one hundred senators were present, and the galleries were packed yet hushed. Vice President Ellen Penn presided from the rostrum, signaling the administration's resolve, if called upon, to break a fifty-fifty tie; as Gage well knew, the Vice President's office in the Senate, a perquisite of her office, had become the center of feverish lobbying by the President's congressional team and Ellen Penn herself. On Gage's behalf, Paul Harshman stood ready to organize the forty-one votes needed to sustain a filibuster, and keep the Masters nomination from coming to a vote. The day would call upon all Gage's stamina and guile; he must banish his concerns about the President, his qualms about Kyle Palmer, his worries about her father, sitting silently behind him.

Standing in the first row, Gage turned to speak to his colleagues. A piece of paper with scribbled notes lay on the varnished mahogany writing desk once used by Henry Clay. But he did not need prompting; he knew the points he wished to make, the passions he needed to arouse, and would simply let this flow. The only awkwardness lay in the first few sentences.

Reining in his tension, he turned toward Chad.

"Before I begin, I wish to note the presence of the senior senator from Ohio, who has come to discharge his public duties despite the personal tragedy which has befallen him." Now Gage faced Palmer directly. "To the condolences we've all expressed, I'd like to add your colleagues' admiration. You honor us, Senator Palmer, by being here."

Pausing, Gage hoped that the tone of welcome, the unfeigned note of sympathy, would reach his wounded rival; as always, but never more uncomfortably, his rivalry with Palmer was commingled with respect. Yet the only reaction he could detect was a faint smile so fleeting and ambiguous that Gage could not decipher it, followed by a look of surprising keenness from a man whose loss remained graven on his face.

Dismissing his worry, Gage turned to his wider audience, the senators and galleries. The silence was complete.

"The time has come," he told them, "to decide whether Judge Caroline Masters should preside over our nation's highest court.

"This is not a time for partisan speeches—our responsibilities are far too grave for that. Just how grave, I submit, the judge herself has made quite clear.

"The Tierney decision—Judge Masters's single most important ruling—tells us what to expect from her.

"It is an expression of judicial arrogance. It rejects the bipartisan will of Congress, and of the American people. It disregards the sanctity of life. It eschews the wisdom of the founding fathers in exchange for a radical philosophy in which judges know best—even when it comes to taking lives."

Abruptly, Gage's voice became quiet, mournful. "In the world of Caroline Masters, God alone knows who and what we will lose. Who among the innocent lives we have striven vainly to protect would find a cure for cancer, or bring peace to a grieving world. How many among them would give a family joy as children and, in the ripeness of time, love children of their own . . ."

.   .   .

In the conference room, Kerry Kilcannon watched intently.

"How many more children," Gage continued, *"however 'flawed' in the view of others, might remind us of our obligation, with a reward and richness all its own, to cherish those less fortunate . . ."*

The door to the conference room opened. Kit Pace appeared and placed a single piece of paper before the President.

Silently, he read it.

"Get this to Senator Hampton," the President directed.

Gage felt himself gaining momentum, his words and thoughts coursing with a passion added to their force. "And how many parents," he asked, "will be deprived of their right to participate in a minor's most important moral decision because Judge Masters—not the family—knows best?

"But I will say no more about this. For the reason to reject this nominee transcends her judicial philosophy, however inimical to our deepest religious, moral, and constitutional traditions. And, I might add, however offensive to her prospective colleagues on the Court."

With slow deliberation, Gage sought out his ultimate audience, the four undecided Republican moderates—Spencer James of Connecticut; Cassie Rollins of Maine; George Felton of Washington; and Clare MacIntire of Kansas—speaking to each of them in turn.

"In judging the personal life of another," he told Clare MacIntire, "one must exercise compassion and restraint. None of us is perfect; none of us entitled to cast the first stone. But when a judge's personal conduct also leads to questions regarding her reliability and truthfulness, we are entitled—we are *compelled*—to examine that conduct."

As he spoke, Senator MacIntire, small and dark, frowned and looked away—wondering, Gage expected, whether she could withstand a primary challenge funded by the Christian Commitment if she voted for Caroline Masters. Turning to Spencer James, Gage continued, "All of us, I'm sure, respect Judge Masters's personal decision that having a child out of wedlock is preferable to taking a child's life—even as we wish that her decision in the Tierney case did not reject this belief so cruelly and completely, in the name of a procedure so barbaric.

"But"—here Gage's voice rose sharply—"what do we say to all the young people on whom we urge abstinence and respect for marriage? What do we say to those we ask to reject the scourge of promiscuity and illegitimacy, youthful experimentation with drugs and alcohol, and the risk of sexually transmitted disease?"

Gage became conscious of how close this might cut to Chad Palmer's private anguish, the remembered pain of raising Kyle. A surreptitious glance revealed only Chad's stony gaze, directed not at Gage, but at some indeterminate middle distance. Gage decided to change his emphasis as smoothly as he could.

"What do we tell them," he asked, "about truthfulness? And *how* can we tell them that a woman who has concealed her past—which many of us deem perjurious—is fit to preside over a legal system based on the universal obligation to tell the truth when sworn to do so, 'so help me God'?"

Kit Pace entered the room again. Briefly glancing at the television, she murmured, "Hokey, but effective."

The President looked up. "Did you get to Hampton?"

"His Chief of Staff. He says Palmer's asked to make a statement. He wants to use Chuck's time."

"Do you know what for?"

Kit shook her head. "No one does. But Chuck could hardly refuse . . ."

"What do we tell them," Gage continued, *"about a judge who rules against the sanctity of life, and in favor of a close friend—the lawyer with whom, only a few weeks before, she shared a private dinner at her home . . ."*

Now Gage faced the galleries, conscious of the millions more who were watching. "In the end, with firmness and clarity, we must say this.

"That her philosophy is alien.

"That her misrepresentations are unworthy.

"That her judicial temperament is questionable.

"That her integrity is compromised.

"That she is *not* fit to be Chief Justice." Gage's voice rose once more. "That to insist on her confirmation is an act of imperiousness and carelessness from which it is our duty as senators—our solemn obligation—to protect the American people.

"The President should never have nominated her. He should never have persisted after all that we have learned. But he has." Pausing, Gage surveyed his colleagues. "And so it falls to us to tell him this: no man—or woman—is above the law. And no woman—or man—should exercise the power of law unless they are fit to do so."

With this, an oblique reference to Kerry's use of the FBI, Gage reached his peroration.

"This is a democracy, and we must face our obligations unafraid. We *must*, if we are men and women of integrity, reject this nominee."

Without more, Gage sat, to an outburst of applause from the galleries, which Ellen Penn gaveled to a ragged halt. He had done his part, he thought with satisfaction—no leader in his memory could have opened this debate as effectively as he just had.

"The Chair," Ellen Penn said crisply, "recognizes the Senior Senator from Illinois."

With his accustomed air of scholarly calm, Chuck Hampton slowly stood. But he must surely feel the tension of the moment, Gage reflected; it was the Minority Leader's duty to speak first on behalf of Caroline Masters.

"I would like to begin," Hampton said, "by reading a wire report from the Associated Press."

His listeners stirred with surprise and, in the case of Macdonald Gage, tension. "It is a statement," Hampton continued, "by Sarah Dash, attorney for Mary Ann Tierney."

Adjusting his glasses, Hampton commenced reading.

"*'This morning, Mary Ann Tierney underwent the procedure to terminate her pregnancy, to protect her ability to have children in the future.*

"*'That procedure is now complete. The attending physician, Dr. Mark Flom, confirms that the fetus had no cerebral development, and no hope of surviving . . .'*"

There were murmurs from the galleries; in consternation, Gage glanced at Clare MacIntire, and saw her rapt attention as Hampton read on.

"*'To further establish the medical facts, we have requested the performance of an autopsy.*

"*'As for Mary Ann Tierney, the procedure was successful. Her capacity to bear children is no longer at risk. For this, we are grateful to the American judicial system, without which she would not have been free to make this difficult—but plainly justified—decision . . .'*"

Breaking the tension, Kerry Kilcannon laughed aloud.

"That should give Gage pause," he said to Clayton. "Did *you* tell her to say all that?"

Clayton shook his head. "No. Dash did it on her own."

"*'Until further notice,'*" Hampton read, "*'Mary Ann has nothing more to say. Her deepest wish is to regain, as much as possible, what she never should have lost: her privacy.'*"

. . .

How, Gage wondered, would Hampton choose to follow this?

Looking up, Hampton said, "The statement speaks for itself. I have nothing more to add."

He paused, seeming to draw a breath. "At this point," he said in a quiet tone, "I yield the floor to my good friend, the Senior Senator from Ohio."

Stunned, Macdonald Gage was powerless to intervene. To the rising cacophony of the galleries, stilled at last by Ellen Penn, Chad Palmer rose to speak.

Thirty

Chad Palmer surveyed his colleagues: Chuck Hampton, openly wondering what Chad intended; Paul Harshman, staring implacably at Chad with his arms folded; his friend Kate Jarman, her face tight with worry. But it was the sight of Macdonald Gage, arranging his features into an expression of beneficence, which turned Chad's anguish into the cold resolve he needed to begin.

"I hope the Senate will indulge me," he began, "while I speak of my daughter's death."

The hush around him deepened. His colleagues looked on with sorrow, tension, alarm, and as though worried that, in his grief, Chad might spin out of control, or perhaps break down entirely. But Gage managed to affect a melancholy calm.

"You know by now," Chad continued, "much of what Kyle lived through. Many of you have faced sorrows too private to share. So it was with Kyle. But only her mother and I can know the depth of her depression, her despair, a self-contempt so searing that often she could not face the world without dulling her own pain.

"Only we can know how hard her mother fought just to keep our daughter alive.

"Only we can know the days and nights, the months and years, her mother clung to hope where there was no hope." Briefly, Chad stopped, his voice choked, and then he stood straighter. "Only we could know the joy we felt when Kyle emerged from darkness.

"Only we could know the rewards of seeing her grow stronger. Above all, only we could know the joy of being able to imagine her with a family of her own."

"You were never *meant* to know this. Nor, any longer, can we."

Looking around him, Chad saw his colleagues' heads bowing, faces fur-

rowed with sympathy. "Her life," Chad continued, "and our dreams for her, vanished in a day—the day that callous and immoral men decided that the private
trauma of a sixteen-year-old girl should be used to destroy her father." Pausing,
Chad spoke more softly yet. "They accomplished too much, and too little. For
Kyle is dead, and I am here. And I know who they are."

Skin clammy, Gage waited. He could sense the fury just below Palmer's tenuous
calm; his fellow senators were transfixed, as though they could not look away.

"They are not within the media," Palmer told his colleagues. "The media
did not steal the consent form from her doctor's files. Nor did the media send it
to a pro-choice leader, hoping *she* would expose as a pro-life 'hypocrite' the
father who remained silent to protect his daughter . . ."

So *that*, Gage thought, was where Taylor had begun. Once again he felt the
visceral fear which had made him avoid Mace Taylor for the last four days, afraid
of what he might learn. "Instead," Chad said with muted irony, "*she* brought it
to the President. None of them imagined, I suppose, that he'd give the document to me.

"'*Take care of your family,*' the President told me. But it was too late." Chad's
voice became muffled, thick with emotion. "Those determined to ruin me gave
a copy of the form to the *Internet Frontier,* and then to Charlie Trask. Within
hours, our daughter was dead."

Glancing about him, Gage saw Kate Jarman gaze at Chad, eyes filled with
sorrow. "Those two copies," Chad said bluntly, "killed her. And, like the envelope delivered to the President, they have been examined by the FBI.

"The President has provided me with the FBI's report, prepared at his direction."

Shocked, Gage felt his throat and stomach constrict. The tension in the
galleries, long suppressed, released itself in a murmur that the Vice President
did not rebuke. Palmer looked down, palms flat on his desk, struggling for
self-control; when he raised his head, his voice trembled with anger.

"By tradition," he continued, "a senator must refrain from attacking other
senators. But no rule protects the past member of this body whose fingerprints
appear on all three documents." Turning, Palmer surveyed the astonished faces
of his colleagues, then said with a chilling mockery of decorum, "Our distinguished former colleague, the Junior Senator from Oklahoma. Senator Mason
Taylor."

The involuntary spasms of noise around him—murmurs, muttered exclamations, a low, almost reverent, "Jesus" from Leo Weller—seemed to come to
Gage from a distance. And then, at last, Palmer turned to face him.

"All of us," he told the Senate, "know Mason Taylor all too well. And so we know the *other* man who is responsible for Kyle's death . . ."

Facing Macdonald Gage, Chad felt the release of emotions as a physical ache. Gage looked back with a stoic resolve; he surely knew that any protest he might make would get no sympathy from Ellen Penn. Despite his fury, Chad forced himself to remain still, until he was certain that the full Senate saw whom he addressed. When he spoke, it was with a terrible softness.

"All of us know," he said to Gage, "who does Taylor's bidding, whose power derives from Taylor's influence, whose ambitions to be President depend on pleasing Taylor's clients." Pausing, Palmer let Gage suffer in the stricken hush. "And all of us know whose aspirations I seemed to threaten, a few short days ago . . ."

Watching, the President felt a silent awe at what he had unleashed.

"*I do not yet know,*" Chad said with grief and anger, "*what punishment he will suffer, in this life or the next. But it is fitting that, from this day forward, every senator who greets him will think of Kyle Palmer . . .*"

"Will they believe him?" Kit Pace asked the President.

Slowly, Kerry nodded. "Most will. The question is what Chad does with that."

On the screen, Chad Palmer's silent stare at Gage was an indictment. Then, with a renewed calm which Kerry knew must cost him dearly, Chad turned, speaking to the others.

"*But I am not here,*" he told them, "*to ask you to mourn my daughter. I will do that, in my own way, for the rest of my life, hour upon hour, as I wonder at the pride and folly which impelled me to ignore the terrible risk to her of continuing in public life . . .*"

Stricken, Gage felt a tide of emotion overtake the Senate, and knew that Palmer—for all his grief—had aroused his colleagues' passions so that he could redirect them. Chad Palmer not only meant them to mourn his daughter; he meant to use her to whatever end he chose.

"Rather," Palmer continued, "I am here to address the Masters nomination, and to ask what we have come to.

"No more can we claim that our politics is simply about ideas, or values, or the clash of competing interests. All too often it is about money—the elegant system of quasi-bribery in which those who finance our campaigns become our stockholders, and men like Mason Taylor demand results." The naked anger returned to Chad's voice. "And if 'results' means ruining whoever stands in the way—for whatever private frailty they can ferret out—then they will use the media to destroy any one of us, and then the next, until the cycle of destruction, turning each of us upon the other, at last drives all decency from public life. And if their aims require a few 'civilian casualties,' they will provide *those*, too."

Chad stopped abruptly, his efforts to control himself palpable. "My daughter," he said more evenly, "is not the only victim, merely the latest and most tragic. In the course of this nomination, this twisted tactic has followed two other women—Mary Ann Tierney and Caroline Masters—into the most private area of their lives: whether to bear a child."

At this, Gage saw, Paul Harshman stared at Palmer, resistant. But others, when Gage turned to them, refused to meet his eyes.

"All three women," Palmer continued, "faced decisions which were painfully individual. Within my own family, we learned how complex that decision can be, how prone to disagreement, how difficult to face."

With this admission, delivered with a softness which drew in the Senate and the galleries, Palmer turned to his party colleagues. "Caroline Masters," he told them, "faced it twice. Once as a young woman and then, half a lifetime later, as a judge.

"In the Tierney case, I disagree with her conclusions. But I must admit to doubts forced on us by Kyle's personal experience. And to one certainty: that our dialogue on abortion—of which I have been part—is rife with dishonesty, distortion, and deception." Chad's voice lowered. "That deception, I believe, pervades the opposition to Judge Masters—distorting the reasons for, and frequency of, late-term abortion. And I fear that this dishonesty will continue as long as abortion is a political, rather than an ethical, debate . . ."

He's done for, Gage thought. But now the battle for his own survival had begun, and perhaps would end, with the vote on Caroline Masters.

For the first time, Chad saw, Kate Jarman gave him a nod of encouragement. It lent him hope; Kate must sense where he was going.

"I believe in our party," Chad said. "We are *not*, by tradition, the party of rule-makers. We are *not* the party of intolerance. We do not believe that government should police us in our private lives. And so, however we view the Tierney case, we should give Judge Masters her due.

"Her decision placed her own privacy at risk. It placed her crowning ambition in doubt. It placed her reputation in the hands of others." Turning to Gage, he spoke with disdain. "It exposed them for who they are, and Judge Masters for who she is. And it places this single ruling in the context of a worthy life."

Now, like Gage before him, he searched the faces of his wavering colleagues—Clare MacIntire, George Felton, Spencer James, and Cassie Rollins. "The Tierney case was complex," he continued. "But our choice today is much clearer. It is between integrity and immorality. It is, for me, a choice between a woman of honor and those who sacrificed my daughter."

In the taut silence, Chad gathered his thoughts. *Yes,* he imagined telling Kyle, *I'm almost done. I hope you approve of me now.*

"Others," he told the Senate, "will say their piece. But once they have, I will move to close debate. And then I will vote to confirm Judge Caroline Masters as Chief Justice of the United States."

For perhaps the last time, the senior senator from Ohio, once so near the presidency, held his colleagues in thrall. "My vote for Caroline Masters," he finished quietly, "will be my final vote in this body. I will be honored if you join me."

Exhausted, Chad sat.

He stared at his desk, thinking of Kyle, then Allie. Gradually, he heard the applause rising from the galleries, then the slow movement of chairs and bodies as a number of his colleagues stood to applaud, until all of the Democrats, and most Republicans, were standing, though for some it was a reluctant act of courtesy. When Gage faced him, still sitting, Chad's lips formed a small and bitter smile.

As the applause began dying, slowly and at last, Gage turned from him, seeking the attention of the chair. His voice was flat, strained. "Madam Vice President, I ask for a recess by unanimous consent . . ."

"For what?" Speaking from his desk, Chad's voice was quiet but audible. "There's nowhere left to hide, Mac."

Above them, Ellen Penn's face was drained of all expression. "The Senate," she said, "will stand in recess until one-thirty." With this, galleries broke into an uproar, above the senators who sat looking in silence from Chad Palmer to Macdonald Gage.

Thirty-one

The next morning, in the news summary Kit Pace gave the President, headlines battled for preeminence: "Tierney Fetus Doomed, Doctor Reports"; "Palmer Resigns, Accusing Gage in Daughter's Death"; "FBI Report Identifies Lobbyist in Leak of Files"; "Gage Charges President with 'Police-State' Tactics"; "Masters Nomination Hangs in Balance." Editorial response was equally varied: ruminations on Mary Ann Tierney's abortion and its meaning; reflections on the degraded state of politics; fulminations for or against Caroline Masters; criticisms of Kerry's use of the FBI. "While we deplore," the *Times* declared, "the tactics suggested by the report, the President's extraconstitutional abuse of the FBI is even more alarming."

"They've found me out," the President said to Clayton, "a tyrant in the making. You'd think they'd have noticed sooner."

In truth, Kerry did not care much, nor did he have time to care. The debate which had resumed in the afternoon, listless and subdued, suggested nothing so much as confusion. So Kerry had manned the phones, as he did this morning, strategizing with Chuck Hampton and pulling undecided senators off the floor. "You can't stall this now," he had said bluntly to Spencer Jones. "A filibuster would be spitting on Kyle Palmer's grave."

He did not thank Chad. He did not need to.

"Don't say a word," Gage said to Mason Taylor. "There's no crime been committed, whatever Palmer and Kilcannon think happened. There's nothing they can do to you."

There was a long silence on the other end of the line. "The little bastard's trying to ruin me," Taylor said softly. "I need friends, Mac. Loyal friends."

Gage's jaw tightened. "You have them, believe me. Just hang tough, and give it time. In six months . . ."

"You'll call me? You need me now, Mac."

It was nine o'clock and there was sweat beneath Gage's armpits. "Let me handle this," he snapped. "*You* need *me,* too."

"Then we both need to win, don't we."

With this, Gage hung up.

Swiftly, he began to calculate. With Palmer's defection, the vote stood—as near as Gage could tell in the confusion—at forty-eight to forty-eight, with the four undecideds frozen by Palmer's speech. But he felt the support for a filibuster eroding beneath him: a new hesitance here; a refusal to commit there; a plea for time to think, or to let emotions subside; a comment that, whatever the merits, the condition of the fetus deprived Gage of the ideological passion needed to refuse Caroline Masters a vote by the full Senate. Palmer had filed a petition to close debate.

Still, there were countless factors which might swing a final vote toward Gage: sincere conviction; pressures from constituents and interest groups; the promise of campaign funds; fear of a primary challenge from the right; dislike for the President; the favors or punishments Gage had at his disposal. But he sensed that, for once, his colleagues feared Kilcannon almost as much as they did Gage himself: not only for the President's ruthlessness, but also for his resourcefulness. They did not want to be standing too close to Gage if Kilcannon proved that Kyle Palmer's death involved him.

The problem was, they *believed* Palmer—not that Gage had imagined she would die, but that Gage knew what Taylor had planned. And Kyle Palmer's death made too many of them squeamish. As Gage discovered when he called Clare MacIntire.

"I had *nothing* to do with this," he insisted. "This is guilt by association."

"I'm sure it is, Mac. But we have to be careful what we're associated *with.*"

"Abortion? Promiscuity? A president who thinks the FBI's his personal Gestapo?"

"Dead girls," Clare answered flatly. "There are sentimentalists who think that puts the rest in a certain perspective. So have a care." Clare paused. "I still don't know how I'll vote. With all this static, I'm trying to stick to the merits."

"Within our party," Gage rejoined, "the merits are pretty clear."

"They were," Clare said thoughtfully.

"Then give me a little more time," Gage urged. "Let Paul stall this, until emotions simmer down."

Clare hesitated. "I'll think about it, Mac. That much, I promise. But nothing more."

Putting down the telephone, Gage could only hope the pressure campaign organized by the Christian Commitment and its allies—faxes, calls, and mail from Clare's prominent supporters in Kansas—would force her into line.

He punched another button, and dialed Spencer James.

At ten o'clock, as Kerry watched on C-SPAN, the Senate debate resumed. For several hours, the speeches continued, one senator after another recapitulating his past position. Yet beneath the surface, there was change.

"The filibuster's evaporating," Chuck Hampton called to say. "I think we'll get our vote."

Shortly before two, Gage pulled Harshman into the cloakroom. "The support for a filibuster's slipping away," Gage said, "I can feel it. If we lose big there, it could hurt us on the final vote."

To Gage's surprise and irritation, Harshman regarded him with something close to contempt. "Chad Palmer," he retorted, "isn't the only senator with principles. I have mine."

By four o'clock, as Kerry watched, all but the four undecideds and Kate Jarman had spoken to the merits of the Masters nomination. Kerry's vote count stood forty-eight to forty-eight when Spencer James yielded to Harshman.

"*It is time,*" Harshman declared, "*to take a deep breath, to sort out reason from emotions. It is time, in candor, to remember that we are grieving for Kyle Palmer, not Caroline Masters.*" His voice rose in contempt. "*It is time to distinguish between an inadvertent tragedy—for which, I am assured, no one here bears responsibility—and a deliberate abuse of power by a president who would intimidate the Senate and its leaders and place us on the road to a police state . . .*"

"Let's have him audited," the President said dryly. "I want to know how much he gives to charity."

The mild joke defused, if only for a moment, the tension in the conference room. Around him, Clayton, Kit, and Adam Shaw smiled but continued to watch.

"I wonder what Palmer's thinking," Clayton murmured.

. . .

Watching Harshman, Chad wavered between anger and fatigue. The night before, sleepless, he had held his grieving wife; now he must listen to this petty, narrow man flaunt his poverty of spirit.

"Only debate," Harshman said sternly, "*extended* debate, and the reflection which it allows us, is worthy of this great deliberative body. This *independent* body, no matter what the President might think.

"We are senators, not servants. We represent our people. And our people do not want us—in a matter so vital to our future and our very moral character—to be rushed to judgment by fear, *or* sorrow, *or* pity.

"We are senators, and the Senate, in its own good time, must work its will."

Shooting Chad a brief look of challenge, Harshman sat to applause from the opponents of Caroline Masters who still crowded the Senate gallery. As Ellen Penn gaveled for silence, Chad caught Kate Jarman's eye, and nodded.

The Vice President, awaiting this, said at once, "The Chair recognizes the Junior Senator from Vermont."

Kate Jarman stood. "There is much I could say," she told her colleagues. "But I will not. I yield to Senator Palmer."

Slowly, Chad rose, gaze sweeping his colleagues and resting last on Harshman, then Gage, the Majority Leader expressionless save for narrowed eyes.

"Indeed," Chad began, "we *are* senators. And most of us are worthy of the name.

"The Majority Leader assures us that the actions of Mason Taylor are a mystery to him. Senator Harshman tells us that this nomination should not be decided on sentiments like grief or shame or anger. I suggest another: self-respect.

"*That* sentiment may not be important to all one hundred of us. But among the great majority, I suspect there will be considerable aversion to hiding behind a filibuster." Pausing, Chad spoke softly. "It is time. Enough has been said, and far too much has been done. We should do what our constituents sent us to do—vote."

With this, Ellen Penn called—as scheduled—for a vote on Chad's petition to close debate.

He sat, foreseeing the outcome. He had made some calls of his own.

"Nice," the President said to Chuck Hampton. "What's the count?"

On the other end, Hampton's voice was muffled; Kerry imagined him in the cloakroom, hunkered in the corner. "To sustain a filibuster? I don't think they've got more than thirty. The only problem is *that* may be their way of having it *both* ways. As far as I know, we've got only forty-eight to actually confirm."

The President thought briefly. "Get me Kate Jarman," he said.

On C-SPAN, the vote to close debate proceeded.

"Mr. Harshman."

"No."

"Mr. Izzo."

"Yes."

"Mr. Jones."

"Yes."

"Ms. MacIntire."

"Yes."

As the total vote reached fifty, the tally on the screen stood at twenty-nine yes's, twenty-one no's. The President experienced a flash of doubt—out of the next fifty votes, he needed thirty-one yes's to reach sixty and close debate.

And then came a string of yes's.

"Mr. Nehlen."

"Yes."

"Mr. Palmer."

Chad, smiling slightly, said, *"Yes."*

The sixty-first "yes," when it came, belonged to an undecided moderate, Cassie Rollins.

"All right," Clayton murmured.

Waiting for Kate Jarman, the President continued to watch. The last vote, giving Chad's motion a total of seventy-one, belonged to Leo Weller.

"I overpaid for *that* one," Kerry observed. "Imagine all those cows, roaming our national parklands."

The telephone rang.

"Hello, Kate," the President said.

"Good afternoon," she answered. "Are you calling to make a decent woman of me, Mr. President?"

Kerry laughed. "I live in hope, Kate. One decent woman deserves another."

In San Francisco, Caroline Masters watched in her penthouse, with Blair Montgomery.

"Thank God for Senator Palmer," Blair said.

But Caroline did not answer—she was too tense. And it was hard to be grateful for what had brought Chad Palmer to this moment.

"Stuck at forty-eight votes to confirm," she murmured. "After all of this."

Kerry put down the telephone. "Kate's waiting," he told Clayton. "Get me to Clare MacIntire."

On the screen, Ellen Penn announced, *"The pending business is the nomination of Judge Caroline Clark Masters to be Chief Justice. The question is, Will the Senate advise and consent to this nomination? The aye's and nay's have been ordered, and the clerk will call the roll."*

"Mr. Allen."

"No."

"Mr. Azoff."

"Yes."

"Ms. Baltry."

"Yes."

Inexorably, the fateful count proceeded, and then the telephone rang.

On the floor, Chad watched the votes fall out, governed by a range of factors from the noble to the crass, the magisterial to the parochial. The first undecided, George Felton, gave him a brief glance of apology, and then looked away.

"No."

Hands folded in front of his belly, Gage nodded in satisfaction. Briefly, Chad shut his eyes.

"Mr. Izzo."

"No."

All Gage needed, Chad realized, was one more vote, and Ellen Penn could not break a tie. From the chair, Ellen gazed down at Kate Jarman.

"Ms. Jarman."

Kate remained sitting, with an inward expression, as though pretending to ignore the tension. To the astonishment of the galleries, she remained silent until the roll call moved on.

Having postponed her vote, she briefly closed her eyes.

Amidst a collective expulsion of breath, the vote proceeded on, the yes's and no's falling into line again.

"Ms. MacIntire," the clerk called out.

. . .

Tense, Gage watched her. One more "no" and it was done.

Hands folded in front of her, Clare MacIntire hesitated, her small dark person the focus of a vast silence.

"Yes," she said firmly.

"Yes," Adam Shaw said under his breath; Kit Pace pumped her fist in the air.

"What did you give her?" Clayton asked the President. "The heavens and earth?"

"Nothing. It seems she despises Gage."

Once more, the vote resumed its inexorable path toward the last undecided, Cassie Rollins. Chad faced her, raising his eyebrows.

This morning, they had met alone.

"I'll miss you," Cassie said. "I wish you weren't going."

It touched him. "You understand, Cassie."

She nodded. "I do. We all do." Then, to his surprise, she smiled a little. "You want my vote, of course. Problem is, what can you do for me once you're gone?"

Chad did not answer. "You know Gage did it, Cassie."

"I don't know that for sure. But I know we should do better." She smiled again. "Consider this a going-away present . . ."

"Ms. Rollins?" the clerk called.

Cassie stood, tall and blond, looking like the former tennis star she was. "*Yes*," she called out, and smiled at Chad Palmer.

Quickly, Gage rose and walked toward Kate Jarman's desk. Kate sat, arms folded, as the roll call ground on toward its inevitable conclusion, save for Kate—fifty no's, forty-nine yes's.

When Gage reached her side, she did not appear to notice him. Touching her shoulder, he whispered, "Kate?"

She looked up at him, eyes cold. "You lose," she said.

Chad watched the roll call reach its end.

Kate Jarman stood. "Madam President?"

Ellen Penn nodded. "The Chair recognizes the Junior Senator from Vermont."

Now Kate Jarman was the focus of an awesome silence. "On the roll call just concluded," Kate asked, "how am I recorded?"

"You are not recorded."

As had Cassie Rollins, Kate Jarman turned to Chad. "I now wish to vote *yes.*"

A deep murmur rose from the gallery. On the floor, senators turned to one another, absorbing what had happened. Only Macdonald Gage was still.

But Chad no longer saw him. Instead he recalled his daughter on their last evening together, filled with hope as she showed her mother and father her portfolio . . .

The Vice President cracked her ivory gavel, returning him to the present.

"The Chair," she said with barely concealed emotion, "votes yes."

Conscious of a moment passing into history, the Vice President paused.

"On this vote," she announced, "the aye's are fifty-one, the nay's are fifty, and the Senate does advise and consent to the nomination of Caroline Clark Masters."

Caroline bent forward, hands covering her eyes. She felt Blair Montgomery's arm around her shoulder.

"You made it," he said. "Was there ever a doubt?"

Whooping, laughing, all speaking at once, the others clustered around the President.

As Kerry stood, Kit embraced him, then Adam Shaw, seized by a sense of moment, solemnly shook his hand. "You just changed the Court, Mr. President."

Kerry smiled. "As I remember, that was the original idea."

He turned to Clayton. Tentative, Clayton touched his shoulder. "Congratulations, Mr. President. You did it."

Others, the President knew, would be waiting in the Oval Office, and he should call the new Chief Justice at once. But he paused for Clayton—for all that had happened, his friend. Softly, he said, "*We* did it, pal. It just took sorting out."

For the first time in weeks, Clayton's guard slipped, and his eyes misted. Quickly, he became stoic. "How should we react?" he asked.

Kerry paused, remembering all he had risked, feeling at last the release of pressure. Then he grinned. "I think it's time for a victory statement in the Rose Garden. The first of many."

"What will you say?"

"That it's a triumph for democracy." Though he smiled, Kerry's voice was quiet again. "Then I'll take some questions. Just enough to crucify Macdonald Gage."

Thirty-two

Tensely waiting with Mary Ann for Martin Tierney, Sarah thought of the first time they had met.

The girl sat rigidly on Sarah's couch. Sarah was not yet used to Mary Ann's comparative slimness, her absence of a belly. Nor, at times, did Mary Ann seem accustomed to it.

"How could I have stood it," she had asked Sarah the night before, "if the baby had been normal?"

Sarah had no answer. But, for the most part, Mary Ann was determined to see herself as right; the outcome of her abortion, Sarah sensed, had changed the balance between Mary Ann and her parents.

"I've talked to your father," Sarah had told her the day before. "They want you to come back."

That was when Mary Ann had asked about the baby.

Now, though, she waited for them. And what else could she do? She had been inundated with offers of help—scholarships, places to live, even offers of adoption. But from strangers. These were her parents, and she was fifteen; in her heart and mind she had nowhere else to go. And so Sarah had not acknowledged that she had asked Martin Tierney what *he* would have done.

There was a brief silence. "Love her," he said quietly. "As before."

But he did not sound convinced—such had been his commitment, at any costs, to preserve his grandson's life. "Still," Sarah said, "you must feel relieved."

This time the silence was far longer. "In some ways," he conceded, "it's better. It's better for all of us. But the outcome will be used to justify late-term abortion. You've already used it, and so has the President, to salvage Caroline Masters. I fear it's opened the floodgates."

"That was the chance you took," Sarah said bluntly, "when you decided to take chances with Mary Ann."

Tierney sighed audibly. "We'll never reconcile our worldviews. So let's not try."

After all the conflict, Sarah thought, nothing between them had changed. "What *did* we learn from this?" she asked.

"Nothing," he answered. "Nothing we didn't already know. We just know different things, and always will."

And so Mary Ann and Sarah attempted desultory chatter until, at last, the buzzer sounded, and Sarah pressed the security button to open the main door. As she did, she was overwhelmed by doubt—whether Mary Ann and her parents could truly reconcile their differences, whether reentering their home would damage her still further, whether parents or child would ever regain their privacy.

Glancing out the window, she saw no reporters on the sidewalk. This much was good: Mary Ann seemed as determined as Sarah not to speak of this in public, to reclaim what normal life she could. The outcome, confirmed by autopsy, was enough for her; Sarah's decision to help the President and Caroline had, to her relief, helped Mary Ann as well.

Turning, Sarah looked at her, poised on the edge of the couch with her suitcase packed beside it, and thought again of how terribly young she was. And, once more, of the first day they had met.

"Well," Sarah said, "we've gone through the worst part."

Seconds from her father's arrival at Sarah's door, Mary Ann looked ever more apprehensive. "I'm still going through it."

This was true, Sarah acknowledged, and there now was little Sarah could do. The doorbell rang.

Quickly, the girl stood, her face tight with anxiety. Sarah embraced her. "I hope it'll be okay," Mary Ann murmured.

Sarah paused for a moment, flooded with her own doubt. "Call me," she said. "Once things settle down."

Mary Ann leaned back, tears filling her eyes. "I love you, Sarah."

Choked with emotion, Sarah held her tight. Then, managing to smile, she released Mary Ann and went to open the door.

Martin Tierney stood there, hands folded in front of him. How strange this must be, Sarah thought: however he felt, his daughter had suffered a trauma, and he had not been at the hospital. Now he gazed past Sarah at his daughter.

"Mary Ann?" It was spoken with such uncertainty that he seemed to question whether she would come with him.

Tentative, she stepped forward.

Her father glanced toward the suitcase. "Is that all you have?"

"Yes." Mary Ann hesitated. "My normal clothes are still at home."

And a normal life, Sarah could only hope.

Martin Tierney picked up the suitcase. "Are you all right?" he asked his daughter.

"Yes. I'm all right."

"Then let's go."

He still had not touched her, nor she him, and Margaret Tierney was not here. The Protection of Life Act, Sarah thought with renewed bitterness, had done its work well. Then, with an uncertainty close to deference, Martin Tierney took his daughter's arm.

Facing Sarah, he merely nodded. Sarah realized that she still hoped for some understanding between them, a clearing of the air, even as she realized that this was not to be. So to Martin Tierney she said nothing. To Mary Ann she repeated, "Whenever you want to, you can call."

The girl seemed to freeze, caught between Sarah and her parents for the last time. And then she smiled, a small, sad movement of the lips, and went with her father.

Sarah watched them from a window, feeling far less relief than she had imagined at the loosening of the bonds which, for seemingly endless weeks, had left her with no other life, and had surely changed the one she had before.

Martin Tierney grasped the suitcase in one hand; the other lightly touched his daughter's elbow. They stopped by a blue Volvo. To Sarah's surprise, the front passenger door opened, and Margaret Tierney got out.

On the sidewalk, Mary Ann was still. Then her mother's encircling arms lightly cradled her shoulder blades. Her forehead touched Mary Ann's.

After a moment, Mary Ann got in the back seat, and the blue Volvo disappeared. Tears came to Sarah's eyes.

But she was free.

Alone, she considered the question which, only in the last few days, had begun to emerge from her subconscious: What now?

The immediate answer was that, tonight, friends she had hardly seen in all this time were taking her out to celebrate; tomorrow, other friends from the firm were having a party at which, she was humorously assured, John Nolan and the executive committee would appear to give her an award. The meaning of the joke was clear: in her accomplishment—and, yes, her fame—Sarah had transcended caring.

She was twenty-nine, a lawyer barely long enough to sign her own brief in the Supreme Court, and she had achieved what most lawyers never would.

She was *free*—and now was free to consider what that meant. It did not, she imagined, likely mean pursuing a partnership at Kenyon & Walker. Somewhere in the last two months, she had realized that the burdens of the Tierney case had obscured the blessings of representing what she believed in.

Perhaps *that* was what this meant to her. She would not, she suspected, ever become a judge; she had made herself too controversial too early. But there was much else she could do: in time, Clayton Slade had intimated, there might be a place at the White House—the President admired her abilities.

Sarah had smiled to herself: she had learned enough to perceive this as seduction—the Chief of Staff had wanted something. But perhaps it was real, as well, and in any case this hardly mattered; regardless of the future, Kerry Kilcannon had turned out to be a president worth helping.

One thing she was sure of. F. Scott Fitzgerald was wrong: there *are* second acts in American lives—and *third* acts, and a thousand permutations in between. Whatever befell her, Sarah believed that she could face it with serenity.

All this, she thought, because of a fifteen-year-old girl.

Thirty-three

Late that afternoon, Macdonald Gage awaited three colleagues who had asked to meet with him in privacy.

For twenty-four hours, Kerry Kilcannon's victory had dominated the news—most strikingly, his impromptu press conference in the Rose Garden. Though by now Gage could have recited much of it from memory, he found himself intently watching clips of Kilcannon's performance on CNN's *Inside Politics*.

The President looked fresh, invigorated. He had begun with the expected: that the confirmation of Caroline Masters had "reasserted the independence of the judiciary by placing integrity above politics." Only when the questions began did his hidden purpose emerge.

"You've been severely criticized," Sam Donaldson called out, "for abusing the investigative powers of the FBI. Wasn't its seizure of documents allegedly passed on by former Senator Taylor a raid in search of a crime?"

In close-up, Kilcannon looked expectant and, Gage thought, faintly amused. "Let's start with what we *know* happened. First, Kyle Palmer's consent form was illegally stolen, violating her right to privacy. Second, three copies of that form were leaked; on each copy, Mason Taylor's prints appear.

"*That*," Kilcannon said with palpable contempt, "is not merely despicable. It is not only the predicate for her death. It suggests a conspiracy to violate Kyle Palmer's civil rights—which is a federal crime.

"I've asked the Justice Department to determine who else may have engaged in this conspiracy and, if warranted, to seek indictments." Kilcannon's eyes were cold, his voice quiet. "I won't forget Kyle Palmer. Before those we've identified try to conceal the involvement of others, they should remember that."

"Does 'others' refer to Senator Gage?" Kelly Wallace of CNN inquired.

The President shrugged slightly. "I'm referring to anyone involved. Whoever they may be."

"But do you think he should remain as Majority Leader?"

The President smiled slightly. "I don't presume to know the results of the Justice Department inquiry, and I certainly don't propose to tell my Republican friends in the Senate who should or should not lead them." Pausing, Kilcannon seemed—or, Gage was certain, pretended—to search for words. "I will simply say this," he finished. "Anyone involved in the death of Kyle Palmer will not be welcome here."

Gage flipped off the television.

It was a made-up crime, he thought angrily—two of the smartest lawyers in Washington had told him it was a stretch, that "conspiracy" was a ruthless prosecutor's way of casting the widest possible net. But in the last twenty-four hours Mace Taylor had not returned his calls.

Fretful, he dialed Taylor again.

Nothing.

Slamming down the telephone, Gage began to pace. He had not *known* what Taylor would do—let alone when or how. His awareness of what *Taylor* knew, and that sooner or later he would use it, did not amount to complicity— let alone "conspiracy." And it was in Taylor's professional interests not to implicate anyone else.

But Taylor *could,* if Kilcannon scared him enough. Taylor could trade Gage for a deal, or for immunity, by lying about Gage's role; the government could not win such a case, but it might leave an imperishable stain. Once more, he regretted his decision to accept Mace Taylor's help, reprised his own well-judged concern that Taylor's methods would entwine him.

Taylor's and—he belatedly realized—Kilcannon's.

"This town," Chad Palmer had told him, *"may wind up littered with the bodies of people who've underrated Kerry Kilcannon."*

All day Gage had heard rumblings—meetings which did not include him; rumors of unrest about which the Majority Whip, his second in command, was dismissive; stories, even, of calls to and from the White House. And now he waited for his visitors: Leo Weller, Paul Harshman, and Kate Jarman.

They were an odd assortment—Weller, a traditional conservative; Harshman, a firebrand with a narrow but zealous following among his peers; Jarman, a representative of the party's embattled moderates. That anything united them enough to request a meeting was worrisome indeed.

Composing himself, Gage called on all his reserves of wisdom and calculation.

Entering, Gage noted with apprehension, they seemed awkward. Harshman did not attempt to smile; Weller's smile was feigned to the point of ghastliness; Kate Jarman was quiet—waiting for someone else to take the lead. With a minimum of small talk, they sat, Kate and Harshman glancing toward Leo Weller.

Weller's twinkling good cheer vanished, replaced by a cool gray-eyed gaze better known to Gage than to the voters of Montana. "I guess you know why we're here," Weller said.

"I have no idea." Gage was pleased that, even now, his tone combined a casual air with a tone of cold command. "Yesterday we lost in the Senate by a single vote. Today Kilcannon's having his little moment. It hardly seems worth a deputation, with all of you as grave as a mortician at grandma's funeral."

"The funeral," Kate Jarman interjected tartly, "is Kyle Palmer's."

"Which I had nothing to do with." Gage bit off his words. "Where's your spine, Kate? Kilcannon's smearing us . . ."

"He's smearing *you*." This time it was Harshman. "As did Palmer, to considerable effect."

"Palmer," Gage snapped. "He talks about the 'cycle of destruction,' while he and Kilcannon conspire to destroy us. That's the only 'conspiracy,' and all of us have to stand up to it."

"Define 'us.'" Leo Weller's voice was melancholy but reasoned. "I'm sure you're right, Mac—Kilcannon's taken your relationship to Taylor, and twisted it. But that worries folks nonetheless."

"Taylor represents a lot of people who're important to us, from the Christian Commitment to the pro-gun folks. Somehow, some way, he funds private investigations that maybe—out of anyone's sight—have crossed a few lines." Weller glanced at Harshman. "Paul's been hearing from our base—political and financial. They don't want Taylor leaned on. They don't want to be tarred with whatever he's done. They want this to go away."

"Speaking of our 'base,'" Kate Jarman said with some distaste, "there's another group I wish *were* part of it—suburban women. They don't like us on abortion, and they don't like us on guns."

"How to put this delicately, Mac. To be seen as destroying the daughter of one of our own, over a legal abortion which should have been private, is not a positive development."

She blamed him, Gage thought angrily. Still composed, he said to Harshman, "We took a stand on principle."

"Against abortion," Harshman said sternly. "Against liberalism, license, and lying. After Kyle Palmer's death, all of that got lost."

Weller summoned his avuncular air. "It may be unfair. But this particular dead mouse, my friend, is lying on your kitchen floor. Folks don't want Taylor indicted."

"What can I do about *that*?"

With this, the others looked to Weller.

"Resign," Weller said at last. His tone was quiet, reluctant. "It's a lot to ask, and all of us hate to ask it. But you don't have the votes to stay."

"And it's for the good of the party, Mac. We believe if you go now, Kilcannon may back off the rest."

So that was it, Gage realized. They had *talked* to Kerry Kilcannon—or, more likely, Clayton Slade. You almost had to laugh.

The little bastard had gotten him.

The next morning, Senator Macdonald Gage's press secretary released a short statement, again deploring the death of Kyle Palmer, denying any involvement in the events preceding it, and resigning as Majority Leader for the sake of the party he held dear.

Thirty-four

On the morning she was to be sworn in as Chief Justice, Caroline Masters and her daughter had breakfast in Caroline's suite at the Hay-Adams.

Later, Jackson Watts would join them, and Blair Montgomery. But both women wanted these few moments alone.

"Two months ago," Caroline said, "I never imagined any of this."

Brett tilted her head, with the questioning, faintly challenging look that Caroline recalled as her mother Nicole's. Quietly, Caroline told her, "I've worried most for you."

With veiled eyes, Brett seemed to regard her coffee cup. "Sometimes, Caroline, I have to remind myself who I am. That's the oddest part—not being exactly who you think you are." When she looked up, her smile was quizzical. "The other funny thing is that I have a piece of you I didn't have before. I feel this irrational pride, like *I* had something to do with who you are."

"You did," Caroline answered. "You do." She hesitated, trying to express what she felt. "I'd look at you, and be so grateful I'd chosen as I did. But it was so painful not to tell you. Now I can."

Looking down again, Brett slowly reached across the table and took her mother's hand. Feeling the light pressure on her fingertips, Caroline closed her eyes.

Soon, they would leave for the White House; after that, Caroline would enter the world of the Supreme Court, so powerful and so little understood. But now, at last, her past had caught up with her present. It was this she would remember most.

· · ·

CNN was carrying the event from the East Room, confident of an audience assured by all the controversy—personal and political—surrounding the confirmation of Caroline Masters.

But Chad Palmer did not watch. The President had invited him; he could not imagine going. He had done his part and now, undistracted, felt overwhelmed by the ugly and enormous fact that his daughter was gone forever. There were no second chances, even to say good-bye.

Sitting in the breakfast room, he heard his wife behind him, and looked up.

She looked pale and faraway; her waking and sleeping were erratic, and she seemed even more detached from the world than he. It reminded him of a harsh reality; however great his loss of Kyle, Allie's was greater. The loss unique to him was a public career turned to ashes in his mouth. And that career, he guessed, and his commitment to it, were a focus of Allie's grief and anger.

"Sit with me," he requested.

Allie did that, clutching the robe at her throat, as if to protect herself from a cold she only imagined. Wordless, she gazed at the *Washington Post* in front of him, its headline declaring "Gage Steps Down as Majority Leader."

Macdonald Gage was feeling at first hand, Chad supposed, the vertiginous swiftness with which a life's ambition can be lost. That Chad found this of minimal satisfaction did not surprise him; no misery on Gage's part could resurrect Kyle Palmer, or heal Allie's wounds. But a kind of justice had been done, with the President's assistance, and Chad and Allie had been spared the poisonous ordeal of watching Gage transcend—even profit by—Kyle's death. For that much he must try to be grateful.

Allie looked up from the newspaper; for the first time since their loss, she seemed to see him. "What will you do now?" she asked.

He considered his answer; the loss of a child, he knew, had ended marriages in far less tragic circumstances.

"I don't know," he said. "For now, just be with you, alone." He touched her face with curled fingers. "You're precious to me, Allie. I don't want anything more to happen to us."

Head bent, she was quiet for a very long time. "You were a great senator," she said at last.

For whatever that's worth to me now, Chad thought. But perhaps it would mean something in years to come; for better or worse, he had helped make Caroline Masters Chief Justice.

"Yes," he answered. "I was."

.   .   .

Sitting between Lara and Caroline Masters in the East Room, President Kerry Kilcannon watched Ellen Penn begin her words of welcome. Ellen had earned the right, Kerry thought, and it gave him a few moments to reflect.

He had been President for two months and seven days.

So much had happened—much by design, and some by chance. He was the agent of Macdonald Gage's destruction. But he would not waste time on this. Gage himself had set events in motion; what had happened to him, a kind of moral recompense, was all too rare in politics. That this had shifted the balance of power in Kerry's favor made it all the better.

As a rival for Kerry, let alone a potential president, Macdonald Gage was through. And so, for very different reasons, was Chad Palmer. The fact that Kerry had triggered Chad's eclipse by inadvertence, and only to protect Caroline Masters, did not entirely salve his conscience.

But Chad's end as a candidate in waiting, Kerry must acknowledge, also served his interests; two months into his presidency, by luck or calculation, his two leading rivals had vanished in an instant. And there still was much that Chad could do. This afternoon Kerry would visit him, to do what little he could to help Chad heal, and to persuade him to remain a senator. If not, in time Kerry and the country would have need of Chad again; a president would always need good people, and there are never enough.

Glancing at Caroline Masters, he absorbed once more the fact that he had won.

But what, exactly?

A fine Chief Justice, certainly. More sway in Congress. The growing belief, never to be undervalued, that Kerry Kilcannon was a president to respect, even fear.

And at what cost?

The deals were easy enough to tally, the human cost far harder to calculate. The world he lived in was ambiguous, a dance of light and shadow, and all the more so for a president. He had used his power to destroy Macdonald Gage; though some might bristle, he had used it openly, in the light of day and subject to judicial review. And though he had used Chad Palmer to further his own ends, Chad had always known this; both had acted as their circumstances, and their natures, demanded—even at the most terrible moments of Chad's grief. As for the many other turning points, fateful in their own way, Kerry had done the best he could. He must learn to be at peace with his decisions, as he was with the results.

In moments, Judge Caroline Masters would become Chief Justice of the United States.

Her daughter sat beside her, with Judge Montgomery from the Ninth Circuit, and her friend Judge Jackson Watts. Sarah Dash, of course, was absent. But Kerry knew that she and Caroline Masters had spoken, and whatever had been said between them seemed to give Caroline pleasure.

He touched Lara's hand. Briefly, Lara smiled at him, and then Ellen Penn invited Judge Masters to the podium.

She stood, tall and commanding, but humble in speech—a few simple words of gratitude, a pledge to serve the law and her fellow citizens as well as she could, and to bring a new spirit of collegiality to the Court which she would lead.

A great ambition, Kerry thought, for a nominee who had been so badly damaged. But she had the talent and the will, and years to make it so.

Smiling, Kerry stepped forward to stand beside Ellen Penn.

A Bible rested on the podium. Placing her hand there, Caroline met his eyes with a small, faintly ironic smile. Perhaps she was thinking, as Kerry was, of the cost; perhaps of the truth of Chad Palmer's favorite maxim, "There are worse things in life than losing an election." Whatever her thoughts, the President knew, they both felt a mixture of regret, sadness, satisfaction, and, in the end, pride at the path they had undertaken together, and that it had led them here.

After this, he would turn, strengthened, to countless other tests, and she would take up her role in another branch of government, far from Kerry's, shaping the law in ways that would touch the lives of others long after they both were gone. But this was a moment to be savored, and shared.

"Ready?" Kerry murmured.

Solemn now, Caroline nodded. Then she drew a breath, and began repeating after the Vice President:

"I, Caroline Clark Masters . . ."

Acknowledgments

When I first conceived *Protect and Defend*, I realized that it required me to grasp a number of complex subjects, among them the politics of a bitter Supreme Court confirmation fight; the workings of the legal system in a case like Mary Ann Tierney's; the fascinating but often arcane machinations of the United States Senate; the legal, moral, and medical issues arising from late-term abortion and the parental consent laws; the dissemination of private conduct through the media to destroy public careers; and the increasing influence of money on our politics. No one person understands all this; certainly—though I'm a former courtroom lawyer who observes politics quite closely—I do not.

This made my research both challenging and rewarding; those with expertise in the numerous facets of this story were generous beyond my expectations. At a minimum, I should discharge my debt by absolving them of blame for any error or biases: all mistakes are mine, and the opinions of any characters are my inventions. In particular, the various political figures who helped me should not be understood as endorsing this book or approving one or another of the often conflicting viewpoints expressed herein.

Having established that the buck stops with me, I'm deeply grateful to all those who made it possible for me to write *Protect and Defend*:

Rich Bond, Mark Childress, Sean Clegg, Ken Duberstein, John Gomperts, C. Boyden Gray, Mandy Grunwald, Harold Ickes, Joel Klein, Peter Knight, Tom Korologos, Mark Paoletta, and Ace Smith all enhanced my understanding of the process and politics of a Supreme Court nomination. The late Dan Dutko and my dear friend Ron Kaufman not only advised me, but introduced me to others who also helped. Another old friend, President George Bush, was kind enough to comment on the nomination process, and a new friend, Bruce Lindsey, was more generous with his time than I could have hoped. And special thanks to President Bill Clinton, who shared his thoughts, and opened doors.

The United States Senate is a place all its own. My guides included Senator

ACKNOWLEDGMENTS

Barbara Boxer, who has fought so hard and so well to bring to light the experiences of women facing late-term abortion, and Senator Bob Dole, by common consensus one of our greatest Senate Majority Leaders. Mathew Baumgart and Diana Huffman gave incisive advice on both substance and procedure. Particularly generous was Mark Gitenstein; I also profited from reading Mark's absorbing study of the Bork nomination, *Matters of Principle.*

There are many facets to any balanced consideration of late-term abortion and the parental consent laws—medical, psychological, ethical, and personal. I am deeply indebted to Claudia Ades, Dr. Nancy Adler, Coreen Costello, Dr. Philip Darney, Dr. Jim Goldberg, Dr. Laurie Green, Erik Parens, and Dr. Laurie Zaben. Central, as well, was a paper written by Erik Parens and Adrienne Asch for the Hastings Center, treating the ethical implications of genetic testing with respect to disability. And special thanks to Dr. Robert Bitonte for all of his time, help, and concern.

Three advocates for the pro-choice movement were kind enough to share their political and philosophical perspectives—Maureen Britell, Judith Lichtman, and Kate Michelman. Several lawyers who represented that perspective in landmark cases were equally helpful: many thanks to Janet Benshoof, Joanne Hustead, Beth Parker, Lori Schecter and, especially, Margaret Crosby. My reading also profited by a survey of pro-choice writings from NARAL, Professor Nadine Strossen, and others.

To my regret, representatives of two leading pro-life groups declined to meet with me; the novel, I am sure, is poorer for it. Therefore, I'm particularly grateful to Robert Melnick, who has represented the pro-life perspective in several important cases, for lending his advice. Douglas Johnson of the National Right to Life Committee also forwarded some materials. Beyond that, I read extensively to deepen my understanding of the likely pro-life perspective in a case such as that of Mary Ann Tierney: particularly helpful were the Parens-Asch paper, Cynthia Gorney's fine book *Articles of Faith,* and Lucinda Franks's *New Yorker* article, "Wonder Kid," as well as a survey of pro-life literature.

Much harder to obtain is an in-depth understanding of judicial procedures and perspectives, and the scope and issues involved on appeal. Thanks to Judges Maxine Chesney and my perceptive friend Judge Thelton Henderson, both of the United States District Court; Judge Robert Henry of the United States Court of Appeals for the Tenth Circuit; former New York State Appellate Judge Milton Mollen; and former Judge Sol Wachtler, Chief Justice of New York's highest court—to whom I'm also indebted for sending me the droll opinion in *Pierce v. Delamater.* Special thanks go to Judge Stephen Reinhardt of the United s Court of Appeals for the Ninth Circuit for his interest and advice.

Some wonderful lawyers and law professors further helped me frame the issues, and plot the course of the Tierney case: Erwin Chemerinsky, Leslie Landau, Stacey Leyton, Deirdre Von Dornum, and, especially, Alan Dershowitz. In preparation, I devoted many hours to a study of the case law; with allowances for a lay audience, I have tried to accurately portray the legal issues and their possible resolution. Here, I should note a change for narrative purposes: unlike most state courts, in the wake of the *Simpson* case the federal courts imposed a ban on television. But my guess is that this ban will not last, and my novel, set in the future, so provides.

There are times when characterization requires more than the exercise of sheer imagination. With his military background, including the impact of kidnapping and imprisonment, Senator Chad Palmer is such a case. Many thanks to those who helped make Chad Palmer who he is: my fellow novelist and valued friend Secretary of Defense William Cohen, NATO Commander General Joseph Ralston, Air Force Vice Chief of Staff General Ed Eberhardt, Colonel Ron Rand, Colonel Bob Stice, Colonel Rowdy Yates, Major J. C. Connors, Larry Benson, Dick Hallion, my cousin Bill Patterson, and my friend Bob Tyrer. I am particularly privileged to have spent time with two former prisoners of war, whose experiences were critical: General Charles Boyd, USAF (Ret.), and Colonel Norman McDaniel, USAF (Ret.).

Finally, others helped me fill in the gaps. Assistant District Attorney Al Giannini introduced me to ninhydrin, Mason Taylor's undoing; Drs. Ken Gottlieb and Rodney Shapiro assisted in shaping Kyle Palmer and Mary Ann Tierney; and Editor in Chief David Talbot of *Salon* magazine helped me think through the journalistic issues raised by Kyle's past, although for himself David might well have concluded that there were sufficient grounds to preserve Kyle's privacy. And literature published by Common Cause, the preeminent public interest lobby, helped provide the background for certain observations about money in politics, as did a reading of the case law on that subject.

One of the needs of any novelist is to share the madness. My talented assistant, Alison Porter Thomas, outdid herself on this book: her detailed, perceptive, and sometimes just plain persistent editorial comments challenged me daily to do better—and, thanks to Alison, every day I did. To give me a further overview I relied on my friend and agent, Fred Hill; my dear friends Anna Chavez and Philip Rotner; and my partner in life, Laurie Patterson. And my splendid publishers, Sonny Mehta and Gina Centrello, not only overcame their initial reservations about the concept of this book, but endorsed the finished novel with an enthusiasm which was both heartening and affirming. All have my warmest thanks.

A NOTE ON THE TYPE

This book was set in Adobe Garamond. Designed for the Adobe Corporation by
Robert Slimbach, the fonts are based on types first cut by Claude Garamond
(c. 1480–1561). Garamond was a pupil of Geoffroy Tory and is believed to have
followed the Venetian models, although he introduced a number of important
differences, and it is to him that we owe the letter we now know as "old style."
He gave to his letters a certain elegance and feeling of movement that won their
creator an immediate reputation and the patronage of Francis I of France.

Composed by
Stratford Publishing Services,
Brattleboro, Vermont